THE WORLD'S CLASSICS
NO NAME

WILLIAM WILKIE COLLINS was born in London in 1824, the son of a popular landscape painter. In 1846 he entered Lincoln's Inn as a law student; in 1851 he was called to the bar, and in the same year met Dickens for the first time. Adopting literature as a profession and collaborating with Dickens, he contributed to *Household Words* and *All the Year Round*. In the latter, in 1862–3, he published *No Name*. Among his best known works are *The Woman in White* (1860) and *The Moonstone* (1868). The 'original' of the woman in white was Mrs Caroline Graves with whom Wilkie Collins lived for most of his life from 1859 until his death, though he had three children by Martha Rudd. He died in 1889.

VIRGINIA BLAIN is a Senior Lecturer in English at Macquarie University in Sydney. She has published a critical edition of *Mr Sponge's Sporting Tour* by R. S. Surtees (Batsford, 1982) and is currently researching Victorian women writers for a forthcoming *Feminist Companion to Literature in English*, co-authored with Patricia Clements and Isobel Grundy.

THE WORLD'S CLASSICS

━━

WILLIAM WILKIE COLLINS

No Name

━━

Edited with an Introduction by
VIRGINIA BLAIN

Oxford   New York
OXFORD UNIVERSITY PRESS
1986

Oxford University Press, Walton Street, Oxford OX2 6DP

Oxford New York Toronto
Delhi Bombay Calcutta Madras Karachi
Petaling Jaya Singapore Hong Kong Tokyo
Nairobi Dar es Salaam Cape Town
Melbourne Auckland

and associated companies in
Beirut Berlin Ibadan Nicosia

Oxford is a trade mark of Oxford University Press

British Library Cataloguing in Publication Data
Collins, Wilkie
No name. — (The Worlds' classics)
I. Title   II. Blain, Virginia
823'.8 [F]   PR4494.N6
ISBN 0-19-281648-9

Library of Congress Cataloging in Publication Data
Collins, Wilkie, 1824-1889.
No name.
(The Worlds' classics)
Bibliography: p.
I. Blain, Virginia, 1945- . II. Title.
PR4494.N6 1986   823'.8   86-12581
ISBN 0-19-281648-9 (pbk.)

Printed in Great Britain by
Hazell Watson & Viney Ltd.
Aylesbury, Bucks

CONTENTS

INTRODUCTION

WILKIE COLLINS published more than thirty novels during a long writing career spanning the forty years from mid-century until his death in 1889. Yet his reputation has rested for over a century upon only two, *The Woman in White* (1860) and *The Moonstone* (1868), and even these have achieved classic status rather as tales of mystery and suspense than as 'serious' Victorian novels. As a result of the popular misconception that Collins was uniquely a writer of mystery stories, some of his other works have been almost entirely lost from view. *No Name* is one of the liveliest and most interesting of these lesser-known novels.

Written in the wake of the popular success of *The Woman in White*, *No Name* tackled a social issue more controversial than that of illegal incarceration in lunatic asylums. As its title implies, this novel revolves upon the issue of illegitimacy, dealing through a complicated plot with the social and moral stigma attaching to 'nameless' female children. From our late twentieth-century viewpoint, its interest is enhanced both by the complexity of its narrative structure and by the particular historical significance of its characterization of women. Collins's heroines tend to be much livelier than those of Dickens, for example, but in the past such a difference was not felt to be especially remarkable. Similarly, the complicatedness of Collins's plots has always been noted, but this characteristic has more often been regarded as a sign of superficiality than as a testimony to sophisticated narrative strategies. In the light of recent critical developments, *No Name* is certainly high on the list of novels calling out for a fresh assessment.

It is well known that Collins himself had no patience with professional critics, preferring to trust to the responses of his large reading public. 'I don't attach much importance to the reviews,' he wrote to Tinsley (publisher of *The Moonstone*) in

1868, '— except as advertisements which are inserted for nothing. But the impression I produce on the general public of readers is the lever that will move anything—provided the impression is favourable. If this book does what my other books have done, in the way of *stimulating the first circle of readers among whom it falls*—that circle will widen to a certainty.'[1] At the time of its first publication, *No Name* was viewed patronizingly by critics as merely a good story relying rather too heavily on its ingenious plot,[2] even though in his Preface Collins had insisted that his new novel, unlike *The Woman in White*, eschewed the element of mystery: 'The only Secret contained in this book, is revealed midway in the first volume.'

There is, however, more than one aspect of plot to be considered here. Apart from the use of suspense—the 'detective story' element—there is a subtler technique operating, whereby melodramatic incident becomes the vehicle for certain aspects of characterization. In denying that his primary aim in *No Name* was to interest readers in the kind of plot that had proved so successful in *The Woman in White*, Collins perhaps meant to draw attention to this subtler side, what he calls 'the train of circumstances by which these foreseen events are brought about' (Preface); in other words, the unconscious motivating influences upon character. In so doing, however, he was disingenuous, as even in this 'non-secretive' novel there is a firm emphasis on suspense, arising from the actions of the characters themselves, several of whom are arch-plotters. As G. Robert Stange has pointed out, Collins proves adept in this novel at balancing a succession of plots and counter-plots with which the characters attempt to ensnare each other, and which grip the reader's interest far more deeply than the outcome of the main

[1] From the letter to W. Tinsley Esq., dated Saturday 11 July 1868. The major portion of this letter is held in the collection at the Pierpont Morgan Library, whose Trustees have kindly given permission for this and subsequent quotations.

[2] E.g.: 'Mr. Wilkie Collins has again produced one of his ingenious puzzles. He has worked out once more a novel that is plot and nothing else but plot', from an unsigned review in *Saturday Review*, reprinted with others in *Wilkie Collins: The Critical Heritage*, ed. Norman Page (London, 1974), p. 136.

plot. 'It would not be far wrong,' Stange wrote, 'to say that the subject of *No Name* is *plotting*. It is a tale of trappers trapping trappers, devised by a novelist who, we are continually reminded, is himself an addictive contriver.'[3]

Certainly the text of *No Name* displays a powerful interweaving of the two aspects of plotting: that is, it demonstrates the special ways in which melodrama can mediate character (and vice versa) while at the same time taking every opportunity for suspenseful endings, whether of short serial episodes (in its first version) or of the three volumes (in its subsequent edition). The shape of three volumes lay dormant within the first (serial) version, invisible until their publication revealed what had been there all along: three well-shaped sections, each with its own inner balance between suspense and climax. So while it is true that this novel gives a new importance to psychological observation, it can still be seen that Collins took great care to suit the design of its plot both to his medium and to his readership. As he makes clear in the letter to Tinsley cited above, he was well aware of the importance of engaging the commitment of the 'first circle' (that is, the readers of the serial version), from whose verbal testimony would spring subsequent sales of the book. And no one knew better than Collins how to produce a 'cliff-hanger' at the end of a weekly instalment. Many episodes in the serial version (published in Dickens's journal *All The Year Round*) end on an upward note of tension or alarm. A significant example occurs in the fortieth episode, which ends like this:

She had read to that point, to that last word and no further, when a hand passed suddenly from behind her between the letter and her eye, and gripped her fast by the wrist in an instant.

She turned with a shriek of terror, and found herself face to face with old Mazey [p. 497].

In the volume edition, there is not even a chapter break at this point, yet as the ending to the last pre-Christmas number (20

[3] See G. Robert Stange's review of the Dover reprint of the American edition of *No Name* in *Nineteenth-Century Fiction*, 34, 1, (1979–80), p. 97.

December 1862), it was clearly designed to sharpen readers' appetites to the point where they might be prepared to buy the book as a Christmas present rather than wait for its ending to be slowly revealed over four more episodes.

Unfortunately, however, plans went awry. Increasing illness towards the end of the year slowed Collins's writing schedule to such an extent that he was not working far enough ahead of time to have his book finished for pre-Christmas publication. It was not until Christmas Eve that he could put down his pen and say 'Done!', as he expressed it in a note to his friend and doctor, Francis Carr Beard, to whom the novel in its volume form is dedicated.[4] Even so, the three-volume edition was on sale only one week later (31 December)—an impressive feat by today's publishing standards.

The first edition of 4,000 copies was sold out on the day of issue. However, this testifies more to Collins's marketing management than to the novel's popularity, for the bulk of the sale was a pre-arranged (and, as it proved, over-optimistic) order from Mudie's Library. Marketing management was an important aspect of professionalism for any writer who hoped to make a living, and Collins, like Dickens, prided himself on his ability to negotiate favourable terms with publishers. He was actually paid the record price of £3,000 for the volume publication by Sampson Low, news of which he relayed excitedly in a letter to his mother on 12 August 1862:

My dear Mother,
. . . I have only today completed the sale of the copyright of "No Name". Low has outbidden everybody—and has offered the most liberal price that has ever been given for the *reprinting* of a work already published periodically—no less a sum than *Three Thousand pounds*!! Add to this, the receipts from "All The Year Round" and from America, and the amount reaches *Four thousand, six hundred*. Not so bad, for story-telling![5]

[4] The letter, dated Tuesday 24 December 1862, gives the exact time of completion as 'two o'clock this morning'. This letter is held in the Morris Parrish Collection in Princeton University Library and is quoted here with the Library's kind permission.

[5] This letter is in the Pierpont Morgan Library.

In fact it was desperately necessary that *No Name* should achieve financial success, for in 1862 Collins was living absolutely hand to mouth, unable to leave his seaside lodgings (taken for the sake of his health) until he had received a publisher's advance with which to settle his bill.[6] In addition, his constant bouts of ill-health were a serious disadvantage to a writer dependent for his livelihood on serial publication; it was during this period that he was prescribed the large doses of laudanum which began a lifelong addiction to opium. Of course, as editor and friend, Dickens gave Collins a great deal of support at this period of difficulty, even offering at one point, when it looked as though Collins might be forced to miss an episode, to 'come to London straight, and do your work. I am quite confident that, with your notes, I could take it up at any time and do it.'[7] This, however, was not to be borne, and Collins managed to muster strength sufficient to finish his novel himself.

Another well-meant but galling interference from Dickens had come in the shape of advice about the title of *No Name*. When Collins intimated that he was having trouble finding a suitable title, Dickens dashed off a list of twenty-seven possibilities, all of which Collins rejected.[8] In fact he never again actively sought Dickens's advice in the way he had done during the early part of the writing of *No Name*—which suggests that with the success of this novel he came to feel himself secure in his own professionalism.

One last instance of this professionalism is worth noting here. As well as conceiving *No Name* simultaneously as serial and

[6] This emerges from a letter written to his friend Charles Ward, in London, from 'The Fort house, Broadstairs', dated 14 October 1862, asking him to 'kindly look at my account . . . to see whether Low has remembered to pay in £125 . . . before I pay for the Fort House'. The letter is in the Pierpont Morgan Library.

[7] See the letter dated 'Tuesday Night, October 14th, 1862', printed in *Letters of Charles Dickens to Wilkie Collins 1851–1870*, selected by Miss Georgina Hogarth, ed. Laurence Hutton (London, 1892), p. 135.

[8] Some examples of Dickens's suggestions are: *The Twig and the Tree*; *Behind the Veil*; *Working in the Dark*; *Magdalen Vanstone*; *The Combe Raven Tragedy*. For the complete list, see Georgina Hogarth's selection of Dickens's letters cited above, pp. 121–2.

three-decker (and of course as the unified whole afforded ultimately by a single volume), Collins also had in mind from the beginning a plan to turn it into a stage play. Again, the form of the work appears to encapsulate this potential, divided as it is into a series of 'Scenes', punctuated by groups of letters. Each of the eight Scenes has a different setting, extending the action from its prelapsarian beginning in rural Somerset as far afield as Dumfries in Scotland, taking in the ancient walls of York, the eroding coast of Suffolk and the misty Essex marshes, as well as several seedy locations in London.

The most interesting effects of these different settings arise from the ways in which they form images of Magdalen's changing state of mind. Partly because of this, and although the air of melodramatic theatricality surrounding many of the important scenes in the novel might have led Collins to believe that he had written a work which would translate effortlessly to the stage, he found when he attempted the task of converting No Name into a play that his material was strangely resistant to such treatment. After many frustrating and fruitless attempts he gave it up, handing the job over to an actor friend, Wybert Reeve, whom he allowed to maul the original story considerably, by greatly reducing the number of characters and completely rearranging the plot.[9] Paradoxically, however, this apparent thwarting of his purpose points to a characteristic of his best fiction that is overlooked by those critics who too easily dismiss his work as containing little of interest beyond a clever plot.

In the translation of No Name to the stage, where it was never a success,[10] the almost caricatured aspects of its art were emphasized, while the subtleties that reside in the detail were lost. This indicates the inadequacy of any view of this novel

---

[9] See the account in Kenneth Robinson's Wilkie Collins: A Biography (London, 1951), p. 174.

[10] Robinson (see note above) claims that the only recorded performances of No Name took place in Melbourne, Australia. But according to the Newcastle Daily Journal of the time, No Name was produced in Newcastle upon Tyne on 26 October 1877, without any indication in the advertisement that this was to be a single performance.

which concentrates on its undoubted dramatic highpoints at the cost of undervaluing its intricate arrangement of characters, actions and settings into complex and dynamic patterns. One major example of such a lost subtlety in the stage version is, ironically enough, an extended reference in the text to a famous stage play, Sheridan's *The Rivals*.

Its use early in the novel as a 'play within a play' appears at first to be merely contrived as a surface effect, but turns out to have particularly suggestive ramifications. It is while the Vanstones are still happily settled in their family home, Combe-Raven, in Somersetshire, quite unconscious of the disasters in store for them, that the Marrables appear on the scene to propose the private theatricals that are destined to throw the novel's heroine, Magdalen Vanstone, and her spineless opposite, Frank Clare, so closely together, and thus indirectly to precipitate the chain of catastrophes that animates the plot.

'Miss Marrable was that hardest of all born tyrants—an only child. She had never granted a constitutional privilege to her oppressed father and mother, since the time when she cut her first tooth' (p. 30). She has no difficulty at all in persuading Magdalen to undertake the part of Lucy in the play, while Magdalen cajoles the passive Frank into the apt role of Faulkland.

While on one level the element of plot contrivance in the introduction of these theatricals is obvious, and indeed heavily emphasized by hints such as: 'What did it mean? . . . Had the idle theatrical scheme, now that it was all over, graver results to answer for than a mischievous waste of time?' (p. 44), on another level, they also have a covert role in foreshadowing the outcome of the story. For when, through the untimely withdrawal of another member of the cast, Magdalen, who plays the pert and cunning Lucy, is asked at short notice to double in the role of the noble and long-suffering Julia, we can read more into the change than simply the opportunity thus afforded her to demonstrate the surprising range of her histrionic powers. The part of Lucy the maid initially allotted to

Magdalen is a small one, though crucial both to the outcome of
the plot of *The Rivals* and to its cynicism. Once it is doubled with
the part of Julia, the two moral extremes of Sheridan's
play—and Collins's novel—are spanned in one person. The fact
that Magdalen's natural talent for drama enables her to act
both these extremes so convincingly is not only a foreshadowing
of her future playing of parts but also an implicit comment on
the whole notion of doubleness which underpins *No Name* and
which, in Collins's next novel, *Armadale*, was to be developed to
its extreme.

In the socially conscious text of *No Name*, the dishonesty of
Sheridan's Lucy is tempered by our awareness of her exploited
class position, while Julia's saintly submissiveness in the face of
masculine absurdity takes on the negative aura of passive
aggression. These modulations are never spelt out in the novel,
but emerge implicitly through the deployment of parallel and
contrast. In taking on the roles of both characters, Magdalen
thus gives expression not only to her own potential for 'good'
(Julia) or 'bad' (Lucy) behaviour, but also to the possibility that
each of these extremes contains within itself the seeds of its own
reversal. Such a deconstructed opposition between 'good' and
'bad' behaviour adds a dimension of subtlety to the text belied
by the conventional binary oppositions of melodrama. Appropriately enough, the character of Magdalen herself is the one
most nearly affected by this complex interplay of contrasting
and parallel forces, for the duality of her early role in *The Rivals*
is echoed in all her subsequent behaviour.

In her relationship with Frank, for instance, so like Faulkand
in his peculiar brand of hypocritical selfishness, Magdalen
re-enacts the part of Julia against the grain of her nature. But
with Noel Vanstone, in some senses Frank's double, she has the
opportunity to wreak revenge in a Lucy-like way, and she does
so with admirable single-mindedness. That she is unaware of
the similarity between the two men which, while never explicit,
is so evident to the reader, adds immeasurably to the
suggestiveness of Magdalen's dual relationship with them both.
It is as though, at some deep level, Magdalen chooses to marry

Noel Vanstone not just to further her plan of revenge but also as a kind of masochistic continuation of her lost relationship with Frank. Both men demand from her a denial of her strength and selfhood that she accepts blindly in the one case, where sexual attraction is a strong factor, but from which she shrinks with abhorrence in the other.

One of Collins's greatest strengths as a writer lies in his ability to take stereotypes and remould them, thereby giving them a twist into some new and unexpected shape which reflects mockingly back on to received social opinions. It is in his characterization rather than in his overt social commentary that Collins best succeeds in the role of subversive. While it is true that his relish for melodrama is not always viewed sympathetically by modern readers, it would be a pity if the exaggerations in his style were allowed completely to over-shadow other aspects of his art which, in a subtler way, also have their roots in melodrama. Magdalen's sister Norah, for instance, although acting the stereotyped part of foil in her conventional 'goodness' (Magdalen uses her as a model for Julia), is shown to be not only morally unimpeachable, but also both dreary and annoying: 'Whether the motive was pride, or sullenness, or distrust of herself, or despair of doing good, the result was not to be mistaken—Norah had resolved on remaining passive for the future' (p. 51). But quite apart from Norah, Collins dishes up a wonderful feast of minor characters in *No Name*, many of whom take life from the ironic variations played on a stock theme.

The wily adventurer Captain Wragge provides one example. With his curly lips and parti-coloured eyes (one green, one brown), he enters the novel as a conventional confidence trickster, trying to extract riddance-money from Mrs Vanstone whom he deviously claims as a relative. But as his character unfolds and, more importantly, as his relationship with Magdalen develops, further dimensions are revealed. A self-confessed swindler—or, as he prefers to call it, 'moral agriculturist' ('" Consult my brother agriculturists in the mere farming line—do they get their crops for the asking? No! they must circumvent arid Nature, exactly as I circumvent sordid Man"' (p. 153))—he lives his life as a parodic form of the capitalist businessman. Obsessed with record-keeping, his accounts of his swindling deals are models of neatness and accuracy: 'everything down in black and white'. Thus he boasts to Magdalen as he shows her what he calls his 'commercial library' of ledgers and accounts:

'Kindly throw your eye over any one of them. I flatter myself there is no such thing as a blot or a careless entry in it from the first page to the last. Look at this room—is there a chair out of place? Not if I know it! Look at *me*. Am I dusty? am I dirty? am I half shaved? Am I, in brief, a speckless pauper, or am I not? Mind! I take no credit to myself; the nature of the man, my dear girl—the nature of the man! [p. 155]'

A comic contrast is set up between Wragge and his wife, the moon-faced giantess with eyes of mild and faded blue (supposedly the model for Lewis Carroll's White Queen), who simultaneously towers over him and cowers beneath the lash of his tongue:

'Tea, captain?' inquired Mrs Wragge, looking submissively down at her husband, whose head when he stood on tiptoe barely reached her shoulder. . . . 'Mrs Wragge is not deaf,' explained the captain. 'She's only a little slow. Constitutionally torpid—if I may use the expression. I am merely loud with her (and I beg you will honour me by being loud too) as a necessary stimulant to her ideas' [pp. 146–7].

Yet the characterization of the Wragges reaches beyond a comedy of stereotypes as their fortunes become entangled with Magdalen's. Although she and Captain Wragge initially join forces out of mutal self-interest, he gradually realizes that he is out of his depth in the strong current of her private obsession with revenge. Once he learns of her plan to ensnare Noel Vanstone into a marriage which will be far more abhorrent to her than to him, even Wragge's cynicism is shaken. Nevertheless, the comedy of his duel of wits with Vanstone's wily housekeeper and protector, Mrs Lecount, is masterly in its balance of humour and tension. Wragge primes himself with absurdly literal facts drawn from a well-known children's science textbook in order to disarm her wariness by pandering to her pride in her late husband's unappreciated scientific achievements. But the comedy gives way eventually to a darker mood, culminating in Magdalen's complete withdrawal from Wragge into a private world of torment and suicidal despair. Although his original plan had been to exploit her needs for his financial gain, in the end it is she who has the upper hand and routs him from the field. He is defeated not by her wits, which scorn his use of cunning, but by her passion, against which he has no weapons.

Another characteristic of Collins's unusual treatment of stereotypes in this novel is the play he makes with suggested or shadow parallels which are effective in their very understatement. For instance, the weak and vacillating Frank Clare, Magdalen's first love, emerges in an unexpectedly sinister light when we gradually become aware of similarities between him and the pale and repellent Noel Vanstone whom Magdalen forces herself to marry. Then again, just as her maid Louisa both draws forth and echoes certain of Magdalen's better qualities, thus emphasizing their female fellowship in misfortune, so the very different Mrs Lecount mirrors some of Magdalen's darker, more obsessive traits through a well-matched clash of wills. Indeed, the shadowy pairing of these two seemingly contrary characters is particularly telling.

Mrs Lecount is much more experienced than Magdalen: she is older, and her cold, manipulative cleverness seems at first the antithesis of Magdalen's volatility. Their first meeting, with Magdalen protected by a disguise and Mrs Lecount by a sinister pet toad, is a suitably guarded one. It sets them up as worthy adversaries for each other.

Snails clung to the sides of the tank . . . on top of the pyramid, there sat solitary, cold as the stone, brown as the stone, motionless as the stone, a little bright-eyed toad. . . .

'Don't be alarmed,' said a woman's voice behind her. 'My pets hurt nobody.'

Magdalen turned, and confronted Mrs Lecount. . . . She found herself in the presence of a lady of mild ingratiating manners, whose

dress was the perfection of neatness, taste, and matronly simplicity. . . . 'And to what circumstances am I indebted for the honour of
this visit?'

'May I inquire, first, if my name happens to be familiar to you?' said
Magdalen, turning towards her as a matter of necessity—but coolly
holding up her handkerchief, at the same time, between her face and
the light [pp. 200–1].

Seeing through each other almost instantly, they artfully
pretend otherwise, and a good deal of tension builds up for the
reader as the battle of wits develops.

On the surface there seems to be no possibility of claiming a
parallelism between Magdalen and Mrs Lecount. The former
so young, so passionate, so idealistic; the latter so experienced,
so well-preserved, so shrewdly calculating. Yet the very
dynamic of their interaction as adversaries sets up a pattern in
which their behaviour comes to mirror each other's. Both find
strength through an inordinate sense of pride and an inflexible
sense of purpose; both are highly intelligent and by nature
independent, although reduced by circumstances to dependency on men they despise; both are obsessed with their own rights
and with receiving what they know to be justice. '"The widow
of Professor Lecompte, sir, takes what is justly hers—and takes
no more!"' declares Mrs Lecount (p. 415), while Magdalen too
is constant in her determination to reap no more than that
which she perceives to be her due as her father's daughter. By
setting up patterns of analogy between two such seemingly
opposite characters, the novel draws attention to the power of
those social and economic forces in mid-nineteenth-century
England which ensured the dependency on men of even the
most courageous, unconventional and independent-minded of
women.

The radicalism of Collins's treatment of women in *No Name*
has never been fully appreciated. William Marshall has made
the claim that: 'Viewed mythically, the Vanstone girls'
disinheritance is essentially that of modern man.'[11] It would be

---

[11] William H. Marshall, *Wilkie Collins* (New York, 1970), p. 69.

more appropriate to see it as the disinheritance of Victorian woman. The dynamic of the novel works in such a way as to illustrate paradigmatically the illegitimacy not only of Magdalen and her sister, but of the claims of any woman in that society to autonomous and self-initiated action. Illegitimacy, with its connotations of allowing no legal inheritance or possession of property, no given social class, no status as a responsible person in the eyes of the law, no legal name, serves here as an evocative and subversive metaphor for the position of all women as non-persons in a patriarchal and patrilineal society.

In that extraordinary section of the book where Collins presents the relationship between Magdalen, raised in the lap of luxury, and her maid Louisa, downtrodden and disregarded, as one of mutual trust and care between two outcast women, he gives words to Magdalen by which she implicitly recognizes that society allows no status to women as persons in their own right. Only through relationship with a man can a woman claim to belong to any particular class in society. As she says to her maid: '"I ask you to sit near me . . . because I wish to speak to you on equal terms. Whatever distinctions there might once have been between us, are now at an end. I am a lonely woman thrown helpless on my own resources, without rank or place in the world"' (p. 446). Her father and husband dead, and with no legal inheritance from either, Magdalen has been turned into a non-person. In showing her refusal to submit to this, or to accept it as anything other than injustice, Collins comes much closer to a true sympathy with the plight of women in Victorian society than Dickens ever did.

At this time, however, the close link with Dickens was still particularly important for Collins, not so much in its mentor-pupil aspect, which is how Dickens saw it, but rather in giving impetus to one of this novel's major themes. It is almost as though Collins wanted to conduct a literary debate with Dickens, begun in *Hide and Seek* (1854), for in again choosing an illegitimate girl as his heroine, he invited further comparison with Dickens's controversial treatment of Esther Summerson in *Bleak House*, first published eight years earlier in 1852–3. Far less sexually reticent in his novels than Dickens, Collins presents Magdalen Vanstone to his readers in terms of unmistakable promise:

The girl's exuberant vitality asserted itself all over her, from head to foot. Her figure—taller than her sister's, taller than the average of woman's height; instinct with such a seductive, serpentine suppleness, so lightly and playfully graceful, that its movement suggested, not unnaturally, the movements of a young cat—her figure was so perfectly developed already that no one who saw her could have supposed that she was only eighteen. She bloomed in the full physical maturity of twenty years or more—bloomed naturally and irresistably, in right of her matchless health and strength [p. 6].

When she is thrust into the world from the protecting shelter of her early home, and faced with the prospect of struggling for her living under the degrading shadow of her recently discovered illegitimacy, Magdalen—unlike Esther, or her own sister Norah—is not one to turn the other cheek. Although she, like them, feels deeply the shame of the social stigma conferred on illegitimate children (and females seem to have borne a more indelible mark of 'inherited' moral and sexual taint), she refuses to take upon herself any guilt for her position. In this refusal lies her extraordinary power, and it is the dangerous attraction of this power that Collins explores in his development of her story. Yet in the end her power deserts her, and she succumbs to a debilitating illness followed closely by a new, and we assume more lasting, romantic attachment.

For, bold as Collins might have been in creating a strong heroine who defies society by fighting for what she believes to be her rights, he shrank from allowing her to win a victory entirely on her own terms. In the end she must be 'rescued' by the love of a good man, in itself a nice reversal of her mother's early 'rescue' of her father from a life of debauchery, and indeed a reversal of the predominant pattern in Victorian novels, where it is generally in the female characters that the saving moral graces lie. Yet it is the ending that most disappoints a modern reader of No Name. For quite opposite reasons, it disappointed—or, rather, scandalized—Victorian readers as well.

That the 'bad' Magdalen, who fought for her rights in what was, in Victorian terms, an entirely disreputable manner (by consciously trading on the power of her sexuality), should be rewarded with a happy and respectable marriage was regarded by the reading public as highly distasteful—so much so that the book was far less successful than *The Woman in White*. As Mrs Oliphant expostulated in an unsigned review in *Blackwood's Magazine*:

Mr. Wilkie Collins, after the skilful and startling complications of the *Woman in White*—his grand effort—has chosen, by way of making his heroine piquant and interesting in his next attempt, to throw her into a career of vulgar and aimless trickery and wickedness, with which it is impossible to have a shadow of sympathy, but from all the pollutions of which he intends us to believe that she emerges, at the cheap cost of a fever, as pure, as high-minded, and as spotless as the most dazzling white of heroines . . . after all her endless deceptions and horrible marriage, it seems quite right to the author that she should be restored to society, and have a good husband and happy home.[12]

That Mrs Oliphant and her kind were not fooled by the novel's final gesture towards propriety is, to a modern view, less a testimony to its failure than to its success. Clearly Collins had succeeded in touching some very sensitive nerves in his portrayal of Magdalen Vanstone. For the subversive, 'sinful' and lively side of this character, given so much space and animated with so much energy earlier in the novel, cannot be easily wiped out for the reader by a 'safe' moral conversion at the end. It is not in the superimposed black and white simplicities that our interest lies. Rather, it is in the detailed elaboration of an array of counterpointed similarities and contrasts between characters that the richest and most living parts of the novel take shape.

VIRGINIA BLAIN

---

[12] Page, op. cit., p. 143.

NOTE ON THE TEXT

No Name was first issued in serial form in *All the Year Round* in forty-four episodes between 15 March 1862 and 17 January 1863. The three-volume edition was published on 31 December 1862 by Sampson Low, Son, and Co. Collins had intended to complete the novel in time for Christmas publication, but was prevented by the illness which had plagued him throughout the second half of the year. Writing against time, often in severe pain, he only put the last words to *No Name* in the early hours of 24 December 1862.[1]

Possibly because of his illness, the serial version was not much revised for the three-volume edition. One notable exception occurs in the First Scene, Chapter XIII, where Collins appears to have made an over-hasty correction of a serious legal error bearing on the plot. An account of this change is given in the Notes. Otherwise the revisions were mainly stylistic, tending to minor local effect rather than major significance. Some heavy hints of foreboding were removed, however, and in the same Chapter XIII an important clue was inserted. The young Andrew Vanstone's saviour from among his superior officers, anonymous in the serial version, was named as Major Kirke; the way was thus paved for the reader to make an early connection between him and his son, the Captain Kirke who redeems Vanstone's daughter.

The 1862 edition had very extensive library sales and as a result was virtually sold out on the first day of issue. Collins was paid what was then considered the extremely large sum of £3000 for the book by Sampson Low, following the enormous success

---

[1] See the letter to Beard cited in the Introduction above (p. x, n. 4). Its evidence is important in helping to scotch the idea that the book *was* in fact published for Christmas 1862 (as, for instance, Baker claims in his 1980 article referred to in n. 3 below), an idea perhaps given currency by the advertisement which appeared in the 13 December number of *All the Year Round* optimistically proclaiming *No Name* to be 'now ready' in three volumes.

of *The Woman in White* in 1860. The 'new edition' of 1863 was a re-issue of the 1862 edition in the same three-volume format, but in 1864 a one-volume edition was published, again by Sampson Low. This edition corrects some printer's errors but there is no evidence to show that Collins made any revisions himself. He did, however, persuade John Millais to produce a fine steel engraving for the frontispiece.

The manuscript

The complete holograph manuscript is held by the King's School, Canterbury, Kent, as part of the Hugh Walpole bequest, and I wish to thank the custodian, Mr D. S. Goodes, for his kindness in making it available to me. It consists of 571 leaves bound into a single quarto volume. Although heavily revised and difficult to read, it is marked up as printer's copy. It differs in many minor respects from the serial version and offers interesting evidence of the novel's evolution. It has long been known that Collins had peculiar difficulty in finding a suitable title for this novel: the manuscript reveals not just that he finally thought of the title after he had written a good portion of the book (this we can deduce from letters) but that he went back and inserted passages explicitly referring to the notion of the Vanstone daughters having 'No Name' while the first serial episodes were in proof.[2] A further important source of evidence about the evolution of *No Name* lies in the correspondence with Dickens, who made detailed comments on certain sections as they were written.[3]

Dramatic adaptation

The division of *No Name* into eight 'Scenes' gives its own indication of Collins's stage orientation, and the last episodes of

[2] For a fuller account see my article, 'The Naming of *No Name*', in the *Wilkie Collins Society Journal*, 4 (1984), pp. 25–9.

[3] For a good discussion of the part Dickens played in shaping the novel, see the article by William Baker, 'Wilkie Collins, Dickens and *No Name*', *Dickens Studies Newsletter*, 11, 2 (June 1980), pp. 49–52.

the serial version in *All the Year Round* are accompanied by the following advertisement:

The author begs to announce that he has protected his right of property (so far as the stage is concerned) in the work of his own invention, by causing a dramatic adaptation of 'No Name' to be written, of which he is the sole proprietor, and which has been published and entered at Stationer's Hall as the law directs.[4]

Owing to his illness, Collins had paid a Mr Bayle Bernard to write this version in five acts. It was formally published in 1863 and a copy deposited in the British Museum, but it was never staged. Its sole purpose was to preserve Collins's copyright, since under the law at that time a novel was not protected from pirated dramatizations unless the author had first registered his or her own adaptation. In 1870 Collins wrote his own stage version in four acts, but felt dissatisfied with it. He subsequently engaged Mr Wybert Reeve to revise it for him, and professed himself happy with the result, but it never achieved success on the stage. (See Introduction, p. xii, n. 9, above.)

The text of this edition

The text of this edition is a photographic reproduction of the 1864 one-volume reprint of the three-volume edition of 1862. The copy photographed was kindly loaned by Clive Hurst for reproduction here. The only other copy I have seen is in the British Library. The 1864 is a good text for reproduction as a number of printer's errors from the first edition were corrected, while only a very few were introduced. In fact this text was used for all subsequent British nineteenth-century reprints. I have compared it with the serial version of 1862–3, the three-volume edition of 1862, and the Harpers American edition of 1873. Although the 1864 text was apparently not corrected by the author, it is more authoritative than the Harpers version, which not only introduced a much larger proportion of substantive errors, but also repunctuated, often with considerable insensitivity.

[4] This appeared first in the number for 27 December 1862.

The only corrections made to this edition have been the silent emendation of the number of Chapter XIV in the Fourth Scene, page 369 (misnumbered XIII in all but the serial version), and the restoration of the folio to page 433 (misnumbered 43 in this copy). Otherwise the integrity of this version remains intact. I have drawn attention in the Notes to a few instances where a printer's error is so plausible as to be misleading. So far as I can judge, the few uncorrected errors that remain are of the order of minor slips of punctuation.

SELECT BIBLIOGRAPHY

BIBLIOGRAPHY

R. V. Andrew, 'A Wilkie Collins Check-List', *English Studies in Africa*, 3 (March 1960), pp. 79–98

Robert P. Ashley, 'Wilkie Collins', in *Victorian Fiction: A Guide to Research*, ed. Lionel Stevenson, 1964, and in *Victorian Fiction: A Second Guide to Research*, ed. George H. Ford, 1978

Kirk H. Beetz, *Wilkie Collins: An Annotated Bibliography, 1889–1976*, 1976

Andrew Gasson, 'Wilkie Collins: A Collector's and Bibliographer's Challenge', *The Private Library*, 3rd ser., 3 (Summer 1980), pp. 51–77

BIOGRAPHY

Wilkie Collins, 'How I Write My Books', *The Globe*, 26 November 1887

——, 'Reminiscences of a Story-teller', *Universal Review*, 1 (May–August 1888), pp. 182–92

Nuel Pharr Davis, *The Life of Wilkie Collins*, 1956

Kenneth Robinson, *Wilkie Collins: A Biography*, 1951 (repr. 1974)

Dorothy L. Sayers, *Wilkie Collins: A Biographical and Critical Study*, ed. E. R. Gregory (uncompleted), 1977

As yet there is no edition of Collins's letters.

CRITICAL STUDIES

R. V. Andrew, *Wilkie Collins: A Critical Survey of his Prose Fiction*, 1979

Robert P. Ashley, *Wilkie Collins*, 1952

William Baker, 'Wilkie Collins, Dickens and *No Name*', *Dickens Studies Newsletter*, 11, 2 (June 1980), pp. 49–52

Virginia Blain, 'Copy-Text and Compromise: Wilkie Collins in the Nineteenth Century and Now', in *Editing Texts*, ed. J. C. Eade, 1985, pp. 54–67

——, 'The Naming of *No Name*', *Wilkie Collins Society Journal*, 4 (1984), pp. 25–9

Sue Lonoff, 'Charles Dickens and Wilkie Collins', *Nineteenth-Century Fiction*, 35 (September 1980), pp. 150–70

——, *Wilkie Collins and His Victorian Readers*, 1982

John Goode, 'Minor Nineteenth-Century Fiction', *Victorian Studies*, 11 (June 1968), pp. 534–8

William H. Marshall, *Wilkie Collins*, 1970

Norman Page (ed.), *Wilkie Collins: The Critical Heritage*, 1974

G. Robert Stange, 'Wilkie Collins, *No Name*', *Nineteenth-Century Fiction*, 34 (June 1979), pp. 96–100

Geoffrey Tillotson, 'Wilkie Collins' *No Name*', *Criticism and the Nineteenth Century*, 1951

Wilkie Collins Society Journal and *Wilkie Collins Society Newsletter*, ed. Kirk H. Beetz, 1981 onwards

A CHRONOLOGY OF
WILLIAM WILKIE COLLINS

[1] N. P. Davis, *The Life of Wilkie Collins*, 1956, pp. 321–2, argues a strong case for the early summer of 1854.

Age

J.E. Millais

NO NAME.

BY

WILKIE COLLINS,

AUTHOR OF "THE WOMAN IN WHITE," "THE DEAD SECRET," ETC., ETC., ETC.

NEW EDITION.

LONDON:

SAMPSON LOW, SON, AND MARSTON,

14 LUDGATE HILL.

1864.

TO

FRANCIS CARR BEARD;*
(FELLOW OF THE ROYAL COLLEGE OF SURGEONS OF ENGLAND)

IN REMEMBRANCE OF THE TIME

WHEN THE CLOSING SCENES OF THIS STORY WERE WRITTEN.

PREFACE.

THE main purpose of this story is to appeal to the reader's interest in a subject, which has been the theme of some of the greatest writers, living and dead—but which has never been, and can never be, exhausted, because it is a subject eternally interesting to all mankind. Here is one more book that depicts the struggle of a human creature, under those opposing influences of Good and Evil, which we have all felt, which we have all known. It has been my aim to make the character of " Magdalen," which personifies this struggle, a pathetic character even in its perversity and its error; and I have tried hard to attain this result by the least obtrusive and the least artificial of all means—by a resolute adherence, throughout, to the truth as it is in Nature. This design was no easy one to accomplish; and it has been a great encouragement to me (during the publication of my story in its periodical form) to know, on the authority of many readers, that the object which I had proposed to myself, I might, in some degree, consider as an object achieved.

Round the central figure in the narrative, other characters will be found grouped, in sharp contrast—contrast, for the most part, in which I have endeavoured to make the element of humour mainly predominant. I have sought to impart this relief to the more serious passages in the book, not only because I believed myself to be justified in doing so by the laws of Art —but because experience has taught me (what the experience of my readers will doubtless confirm) that there is no such moral phenomenon as unmixed tragedy to be found in the world around us. Look where we may, the dark threads and the light cross each other perpetually in the texture of human life.

To pass from the Characters to the Story, it will be seen that the narrative related in these pages has been constructed on a plan, which differs from the plan followed in my last novel, and in some other of my works published at an earlier date. The only Secret contained in this book, is revealed midway in the first volume. From that point, all the main events of the story are purposely foreshadowed, before they take place—my present design being to rouse the reader's interest in following the train of circumstances by which these foreseen events are brought about. In trying this new ground, I am not turning my back in doubt on the ground which I have passed over already. My one object in following a new course, is to enlarge the range of my studies in the art of writing fiction, and to vary the form in which I make my appeal to the reader, as attractively as I can.

There is no need for me to add more to these few prefatory words than is here written. What I might otherwise have wished to say in this place, I have endeavoured to make the book itself say for me.

Harley Street,
November, 1862.

N O   N A M E.

THE FIRST SCENE.

COMBE-RAVEN, SOMERSETSHIRE.

——◇◆◇——

CHAPTER I.

THE hands on the hall-clock pointed to half-past six in the morning. The house was a country residence in West Somersetshire, called Combe-Raven. The day was the fourth of March, and the year was eighteen hundred and forty-six.*

No sounds but the steady ticking of the clock, and the lumpish snoring of a large dog stretched on a mat outside the dining-room door, disturbed the mysterious morning stillness of hall and staircase. Who we·e the sleepers hidden in the upper regions? Let the house reveal its own secrets; and, one by one, as they descend the stairs from their beds, let the sleepers disclose themselves.

As the clock pointed to a quarter to seven, the dog woke and shook himself. After waiting in vain for the footman, who was accustomed to let him out, the animal wandered restlessly from one closed door to another on the ground floor; and, returning to his mat in great perplexity, appealed to the sleeping family, with a long and melancholy howl.

Before the last notes of the dog's remonstrance had died away, the oaken stairs in the higher regions of the house creaked under slowly-descending footsteps. In a minute more the first of the female servants made her appearance, with a dingy woollen shawl over her shoulders—for the March morning was bleak; and rheumatism and the cook were old acquaintances. Receiving the dog's first cordial advances with the worst possible grace, the cook slowly opened the hall door, and let the animal out. It was a wild morning. Over a spacious lawn, and behind a black plantation of firs, the rising sun rent its way upward through piles of ragged grey cloud; heavy drops of rain fell few and far between; the March wind shuddered round the corners of the house, and the wet trees swayed wearily.

Seven o'clock struck; and the signs of domestic life began to show themselves in more rapid succession.

The housemaid came down—tall and slim, with the state of the spring temperature written redly on her nose. The lady's-maid followed—young, smart, plump, and sleepy. The kitchen-maid came next—afflicted with the face-ache, and making no secret of her sufferings. Last of all, the footman appeared, yawning disconsolately; the living picture of a man who felt that he had been defrauded of his fair night's rest.

The conversation of the servants, when they assembled before the slowly-lighting kitchen fire, referred to a recent family event, and turned at starting on this question: Had Thomas, the footman, seen anything of the concert at Clifton, at which his master and the two young ladies had been present on the previous night? Yes; Thomas had heard the concert; he had been paid for to go in at the back; it was a loud concert; it was a hot concert; it was described at the top of the bills as Grand; whether it was worth travelling sixteen miles to hear by railway, with the additional hardship of going back nineteen miles by road, at half-past one in the morning—was a question which he would leave his master and the young ladies to decide; his own opinion, in the mean time, being unhesitatingly, No. Further inquiries, on the part of all the female servants in succession, elicited no additional information of any sort. Thomas could hum none of the songs, and could describe none of the ladies' dresses. His audience accordingly gave him up in despair; and the kitchen small-talk flowed back into its ordinary channels, until the clock struck eight, and startled the assembled servants into separating for their morning's work.

A quarter-past eight, and nothing happened. Half-past—and more signs of life appeared from the bedroom regions. The next member of the family who came down stairs was Mr. Andrew Vanstone, the master of the house.

Tall, stout, and upright—with bright blue eyes, and healthy florid complexion—his brown plush shooting-jacket carelessly buttoned awry; his vixenish little Scotch terrier barking unrebuked at his heels; one hand thrust into his waistcoat pocket, and the other smacking the banisters cheerfully as he came down stairs humming a tune—Mr. Vanstone showed his character on the surface of him freely to all men. An easy, hearty, handsome, good-humoured gentleman, who walked on the sunny side of the way of life, and who asked nothing better than to meet all his fellow-passengers in this world on the sunny side, too. Estimating him by years, he had turned fifty. Judging him by lightness of heart, strength of constitution, and capacity for enjoyment, he was no older than most men who have only turned thirty.

"Thomas!" cried Mr. Vanstone, taking up his old felt hat and his thick walking-stick from the hall table. "Breakfast, this morning, at ten. The

young ladies are not likely to be down earlier after the concert last night.—
By-the-by, how did you like the concert, yourself, eh? You thought it
was Grand? Quite right; so it was. Nothing but Crash-Bang, varied
now and then by Bang-Crash; all the women dressed within an inch of
their lives; smothering heat, blazing gas, and no room for anybody—yes,
yes, Thomas: Grand's the word for it, and Comfortable isn't." With that
expression of opinion, Mr. Vanstone whistled to his vixenish terrier; flourished his stick at the hall door in cheerful defiance of the rain; and set off
through wind and weather for his morning walk.

The hands, stealing their steady way round the dial of the clock, pointed
to ten minutes to nine. Another member of the family appeared on the
stairs—Miss Garth, the governess.

No observant eyes could have surveyed Miss Garth without seeing at
once that she was a north-countrywoman. Her hard-featured face; her
masculine readiness and decision of movement; her obstinate honesty of
look and manner, all proclaimed her border birth and border training.
Though little more than forty years of age, her hair was quite grey; and
she wore over it the plain cap of an old woman. Neither hair nor head-
dress was out of harmony with her face—it looked older than her years:
the hard handwriting of trouble had scored it heavily at some past time.
The self-possession of her progress down the stairs, and the air of habitual
authority with which she looked about her, spoke well for her position in Mr.
Vanstone's family. This was evidently not one of the forlorn, persecuted,
pitiably dependent order of governesses. Here was a woman who lived on
ascertained and honourable terms with her employers—a woman who looked
capable of sending any parents in England to the right-about, if they failed
to rate her at her proper value.

"Breakfast at ten?" repeated Miss Garth, when the footman had answered the bell, and had mentioned his master's orders. "Ha! I thought
what would come of that concert last night. When people who live in the
country patronize public amusements, public amusements return the compliment by upsetting the family afterwards for days together. You're
upset, Thomas, I can see—your eyes are as red as a ferret's, and your cravat
looks as if you had slept in it. Bring the kettle at a quarter to ten—and if
you don't get better in the course of the day, come to me, and I'll give you
a dose of physic. That's a well-meaning lad, if you only let him alone,"
continued Miss Garth, in soliloquy, when Thomas had retired; "but he's
not strong enough for concerts twenty miles off. They wanted *me* to go
with them last night. Yes: catch me!"

Nine o'clock struck; and the minute hand stole on to twenty minutes
past the hour, before any more footsteps were heard on the stairs. At the
end of that time, two ladies appeared, descending to the breakfast-room together—Mrs. Vanstone and her eldest daughter.

If the personal attractions of Mrs. Vanstone, at an earlier period of life, had depended solely on her native English charms of complexion and freshness, she must have long since lost the last relics of her fairer self. But her beauty, as a young woman, had passed beyond the average national limits; and she still preserved the advantage of her more exceptional personal gifts. Although she was now in her forty-fourth year; although she had been tried, in bygone times, by the premature loss of more than one of her children, and by long attacks of illness which had followed those bereavements of former years—she still preserved the fair proportion and subtle delicacy of feature, once associated with the all-adorning brightness and freshness of beauty, which had left her never to return. Her eldest child, now descending the stairs by her side, was the mirror in which she could look back, and see again the reflection of her own youth. There, folded thick on the daughter's head, lay the massive dark hair, which, on the mother's, was fast turning grey. There, in the daughter's cheek, glowed the lovely dusky red which had faded from the mother's to bloom again no more. Miss Vanstone had already reached the first maturity of womanhood: she had completed her six-and-twentieth year. Inheriting the dark majestic character of her mother's beauty, she had yet hardly inherited all its charms. Though the shape of her face was the same, the features were scarcely so delicate, their proportion was scarcely so true. She was not so tall. She had the dark-brown eyes of her mother—full and soft, with the steady lustre in them which Mrs. Vanstone's eyes had lost—and yet there was less interest, less refinement and depth of feeling in her expression: it was gentle and feminine, but clouded by a certain quiet reserve, from which her mother's face was free. If we dare to look closely enough, may we not observe, that the moral force of character and the higher intellectual capacities in parents seem often to wear out mysteriously in the course of transmission to children? In these days of insidious nervous exhaustion and subtly-spreading nervous malady, is it not possible that the same rule may apply, less rarely than we are willing to admit, to the bodily gifts as well?

The mother and daughter slowly descended the stairs together—the first dressed in dark brown, with an Indian shawl thrown over her shoulders; the second more simply attired in black, with a plain collar and cuffs, and a dark orange-coloured ribbon over the bosom of her dress. As they crossed the hall, and entered the breakfast-room, Miss Vanstone was full of the all-absorbing subject of the last night's concert.

"I am so sorry, mamma, you were not with us," she said. "You have been so strong and so well ever since last summer—you have felt so many years younger, as you said yourself—that I am sure the exertion would not have been too much for you."

"Perhaps not, my love—but it was as well to keep on the safe side."

"Quite as well," remarked Miss Garth, appearing at the breakfast-room door. " Look at Norah (good morning, my dear)—look, I say, at Norah. A perfect wreck; a living proof of your wisdom and mine in staying at home. The vile gas, the foul air, the late hours—what can you expect? She's not made of iron, and she suffers accordingly. No, my dear, you needn't deny it. I see you've got a headache."

Norah's dark, handsome face brightened into a smile—then lightly clouded again with its accustomed quiet reserve.

" A very little headache; not half enough to make me regret the concert," she said, and walked away by herself to the window.

On the far side of a garden and paddock, the view overlooked a stream, some farm-buildings which lay beyond, and the opening of a wooded rocky pass (called, in Somersetshire, a Combe), which here cleft its way through the hills that closed the prospect. A winding strip of road was visible, at no great distance, amid the undulations of the open ground; and along this strip the stalwart figure of Mr. Vanstone was now easily recognizable, returning to the house from his morning walk. He flourished his stick gaily, as he observed his eldest daughter at the window. She nodded and waved her hand in return, very gracefully and prettily—but with something of old-fashioned formality in her manner, which looked strangely in so young a woman, and which seemed out of harmony with a salutation addressed to her father.

The hall-clock struck the adjourned breakfast-hour. When the minute-hand had recorded the lapse of five minutes more, a door banged in the bedroom regions—a clear young voice was heard singing blithely—light rapid footsteps pattered on the upper stairs, descended with a jump to the landing, and pattered again, faster than ever, down the lower flight. In another moment, the youngest of Mr. Vanstone's two daughters (and two only surviving children) dashed into view on the dingy old oaken stairs, with the suddenness of a flash of light; and clearing the last three steps into the hall at a jump, presented herself breathless in the breakfast-room, to make the family circle complete.

By one of those strange caprices of Nature, which science leaves still unexplained, the youngest of Mr. Vanstone's children presented no recognizable resemblance to either of her parents. How had she come by her hair? how had she come by her eyes? Even her father and mother had asked themselves those questions, as she grew up to girlhood, and had been sorely perplexed to answer them. Her hair was of that purely light-brown hue, unmixed with flaxen, or yellow, or red—which is oftener seen on the plumage of a bird than on the head of a human being. It was soft and plentiful, and waved downward from her low forehead in regular folds—but, to some tastes, it was dull and dead, in its absolute want of glossiness, in its monotonous purity of plain light colour. Her eyebrows and eyelashes were just a shade darker than her hair, and seemed made expressly for those violet-blue eyes, which assert their most irresistible charm when associated with a fair complexion. But it was here exactly that the promise of her face failed of performance in the most startling manner. The eyes, which should have been dark, were incomprehensibly and discordantly light: they were of that nearly colourless grey, which, though little attractive in itself, possesses the rare compensating merit of interpreting the finest gradations of thought, the gentlest changes of feeling, the deepest trouble of passion, with a subtle transparency of expression which no darker eyes can rival. Thus quaintly self-contradictory in the upper part of her face, she was hardly less at variance with established ideas of harmony in the lower. Her lips had the true feminine delicacy of form, her cheeks the lovely roundness and smoothness of youth—but the mouth was too large and firm, the chin too square and massive for her sex and age. Her complexion partook of the pure monotony of tint which characterized her hair—it was of the same soft warm creamy fairness all over, without a tinge of colour in the cheeks, except on occasions of unusual bodily exertion, or sudden mental disturbance. The whole countenance—so remarkable in its strongly-opposed characteristics—was rendered additionally striking by its extraordinary mobility. The large, electric, light-grey eyes were hardly ever in repose; all varieties of expression followed each other over the plastic, ever-changing face, with a giddy rapidity which left sober analysis far behind in the race. The girl's exuberant vitality asserted itself all over her, from head to foot. Her figure—taller than her sister's, taller than the average of woman's height; instinct with such a seductive, serpentine suppleness, so lightly and playfully graceful, that its movements suggested, not unnaturally, the movements of a young cat—her figure was so perfectly developed already that no one who saw her could have supposed that she was only eighteen. She bloomed in the full physical maturity of twenty years or more—bloomed naturally and irresistibly, in right of her matchless health and strength. Here, in truth, lay the mainspring of this strangely-constituted organization. Her headlong course down the house stairs; the brisk activity of all her movements; the incessant sparkle of expression in her face; the enticing gaiety which took the hearts of the quietest people by storm—even the reckless delight in bright colours, which showed itself in her brilliantly-striped morning dress, in her fluttering ribbons, in the large scarlet rosettes on her smart little shoes—all sprang alike from the same source; from the overflowing physical health which strengthened every muscle, braced every nerve, and set the warm young blood tingling through her veins, like the blood of a growing child.

On her entry into the breakfast-room, she was saluted with the customary remonstrance which her flighty disregard of all punctuality habitually provoked from the long-suffering household authorities. In Miss Garth's favourite phrase, "Magdalen was born with all the senses—except a sense of order."

Magdalen!* It was a strange name to have given her? Strange, indeed; and yet, chosen under no extraordinary circumstances. The name had been borne by one of Mr. Vanstone's sisters, who had died in early youth; and, in affectionate remembrance of her, he had called his second daughter by it—just as he had called his eldest daughter Norah, for his wife's sake. Magdalen! Surely, the grand old Bible name—suggestive of a sad and sombre dignity; recalling, in its first association, mournful ideas of penitence and seclusion—had been here, as events had turned out, inappropriately bestowed? Surely, this self-contradictory girl had perversely accomplished one contradiction more, by developing into a character which was out of all harmony with her own christian name!

"Late again!" said Mrs. Vanstone, as Magdalen breathlessly kissed her.

"Làte again!" chimed in Miss Garth, when Magdalen came her way next. "Well?" she went on, taking the girl's chin familiarly in her hand, with a half-satirical, half-fond attention which betrayed that the youngest daughter, with all her faults, was the governess's favourite—"Well? and what has the concert done for *you*? What form of suffering has dissipation inflicted on *your* system, this morning?"

"Suffering!" repeated Magdalen, recovering her breath, and the use of her tongue with it. "I don't know the meaning of the word: if there's anything the matter with me, I'm too well. Suffering! I'm ready for another concert to-night, and a ball to-morrow, and a play the day after. Oh," cried Magdalen, dropping into a chair and crossing her hands rapturously on the table, "how I do like pleasure!"

"Come! that's explicit at any rate," said Miss Garth. "I think Pope must have had you in his mind, when he wrote his famous lines:

"'Men some to business, some to pleasure take,
    But every woman is at heart a rake.'*

"The deuce she is!" cried Mr. Vanstone, entering the room while Miss Garth was making her quotation, with the dogs at his heels. "Well; live and learn. If you're all rakes, Miss Garth, the sexes are turned topsy-turvy with a vengeance; and the men will have nothing left for it, but to stop at home and darn the stockings.—Let's have some breakfast."

"How-d'ye-do, papa?" said Magdalen, taking Mr. Vanstone as boisterously round the neck, as if he belonged to some larger order of Newfoundland dog, and was made to be romped with at his daughter's convenience. "I'm the rake Miss Garth means; and I want to go to another concert—or a play, if you like—or a ball, if you prefer it—or, anything else in the way of amusement that puts me into a new dress, and plunges me into a crowd of people, and illuminates me with plenty of light, and sets me in a tingle of excitement all over, from head to foot. Anything will do, as long as it doesn't send us to bed at eleven o'clock."

Mr. Vanstone sat down composedly under his daughter's flow of language, like a man who was well used to verbal inundation from that quarter. "If I am to be allowed my choice of amusements next time," said the worthy gentleman, "I think a play will suit me better than a concert. The girls enjoyed themselves amazingly, my dear," he continued, addressing his wife. "More than I did, I must say. It was altogether above my mark. They played one piece of music which lasted forty minutes. It stopped three times by the way; and we all thought it was done each time, and clapped our hands, rejoiced to be rid of it. But on it went again, to our great surprise and mortification, till we gave it up in despair, and all wished ourselves at Jericho. Norah, my dear! when we had Crash-Bang for forty minutes, with three stoppages by the way, what did they call it?"

"A Symphony, papa," replied Norah.

"Yes, you darling old Goth, a Symphony by the great Beethoven!" added Magdalen. "How can you say you were not amused? Have you forgotten the yellow-looking foreign woman, with the unpronounceable name? Don't you remember the faces she made when she sang? and the way she curtseyed and curtseyed, till she cheated the foolish people into crying encore? Look here, mamma—look here, Miss Garth!"

She snatched up an empty plate from the table, to represent a sheet of music, held it before her in the established concert-room position, and produced an imitation of the unfortunate singer's grimaces and curtseyings, so accurately and quaintly true to the original, that her father roared with laughter; and even the footman (who came in at that moment, with the post-bag) rushed out of the room again, and committed the indecorum of echoing his master audibly on the other side of the door.

"Letters, papa. I want the key," said Magdalen, passing from the imitation at the breakfast-table to the post-bag on the sideboard, with the easy abruptness which characterized all her actions.

Mr. Vanstone searched his pockets and shook his head. Though his youngest daughter might resemble him in nothing else, it was easy to see where Magdalen's unmethodical habits came from.

"I dare say I have left it in the library, along with my other keys," said Mr. Vanstone. "Go and look for it, my dear."

"You really should check Magdalen," pleaded Mrs. Vanstone, addressing her husband, when her daughter had left the room. "Those habits of mimicry are growing on her; and she speaks to you with a levity which it is positively shocking to hear."

"Exactly what I have said myself, till I am tired of repeating it," remarked Miss Garth. "She treats Mr. Vanstone as if he was a kind of younger brother of hers."

"You are kind to us in everything else, papa; and you make kind allowance for Magdalen's high spirits—don't you?" said the quiet Norah, taking her father's part and her sister's, with so little show of resolution on the surface, that few observers would have been sharp enough to detect the genuine substance beneath it.

"Thank you, my dear," said good-natured Mr. Vanstone. "Thank you, for a very pretty speech. As for Magdalen," he continued, addressing his wife and Miss Garth, "she's an unbroken filly. Let her caper and kick in the paddock to her heart's content. Time enough to break her to harness, when she gets a little older."

The door opened, and Magdalen returned with the key. She unlocked the post-bag at the sideboard and poured out the letters in a heap. Sorting them gaily in less than a minute, she approached the breakfast-table with both hands full; and delivered the letters all round with the business-like rapidity of a London postman.

"Two for Norah," she announced, beginning with her sister. "Three for Miss Garth. None for mamma. One for me. And the other six all for papa. You lazy old darling, you hate answering letters, don't you?" pursued Magdalen, dropping the postman's character, and assuming the daughter's. "How you will grumble and fidget in the study! and how you will wish there were no such things as letters in the world! and how red your nice old bald head will get at the top with the worry of writing the answers; and how many of the answers you will leave until to-morrow after all! *The Bristol Theatre's open, papa*," she whispered, slily and suddenly in her father's ear; "'I saw it in the newspaper when I went to the library to get the key. Let's go to-morrow night!'"

While his daughter was chattering, Mr. Vanstone was mechanically sorting his letters. He turned over the first four, in succession, and looked carelessly at the addresses. When he came to the fifth, his attention, which had hitherto wandered towards Magdalen, suddenly became fixed on the post-mark of the letter.

Stooping over him, with her head on his shoulder, Magdalen could see the post-mark as plainly as her father saw it:—NEW ORLEANS.

"An American letter, papa!" she said. "Who do you know at New Orleans?"

Mrs. Vanstone started, and looked eagerly at her husband, the moment Magdalen spoke those words.

Mr. Vanstone said nothing. He quietly removed his daughter's arm from his neck, as if he wished to be free from all interruption. She returned accordingly to her place at the breakfast-table. Her father, with the letter in his hand, waited a little before he opened it; her mother looking at him, the while, with an eager expectant attention, which attracted Miss Garth's notice, and Norah's, as well as Magdalen's.

After a minute or more of hesitation, Mr. Vanstone opened the letter.

His face changed colour the instant he read the first lines; his cheeks fading to a dull, yellow-brown hue, which would have been ashy paleness in a less florid man; and his expression becoming saddened and overclouded in a moment. Norah and Magdalen, watching anxiously, saw nothing but the change that passed over their father. Miss Garth alone observed the effect which that change produced on the attentive mistress of the house.

It was not the effect which she, or any one, could have anticipated. Mrs. Vanstone looked excited rather than alarmed. A faint flush rose on her cheeks—her eyes brightened—she stirred the tea round and round in her cup in a restless impatient manner which was not natural to her.

Magdalen, in her capacity of spoilt child, was, as usual, the first to break the silence.

"What *is* the matter, papa?" she asked.

"Nothing," said Mr. Vanstone, sharply, without looking up at her.

"I'm sure there must be something," persisted Magdalen. "I'm sure there is bad news, papa, in that American letter."

"There is nothing in the letter that concerns *you*," said Mr. Vanstone.

It was the first direct rebuff that Magdalen had ever received from her father. She looked at him with an incredulous surprise, which would have been irresistibly absurd under less serious circumstances.

Nothing more was said. For the first time, perhaps, in their lives, the family sat round the breakfast-table in painful silence. Mr. Vanstone's hearty morning appetite, like his hearty morning spirits, was gone. He absently broke off some morsels of dry toast from the rack near him, absently finished his first cup of tea—then asked for a second, which he left before him untouched.

"Norah," he said, after an interval, "you needn't wait for me. Magdalen, my dear, you can go when you like."

His daughters rose immediately; and Miss Garth considerately followed their example. When an easy-tempered man does assert himself in his family, the rarity of the demonstration invariably has its effect; and the will of that easy-tempered man is Law.

"What can have happened?" whispered Norah, as they closed the breakfast-room door, and crossed the hall.

"What does papa mean by being cross with Me?" exclaimed Magdalen, chafing under a sense of her own injuries.

"May I ask what right you had to pry into your father's private affairs?" retorted Miss Garth.

"Right?" repeated Magdalen. "I have no secrets from papa—what business has papa to have secrets from me! I consider myself insulted."

"If you considered yourself properly reproved for not minding your own business," said the plain-spoken Miss Garth, "you would be a trifle nearer the truth. Ah! you are like all the rest of the girls in the present day. Not one in a hundred of you knows which end of her's uppermost."

The three ladies entered the morning-room; and Magdalen acknowledged Miss Garth's reproof by banging the door.

Half an hour passed, and neither Mr. Vanstone nor his wife left the breakfast-room. The servant, ignorant of what had happened, went in to clear the table—found his master and mistress seated close together in deep consultation—and immediately went out again. Another quarter of an hour elapsed before the breakfast-room door was opened, and the private conference of the husband and wife came to an end.

"I hear mamma in the hall," said Norah. "Perhaps she is coming to tell us something."

Mrs. Vanstone entered the morning-room as her daughter spoke. The colour was deeper on her cheeks, and the brightness of half-dried tears glistened in her eyes; her step was more hasty, all her movements were quicker than usual.

"I bring news, my dears, which will surprise you," she said, addressing her daughters. "Your father and I are going to London to-morrow."

Magdalen caught her mother by the arm in speechless astonishment; Miss Garth dropped her work on her lap; even the sedate Norah started to her feet, and amazedly repeated the words, "Going to London!"

"Without us?" added Magdalen.

"Your father and I are going alone," said Mrs. Vanstone. "Perhaps, for as long as three weeks—but not longer. We are going "—she hesitated —" we are going on important family business. Don't hold me, Magdalen. This is a sudden necessity—I have a great deal to do to-day—many things to set in order before to-morrow. There, there, my love, let me go."

She drew her arm away; hastily kissed her youngest daughter on the forehead; and at once left the room again. Even Magdalen saw that her mother was not to be coaxed into hearing or answering any more questions.

The morning wore on, and nothing was seen of Mr. Vanstone. With the reckless curiosity of her age and character, Magdalen, in defiance of Miss Garth's prohibition and her sister's remonstrances, determined to go to the study, and look for her father there. When she tried the door, it was locked on the inside. She said, "It's only me, papa;" and waited for the answer. "I'm busy now, my dear," was the answer. "Don't disturb me."

Mrs. Vanstone was, in another way, equally inaccessible. She remained in her own room, with the female servants about her, immersed in endless preparations for the approaching departure. The servants, little used in that family to sudden resolutions and unexpected orders, were awkward and confused in obeying directions. They ran from room to room unnecessarily, and lost time and patience in jostling each other on the stairs. If a stranger had entered the house, that day, he might have imagined that an unexpected disaster had happened in it, instead of an unexpected necessity for a journey to London. Nothing proceeded in its ordinary routine. Magdalen, who was accustomed to pass the morning at the piano, wandered restlessly about the staircases and passages, and in and out of doors when there were glimpses of fine weather. Norah, whose fondness for reading had passed into a family proverb, took up book after book from table and shelf, and laid them down again, in despair of fixing her attention. Even Miss Garth felt the all-pervading influence of the household disorganization, and sat alone by the morning-room fire, with her head shaking ominously and her work laid aside.

"Family affairs?" thought Miss Garth, pondering over Mrs. Vanstone's vague explanatory words. "I have lived twelve years at Combe-Raven; and these are the first family affairs which have got between the parents and the children, in all my experience. What does it mean? Change? I suppose I'm getting old. I don't like change."

CHAPTER II.

AT ten o'clock the next morning, Norah and Magdalen stood alone in the hall at Combe-Raven, watching the departure of the carriage which took their father and mother to the London train.

Up to the last moment, both the sisters had hoped for some explanation of that mysterious "family business" to which Mrs. Vanstone had so briefly alluded on the previous day. No such explanation had been offered. Even the agitation of the leave-taking, under circumstances entirely new in the home experience of the parents and children, had not shaken the resolute discretion of Mr. and Mrs. Vanstone. They had gone—with the warmest testimonies of affection, with farewell embraces fervently reiterated again and again—but without dropping one word, from first to last, of the nature of their errand.

As the grating sound of the carriage-wheels ceased suddenly at a turn in the road, the sisters looked one another in the face; each feeling, and each betraying in her own way, the dreary sense that she was openly excluded, for the first time, from the confidence of her parents. Norah's customary reserve strengthened into sullen silence—she sat down in one of the hall chairs, and looked out frowningly through the open house-door. Magdalen, as usual when her temper was ruffled, expressed her dissatisfaction in the plainest terms. "I don't care who knows it—I think we are both of us shamefully ill-used!" With those words, the young lady followed her sister's example, by seating herself on a hall chair, and looking aimlessly out through the open house-door.

Almost at the same moment, Miss Garth entered the hall, from the morning-room. Her quick observation showed her the necessity for interfering to some practical purpose; and her ready good sense at once pointed the way.

"Look up, both of you, if you please, and listen to me," said Miss Garth. "If we are all three to be comfortable and happy together, now we are alone, we must stick to our usual habits and go on in our regular way. There is the state of things in plain words. Accept the situation—as the French say. Here am I to set you the example. I have just ordered an excellent dinner at the customary hour. I am going to the medicine-chest, next, to physic the kitchen-maid; an unwholesome girl, whose face-ache is all stomach. In the mean time, Norah, my dear, you will find your work and your books, as usual, in the library. Magdalen, suppose you leave off tying your handkerchief into knots, and use your fingers on the keys of the piano instead? We'll lunch at one, and take the dogs out afterwards. Be as brisk and cheerful both of you as I am. Come, rouse up directly. If I see those gloomy faces any longer, as sure as my name's Garth, I'll give your mother written warning, and go back to my friends by the mixed train at twelve forty."

Concluding her address of expostulation in those terms, Miss Garth led Norah to the library door, pushed Magdalen into the morning-room, and went on her own way sternly to the regions of the medicine-chest.

In this half-jesting, half-earnest manner, she was accustomed to maintain a sort of friendly authority over Mr. Vanstone's daughters, after her proper functions as governess had necessarily come to an end. Norah, it is needless to say, had long since ceased to be her pupil; and Magdalen had, by this time, completed her education. But Miss Garth had lived too long and too intimately under Mr. Vanstone's roof to be parted with, for any purely formal considerations; and the first hint at going away which she had thought it her duty to drop, was dismissed with such affectionate warmth of protest, that she never repeated it again, except in jest. The entire management of the household was, from that time forth, left in her hands; and to those duties she was free to add what companionable assistance she could render to Norah's reading, and what friendly superintendence she could still exercise over Magdalen's music. Such were the terms on which Miss Garth was now a resident in Mr. Vanstone's family.

Towards the afternoon the weather improved. At half-past one the sun was shining brightly; and the ladies left the house, accompanied by the dogs, to set forth on their walk.

They crossed the stream, and ascended by the little rocky pass to the hills beyond; then diverged to the left, and returned by a cross-road which led through the village of Combe-Raven.

As they came in sight of the first cottages, they passed a man, hanging about the road, who looked attentively, first at Magdalen, then at Norah. They merely observed that he was short, that he was dressed in black, and that he was a total stranger to them—and continued their homeward walk, without thinking more about the loitering foot-passenger whom they had met on their way back.

After they had left the village, and had entered the road which led straight to the house, Magdalen surprised Miss Garth by announcing that the stranger in black had turned, after they had passed him, and was now following them. "He keeps on Norah's side of the road," she added, mischievously. "I'm not the attraction—don't blame *me*."

Whether the man was really following them, or not, made little difference, for they were now close to the house. As they passed through the lodge-gates, Miss Garth looked round, and saw that the stranger was quickening his pace, apparently with the purpose of entering into conversation. Seeing this, she at once directed the young ladies to go on to the house with the dogs, while she herself waited for events at the gate.

There was just time to complete this discreet arrangement, before the stranger reached the lodge. He took off his hat to Miss Garth politely, as she turned round. What did he look like, on the face of him? He looked like a clergyman in difficulties.

Taking his portrait, from top to toe, the picture of him began with a tall hat, broadly encircled by a mourning band of crumpled crape. Below the hat was a lean, long, sallow face, deeply pitted with the small-pox, and characterized, very remarkably, by eyes of two different colours—one bilious green, one bilious brown, both sharply intelligent. His hair was iron-grey, carefully brushed round at the temples. His cheeks and chin were in the bluest bloom of smooth shaving; his nose was short Roman; his lips long, thin, and supple, curled up at the corners with a mildly-humorous smile. His white cravat was high, stiff, and dingy; the collar, higher, stiffer, and dingier, projected its rigid points on either side beyond his chin. Lower down, the lithe little figure of the man was arrayed throughout in sober-shabby black. His frock-coat was buttoned tight round the waist, and left to bulge open majestically at the chest. His hands were covered with black cotton gloves, neatly darned at the fingers; his umbrella, worn down at the ferule to the last quarter of an inch, was carefully preserved, nevertheless, in an oilskin case. The front view of him was the view in which he looked oldest; meeting him face to face, he might have been estimated at fifty or more. Walking behind him, his back and shoulders were almost young enough to have passed for five-and-thirty. His manners were distinguished by a grave serenity. When he opened his lips, he spoke in a rich bass voice, with an easy flow of language, and a strict attention to the elocutionary claims of words in more than one syllable. Persuasion distilled from his mildly-curling lips; and, shabby as he was, perennial flowers of courtesy bloomed all over him from head to foot.

"This is the residence of Mr. Vanstone, I believe?" he began, with a circular wave of his hand in the direction of the house. "Have I the honour of addressing a member of Mr. Vanstone's family?"

"Yes," said the plain-spoken Miss Garth. "You are addressing Mr. Vanstone's governess."

The persuasive man fell back a step—admired Mr. Vanstone's governess—advanced a step again—and continued the conversation.

"And the two young ladies," he went on, "the two young ladies who were walking with you, are doubtless Mr. Vanstone's daughters? I recognized the darker of the two, and the elder as I apprehend, by her likeness to her handsome mother. The younger lady——"

"You are acquainted with Mrs. Vanstone, I suppose?" said Miss Garth, interrupting the stranger's flow of language, which, all things considered, was beginning, in her opinion, to flow rather freely. The stranger acknowledged the interruption by one of his polite bows, and submerged Miss Garth in his next sentence as if nothing had happened.

"The younger lady," he proceeded, "takes after her father, I presume? I assure you, her face struck me. Looking at it with my friendly interest in the family, I thought it very remarkable. I said to myself—Charming, Characteristic, Memorable. Not like her sister, not like her mother. No doubt, the image of her father?"

Once more Miss Garth attempted to stem the man's flow of words. It was plain that he did not know Mr. Vanstone, even by sight—otherwise, he would never have committed the error of supposing that Magdalen took after her father. Did he know Mrs. Vanstone any better? He had left Miss Garth's question on that point unanswered. In the name of wonder, who was he? Powers of impudence! what did he want?

"You may be a friend of the family, though I don't remember your face," said Miss Garth. "What may your commands be, if you please? Did you come here to pay Mrs. Vanstone a visit?"

"I had anticipated the pleasure of communicating with Mrs. Vanstone," answered this inveterately evasive and inveterately civil man. "How is she?"

"Much as usual," said Miss Garth, feeling her resources of politeness fast failing her.

"Is she at home?"

"No."

"Out for long?"

"Gone to London with Mr. Vanstone."

The man's long face suddenly grew longer. His bilious brown eye looked disconcerted, and his bilious green eye followed its example. His manner became palpably anxious; and his choice of words was more carefully selected than ever.

"Is Mrs. Vanstone's absence likely to extend over any very lengthened period?" he inquired.

"It will extend over three weeks," replied Miss Garth. "I think you have now asked me questions enough," she went on, beginning to let her temper get the better of her at last. "Be so good, if you please, as to mention your business and your name. If you have any message to leave for Mrs. Vanstone, I shall be writing to her by to-night's post, and I can take charge of it."

"A thousand thanks! A most valuable suggestion. Permit me to take advantage of it immediately."

He was not in the least affected by the severity of Miss Garth's looks and language—he was simply relieved by her proposal, and he showed it with the most engaging sincerity. This time, his bilious green eye took the initiative, and set his bilious brown eye the example of recovered serenity. His curling lips took a new twist upwards; he tucked his umbrella briskly under his arm; and produced from the breast of his coat a large old-fashioned black pocket-book. From this he took a pencil and a card—hesitated and considered for a moment—wrote rapidly on the card—and placed it, with the politest alacrity, in Miss Garth's hand.

"I shall feel personally obliged, if you will honour me by enclosing that card in your letter," he said. "There is no necessity for my troubling you additionally with a message. My name will be quite sufficient to recall a little family matter to Mrs. Vanstone, which has no doubt escaped her memory. Accept my best thanks. This has been a day of agreeable surprises to me. I have found the country hereabouts remarkably pretty; I have seen Mrs. Vanstone's two charming daughters; I have become acquainted with an honoured preceptress in Mr. Vanstone's family. I congratulate myself—I apologize for occupying your valuable time—I beg my renewed acknowledgments—I wish you good morning."

He raised his tall hat. His brown eye twinkled, his green eye twinkled, his curly lips smiled sweetly. In a moment, he turned on his heel. His youthful back appeared to the best advantage; his active little legs took him away trippingly in the direction of the village. One, two, three—and he reached the turn in the road. Four, five, six—and he was gone.

Miss Garth looked down at the card in her hand, and looked up again in blank astonishment. The name and address of the clerical-looking stranger (both written in pencil) ran as follows:—

Captain Wragge.   Post-office, Bristol.

CHAPTER III.

WHEN she returned to the house, Miss Garth made no attempt to conceal her unfavourable opinion of the stranger in black. His object was, no doubt, to obtain pecuniary assistance from Mrs. Vanstone. What the nature of his claim on her might be, seemed less intelligible—unless it was the claim of a poor relation. Had Mrs. Vanstone ever mentioned, in the presence of her daughters, the name of Captain Wragge? Neither of them recollected to have heard it before. Had Mrs. Vanstone ever referred to any poor relations who were dependent on her? On the contrary, she had mentioned of late years that she doubted having any relations at all who were still living. And yet, Captain Wragge had plainly declared that the name on his card would recall "a family matter" to Mrs. Vanstone's memory. What did it mean? A false statement, on the stranger's part, without any intelligible reason for making it? Or a second mystery, following close on the heels of the mysterious journey to London?

All the probabilities seemed to point to some hidden connection between the "family affairs" which had taken Mr. and Mrs. Vanstone so suddenly from home, and the "family matter" associated with the name of Captain Wragge. Miss Garth's doubts thronged back irresistibly on her mind, as she sealed her letter to Mrs. Vanstone, with the captain's card added by way of enclosure.

By return of post the answer arrived.

Always the earliest riser among the ladies of the house, Miss Garth was alone in the breakfast-room when the letter was brought in. Her first glance at its contents convinced her of the necessity of reading it carefully through in retirement, before any embarrassing questions could be put to her. Leaving a message with the servant requesting Norah to make the tea that morning, she went upstairs at once to the solitude and security of her own room.

Mrs. Vanstone's letter extended to some length. The first part of it referred to Captain Wragge, and entered unreservedly into all necessary explanations relating to the man himself and to the motive which had brought him to Combe-Raven.

It appeared from Mrs. Vanstone's statement that her mother had been twice married. Her mother's first husband had been a certain Doctor Wragge—a widower with young children; and one of those children was now the unmilitary-looking captain, whose address was "Post-office, Bristol." Mrs. Wragge had left no family by her first husband; and had afterwards married Mrs. Vanstone's father. Of that second marriage Mrs. Vanstone herself was the only issue. She had lost both her parents

while she was still a young woman; and, in course of years, her mother's
family connections (who were then her nearest surviving relatives) had
been one after another removed by death. She was left, at the present
writing, without a relation in the world—excepting perhaps certain cousins
whom she had never seen, and of whose existence even, at the present
moment, she possessed no positive knowledge.

Under these circumstances, what family claim had Captain Wragge on
Mrs. Vanstone?

None whatever. As the son of her mother's first husband, by that
husband's first wife, not even the widest stretch of courtesy could have
included him at any time in the list of Mrs. Vanstone's most distant
relations. Well knowing this (the letter proceeded to say), he had nevertheless persisted in forcing himself upon her as a species of family connection; and she had weakly sanctioned the intrusion, solely from the
dread that he would otherwise introduce himself to Mr. Vanstone's notice,
and take unblushing advantage of Mr. Vanstone's generosity. Shrinking,
naturally, from allowing her husband to be annoyed, and probably cheated
as well, by any person, who claimed, however preposterously, a family
connection with herself, it had been her practice, for many years past, to
assist the captain from her own purse, on the condition that he should
never come near the house, and that he should not presume to make
any application whatever to Mr. Vanstone.

Readily admitting the imprudence of this course, Mrs. Vanstone further
explained that she had perhaps been the more inclined to adopt it, through
having been always accustomed, in her early days, to see the captain living
now upon one member, and now upon another, of her mother's family.
Possessed of abilities which might have raised him to distinction, in almost
any career that he could have chosen, he had nevertheless, from his youth
upwards, been a disgrace to all his relatives. He had been expelled the
militia regiment in which he once held a commission. He had tried one
employment after another, and had discreditably failed in all. He had
lived on his wits, in the lowest and basest meaning of the phrase. He had
married a poor ignorant woman, who had served as a waitress at some low
eating-house, who had unexpectedly come into a little money, and whose
small inheritance he had mercilessly squandered to the last farthing. In
plain terms, he was an incorrigible scoundrel; and he had now added one
more to the list of his many misdemeanours, by impudently breaking the
conditions on which Mrs. Vanstone had hitherto assisted him. She had
written at once to the address indicated on his card, in such terms and to
such purpose as would prevent him, she hoped and believed, from ever
venturing near the house again. Such were the terms in which Mrs.
Vanstone concluded that first part of her letter which referred exclusively
to Captain Wragge.

Although the statement thus presented implied a weakness in Mrs. Vanstone's character which Miss Garth, after many years of intimate experience, had never detected, she accepted the explanation as a matter of course; receiving it all the more readily, inasmuch as it might, without impropriety, be communicated in substance to appease the irritated curiosity of the two young ladies. For this reason especially, she perused the first half of the letter with an agreeable sense of relief. Far different was the impression produced on her, when she advanced to the second half, and when she had read it to the end.

The second part of the letter was devoted to the subject of the journey to London.

Mrs. Vanstone began by referring to the long and intimate friendship which had existed between Miss Garth and herself. She now felt it due to that friendship to explain confidentially the motive which had induced her to leave home with her husband. Miss Garth had delicately refrained from showing it, but she must naturally have felt, and must still be feeling, great surprise at the mystery in which their departure had been involved; and she must doubtless have asked herself why Mrs. Vanstone should have been associated with family affairs which (in her independent position as to relatives) must necessarily concern Mr. Vanstone alone.

Without touching on those affairs, which it was neither desirable nor necessary to do, Mrs. Vanstone then proceeded to say that she would at once set all Miss Garth's doubts at rest, so far as they related to herself, by one plain acknowledgment. Her object in accompanying her husband to London was to see a certain celebrated physician, and to consult him privately on a very delicate and anxious matter connected with the state of her health. In plainer terms still, this anxious matter meant nothing less than the possibility that she might again become a mother.

When the doubt had first suggested itself, she had treated it as a mere delusion. The long interval that had elapsed since the birth of her last child; the serious illness which had afflicted her after the death of that child in infancy; the time of life at which she had now arrived—all inclined her to dismiss the idea as soon as it arose in her mind. It had returned again and again in spite of her. She had felt the necessity of consulting the highest medical authority; and had shrunk, at the same time, from alarming her daughters, by summoning a London physician to the house. The medical opinion, sought under the circumstances already mentioned, had now been obtained. Her doubt was confirmed as a certainty; and the result, which might be expected to take place towards the end of the summer, was, at her age and with her constitutional peculiarities, a subject for serious future anxiety, to say the least of it. The physician had done his best to encourage her; but she had understood

the drift of his questions more clearly than he supposed, and she knew that
he looked to the future with more than ordinary doubt.

Having disclosed these particulars, Mrs. Vanstone requested that they
might be kept a secret between her correspondent and herself. She had felt
unwilling to mention her suspicions to Miss Garth, until those suspicions
had been confirmed—and she now recoiled, with even greater reluctance,
from allowing her daughters to be in any way alarmed about her. It would
be best to dismiss the subject for the present, and to wait hopefully till the
summer came. In the mean time they would all, she trusted, be happily
reunited on the twenty-third of the month, which Mr. Vanstone had fixed
on as the day for their return. With this intimation, and with the
customary messages, the letter, abruptly and confusedly, came to an end.

For the first few minutes, a natural sympathy for Mrs. Vanstone was the
only feeling of which Miss Garth was conscious after she had laid the letter
down. Ere long, however, there rose obscurely on her mind a doubt which
perplexed and distressed her. Was the explanation which she had just
read, really as satisfactory and as complete as it professed to be? Testing
it plainly by facts, surely not.

On the morning of her departure, Mrs. Vanstone had unquestionably left
the house in good spirits. At her age, and in her state of health, were good
spirits compatible with such an errand to a physician as the errand on which
she was bent? Then, again, had that letter from New Orleans, which had
necessitated Mr. Vanstone's departure, no share in occasioning his wife's
departure as well? Why, otherwise, had she looked up so eagerly the
moment her daughter mentioned the post-mark. Granting the avowed
motive for her journey—did not her manner, on the morning when the
letter was opened, and again on the morning of departure, suggest the
existence of some other motive which her letter kept concealed?

If it was so, the conclusion that followed was a very distressing one.
Mrs. Vanstone, feeling what was due to her long friendship with Miss
Garth, had apparently placed the fullest confidence in her, on one subject,
by way of unsuspiciously maintaining the strictest reserve towards her on
another. Naturally frank and straightforward in all her own dealings,
Miss Garth shrank from plainly pursuing her doubts to this result: a
want of loyalty towards her tried and valued friend seemed implied in the
mere dawning of it on her mind.

She locked up the letter in her desk; roused herself resolutely to
attend to the passing interests of the day; and went down stairs again to
the breakfast-room. Amid many uncertainties, this at least was clear:
Mr. and Mrs. Vanstone were coming back on the twenty-third of the month.
Who could say what new revelations might not come back with them?

CHAPTER IV.

No new revelations came back with them : no anticipations associated with their return were realized. On the one forbidden subject of their errand in London, there was no moving either the master or the mistress of the house. Whatever their object might have been, they had to all appearance successfully accomplished it—for they both returned in perfect possession of their every-day looks and manners. Mrs. Vanstone's spirits had subsided to their natural quiet level; Mr. Vanstone's imperturbable cheerfulness sat as easily and indolently on him as usual. This was the one noticeable result of their journey—this, and no more. Had the household revolution run its course already ? Was the secret, thus far hidden impenetrably, hidden for ever ?

Nothing in this world is hidden for ever. The gold which has lain for centuries unsuspected in the ground, reveals itself one day on the surface. Sand turns traitor, and betrays the footstep that has passed over it; water gives back to the tell-tale surface the body that has been drowned. Fire itself leaves the confession, in ashes, of the substance consumed in it. Hate breaks its prison-secrecy in the thoughts, through the doorway of the eyes; and Love finds the Judas who betrays it by a kiss. Look where we will, the inevitable law of revelation is one of the laws of nature : the lasting preservation of a secret is a miracle which the world has never yet seen.

How was the secret now hidden in the household at Combe-Raven doomed to disclose itself ? Through what coming event in the daily lives of the father, the mother, and the daughters, was the law of revelation destined to break the fatal way to discovery ? The way opened (unseen by the parents, and unsuspected by the children) through the first event that happened after Mr. and Mrs. Vanstone's return—an event which presented, on the surface of it, no interest of greater importance than the trivial social ceremony of a morning call.

Three days after the master and mistress of Combe-Raven had come back, the female members of the family happened to be assembled together in the morning-room. The view from the windows looked over the flower-garden and shrubbery ; this last being protected at its outward extremity by a fence, and approached from the lane beyond by a wicket-gate. During an interval in the conversation, the attention of the ladies was suddenly attracted to this gate, by the sharp sound of the iron latch falling in its socket. Some one had entered the shrubbery from the lane ; and Magdalen at once placed herself at the window to catch the first sight of the visitor through the trees.

After a few minutes, the figure of a gentleman became visible, at the point where the shrubbery path joined the winding garden-walk which led to the house. Magdalen looked at him attentively, without appearing, at first, to know who he was. As he came nearer, however, she started in astonishment; and turning quickly to her mother and sister, proclaimed the gentleman in the garden to be no other than "Mr. Francis Clare."

The visitor thus announced, was the son of Mr. Vanstone's oldest associate and nearest neighbour.

Mr. Clare the elder inhabited an unpretending little cottage, situated just outside the shrubbery-fence which marked the limit of the Combe-Raven grounds. Belonging to the younger branch of a family of great antiquity, the one inheritance of importance that he had derived from his ancestors, was the possession of a magnificent library, which not only filled all the rooms in his modest little dwelling, but lined the staircases and passages as well. Mr. Clare's books represented the one important interest of Mr. Clare's life. He had been a widower for many years past, and made no secret of his philosophical resignation to the loss of his wife. As a father, he regarded his family of three sons in the light of a necessary domestic evil, which perpetually threatened the sanctity of his study and the safety of his books. When the boys went to school, Mr. Clare said "good-bye" to them—and "thank God" to himself. As for his small income, and his still smaller domestic establishment, he looked at them both from the same satirically indifferent point of view. He called himself a pauper with a pedigree. He abandoned the entire direction of his household to the slatternly old woman who was his only servant, on the condition that she was never to venture near his books, with a duster in her hand, from one year's end to the other. His favourite poets were Horace and Pope; his chosen philosophers, Hobbes and Voltaire. He took his exercise and his fresh air under protest; and always walked the same distance to a yard, on the ugliest high-road in the neighbourhood. He was crooked of back, and quick of temper. He could digest radishes, and sleep after green tea. His views of human nature were the views of Diogenes, tempered by Rochefoucault;* his personal habits were slovenly in the last degree; and his favourite boast was that he had outlived all human prejudices.

Such was this singular man, in his more superficial aspects. What nobler qualities he might possess below the surface, no one had ever discovered. Mr. Vanstone, it is true, stoutly asserted that "Mr. Clare's worst side was his outside"—but, in this expression of opinion, he stood alone among his neighbours. The association between these two widely-dissimilar men had lasted for many years, and was almost close enough to be called a friendship. They had acquired a habit of meeting to smoke together on certain evenings in the week, in the cynic-philosopher's study, and of there disputing on every imaginable subject—Mr. Vanstone flourishing the stout cudgels of assertion, and Mr. Clare meeting him with the keen edged-tools of sophistry. They generally quarrelled at night, and met on the neutral ground of the shrubbery to be reconciled together the next morning. The bond of intercourse thus curiously established between them, was strengthened on Mr. Vanstone's side by a hearty interest in his neighbour's three sons—an interest by which those sons benefited all the more importantly, seeing that one of the prejudices which their father had outlived, was a prejudice in favour of his own children.

"I look at those boys," the philosopher was accustomed to say, "with a perfectly impartial eye; I dismiss the unimportant accident of their birth from all consideration; and I find them below the average in every respect. The only excuse which a poor gentleman has for presuming to exist in the nineteenth century, is the excuse of extraordinary ability. My boys have been addle-headed from infancy. If I had any capital to give them, I should make Frank a butcher, Cecil a baker, and Arthur a grocer—those being the only human vocations I know of which are certain to be always in request. As it is, I have no money to help them with; and they have no brains to help themselves. They appear to me to be three human superfluities in dirty jackets and noisy boots; and, unless they clear themselves off the community by running away, I don't myself profess to see what is to be done with them."

Fortunately for the boys, Mr. Vanstone's views were still fast imprisoned in the ordinary prejudices. At his intercession, and through his influence, Frank, Cecil, and Arthur were received on the foundation of a well-reputed grammar-school.* In holiday time they were mercifully allowed the run of Mr. Vanstone's paddock; and were humanized and refined by association, indoors, with Mrs. Vanstone and her daughters. On these occasions, Mr. Clare used sometimes to walk across from his cottage (in his dressing-gown and slippers), and look at the boys disparagingly, through the window or over the fence, as if they were three wild animals whom his neighbour was attempting to tame. "You and your wife are excellent people," he used to say to Mr. Vanstone. "I respect your honest prejudices in favour of those boys of mine with all my heart. But you are *so* wrong about them—you are indeed! I wish to give no offence; I speak quite impartially—but mark my words, Vanstone: they'll all three turn out ill, in spite of everything you can do to prevent it."

In later years, when Frank had reached the age of seventeen, the same curious shifting of the relative positions of parent and friend between the two neighbours, was exemplified more absurdly than ever. A civil engineer in the north of England, who owed certain obligations to Mr. Vanstone,

expressed his willingness to take Frank under superintendence, on terms of
the most favourable kind. When this proposal was received, Mr. Clare, as
usual, first shifted his own character as Frank's father on Mr. Vanstone's
shoulders—and then moderated his neighbour's parental enthusiasm from
the point of view of an impartial spectator.

"It's the finest chance for Frank that could possibly have happened,"
cried Mr. Vanstone, in a glow of fatherly enthusiasm.

"My good fellow, he won't take it," retorted Mr. Clare, with the icy
composure of a disinterested friend.

"But he *shall* take it," persisted Mr. Vanstone.

"Say he shall have a mathematical head," rejoined Mr. Clare; "say he
shall possess industry, ambition, and firmness of purpose. Pooh! pooh!
you don't look at him with my impartial eyes. I say, No mathematics,
no industry, no ambition, no firmness of purpose. Frank is a compound of
negatives—and there they are."

"Hang your negatives!" shouted Mr. Vanstone. "I don't care a rush
for negatives, or affirmatives either. Frank shall have this splendid
chance; and I'll lay you any wager you like he makes the best of it."

"I am not rich enough to lay wagers usually," replied Mr. Clare; "but
I think I have got a guinea about the house somewhere; and I'll lay you
that guinea Frank comes back on our hands like a bad shilling."

"Done!" said Mr. Vanstone. "No: stop a minute! I won't do the
lad's character the injustice of backing it at even money. I'll lay you five
to one Frank turns up trumps in this business! You ought to be ashamed
of yourself for talking of him as you do. What sort of hocus-pocus you
bring it about by, I don't pretend to know; but you always end in making
me take his part, as if I was his father instead of you. Ah, yes! give you
time, and you'll defend yourself. I won't give you time; I won't have
any of your special-pleading. Black's white according to you. I don't
care: it's black for all that. You may talk nineteen to the dozen—·I shall
write to my friend and say Yes, in Frank's interests, by to-day's post."

Such were the circumstances under which Mr. Francis Clare departed
for the north of England, at the age of seventeen, to start in life as a civil
engineer.

From time to time, Mr. Vanstone's friend communicated with him on
the subject of the new pupil. Frank was praised, as a quiet, gentlemanlike, interesting lad—but he was also reported to be rather slow at acquir-
ing the rudiments of engineering science. Other letters, later in date,
described him as a little too ready to despond about himself; as having
been sent away, on that account, to some new railway works, to see if
change of scene would rouse him; and as having benefited in every respect
by the experiment—except perhaps in regard to his professional studies,
which still advanced but slowly. Subsequent communications announced

his departure, under care of a trustworthy foreman, for some public works in Belgium; touched on the general benefit he appeared to derive from this new change; praised his excellent manners and address, which were of great assistance in facilitating business communications with the foreigners —and passed over in ominous silence the main question of his actual progress in the acquirement of knowledge. These reports, and many others which resembled them, were all conscientiously presented by Frank's friend to the attention of Frank's father. On each occasion, Mr. Clare exulted over Mr. Vanstone; and Mr. Vanstone quarrelled with Mr. Clare. "One of these days, you'll wish you hadn't laid that wager," said the cynic philosopher. "One of these days, I shall have the blessed satisfaction of pocketing your guinea," cried the sanguine friend. Two years had then passed since Frank's departure. In one year more, results asserted themselves, and settled the question.

Two days after Mr. Vanstone's return from London, he was called away from the breakfast-table before he had found time enough to look over his letters, delivered by the morning's post. Thrusting them into one of the pockets of his shooting-jacket, he took the letters out again, at one grasp, to read them when occasion served, later in the day. The grasp included the whole correspondence, with one exception—that exception being a final report from the civil engineer, which notified the termination of the connection between his pupil and himself, and the immediate return of Frank to his father's house.

While this important announcement lay unsuspected in Mr. Vanstone's pocket, the object of it was travelling home, as fast as railways could take him. At half-past ten at night, while Mr. Clare was sitting in studious solitude over his books and his green tea, with his favourite black cat to keep him company, he heard footsteps in the passage—the door opened—and Frank stood before him.

Ordinary men would have been astonished. But the philosopher's composure was not to be shaken by any such trifle as the unexpected return of his eldest son. He could not have looked up more calmly from his learned volume, if Frank had been absent for three minutes instead of three years.

"Exactly what I predicted," said Mr. Clare. "Don't interrupt me by making explanations; and don't frighten the cat. If there is anything to eat in the kitchen, get it and go to bed. You can walk over to Combe-Raven to-morrow, and give this message from me to Mr. Vanstone:— 'Father's compliments, sir, and I have come back upon your hands like a bad shilling, as he always said I should. He keeps his own guinea, and takes your five; and he hopes you'll mind what he says to you another time.' That is the message. Shut the door after you. Good-night."

Under these unfavourable auspices, Mr. Francis Clare made his appearance the next morning in the grounds at Combe-Raven; and, something doubtful of the reception that might await him, slowly approached the precincts of the house.

It was not wonderful that Magdalen should have failed to recognize him when he first appeared in view. He had gone away a backward lad of seventeen; he returned a young man of twenty. His slim figure had now acquired strength and grace, and had increased in stature to the medium height. The small regular features, which he was supposed to have inherited from his mother, were rounded and filled out, without having lost their remarkable delicacy of form. His beard was still in its infancy; and nascent lines of whisker traced their modest way sparely down his cheeks. His gentle wandering brown eyes would have looked to better advantage in a woman's face—they wanted spirit and firmness to fit them for the face of a man. His hands had the same wandering habit as his eyes; they were constantly changing from one position to another, constantly twisting and turning any little stray thing they could pick up. He was undeniably handsome, graceful, well bred—but no close observer could look at him, without suspecting that the stout old family stock had begun to wear out in the later generations, and that Mr. Francis Clare had more in him of the shadow of his ancestors than of the substance.

When the astonishment caused by his appearance had partially subsided, a search was instituted for the missing report. It was found in the remotest recesses of Mr. Vanstone's capacious pocket, and was read by that gentleman on the spot.

The plain facts, as stated by the engineer, were briefly these. Frank was not possessed of the necessary abilities to fit him for his new calling; and it was useless to waste time, by keeping him any longer in an employment for which he had no vocation. This, after three years' trial, being the conviction on both sides, the master had thought it the most straightforward course for the pupil to go home, and candidly place results before his father and his friends. In some other pursuit, for which he was more fit and in which he could feel an interest, he would no doubt display the industry and perseverance which he had been too much discouraged to practise in the profession that he had now abandoned. Personally, he was liked by all who knew him; and his future prosperity was heartily desired by the many friends whom he had made in the north. Such was the substance of the report, and so it came to an end.

Many men would have thought the engineer's statement rather too carefully worded; and, suspecting him of trying to make the best of a bad case, would have entertained serious doubts on the subject of Frank's future. Mr. Vanstone was too easy-tempered and sanguine—and too anxious as well, not to yield his old antagonist an inch more ground than he could help—to look at the letter from any such unfavourable point of view. Was it Frank's fault if he had not got the stuff in him that engineers were made of? Did no other young men ever begin life with a false start? Plenty began in that way, and got over it, and did wonders afterwards. With these commentaries on the letter, the kind-hearted gentleman patted Frank on the shoulder. "Cheer up, my lad!" said Mr. Vanstone. "We will be even with your father one of these days, though he *has* won the wager this time!"

The example thus set by the master of the house, was followed at once by the family—with the solitary exception of Norah, whose incurable formality and reserve expressed themselves, not too graciously, in her distant manner towards the visitor. The rest, led by Magdalen (who had been Frank's favourite playfellow in past times) glided back into their old easy habits with him, without an effort. He was "Frank" with all of them but Norah, who persisted in addressing him as "Mr. Clare." Even the account he was now encouraged to give of the reception accorded to him by his father, on the previous night, failed to disturb Norah's gravity. She sat with her dark handsome face steadily averted, her eyes cast down, and the rich colour in her cheeks warmer and deeper than usual. All the rest, Miss Garth included, found old Mr. Clare's speech of welcome to his son, quite irresistible. The noise and merriment were at their height, when the servant came in, and struck the whole party dumb by the announcement of visitors in the drawing-room. "Mr. Marrable, Mrs. Marrable, and Miss Marrable; Evergreen Lodge, Clifton."

Norah rose as readily as if the new arrivals had been a relief to her mind. Mrs. Vanstone was the next to leave her chair. These two went away first, to receive the visitors. Magdalen, who preferred the society of her father and Frank, pleaded hard to be left behind; but Miss Garth, after granting five minutes' grace, took her into custody, and marched her out of the room. Frank rose to take his leave.

"No, no," said Mr. Vanstone, detaining him. "Don't go. These people won't stop long. Mr. Marrable's a merchant at Bristol. I've met him once or twice, when the girls forced me to take them to parties at Clifton. Mere acquaintances, nothing more. Come and smoke a cigar in the greenhouse. Hang all visitors—they worry one's life out. I'll appear at the last moment with an apology; and you shall follow me at a safe distance, and be a proof that I was really engaged."

Proposing this ingenious stratagem, in a confidential whisper, Mr. Vanstone took Frank's arm, and led him round the house by the back way. The first ten minutes of seclusion in the conservatory, passed without events of any kind. At the end of that time, a flying figure in bright garments, flashed upon the two gentlemen through the glass—the door was flung open—flower-pots fell in homage to passing petticoats—and Mr. Vanstone's youngest daughter ran up to him at headlong speed, with every external appearance of having suddenly taken leave of her senses.

"Papa! the dream of my whole life is realized," she said, as soon as she could speak. "I shall fly through the roof of the greenhouse, if somebody doesn't hold me down. The Marrables have come here with an invitation. Guess, you darling—guess what they're going to give at Evergreen Lodge!"

"A ball," said Mr. Vanstone, without a moment's hesitation.

"Private Theatricals!!!" cried Magdalen, her clear young voice ringing through the conservatory like a bell; her loose sleeves falling back, and showing her round white arms to the dimpled elbows, as she clapped her hands ecstatically in the air. "The Rivals, is the play, papa—the Rivals by the famous what's-his-name*—and they want ME to act! The one thing in the whole universe that I long to do most. It all depends on you. Mamma shakes her head; and Miss Garth looks daggers; and Norah's as sulky as usual—but if you say Yes, they must all three give way, and let me do as I like. Say yes," she pleaded, nestling softly up to her father, and pressing her lips with a fond gentleness to his ear, as she whispered the next words. "Say Yes—and I'll be a good girl for the rest of my life."

"A good girl?" repeated Mr. Vanstone—"A mad girl, I think you must mean. Hang these people, and their theatricals! I shall have to go indoors, and see about this matter. You needn't throw away your cigar, Frank. You're well out of the business, and you can stop here."

"No, he can't," said Magdalen. "He's in the business, too."

Mr. Francis Clare had hitherto remained modestly in the background. He now came forward, with a face expressive of speechless amazement.

"Yes," continued Magdalen, answering his blank look of inquiry with perfect composure. "You are to act. Miss Marrable and I have a turn for business, and we settled it all in five minutes. There are two parts in the play left to be filled. One is Lucy, the waiting-maid; which is the character I have undertaken—with papa's permission," she added, slily pinching her father's arm; "and he won't say No, will he? First, because he's a darling; secondly, because I love him, and he loves me; thirdly, because there is never any difference of opinion between us (is there?); fourthly, because I give him a kiss, which naturally stops his mouth and settles the whole question. Dear me, I'm wandering. Where was I just now? Oh, yes! explaining myself to Frank——"

"I beg your pardon," began Frank, attempting, at this point, to enter his protest.

"The second character in the play," pursued Magdalen, without taking the smallest notice of the protest, "is Falkland—a jealous lover, with a fine flow of language. Miss Marrable and I discussed Falkland privately on the window-seat while the rest were talking. She is a delightful girl—so impulsive, so sensible, so entirely unaffected. She confided in me. She said, 'One of our miseries is that we can't find a gentleman who will grapple with the hideous difficulties of Falkland.' Of course I soothed her. Of course I said, 'I've got the gentleman, and he shall grapple immediately.' —'Oh heavens! who is he?'—'Mr. Francis Clare.'—'And where is he?' —'In the house at this moment.'—'Will you be so very charming, Miss Vanstone, as to fetch him?'—'I'll fetch him, Miss Marrable, with the greatest pleasure.' I left the window-seat—I rushed into the morning-room—I smelt cigars—I followed the smell—and here I am."

"It's a compliment, I know, to be asked to act," said Frank, in great embarrassment. "But I hope you and Miss Marrable will excuse me——"

"Certainly not. Miss Marrable and I are both remarkable for the firmness of our characters. When we say Mr. So-and-So is positively to act the part of Falkland, we positively mean it. Come in, and be introduced."

"But I never tried to act. I don't know how."

"Not of the slightest consequence. If you don't know how, come to me, and I'll teach you."

"You!" exclaimed Mr. Vanstone. "What do you know about it?"

"Pray, papa, be serious! I have the strongest internal conviction that I could act every character in the play—Falkland included. Don't let me have to speak a second time, Frank. Come and be introduced."

She took her father's arm, and moved on with him to the door of the greenhouse. At the steps, she turned and looked round to see if Frank was following her. It was only the action of a moment; but in that moment her natural firmness of will rallied all its resources—strengthened itself with the influence of her beauty—commanded—and conquered. She looked lovely: the flush was tenderly bright in her cheeks; the radiant pleasure shone and sparkled in her eyes; the position of her figure, turned suddenly from the waist upwards, disclosed its delicate strength, its supple firmness, its seductive serpentine grace. "Come!" she said, with a co-quettish beckoning action of her head. "Come, Frank!"

Few men of forty would have resisted her, at that moment. Frank was twenty last birthday. In other words, he threw aside his cigar, and followed her out of the greenhouse.

As he turned, and closed the door—in the instant when he lost sight of her—his disinclination to be associated with the private theatricals revived. At the foot of the house-steps he stopped again; plucked a twig from a plant near him; broke it in his hand; and looked about him uneasily, on this side, and on that. The path to the left led back to his father's cottage—the way of escape lay open. Why not take it?

While he still hesitated, Mr. Vanstone and his daughter reached the top of the steps. Once more, Magdalen looked round; looked with her resistless beauty, with her all-conquering smile. She beckoned again; and again he followed her—up the steps, and over the threshold. The door closed on them.

So, with a trifling gesture of invitation on one side, with a trifling act of compliance on the other: so—with no knowledge in his mind, with no thought in hers, of the secret still hidden under the journey to London—they took the way which led to that secret's discovery, through many a darker winding that was yet to come.

CHAPTER V.

MR. VANSTONE's inquiries into the proposed theatrical entertainment at Evergreen Lodge were answered by a narrative of dramatic disasters; of which Miss Marrable impersonated the innocent cause, and in which her father and mother played the parts of chief victims.

Miss Marrable was that hardest of all born tyrants—an only child. She had never granted a constitutional privilege to her oppressed father and mother, since the time when she cut her first tooth. Her seventeenth birthday was now near at hand; she had decided on celebrating it by acting a play; had issued her orders accordingly; and had been obeyed by her docile parents as implicitly as usual. Mrs. Marrable gave up the drawing-room to be laid waste for a stage and a theatre. Mr. Marrable secured the services of a respectable professional person to drill the young ladies and gentlemen, and to accept all the other responsibilities, incidental to creating a dramatic world out of a domestic chaos. Having further accustomed themselves to the breaking of furniture and the staining of walls—to thumping, tumbling, hammering, and screaming; to doors always banging, and to footsteps perpetually running up and down stairs—the nominal master and mistress of the house fondly believed that their chief troubles were over. Innocent and fatal delusion! It is one thing in private society to set up the stage and choose the play—it is another thing altogether to find the actors. Hitherto, only the small preliminary annoyances proper to the occasion had shown themselves at Evergreen Lodge. The sound and serious troubles were all to come.

"The Rivals" having been chosen as the play, Miss Marrable, as a matter of course, appropriated to herself the part of "Lydia Languish." One of her favoured swains next secured "Captain Absolute," and another laid violent hands on "Sir Lucius O'Trigger." These two were followed by an accommodating spinster-relative, who accepted the heavy dramatic responsibility of "Mrs. Malaprop"—and there the theatrical proceedings came to a pause. Nine more speaking characters were left to be fitted with representatives; and with that unavoidable necessity the serious troubles began.

All the friends of the family suddenly became unreliable people, for the first time in their lives. After encouraging the idea of the play, they declined the personal sacrifice of acting in it—or, they accepted characters, and then broke down in the effort to study them—or they volunteered to take the parts which they knew were already engaged, and declined the parts which were waiting to be acted—or they were afflicted with weak constitutions, and mischievously fell ill when they were wanted at rehearsal —or they had Puritan relatives in the background, and, after slipping into their parts cheerfully at the week's beginning, oozed out of them penitently, under serious family pressure, at the week's end. Meanwhile, the carpenters hammered and the scenes rose. Miss Marrable, whose temperament was sensitive, became hysterical under the strain of perpetual anxiety; the family doctor declined to answer for the nervous consequences if something was not done. Renewed efforts were made in every direction. Actors and actresses were sought with a desperate disregard of all considerations of personal fitness. Necessity, which knows no law, either in the drama or out of it, accepted a lad of eighteen as the representative of "Sir Anthony Absolute;" the stage-manager undertaking to supply the necessary wrinkles from the illimitable resources of theatrical art. A lady whose age was unknown, and whose personal appearance was stout—but whose heart was in the right place—volunteered to act the part of the sentimental "Julia," and brought with her the dramatic qualification of habitually wearing a wig in private life. Thanks to these vigorous measures, the play was at last supplied with representatives—always excepting the two unmanageable characters of "Lucy" the waiting-maid, and "Falkland," Julia's jealous lover. Gentlemen came; saw Julia at rehearsal; observed her stoutness and her wig; omitted to notice that her heart was in the right place; quailed at the prospect, apologized, and retired. Ladies read the part of "Lucy;" remarked that she appeared to great advantage in the first half of the play, and faded out of it altogether in the latter half; objected to pass from the notice of the audience in that manner, when all the rest had a chance of distinguishing themselves to the end; shut up the book, apologized, and retired. In eight days more the night of performance would arrive; a phalanx of social martyrs two hundred strong, had been convened to witness it; three full rehearsals were absolutely necessary; and two characters in the play were not filled yet. With this lamentable story, and with the humblest apologies for presuming on a slight acquaintance, the Marrables appeared at Combe-Raven, to appeal to the young ladies for a "Lucy," and to the universe for a "Falkland," with the mendicant pertinacity of a family in despair.

This statement of circumstances—addressed to an audience which included a father of Mr. Vanstone's disposition, and a daughter of Magdalen's temperament—produced the result which might have been anticipated from the first.

Either misinterpreting, or disregarding, the ominous silence preserved

by his wife and Miss Garth, Mr. Vanstone not only gave Magdalen permission to assist the forlorn dramatic company, but accepted an invitation
to witness the performance for Norah and himself. Mrs. Vanstone declined accompanying them on account of her health: and Miss Garth only
engaged to make one among the audience, conditionally on not being
wanted at home. The "parts" of "Lucy" and "Falkland" (which the
distressed family carried about with them everywhere, like incidental
maladies) were handed to their representatives on the spot. Frank's faint
remonstrances were rejected without a hearing; the days and hours of
rehearsal were carefully noted down on the covers of the parts; and the
Marrables took their leave, with a perfect explosion of thanks—father,
mother, and daughter sowing their expressions of gratitude broadcast, from
the drawing-room door to the garden-gates.

As soon as the carriage had driven away, Magdalen presented herself to
the general observation under an entirely new aspect.

"If any more visitors call to-day," she said, with the profoundest gravity
of look and manner, "I am not at home. This is a far more serious
matter than any of you suppose. Go somewhere by yourself, Frank, and
read over your part, and don't let your attention wander if you can possibly
help it. I shall not be accessible before the evening. If you will come
here—with papa's permission—after tea, my views on the subject of
Falkland will be at your disposal. Thomas! whatever else the gardener
does, he is not to make any floricultural noises under my window. For
the rest of the afternoon, I shall be immersed in study—and the quieter
the house is, the more obliged I shall feel to everybody."

Before Miss Garth's battery of reproof could open fire, before the first
outburst of Mr. Vanstone's hearty laughter could escape his lips, she bowed
to them with imperturbable gravity; ascended the house-steps for the first
time in her life, at a walk instead of a run; and retired then and there to
the bedroom regions. Frank's helpless astonishment at her disappearance,
added a new element of absurdity to the scene. He stood first on one leg
and then on the other; rolling and unrolling his part, and looking piteously
in the faces of the friends about him. "I know I can't do it," he said.
"May I come in after tea, and hear Magdalen's views? Thank you—I'll
look in about eight. Don't tell my father about this acting, please: I
should never hear the last of it." Those were the only words he had spirit
enough to utter. He drifted away aimlessly in the direction of the shrubbery, with the part hanging open in his hand—the most incapable of
Falklands, and the most helpless of mankind.

Frank's departure left the family by themselves, and was the signal
accordingly for an attack on Mr. Vanstone's inveterate carelessness in the
exercise of his paternal authority.

"What could you possibly be thinking of, Andrew, when you gave your consent?" said Mrs. Vanstone. "Surely my silence was a sufficient warning to you to say No?"

"A mistake, Mr. Vanstone," chimed in Miss Garth. "Made with the best intentions—but a mistake for all that."

"It may be a mistake," said Norah, taking her father's part, as usual. "But I really don't see how papa, or any one else, could have declined, under the circumstances."

"Quite right, my dear," observed Mr. Vanstone. "The circumstances, as you say, were dead against me. Here were these unfortunate people in a scrape on one side; and Magdalen, on the other, mad to act. I couldn't say I had methodistical objections—I've nothing methodistical about me. What other excuse could I make? The Marrables are respectable people, and keep the best company in Clifton. What harm can she get in their house? If you come to prudence and that sort of thing—why shouldn't Magdalen do what Miss Marrable does? There! there! let the poor things act, and amuse themselves. We were their age once—and it's no use making a fuss—and that's all I've got to say about it."

With that characteristic defence of his own conduct, Mr. Vanstone sauntered back to the greenhouse to smoke another cigar.

"I didn't say so to papa," said Norah, taking her mother's arm on the way back to the house, "but the bad result of the acting, in my opinion, will be the familiarity it is sure to encourage between Magdalen and Francis Clare."

"You are prejudiced against Frank, my love," said Mrs. Vanstone.

Norah's soft, secret, hazel eyes sank to the ground; she said no more. Her opinions were unchangeable—but she never disputed with anybody. She had the great failing of a reserved nature—the failing of obstinacy; and the great merit—the merit of silence. "What is your head running on now?" thought Miss Garth, casting a sharp look at Norah's dark, downcast face. "You're one of the impenetrable sort. Give me Magdalen, with all her perversities; I can see daylight through her. You're as dark as night."

The hours of the afternoon passed away, and still Magdalen remained shut up in her own room. No restless footsteps pattered on the stairs; no nimble tongue was heard chattering here, there, and everywhere, from the garret to the kitchen—the house seemed hardly like itself, with the one ever-disturbing element in the family serenity suddenly withdrawn from it. Anxious to witness, with her own eyes, the reality of a transformation in which past experience still inclined her to disbelieve, Miss Garth ascended to Magdalen's room, knocked twice at the door, received no answer, opened it, and looked in.

There sat Magdalen, in an arm-chair before the long looking-glass, with all her hair let down over her shoulders; absorbed in the study of her part;

and comfortably arrayed in her morning wrapper, until it was time to
dress for dinner. And there behind her sat the lady's-maid, slowly combing out the long heavy locks of her young mistress's hair, with the sleepy
resignation of a woman who had been engaged in that employment for
some hours past. The sun was shining ; and the green shutters outside the
window were closed. The dim light fell tenderly on the two quiet seated
figures ; on the little white bed, with the knots of rose-coloured ribbon
which looped up its curtains, and the bright dress for dinner laid ready
across it ; on the gaily painted bath, with its pure lining of white enamel ;
on the toilet-table with its sparkling trinkets, its crystal bottles, its silver
bell with Cupid for a handle, its litter of little luxuries that adorn the
shrine of a woman's bedchamber. The luxurious tranquillity of the scene ;
the cool fragrance of flowers and perfumes in the atmosphere ; the rapt
attitude of Magdalen, absorbed over her reading ; the monotonous regularity
of movement in the maid's hand and arm, as she drew the comb smoothly
through and through her mistress's hair—all conveyed the same soothing
impression of drowsy delicious quiet. On one side of the door were the
broad daylight, and the familiar realities of life. On the other, was the
dreamland of Elysian serenity—the sanctuary of unruffled repose.

Miss Garth paused on the threshold, and looked into the room in
silence.

Magdalen's curious fancy for having her hair combed at all times and
seasons, was among the peculiarities of her character which were notorious
to everybody in the house. It was one of her father's favourite jokes, that
she reminded him, on such occasions, of a cat having her back stroked,
and that he always expected, if the combing were only continued long
enough, to hear her *purr*. Extravagant as it may seem, the comparison
was not altogether inappropriate. The girl's fervid temperament intensified
the essentially feminine pleasure that most women feel in the passage of the
comb through their hair, to a luxury of sensation which absorbed her in
enjoyment, so serenely self-demonstrative, so drowsily deep, that it did
irresistibly suggest a pet cat's enjoyment under a caressing hand. Intimately as Miss Garth was acquainted with this peculiarity in her pupil,
she now saw it asserting itself for the first time, in association with mental
exertion of any kind on Magdalen's part. Feeling, therefore, some curiosity
to know how long the combing and the studying had gone on together,
she ventured on putting the question, first to the mistress ; and (receiving
no answer in that quarter) secondly to the maid.

"All the afternoon, Miss, off and on," was the weary answer. "Miss
Magdalen says it soothes her feelings and clears her mind."

Knowing by experience that interference would be hopeless, under these
circumstances, Miss Garth turned sharply and left the room. She smiled
when she was outside on the landing. The female mind does occasionally

—though not often—project itself into the future. Miss Garth was prophetically pitying Magdalen's unfortunate husband.

Dinner-time presented the fair student to the family eye in the same mentally absorbed aspect. On all ordinary occasions Magdalen's appetite would have terrified those feeble sentimentalists, who affect to ignore the all-important influence which female feeding exerts in the production of female beauty. On this occasion, she refused one dish after another with a resolution which implied the rarest of all modern martyrdoms—gastric martyrdom. "I have conceived the part of Lucy," she observed, with the demurest gravity. "The next difficulty is to make Frank conceive the part of Falkland. I see nothing to laugh at—you would all be serious enough if you had my responsibilities. No, papa—no wine to-day, thank you. I must keep my intelligence clear. Water, Thomas—and a little more jelly, I think, before you take it away."

When Frank presented himself in the evening, ignorant of the first elements of his part, she took him in hand, as a middle-aged schoolmistress might have taken in hand a backward little boy. The few attempts he made to vary the sternly practical nature of the evening's occupation by slipping in compliments sidelong, she put away from her with the contemptuous self-possession of a woman of twice her age. She literally forced him into his part. Her father fell asleep in his chair. Mrs. Vanstone and Miss Garth lost their interest in the proceedings, retired to the farther end of the room, and spoke together in whispers. It grew later and later ; and still Magdalen never flinched from her task—still, with equal perseverance, Norah, who had been on the watch all through the evening, kept on the watch to the end. The distrust darkened and darkened on her face as she looked at her sister and Frank ; as she saw how close they sat together, devoted to the same interest and working to the same end. The clock on the mantelpiece pointed to half-past eleven, before Lucy the resolute, permitted Falkland the helpless to shut up his task-book for the night. "She's wonderfully clever, isn't she ?" said Frank, taking leave of Mr. Vanstone at the hall-door. "I'm to come to-morrow, and hear more of her views—if you have no objection. I shall never do it ; don't tell her I said so. As fast as she teaches me one speech, the other goes out of my head. Discouraging, isn't it? Good night."

The next day but one was the day of the first full rehearsal. On the previous evening Mrs. Vanstone's spirits had been sadly depressed. At a private interview with Miss Garth, she had referred again, of her own accord, to the subject of her letter from London—had spoken self-reproachfully of her weakness in admitting Captain Wragge's impudent claim to a family connection with her—and had then reverted to the state of her health, and to the doubtful prospect that awaited her in the coming summer, in a tone of despondency which it was very distressing to hear. Anxious to cheer her spirits, Miss Garth had changed the conversation as soon as possible—had referred to the approaching theatrical performance—and had relieved Mrs. Vanstone's mind of all anxiety in that direction, by announcing her intention of accompanying Magdalen to each rehearsal, and of not losing sight of her until she was safely back again in her father's house. Accordingly, when Frank presented himself at Combe-Raven on the eventful morning, there stood Miss Garth, prepared—in the interpolated character of Argus*—to accompany Lucy and Falkland to the scene of trial. The railway conveyed the three, in excellent time, to Evergreen Lodge; and at one o'clock the rehearsal began.

CHAPTER VI.

" I hope Miss Vanstone knows her part?" whispered Mrs. Marrable, anxiously addressing herself to Miss Garth, in a corner of the theatre.

" If airs and graces make an actress, ma'am, Magdalen's performance will astonish us all." With that reply, Miss Garth took out her work, and seated herself, on guard, in the centre of the pit.

The manager perched himself, book in hand, on a stool close in front of the stage. He was an active little man, of a sweet and cheerful temper; and he gave the signal to begin, with as patient an interest in the proceedings as if they had caused him no trouble in the past, and promised him no difficulty in the future. The two characters which open the comedy of The Rivals, " Fag," and the " Coachman," appeared on the scene—looked many sizes too tall for their canvas background, which represented a " Street in Bath"—exhibited the customary inability to manage their own arms, legs, and voices—went out severally at the wrong exits—and expressed their perfect approval of results, so far, by laughing heartily behind the scenes. " Silence, gentlemen, if you please," remonstrated the cheerful manager. " As loud as you like *on* the stage, but the audience mustn't hear you *off* it. Miss Marrable ready? Miss Vanstone ready? Easy there with the ' Street in Bath ;' it's going up crooked ! Face this way, Miss Marrable ; full face, if you please. Miss Vanstone——" he checked himself suddenly. " Curious," he said, under his breath—" she fronts the audience of her own accord !" Lucy opened the scene in these words : " Indeed, ma'am, I traversed half the town in search of it: I don't believe there's a circulating library in Bath I haven't been at." The manager started in his chair. " My heart alive! she speaks out without telling !" The dialogue went on. Lucy produced the novels for Miss Lydia Languish's private reading from under her cloak. The manager rose excitably to his feet. Marvellous! No hurry with the books; no dropping them. She looked at the titles before she announced them to her mistress; she set down "Humphry Clinker" on "The Tears of Sensibility" with a smart little smack which pointed the antithesis. One moment—and she announced Julia's visit; another—and she dropped the brisk waiting-maid's curtsey; a third —and she was off the stage on the side set down for her in the book. The manager wheeled round on his stool, and looked hard at Miss Garth. "I beg your pardon, ma'am," he said. "Miss Marrable told me, before we began, that this was the young lady's first attempt. It can't be surely?"

"It is," replied Miss Garth, reflecting the manager's look of amazement on her own face. Was it possible that Magdalen's unintelligible industry in the study of her part, really sprang from a serious interest in her occupation—an interest which implied a natural fitness for it?

The rehearsal went on. The stout lady with the wig (and the excellent heart) personated the sentimental Julia from an inveterately tragic point of view, and used her handkerchief distractedly in the first scene. The spinster-relative felt Mrs. Malaprop's mistakes in language so seriously, and took such extraordinary pains with her blunders, that they sounded more like exercises in elocution than anything else. The unhappy lad who led the forlorn hope of the company, in the person of "Sir Anthony Absolute," expressed the age and irascibility of his character by tottering incessantly at the knees, and thumping the stage perpetually with his stick. Slowly and clumsily, with constant interruptions, and interminable mistakes, the first act dragged on, until Lucy appeared again to end it in soliloquy, with the confession of her assumed simplicity and the praise of her own cunning.

Here, the stage artifice of the situation presented difficulties which Magdalen had not encountered in the first scene—and here, her total want of experience led her into more than one palpable mistake. The stage-manager, with an eagerness which he had not shown in the case of any other member of the company, interfered immediately, and set her right. At one point she was to pause, and take a turn on the stage—she did it. At another, she was to stop, toss her head, and look pertly at the audience —she did it. When she took out the paper to read the list of the presents she had received, could she give it a tap with her finger (Yes)? And lead off with a little laugh (Yes—after twice trying)? Could she read the different items with a sly look at the end of each sentence, straight at the pit (Yes, straight at the pit, and as sly as you please)? The manager's cheerful face beamed with approval. He tucked the play under his arm, and clapped his hands gaily; the gentlemen, clustered together behind the scenes, followed his example; the ladies looked at each other with dawning doubts whether they had not better have left the new recruit in the retirement of private life. Too deeply absorbed in the business of the stage to heed any of them, Magdalen asked leave to repeat the soliloquy, and make quite sure of her own improvement. She went all through it again, without a mistake, this time, from beginning to end; the manager celebrating her attention to his directions by an outburst of professional approbation, which escaped him in spite of himself. "She can take a hint!" cried the little man, with a hearty smack of his hand on the prompt-book. "She's a born actress, if ever there was one yet!"

"I hope not," said Miss Garth to herself, taking up the work which had dropped into her lap, and looking down at it in some perplexity. Her worst apprehension of results in connection with the theatrical enterprise, had foreboded levity of conduct with some of the gentlemen—she had not bargained for this. Magdalen, in the capacity of a thoughtless girl, was comparatively easy to deal with. Magdalen, in the character of a born actress, threatened serious future difficulties.

The rehearsal proceeded. Lucy returned to the stage for her scenes in the second act (the last in which she appears) with Sir Lucius and Fag. Here, again, Magdalen's inexperience betrayed itself—and here once more her resolution in attacking and conquering her own mistakes astonished everybody. "Bravo!" cried the gentlemen behind the scenes, as she steadily trampled down one blunder after another. "Ridiculous!" said the ladies, "with such a small part as hers." "Heaven forgive me!" thought Miss Garth, coming round unwillingly to the general opinion. "I almost wish we were Papists, and had a convent to put her in to-morrow." One of Mr. Marrable's servants entered the theatre as that desperate aspiration escaped the governess. She instantly sent the man behind the scenes with a message:—"Miss Vanstone has done her part in the rehearsal: request her to come here, and sit by me." The servant returned with a polite apology:—"Miss Vanstone's kind love, and she begs to be excused—she's prompting Mr. Clare." She prompted him to such purpose that he actually got through his part. The performances of the other gentlemen were obtrusively imbecile. Frank was just one degree better—he was modestly incapable; and he gained by comparison. "Thanks to Miss Vanstone," observed the manager, who had heard the prompting. "She pulled him through. We shall be flat enough at night, when the drop falls on the second act, and the audience have seen the last of her. It's a thousand pities she hasn't got a better part!"

"It's a thousand mercies she's no more to do than she has," muttered Miss Garth, overhearing him. "As things are, the people can't well turn her head with applause. She's out of the play in the second act—that's one comfort!"

No well-regulated mind ever draws its inferences in a hurry; Miss Garth's mind was well regulated; therefore, logically speaking, Miss

Garth ought to have been superior to the weakness of rushing at conclusions. She had committed that error, nevertheless, under present circumstances. In plainer terms, the consoling reflection which had just
occurred to her, assumed that the play had by this time survived all its
disasters, and entered on its long-deferred career of success. The play had
done nothing of the sort. Misfortune and the Marrable family had not
parted company yet.

When the rehearsal was over, nobody observed that the stout lady with
the wig privately withdrew herself from the company; and when she was
afterwards missed from the table of refreshments, which Mr. Marrable's
hospitality kept ready spread in a room near the theatre, nobody imagined
that there was any serious reason for her absence. It was not till the
ladies and gentlemen assembled for the next rehearsal, that the true state
of the case was impressed on the minds of the company. At the appointed
hour no Julia appeared. In her stead, Mrs. Marrable portentously approached the stage, with an open letter in her hand. She was naturally a
lady of the mildest good breeding: she was mistress of every bland con-
ventionality in the English language—but disasters and dramatic influences
combined, threw even this harmless matron off her balance at last. For
the first time in her life Mrs. Marrable indulged in vehement gesture, and
used strong language. She handed the letter sternly, at arm's length, to
her daughter. "My dear," she said, with an aspect of awful composure,
"we are under a Curse." Before the amazed dramatic company could
petition for an explanation, she turned, and left the room. The manager's
professional eye followed her out respectfully—he looked as if he approved
of the exit, from a theatrical point of view.

What new misfortune had befallen the play? The last and worst of all
misfortunes had assailed it. The stout lady had resigned her part.

Not maliciously. Her heart, which had been in the right place throughout, remained inflexibly in the right place still. Her explanation of the
circumstances proved this, if nothing else did. The letter began with a
statement:—She had overheard, at the last rehearsal (quite unintentionally)
personal remarks of which she was the subject. They might, or might not
have had reference to her—Hair; and her—Figure. She would not distress Mrs. Marrable by repeating them. Neither would she mention
names, because it was foreign to her nature to make bad worse. The
only course at all consistent with her own self-respect, was to resign
her part. She enclosed it accordingly to Mrs. Marrable, with many
apologies for her presumption in undertaking a youthful character, at—
what a gentleman was pleased to term—her Age; and with what two
ladies were rude enough to characterize as her disadvantages of—Hair, and
—Figure. A younger and more attractive representative of Julia, would
no doubt be easily found. In the mean time, all persons concerned had

her full forgiveness, to which she would only beg leave to add her best and kindest wishes for the success of the play.

In four nights more the play was to be performed. If ever any human enterprise stood in need of good wishes to help it, that enterprise was un-questionably the theatrical entertainment at Evergreen Lodge!

One arm-chair was allowed on the stage; and, into that arm-chair, Miss Marrable sank, preparatory to a fit of hysterics. Magdalen stepped forward at the first convulsion; snatched the letter from Miss Marrable's hand; and stopped the threatened catastrophe.

"She's an ugly, bald-headed, malicious, middle-aged wretch," said Magdalen, tearing the letter into fragments, and tossing them over the heads of the company. "But I can tell her one thing—she sha'n't spoil the play. I'll act Julia."

"Bravo!" cried the chorus of gentlemen—the anonymous gentleman who had helped to do the mischief (otherwise Mr. Francis Clare) loudest of all

"If you want the truth, I don't shrink from owning it," continued Magdalen. "I'm one of the ladies she means. I said she had a head like a mop, and a waist like a bolster. So she has."

"I am the other lady," added the spinster-relative. "But *I* only said she was too stout for the part."

"I am the gentleman," chimed in Frank, stimulated by the force of example. "I said nothing—I only agreed with the ladies."

Here Miss Garth seized her opportunity, and addressed the stage loudly from the pit.

"Stop! stop!" she said. "You can't settle the difficulty that way. If Magdalen plays Julia, who is to play Lucy?"

Miss Marrable sank back in the arm-chair, and gave way to the second convulsion.

"Stuff and nonsense!" cried Magdalen, "the thing's simple enough. I'll act Julia and Lucy both together."

The manager was consulted on the spot. Suppressing Lucy's first entrance, and turning the short dialogue about the novels into a soliloquy for Lydia Languish, appeared to be the only changes of importance neces-sary to the accomplishment of Magdalen's project. Lucy's two telling scenes at the end of the first and second acts, were sufficiently removed from the scenes in which Julia appeared, to give time for the necessary transformations in dress. Even Miss Garth, though she tried hard to find them, could put no fresh obstacles in the way. The question was settled in five minutes, and the rehearsal went on; Magdalen learning Julia's stage situations with the book in her hand, and announcing afterwards, on the journey home, that she proposed sitting up all night to study the new part. Frank thereupon expressed his fears that she would have no time left to help him through his theatrical difficulties. She tapped him on the shoulder coquettishly with her part. "You foolish fellow, how am I to do without you? You're Julia's jealous lover; you're always making Julia cry. Come to-night, and make me cry at tea-time. You haven't got a venomous old woman in a wig to act with now. It's *my* heart you're to break—and of course I shall teach you how to do it."

The four days' interval passed busily in perpetual rehearsals, public and private. The night of performance arrived; the guests assembled; the great dramatic experiment stood on its trial. Magdalen had made the most of her opportunities; she had learnt all that the manager could teach her in the time. Miss Garth left her when the overture began, sitting apart in a corner behind the scenes, serious and silent, with her smelling-bottle in one hand, and her book in the other, resolutely training herself for the coming ordeal, to the very last.

The play began, with all the proper accompaniments of a theatrical performance in private life; with a crowded audience, an African temperature, a bursting of heated lamp-glasses, and a difficulty in drawing up the curtain. "Fag," and "the Coachman," who opened the scene, took leave of their memories as soon as they stepped on the stage; left half their dialogue unspoken; came to a dead pause; were audibly entreated by the invisible manager to "come off;" and went off accordingly, in every respect sadder and wiser men than when they went on. The next scene disclosed Miss Marrable as "Lydia Languish," gracefully seated, very pretty, beautifully dressed, accurately mistress of the smallest words in her part; possessed, in short, of every personal resource—except her voice. The ladies admired, the gentlemen applauded. Nobody heard anything, but the words "Speak up, Miss," whispered by the same voice which had already entreated Fag and the Coachman to "come off." A responsive titter rose among the younger spectators; checked immediately by magnanimous applause. The temperature of the audience was rising to Blood Heat—but the national sense of fair play was not boiled out of them yet.

In the midst of the demonstration, Magdalen quietly made her first entrance, as "Julia." She was dressed very plainly in dark colours, and wore her own hair; all stage adjuncts and alterations (excepting the slightest possible touch of rouge on her cheeks) having been kept in reserve, to disguise her the more effectually in her second part. The grace and simplicity of her costume, the steady self-possession with which she looked out over the eager rows of faces before her, raised a low hum of approval and expectation. She spoke—after suppressing a momentary tremor—with a quiet distinctness of utterance which reached all ears, and which at once confirmed the favourable impression that her appearance had produced. The one member of the audience who looked at her and

listened to her coldly, was ner elder sister. Before the actress of the
evening had been five minutes on the stage, Norah detected, to her own
indescribable astonishment, that Magdalen had audaciously individualized
the feeble amiability of "Julia's" character, by seizing no less a person
than herself as the model to act it by. She saw all her own little formal
peculiarities of manner and movement, unblushingly reproduced—and even
the very tone of her voice so accurately mimicked from time to time, that
the accents startled her as if she was speaking herself, with an echo on the
stage. The effect of this cool appropriation of Norah's identity to theatrical
purposes, on the audience—who only saw results—asserted itself in a storm
of applause on Magdalen's exit. She had won two incontestable triumphs
in her first scene. By a dexterous piece of mimicry, she had made a living
reality of one of the most insipid characters in the English drama ; and she
had roused to enthusiasm an audience of two hundred exiles from the
blessings of ventilation, all simmering together in their own animal heat.
Under the circumstances, where is the actress by profession who could
have done much more?

But the event of the evening was still to come. Magdalen's disguised
reappearance at the end of the act, in the character of "Lucy"—with false
hair and false eyebrows, with a bright-red complexion and patches on her
cheeks, with the gayest colours flaunting in her dress, and the shrillest
vivacity of voice and manner—fairly staggered the audience. They looked
down at their programmes, in which the representative of Lucy figured
under an assumed name ; looked up again at the stage ; penetrated the
disguise ; and vented their astonishment in another round of applause,
louder and heartier even than the last. Norah herself could not deny this
time, that the tribute of approbation had been well deserved. There,
forcing its way steadily through all the faults of inexperience—there,
plainly visible to the dullest of the spectators, was the rare faculty of
dramatic impersonation, expressing itself in every look and action of this
girl of eighteen, who now stood on a stage for the first time in her life.
Failing in many minor requisites of the double task which she had undertaken, she succeeded in the one important necessity of keeping the main
distinctions of the two characters thoroughly apart. Everybody felt that
the difficulty lay here—everybody saw the difficulty conquered—everybody echoed the manager's enthusiasm at rehearsal, which had hailed her
as a born actress.

When the drop-scene descended for the first time, Magdalen had concentrated in herself the whole interest and attraction of the play. The audience
politely applauded Miss Marrable, as became the guests assembled in her
father's house : and good-humouredly encouraged the remainder of the
company, to help them through a task for which they were all, more or
less, palpably unfit. But, as the play proceeded, nothing roused them to

any genuine expression of interest when Magdalen was absent from the scene. There was no disguising it : Miss Marrable and her bosom friends had been all hopelessly cast in the shade by the new recruit whom they had summoned to assist them, in the capacity of forlorn hope. And this on Miss Marrable's own birthday! and this in her father's house! and this after the unutterable sacrifices of six weeks past! Of all the domestic disasters which the thankless theatrical enterprise had inflicted on the Marrable family, the crowning misfortune was now consummated by Magdalen's success.

Leaving Mr. Vanstone and Norah, on the conclusion of the play, among the guests in the supper-room, Miss Garth went behind the scenes; ostensibly anxious to see if she could be of any use; really bent on ascertaining whether Magdalen's head had been turned by the triumphs of the evening. It would not have surprised Miss Garth if she had discovered her pupil in the act of making terms with the manager for her forthcoming appearance in a public theatre. As events really turned out, she found Magdalen on the stage, receiving, with gracious smiles, a card which the manager presented to her with a professional bow. Noticing Miss Garth's mute look of inquiry, the civil little man hastened to explain that the card was his own, and that he was merely asking the favour of Miss Vanstone's recommendation at any future opportunity.

"This is not the last time the young lady will be concerned in private theatricals, I'll answer for it," said the manager. "And if a superintendent is wanted on the next occasion, she has kindly promised to say a good word for me. I am always to be heard of, Miss, at that address." Saying those words, he bowed again, and discreetly disappeared.

Vague suspicions beset the mind of Miss Garth, and urged her to insist on looking at the card. No more harmless morsel of pasteboard was ever passed from one hand to another. The card contained nothing but the manager's name, and, under it, the name and address of a theatrical agent in London.

"It is not worth the trouble of keeping," said Miss Garth.

Magdalen caught her hand, before she could throw the card away—possessed herself of it the next instant—and put it in her pocket.

"I promised to recommend him," she said—"and that's one reason for keeping his card. If it does nothing else, it will remind me of the happiest evening of my life—and that's another. Come!" she cried, throwing her arms round Miss Garth with a feverish gaiety—"congratulate me on my success!"

"I will congratulate you when you have got over it," said Miss Garth.

In half an hour more, Magdalen had changed her dress; had joined the guests; and had soared into an atmosphere of congratulation, high above the reach of any controlling influence that Miss Garth could exercise.

Frank, dilatory in all his proceedings, was the last of the dramatic company
who left the precincts of the stage. He made no attempt to join Magdalen
in the supper-room—but he was ready in the hall, with her cloak, when the
carriages were called and the party broke up.

"Oh, Frank!" she said, looking round at him, as he put the cloak on her
shoulders, "I am so sorry it's all over! Come to-morrow morning, and
let's talk about it by ourselves."

"In the shrubbery at ten?" asked Frank in a whisper.

She drew up the hood of her cloak, and nodded to him gaily. Miss
Garth, standing near, noticed the looks that passed between them, though
the disturbance made by the parting guests prevented her from hearing
the words. There was a soft, underlying tenderness in Magdalen's assumed
gaiety of manner—there was a sudden thoughtfulness in her face, a confidential readiness in her hand, as she took Frank's arm and went out to the
carriage. What did it mean? Had her passing interest in him, as her
stage-pupil, treacherously sown the seeds of any deeper interest in him, as
a man? Had the idle theatrical scheme, now that it was all over, graver
results to answer for than a mischievous waste of time?

The lines on Miss Garth's face deepened and hardened: she stood lost
among the fluttering crowd around her. Norah's warning words, addressed
to Mrs. Vanstone in the garden, recurred to her memory—and now, for
the first time, the idea dawned on her that Norah had seen consequences in
their true light.

CHAPTER VII.

EARLY the next morning Miss Garth and Norah met in the garden, and
spoke together privately. The only noticeable result of the interview, when
they presented themselves at the breakfast-table, appeared in the marked
silence which they both maintained on the topic of the theatrical performance. Mrs. Vanstone was entirely indebted to her husband and to her
youngest daughter for all that she heard of the evening's entertainment.
The governess and the elder daughter had evidently determined on letting
the subject drop.

After breakfast was over, Magdalen proved to be missing, when the
ladies assembled as usual in the morning-room. Her habits were so little
regular that Mrs. Vanstone felt neither surprise nor uneasiness at her
absence. Miss Garth and Norah looked at one another significantly, and
waited in silence. Two hours passed—and there were no signs of Magdalen. Norah rose, as the clock struck twelve, and quietly left the room to
look for her.

She was not up-stairs, dusting her jewelry and disarranging her dresses.

She was not in the conservatory, not in the flower-garden; not in the kitchen teasing the cook; not in the yard playing with the dogs. Had she, by any chance, gone out with her father? Mr. Vanstone had announced his intention, at the breakfast-table, of paying a morning visit to his old ally, Mr. Clare, and of rousing the philosopher's sarcastic indignation by an account of the dramatic performance. None of the other ladies at Combe-Raven ever ventured themselves inside the cottage. But Magdalen was reckless enough for anything—and Magdalen might have gone there. As the idea occurred to her, Norah entered the shrubbery.

At the second turning, where the path among the trees wound away out of sight of the house, she came suddenly face to face with Magdalen and Frank : they were sauntering towards her, arm-in-arm ; their heads close together, their conversation apparently proceeding in whispers. They looked suspiciously handsome and happy. At the sight of Norah, both started, and both stopped. Frank confusedly raised his hat, and turned back in the direction of his father's cottage. Magdalen advanced to meet her sister, carelessly swinging her closed parasol from side to side, carelessly humming an air from the overture which had preceded the rising of the curtain on the previous night.

"Luncheon time already !" she said, looking at her watch. "Surely not ?"

"Have you and Mr. Francis Clare been alone in the shrubbery since ten o'clock ?" asked Norah.

"*Mr.* Francis Clare ! How ridiculously formal you are. Why don't you call him Frank ?"

"I asked you a question, Magdalen."

"Dear me, how black you look this morning ! I'm in disgrace, I suppose. Haven't you forgiven me yet for my acting last night ? I couldn't help it, love; I should have made nothing of Julia, if I hadn't taken you for my model. It's quite a question of Art. In your place, I should have felt flattered by the selection."

"In *your* place, Magdalen, I should have thought twice before I mimicked my sister to an audience of strangers."

"That's exactly why I did it—an audience of strangers. How were they to know ? Come ! come ! don't be angry. You are eight years older than I am—you ought to set me an example of good humour."

"I will set you an example of plain-speaking. I am more sorry than I can say, Magdalen, to meet you as I met you here just now !"

"What next, I wonder ? You meet me in the shrubbery at home, talking over the private theatricals with my old playfellow, whom I knew when I was no taller than this parasol. And that is a glaring impropriety, is it ? Honi soit qui mal y pense. You wanted an answer a minute ago —there it is for you, my dear, in the choicest Norman-French."

"I am in earnest about this, Magdalen——"

"Not a doubt of it. Nobody can accuse you of ever making jokes."

"I am seriously sorry——"

"Oh dear!"

"It is quite useless to interrupt me. I have it on my conscience to tell you—and I *will* tell you—that I am sorry to see how this intimacy is growing. I am sorry to see a secret understanding established already between you and Mr. Francis Clare."

"Poor Frank! How you do hate him to be sure. What on earth has he done to offend you?"

Norah's self-control began to show signs of failing her. Her dark cheeks glowed, her delicate lips trembled, before she spoke again. Magdalen paid more attention to her parasol than to her sister. She tossed it high in the air, and caught it. "Once!" she said—and tossed it up again. "Twice!"—and she tossed it higher. "Thrice——!" Before she could catch it for the third time, Norah seized her passionately by the arm, and the parasol dropped to the ground between them.

"You are treating me heartlessly," she said. "For shame, Magdalen—for shame!"

The irrepressible outburst of a reserved nature, forced into open self-assertion in its own despite, is of all moral forces the hardest to resist. Magdalen was startled into silence. For a moment, the two sisters—so strangely dissimilar in person and character—faced one another, without a word passing between them. For a moment, the deep brown eyes of the elder, and the light grey eyes of the younger, looked into each other with steady unyielding scrutiny on either side. Norah's face was the first to change; Norah's head was the first to turn away. She dropped her sister's arm, in silence. Magdalen stooped, and picked up her parasol.

"I try to keep my temper," she said, "and you call me heartless for doing it. You always were hard on me, and you always will be."

Norah clasped her trembling hands fast in each other. "Hard on you!" she said, in low, mournful tones—and sighed bitterly.

Magdalen drew back a little, and mechanically dusted the parasol with the end of her garden cloak.

"Yes!" she resumed, doggedly. "Hard on me, and hard on Frank."

"Frank!" repeated Norah, advancing on her sister, and turning pale as suddenly as she had turned red. "Do you talk of yourself and Frank as if your interests were One already? Magdalen! if I hurt *you*, do I hurt *him*? Is he so near and so dear to you as that?"

Magdalen drew farther and farther back. A twig from a tree near caught her cloak; she turned petulantly, broke it off, and threw it on the ground. "What right have you to question me?" she broke out on a sudden. "Whether I like Frank, or whether I don't, what interest is it of yours?" As she said the words, she abruptly stepped forward to pass her sister, and return to the house.

Norah, turning paler and paler, barred the way to her. "If I hold you by main force," she said, "you shall stop and hear me. I have watched this Francis Clare; I know him better than you do. He is unworthy of a moment's serious feeling on your part; he is unworthy of our dear, good, kind-hearted father's interest in him. A man with any principle, any honour, any gratitude, would not have come back as he has come back, disgraced—yes! disgraced by his spiritless neglect of his own duty. I watched his face while the friend who has been better than a father to him, was comforting and forgiving him with a kindness he had not deserved: I watched his face, and I saw no shame, and no distress in it— I saw nothing but a look of thankless, heartless relief. He is selfish, he is ungrateful, he is ungenerous—he is only twenty, and he has the worst failings of a mean old age already. And this is the man I find you meeting in secret—the man who has taken such a place in your favour that you are deaf to the truth about him, even from *my* lips! Magdalen! this will end ill. For God's sake, think of what I have said to you, and control yourself before it is too late!" She stopped, vehement and breathless, and caught her sister anxiously by the hand.

Magdalen looked at her in unconcealed astonishment.

"You are so violent," she said, "and so unlike yourself that I hardly know you. The more patient I am, the more hard words I get for my pains. You have taken a perverse hatred to Frank; and you are unreasonably angry with me, because I won't hate him too. Don't, Norah! you hurt my hand."

Norah pushed the hand from her, contemptuously. "I shall never hurt your heart," she said—and suddenly turned her back on Magdalen as she spoke the words.

There was a momentary pause. Norah kept her position. Magdalen looked at her perplexedly—hesitated—then walked away by herself towards the house.

At the turn in the shrubbery path, she stopped, and looked back uneasily. "Oh, dear, dear!" she thought to herself, "why didn't Frank go when I told him?" She hesitated, and went back a few steps. "There's Norah standing on her dignity, as obstinate as ever." She stopped again. "What had I better do? I hate quarrelling: I think I'll make it up." She ventured close to her sister, and touched her on the shoulder. Norah never moved. "It's not often she flies into a passion," thought Magdalen, touching her again; "but when she does, what a time it lasts her!— Come!" she said, "give me a kiss, Norah, and make it up. Won't you let me get at any part of you, my dear, but the back of your neck? Well, it's a very nice neck—it's better worth kissing than mine—and there the kiss is, in spite of you!"

She caught fast hold of Norah from behind, and suited the action to the word, with a total disregard of all that had just passed, which her sister was far from emulating. Hardly a minute since, the warm outpouring of Norah's heart had burst through all obstacles. Had the icy reserve frozen her up again already! It was hard to say. She never spoke; she never changed her position—she only searched hurriedly for her handkerchief. As she drew it out, there was a sound of approaching footsteps in the inner recesses of the shrubbery. A Scotch terrier scampered into view; and a cheerful voice sang the first lines of the glee in 'As You Like It.' "It's papa!" cried Magdalen. "Come, Norah—come and meet him."

Instead of following her sister, Norah pulled down the veil of her garden hat; turned in the opposite direction; and hurried back to the house.

She ran up to her own room, and locked herself in. She was crying bitterly.

CHAPTER VIII.

WHEN Magdalen and her father met in the shrubbery, Mr. Vanstone's face showed plainly that something had happened to please him, since he had left home in the morning. He answered the question which his daughter's curiosity at once addressed to him, by informing her that he had just come from Mr. Clare's cottage; and that he had picked up, in that un-promising locality, a startling piece of news for the family at Combe-Raven.

On entering the philosopher's study, that morning, Mr. Vanstone had found him still dawdling over his late breakfast, with an open letter by his side, in place of the book which, on other occasions, lay ready to his hand at meal-times. He held up the letter, the moment his visitor came into the room; and abruptly opened the conversation by asking Mr. Vanstone if his nerves were in good order, and if he felt himself strong enough for the shock of an overwhelming surprise.

"Nerves?" repeated Mr. Vanstone. "Thank God, I know nothing about my nerves. If you have got anything to tell me, shock or no shock, out with it on the spot."

Mr. Clare held the letter a little higher, and frowned at his visitor across the breakfast-table. "What have I always told you?" he asked, with his sourest solemnity of look and manner.

"A great deal more than I could ever keep in my head," answered Mr. Vanstone.

"In your presence and out of it," continued Mr. Clare, "I have always maintained that the one important phenomenon presented by modern society is—the enormous prosperity of Fools. Show me an individual Fool, and I will show you an aggregate Society which gives that highly-favoured personage nine chances out of ten—and grudges the tenth to the wisest man in existence. Look where you will, in every high place there sits an Ass, settled beyond the reach of all the greatest intellects in this world to pull him down. Over our whole social system, complacent Imbecility rules supreme—snuffs out the searching light of Intelligence, with total impunity—and hoots, owl-like, in answer to every form of protest, See how well we all do in the dark ! One of these days that audacious assertion will be practically contradicted ; and the whole rotten system of modern society will come down with a crash."

" God forbid !" cried Mr. Vanstone, looking about him as if the crash was coming already.

" With a crash !" repeated Mr. Clare. " There is my theory, in few words. Now for the remarkable application of it, which this letter suggests. Here is my lout of a boy——"

" You don't mean that Frank has got another chance !" exclaimed Mr. Vanstone.

" Here is this perfectly hopeless booby, Frank," pursued the philosopher. " He has never done anything in his life to help himself, and as a necessary consequence, Society is in a conspiracy to carry him to the top of the tree. He has hardly had time to throw away that chance you gave him, before this letter comes, and puts the ball at his foot for the second time. My rich cousin (who is intellectually fit to be at the tail of the family, and who is therefore as a matter of course, at the head of it), has been good enough to remember my existence ; and has offered his influence to serve my eldest boy. Read his letter, and then observe the sequence of events. My rich cousin is a booby who thrives on landed property ; he has done something for another booby who thrives on Politics, who knows a third booby who thrives on Commerce, who can do something for a fourth booby, thriving at present on nothing, whose name is Frank. So the mill goes. So the cream of all human rewards is sipped in endless succession by the Fools. I shall pack Frank off to-morrow. In course of time, he'll come back again on our hands like a bad shilling : more chances will fall in his way, as a necessary consequence of his meritorious imbecility. Years will go on—I may not live to see it, no more may you—it doesn't matter ; Frank's future is equally certain either way—put him into the army, the church, politics, what you please, and let him drift : he'll end in being a general, a bishop, or a minister of state, by dint of the great modern qualification of doing nothing whatever to deserve his place." With this summary of his son's worldly prospects, Mr. Clare tossed the letter contemptuously across the table, and poured himself out another cup of tea.

Mr. Vanstone read the letter with eager interest and pleasure. It was written in a tone of somewhat elaborate cordiality ; but the practical advantages which it placed at Frank's disposal were beyond all doubt. The writer had the means of using a friend's interest—interest of no ordi-

nary kind—with a great Mercantile Firm in the City; and he had at once
exerted this influence in favour of Mr. Clare's eldest boy. Frank would
be received in the office on a very different footing from the footing of an
ordinary clerk; he would be "pushed on" at every available opportunity;
and the first "good thing" the House had to offer either at home or
abroad, would be placed at his disposal. If he possessed fair abilities and
showed common diligence in exercising them, his fortune was made; and
the sooner he was sent to London to begin, the better for his own interests
it would be.

"Wonderful news!" cried Mr. Vanstone, returning the letter. "I'm
delighted—I must go back and tell them at home. This is fifty times the
chance that mine was. What the deuce do you mean by abusing Society?
Society has behaved uncommonly well, in my opinion. Where's Frank?"

"Lurking," said Mr. Clare. "It is one of the intolerable peculiarities
of louts that they always lurk. I haven't seen *my* lout this morning. If
you meet with him anywhere, give him a kick, and say I want him."

Mr. Clare's opinion of his son's habits might have been expressed more
politely as to form; but, as to substance, it happened, on that particular
morning, to be perfectly correct. After leaving Magdalen, Frank had
waited in the shrubbery, at a safe distance, on the chance that she might
detach herself from her sister's company, and join him again. Mr. Vanstone's appearance immediately on Norah's departure, instead of encouraging him to show himself, had determined him on returning to the
cottage. He walked back discontentedly; and so fell into his father's
clutches, totally unprepared for the pending announcement, in that formidable quarter, of his departure for London.

In the mean time, Mr. Vanstone had communicated his news—in the
first place, to Magdalen, and afterwards, on getting back to the house, to
his wife and Miss Garth. He was too unobservant a man to notice that
Magdalen looked unaccountably startled, and Miss Garth unaccountably
relieved, by his announcement of Frank's good fortune. He talked on
about it, quite unsuspiciously, until the luncheon-bell rang—and then, for
the first time, he noticed Norah's absence. She sent a message down
stairs, after they had assembled at the table, to say that a headache was
keeping her in her own room. When Miss Garth went up shortly afterwards to communicate the news about Frank, Norah appeared, strangely
enough, to feel very little relieved by hearing it. Mr. Francis Clare had
gone away on a former occasion (she remarked) and had come back. He
might come back again, and sooner than they any of them thought for.
She said no more on the subject than this: she made no reference to what
had taken place in the shrubbery. Her unconquerable reserve seemed to
have strengthened its hold on her since the outburst of the morning. She

met Magdalen, later in the day, as if nothing had happened: no formal reconciliation took place between them. It was one of Norah's peculiarities to shrink from all reconciliations that were openly ratified, and to take her shy refuge in reconciliations that were silently implied. Magdalen saw plainly, in her look and manner, that she had made her first and last protest. Whether the motive was pride, or sullenness, or distrust of herself, or despair of doing good, the result was not to be mistaken—Norah had resolved on remaining passive for the future.

Later in the afternoon, Mr. Vanstone suggested a drive to his eldest daughter, as the best remedy for her headache. She readily consented to accompany her father; who, thereupon, proposed, as usual, that Magdalen should join them. Magdalen was nowhere to be found. For the second time that day, she had wandered into the grounds by herself. On this occasion, Miss Garth—who, after adopting Norah's opinions, had passed from the one extreme of overlooking Frank altogether, to the other extreme of believing him capable of planning an elopement at five minutes' notice—volunteered to set forth immediately, and do her best to find the missing young lady. After a prolonged absence, she returned unsuccessful—with the strongest persuasion in her own mind that Magdalen and Frank had secretly met one another somewhere, but without having discovered the smallest fragment of evidence to confirm her suspicions. By this time, the carriage was at the door, and Mr. Vanstone was unwilling to wait any longer. He and Norah drove away together; and Mrs. Vanstone and Miss Garth sat at home over their work.

In half an hour more, Magdalen composedly walked into the room. She was pale and depressed. She received Miss Garth's remonstrances with a weary inattention; explained carelessly that she had been wandering in the wood; took up some books, and put them down again; sighed impatiently; and went away upstairs to her own room.

"I think Magdalen is feeling the reaction, after yesterday," said Mrs. Vanstone, quietly. "It is just as we thought. Now the theatrical amusements are all over, she is fretting for more."

Here was an opportunity of letting in the light of truth on Mrs. Vanstone's mind, which was too favourable to be missed. Miss Garth questioned her conscience, saw her chance, and took it on the spot.

"You forget," she rejoined, "that a certain neighbour of ours is going away to-morrow. Shall I tell you the truth? Magdalen is fretting over the departure of Francis Clare."

Mrs. Vanstone looked up from her work, with a gentle smiling surprise.

"Surely not?" she said. "It is natural enough that Frank should be attracted by Magdalen—but I can't think that Magdalen returns the feeling. Frank is so very unlike her; so quiet and undemonstrative; so dull and helpless, poor fellow, in some things. He is handsome, I know;

but he is so singularly unlike Magdalen, that I can't think it possible—I can't indeed."

"My dear good lady!" cried Miss Garth, in great amazement; "do you really suppose that people fall in love with each other on account of similarities in their characters? In the vast majority of cases, they do just the reverse. Men marry the very last women, and women the very last men, whom their friends would think it possible they could care about. Is there any phrase that is oftener on all our lips than 'What can have made Mr. So-and-So marry that woman?'—or 'How could Mrs. So-and-So throw herself away on that man?' Has all your experience of the world never yet shown you that girls take perverse fancies for men who are totally unworthy of them?"

"Very true," said Mrs. Vanstone, composedly. "I forgot that. Still it seems unaccountable, doesn't it?"

"Unaccountable, because it happens every day!" retorted Miss Garth, good-humouredly. "I know a great many excellent people who reason against plain experience in the same way—who read the newspapers in the morning, and deny in the evening that there is any romance for writers or painters to work upon in modern life. Seriously, Mrs. Vanstone, you may take my word for it—thanks to those wretched theatricals, Magdalen is going the way with Frank that a great many young ladies have gone before her. He is quite unworthy of her; he is, in almost every respect, her exact opposite—and, without knowing it herself, she has fallen in love with him on that very account. She is resolute and impetuous, clever and domineering; she is not one of those model women who want a man to look up to, and to protect them—her beau-ideal (though she may not think it herself) is a man she can henpeck. Well! one comfort is, there are far better men, even of that sort, to be had than Frank. It's a mercy he is going away, before we have more trouble with them, and before any serious mischief is done."

"Poor Frank!" said Mrs. Vanstone, smiling compassionately. "We have known him since he was in jackets, and Magdalen in short frocks. Don't let us give him up yet. He may do better this second time."

Miss Garth looked up in astonishment.

"And suppose he does better?" she asked. "What then?"

Mrs. Vanstone cut off a loose thread in her work, and laughed outright

"My good friend," she said, "there is an old farm-yard proverb which warns us not to count our chickens before they are hatched. Let us wait a little before we count ours."

It was not easy to silence Miss Garth, when she was speaking under the influence of a strong conviction; but this reply closed her lips. She resumed her work; and looked, and thought, unutterable things.

Mrs. Vanstone's behaviour was certainly remarkable under the circumstances. Here, on one side, was a girl—with great personal attractions, with rare pecuniary prospects, with a social position which might have justified the best gentleman in the neighbourhood in making her an offer of marriage—perversely casting herself away on a penniless idle young fellow, who had failed at his first start in life, and who, even if he succeeded in his second attempt, must be for years to come in no position to marry a young lady of fortune on equal terms. And there, on the other side, was that girl's mother, by no means dismayed at the prospect of a connection which was, to say the least of it, far from desirable; by no means certain, judging her by her own words and looks, that a marriage between Mr. Vanstone's daughter and Mr. Clare's son might not prove to be as satisfactory a result of the intimacy between the two young people, as the parents on both sides could possibly wish for! It was perplexing in the extreme. It was almost as unintelligible as that past mystery—that forgotten mystery now—of the journey to London.

In the evening, Frank made his appearance, and announced that his father had mercilessly sentenced him to leave Combe-Raven by the parliamentary train the next morning. He mentioned this circumstance with an air of sentimental resignation; and listened to Mr. Vanstone's boisterous rejoicings over his new prospects, with a mild and mute surprise. His gentle melancholy of look and manner greatly assisted his personal advantages. In his own effeminate way, he was more handsome than ever, that evening. His soft brown eyes wandered about the room with a melting tenderness; his hair was beautifully brushed; his delicate hands hung over the arms of his chair with a languid grace. He looked like a convalescent Apollo. Never, on any previous occasion, had he practised more successfully the social art which he habitually cultivated—the art of casting himself on society in the character of a well-bred Incubus, and conferring an obligation on his fellow-creatures by allowing them to sit under him. It was undeniably a dull evening. All the talking fell to the share of Mr. Vanstone, and Miss Garth. Mrs. Vanstone was habitually silent; Norah kept herself obstinately in the background; Magdalen was quiet and undemonstrative beyond all former precedent. From first to last, she kept rigidly on her guard. The few meaning looks that she cast on Frank, flashed at him like lightning, and were gone before any one else could see them. Even when she brought him his tea; and, when in doing so, her self-control gave way under the temptation which no woman can resist—the temptation of touching the man she loves—even then, she held the saucer so dexterously that it screened her hand. Frank's self-possession was far less steadily disciplined; it only lasted as long as he remained passive. When he rose to go; when he felt the warm clinging pressure of Magdalen's fingers round his hand, and the lock of her hair which she

slipped into it at the same moment, he became awkward and confused.
He might have betrayed Magdalen and betrayed himself, but for Mr. Vanstone, who innocently covered his retreat by following him out, and patting
him on the shoulder all the way. " God bless you, Frank !" cried the
friendly voice that never had a harsh note in it for anybody. " Your fortune's waiting for you. Go in, my boy—go in and win."

" Yes," said Frank. " Thank you. It will be rather difficult to go in
and win, at first. Of course, as you have always told me, a man's business
is to conquer his difficulties, and not to talk about them. At the same
time, I wish I didn't feel quite so loose as I do in my figures. It's discouraging to feel loose in one's figures.—Oh, yes; I'll write and tell you
how I get on. I'm very much obliged by your kindness, and very sorry I
couldn't succeed with the engineering. I think I should have liked engineering better than trade. It can't be helped now, can it? Thank you,
again. Good-bye."

So he drifted away into the misty commercial future—as aimless, as
helpless, as gentlemanlike as ever.

CHAPTER IX.

THREE months passed. During that time, Frank remained in London ;
pursuing his new duties, and writing occasionally to report himself to Mr.
Vanstone, as he had promised.

His letters were not enthusiastic on the subject of mercantile occupations.
He described himself as being still painfully loose in his figures. He was
also more firmly persuaded than ever—now when it was unfortunately too
late—that he preferred engineering to trade. In spite of this conviction ;
in spite of headaches caused by sitting on a high stool and stooping over
ledgers in unwholesome air ; in spite of want of society, and hasty breakfasts, and bad dinners at chop-houses, his attendance at the office was
regular, and his diligence at the desk unremitting. The head of the department in which he was working might be referred to if any corrobora-
tion of this statement was desired. Such was the general tenour of the
letters ; and Frank's correspondent, and Frank's father differed over them,
as widely as usual. Mr. Vanstone accepted them, as proofs of the steady
development of industrious principles in the writer. Mr. Clare took his
own characteristically opposite view. " These London men," said the
philosopher, " are not to be trifled with by louts. They have got Frank
by the scruff of the neck—he can't wriggle himself free—and he makes a
merit of yielding to sheer necessity."

The three months' interval of Frank's probation in London, passed less
cheerfully than usual in the household at Combe-Raven.

As the summer came nearer and nearer, Mrs. Vanstone's spirits, in spite of her resolute efforts to control them, became more and more depressed. "I do my best," she said to Miss Garth; "I set an example of cheerfulness to my husband and my children—but I dread July." Norah's secret misgivings on her sister's account rendered her more than usually serious and uncommunicative, as the year advanced. Even Mr. Vanstone, when July drew nearer, lost something of his elasticity of spirit. He kept up appearances in his wife's presence—but, on all other occasions, there was now a perceptible shade of sadness in his look and manner. Magdalen was so changed, since Frank's departure, that she helped the general depression, instead of relieving it. All her movements had grown languid; all her usual occupations were pursued with the same weary indifference; she spent hours alone in her own room; she lost her interest in being brightly and prettily dressed; her eyes were heavy, her nerves were irritable, her complexion was altered visibly for the worse—in one word, she had become an oppression and a weariness to herself and to all about her. Stoutly as Miss Garth contended with these growing domestic difficulties, her own spirits suffered in the effort. Her memory reverted, oftener and oftener, to the March morning when the master and mistress of the house had departed for London, and when the first serious change, for many a year past, had stolen over the family atmosphere. When was that atmosphere to be clear again? When were the clouds of change to pass off before the returning sunshine of past and happier times?

The spring and the early summer wore away. The dreaded month of July came, with its airless nights, its cloudless mornings, and its sultry days.

On the fifteenth of the month, an event happened which took every one but Norah by surprise. For the second time, without the slightest apparent reason—for the second time, without a word of warning beforehand—Frank suddenly reappeared at his father's cottage!

Mr. Clare's lips opened to hail his son's return, in the old character of the "bad shilling;" and closed again without uttering a word. There was a portentous composure in Frank's manner which showed that he had other news to communicate than the news of his dismissal. He answered his father's sardonic look of inquiry, by at once explaining that a very important proposal for his future benefit had been made to him, that morning, at the office. His first idea had been to communicate the details in writing; but the partners had, on reflection, thought that the necessary decision might be more readily obtained by a personal interview with his father and his friends. He had laid aside the pen accordingly; and had resigned himself to the railway on the spot.

After this preliminary statement, Frank proceeded to describe the proposal which his employers had addressed to him, with every external appearance of viewing it in the light of an intolerable hardship.

The great firm in the City had obviously made a discovery in relation to their clerk, exactly similar to the discovery which had formerly forced itself on the engineer in relation to his pupil. The young man, as they politely phrased it, stood in need of some special stimulant to stir him up. His employers (acting under a sense of their obligation to the gentleman by whom Frank had been recommended) had considered the question carefully, and had decided that the one premising use to which they could put Mr. Francis Clare, was to send him forthwith into another quarter of the globe.

As a consequence of this decision, it was now therefore proposed, that he should enter the house of their correspondents in China; that he should remain there, familiarizing himself thoroughly on the spot with the tea-trade and the silk-trade for five years; and that he should return, at the expiration of this period, to the central establishment in London. If he made a fair use of his opportunities in China, he would come back, while still a young man, fit for a position of trust and emolument, and justified in looking forward, at no distant date, to a time when the House would assist him to start in business for himself. Such were the new prospects which— to adopt Mr. Clare's theory—now forced themselves on the ever-reluctant, ever-helpless, and ever-ungrateful Frank. There was no time to be lost. The final answer was to be at the office on "Monday, the twentieth:" the correspondents in China were to be written to by the mail on that day; and Frank was to follow the letter by the next opportunity, or to resign his chance in favour of some more enterprising young man.

Mr. Clare's reception of this extraordinary news was startling in the extreme. The glorious prospect of his son's banishment to China appeared to turn his brain. The firm pedestal of his philosophy sank under him; the prejudices of society recovered their hold on his mind. He seized Frank by the arm, and actually accompanied him to Combe-Raven, in the amazing character of a visitor to the house!

"Here I am with my lout," said Mr. Clare, before a word could be uttered by the astonished family. "Hear his story, all of you. It has reconciled me, for the first time in my life, to the anomaly of his existence." Frank ruefully narrated the Chinese proposal for the second time, and attempted to attach to it his own supplementary statement of objections and difficulties. His father stopped him at the first word, pointed peremptorily south-eastward (from Somersetshire to China); and said, without an instant's hesitation: "Go!" Mr. Vanstone, basking in golden visions of his young friend's future, echoed that monosyllabic decision with all his heart. Mrs. Vanstone, Miss Garth, even Norah herself, spoke to the same purpose. Frank was petrified by an absolute unanimity of opinion which he had not anticipated; and Magdalen was caught, for once in her life, at the end of all her resources.

So far as practical results were concerned, the sitting of the family council began and ended with the general opinion that Frank must go. Mr. Vanstone's faculties were so bewildered by the son's sudden arrival, the father's unexpected visit, and the news they both brought with them, that he petitioned for an adjournment, before the necessary arrangements connected with his young friend's departure were considered in detail. "Suppose we all sleep upon it?" he said. "To-morrow, our heads will feel a little steadier; and to-morrow will be time enough to decide all uncertainties." This suggestion was readily adopted; and all further proceedings stood adjourned until the next day.

That next day was destined to decide more uncertainties than Mr. Vanstone dreamed of.

Early in the morning, after making tea by herself as usual, Miss Garth took her parasol, and strolled into the garden. She had slept ill; and ten minutes in the open air before the family assembled at breakfast, might help to compensate her, as she thought, for the loss of her night's rest.

She wandered to the outermost boundary of the flower-garden, and then returned by another path, which led back, past the side of an ornamental summer-house commanding a view over the fields from a corner of the lawn. A slight noise—like, and yet not like, the chirruping of a bird— caught her ear, as she approached the summer-house. She stepped round to the entrance; looked in; and discovered Magdalen and Frank seated close together. To Miss Garth's horror, Magdalen's arm was unmistakably round Frank's neck; and, worse still, the position of her face at the moment of discovery, showed beyond all doubt, that she had just been offering to the victim of Chinese commerce, the first and foremost of all the consolations which a woman can bestow on a man. In plainer words, she had just given Frank a kiss.

In the presence of such an emergency as now confronted her, Miss Garth felt instinctively that all ordinary phrases of reproof would be phrases thrown away.

"I presume," she remarked, addressing Magdalen with the merciless self-possession of a middle-aged lady, unprovided for the occasion with any kissing remembrances of her own. "I presume (whatever excuses your effrontery may suggest) you will not deny that my duty compels me to mention what I have just seen to your father?"

"I will save you the trouble," replied Magdalen, composedly. "I will mention it to him myself."

With those words, she looked round at Frank, standing trebly helpless in a corner of the summer-house. "You shall hear what happens," she said, with her bright smile. "And so shall you," she added for Miss Garth's especial benefit, as she sauntered past the governess, on her way back to the breakfast-table. The eyes of Miss Garth followed her indignantly; and Frank slipped out on his side, at that favourable opportunity.

Under these circumstances, there was but one course that any respectable woman could take—she could only shudder. Miss Garth registered her protest in that form, and returned to the house.

When breakfast was over, and when Mr. Vanstone's hand descended to his pocket in search of his cigar-case, Magdalen rose; looked significantly at Miss Garth; and followed her father into the hall.

"Papa," she said, "I want to speak to you this morning—in private."

"Ay! ay!" returned Mr. Vanstone. "What about, my dear?"

"About——" Magdalen hesitated, searched for a satisfactory form of expression, and found it. "About business, papa," she said.

Mr. Vanstone took his garden hat from the hall table—opened his eyes in mute perplexity—attempted to associate in his mind the two extravagantly dissimilar ideas of Magdalen and "business"—failed—and led the way resignedly into the garden.

His daughter took his arm, and walked with him to a shady seat at a convenient distance from the house. She dusted the seat with her smart silk apron, before her father occupied it. Mr. Vanstone was not accustomed to such an extraordinary act of attention as this. He sat down, looking more puzzled than ever. Magdalen immediately placed herself on his knee, and rested her head comfortably on his shoulder.

"Am I heavy, papa?" she asked.

"Yes, my dear, you are," said Mr. Vanstone—"but not too heavy for *me*. Stop on your perch, if you like it. Well? And what may this business happen to be?"

"It begins with a question."

"Ah, indeed? That doesn't surprise me. Business with your sex, my dear, always begins with questions. Go on."

"Papa! do you ever intend allowing me to be married?"

Mr. Vanstone's eyes opened wider and wider. The question, to use his own phrase, completely staggered him.

"This is business with a vengeance!" he said. "Why, Magdalen! what have you got in that harum-scarum head of yours now?"

"I don't exactly know, papa. Will you answer my question?"

"I will if I can, my dear; you rather stagger me. Well, I don't know. Yes; I suppose I must let you be married, one of these days—if we can find a good husband for you. How hot your face is! Lift it up, and let the air blow over it. You won't? Well—have your own way. If talking of business means tickling your cheek against my whisker, I've nothing to say against it. Go on, my dear. What's the next question? Come to the point!"

She was far too genuine a woman to do anything of the sort. She skirted round the point, and calculated her distance to the nicety of a hair's breadth.

"We were all very much surprised, yesterday—were we not, papa? Frank is wonderfully lucky, isn't he?"

"He's the luckiest dog I ever came across," said Mr. Vanstone. "But what has that got to do with this business of yours? I dare say you see your way, Magdalen. Hang me, if I can see mine!"

She skirted a little nearer.

"I suppose he will make his fortune in China?" she said. "It's a long way off, isn't it? Did you observe, papa, that Frank looked sadly out of spirits yesterday?"

"I was so surprised by the news," said Mr. Vanstone, "and so staggered by the sight of old Clare's sharp nose in my house, that I didn't much notice. Now you remind me of it—yes. I don't think Frank took kindly to his own good luck; not kindly at all."

"Do you wonder at that, papa?"

"Yes, my dear; I do, rather."

"Don't you think it's hard to be sent away for five years, to make your fortune among hateful savages, and lose sight of your friends at home for all that long time? Don't you think Frank will miss us, sadly? Don't you, papa?—don't you?"

"Gently, Magdalen! I'm a little too old for those long arms of yours to throttle me in fun.—You're right, my love. Nothing in this world, without a drawback. Frank *will* miss his friends in England: there's no denying that."

"You always liked Frank. And Frank always liked you."

"Yes, yes—a good fellow; a quiet, good fellow. Frank and I have always got on smoothly together."

"You have got on like father and son, haven't you?"

"Certainly, my dear."

"Perhaps you will think it harder on him when he has gone, than you think it now?"

"Likely enough, Magdalen; I don't say no."

"Perhaps you will wish he had stopped in England? Why shouldn't he stop in England, and do as well as if he went to China?"

"My dear! he has no prospects in England. I wish he had, for his own sake. I wish the lad well, with all my heart."

"May I wish him well, too, papa—with all *my* heart?"

"Certainly, my love—your old playfellow—why not? What's the matter? God bless my soul, what is the girl crying about? One would think Frank was transported for life. You goose! You know, as well as I do, he is going to China to make his fortune."

"He doesn't want to make his fortune—he might do much better."

" The deuce he might !   How—I should like to know ?"

" I'm afraid to tell you. I'm afraid you'll laugh at me. Will you promise not to laugh at me ?"

" Anything to please you, my dear. Yes: I promise. Now then, out with it ! How might Frauk do better ?"

" He might marry Me."

If the summer-scene which then spread before Mr. Vanstone's eyes, had suddenly changed to a dreary winter view—if the trees had lost all their leaves, and the green fields had turned white with snow, in an instant—his face could hardly have expressed greater amazement than it displayed, when his daughter's faltering voice spoke those four last words. He tried to look at her—but she steadily refused him the opportunity : she kept her face hidden over his shoulder. Was she in earnest ? His cheek, still wet with her tears, answered for her. There was a long pause of silence ; she waited—with unaccustomed patience, she waited for him to speak. He roused himself, and spoke these words only :—" You surprise me, Magdalen ; you surprise me, more than I can say."

At the altered tone of his voice—altered to a quiet fatherly seriousness —Magdalen's arms clung round him closer than before.

" Have I disappointed you, papa ?" she asked faintly. " Don't say I have disappointed you ! Who am I to tell my secret to, if not to you ? Don't let him go—don't ! don't ! You will break his heart. He is afraid to tell his father ; he is even afraid *you* might be angry with him. There is nobody to speak for us, except—except me. Oh, don't let him go ! Don't for his sake—" she whispered the next words in a kiss—" Don't for Mine !"

Her father's kind face saddened ; he sighed, and patted her fair head tenderly. " Hush, my love," he said, almost in a whisper ; " hush !" She little knew what a revelation every word, every action that escaped her, now opened before him. She had made him her grown-up playfellow, from her childhood to that day. She had romped with him in her frocks, she had gone on romping with him in her gowns. He had never been long enough separated from her to have the external changes in his daughter forced on his attention. His artless fatherly experience of her, had taught him that she was a taller child in later years—and had taught him little more. And now, in one breathless instant, the conviction that she was a woman rushed over his mind. He felt it in the trouble of her bosom pressed against his ; in the nervous thrill of her arms clasped around his neck. The Magdalen of his innocent experience, a woman—with the master-passion of her sex in possession of her heart already !

" Have you thought long of this, my dear ?" he asked, as soon as he could speak composedly. " Are you sure—— ?"

She answered the question before he could finish it.

" Sure I love him ?" she said. " Oh what words can say Yes for me as I want to say it! I love him——!" Her voice faltered softly; and her answer ended in a sigh.

"You are very young. You and Frank, my love, are both very young."

She raised her head from his shoulder for the first time. The thought and its expression flashed from her at the same moment.

"Are we much younger than you and mamma were?" she asked, smiling through her tears.

She tried to lay her head back in its old position; but as she spoke those words, her father caught her round the waist—forced her, before she was aware of it, to look him in the face—and kissed her, with a sudden outburst of tenderness which brought the tears thronging back thickly into her eyes. "Not much younger, my child," he said, in low, broken tones —"not much younger than your mother and I were." He put her away from him, and rose from the seat, and turned his head aside quickly. "Wait here, and compose yourself; I will go indoors and speak to your mother." His voice trembled over those parting words: and he left her without once looking round again.

She waited—waited a weary time; and he never came back. At last, her growing anxiety urged her to follow him into the house. A new timidity throbbed in her heart, as she doubtingly approached the door. Never had she seen the depths of her father's simple nature, stirred as they had been stirred by her confession. She almost dreaded her next meeting with him. She wandered softly to and fro in the hall, with a shyness unaccountable to herself; with a terror of being discovered and spoken to by her sister or Miss Garth, which made her nervously susceptible to the slightest noises in the house. The door of the morning-room opened, while her back was turned towards it. She started violently, as she looked round and saw her father in the hall: her heart beat faster and faster, and she felt herself turning pale. A second look at him, as he came nearer, reassured her. He was composed again, though not so cheerful as usual. She noticed that he advanced and spoke to her with a forbearing gentleness, which was more like his manner to her mother, than his ordinary manner to herself.

"Go in, my love," he said, opening the door for her which he had just closed. "Tell your mother all you have told me—and more, if you have more to say. She is better prepared for you than I was. We will take to-day to think of it, Magdalen; and to-morrow you shall know, and Frank shall know, what we decide."

Her eyes brightened, as they looked into his face, and saw the decision there already, with the double penetration of her womanhood and her love. Happy, and beautiful in her happiness, she put his hand to her lips, and went, without hesitation, into the morning-room. There, her father's words had smoothed the way for her: there, the first shock of the surprise was past and over, and only the pleasure of it remained. Her mother had been her age once ; her mother would know how fond she was of Frank. So the coming interview was anticipated in her thoughts ; and—except that there was an unaccountable appearance of restraint in Mrs. Vanstone's first reception of her—was anticipated aright. After a little, the mother's questions came more and more unreservedly from the sweet, unforgotten experience of the mother's heart. She lived again through her own young days of hope and love in Madgalen's replies.

The next morning, the all-important decision was announced in words. Mr. Vanstone took his daughter up-stairs into her mother's room, and there placed before her the result of the yesterday's consultation, and of the night's reflection which had followed it. He spoke with perfect kindness and self-possession of manner—but in fewer and more serious words than usual ; and he held his wife's hand tenderly in his own, all through the interview.

He informed Magdalen that neither he nor her mother felt themselves justified in blaming her attachment to Frank. It had been, in part perhaps, the natural consequence of her childish familiarity with him ; in part, also, the result of the closer intimacy between them which the theatrical entertainment had necessarily produced. At the same time, it was now the duty of her parents to put that attachment, on both sides, to a proper test —for her sake, because her happy future was their dearest care ; for Frank's sake, because they were bound to give him the opportunity of showing himself worthy of the trust confided in him. They were both conscious of being strongly prejudiced in Frank's favour. His father's eccentric conduct had made the lad the object of their compassion and their care from his earliest years. He (and his younger brothers) had almost filled the places to them of those other children of their own whom they had lost. Although they firmly believed their good opinion of Frank to be well founded —still, in the interest of their daughter's happiness, it was necessary to put that opinion firmly to the proof, by fixing certain conditions, and by interposing a year of delay between the contemplated marriage and the present time.

During that year, Frank was to remain at the office in London ; his employers being informed beforehand that family circumstances prevented his accepting their offer of employment in China. He was to consider this concession as a recognition of the attachment between Magdalen and himself, on certain terms only. If, during the year of probation, he failed to justify the confidence placed in him—a confidence which had led Mr. Vanstone to take unreservedly upon himself the whole responsibility of Frank's future prospects—the marriage scheme was to be considered, from that moment, as at an end. If, on the other hand, the result to which Mr. Vanstone confidently looked forward, really occurred—if Frank's probationary year proved his claim to the most precious trust that could be placed in his hands---then, Magdalen herself should reward him with all that a woman can bestow; and the future which his present employers had placed before him as the result of a five years' residence in China, should be realized in one year's time, by the dowry of his young wife.

As her father drew that picture of the future, the outburst of Magdalen's gratitude could no longer be restrained. She was deeply touched---she spoke from her inmost heart. Mr. Vanstone waited until his daughter and his wife were composed again; and then added the last words of explanation which were now left for him to speak.

"You understand, my love," he said, "that I am not anticipating Frank's living in idleness on his wife's means? My plan for him is that he should still profit by the interest which his present employers take in him. Their knowledge of affairs in the City, will soon place a good partnership at his disposal---and you will give him the money to buy it out of hand. I shall limit the sum, my dear, to half your fortune; and the other half I shall have settled upon yourself. We shall all be alive and hearty, I hope" ---he looked tenderly at his wife as he said those words---"all alive and hearty at the year's end. But if I am gone, Magdalen, it will make no difference. My will---made long before I ever thought of having a son-in-law---divides my fortune into two equal parts. One part goes to your mother; and the other part is fairly divided between my children. You will have your share on your wedding-day (and Norah will have hers when she marries) from my own hand, if I live; and under my will if I die. There! there! no gloomy faces," he said, with a momentary return of his every-day good spirits. "Your mother and I mean to live and see Frank a great merchant. I shall leave you, my dear, to enlighten the son on our new projects, while I walk over to the cottage——"

He stopped; his eyebrows contracted a little; and he looked aside hesitatingly at Mrs. Vanstone.

"What must you do at the cottage, papa?" asked Magdalen, after having vainly waited for him to finish the sentence of his own accord.

"I must consult Frank's father," he replied. "We must not forget that Mr. Clare's consent is still wanting to settle this matter. And as time presses, and we don't know what difficulties he may not raise, the sooner I see him the better."

He gave that answer in low, altered tones; and rose from his chair in a half-reluctant, half-resigned manner, which Magdalen observed with secret alarm.

She glanced inquiringly at her mother. To all appearance, Mrs. Vanstone had been alarmed by the change in him also. She looked anxious and uneasy; she turned her face away on the sofa pillow---turned it suddenly, as if she was in pain.

"Are you not well, mamma?" asked Magdalen.

"Quite well, my love," said Mrs. Vanstone, shortly and sharply, without turning round. "Leave me a little—I only want rest."

Magdalen went out with her father.

"Papa!" she whispered anxiously, as they descended the stairs. "You don't think Mr. Clare will say No?"

"I can't tell beforehand," answered Mr. Vanstone. "I hope he will say Yes."

"There is no reason why he should say anything else—is there?"

She put the question faintly, while he was getting his hat and stick; and he did not appear to hear her. Doubting whether she should repeat it or not, she accompanied him as far as the garden, on his way to Mr. Clare's cottage. He stopped her on the lawn, and sent her back to the house.

"You have nothing on your head, my dear," he said. "If you want to be in the garden, don't forget how hot the sun is—don't come out without your hat."

He walked on towards the cottage.

She waited a moment, and looked after him. She missed the customary flourish of his stick; she saw his little Scotch terrier, who had run out at his heels, barking and capering about him unnoticed. He was out of spirits: he was strangely out of spirits. What did it mean?

CHAPTER X.

On returning to the house, Magdalen felt her shoulder suddenly touched from behind, as she crossed the hall. She turned, and confronted her sister. Before she could ask any questions, Norah confusedly addressed her, in these words: "I beg your pardon; I beg you to forgive me."

Magdalen looked at her sister in astonishment. All memory, on her side, of the sharp words which had passed between them in the shrubbery, was lost in the new interests that now absorbed her; lost as completely as if the angry interview had never taken place. "Forgive you!" she repeated, amazedly. "What for?"

"I have heard of your new prospects," pursued Norah, speaking with a mechanical submissiveness of manner which seemed almost ungracious; "I wished to set things right between us; I wished to say I was sorry for what happened. Will you forget it? Will you forget and forgive what happened in the shrubbery?" She tried to proceed; but her inveterate reserve —or, perhaps, her obstinate reliance on her own opinions—silenced her at those last words. Her face clouded over on a sudden. Before her sister could answer her, she turned away abruptly and ran up-stairs.

The door of the library opened, before Magdalen could follow her; and Miss Garth advanced to express the sentiments proper to the occasion.

They were not the mechanically-submissive sentiments which Magdalen had just heard. Norah had struggled against her rooted distrust of Frank, in deference to the unanswerable decision of both her parents in his favour; and had suppressed the open expression of her antipathy, though the feeling itself remained unconquered. Miss Garth had made no such concession to the master and mistress of the house. She had hitherto held the position of a high authority on all domestic questions; and she flatly declined to get off her pedestal in deference to any change in the family circumstances, no matter how amazing or how unexpected that change might be.

"Pray accept my congratulations," said Miss Garth, bristling all over with implied objections to Frank—"my congratulations, *and* my apologies. When I caught you kissing Mr. Francis Clare in the summer-house, I had no idea you were engaged in carrying out the intentions of your parents. I offer no opinion on the subject. I merely regret my own accidental appearance in the character of an Obstacle to the course of true love—which appears to run smooth in summer-houses, whatever Shakespeare may say to the contrary. Consider me for the future, if you please, as an Obstacle removed. May you be happy!" Miss Garth's lips closed on that last sentence like a trap; and Miss Garth's eyes looked ominously prophetic into the matrimonial future.

If Magdalen's anxieties had not been far too serious to allow her the customary free use of her tongue, she would have been ready on the instant, with an appropriately satirical answer. As it was, Miss Garth simply irritated her. "Pooh!" she said—and ran up-stairs to her sister's room.

She knocked at the door, and there was no answer. She tried the door, and it resisted her from the inside. The sullen unmanageable Norah was locked in.

Under other circumstances, Magdalen would not have been satisfied with knocking—she would have called through the door loudly and more loudly, till the house was disturbed, and she had carried her point. But the doubts and fears of the morning had unnerved her already. She went down-stairs again softly, and took her hat from the stand in the hall. "He told me to put my hat on," she said to herself, with a meek filial docility which was totally out of her character.

She went into the garden, on the shrubbery side; and waited there to catch the first sight of her father on his return. Half an hour passed; forty minutes passed—and then his voice reached her from among the distant trees. "Come in to heel!" she heard him call out loudly to the dog. Her face turned pale. "He's angry with Snap!" she exclaimed to herself in a whisper. The next minute he appeared in view; walking rapidly, with his head down, and Snap at his heels in disgrace. The sudden excess of her alarm as she observed those ominous signs of something wrong rallied her natural energy, and determined her desperately on knowing the worst.

She walked straight forward to meet her father.

" Your face tells your news," she said faintly. " Mr. Clare has been as heartless as usual—Mr. Clare has said, No?"

Her father turned on her with a sudden severity, so entirely unparalleled in her experience of him, that she started back in downright terror.

" Magdalen!" he said; " whenever you speak of my old friend and neighbour again, bear this in mind. Mr. Clare has just laid me under an obligation which I shall remember gratefully to the end of my life."

He stopped suddenly, after saying those remarkable words. Seeing that he had startled her, his natural kindness prompted him instantly to soften the reproof, and to end the suspense from which she was plainly suffering. " Give me a kiss, my love," he resumed; " and I'll tell you in return that Mr. Clare has said—YES."

She attempted to thank him; but the sudden luxury of relief was too much for her. She could only cling round his neck in silence. He felt her trembling from head to foot, and said a few words to calm her. At the altered tones of his master's voice, Snap's meek tail reappeared fiercely from between his legs; and Snap's lungs modestly tested his position with a brief experimental bark. The dog's quaintly appropriate assertion of himself on his old footing, was the interruption of all others which was best fitted to restore Magdalen to herself. She caught the shaggy little terrier up in her arms, and kissed *him* next. " You darling," she exclaimed, " you're almost as glad as I am!" She turned again to her father, with a look of tender reproach. " You frightened me, papa," she said. " You were so unlike yourself."

" I shall be right again, to-morrow, my dear. I am a little upset to-day."

" Not by me?"

" No, no."

" By something you have heard at Mr. Clare's?"

" Yes—nothing you need alarm yourself about; nothing that won't wear off by to-morrow. Let me go now, my dear, I have a letter to write; and I want to speak to your mother."

He left her, and went on to the house. Magdalen lingered a little on the lawn, to feel all the happiness of her new sensations—then turned away towards the shrubbery, to enjoy the higher luxury of communicating them. The dog followed her. She whistled, and clapped her hands. " Find him!" she said, with beaming eyes. " Find Frank!" Snap scampered into the shrubbery, with a bloodthirsty snarl at starting. Perhaps he had mistaken his young mistress, and considered himself her emissary in search of a rat?

Meanwhile Mr. Vanstone entered the house. He met his wife, slowly descending the stairs, and advanced to give her his arm. "How has it ended?" she asked anxiously, as he led her to the sofa.

"Happily—as we hoped it would," answered her husband. "My old friend has justified my opinion of him."

"Thank God!" said Mrs. Vanstone, fervently. "Did you feel it, love?" she asked, as her husband arranged the sofa pillows—"did you feel it as painfully as I feared you would?"

"I had a duty to do, my dear—and I did it."

After replying in those terms, he hesitated. Apparently, he had something more to say—something, perhaps, on the subject of that passing uneasiness of mind, which had been produced by his interview with Mr. Clare, and which Magdalen's questions had obliged him to acknowledge. A look at his wife decided his doubts in the negative. He only asked if she felt comfortable; and then turned away to leave the room.

"Must you go?" she asked.

"I have a letter to write, my dear."

"Anything about Frank?"

"No: to-morrow will do for that. A letter to Mr. Pendril. I want him here immediately."

"Business, I suppose?"

"Yes, my dear—business."

He went out, and shut himself into the little front room, close to the hall-door, which was called his study. By nature and habit the most procrastinating of letter-writers, he now inconsistently opened his desk and took up the pen without a moment's delay. His letter was long enough to occupy three pages of note-paper; it was written with a readiness of expression and a rapidity of hand which seldom characterized his proceedings when engaged over his ordinary correspondence. He wrote the address as follows, "Immediate:—William Pendril, Esq., Serle Street, Lincoln's Inn, London"—then pushed the letter away from him, and sat at the table, drawing lines on the blotting-paper with his pen, lost in thought. "No," he said to himself; "I can do nothing more till Pendril comes." He rose; his face brightened as he put the stamp on the envelope. The writing of the letter had sensibly relieved him, and his whole bearing showed it as he left the room.

On the door-step, he found Norah and Miss Garth, setting forth together for a walk.

"Which way are you going?" he asked. "Anywhere near the post-office? I wish you would post this letter for me, Norah. It is very important—so important, that I hardly like to trust it to Thomas as usual."

Norah at once took charge of the letter.

"If you look, my dear," continued her father, "you will see that I am writing to Mr. Pendril. I expect him here to-morrow afternoon. Will

you give the necessary directions, Miss Garth? Mr. Pendril will sleep here
to-morrow night, and stay over Sunday.—Wait a minute! To-day is
Friday. Surely I had an engagement for Saturday afternoon?" He consulted his pocket-book, and read over one of the entries, with a look of
annoyance. "Grailsea Mill, three o'clock, Saturday. Just the time when
Pendril will be here; and I *must* be at home to see him. How can I
manage it? Monday will be too late for my business at Grailsea. I'll go
to-day, instead; and take my chance of catching the miller at his dinner-
time." He looked at his watch. "No time for driving; I must do it by
railway. If I go at once, I shall catch the down train at our station, and get
on to Grailsea. Take care of the letter, Norah. I won't keep dinner waiting;
if the return train doesn't suit, I'll borrow a gig, and get back in that way."

As he took up his hat, Magdalen appeared at the door, returning from
her interview with Frank. The hurry of her father's movements attracted
her attention; and she asked him where he was going.

"To Grailsea," replied Mr. Vanstone. "Your business, Miss Magdalen,
has got in the way of mine—and mine must give way to it."

He spoke those parting words in his old hearty manner; and left them,
with the old characteristic flourish of his trusty stick.

"My business!" said Magdalen. "I thought my business was done."

Miss Garth pointed significantly to the letter in Norah's hand. "Your
business, beyond all doubt," she said. " Mr. Pendril is coming to-morrow;
and Mr. Vanstone seems remarkably anxious about it. Law, and its
attendant troubles already! Governesses who look in at summer-house
doors are not the only obstacles to the course of true love. Parchment is
sometimes an obstacle. I hope you may find Parchment as pliable as I
am—I wish you well through it. Now, Norah!"

Miss Garth's second shaft struck as harmless as the first. Magdalen had
returned to the house, a little vexed; her interview with Frank having
been interrupted by a messenger from Mr. Clare, sent to summon the son
into the father's presence. Although it had been agreed at the private
interview between Mr. Vanstone and Mr. Clare, that the questions discussed that morning should not be communicated to the children, until the
year of probation was at an end—and although, under these circumstances,
Mr. Clare had nothing to tell Frank which Magdalen could not communicate
to him much more agreeably—the philosopher was not the less resolved on
personally informing his son of the parental concession which rescued him
from Chinese exile. The result was a sudden summons to the cottage,
which startled Magdalen, but which did not appear to take Frank by
surprise. His filial experience penetrated the mystery of Mr. Clare's
motives easily enough. "When my father's in spirits," he said, sulkily,
"he likes to bully me about my good luck. This message means that he's
going to bully me now."

"Don't go," suggested Magdalen.

"I must," rejoined Frank. "I shall never hear the last of it, if I don't. He's primed and loaded, and he means to go off. He went off, once, when the engineer took me; he went off, twice, when the office in the City took me; and he's going off, thrice, now *you've* taken me. If it wasn't for you, I should wish I had never been born. Yes; your father's been kind to me, I know—and I should have gone to China, if it hadn't been for him. I'm sure I'm very much obliged. Of course, we have no right to expect anything else—still it's discouraging to keep us waiting a year, isn't it?"

Magdalen stopped his mouth by a summary process, to which even Frank submitted gratefully. At the same time, she did not forget to set down his discontent to the right side. "How fond he is of me!" she thought. "A year's waiting is quite a hardship to him." She returned to the house, secretly regretting that she had not heard more of Frank's complimentary complaints. Miss Garth's elaborate satire, addressed to her while she was in this frame of mind, was a purely gratuitous waste of Miss Garth's breath. What did Magdalen care for satire? What do Youth and Love ever care for except themselves? She never even said as much as "Pooh!" this time. She laid aside her hat in serene silence, and sauntered languidly into the morning-room to keep her mother company. She lunched on dire forebodings of a quarrel between Frank and his father, with accidental interruptions in the shape of cold chicken and cheese-cakes. She trifled away half an hour at the piano; and played, in that time, selections from the Songs of Mendelssohn, the Mazurkas of Chopin, the Operas of Verdi, and the Sonatas of Mozart—all of whom had combined together on this occasion, and produced one immortal work, entitled "Frank." She closed the piano and went up to her room, to dream away the hours luxuriously in visions of her married future. The green shutters were closed, the easy-chair was pushed in front of the glass, the maid was summoned as usual; and the comb assisted the mistress's reflections, through the medium of the mistress's hair, till heat and idleness asserted their narcotic influences together, and Magdalen fell asleep.

It was past three o'clock when she woke. On going down stairs again she found her mother, Norah, and Miss Garth all sitting together enjoying the shade and the coolness under the open portico in front of the house.

Norah had the railway time-table in her hand. They had been discussing the chances of Mr. Vanstone's catching the return train, and getting back in good time. That topic had led them, next, to his business errand at Grailsea—an errand of kindness, as usual; undertaken for the benefit of the miller, who had been his old farm-servant, and who was now hard pressed by serious pecuniary difficulties. From this they had glided insensibly into a subject often repeated among them, and never exhausted by repetition—the praise of Mr. Vanstone himself. Each one of the three had some experience of her own to relate of his simple, generous nature. The conversation seemed to be almost painfully interesting to his wife. She was too near the time of her trial now, not to feel nervously sensitive to the one subject which always held the foremost place in her heart. Her eyes overflowed as Magdalen joined the little group under the portico; her frail hand trembled, as it signed to her youngest daughter to take the vacant chair by her side. "We were talking of your father," she said, softly. "Oh, my love, if your married life is only as happy——" Her voice failed her; she put her handkerchief hurriedly over her face, and rested her head on Magdalen's shoulder. Norah looked appealingly to Miss Garth; who at once led the conversation back to the more trivial subject of Mr. Vanstone's return. "We have all been wondering," she said, with a significant look at Magdalen, "whether your father will leave Grailsea in time to catch the train—or whether he will miss it, and be obliged to drive back. What do you say?"

"I say, papa will miss the train," replied Magdalen, taking Miss Garth's hint with her customary quickness. "The last thing he attends to at Grailsea, will be the business that brings him there. Whenever he has business to do, he always puts it off to the last moment, doesn't he, mamma?"

The question roused her mother exactly as Magdalen had intended it should. "Not when his errand is an errand of kindness," said Mrs. Vanstone. "He has gone to help the miller, in a very pressing difficulty——"

"And don't you know what he'll do?" persisted Magdalen. "He'll romp with the miller's children, and gossip with the mother, and hob-and-nob with the father. At the last moment, when he has got five minutes left to catch the train, he'll say, 'Let's go into the counting-house, and look at the books.' He'll find the books dreadfully complicated; he'll suggest sending for an accountant; he'll settle the business off-hand, by lending the money in the mean time; he'll jog back comfortably in the miller's gig; and he'll tell us all how pleasant the lanes were in the cool of the evening."

The little character-sketch which these words drew, was too faithful a likeness not to be recognized. Mrs. Vanstone showed her appreciation of it by a smile. "When your father returns," she said, "we will put your account of his proceedings to the test. I think," she continued, rising languidly from her chair, "I had better go in-doors again now, and rest on the sofa till he comes back."

The little group under the portico broke up. Magdalen slipped away into the garden to hear Frank's account of the interview with his father. The other three ladies entered the house together. When Mrs. Vanstone was comfortably established on the sofa, Norah and Miss Garth left her to repose, and withdrew to the library to look over the last parcel of books from London.

It was a quiet, cloudless summer's day. The heat was tempered by a light western breeze; the voices of labourers at work in a field near, reached the house cheerfully; the clock-bell of the village church as it struck the quarters, floated down the wind with a clearer ring, a louder melody than usual. Sweet odours from field and flower-garden, stealing in at the open windows, filled the house with their fragrance; and the birds in Norah's aviary up-stairs, sang the song of their happiness exultingly in the sun.

As the church clock struck the quarter past four, the morning-room door opened; and Mrs. Vanstone crossed the hall alone. She had tried vainly to compose herself. She was too restless to lie still, and sleep. For a moment, she directed her steps towards the portico—then turned, and looked about her, doubtful where to go, or what to do next. While she was still hesitating, the half-open door of her husband's study attracted her attention. The room seemed to be in sad confusion. Drawers were left open; coats and hats, account-books and papers, pipes and fishing-rods were all scattered about together. She went in, and pushed the door to— but so gently that she still left it ajar. "It will amuse me to put his room to rights," she thought to herself. "I should like to do something for him, before I am down on my bed helpless." She began to arrange his drawers; and found his banker's book lying open in one of them. "My poor dear, how careless he is! The servants might have seen all his affairs, if I had not happened to have looked in." She set the drawers right; and then turned to the multifarious litter on a side table. A little old-fashioned music-book appeared among the scattered papers, with her name written in it, in faded ink. She blushed like a young girl in the first happiness of the discovery. "How good he is to me! He remembers my poor old music-book, and keeps it for my sake." As she sat down by the table and opened the book, the bygone time came back to her in all its tenderness. The clock struck the half-hour, struck the three-quarters—and still she sat there, with the music-book on her lap, dreaming happily over the old songs; thinking gratefully of the golden days when his hand had turned the pages for her, when his voice had whispered the words which no woman's memory ever forgets.

Norah roused herself from the volume she was reading, and glanced at the clock on the library mantelpiece.

"If papa comes back by railway," she said, "he will be here in ten minutes."

Miss Garth started, and looked up drowsily from the book which was just dropping out of her hand.

"I don't think he will come by train," she replied. "He will jog back— as Magdalen flippantly expressed it—in the miller's gig."

As she said the words, there was a knock at the library door. The footman appeared, and addressed himself to Miss Garth.

"A person wishes to see you, ma'am."

"Who is it?"

"I don't know, ma'am. A stranger to me—a respectable-looking man —and he said he particularly wished to see you."

Miss Garth went out into the hall. The footman closed the library door after her; and withdrew down the kitchen stairs.

The man stood just inside the door, on the mat. His eyes wandered, his face was pale—he looked ill; he looked frightened. He trifled nervously with his cap, and shifted it backwards and forwards, from one hand to the other.

"You wanted to see me?" said Miss Garth.

"I beg your pardon ma'am.—You are not Mrs. Vanstone, are you?"

"Certainly not. I am Miss Garth. Why do you ask the question?"

"I am employed in the clerk's office at Grailsea Station——"

"Yes?"

"I am sent here——"

He stopped again. His wandering eyes looked down at the mat, and his restless hands wrung his cap harder and harder. He moistened his dry lips, and tried once more.

"I am sent here on a very serious errand."

"Serious to *me*?"

"Serious to all in this house."

Miss Garth took one step nearer to him—took one steady look at his face. She turned cold in the summer heat. "Stop!" she said, with a sudden distrust, and glanced aside anxiously at the door of the morning-room. It was safely closed. "Tell me the worst; and don't speak loud. There has been an accident. Where?"

"On the railway. Close to Grailsea Station."

"The up-train, to London?"

"No : the down-train at one-fifty——"

"God Almighty help us! The train Mr. Vanstone travelled by to Grailsea?"

"The same. I was sent here by the up-train : the line was just cleared in time for it. They wouldn't write—they said I must see 'Miss Garth,' and tell her. There are seven passengers badly hurt; and two——"

The next word failed on his lips; he raised his hand in the dead silence. With eyes that opened wide in horror, he raised his hand and pointed over Miss Garth's shoulder.

She turned a little, and looked back.

Face to face with her, on the threshold of the study door, stood the mistress of the house. She held her old music-book clutched fast mechanically in both hands. She stood, the spectre of herself. With a dreadful vacancy in her eyes, with a dreadful stillness in her voice, she repeated the man's last words:

"Seven passengers badly hurt; and two——"

Her tortured fingers relaxed their hold; the book dropped from them; she sank forward heavily. Miss Garth caught her before she fell—caught her, and turned upon the man, with the wife's swooning body in her arms, to hear the husband's fate.

"The harm is done," she said: "you may speak out. Is he wounded, or dead?"

"Dead."

CHAPTER XI.

THE sun sank lower; the western breeze floated cool and fresh into the house. As the evening advanced, the cheerful ring of the village clock came nearer and nearer. Field and flower-garden felt the influence of the hour, and shed their sweetest fragrance. The birds in Norah's aviary sunned themselves in the evening stillness, and sang their farewell gratitude to the dying day.

Staggered in its progress for a time only, the pitiless routine of the house went horribly on its daily way. The panic-stricken servants took their blind refuge in the duties proper to the hour. The footman softly laid the table for dinner. The maid sat waiting in senseless doubt, with the hot-water jugs for the bedrooms ranged near her in their customary row. The gardener, who had been ordered to come to his master, with vouchers for money that he had paid in excess of his instructions, said his character was dear to him, and left the vouchers at his appointed time. Custom that never yields, and Death that never spares, met on the wreck of human happiness—and Death gave way.

Heavily the thunder-clouds of Affliction had gathered over the house—heavily, but not at their darkest yet. At five, that evening, the shock of the calamity had struck its blow. Before another hour had passed, the disclosure of the husband's sudden death was followed by the suspense of the wife's mortal peril. She lay helpless on her widowed bed; her own life, and the life of her unborn child, trembling in the balance.

But one mind still held possession of its resources—but one guiding spirit now moved helpfully in the house of mourning.

If Miss Garth's early days had been passed as calmly and as happily as her later life at Combe-Raven, she might have sunk under the cruel necessities of the time. But the governess's youth had been tried in the ordeal of family affliction; and she met her terrible duties with the steady courage of a woman who had learnt to suffer. Alone, she had faced the trial of telling the daughters that they were fatherless. Alone, she now struggled to sustain them, when the dreadful certainty of their bereavement was at last impressed on their minds.

Her least anxiety was for the elder sister. The agony of Norah's grief had forced its way outward to the natural relief of tears. It was not so with Magdalen. Tearless and speechless, she sat in the room where the revelation of her father's death had first reached her; her face, unnaturally petrified by the sterile sorrow of old age—a white changeless blank, fearful to look at. Nothing roused, nothing melted her. She only said "Don't speak to me; don't touch me. Let me bear it by myself"—and fell silent again. The first great grief which had darkened the sisters' lives, had, as it seemed, changed their every-day characters already.

The twilight fell, and faded; and the summer night came brightly. As the first carefully shaded light was kindled in the sick-room, the physician who had been summoned from Bristol, arrived to consult with the medical attendant of the family. He could give no comfort: he could only say, "We must try, and hope. The shock which struck her, when she overheard the news of her husband's death, has prostrated her strength at the time when she needed it most. No effort to preserve her shall be neglected. I will stay here for the night."

He opened one of the windows to admit more air as he spoke. The view overlooked the drive in front of the house, and the road outside. Little groups of people were standing before the lodge-gates, looking in. "If those persons make any noise," said the doctor, "they must be warned away." There was no need to warn them: they were only the labourers who had worked on the dead man's property, and here and there some women and children from the village. They were all thinking of him— some talking of him—and it quickened their sluggish minds to look at his house. The gentlefolks thereabouts were mostly kind to them (the men said), but none like *him*. The women whispered to each other of his comforting ways, when he came into their cottages. "He was a cheerful man, poor soul; and thoughtful of us, too: he never came in, and stared at meal times; the rest of 'em help us, and scold us—all *he* ever said was, better luck next time." So they stood, and talked of him, and looked at his house and grounds, and moved off clumsily by twos and threes, with the dim sense that the sight of his pleasant face would never comfort them again. The dullest head among them knew, that night, that the hard ways of poverty would be all the harder to walk on now he was gone.

A little later, news was brought to the bedchamber door that old Mr. Clare had come alone to the house, and was waiting in the hall below, to hear what the physician said. Miss Garth was not able to go down to him her~·'· she sent a message. He said to the servant, "I'll come, and ask again, in two hours' time"—and went out slowly. Unlike other men in all things else, the sudden death of his old friend had produced no discernible change in him. The feeling implied in the errand of inquiry that had brought him to the house, was the one betrayal of human sympathy which escaped the rugged, impenetrable old man.

He came again, when the two hours had expired; and this time Miss Garth saw him.

They shook hands in silence. She waited; she nerved herself to hear him speak of his lost friend. No: he never mentioned the dreadful accident, he never alluded to the dreadful death. He said these words, "Is she better, or worse?" and said no more. Was the tribute of his grief for the husband, sternly suppressed under the expression of his anxiety for the wife? The nature of the man, unpliably antagonistic to the world and the world's customs, might justify some such interpretation of his conduct as this. He repeated his question, "Is she better, or worse?"

Miss Garth answered him:—

"No better; if there is any change, it is a change for the worse."

They spoke those words at the window of the morning-room which opened on the garden. Mr. Clare paused, after hearing the reply to his inquiry, stepped out on to the walk, then turned on a sudden, and spoke again:

"Has the doctor given her up?" he asked.

"He has not concealed from us that she is in danger. We can only pray for her."

The old man laid his hand on Miss Garth's arm as she answered him, and looked her attentively in the face.

"You believe in prayer?" he said.

Miss Garth drew sorrowfully back from him.

"You might have spared me that question, sir, at such a time as this."

He took no notice of her answer; his eyes were still fastened on her face.

"Pray!" he said. "Pray as you never prayed before, for the preservation of Mrs. Vanstone's life."

He left her. His voice and manner implied some unutterable dread of the future, which his words had not confessed. Miss Garth followed him into the garden, and called to him. He heard her, but he never turned back: he quickened his pace, as if he desired to avoid her. She watched him across the lawn in the warm summer moonlight. She saw his white withered hands, saw then suddenly against the black background of the shrubbery, raised and wrung above his head. They dropped—the trees shrouded him in darkness—he was gone.

Miss Garth went back to the suffering woman, with the burden on her mind of one anxiety more.

It was then past eleven o'clock. Some little time had elapsed ... she had seen the sisters, and spoken to them. The inquiries she addressed to one of the female servants, only elicited the information that they were both in their rooms. She delayed her return to the mother's bedside to say her parting words of comfort to the daughters, before she left them for the night. Norah's room was the nearest. She softly opened the door and looked in. The kneeling figure by the bedside, told her that God's help had found the fatherless daughter in her affliction. Grateful tears gathered in her eyes as she looked : she softly closed the door, and went on to Magdalen's room. There, doubt stayed her feet at the threshold ; and she waited for a moment before going in.

A sound in the room caught her ear—the monotonous rustling of a woman's dress, now distant, now near ; passing without cessation from end to end over the floor—a sound which told her that Magdalen was pacing to and fro in the secrecy of her own chamber. Miss Garth knocked. The rustling ceased ; the door was opened, and the sad young face confronted her, locked in its cold despair; the large light eyes looked mechanically into hers, as vacant and as tearless as ever.

That look wrung the heart of the faithful woman, who had trained her and loved her from a child. She took Magdalen tenderly in her arms.

"Oh, my love," she said, "no tears yet ! Oh, if I could see you as I have seen Norah ! Speak to me, Magdalen—try if you can speak to me."

She tried, and spoke :

"Norah," she said, "feels no remorse. He was not serving Norah's interests when he went to his death : he was serving mine."

With that terrible answer, she put her cold lips to Miss Garth's cheek.

"Let me bear it by myself," she said, and gently closed the door.

Again Miss Garth waited at the threshold, and again the sound of the rustling dress passed to and fro—now far, now near—to and fro with a cruel, mechanical regularity, that chilled the warmest sympathy, and daunted the boldest hope.

The night passed. It had been agreed, if no change for the better showed itself by the morning, that the London physician whom Mrs. Vanstone had consulted some months since, should be summoned to the house on the next day. No change for the better appeared; and the physician was sent for.

As the morning advanced, Frank came to make inquiries, from the cottage. Had Mr. Clare intrusted to his son the duty which he had personally performed on the previous day, through reluctance to meet Miss Garth again after what he had said to her? It might be so. Frank could throw no light on the subject ; he was not in his father's confidence.

He looked pale and bewildered. His first inquiries after Magdalen, showed how his weak nature had been shaken by the catastrophe. He was not capable of framing his own questions: the words faltered on his lips, and the ready tears came into his eyes. Miss Garth's heart warmed to him for the first time. Grief has this that is noble in it—it accepts all sympathy, come whence it may. She encouraged the lad by a few kind words, and took his hand at parting.

Before noon, Frank returned with a second message. His father desired to know whether Mr. Pendril was not expected at Combe-Raven on that day. If the lawyer's arrival was looked for, Frank was directed to be in attendance at the station, and to take him to the cottage, where a bed would be placed at his disposal. This message took Miss Garth by surprise. It showed that Mr. Clare had been made acquainted with his dead friend's purpose of sending for Mr. Pendril. Was the old man's thoughtful offer of hospitality, another indirect expression of the natural human distress which he perversely concealed? or was he aware of some secret necessity for Mr. Pendril's presence, of which the bereaved family had been kept in total ignorance? Miss Garth was too heart-sick and hopeless to dwell on either question. She told Frank that Mr. Pendril had been expected at three o'clock, and sent him back with her thanks.

Shortly after his departure, such anxieties on Magdalen's account as her mind was now able to feel, were relieved by better news than her last night's experience had inclined her to hope for. Norah's influence had been exerted to rouse her sister: and Norah's patient sympathy had set the prisoned grief free. Magdalen had suffered severely—suffered inevitably, with such a nature as hers—in the effort that relieved her. The healing tears had not come gently; they had burst from her with a torturing, passionate vehemence—but Norah had never left her till the struggle was over, and the calm had come. These better tidings encouraged Miss Garth to withdraw to her own room, and to take the rest which she needed sorely. Worn out in body and mind, she slept from sheer exhaustion—slept heavily and dreamlessly for some hours. It was between three and four in the afternoon, when she was roused by one of the female servants. The woman had a note in her hand—a note left by Mr. Clare the younger, with a message desiring that it might be delivered to Miss Garth immediately. The name written in the lower corner of the envelope was " William Pendril." The lawyer had arrived.

Miss Garth opened the note. After a few first sentences of sympathy and condolence, the writer announced his arrival at Mr. Clare's; and then proceeded, apparently in his professional capacity, to make a very startling request.

"If," he wrote, "any change for the better in Mrs. Vanstone should take place—whether it is only an improvement for the time, or whether it

is the permanent improvement for which we all hope—in either case, I
entreat you to let me know of it immediately. It is of the last importance
that I should see her, in the event of her gaining strength enough to give
me her attention for five minutes, and of her being able at the expiration
of that time to sign her name. May I beg that you will communicate my
request, in the strictest confidence, to the medical men in attendance?
They will understand, and you will understand, the vital importance I
attach to this interview, when I tell you that I have arranged to defer to it
all other business claims on me; and that I hold myself in readiness to
obey your summons, at any hour of the day or night."

In those terms the letter ended. Miss Garth read it twice over. At
the second reading, the request which the lawyer now addressed to her, and
the farewell words which had escaped Mr. Clare's lips the day before, connected themselves vaguely in her mind. There was some other serious
interest in suspense, known to Mr. Pendril and known to Mr. Clare,
besides the first and foremost interest of Mrs. Vanstone's recovery. Whom
did it affect? The children? Were they threatened by some new calamity
which their mother's signature might avert? What did it mean? Did
it mean that Mr. Vanstone had died without leaving a will?

In her distress and confusion of mind, Miss Garth was incapable of
reasoning with herself, as she might have reasoned at a happier time. She
hastened to the ante-chamber of Mrs. Vanstone's room; and, after explaining Mr. Pendril's position towards the family, placed his letter in the
hands of the medical men. They both answered without hesitation, to
the same purpose. Mrs. Vanstone's condition rendered any such interview
as the lawyer desired, a total impossibility. If she rallied from her present
prostration, Miss Garth should be at once informed of the improvement. In
the mean time, the answer to Mr. Pendril might be conveyed in one word
—Impossible.

"You see what importance Mr. Pendril attaches to the interview?" said
Miss Garth.

Yes: both the doctors saw it.

"My mind is lost and confused, gentlemen, in this dreadful suspense.
Can you either of you guess why the signature is wanted? or what the
object of the interview may be? I have only seen Mr. Pendril when he
has come here on former visits: I have no claim to justify me in questioning him. Will you look at the letter again? Do you think it implies
that Mr. Vanstone has never made a will?"

"I think it can hardly imply that," said one of the doctors. "But,
even supposing Mr. Vanstone to have died intestate, the law takes due care
of the interests of his widow and his children——"

"Would it do so," interposed the other medical man, "if the property
happened to be in land?"

"I am not sure in that case. Do you happen to know, Miss Garth, whether Mr. Vanstone's property was in money or in land?"

"In money," replied Miss Garth. "I have heard him say so on more than one occasion."

"Then I can relieve your mind by speaking from my own experience. The law if he has died intestate, gives a third of his property to his widow, and divides the rest equally among his children."

"But if Mrs. Vanstone——?"

"If Mrs. Vanstone should die," pursued the doctor, completing the question which Miss Garth had not the heart to conclude for herself, "I believe I am right in telling you that the property would, as a matter of legal course, go to the children. Whatever necessity there may be for the interview which Mr. Pendril requests, I can see no reason for connecting it with the question of Mr. Vanstone's presumed intestacy. But, by all means, put the question, for the satisfaction of your own mind, to Mr. Pendril himself."

Miss Garth withdrew to take the course which the doctor advised. After communicating to Mr. Pendril the medical decision which, thus far, refused him the interview that he sought, she added a brief statement of the legal question she had put to the doctors ; and hinted delicately at her natural anxiety to be informed of the motives which had led the lawyer to make his request. The answer she received was guarded in the extreme : it did not impress her with a favourable opinion of Mr. Pendril. He confirmed the doctors' interpretation of the law, in general terms only ; expressed his intention of waiting at the cottage, in the hope that a change for the better might yet enable Mrs. Vanstone to see him ; and closed his letter without the slightest explanation of his motives, and without a word of reference to the question of the existence, or the non-existence, of Mr. Vanstone's will.

The marked caution of the lawyer's reply dwelt uneasily on Miss Garth's mind, until the long-expected event of the day recalled all her thoughts to her one absorbing anxiety on Mrs. Vanstone's account.

Early in the evening, the physician from London arrived. He watched long by the bedside of the suffering woman ; he remained longer still in consultation with his medical brethren ; he went back again to the sick room, before Miss Garth could prevail on him to communicate to her the opinion at which he had arrived.

When he came out into the ante-chamber for the second time, he silently took a chair by her side. She looked in his face; and the last faint hope died in her before he opened his lips.

"I must speak the hard truth," he said gently. "All that *can* be done, *has* been done. The next four-and-twenty hours, at most, will end your suspense. If Nature makes no effort in that time—I grieve to say it—you must prepare yourself for the worst."

Those words said all: they were prophetic of the end.

The night passed; and she lived through it. The next day came; and she lingered on till the clock pointed to five. At that hour the tidings of her husband's death had dealt the mortal blow. When the hour came round again, the mercy of God let her go to him in the better world. Her daughters were kneeling at the bedside, as her spirit passed away. She left them unconscious of their presence; mercifully and happily insensible to the pang of the last farewell.

Her child survived her till the evening was on the wane, and the sunset was dim in the quiet western heaven. As the darkness came, the light of the frail little life—faint and feeble from the first—flickered, and went out. All that was earthly of mother and child lay, that night, on the same bed. The Angel of Death had done his awful bidding; and the two Sisters were left alone in the world.

CHAPTER XII.

EARLIER than usual, on the morning of Thursday, the twenty-third of July, Mr. Clare appeared at the door of his cottage, and stepped out into the little strip of garden attached to his residence.

After he had taken a few turns backwards and forwards, alone, he was joined by a spare, quiet, gray-haired man, whose personal appearance was totally devoid of marked character of any kind; whose inexpressive face and conventionally-quiet manner presented nothing that attracted approval, and nothing that inspired dislike. This was Mr. Pendril—this was the man, on whose lips hung the future of the orphans at Combe-Raven.

"The time is getting on," he said, looking towards the shrubbery, as he joined Mr. Clare. "My appointment with Miss Garth is for eleven o'clock: it only wants ten minutes of the hour."

"Are you to see her alone?" asked Mr. Clare.

"I left Miss Garth to decide—after warning her, first of all, that the circumstances I am compelled to disclose are of a very serious nature."

"And *has* she decided?"

"She writes me word that she mentioned my appointment, and repeated the warning I had given her to both the daughters. The elder of the two shrinks—and who can wonder at it?—from any discussion connected with the future, which requires her presence so soon as the day after the funeral. The younger one appears to have expressed no opinion on the subject. As I understand it, she suffers herself to be passively guided by her sister's example. My interview, therefore, will take place with Miss Garth alone—and it is a very great relief to me to know it."

He spoke the last words with more emphasis and energy than seemed habitual to him. Mr. Clare stopped, and looked at his guest attentively.

"You are almost as old as I am, sir," he said. "Has all your long experience as a lawyer not hardened you yet?"

"I never knew how little it had hardened me," replied Mr. Pendril, quietly, "until I returned from London yesterday to attend the funeral. I was not warned that the daughters had resolved on following their parents to the grave. I think their presence made the closing scene of this dreadful calamity doubly painful, and doubly touching. You saw how the great concourse of people were moved by it—and *they* were in ignorance of the truth; *they* knew nothing of the cruel necessity which takes me to the house this morning. The sense of that necessity—and the sight of those poor girls at the time when I felt my hard duty towards them most painfully—shook me, as a man of my years and my way of life, is not often shaken by any distress in the present, or any suspense in the future. I have not recovered it this morning: I hardly feel sure of myself yet."

"A man's composure—when he is a man like you—comes with the necessity for it," said Mr. Clare. "You must have had duties to perform as trying in their way as the duty that lies before you this morning.'

Mr. Pendril shook his head. "Many duties as serious; many stories more romantic. No duty so trying; no story so hopeless, as this."

With those words they parted. Mr. Pendril left the garden for the shrubbery path which led to Combe-Raven. Mr. Clare returned to the cottage.

On reaching the passage, he looked through the open door of his little parlour, and saw Frank sitting there in idle wretchedness, with his head resting wearily on his hand.

"I have had an answer from your employers in London," said Mr. Clare. "In consideration of what has happened, they will allow the offer they made you to stand over for another month."

Frank changed colour, and rose nervously from his chair.

"Are my prospects altered?" he asked. "Are Mr. Vanstone's plans for me not to be carried out? He told Magdalen his will had provided for her. She repeated his words to me; she said I ought to know all that his goodness and generosity had done for both of us. How can his death make a change? Has anything happened?"

"Wait till Mr. Pendril comes back from Combe-Raven," said his father. "Question him—don't question me."

The ready tears rose in Frank's eyes.

"You won't be hard on me?" he pleaded, faintly. "You won't expect me to go back to London without seeing Magdalen first?"

Mr. Clare looked thoughtfully at his son; and considered a little before he replied.

"You may dry your eyes," he said. "You shall see Magdalen before you go back."

He left the room, after making that reply, and withdrew to his study. The books lay ready to his hand as usual. He opened one of them, and set himself to read in the customary manner. But his attention wandered; and his eyes strayed away from time to time, to the empty chair opposite —the chair in which his old friend and gossip had sat and wrangled with him good-humouredly for many and many a year past. After a struggle with himself, he closed the book. "Damn the chair!" he said: "it *will* talk of him; and I must listen." He reached down his pipe from the wall, and mechanically filled it with tobacco. His hand shook, his eyes wandered back to the old place; and a heavy sigh came from him unwillingly. That empty chair was the only earthly argument for which he had no answer: his heart owned its defeat, and moistened his eyes in spite of him. "He has got the better of me at last," said the rugged old man. "There is one weak place left in me still—and *he* has found it."

Meanwhile, Mr. Pendril entered the shrubbery, and followed the path which led to the lonely garden and the desolate house. He was met at the door by the man-servant, who was apparently waiting in expectation of his arrival.

"I have an appointment with Miss Garth. Is she ready to see me?"

"Quite ready, sir."

"Is she alone?"

"Yes, sir."

"In the room which was Mr. Vanstone's study?"

"In that room, sir."

The servant opened the door; and Mr. Pendril went in.

The governess stood alone at the study window. The morning was oppressively hot, and she threw up the lower sash to admit more air into the room, as Mr. Pendril entered it.

They bowed to each other with a formal politeness, which betrayed on either side an uneasy sense of restraint. Mr. Pendril was one of the many men who appear superficially to the worst advantage, under the influence of strong mental agitation which it is necessary for them to control. Miss Garth, on her side, had not forgotten the ungraciously guarded terms in which the lawyer had replied to her letter; and the natural anxiety which she had felt on the subject of the interview, was not relieved by any favourable opinion of the man who sought it. As they confronted each other in the silence of the summer's morning—both dressed in black; Miss Garth's hard features, gaunt and haggard with grief; the lawyer's cold, colourless face, void of all marked expression, suggestive of a business embarrassment and of nothing more—it would have been hard to find two persons less attractive externally to any ordinary sympathies than the two who had now met together, the one to tell, the other to hear, the secrets of the dead.

"I am sincerely sorry, Miss Garth, to intrude on you at such a time as this. But circumstances, as I have already explained, leave me no other choice."

"Will you take a seat, Mr. Pendril? You wished to see me in this room, I believe?"

"Only in this room, because Mr. Vanstone's papers are kept here, and I may find it necessary to refer to some of them."

After that formal interchange of question and answer, they sat down on either side of a table placed close under the window. One waited to speak, the other waited to hear. There was a momentary silence. Mr. Pendril broke it by referring to the young ladies, with the customary inquiries, and the customary expressions of sympathy. Miss Garth answered him with the same ceremony, in the same conventional tone. There was a second pause of silence. The humming of flies among the evergreen shrubs under the window, penetrated drowsily into the room; and the tramp of a heavy-footed cart-horse, plodding along the high-road beyond the garden, was as plainly audible in the stillness, as if it had been night.

The lawyer roused his flagging resolution, and spoke to the purpose when he spoke next.

"You have some reason, Miss Garth," he began, "to feel not quite satisfied with my past conduct towards you, in one particular. During Mrs. Vanstone's fatal illness, you addressed a letter to me, making certain inquiries; which, while she lived, it was impossible for me to answer. Her deplorable death releases me from the restraint which I had imposed on myself, and permits—or, more properly, obliges me to speak. You shall know what serious reasons I had for waiting day and night in the hope of obtaining that interview which unhappily never took place; and in justice to Mr. Vanstone's memory, your own eyes shall inform you that he made his will."

He rose; unlocked a little iron safe in the corner of the room; and returned to the table with some folded sheets of paper, which he spread open under Miss Garth's eyes. When she had read the first words, "In the name of God, Amen," he turned the sheet, and pointed to the end of the next page. She saw the well-known signature: "Andrew Vanstone." She saw the customary attestations of the two witnesses; and the date of the document, reverting to a period of more than five years since. Having thus convinced her of the formality of the will, the lawyer interposed before she could question him, and addressed her in these words:

"I must not deceive you," he said. "I have my own reasons for producing this document."

"What reasons, sir?"

"You shall hear them. When you are in possession of the truth,

these pages may help to preserve your respect for Mr. Vanstone's memory——"

Miss Garth started back in her chair.

"What do you mean?" she asked, with a stern straightforwardness.

He took no heed of the question; he went on as if she had not interrupted him.

"I have a second reason," he continued, "for showing you the will. If
I can prevail on you to read certain clauses in it, under my superintendence, you will make your own discovery of the circumstances which I am
here to disclose—circumstances so painful, that I hardly know how to
communicate them to you with my own lips."

Miss Garth looked him steadfastly in the face.

"Circumstances, sir, which affect the dead parents, or the living
children?"

"Which affect the dead and the living both," answered the lawyer.
"Circumstances, I grieve to say, which involve the future of Mr. Vanstone's unhappy daughters."

"Wait," said Miss Garth, "wait a little." She pushed her grey hair
back from her temples, and struggled with the sickness of heart, the
dreadful faintness of terror, which would have overpowered a younger, or
a less resolute woman. Her eyes dim with watching, weary with grief,
searched the lawyer's unfathomable face. "His unhappy daughters?" she
repeated to herself, vacantly. "He talks as if there was some worse
calamity than the calamity which has made them orphans." She paused
once more; and rallied her sinking courage. "I will not make your hard
duty, sir, more painful to you than I can help," she resumed. "Show me
the place in the will. Let me read it, and know the worst."

Mr. Pendril turned back to the first page, and pointed to a certain place
in the cramped lines of writing. "Begin here," he said.

She tried to begin; she tried to follow his finger, as she had followed
it already to the signatures and the dates. But her senses seemed to share
the confusion of her mind—the words mingled together, and the lines swam
before her eyes.

"I can't follow you," she said. "You must tell it, or read it to me."
She pushed her chair back from the table, and tried to collect herself.
"Stop!" she exclaimed, as the lawyer, with visible hesitation and reluctance, took the papers in his own hand. "One question, first. Does his
will provide for his children?"

"His will provided for them, when he made it."

"When he made it?" (Something of her natural bluntness broke out
in her manner as she repeated the answer.) "Does it provide for them
now?"

"It does not."

She snatched the will from his hand, and threw it into a corner of the room. "You mean well," she said; "you wish to spare me—but you are wasting your time, and my strength. If the will is useless, there let it lie. Tell me the truth, Mr. Pendril—tell it plainly, tell it instantly, in your own words!"

He felt that it would be useless cruelty to resist that appeal. There was no merciful alternative but to answer it on the spot.

"I must refer you to the spring of the present year, Miss Garth. Do you remember the fourth of March?"

Her attention wandered again; a thought seemed to have struck her at the moment when he spoke. Instead of answering his inquiry, she put a question of her own.

"Let me break the news to myself," she said—"let me anticipate you, if I can. His useless will, the terms in which you speak of his daughters, the doubt you seem to feel of my continued respect for his memory, have opened a new view to me. Mr. Vanstone has died a ruined man—is that what you had to tell me?"

"Far from it. Mr. Vanstone has died, leaving a fortune of more than eighty thousand pounds—a fortune invested in excellent securities. He lived up to his income, but never beyond it; and all his debts added together would not reach two hundred pounds. If he had died a ruined man, I should have felt deeply for his children—but I should not have hesitated to tell you the truth, as I am hesitating now. Let me repeat a question which escaped you, I think, when I first put it. Carry your mind back to the spring of this year. Do you remember the fourth of March?"

Miss Garth shook her head. "My memory for dates is bad at the best of times," she said. "I am too confused to exert it at a moment's notice. Can you put your question in no other form?"

He put it in this form:—

"Do you remember any domestic event in the spring of the present year, which appeared to affect Mr. Vanstone more seriously than usual?"

Miss Garth leaned forward in her chair, and looked eagerly at Mr. Pendril across the table. "The journey to London!" she exclaimed. "I distrusted the journey to London from the first! Yes! I remember Mr. Vanstone receiving a letter—I remember his reading it, and looking so altered from himself that he startled us all."

"Did you notice any apparent understanding between Mr. and Mrs. Vanstone, on the subject of that letter?"

"Yes: I did. One of the girls—it was Magdalen—mentioned the postmark; some place in America. It all comes back to me, Mr. Pendril. Mrs. Vanstone looked excited and anxious, the moment she heard the place named. They went to London together the next day; they explained nothing to their daughters, nothing to me. Mrs. Vanstone said the journey was for family affairs. I suspected something wrong; I couldn't tell what. Mrs. Vanstone wrote to me from London, saying that her object was to consult a physician on the state of her health, and not to alarm her daughters by telling them. Something in the letter rather hurt me at the time. I thought there might be some other motive that she was keeping from me. Did I do her wrong?"

"You did her no wrong. There *was* a motive which she was keeping from you. In revealing that motive, I reveal the painful secret which brings me to this house. All that I could do to prepare you, I have done. Let me now tell the truth in the plainest and fewest words. When Mr. and Mrs. Vanstone left Combe-Raven, in the March of the present year——"

Before he could complete the sentence, a sudden movement of Miss Garth's interrupted him. She started violently, and looked round towards the window. "Only the wind among the leaves," she said, faintly. "My nerves are so shaken, the least thing startles me. Speak out, for God's sake! When Mr. and Mrs. Vanstone left this house, tell me in plain words—why did they go to London?"

In plain words, Mr. Pendril told her:

"They went to London to be married."

With that answer he placed a slip of paper on the table. It was the marriage certificate of the dead parents, and the date it bore was March the twentieth, eighteen hundred and forty-six.

Miss Garth neither moved nor spoke. The certificate lay beneath her unnoticed. She sat with her eyes rooted on the lawyer's face; her mind stunned, her senses helpless. He saw that all his efforts to break the shock of the discovery had been efforts made in vain; he felt the vital import-ance of rousing her, and firmly and distinctly repeated the fatal words.

"They went to London to be married," he said. "Try to rouse your-self: try to realize the plain fact first: the explanation shall come after-wards. Miss Garth, I speak the miserable truth! In the spring of this year they left home; they lived in London for a fortnight, in the strictest retirement; they were married by licence at the end of that time. There is a copy of the certificate, which I myself obtained on Monday last. Read the date of the marriage for yourself. It is Friday, the twentieth of March—the March of this present year."

As he pointed to the certificate, that faint breath of air among the shrubs beneath the window, which had startled Miss Garth, stirred the leaves once more. He heard it himself, this time; and turned his face, so as to let the breeze play upon it. No breeze came; no breath of air that was strong enough for him to feel, floated into the room.

Miss Garth roused herself mechanically, and read the certificate. It seemed to produce no distinct impression on her : she laid it on one side, in a lost bewildered manner. "Twelve years," she said, in low hopeless tones—"twelve quiet happy years I lived with this family. Mrs. Vanstone was my friend ; my dear, valued friend—my sister, I might almost say. I can't believe it. Bear with me a little, sir, I can't believe it yet."

"I shall help you to believe it, when I tell you more," said Mr. Pendril —"you will understand me better when I take you back to the time of Mr. Vanstone's early life. I won't ask for your attention just yet. Let us wait a little, until you recover yourself."

They waited a few minutes. The lawyer took some letters from his pocket, referred to them attentively, and put them back again. "Can you listen to me, now?" he asked kindly. She bowed her head in answer. Mr. Pendril considered with himself for a moment. "I must caution you on one point," he said. "If the aspect of Mr. Vanstone's character which I am now about to present to you, seems in some respects at variance with your later experience, bear in mind that when you first knew him twelve years since, he was a man of forty ; and that, when I first knew him, he was a lad of nineteen."

His next words raised the veil, and showed the irrevocable Past.

CHAPTER XIII.

"THE fortune which Mr. Vanstone possessed when you knew him" (the lawyer began) "was part, and part only, of the inheritance which fell to him on his father's death. Mr. Vanstone the elder, was a manufacturer in the North of England. He married early in life ; and the children of the marriage were either six, or seven in number—I am not certain which. First, Michael, the eldest son, still living, and now an old man turned seventy. Secondly, Selina, the eldest daughter, who married in after-life, and who died ten or eleven years ago. After those two, came other sons and daughters whose early deaths make it unnecessary to mention them particularly. The last and by many years the youngest of the children was Andrew, whom I first knew, as I told you, at the age of nineteen. My father was then on the point of retiring from the active pursuit of his profession ; and, in succeeding to his business, I also succeeded to his connection with the Vanstones, as the family solicitor.

"At that time, Andrew had just started in life by entering the army. After little more than a year of home-service, he was ordered out with his regiment to Canada. When he quitted England, he left his father and his elder brother Michael seriously at variance. I need not detain you by entering into the cause of the quarrel. I need only tell you that the elder Mr. Vanstone, with many excellent qualities, was a man of fierce and intractable temper. His eldest son had set him at defiance, under circumstances which might have justly irritated a father of far milder character ; and he declared, in the most positive terms, that he would never see Michael's face again. In defiance of my entreaties, and of the entreaties of his wife, he tore up, in our presence, the will which provided for Michael's share in the paternal inheritance. Such was the family position, when the younger son left home for Canada.

" Some months after Andrew's arrival with his regiment at Quebec, he became acquainted with a woman of great personal attractions, who came, or said she came, from one of the southern states of America. She obtained an immediate influence over him : and she used it to the basest purpose. You knew the easy, affectionate, trusting nature of the man, in later life— you can imagine how thoughtlessly he acted on the impulses of his youth. It is useless to dwell on this lamentable part of the story. He was just twenty-one : he was blindly devoted to a worthless woman ; and she led him on, with merciless cunning, till it was too late to draw back. In one word, he committed the fatal error of his life : he married her.

" She had been wise enough in her own interests to dread the influence of his brother officers, and to persuade him, up to the period of the marriage ceremony, to keep the proposed union between them a secret. She could do this ; but she could not provide against the results of accident. Hardly three months had passed, when a chance disclosure exposed the life she had led, before her marriage. But one alternative was left to her husband—the alternative of instantly separating from her.

" The effect of the discovery on the unhappy boy—for a boy in disposition he still was—may be judged by the event which followed the exposure. One of Andrew's superior officers—a certain Major Kirke, if I remember right—found him in his quarters, writing to his father a confession of the disgraceful truth, with a loaded pistol by his side. That officer saved the lad's life from his own hand ; and hushed up the scandalous affair, by a compromise. The marriage being a perfectly legal one, and the wife's misconduct prior to the ceremony, giving her husband no claim to his release from her by divorce, it was only possible to appeal to her sense of her own interests. A handsome annual allowance was secured to her, on condition that she returned to the place from which she had come ; that she never appeared in England ; and that she ceased to use her husband's name. Other stipulations were added to these. She accepted them all ; and measures were privately taken to have her well looked after in the place of her retreat. What life she led there, and whether she performed all the conditions imposed on her, I cannot say. I can only tell you that she never, to my knowledge, came to England ; that she never annoyed Mr.

Vanstone; and that the annual allowance was paid her, through a local agent in America, to the day of her death. All that she wanted in marrying him was money; and money she got.

"In the mean time, Andrew had left the regiment. Nothing would induce him to face his brother-officers after what had happened. He sold out, and returned to England. The first intelligence which reached him on his return, was the intelligence of his father's death. He came to my office in London, before going home, and there learnt from my lips how the family quarrel had ended.

"The will which Mr. Vanstone the elder had destroyed in my presence, had not been, so far as I knew, replaced by another. When I was sent for, in the usual course, on his death, I fully expected that the law would be left to make the customary division among his widow and his children. To my surprise, a will appeared among his papers, correctly drawn and executed, and dated about a week after the period when the first will had been destroyed. He had maintained his vindictive purpose against his eldest son; and had applied to a stranger for the professional assistance which I honestly believe he was ashamed to ask for at my hands.

"It is needless to trouble you with the provisions of the will in detail. There were the widow, and three surviving children to be provided for. The widow received a life-interest only, in a portion of the testator's property. The remaining portion was divided between Andrew and Selina—two-thirds to the brother; one-third to the sister. On the mother's death, the money from which her income had been derived, was to go to Andrew and Selina, in the same relative proportions as before—five thousand pounds having been first deducted from the sum, and paid to Michael, as the sole legacy left by the implacable father to his eldest son.

"Speaking in round numbers, the division of property, as settled by the will, stood thus. Before the mother's death, Andrew had seventy thousand pounds; Selina had thirty-five thousand pounds; Michael—had nothing. After the mother's death, Michael had five thousand pounds, to set against Andrew's inheritance augmented to one hundred thousand, and Selina's inheritance increased to fifty thousand.—Do not suppose that I am dwelling unnecessarily on this part of the subject. Every word I now speak bears on interests still in suspense, which vitally concern Mr. Vanstone's daughters. As we get on from past to present, keep in mind the terrible inequality of Michael's inheritance and Andrew's inheritance. The harm done by that vindictive will is, I greatly fear, not over yet.

"Andrew's first impulse, when he heard the news which I had to tell him, was worthy of the open, generous nature of the man. He at once proposed to divide his inheritance with his elder brother. But there was one serious obstacle in the way. A letter from Michael was waiting for him at my office, when he came there; and that letter charged him with

being the original cause of estrangement between his father and his elder
brother. The efforts which he had made—bluntly and incautiously, I
own ; but with the purest and kindest intentions, as I know—to compose
the . quarrel before leaving home, were perverted by the vilest miscon-
struction, to support an accusation of treachery and falsehood which would
have stung any man to the quick. Andrew felt, what I felt, that if these
imputations were not withdrawn, before his generous intentions towards
his brother took effect, the mere fact of their execution would amount to a
practical acknowledgment of the justice of Michael's charge against him.
He wrote to his brother in the most forbearing terms. The answer received
was as offensive as words could make it. Michael had inherited his father's
temper, unredeemed by his father's better qualities : his second letter reiterated the charges contained in the first, and declared that he would only
accept the offered division as an act of atonement and restitution on
Andrew's part. I next wrote to the mother, to use her influence. She
was herself aggrieved at being left with nothing more than a life interest in
her husband's property ; she sided resolutely with Michael ; and she stig-
matized Andrew's proposal as an attempt to bribe her eldest son into with-
drawing a charge against his brother, which that brother knew to be true.
After this last repulse, nothing more could be done. Michael withdrew to
the Continent ; and his mother followed him there. She lived long enough,
and saved money enough out of her income, to add considerably, at her
death, to her elder son's five thousand pounds. He had previously still
further improved his pecuniary position by an advantageous marriage ; and
he is now passing the close of his days either in France or Switzerland—a
widower, with one son. We shall return to him shortly. In the mean
time, I need only tell you that Andrew and Michael never again met—
never again communicated, even by writing. To all intents and purposes,
they were dead to each other, from those early days to the present
time.

"You can now estimate what Andrew's position was when he left his
profession and returned to England. Possessed of a fortune, he was alone
in the world ;—his future destroyed at the fair outset of life ; his mother
and brother estranged from him ; his sister lately married, with interests
and hopes in which he had no share. Men of firmer mental calibre might
have found refuge from such a situation as this, in an absorbing intellectual
pursuit. He was not capable of the effort ; all the strength of his character
lay in the affections he had wasted. His place in the world was that quiet
place at home, with wife and children to make his life happy, which he had
lost for ever. To look back was more than he dare. To look forward was
more than he could. In sheer despair, he let his own impetuous youth
drive him on ; and cast himself into the lowest dissipations of a London
life.

"A woman's falsehood had driven him to his ruin. A woman's love saved him at the outset of his downward career. Let us not speak of her harshly—for we laid her with him yesterday in the grave.

"You, who only knew Mrs. Vanstone in later life, when illness and sorrow and secret care had altered and saddened her, can form no adequate idea of her attractions of person and character when she was a girl of seventeen. I was with Andrew when he first met her. I had tried to rescue him for one night at least, from degrading associates and degrading pleasures, by persuading him to go with me to a ball given by one of the great City Companies. There, they met. She produced a strong impression on him, the moment he saw her. To me, as to him, she was a total stranger. An introduction to her, obtained in the customary manner, informed him that she was the daughter of one Mr. Blake. The rest he discovered from herself. They were partners in the dance (unobserved in that crowded ball-room), all through the evening.

"Circumstances were against her from the first. She was unhappy at home. Her family and friends occupied no recognized station in life : they were mean, underhand people, in every way unworthy of her. It was her first ball—it was the first time she had ever met with a man who had the breeding, the manners, and the conversation of a gentleman. Are these excuses for her, which I have no right to make ? If we have any human feeling for human weakness, surely not !

"The meeting of that night, decided their future. When other meetings had followed, when the confession of her love had escaped her, he took the one course of all others (took it innocently and unconsciously), which was most dangerous to them both. His frankness and his sense of honour forbade him to deceive her : he opened his heart, and told her the truth. She was a generous, impulsive girl ; she had no home ties strong enough to plead with her ; she was passionately fond of him—and he had made that appeal to her pity, which, to the eternal honour of women, is the hardest of all appeals for them to resist. She saw, and saw truly, that she alone stood between him and his ruin. The last chance of his rescue hung on her decision. She decided ; and saved him.

"Let me not be misunderstood ; let me not be accused of trifling with the serious social question on which my narrative forces me to touch. I will defend her memory by no false reasoning—I will only speak the truth. It is the truth that she snatched him from mad excesses which must have ended in his early death. It is the truth that she restored him to that happy home-existence which you remember so tenderly—which *he* remembered so gratefully that, on the day when he was free, he made her his wife. Let strict morality claim its right, and condemn her early fault. I have read my New Testament to little purpose indeed, if Christian mercy may not soften the hard sentence against her—if Christian charity may not find a plea for her memory in the love and fidelity, the suffering and the sacrifice of her whole life.

"A few words more will bring us to a later time, and to events which have happened within your own experience.

"I need not remind you that the position in which Mr. Vanstone was now placed, could lead in the end to but one result—to a disclosure, more or less inevitable, of the truth.   Attempts were made to keep the hopeless misfortune of his life a secret from Miss Blake's family; and, as a matter of course, those attempts failed before the relentless scrutiny of her father and her friends.   What might have happened if her relatives had been, what is termed, 'respectable,' I cannot pretend to say.   As it was, they were people who could (in the common phrase) be conveniently treated with. The only survivor of the family at the present time, is a scoundrel calling himself Captain Wragge.   When I tell you that he privately extorted the price of his silence from Mrs. Vanstone, to the last; and when I add that his conduct presents no extraordinary exception to the conduct, in their lifetime, of the other relatives—you will understand what sort of people I had to deal with in my client's interests, and how their assumed indignation was appeased.

"Having, in the first instance, left England for Ireland, Mr. Vanstone and Miss Blake remained there afterwards for some years.   Girl as she was, she faced her position and its necessities without flinching.   Having once resolved to sacrifice her life to the man she loved; having quieted her conscience by persuading herself that his marriage was a legal mockery, and that she was 'his wife in the sight of Heaven;' she set herself from the first to accomplish the one foremost purpose of so living with him, in the world's eye, as never to raise the suspicion that she was not his lawful wife.   The women are few indeed, who cannot resolve firmly, scheme patiently, and act promptly, where the dearest interests of their lives are concerned.   Mrs. Vanstone—she has a right now, remember, to that name —Mrs. Vanstone had more than the average share of a woman's tenacity and a woman's tact; and she took all the needful precautions, in those early days, which her husband's less ready capacity had not the art to devise — precautions to which they were largely indebted for the preservation of their secret in later times.

"Thanks to these safeguards, not a shadow of suspicion followed them when they returned to England.   They first settled in Devonshire, merely because they were far removed there from that northern county in which Mr. Vanstone's family and connections had been known.   On the part of his surviving relatives, they had no curious investigations to dread.   He was totally estranged from his mother and his elder brother.   His married sister had been forbidden by her husband (who was a clergyman) to hold any communication with him, from the period when he had fallen into the deplorable way of life which I have described as following his return from Canada. Other relations he had none. When he and Miss Blake left Devonshire, their next change of residence was to this house. Neither courting, nor avoiding notice; simply happy in themselves, in their children, and in their quiet rural life; unsuspected by the few neighbours who formed their modest circle of acquaintance to be other than what they seemed—the truth in their case, as in the cases of many others, remained undiscovered until accident forced it into the light of day.

"If, in your close intimacy with them, it seems strange that they should never have betrayed themselves, let me ask you to consider the circumstances, and you will understand the apparent anomaly. Remember that they had been living as husband and wife, to all intents and purposes (except that the marriage service had not been read over them) for fifteen years before you came into the house; and bear in mind, at the same time, that no event occurred to disturb Mr. Vanstone's happiness in the present, to remind him of the past, or to warn him of the future, until the announcement of his wife's death reached him, in that letter from America which you saw placed in his hand. From that day forth—when a past which *he* abhorred was forced back to his memory; when a future which *she* had never dared to anticipate was placed within her reach—you will soon perceive, if you have not perceived already, that they both betrayed themselves, time after time; and that your innocence of all suspicion, and their children's innocence of all suspicion, alone prevented you from discovering the truth.

"The sad story of the past is now as well known to you as to me. I have had hard words to speak. God knows I have spoken them with true sympathy for the living, with true tenderness for the memory of the dead."

He paused, turned his face a little away, and rested his head on his hand, in the quiet undemonstrative manner which was natural to him. Thus far, Miss Garth had only interrupted his narrative by an occasional word, or by a mute token of her attention. She made no effort to conceal her tears; they fell fast and silently over her wasted cheeks, as she looked up and spoke to him. "I have done you some injury, sir, in my thoughts," she said, with a noble simplicity. "I know you better now. Let me ask your forgiveness; let me take your hand."

Those words, and the action which accompanied them, touched him deeply. He took her hand in silence. She was the first to speak, the first to set the example of self-control. It is one of the noble instincts of women, that nothing more powerfully rouses them to struggle with their own sorrow than the sight of a man's distress. She quietly dried her tears; she quietly drew her chair round the table so as to sit nearer to him when she spoke again.

"I have been sadly broken, Mr. Pendril, by what has happened in this house," she said, "or I should have borne what you have told me, better than I have borne it to-day. Will you let me ask one question, before you go on? My heart aches for the children of my love—more than ever my children now. Is there no hope for their future? Are they left with no prospect but poverty before them?"

The lawyer hesitated before he answered the question.

"They are left dependent," he said, at last, "on the justice and the mercy of a stranger."

"Through the misfortune of their birth?"

"Through the misfortunes which have followed the marriage of their parents."

With that startling answer he rose, took up the will from the floor, and restored it to its former position on the table between them.

"I can only place the truth before you," he resumed, "in one plain form of words. The marriage has destroyed this will, and has left Mr. Vanstone's daughters dependent on their uncle."

As he spoke, the breeze stirred again among the shrubs under the window.

"On their uncle?" repeated Miss Garth. She considered for a moment, and laid her hand suddenly on Mr. Pendril's arm. "Not on Michael Vanstone!"

"Yes: on Michael Vanstone."

Miss Garth's hand still mechanically grasped the lawyer's arm. Her whole mind was absorbed in the effort to realize the discovery which had now burst on her.

"Dependent on Michael Vanstone!" she said to herself. "Dependent on their father's bitterest enemy? How can it be?"

"Give me your attention for a few minutes more," said Mr. Pendril, "and you shall hear. The sooner we can bring this painful interview to a close, the sooner I can open communications with Mr. Michael Vanstone, and the sooner you will know what he decides on doing for his brother's orphan daughters. I repeat to you that they are absolutely dependent on him. You will most readily understand how and why, if we take up the chain of events where we last left it—at the period of Mr. and Mrs. Vanstone's marriage."

"One moment, sir," said Miss Garth. "Were you in the secret of that marriage at the time when it took place?"

"Unhappily, I was not. I was away from London—away from England at the time. If Mr. Vanstone had been able to communicate with me when the letter from America announced the death of his wife, the fortunes of his daughters would not have been now at stake."

He paused: and before proceeding further, looked once more at the letters which he had consulted at an earlier period of the interview. He took one letter from the rest, and put it on the table by his side.

"At the beginning of the present year," he resumed, "a very serious business necessity, in connection with some West Indian property possessed by an old client and friend of mine, required the presence either of myself, or of one of my two partners, in Jamaica. One of the two could not be spared: the other was not in health to undertake the voyage. There was no choice left but for me to go. I wrote to Mr. Vanstone, telling him that I should leave England at the end of February, and that the nature of the business which took me away afforded little hope of my getting back from the West Indies before June. My letter was not written with any special motive. I merely thought it right—seeing that my partners were not admitted to my knowledge of Mr. Vanstone's private affairs—to warn him of my absence, as a measure of formal precaution which it was right to take. At the end of February I left England, without having heard from him. I was on the sea when the news of his wife's death reached him, on the fourth of March; and I did not return until the middle of last June."

"You warned him of your departure," interposed Miss Garth. "Did you not warn him of your return?"

"Not personally. My head-clerk sent him one of the circulars which were despatched from my office, in various directions, to announce my return. It was the first substitute I thought of, for the personal letter which the pressure of innumerable occupations, all crowding on me together after my long absence, did not allow me leisure to write. Barely a month later, the first information of his marriage reached me in a letter from himself, written on the day of the fatal accident. The circumstances which induced him to write, arose out of an event in which you must have taken some interest—I mean the attachment between Mr. Clare's son and Mr. Vanstone's youngest daughter."

"I cannot say that I was favourably disposed towards that attachment at the time," replied Miss Garth. "I was ignorant then of the family secret: I know better now."

"Exactly. The motive which you can now appreciate is the motive that leads us to the point. The young lady herself (as I have heard from the elder Mr. Clare, to whom I am indebted for my knowledge of the circumstances in detail) confessed her attachment to her father, and innocently touched him to the quick by a chance reference to his own early life. He had a long conversation with Mrs. Vanstone, at which they both agreed that Mr. Clare must be privately informed of the truth, before the attachment between the two young people was allowed to proceed further. It was painful in the last degree, both to husband and wife, to be reduced to this alternative. But they were resolute, honourably resolute, in making the sacrifice of their own feelings; and Mr. Vanstone betook himself on the spot to Mr. Clare's cottage.—You no doubt observed a remarkable change in Mr. Vanstone's manner on that day; and you can now account for it?"

Miss Garth bowed her head; and Mr. Pendril went on.

"You are sufficiently acquainted with Mr. Clare's contempt for all social prejudices," he continued, "to anticipate his reception of the confession which his neighbour addressed to him. Five minutes after the interview had begun, the two old friends were as easy and unrestrained together as usual. In the course of conversation, Mr. Vanstone mentioned the pecuniary arrangement which he had made for the benefit of his daughter and of her future husband—and, in doing so, he naturally referred to his will, here, on the table between us. Mr. Clare, remembering that his friend had been married in the March of that year, at once asked when the will had been executed; received the reply that it had been made five years since; and, thereupon, astounded Mr. Vanstone by telling him bluntly that the document was waste paper in the eye of the law. Up to that moment, he, like many other persons, had been absolutely ignorant that a man's marriage is, legally, as well as socially, considered to be the most important event in his life; that it destroys the validity of any will which he may have made as a single man; and that it renders absolutely necessary the entire reassertion of his testamentary intentions in the character of a husband. The statement of this plain fact appeared to overwhelm Mr. Vanstone. Declaring that his friend had laid him under an obligation which he should remember to his dying day, he at once left the cottage, at once returned home, and wrote me this letter:"

He handed the letter open to Miss Garth. In tearless, speechless grief, she read these words:

"MY DEAR PENDRIL,—Since we last wrote to each other, an extraordinary change has taken place in my life. About a week after you went away, I received news from America which told me that I was free. Need I say what use I made of that freedom? Need I say that the mother of my children is now my Wife?

"If you are surprised at not having heard from me the moment you got back, attribute my silence, in great part—if not altogether—to my own total ignorance of the legal necessity for making another will. Not half an hour since, I was enlightened for the first time (under circumstances which I will mention when we meet) by my old friend, Mr. Clare. Family anxieties have had something to do with my silence, as well. My wife's confinement is close at hand; and, besides this serious anxiety, my second daughter is just engaged to be married. Until I saw Mr. Clare to-day, these matters so filled my mind that I never thought of writing to you, during the one short month which is all that has passed since I got news of your return. Now I know that my will must be made again, I write instantly. For God's sake, come on the day when you receive this—come and relieve me from the dreadful thought that my two darling girls are at this moment unprovided for. If anything happened to me, and if my desire to do their mother justice, ended (through my miserable ignorance of the law) in leaving Norah and Magdalen disinherited, I should not rest in my grave! Come, at any cost, to yours ever,   "A. V."

"On the Saturday morning," Mr. Pendril resumed, "those lines reached me. I instantly set aside all other business, and drove to the railway. At the London terminus, I heard the first news of the Friday's accident; heard it, with conflicting accounts of the numbers and names of the passengers killed. At Bristol, they were better informed; and the dreadful truth about Mr. Vanstone was confirmed. I had time to recover myself, before I reached your station here, and found Mr. Clare's son waiting for me. He took me to his father's cottage; and there, without losing a moment, I drew out Mrs. Vanstone's will. My object was to secure the only provision for her daughters which it was now possible to make. Mr. Vanstone having died intestate, a third of his fortune would go to his widow; and the rest would be divided among his next of kin. As children born out of wedlock,* Mr. Vanstone's daughters, under the circumstances of their father's death, had no more claim to a share in his property, than the daughters of one of his labourers in the village. The one chance left, was that their mother might sufficiently recover to leave her third share to them, by will, in the event of her decease. Now you know why I wrote to you to ask for that interview—why I waited day and night, in the hope of receiving a summons to the house. I was sincerely sorry to send back such an answer to your note of inquiry as I was compelled to write. But while there was a chance of the preservation of Mrs. Vanstone's life, the secret of the marriage was hers, not mine; and every consideration of delicacy forbade me to disclose it."

"You did right, sir," said Miss Garth; "I understand your motives, and respect them."

"My last attempt to provide for the daughters," continued Mr. Pendril, "was, as you know, rendered unavailing by the dangerous nature of Mrs. Vanstone's illness. Her death left the infant who survived her by a few hours (the infant born, you will remember, in lawful wedlock) possessed, in due legal course, of the whole of Mr. Vanstone's fortune. On the child's death—if it had only outlived the mother by a few seconds, instead of a few hours, the result would have been the same—the next of kin to the legitimate offspring took the money; and that next of kin is the infant's paternal uncle, Michael Vanstone. The whole fortune of eighty thousand pounds has virtually passed into his possession already."

"Are there no other relations?" asked Miss Garth. "Is there no hope from any one else?"

"There are no other relations with Michael Vanstone's claim," said the lawyer. "There are no grandfathers or grandmothers of the dead child (on the side of either of the parents) now alive. It was not likely there should be, considering the ages of Mr. and Mrs. Vanstone, when they died. But it is a misfortune to be reasonably lamented that no other uncles or aunts survive. There are cousins alive; a son and two daughters of that elder sister of Mr. Vanstone's, who married Archdeacon Bartram, and who died, as I told you, some years since. But their interest is superseded by the interest of the nearer blood. No, Miss Garth; we must look facts as they are resolutely in the face. Mr. Vanstone's daughters are Nobody's Children; and the law leaves them helpless at their uncle's mercy."

"A cruel law, Mr. Pendril—a cruel law in a Christian country."

"Cruel as it is, Miss Garth, it stands excused by a shocking peculiarity in this case. I am far from defending the law of England, as it affects illegitimate offspring. On the contrary, I think it a disgrace to the nation. It visits the sins of the parents on the children; it encourages vice by depriving fathers and mothers of the strongest of all motives for making the atonement of marriage; and it claims to produce these two abominable results in the names of morality and religion. But it has no extraordinary oppression to answer for, in the case of these unhappy girls. The more merciful and Christian law of other countries, which allows the marriage of the parents to make the children legitimate, has no mercy on *these* children. The accident of their father having been married, when he first met with their mother, has made them the outcasts of the whole social community: it has placed them out of the pale of the Civil Law of Europe. I tell you the hard truth—it is useless to disguise it. There is no hope, if we look back at the past: there may be hope, if we look on to the future. The best service which I can now render you, is to shorten the period of your suspense. In less than an hour I shall be on my way back to London. Immediately on my arrival I will ascertain the speediest means of communicating with Mr. Michael Vanstone; and will let you know the result. Sad as the position of the two sisters now is, we must look at it on its best side; we must not lose hope."

"Hope?" repeated Miss Garth. "Hope from Michael Vanstone!"

"Yes; hope from the influence on him of time, if not from the influence of mercy. As I have already told you, he is now an old man; he cannot, in the course of nature, expect to live much longer. If he looks back to the period when he and his brother were first at variance, he must look oack through thirty years. Surely, these are softening influences which must affect any man? Surely, his own knowledge of the shocking circumstances under which he has become possessed of this money, will plead with him, if nothing else does?"

"I will try to think as you do, Mr. Pendril—I will try to hope for the best. Shall we be left long in suspense before the decision reaches us?"

"I trust not. The only delay on my side will be caused by the necessity of discovering the place of Michael Vanstone's residence on the Continent. I think I have the means of meeting this difficulty successfully; and the moment I reach London, those means shall be tried."

He took up his hat; and then returned to the table on which the father's last letter, and the father's useless will, were lying side by side. After a moment's consideration, he placed them both in Miss Garth's hands.

"It may help you in breaking the hard truth to the orphan sisters," he said, in his quiet, self-repressed way, "if they can see how their father refers to them in his will—if they can read his letter to me, the last he ever wrote. Let these tokens tell them that the one idea of their father's life, was the idea of making atonement to his children. 'They may think bitterly of their birth,' he said to me, at the time when I drew this useless will; 'but they shall never think bitterly of *me*. I will cross them in nothing: they shall never know a sorrow that I can spare them, or a want which I will not satisfy.' He made me put those words in his will, to plead for him when the truth which he had concealed from his children in his lifetime, was revealed to them after his death. No law can deprive his daughters of the legacy of his repentance and his love. I leave the will and the letter to help you: I give them both into your care."

He saw how his parting kindness touched her, and thoughtfully hastened the farewell. She took his hand in both her own, and murmured a few broken words of gratitude. "Trust me to do my best," he said—and, turning away with a merciful abruptness, left her. In the broad, cheerful sunshine, he had come in to reveal the fatal truth. In the broad, cheerful sunshine—that truth disclosed—he went out.

CHAPTER XIV.

IT was nearly an hour past noon, when Mr. Pendril left the house. Miss Garth sat down again at the table alone; and tried to face the necessity which the event of the morning now forced on her.

Her mind was not equal to the effort. She tried to lessen the strain on it—to lose the sense of her own position—to escape from her thoughts for a few minutes only. After a little, she opened Mr. Vanstone's letter, and mechanically set herself to read it through once more.

One by one, the last words of the dead man fastened themselves more

and more firmly on her attention. The unrelieved solitude, the unbroken
silence, helped their influence on her mind, and opened it to those very
impressions of past and present which she was most anxious to shun. As
she reached the melancholy lines which closed the letter, she found herself
—insensibly, almost unconsciously, at first—tracing the fatal chain of
events, link by link backwards, until she reached its beginning in the contemplated marriage between Magdalen and Francis Clare.

That marriage had taken Mr. Vanstone to his old friend, with the
confession on his lips which would otherwise never have escaped them.
Thence came the discovery which had sent him home to summon the
lawyer to the house. That summons, again, had produced the inevitable
acceleration of the Saturday's journey to Friday; the Friday of the fatal
accident, the Friday when he went to his death. From his death, followed
the second bereavement which had made the house desolate; the helpless
position of the daughters whose prosperous future had been his dearest care;
the revelation of the secret which had overwhelmed her that morning; the
disclosure, more terrible still, which she now stood committed to make to
the orphan sisters. For the first time, she saw the whole sequence of
events—saw it as plainly as the cloudless blue of the sky, and the green
glow of the trees in the sunlight outside.

How—when could she tell them? Who could approach them with the
disclosure of their own illegitimacy, before their father and mother had
been dead a week? Who could speak the dreadful words, while the first
tears were wet on their cheeks, while the first pang of separation was at its
keenest in their hearts, while the memory of the funeral was not a day old
yet? Not their last friend left; not the faithful woman whose heart bled
for them. No! silence for the present time, at all risks—merciful silence,
for many days to come!

She left the room, with the will and the letter in her hand—with the
natural, human pity at her heart, which sealed her lips and shut her eyes
resolutely to the future. In the hall, she stopped and listened. Not a
sound was audible. She softly ascended the stairs, on her way to her own
room, and passed the door of Norah's bed-chamber. Voices inside, the
voices of the two sisters, caught her ear. After a moment's consideration,
she checked herself, turned back, and quickly descended the stairs again.
Both Norah and Magdalen knew of the interview between Mr. Pendril and
herself: she had felt it her duty to show them his letter, making the
appointment. Could she excite their suspicion by locking herself up from
them in her room, as soon as the lawyer had left the house? Her hand
trembled on the banister; she felt that her face might betray her. The
self-forgetful fortitude, which had never failed her until that day, had been
tried once too often—had been tasked beyond its powers at last.

At the hall-door, she reflected for a moment again, and went into the garden ; directing her steps to a rustic bench and table placed out of sight of the house, among the trees. In past times, she had often sat there, with Mrs. Vanstone on one side, with Norah on the other, with Magdalen and the dogs romping on the grass. Alone, she sat there now—the will and the letter, which she dared not trust out of her own possession, laid on the table—her head bowed over them ; her face hidden in her hands. Alone, she sat there, and tried to rouse her sinking courage.

Doubts thronged on her of the dark days to come ; dread beset her of the hidden danger which her own silence towards Norah and Magdalen, might store up in the near future. The accident of a moment might suddenly reveal the truth. Mr. Pendril might write, might personally address himself to the sisters, in the natural conviction that she had enlightened them. Complications might gather round them at a moment's notice ; unforeseen necessities might arise for immediately leaving the house. She saw all these perils—and still the cruel courage to face the worst, and speak, was as far from her as ever. Ere long, the thickening conflict of her thoughts forced its way outward for relief, in words and actions. She raised her head, and beat her hand helplessly on the table.

"God help me, what am I to do!" she broke out. "How am I to tell them?"

"There is no need to tell them," said a voice, behind her. "They know it already."

She started to her feet; and looked round. It was Magdalen who stood before her—Magdalen who had spoken those words.

Yes, there was the graceful figure, in its mourning garments, standing out tall and black and motionless against the leafy background. There was Magdalen herself, with a changeless stillness on her white face; with an icy resignation in her steady grey eyes.

"We know it already," she repeated, in clear, measured tones. "Mr. Vanstone's daughters are Nobody's Children ; and the law leaves them helpless at their uncle's mercy."

So, without a tear on her cheeks, without a faltering tone in her voice, she repeated the lawyer's own words, exactly as he had spoken them. Miss Garth staggered back a step, and caught at the bench to support herself. Her head swam ; she closed her eyes in a momentary faintness. When they opened again, Magdalen's arm was supporting her, Magdalen's breath fanned her cheek, Magdalen's cold lips kissed her. She drew back from the kiss; the touch of the girl's lips thrilled her with terror.

As soon as she could speak, she put the inevitable question. "You heard us," she said. "Where?"

"Under the open window."

"All the time?"

"From beginning to end."

She had listened—this girl of eighteen, in the first week of her orphanage, had listened to the whole terrible revelation, word by word, as it fell from the lawyer's lips; and had never once betrayed herself! From first to last, the only movements which had escaped her, had been movements guarded enough and slight enough to be mistaken for the passage of the summer breeze through the leaves!

"Don't try to speak yet," she said, in softer and gentler tones. "Don't look at me with those doubting eyes. What wrong have I done? When Mr. Pendril wished to speak to you about Norah and me, his letter gave us our choice to be present at the interview, or to keep away. If my elder sister decided to keep away, how could I come? How could I hear my own story, except as I did? My listening has done no harm. It has done good—it has saved you the distress of speaking to us. You have suffered enough for us already; it is time we learnt to suffer for ourselves. I have learnt. And Norah is learning."

"Norah!"

"Yes. I have done all I could to spare you. I have told Norah."

She had told Norah! Was this girl, whose courage had faced the terrible necessity from which a woman old enough to be her mother had recoiled, the girl Miss Garth had brought up? the girl whose nature she had believed to be as well known to her as her own?

"Magdalen!" she cried out passionately, "you frighten me!"

Magdalen only sighed, and turned wearily away.

"Try not to think worse of me than I deserve," she said. "I can't cry. My heart is numbed."

She moved away slowly over the grass. Miss Garth watched the tall black figure gliding away alone, until it was lost among the trees. While it was in sight, she could think of nothing else. The moment it was gone, she thought of Norah. For the first time, in her experience of the sisters, her heart led her instinctively to the elder of the two.

Norah was still in her own room. She was sitting on the couch by the window, with her mother's old music-book—the keepsake which Mrs. Vanstone had found in her husband's study, on the day of her husband's death—spread open on her lap. She looked up from it with such quiet sorrow, and pointed with such ready kindness to the vacant place at her side, that Miss Garth doubted for the moment whether Magdalen had spoken the truth. "See," said Norah, simply, turning to the first leaf in the music-book. "My mother's name written in it, and some verses to my father on the next page. We may keep this for ourselves, if we keep nothing else." She put her arm round Miss Garth's neck; and a faint tinge of colour stole over her cheeks. "I see anxious thoughts in your face," she whispered. "Are you anxious about me? Are you doubting whether I have heard it? I have heard the whole truth. I might have felt it bitterly, later; it is too soon to feel it now. You have seen Magdalen? She went out to find you—where did you leave her?"

"In the garden. I couldn't speak to her; I couldn't look at her. Magdalen has frightened me."

Norah rose hurriedly; rose, startled and distressed by Miss Garth's reply.

"Don't think ill of Magdalen," she said. "Magdalen suffers in secret more than I do. Try not to grieve over what you have heard about us this morning. Does it matter who we are, or what we keep or lose? What loss is there for us, after the loss of our father and mother? Oh, Miss Garth, *there* is the only bitterness! What did we remember of them, when we laid them in the grave yesterday? Nothing but the love they gave us—the love we must never hope for again. What else can we remember to-day? What change can the world, and the world's cruel laws, make in *our* memory of the kindest father, the kindest mother, that children ever had!" She stopped: struggled with her rising grief; and quietly, resolutely, kept it down. "Will you wait here?" she said, "while I go and bring Magdalen back? Magdalen was always your favourite: I want her to be your favourite still." She laid the music-book gently on Miss Garth's lap—and left the room.

"Magdalen was always your favourite."

Tenderly as they had been spoken, those words fell reproachfully on Miss Garth's ear. For the first time in the long companionship of her pupils and herself, a doubt whether she, and all those about her, had not been fatally mistaken in their relative estimate of the sisters, now forced itself on her mind.

She had studied the natures of her two pupils in the daily intimacy of twelve years. Those natures, which she believed herself to have sounded through all their depths, had been suddenly tried in the sharp ordeal of affliction. How had they come out from the test? As her previous experience had prepared her to see them? No: in flat contradiction to it.

What did such a result as this imply?

Thoughts came to her, as she asked herself that question, which have startled and saddened us all.

Does there exist in every human being, beneath that outward and visible character which is shaped into form by the social influences surrounding us, an inward, invisible disposition, which is part of ourselves; which education may indirectly modify, but can never hope to change? Is the philosophy which denies this, and asserts that we are born with dispositions like blank sheets of paper, a philosophy which has failed to remark that we are not born with blank faces—a philosophy which has never compared together two infants of a few days old, and has never observed that those infants are not born with blank tempers for mothers and nurses to fill up at will? Are there, infinitely varying with each individual, inbred forces of Good and Evil in all of us, deep down below the reach of mortal encouragement and mortal repression—hidden Good and hidden Evil, both alike at the mercy of the liberating opportunity and the sufficient temptation? Within these earthly limits, is earthly Circumstance ever the key; and can no human vigilance warn us beforehand of the forces imprisoned in ourselves which that key *may* unlock?

For the first time, thoughts such as these rose darkly—as shadowy and terrible possibilities—in Miss Garth's mind. For the first time, she associated those possibilities with the past conduct and characters, with the future lives and fortunes of the orphan-sisters.

Searching, as in a glass darkly, into the two natures, she felt her way, doubt by doubt, from one possible truth to another. It might be, that the upper surface of their characters was all that she had, thus far, plainly seen in Norah and Magdalen. It might be, that the unalluring secrecy and reserve of one sister, the all-attractive openness and high spirits of the other, were more or less referable, in each case, to those physical causes which work towards the production of moral results. It might be, that under the surface so formed—a surface which there had been nothing, hitherto, in the happy, prosperous, uneventful lives of the sisters to disturb—forces of inborn and inbred disposition had remained concealed, which the shock of the first serious calamity in their lives had now thrown up into view. Was this so? Was the promise of the future shining with prophetic light through the surface-shadow of Norah's reserve; and darkening with prophetic gloom, under the surface-glitter of Magdalen's bright spirits? If the life of the elder sister was destined henceforth to be the ripening ground of the undeveloped Good that was in her—was the life of the younger doomed to be the battle-field of mortal conflict with the roused forces of Evil in herself?

On the brink of that terrible conclusion, Miss Garth shrank back in dismay. Her heart was the heart of a true woman. It accepted the conviction which raised Norah higher in her love: it rejected the doubt which threatened to place Magdalen lower. She rose and paced the room impatiently; she recoiled with an angry suddenness from the whole train of thought in which her mind had been engaged but the moment before. What if there were dangerous elements in the strength of Magdalen's character—was it not her duty to help the girl against herself? How had she performed that duty? She had let herself be governed by first fears and first impressions; she had never waited to consider whether Magdalen's openly acknowledged action of that morning might not imply a self-sacrificing fortitude, which promised, in after-life, the noblest and the most enduring results. She had let Norah go and speak those words of tender remonstrance, which she should first have spoken herself. "Oh!" she thought bitterly, "how long I have lived in the world, and how little I have known of my own weakness and wickedness until to-day!"

The door of the room opened. Norah came in, as she had gone out, alone.

"Do you remember leaving anything on the little table by the garden-seat?" she asked, quietly.

Before Miss Garth could answer the question, she held out her father's will, and her father's letter.

"Magdalen came back after you went away," she said, "and found these last relics. She heard Mr. Pendril say they were her legacy and mine. When I went into the garden, she was reading the letter. There was no need for me to speak to her; our father had spoken to her from his grave. See how she has listened to him!"

She pointed to the letter. The traces of heavy tear-drops lay thick over the last lines of the dead man's writing.

"*Her* tears," said Norah, softly.

Miss Garth's head drooped low, over the mute revelation of Magdalen's return to her better self.

"Oh, never doubt her again!" pleaded Norah. "We are alone, now— we have our hard way through the world to walk on as patiently as we can. If Magdalen ever falters and turns back, help her for the love of old times; help her against herself."

"With all my heart and strength—as God shall judge me, with the devotion of my whole life!" In those fervent words Miss Garth answered. She took the hand which Norah held out to her, and put it, in sorrow and humility, to her lips. "Oh, my love, forgive me! I have been miserably blind—I have never valued you as I ought!"

Norah gently checked her before she could say more; gently whispered, "Come with me into the garden—come, and help Magdalen to look patiently to the future."

The future! Who could see the faintest glimmer of it? Who could see anything but the ill-omened figure of Michael Vanstone, posted darkly on the verge of the present time—and closing all the prospect that lay beyond him?

CHAPTER XV.

On the next morning but one, news was received from Mr. Pendril. The place of Michael Vanstone's residence on the Continent had been discovered. He was living at Zurich ; and a letter had been despatched to him, at that place, on the day when the information was obtained. In the course of the coming week an answer might be expected, and the purport of it should be communicated forthwith to the ladies at Combe-Raven.

Short as it was, the interval of delay passed wearily. Ten days elapsed before the expected answer was received ; and when it came at last, it proved to be, strictly speaking, no answer at all. Mr. Pendril had been merely referred to an agent in London who was in possession of Michael Vanstone's instructions. Certain difficulties had been discovered in connection with those instructions, which had produced the necessity of once more writing to Zurich. And there " the negociations" rested again for the present.

A second paragraph in Mr. Pendril's letter contained another piece of intelligence entirely new. Mr. Michael Vanstone's son (and only child), Mr. Noel Vanstone, had recently arrived in London, and was then staying in lodgings occupied by his cousin, Mr. George Bartram. Professional considerations had induced Mr. Pendril to pay a visit to the lodgings. He had been very kindly received by Mr. Bartram ; but had been informed by that gentleman that his cousin was not then in a condition to receive visitors. Mr. Noel Vanstone had been suffering, for some years past, from a wearing and obstinate malady ; he had come to England expressly to obtain the best medical advice, and he still felt the fatigue of the journey so severely as to be confined to his bed. Under these circumstances, Mr. Pendril had no alternative but to take his leave. An interview with Mr. Noel Vanstone might have cleared up some of the difficulties in connection with his father's instructions. As events had turned out, there was no help for it but to wait for a few days more.

The days passed, the empty days of solitude and suspense. At last, a third letter from the lawyer announced the long-delayed conclusion of the correspondence. The final answer had been received from Zurich ; and Mr. Pendril would personally communicate it at Combe-Raven, on the afternoon of the next day.

That next day was Wednesday, the twelfth of August. The weather had changed in the night : and the sun rose watery through mist and cloud. By noon, the sky was overcast at all points ; the temperature was sensibly colder ; and the rain poured down, straight and soft and steady, on the thirsty earth. Towards three o'clock, Miss Garth and Norah entered the morning-room, to await Mr. Pendril's arrival. They were joined shortly afterwards by Magdalen. In half an hour more, the familiar fall of the iron latch in the socket, reached their ears from the fence beyond the shrubbery. Mr. Pendril and Mr. Clare advanced into view along the garden-path, walking arm in arm through the rain, sheltered by the same umbrella. The lawyer bowed as they passed the windows; Mr. Clare walked straight on, deep in his own thoughts; noticing nothing.

After a delay which seemed interminable; after a weary scraping of wet feet on the hall mat; after a mysterious, muttered interchange of question and answer outside the door, the two came in—Mr. Clare leading the way. The old man walked straight up to the table, without any preliminary greeting; and looked across it at the three women, with a stern pity for them, in his rugged wrinkled face.

"Bad news," he said. "I am an enemy to all unnecessary suspense. Plainness is kindness in such a case as this. I mean to be kind—and I tell you plainly—bad news."

Mr. Pendril followed him. He shook hands, in silence, with Miss Garth and the two sisters; and took a seat near them. Mr. Clare placed himself apart on a chair by the window. The grey rainy light fell soft and sad on the faces of Norah and Magdalen, who sat together opposite to him. Miss Garth had placed herself a little behind them, in partial shadow; and the lawyer's quiet face was seen in profile, close beside her. So the four occupants of the room appeared to Mr. Clare, as he sat apart in his corner; his long claw-like fingers interlaced on his knee; his dark vigilant eyes fixed searchingly now on one face, now on another. The dripping rustle of the rain among the leaves, and the clear ceaseless tick of the clock on the mantelpiece, made the minute of silence which followed the settling of the persons present in their places, indescribably oppressive. It was a relief to every one, when Mr. Pendril spoke.

"Mr. Clare has told you already," he began, "that I am the bearer of bad news. I am grieved to say, Miss Garth, that your doubts, when I last saw you, were better founded than my hopes. What that heartless elder brother was in his youth, he is still in his old age. In all my unhappy experience of the worst side of human nature, I have never met with a man so utterly dead to every consideration of mercy, as Michael Vanstone."

"Do you mean that he takes the whole of his brother's fortune, and makes no provision whatever for his brother's children?" asked Miss Garth.

"He offers a sum of money for present emergencies," replied Mr. Pendril, "so meanly and disgracefully insufficient, that I am ashamed to mention it."

"And nothing for the future?"

"Absolutely nothing."

As that answer was given, the same thought passed, at the same moment, through Miss Garth's mind and through Norah's. The decision which deprived both the sisters alike of the resources of fortune, did not end there for the younger of the two. Michael Vanstone's merciless resolution had virtually pronounced the sentence which dismissed Frank to China, and which destroyed all present hope of Magdalen's marriage. As the words passed the lawyer's lips, Miss Garth and Norah looked at Magdalen anxiously. Her face turned a shade paler—but not a feature of it moved; not a word escaped her. Norah, who held her sister's hand in her own, felt it tremble for a moment, and then turn cold—and that was all.

"Let me mention plainly what I have done," resumed Mr. Pendril; "I am very desirous you should not think that I have left any effort untried. When I wrote to Michael Vanstone, in the first instance, I did not confine myself to the usual formal statement. I put before him, plainly and earnestly, every one of the circumstances under which he has become possessed of his brother's fortune. When I received the answer, referring me to his written instructions to his lawyer in London—and when a copy of those instructions was placed in my hands—I positively declined, on becoming acquainted with them, to receive the writer's decision as final. I induced the solicitor on the other side, to accord us a further term of delay; I attempted to see Mr. Noel Vanstone in London for the purpose of obtaining his intercession; and, failing in that, I myself wrote to his father for the second time. The answer referred me, in insolently curt terms, to the instructions already communicated; declared those instructions to be final; and declined any further correspondence with me. There is the beginning and the end of the negociation. If I have overlooked any means of touching this heartless man—tell me, and those means shall be tried."

He looked at Norah. She pressed her sister's hand encouragingly, and answered for both of them.

"I speak for my sister, as well as for myself," she said, with her colour a little heightened, with her natural gentleness of manner just touched by a quiet, uncomplaining sadness. "You have done all that could be done, Mr. Pendril. We have tried to restrain ourselves from hoping too confidently; and we are deeply grateful for your kindness, at a time when kindness is sorely needed by both of us."

Magdalen's hand returned the pressure of her sister's—withdrew itself—trifled for a moment impatiently with the arrangement of her dress—then suddenly moved the chair closer to the table. Leaning one arm on it (with the hand fast clenched), she looked across at Mr. Pendril. Her face, always remarkable for its want of colour, was now startling to contemplate, in its blank bloodless pallor. But the light in her large grey eyes was bright and steady as ever; and her voice, though low in tone, was clear and resolute in accent as she addressed the lawyer in these terms:—

" I understood you to say, Mr. Pendril, that my father's brother had sent his written orders to London, and that you had a copy. Have you preserved it?"

" Certainly."

" Have you got it about you?"

" I have."

" May I see it?"

Mr. Pendril hesitated, and looked uneasily from Magdalen to Miss Garth, and from Miss Garth back again to Magdalen.

" Pray oblige me by not pressing your request," he said. " It is surely enough that you know the result of the instructions. Why should you agitate yourself to no purpose by reading them? They are expressed so cruelly; they show such abominable want of feeling, that I really cannot prevail upon myself to let you see them."

" I am sensible of your kindness, Mr. Pendril, in wishing to spare me pain. But I can bear pain; I promise to distress nobody. Will you excuse me if I repeat my request?"

She held out her hand—the soft, white, virgin hand that had touched nothing to soil it or harden it yet.

" Oh, Magdalen, think again!" said Norah.

" You distress Mr. Pendril," added Miss Garth; " you distress us all."

" There can be no end gained," pleaded the lawyer—" forgive me for saying so—there can really be no useful end gained by my showing you the instructions."

(" Fools!" said Mr. Clare to himself. " Have they no eyes to see that she means to have her own way?")

" Something tells me there *is* an end to be gained," persisted Magdalen. " This decision is a very serious one. It is more serious to me——" She looked round at Mr. Clare, who sat closely watching her, and instantly looked back again, with the first outward betrayal of emotion which had escaped her yet. " It is even more serious to me," she resumed, " for private reasons—than it is to my sister. I know nothing yet, but that our father's brother has taken our fortunes from us. He must have some motives of his own for such conduct as that. It is not fair to him, or fair to us, to keep those motives concealed. He has deliberately robbed Norah, and robbed me; and I think we have a right, if we wish it, to know why?"

" I don't wish it," said Norah.

" I do," said Magdalen; and, once more, she held out her hand.

At this point, Mr. Clare roused himself, and interfered for the first time.

" You have relieved your conscience," he said, addressing the lawyer. " Give her the right she claims. It *is* her right—if she will have it."

M . Pendril quietly took the written instructions from his pocket. " I have warned you," he said—and handed the papers across the table, without another word. One of the pages of writing was folded down at the corner; and, at that folded page, the manuscript opened, when Magdalen first turned the leaves. "Is this the place which refers to my sister and myself?" she inquired. Mr. Pendril bowed; and Magdalen smoothed out the manuscript before her, on the table.

"Will you decide, Norah?" she asked, turning to her sister. "Shall I read this aloud, or shall I read it to myself?"

"To yourself," said Miss Garth; answering for Norah, who looked at her in mute perplexity and distress.

"It shall be as you wish," said Magdalen. With that reply, she turned again to the manuscript, and read these lines:—

" . . . . . You are now in possession of my wishes in relation to the property in money, and to the sale of the furniture, carriages, horses, and so forth. The last point left, on which it is necessary for me to instruct you, refers to the persons inhabiting the house, and to certain preposterous claims on their behalf, set up by a solicitor named Pendril; who has no doubt interested reasons of his own for making application to me.

"I understand that my late brother has left two illegitimate children; both of them young women, who are of an age to earn their own livelihood. Various considerations, all equally irregular, have been urged in respect to these persons, by the solicitor representing them. Be so good as to tell him that neither you nor I have anything to do with questions of mere sentiment; and then state plainly, for his better information, what the motives are which regulate my conduct, and what the provision is which I feel myself justified in making for the two young women. Your instructions on both these points, you will find detailed in the next paragraph.

"I wish the persons concerned, to know, once for all, how I regard the circumstances which have placed my late brother's property at my disposal. Let them understand that I consider those circumstances to be a Providential interposition, which has restored to me the inheritance that ought always to have been mine. I receive the money, not only as my right, but also as a proper compensation for the injustice which I suffered from my father, and a proper penalty paid by my younger brother for the vile intrigue by which he succeeded in disinheriting me. His conduct, when a young man, was uniformly discreditable in all the relations of life; and what it then was, it continued to be (on the showing of his own legal representative) after the time when I ceased to hold any communication with him. He appears to have systematically imposed a woman on Society as his wife, who was not his wife; and to have completed the outrage on morality by afterwards marrying her. Such conduct as this, has called down a Judgment on himself and his children. I will not invite retribution on my own head, by assisting those children to continue the imposition which their parents practised, and by helping them to take a place in the world to which they are not entitled. Let them, as becomes their birth, gain their bread in situations. If they show themselves disposed to accept their proper position, I will assist them to start virtuously in life, by a present of one hundred pounds each. This sum I authorise you to pay them, on their personal application, with the necessary acknowledgment of receipt; and on the express understanding that the transaction, so completed, is to be the beginning and the end of my connection with them. The arrangements under which they quit the house, I leave to your discretion; and I have only to add that my decision on this matter, as on all other matters, is positive and final."

Line by line—without once looking up from the pages before her—Magdalen read those atrocious sentences through, from beginning to end. The other persons assembled in the room, all eagerly looking at her together, saw the dress rising and falling faster and faster over her bosom—saw the hand in which she lightly held the manuscript at the outset, close unconsciously on the paper, and crush it, as she advanced nearer and nearer to the end—but detected no other outward signs of what was passing within her. As soon as she had done, she silently pushed the manuscript away, and put her hands on a sudden over her face. When she withdrew them, all the four persons in the room noticed a change in her. Something in her expression had altered, subtly and silently; something which made the familiar features suddenly look strange, even to her sister and Miss Garth; something, through all after years, never to be forgotten in connection with that day—and never to be described.

The first words she spoke were addressed to Mr. Pendril.

"May I ask one more favour," she said, "before you enter on your business arrangements?"

Mr. Pendril replied ceremoniously by a gesture of assent. Magdalen's resolution to possess herself of the Instructions, did not appear to have produced a favourable impression on the lawyer's mind.

"You mentioned what you were so kind as to do, in our interests, when you first wrote to Mr. Michael Vanstone," she continued. "You said you had told him all the circumstances. I want—if you will allow me—to be made quite sure of what he really knew about us when he sent these orders to his lawyer. Did he know that my father had made a will, and that he had left our fortunes to my sister and myself?"

"He did know it," said Mr. Pendril.

"Did you tell him how it happened that we are left in this helpless position?"

"I told him that your father was entirely unaware, when he married, of the necessity for making another will."

"And that another will would have been made, after he saw Mr. Clare, but for the dreadful misfortune of his death?"

"He knew that, also."

"Did he know that my father's untiring goodness and kindness to both of us——"

Her voice faltered for the first time: she sighed, and put her hand to her head wearily. Norah spoke entreatingly to her; Miss Garth spoke entreatingly to her; Mr. Clare sat silent, watching her more and more earnestly. She answered her sister's remonstrance with a faint smile. "I will keep my promise," she said; "I will distress nobody." With that reply, she turned again to Mr. Pendril; and steadily reiterated the question —but in another form of words.

"Did Mr. Michael Vanstone know that my father's great anxiety was to make sure of providing for my sister and myself?"

"He knew it in your father's own words. I sent him an extract from your father's last letter to me."

"The letter which asked you to come for God's sake, and relieve him from the dreadful thought that his daughters were unprovided for? The letter which said he should not rest in his grave if he left us disinherited?"

"That letter and those words."

She paused, still keeping her eyes steadily fixed on the lawyer's face.

"I want to fasten it all in my mind," she said, "before I go on. Mr. Michael Vanstone knew of the first will; he knew what prevented the making of the second will; he knew of the letter, and he read the words. What did he know of besides? Did you tell him of my mother's last illness? Did you say that her share in the money would have been left to us, if she could have lifted her dying hand in your presence? Did you try to make him ashamed of the cruel law which calls girls in our situation Nobody's Children, and which allows him to use us as he is using us now?"

"I put all those considerations to him. I left none of them doubtful; I left none of them out."

She slowly reached her hand to the copy of the Instructions; and slowly folded it up again, in the shape in which it had been presented to her. "I am much obliged to you, Mr. Pendril." With those words, she bowed, and gently pushed the manuscript back across the table; then turned to her sister.

"Norah," she said, "if we both of us live to grow old, and if you ever forget all that we owe to Michael Vanstone—come to me, and I will remind you."

She rose and walked across the room by herself to the window. As she passed Mr. Clare, the old man stretched out his claw-like fingers, and caught her fast by the arm before she was aware of him.

"What is this mask of yours hiding?" he asked, forcing her to bend to him, and looking close into her face. "Which of the extremes of human temperature does your courage start from—the dead cold or the white hot?"

She shrank back from him; and turned away her head in silence. She would have resented that unscrupulous intrusion on her own thoughts from any man alive but Frank's father. He dropped her arm as suddenly as he had taken it, and let her go on to the window. "No," he said to himself, "not the cold extreme, whatever else it may be. So much the worse for her, and for all belonging to her."

There was a momentary pause. Once more the dripping rustle of the rain, and the steady ticking of the clock filled up the gap of silence. Mr. Pendril put the Instructions back in his pocket, considered a little; and, turning towards Norah and Miss Garth, recalled their attention to the present and pressing necessities of the time.

"Our consultation has been needlessly prolonged," he said, "by painful references to the past. We shall be better employed in settling our arrangements for the future. I am obliged to return to town this evening. Pray let me hear how I can best assist you; pray tell me what trouble and what responsibility I can take off your hands."

For the moment, neither Norah nor Miss Garth seemed to be capable of answering him. Magdalen's reception of the news which annihilated the marriage prospect that her father's own lips had placed before her not a month since, had bewildered and dismayed them alike. They had summoned their courage to meet the shock of her passionate grief, or to face the harder trial of witnessing her speechless despair. But they were not prepared for her invincible resolution to read the Instructions; for the terrible questions which she had put to the lawyer; for her immovable determination to fix all the circumstances in her mind, under which Michael Vanstone's decision had been pronounced. There she stood at the window, an unfathomable mystery to the sister who had never been parted from her, to the governess who had trained her from a child. Miss Garth remembered the dark doubts which had crossed her mind, on the day when she and Magdalen had met in the garden. Norah looked forward to the coming time, with the first serious dread of it on her sister's account, which she had felt yet. Both had hitherto remained passive, in despair of knowing what to do. Both were now silent, in despair of knowing what to say.

Mr. Pendril patiently and kindly helped them, by returning to the subject of their future plans for the second time.

"I am sorry to press any business matters on your attention," he said, "when you are necessarily unfitted to deal with them. But I must take my instructions back to London with me to-night. With reference, in the first place, to the disgraceful pecuniary offer, to which I have already alluded. The younger Miss Vanstone having read the Instructions, needs no further information from my lips. The elder will, I hope, excuse me if I tell her (what I should be ashamed to tell her, but that it is a matter of necessity), that Mr. Michael Vanstone's provision for his brother's children, begins and ends with an offer to each of them of one hundred pounds."

Norah's face crimsoned with indignation. She started to her feet, as if Michael Vanstone had been present in the room, and had personally insulted her.

"I see," said the lawyer, wishing to spare her; "I may tell Mr. Michael Vanstone you refuse the money."

"Tell him," she broke out passionately, "if I was starving by the road-side, I wouldn't touch a farthing of it !"

"Shall I notify your refusal also ?" asked Mr. Pendril, speaking to Magdalen next.

She turned round from the window—but kept her face in shadow, by standing close against it with her back to the light.

"Tell him, on my part," she said, "to think again, before he starts me in life with a hundred pounds. I will give him time to think." She spoke those strange words, with a marked emphasis ; and turning back quickly to the window, hid her face from the observation of every one in the room.

"You both refuse the offer," said Mr. Pendril, taking out his pencil, and making his professional note of the decision. As he shut up his pocket-book, he glanced towards Magdalen doubtfully. She had roused in him the latent distrust which is a lawyer's second nature : he had his suspicions of her looks; he had his suspicions of her language. Her sister seemed to have more influence over her than Miss Garth. He resolved to speak privately to her sister before he went away.

While the idea was passing through his mind, his attention was claimed by another question from Magdalen.

"Is he an old man ?" she asked, suddenly, without turning round from the window.

"If you mean Mr. Michael Vanstone, he is seventy-five, or seventy-six years of age."

"You spoke of his son, a little while since. Has he any other sons—or daughters ?"

"None."

"Do you know anything of his wife ?"

"She has been dead for many years."

There was a pause. "Why do you ask these questions ?" said Norah.

"I beg your pardon," replied Magdalen, quietly ; "I won't ask any more."

For the third time, Mr. Pendril returned to the business of the interview.

"The servants must not be forgotten," he said. "They must be settled with and discharged : I will give them the necessary explanation before I leave. As for the house, no questions connected with it need trouble you. The carriages and horses, the furniture and plate, and so on, must simply be left on the premises to await Mr. Michael Vanstone's further orders. But any possessions, Miss Vanstone, personally belonging to you or to your sister—your jewelry and dresses, and any little presents which may have been made to you—are entirely at your disposal. With regard to the time of your departure, I understand that a month, or more, will elapse before Mr. Michael Vanstone can leave Zurich; and I am sure I only do his solicitor justice in saying——"

"Excuse me, Mr. Pendril," interposed Norah; "I think I understand, from what you have just said, that our house and everything in it belongs to——?" She stopped, as if the mere utterance of the man's name was abhorrent to her.

"To Michael Vanstone," said Mr. Pendril. "The house goes to him with the rest of the property."

"Then I, for one, am ready to leave it to-morrow !"

Magdalen started at the window, as her sister spoke, and looked at Mr. Clare, with the first open signs of anxiety and alarm which she had shown yet.

"Don't be angry with me," she whispered, stooping over the old man with a sudden humility of look, and a sudden nervousness of manner. "I can't go, without seeing Frank first !"

"You shall see him," replied Mr. Clare. "I am here to speak to you about it, when the business is done."

"It is quite unnecessary to hurry your departure, as you propose," continued Mr. Pendril, addressing Norah. "I can safely assure you that a week hence will be time enough."

"If this is Mr. Michael Vanstone's house," repeated Norah, "I am ready to leave it to-morrow."

She impatiently quitted her chair ; and seated herself farther away on the sofa. As she laid her hand on the back of it, her face changed. There, at the head of the sofa, were the cushions which had supported her mother, when she lay down for the last time to repose. There, at the foot of the sofa, was the clumsy, old-fashioned arm-chair, which had been her father's favourite seat on rainy days, when she and her sister used to amuse him at the piano opposite, by playing his favourite tunes. A heavy sigh, which she tried vainly to repress, burst from her lips. "Oh," she thought, "I had forgotten these old friends ! How shall we part from them when the time comes !"

"May I inquire, Miss Vanstone, whether you and your sister have formed any definite plans for the future ?" asked Mr. Pendril. "Have you thought of any place of residence ?"

"I may take it on myself, sir," said Miss Garth, "to answer your question for them. When they leave this house they leave it with me. My home is their home; and my bread is their bread. Their parents honoured me, trusted me, and loved me. For twelve happy years they never let me remember that I was their governess, they only let me know myself as their companion and their friend. My memory of them is the memory of unvarying gentleness and generosity; and my life shall pay the debt of my gratitude to their orphan children."

Norah rose hastily from the sofa; Magdalen impetuously left the window. For once, there was no contrast in the conduct of the sisters. For once, the same impulse moved their hearts, the same earnest feeling inspired their words. Miss Garth waited until the first outburst of emotion had passed away; then rose; and taking Norah and Magdalen each by the hand, addressed herself to Mr. Pendril and Mr. Clare. She spoke with perfect self-possession; strong in her artless unconsciousness of her own good action.

"Even such a trifle as my own story," she said, "is of some importance at such a moment as this. I wish you both, gentlemen, to understand that I am not promising more to the daughters of your old friend than I can perform. When I first came to this house, I entered it under such independent circumstances as are not common in the lives of governesses. In my younger days, I was associated in teaching with my elder sister: we established a school in London, which grew to be a large and prosperous one. I only left it and became a private governess, because the heavy responsibility of the school was more than my strength could bear. I left my share in the profits untouched, and I possess a pecuniary interest in our establishment to this day. That is my story, in few words. When we leave this house, I propose that we shall go back to the school in London, which is still prosperously directed by my elder sister. We can live there as quietly as we please, until time has helped us to bear our affliction better than we can bear it now. If Norah's and Magdalen's altered prospects oblige them to earn their own independence, I can help them to earn it, as a gentleman's daughters should. The best families in this land are glad to ask my sister's advice where the interests of their children's home-training are concerned; and I answer, beforehand, for her hearty desire to serve Mr. Vanstone's daughters, as I answer for my own. That is the future which my gratitude to their father and mother, and my love for themselves, now offers to them. If you think my proposal, gentlemen, a fit and fair proposal—and I see in your faces that you do—let us not make the hard necessities of our position harder still, by any useless delay in meeting them at once. Let us do what we must do; let us act on Norah's decision, and leave this house to-morrow. You mentioned the servants, just now, Mr. Pendril: I am ready to call them together in the next room, and to assist you in the settlement of their claims, whenever you please."

Without waiting for the lawyer's answer, without leaving the sisters time to realize their own terrible situation, she moved at once towards the door. It was her wise resolution to meet the coming trial by doing much, and saying little. Before she could leave the room, Mr. Clare followed, and stopped her on the threshold.

"I never envied a woman's feelings before," said the old man. "It may surprise you to hear it; but I envy yours. Wait! I have something more to say. There is an obstacle still left—the everlasting obstacle of Frank. Help me to sweep him off. Take the elder sister along with you and the lawyer; and leave me here to have it out with the younger. I want to see what metal she's really made of."

While Mr. Clare was addressing these words to Miss Garth, Mr. Pendril had taken the opportunity of speaking to Norah. "Before I go back to town," he said, "I should like to have a word with you in private. From what has passed to-day, Miss Vanstone, I have formed a very high opinion of your discretion; and, as an old friend of your father's, I want to take the freedom of speaking to you about your sister."

Before Norah could answer, she was summoned, in compliance with Mr. Clare's request, to the conference with the servants. Mr. Pendril followed Miss Garth, as a matter of course. When the three were out in the hall, Mr. Clare re-entered the room, closed the door, and signed peremptorily to Magdalen to take a chair.

She obeyed him in silence. He took a turn up and down the room, with his hands in the side pockets of the long, loose, shapeless coat which he habitually wore.

"How old are you?" he said, stopping suddenly, and speaking to her with the whole breadth of the room between them.

"I was eighteen last birthday," she answered humbly, without looking up at him.

"You have shown extraordinary courage for a girl of eighteen. Have you got any of that courage left?"

She clasped her hands together, and wrung them hard. A few tears gathered in her eyes, and rolled slowly over her cheeks.

"I can't give Frank up," she said faintly. "You don't care for me, I know; but you used to care for my father. Will you try to be kind to me for my father's sake?"

The last words died away in a whisper; she could say no more. Never had she felt the illimitable power which a woman's love possesses of absorbing into itself every other event, every other joy or sorrow of her life, as she felt it then. Never had she so tenderly associated Frank with the memory of her lost parents, as at that moment. Never had the impenetrable atmosphere of illusion through which women behold the man of their choice—the atmosphere which had blinded her to all that was weak, selfish, and mean in Frank's nature—surrounded him with a brighter halo than now, when she was pleading with the father for the possession of the son. "Oh, don't ask me to give him up!" she said, trying to take courage, and shuddering from head to foot. In the next instant, she flew to the opposite extreme, with the suddenness of a flash of lightning. "I won't give him up!" she burst out violently. "No! not if a thousand fathers ask me!"

"I am one father," said Mr. Clare. "And I don't ask you."

In the first astonishment and delight of hearing those unexpected words, she started to her feet, crossed the room, and tried to throw her arms round his neck. She might as well have attempted to move the house from its foundations. He took her by the shoulders and put her back in her chair. His inexorable eyes looked her into submission; and his lean forefinger shook at her warningly, as if he was quieting a fractious child.

"Hug Frank," he said; "don't hug me. I haven't done with you yet: when I have, you may shake hands with me, if you like. Wait, and compose yourself."

He left her. His hands went back into his pockets, and his monotonous march up and down the room began again.

"Ready?" he asked, stopping short after a while. She tried to answer. "Take two minutes more," he said, and resumed his walk with the regularity of clockwork. "These are the creatures," he thought to himself, "into whose keeping men otherwise sensible, give the happiness of their lives. Is there any other object in creation, I wonder, which answers its end as badly as a woman does?"

He stopped before her once more. Her breathing was easier; the dark flush on her face was dying out again.

"Ready?" he repeated. "Yes; ready at last. Listen to me; and let's get it over. I don't ask you to give Frank up. I ask you to wait."

"I will wait," she said. "Patiently, willingly."

"Will you make Frank wait?"

"Yes."

"Will you send him to China?"

Her head drooped upon her bosom, and she clasped her hands again, in silence. Mr. Clare saw where the difficulty lay, and marched straight up to it on the spot.

"I don't pretend to enter into your feelings for Frank, or Frank's for you," he said. "The subject doesn't interest me. But I *do* pretend to state two plain truths. It is one plain truth that you can't be married till you have money enough to pay for the roof that shelters you, the clothes that cover you, and the victuals you eat. It is another plain truth that you can't find the money; that I can't find the money; and that Frank's only chance of finding it, is going to China. If I tell him to go, he'll sit in a corner and cry. If I insist, he'll say Yes, and deceive me. If I go a step further, and see him on board ship with my own eyes—he'll slip off in the pilot's boat, and sneak back secretly to you. That's his disposition."

"No!" said Magdalen. "It's not his disposition; it's his love for Me."

"Call it what you like," retorted Mr. Clare. "Sneak or Sweetheart—he's too slippery, in either capacity, for my fingers to hold him. My shutting the door won't keep him from coming back. Your shutting the door will. Have you the courage to shut it? Are you fond enough of him not to stand in his light?"

"Fond! I would die for him!"

"Will you send him to China?"

She sighed bitterly.

"Have a little pity for me," she said. "I have lost my father; I have lost my mother; I have lost my fortune—and now I am to lose Frank. You don't like women, I know; but try to help me with a little pity. I don't say it's not for his own interests to send him to China; I only say it's hard—very, very hard on *me*."

Mr. Clare had been deaf to her violence, insensible to her caresses, blind to her tears; but under the tough integument of his philosophy, he had a heart—and it answered that hopeless appeal; it felt those touching words.

"I don't deny that your case is a hard one," he said. "I don't want to make it harder: I only ask you to do in Frank's interests, what Frank is too weak to do for himself. It's no fault of yours; it's no fault of mine—but it's not the less true, that the fortune you were to have brought him, has changed owners."

She suddenly looked up, with a furtive light in her eyes, with a threatening smile on her lips.

"It may change owners again," she said.

Mr. Clare saw the alteration in her expression, and heard the tones of her voice. But the words were spoken low; spoken as if to herself—they failed to reach him across the breadth of the room. He stopped instantly in his walk, and asked what she had said.

"Nothing," she answered, turning her head away towards the window, and looking out mechanically at the falling rain. "Only my own thoughts."

Mr. Clare resumed his walk, and returned to his subject.

"It's your interest," he went on, "as well as Frank's interest, that he should go. He may make money enough to marry you in China; he can't make it here. If he stops at home, he'll be the ruin of both of you. He'll shut his eyes to every consideration of prudence, and pester you to marry him; and when he has carried his point, he will be the first to turn round afterwards, and complain that you're a burden on him. Hear me out! You're in love with Frank—I'm not, and I know him. Put you two together often enough; give him time enough to hug, cry, pester, and plead; and I'll tell you what the end will be—you'll marry him."

He had touched the right string at last. It rung back in answer, before he could add another word.

"You don't know me," she said firmly. "You don't know what I can suffer for Frank's sake. He shall never marry me, till I can be what my father said I should be—the making of his fortune. He shall take no burden, when he takes me; I promise you that! I'll be the good angel of Frank's life; I'll not go a penniless girl to him, and drag him down." She abruptly left her seat, advanced a few steps towards Mr. Clare, and stopped in the middle of the room. Her arms fell helpless on either side of her; and she burst into tears. "He shall go," she said.—"If my heart breaks in doing it, I'll tell him to-morrow that we must say Good-bye!"

Mr. Clare at once advanced to meet her, and held out his hand.

"I'll help you," he said. "Frank shall hear every word that has passed between us. When he comes to-morrow, he shall know, beforehand, that he comes to say God-bye."

She took his hand in both her own—hesitated—looked at him—and pressed it to her bosom. "May I ask a favour of you, before you go?" she said, timidly. He tried to take his hand from her; but she knew her advantage, and held it fast. "Suppose there should be some change for the better?" she went on. "Suppose I could come to Frank, as my father said I should come to him——?"

Before she could complete the question, Mr. Clare made a second effort, and withdrew his hand. "As your father said you should come to him?" he repeated, looking at her attentively.

"Yes," she replied. "Strange things happen sometimes. If strange things happen to *me*, will you let Frank come back before the five years are out?"

What did she mean? Was she clinging desperately to the hope of melting Michael Vanstone's heart? Mr. Clare could draw no other con-clusion from what she had just said to him. At the beginning of the interview, he would have roughly dispelled her delusion. At the end of the interview, he left her compassionately in possession of it.

"You are hoping against all hope," he said; "but if it gives you courage, hope on. If this impossible good fortune of yours ever happens, tell me; and Frank shall come back. In the mean time——"

"In the mean time," she interposed sadly, "you have my promise."

Once more, Mr. Clare's sharp eyes searched her face attentively.

"I will trust your promise," he said. "You shall see Frank to-morrow."

She went back thoughtfully to her chair, and sat down again in silence. Mr. Clare made for the door, before any formal leave-taking could pass between them. "Deep!" he thought to himself, as he looked back at her before he went out; "only eighteen; and too deep for my sounding!"

In the hall, he found Norah, waiting anxiously to hear what had happened.

"Is it all over?" she asked. "Does Frank go to China?"

"Be careful how you manage that sister of yours," said Mr. Clare, without noticing the question. "She has one great misfortune to contend with: she's not made for the ordinary jog-trot of a woman's life. I don't say I can see straight to the end of the good or the evil in her—I only warn you, her future will be no common one."

An hour later, Mr. Pendril left the house; and, by that night's post, Miss Garth despatched a letter to her sister in London.

THE END OF THE FIRST SCENE.

BETWEEN THE SCENES.

PROGRESS OF THE STORY THROUGH THE POST.

I.

FROM NORAH VANSTONE TO MR. PENDRIL.

"Westmoreland House, Kensington,
"August 14th, 1846.

"DEAR MR. PENDRIL,—

"The date of this letter will show you that the last of many hard partings is over. We have left Combe-Raven; we have said farewell to home.

"I have been thinking seriously of what you said to me, on Wednesday, before you went back to town. I entirely agree with you, that Miss Garth is more shaken by all she has gone through for our sakes, than she is herself willing to admit; and that it is my duty, for the future, to spare her all the anxiety that I can, on the subject of my sister and myself. This is very little to do for our dearest friend, for our second mother. Such as it is, I will do it with all my heart.

"But, forgive me for saying that I am as far as ever from agreeing with you about Magdalen. I am so sensible, in our helpless position, of the importance of your assistance; so anxious to be worthy of the interest of my father's trusted adviser and oldest friend, that I feel really and truly disappointed with myself for differing with you—and yet I do differ. Magdalen is very strange, very unaccountable, to those who don't know her intimately. I can understand that she has innocently misled you; and that she has presented herself, perhaps, under her least favourable aspect. But, that the clue to her language and her conduct on Wednesday last, is to be found in such a feeling towards the man who has ruined us, as the feeling at which you hinted, is what I cannot and will not believe of my sister. If you knew, as I do, what a noble nature she has, you would not be surprised at this obstinate resistance of mine to your opinion. Will you try to alter it? I don't mind what Mr. Clare says: he believes in nothing. But I attach a very serious importance to what *you* say; and, kind as I know your motives to be, it distresses me to think you are doing Magdalen an injustice.

"Having relieved my mind of this confession, I may now come to the proper object of my letter. I promised, if you could not find leisure time to visit us to-day, to write and tell you all that happened after you left us. The day has passed, without our seeing you. So I open my writing-case, and perform my promise.

"I am sorry to say that three of the women-servants—the housemaid, the kitchenmaid, and even our own maid (to whom I am sure we have always been kind)—took advantage of your having paid them their wages to pack up and go, as soon as your back was turned. They came to say good-bye with as much ceremony, and as little feeling, as if they were leaving the house under ordinary circumstances. The cook, for all her violent temper, behaved very differently: she sent up a message to say that she would stop and help us to the last. And Thomas (who has never yet been in any other place than ours) spoke so gratefully of my dear father's unvarying kindness to him; and asked so anxiously to be allowed to go on serving us, while his little savings lasted, that Magdalen and I forgot all formal considerations, and both shook hands with him. The poor lad went out of the room crying. I wish him well; I hope he will find a kind master and a good place.

"The long, quiet, rainy evening out of doors—our last evening at Combe-Raven—was a sad trial to us. I think winter-time would have weighed less on our spirits: the drawn curtains, and the bright lamps, and the companionable fires would have helped us. We were only five in the house altogether—after having once been so many! I can't tell you how dreary the grey daylight looked, towards seven o'clock, in the lonely rooms, and on the noiseless staircase. Surely, the prejudice in favour of long summer evenings, is the prejudice of happy people? We did our best. We kept ourselves employed, and Miss Garth helped us. The prospect of preparing for our departure, which had seemed so dreadful earlier in the day, altered into the prospect of a refuge from ourselves, as the evening came on. We each tried at first to pack up in our own rooms—but the loneliness was more than we could bear. We carried all our possessions down stairs, and heaped them on the large dining-table, and so made our preparations together, in the same room. I am sure we have taken nothing away which does not properly belong to us.

"Having already mentioned to you my own conviction that Magdalen was not herself when you saw her on Wednesday, I feel tempted to stop here, and give you an instance in proof of what I say. The little circumstance happened on Wednesday night, just before we went up to our rooms.

"After we had packed our dresses and our birthday presents, our books and our music, we began to sort our letters, which had got confused from being all placed on the table together. Some of my letters were mixed with Magdalen's, and some of hers with mine. Among these last, I found a card, which had been given to my sister early in the year, by an actor who managed an amateur theatrical performance in which she took a part. The man had given her the card, containing his name and address, in the belief that she would be invited to many more amusements of the same kind, and in the hope that she would recommend him as a superintendent on future occasions. I only relate these trifling particulars to show you how little worth keeping such a card could be, in such circumstances as ours. Naturally enough, I threw it away from me across the table, meaning to throw it on the floor. It fell short, close to the place in which Magdalen was sitting. She took it up, looked at it, and immediately declared that she would not have had this perfectly worthless thing destroyed for the world. She was almost angry with me, for having thrown it away; almost angry with Miss Garth for asking what she could possibly want with it! Could there be any plainer proof than this, that our misfortunes—falling so much more heavily on her than on me—have quite unhinged her, and worn her out? Surely her words and looks are not to be interpreted against her, when she is not sufficiently mistress of herself to exert her natural judgment—when she shows the unreasonable petulance of a child on a question which is not of the slightest importance.

"A little after eleven we went upstairs to try if we could get some rest.

"I drew aside the curtain of my window, and looked out. Oh, what a cruel last night it was; no moon, no stars; such deep darkness, that not one of the dear familiar objects in the garden was visible when I looked for them; such deep stillness, that even my own movements about the room almost frightened me! I tried to lie down and sleep, but the sense of loneliness came again, and quite overpowered me. You will say I am old enough, at six-and-twenty, to have exerted more control over myself. I hardly know how it happened, but I stole into Magdalen's room, just as I used to steal into it, years and years ago, when we were children. She was not in bed; she was sitting with her writing materials before her, thinking. I said I wanted to be with her the last night; and she kissed me, and told me to lie down, and promised soon to follow me. My mind was a little quieted, and I fell asleep. It was daylight when I woke—and the first sight I saw was Magdalen, still sitting in the chair, and still thinking. She had never been to bed; she had not slept all through the night.

"'I shall sleep when we have left Combe-Raven,' she said. 'I shall be better when it is all over, and I have bid Frank good-bye.' She had in her hand our father's will, and the letter he wrote to you; and when she had done speaking, she gave them into my possession. I was the eldest (she said), and those last precious relics ought to be in my keeping. I tried to propose to her that we should divide them; but she shook her head. 'I have copied for myself,' was her answer, 'all that he says of us in the will, and all that he says in the letter.' She told me this, and took from her bosom a tiny white silk bag, which she had made in the night, and in which she had put the extracts, so as to keep them always about her. 'This tells me in his own words what his last wishes were for both of us,' she said; 'and this is all I want for the future.'

"These are trifles to dwell on; and I am almost surprised at myself for not feeling ashamed to trouble you with them. But, since I have known what your early connection was with my father and mother, I have learnt to think of you (and, I suppose, to write to you) as an old friend. And, besides, I have it so much at heart to change your opinion of Magdalen, that I can't help telling you the smallest things about her which may, in my judgment, end in making you think of her as I do.

"When breakfast-time came (on Thursday morning) we were surprised to find a strange letter on the table. Perhaps, I ought to mention it to you, in case of any future necessity for your interference. It was addressed to Miss Garth, on paper with the deepest mourning border round it; and the writer was the same man who followed us on our way home from a walk, one day last spring—Captain Wragge. His object appears to be, to assert once more his audacious claim to a family connection with my poor mother, under cover of a letter of condolence, which it is an insolence in such a person to have written at all. He expresses as much sympathy— on his discovery of our affliction in the newspaper—as if he had been really intimate with us; and he begs to know, in a postscript (being evidently in total ignorance of all that has really happened), whether it is thought desirable that he should be present, among the other relatives, at the reading of the will! The address he gives, at which letters will reach him for the next fortnight, is, 'Post-office, Birmingham.' This is all I have to tell you on the subject. Both the letter and the writer seem to me to be equally unworthy of the slightest notice, on our part or on yours.

"After breakfast, Magdalen left us, and went by herself into the morning-room. The weather being still showery, we had arranged that Francis Clare should see her in that room, when he presented himself to take his leave. I was upstairs when he came; and I remained upstairs for more than half an hour afterwards, sadly anxious, as you may well believe, on Magdalen's account.

"At the end of the half-hour, or more, I came downstairs. As I reached the landing, I suddenly heard her voice, raised entreatingly, and calling on him by his name—then loud sobs—then a frightful laughing and screaming, both together, that rang through the house. I instantly ran into the room; and found Magdalen on the sofa in violent hysterics, and Frank standing staring at her, with a lowering angry face, biting his nails.

"I felt so indignant—without knowing plainly why, for I was ignorant of course of what had passed at the interview—that I took Mr. Francis Clare by the shoulders, and pushed him out of the room. I am careful to tell you how I acted towards him, and what led to it; because I understand that he is excessively offended with me, and that he is likely to mention elsewhere, what he calls, my unladylike violence towards him. If he should mention it to you, I am anxious to acknowledge, of my own accord, that I forgot myself—not, I hope you will think, without some provocation.

"I pushed him into the hall, leaving Magdalen, for the moment, to Miss Garth's care. Instead of going away, he sat down sulkily on one of the hall chairs. 'May I ask the reason of this extraordinary violence?' he inquired, with an injured look. 'No,' I said. 'You will be good enough to imagine the reason for yourself, and to leave us immediately, if you please.' He sat doggedly in the chair, biting his nails, and considering. 'What have I done to be treated in this unfeeling manner?' he asked, after a while. 'I can enter into no discussion with you,' I answered; 'I can only request you to leave us. If you persist in waiting to see my sister again, I will go to the cottage myself, and appeal to your father.' He got up in a great hurry at those words. 'I have been infamously used in this business,' he said. 'All the hardships and the sacrifices have fallen to my share. I'm the only one among you who has any heart: all the rest are as hard as stones—Magdalen included. In one breath she says she loves me, and in another, she tells me to go to China. What have I done to be treated with this heartless inconsistency? I'm consistent myself—I only want to stop at home—and (what's the consequence?) you're all against

me !' In that manner, he grumbled his way down the steps, and so I saw
the last of him. This was all that passed between us. If he gives you any
other account of it, what he says will be false. He made no attempt to
return. An hour afterwards, his father came alone to say good-bye. He
saw Miss Garth and me, but not Magdalen ; and he told us he would take
the necessary measures, with your assistance, for having his son properly
looked after in London, and seen safely on board the vessel when the time
came. It was a short visit, and a sad leave-taking. Even Mr. Clare was
sorry, though he tried hard to hide it.

"We had barely two hours, after Mr. Clare had left us, before it would
be time to go. I went back to Magdalen, and found her quieter and
better; though terribly pale and exhausted, and oppressed, as I fancied, by
thoughts which she could not prevail on herself to communicate. She
would tell me nothing then—she has told me nothing since—of what
passed between herself and Francis Clare. When I spoke of him angrily
(feeling as I did that he had distressed and tortured her, when she ought
to have had all the encouragement and comfort from him that man could
give), she refused to hear me : she made the kindest allowances, and the
sweetest excuses for him ; and laid all the blame of the dreadful state in
which I had found her, entirely on herself. Was I wrong in telling you
that she had a noble nature ? And won't you alter your opinion when you
read these lines ?

"We had no friends to come and bid us good-bye; and our few acquaintances were too far from us—perhaps too indifferent about us—to call. We
employed the little leisure left, in going over the house together for the last
time. We took leave of our old schoolroom, our bedrooms, the room where
our mother died, the little study where our father used to settle his accounts
and write his letters—feeling towards them, in our forlorn situation, as
other girls might have felt at parting with old friends. From the house,
in a gleam of fine weather, we went into the garden, and gathered our last
nosegay ; with the purpose of drying the flowers when they begin to
wither, and keeping them in remembrance of the happy days that are gone.
When we had said good-bye to the garden, there was only half an hour
left. We went together to the grave ; we knelt down, side by side, in
silence, and kissed the sacred ground. I thought my heart would have
broken. August was the month of my mother's birthday ; and, this time
last year, my father and Magdalen and I were all consulting in secret what
present we could make to surprise her with on the birthday morning.

"If you had seen how Magdalen suffered, you would never doubt her
again. I had to take her from the last resting-place of our father and
mother, almost by force. Before we were out of the churchyard, she broke
from me, and ran back. She dropped on her knees at the grave; tore up
from it passionately a handful of grass ; and said something to herself, at

tne same moment, which, though I followed her instantly, I did not get near enough to hear. She turned on me in such a frenzied manner, when I tried to raise her from the ground—she looked at me with such a fearful wildness in her eyes—that I felt absolutely terrified at the sight of her. To my relief, the paroxysm left her as suddenly as it had come. She thrust away the tuft of grass into the bosom of her dress, and took my arm and hurried with me out of the churchyard. I asked her why she had gone back—I asked what those words were, which she had spoken at the grave. 'A promise to our dead father,' she answered, with a momentary return of the wild look and the frenzied manner which had startled me already. I was afraid to agitate her by saying more; I left all other questions to be asked at a fitter and a quieter time. You will understand from this, how terribly she suffers, how wildly and strangely she acts under violent agitation; and you will not interpret against her what she said or did, when you saw her on Wednesday last.

"We only returned to the house, in time to hasten away from it to the train. Perhaps, it was better for us so—better that we had only a moment left to look back, before the turn in the road hid the last of Combe-Raven from our view. There was not a soul we knew at the station; nobody to stare at us, nobody to wish us good-bye. The rain came on again, as we took our seats in the train. What we felt at the sight of the railway; what horrible remembrances it forced on our minds of the calamity which has made us fatherless—I cannot, and dare not, tell you. I have tried anxiously not to write this letter in a gloomy tone; not to return all your kindness to us by distressing you with our grief. Perhaps I have dwelt too long already on the little story of our parting from home? I can only say in excuse, that my heart is full of it; and what is not in my heart my pen won't write.

"We have been so short a time in our new abode, that I have nothing more to tell you—except that Miss Garth's sister has received us with the heartiest kindness. She considerately leaves us to ourselves, until we are fitter than we are now to think of our future plans, and to arrange as we best can for earning our own living. The house is so large, and the position of our rooms has been so thoughtfully chosen, that I should hardly know—except when I hear the laughing of the younger girls in the garden —that we were living in a school.

"With kindest and best wishes from Miss Garth and my sister, believe me, dear Mr. Pendril, gratefully yours,

"NORAH VANSTONE."

II.

From Miss Garth to Mr. Pendril.

"Westmoreland House, Kensington,
"September 23rd, 1846.

" MY DEAR SIR,—

"I write these lines in such misery of mind as no words can describe. Magdalen has deserted us. At an early hour this morning, she secretly left the house ; and she has not been heard of since.

"I would come and speak to you personally ; but I dare not leave Norah. I must try to control myself ; I must try to write.

"Nothing happened yesterday, to prepare me, or to prepare Norah, for this last—I had almost said, this worst—of all our afflictions. The only alteration we either of us noticed in the unhappy girl, was an alteration for the better when we parted for the night. She kissed me, which she has not done latterly ; and she burst out crying, when she embraced her sister next. We had so little suspicion of the truth, that we thought these signs of renewed tenderness and affection, a promise of better things for the future.

"This morning, when her sister went into her room, it was empty, and a note in her handwriting, addressed to Norah, was lying on the dressing-table. I cannot prevail on Norah to part with the note ; I can only send you the enclosed copy of it. You will see that it affords no clue to the direction she has taken.

"Knowing the value of time, in this dreadful emergency, I examined her room, and (with my sister's help) questioned the servants, immediately on the news of her absence reaching me. Her wardrobe was empty ; and all her boxes but one, which she has evidently taken away with her, are empty too. We are of opinion that she has privately turned her dresses and jewelry into money ; that she had the one trunk she took with her, removed from the house yesterday ; and that she left us this morning, on foot. The answers given by one of the servants are so unsatisfactory, that we believe the woman has been bribed to assist her ; and has managed all those arrangements for her flight, which she could not have safely undertaken by herself.

"Of the immediate object with which she has left us, I entertain no doubt.

"I have reasons (which I can tell you at a fitter time) for feeling assured that she has gone away, with the intention of trying her fortune on the stage. She has in her possession the card of an actor by profession, who superintended an amateur theatrical performance at Clifton, in which she took part ; and to him she has gone to help her. I saw the card at the time; and I know the actor's name to be Huxtable. The address, I cannot call to mind quite so correctly; but I am almost sure it was at some theatrical place, in Bow Street, Covent Garden. Let me entreat you not to lose a moment in sending to make the necessary inquiries; the first trace of her will, I firmly believe, be found at that address.

"If we had nothing worse to dread than her attempting to go on the stage, I should not feel the distress and dismay which now overpower me. Hundreds of other girls have acted as recklessly as she has acted, and have not ended ill after all. But my fears for Magdalen do not begin and end with the risk she is running at present.

"There has been something weighing on her mind ever since we left Combe-Raven—weighing far more heavily for the last six weeks than at first. Until the period when Francis Clare left England, I am persuaded she was secretly sustained by the hope that he would contrive to see her again. From the day when she knew that the measures you had taken for preventing this had succeeded; from the day when she was assured that the ship had really taken him away, nothing has roused, nothing has interested her. She has given herself up, more and more hopelessly, to her own brooding thoughts; thoughts which I believe first entered her mind, on the day when the utter ruin of the prospects on which her marriage depended was made known to her. She has formed some desperate project of contesting the possession of her father's fortune with Michael Vanstone; and the stage career which she has gone away to try, is nothing more than a means of freeing herself from all home-dependence, and of enabling her to run what mad risks she pleases, in perfect security from all home-control. What it costs me to write of her in these terms, I must leave you to imagine. The time has gone by when any consideration of distress to my own feelings can weigh with me. Whatever I can say which will open your eyes to the real danger, and strengthen your conviction of the instant necessity of averting it, I say in despite of myself, without hesitation and without reserve.

"One word more, and I have done.

"The last time you were so good as to come to this house, do you remember how Magdalen embarrassed and distressed us, by questioning you about her right to bear her father's name? Do you remember her persisting in her inquiries, until she had forced you to acknowledge that, legally speaking, she and her sister had No Name?* I venture to remind you of this, because you have the affairs of hundreds of clients to think of, and you might well have forgotten the circumstance. Whatever natural reluctance she might otherwise have had to deceiving us, and degrading herself, by the use of an assumed name, that conversation with you is certain to have removed. We must discover her, by personal description —we can trace her in no other way.

"I can think of nothing more to guide your decision in our deplorable emergency. For God's sake, let no expense and no efforts be spared. My letter ought to reach you by ten o'clock this morning, at the latest. Let me have one line in answer, to say you will act instantly for the best. My only hope of quieting Norah is to show her a word of encouragement from your pen. Believe me, dear sir, yours sincerely and obliged,

"HARRIET GARTH."

III.

FROM MAGDALEN TO NORAH (ENCLOSED IN THE PRECEDING LETTER).

"MY DARLING,—

"Try to forgive me. I have struggled against myself, till I am worn out in the effort. I am the wretchedest of living creatures. Our quiet life here, maddens me; I can bear it no longer, I must go. If you knew what my thoughts are; if you knew how hard I have fought against them, and how horribly they have gone on haunting me in the lonely quiet of this house, you would pity and forgive me. Oh, my love, don't feel hurt at my not opening my heart to you as I ought! I dare not open it. I dare not show myself to you as I really am.

"Pray don't send and seek after me; I will write and relieve all your anxieties. You know, Norah, we must get our living for ourselves; I have only gone to get mine in the manner which is fittest for me. Whether I succeed, or whether I fail, I can do myself no harm, either way. I have no position to lose, and no name to degrade. Don't doubt I love you— don't let Miss Garth doubt my gratitude. I go away miserable at leaving you; but I must go. If I had loved you less dearly, I might have had the courage to say this in your presence—but how could I trust myself to resist your persuasions, and to bear the sight of your distress? Farewell, my darling! Take a thousand kisses from me, my own best dearest love, till we meet again.

"MAGDALEN."

IV.

FROM SERGEANT BULMER (OF THE DETECTIVE POLICE) TO MR. PENDRIL.

"Scotland Yard,
"September 29th, 1846.

"SIR,—

"Your clerk informs me that the parties interested in our inquiry after the missing young lady, are anxious for news of the same. I went to your office to speak to you about the matter to-day. Not having found you, and not being able to return and try again to-morrow, I write these lines to save delay, and to tell you how we stand thus far.

"I am sorry to say, no advance has been made since my former report. The trace of the young lady which we found nearly a week since, still remains the last trace discovered of her. This case seems a mighty simple one looked at from a distance. Looked at close, it alters very considerably for the worse, and becomes, to speak the plain truth—a Poser.

"This is how we now stand:

"We have traced the young lady to the theatrical agent's in Bow Street. We know that at an early hour on the morning of the twenty-third, the agent was called down stairs, while he was dressing, to speak to a young lady in a cab at the door. We know that, on her production of Mr. Huxtable's card, he wrote on it Mr. Huxtable's address in the country, and heard her order the cabman to drive to the Great Northern terminus. We believe she left by the nine o'clock train. We followed her by the twelve o'clock train. We have ascertained that she called, at half-past two, at Mr. Huxtable's lodgings; that she found he was away, and not expected back till eight in the evening; that she left word she would call again at eight; and that she never returned. Mr. Huxtable's statement is—he and the young lady have never set eyes on each other. The first consideration which follows, is this:—Are we to believe Mr. Huxtable? I have carefully inquired into his character; I know as much, or more, about him than he knows about himself; and my opinion is, that we *are* to believe him. To the best of my knowledge, he is a perfectly honest man.

"Here, then, is the hitch in the case. The young lady sets out with a certain object before her. Instead of going on to the accomplishment of that object, she stops short of it. Why has she stopped? and where? Those are, unfortunately, just the questions which we can't answer yet.

"My own opinion of the matter is briefly as follows:—I don't think she has met with any serious accident. Serious accidents in nine cases out of ten, discover themselves. My own notion is, that she has fallen into the hands of some person or persons, interested in hiding her away, and sharp enough to know how to set about it. Whether she is in their charge, with or without her own consent, is more than I can undertake to say at present. I don't wish to raise false hopes or false fears; I wish to stop short at the opinion I have given already.

"In regard to the future, I may tell you that I have left one of my men in daily communication with the authorities. I have also taken care to have the handbills offering a reward for the discovery of her, widely circulated. Lastly, I have completed the necessary arrangements for seeing the playbills of all country theatres, and for having the dramatic companies well looked after. Some years since, this would have cost a serious expenditure of time and money. Luckily for our purpose, the country theatres

are in a bad way.* Excepting the large cities, hardly one of them is open;
and we can keep our eye on them, with little expense and less difficulty.

"These are the steps which I think it needful to take at present. If you
are of another opinion, you have only to give me your directions, and I will
carefully attend to the same. I don't by any means despair of our finding
the young lady, and bringing her back to her friends safe and well. Please
to tell them so; and allow me to subscribe myself, yours respectfully,

"ABRAHAM BULMER."

V.

ANONYMOUS LETTER ADDRESSED TO MR. PENDRIL.

" SIR,—

"A word to the wise. The friends of a certain young lady are
wasting time and money to no purpose. Your confidential clerk and your
detective policeman are looking for a needle in a bottle of hay.* This is the
ninth of October, and they have not found her yet: they will as soon find
the North-West Passage.* Call your dogs off; and you may hear of the
young lady's safety under her own hand. The longer you look for her, the
longer she will remain, what she is now—lost."

[The preceding letter is thus endorsed, in Mr. Pendril's handwriting :—
"No apparent means of tracing the enclosed to its source. Post-mark,
'Charing Cross.' Stationer's stamp cut off the inside of the envelope.
Handwriting, probably a man's, in disguise. Writer, whoever he is, cor-
rectly informed. No further trace of the younger Miss Vanstone discovered
yet."]

THE SECOND SCENE.

SKELDERGATE, YORK.

———

CHAPTER I.

In that part of the city of York, which is situated on the western bank of the Ouse, there is a narrow street, called Skeldergate, running nearly north and south, parallel with the course of the river. The postern by which Skeldergate was formerly approached, no longer exists; and the few old houses left in the street, are disguised in melancholy modern costume of whitewash and cement. Shops of the smaller and poorer order, intermixed here and there with dingy warehouses and joyless private residences of red brick, compose the present aspect of Skeldergate. On the riverside the houses are separated, at intervals, by lanes running down to the water, and disclosing lonely little plots of open ground, with the masts of sailing barges rising beyond. At its southward extremity, the street ceases on a sudden, and the broad flow of the Ouse, the trees, the meadows, the public-walk on one bank and the towing-path on the other, open to view.

Here, where the street ends, and on the side of it farthest from the river, a narrow little lane leads up to the paved footway surmounting the ancient Walls of York. The one small row of buildings, which is all that the lane possesses, is composed of cheap lodging-houses, with an opposite view, at the distance of a few feet, of a portion of the massive city wall. This place is called Rosemary Lane. Very little light enters it; very few people live in it; the floating population of Skeldergate passes it by; and visitors to the Walk on the Walls, who use it as the way up or the way down, get out of the dreary little passage as fast as they can.

The door of one of the houses in this lost corner of York, opened softly on the evening of the twenty-third of September, eighteen hundred and forty-six; and a solitary individual of the male sex sauntered into Skeldergate from the seclusion of Rosemary Lane.

Turning northward, this person directed his steps towards the bridge over the Ouse and the busy centre of the city. He bore the external appearance of respectable poverty; he carried a gingham umbrella, preserved in an oilskin case; he picked his steps, with the neatest avoidance of all dirty places on the pavement; and he surveyed the scene around him with eyes of two different colours—a bilious brown eye on the look out for employment, and a bilious green eye in a similar predicament. In plainer terms, the stranger from Rosemary Lane was no other than—Captain Wragge.

Outwardly speaking, the captain had not altered for the better, since the memorable spring day when he had presented himself to Miss Garth at the lodge-gate at Combe-Raven. The railway mania of that famous year had attacked even the wary Wragge; had withdrawn him from his customary pursuits; and had left him prostrate in the end, like many a better man. He had lost his clerical appearance—he had faded with the autumn leaves. His crape hat-band had put itself in brown mourning for its own bereavement of black. His dingy white collar and cravat had died the death of old linen, and had gone to their long home at the paper-maker's, to live again one day in quires at a stationer's shop. A grey shooting-jacket in the last stage of woollen atrophy, replaced the black frock-coat of former times, and, like a faithful servant, kept the dark secret of its master's linen from the eyes of a prying world. From top to toe, every square inch of the captain's clothing was altered for the worse; but the man himself remained unchanged—superior to all forms of moral mildew, impervious to the action of social rust. He was as courteous, as persuasive, as blandly dignified as ever. He carried his head as high without a shirt collar as ever he had carried it with one. The threadbare black handkerchief round his neck, was perfectly tied; his rotten old shoes were neatly blacked; he might have compared chins, in the matter of smooth shaving, with the highest church dignitary in York. Time, change, and poverty, had all attacked the captain together; and had all failed alike to get him down on the ground. He paced the streets of York, a man superior to clothes and circumstances; his vagabond varnish as bright on him as ever.

Arrived at the bridge, Captain Wragge stopped, and looked idly over the parapet at the barges in the river. It was plainly evident that he had no particular destination to reach, and nothing whatever to do. While he was still loitering, the clock of York Minster chimed the half-hour past five. Cabs rattled by him over the bridge on their way to meet the train from London, at twenty minutes to six. After a moment's hesitation, the captain sauntered after the cabs. When it is one of a man's regular habits to live upon his fellow-creatures, that man is always more or less fond of haunting large railway stations. Captain Wragge gleaned the human field; and on that unoccupied afternoon, the York terminus was as likely a corner to look about in as any other.

He reached the platform a few minutes after the train had arrived. That entire incapability of devising administrative measures for the management of large crowds, which is one of the national characteristics of Englishmen in authority, is nowhere more strikingly exemplified than at

York. Three different lines of railway assemble three passenger mobs, from morning to night, under one roof; and leave them to raise a travellers' riot, with all the assistance which the bewildered servants of the company can render to increase the confusion. The customary disturbance was rising to its climax as Captain Wragge approached the platform. Dozens of different people were trying to attain dozens of different objects, in dozens of different directions, all starting from the same common point, and all equally deprived of the means of information. A sudden parting of the crowd, near the second-class carriages, attracted the captain's curiosity. He pushed his way in; and found a decently-dressed man—assisted by a porter and a policeman—attempting to pick up some printed bills scattered from a paper parcel, which his frenzied fellow-passengers had knocked out of his hand.

Offering his assistance in this emergency, with the polite alacrity which marked his character, Captain Wragge observed the three startling words, "Fifty Pounds Reward," printed in capital letters on the bills which he assisted in recovering; and instantly secreted one of them, to be more closely examined at the first convenient opportunity. As he crumpled up the bill in the palm of his hand, his parti-coloured eyes fixed with hungry interest on the proprietor of the unlucky parcel. When a man happens not to be possessed of fifty pence in his own pocket, if his heart is in the right place, it bounds, if his mouth is properly constituted, it waters, at the sight of another man who carries about with him a printed offer of fifty pounds sterling, addressed to his fellow-creatures.

The unfortunate traveller wrapped up his parcel as he best might, and made his way off the platform; after addressing an inquiry to the first official victim of the day's passenger-traffic, who was sufficiently in possession of his senses to listen to it. Leaving the station for the river-side, which was close at hand, the stranger entered the ferry-boat at the North Street Postern.* The captain, who had carefully dogged his steps thus far, entered the boat also; and employed the short interval of transit to the opposite bank, in a perusal of the handbill which he had kept for his own private enlightenment. With his back carefully turned on the traveller, Captain Wragge now possessed his mind of the following lines:—

"Fifty Pounds Reward.

"Left her home, in London, early on the morning of September 23rd, 1846, A Young Lady. Age—eighteen. Dress—deep mourning. Personal appearance—hair of a very light brown; eyebrows and eyelashes darker; eyes light grey; complexion strikingly pale; lower part of her face large and full; tall upright figure; walks with remarkable grace and ease; speaks with openness and resolution; has the manners and habits of a refined, cultivated lady. Personal marks—two little moles, close together, on the left side of the neck. Mark on the under clothing—'Magdalen Vanstone.' Is supposed to have joined, or attempted to join, under an assumed name, a theatrical company now performing at York. Had, when she left London, one black box, and no other luggage. Whoever will give such information as will restore her to her friends, shall receive the above Reward. Apply at the office of Mr. Harkness, solicitor, Coney Street, York. Or to Messrs. Wyatt, Pendril, and Gwilt, Serle Street, Lincoln's Inn, London."

Accustomed as Captain Wragge was to keep the completest possession of himself, in all human emergencies, his own profound astonishment, when the course of his reading brought him to the mark on the linen of the missing young lady, betrayed him into an exclamation of surprise which even startled the ferryman. The traveller was less observant; his whole attention was fixed on the opposite bank of the river, and he left the boat hastily, the moment it touched the landing-place. Captain Wragge recovered himself, pocketed the handbill, and followed his leader for the second time.

The stranger directed his steps to the nearest street which ran down to the river ; compared a note in his pocket-book with the numbers of the houses on the left-hand side, stopped at one of them, and rang the bell. The captain went on to the next house; affected to ring the bell, in his turn ; and stood with his back to the traveller—in appearance, waiting to be let in ; in reality, listening with all his might for any scraps of dialogue which might reach his ears on the opening of the door behind him.

The door was answered with all due alacrity, and a sufficiently instructive interchange of question and answer on the threshold, rewarded the dexterity of Captain Wragge.

" Does Mr. Huxtable live here?" asked the traveller.

" Yes, sir," was the answer, in a woman's voice.

" Is he at home ?"

" Not at home, now, sir ; but he will be in again at eight to-night."

" I think a young lady called here early in the day, did she not ?"

" Yes ; a young lady came this afternoon."

" Exactly ; I come on the same business. Did she see Mr. Huxtable ?"

" No, sir ; he has been away all day. The young lady told me she would come back at eight o'clock."

" Just so. I will call and see Mr. Huxtable at the same time."

" Any name, sir ?"

" No ; say a gentleman called on theatrical business—that will be enough. Wait one minute, if you please. I am a stranger in York ; will you kindly tell me which is the way to Coney Street ?"

The woman gave the required information; the door closed, and the stranger hastened away in the direction of Coney Street.

On this occasion, Captain Wragge made no attempt to follow him. The handbill revealed plainly enough that the man's next object was to complete the necessary arrangements with the local solicitor, on the subject of the promised reward.

Having seen and heard enough for his immediate purpose, the captain retraced his steps down the street, turned to the right, and entered on the Esplanade, which, in that quarter of the city, borders the river-side between the swimming-baths and Lendal Tower. "This is a family matter," said Captain Wragge to himself, persisting, from sheer force of habit, in the old assertion of his relationship to Magdalen's mother; "I must consider it in all its bearings." He tucked the umbrella under his arm, crossed his hands behind him, and lowered himself gently into the abyss of his own reflections. The order and propriety observable in the captain's shabby garments, accurately typified the order and propriety which distinguished the operations of the captain's mind. It was his habit always to see his way before him through a neat succession of alternatives—and so he saw it now.

Three courses were open to him in connection with the remarkable discovery which he had just made. The first course was to do nothing in the matter at all. Inadmissible, on family grounds: equally inadmissible on pecuniary grounds: rejected accordingly. The second course was to deserve the gratitude of the young lady's friends, rated at fifty pounds. The third course was by a timely warning, to deserve the gratitude of the young lady herself, rated—at an unknown figure. Between these two last alternatives, the wary Wragge hesitated; not from doubt of Magdalen's pecuniary resources, for he was totally ignorant of the circumstances which had deprived the sisters of their inheritance—but from doubt whether an obstacle, in the shape of an undiscovered gentleman, might not be privately connected with her disappearance from home. After mature reflection, he determined to pause, and be guided by circumstances. In the mean time, the first consideration was to be beforehand with the messenger from London, and to lay hands securely on the young lady herself.

"I feel for this misguided girl," mused the captain, solemnly strutting backwards and forwards by the lonely river-side. "I always have looked upon her—I always shall look upon her—in the light of a niece."

Where was the adopted relative at that moment? In other words, how was a young lady, in Magdalen's critical position, likely to while away the hours until Mr. Huxtable's return? If there was an obstructive gentleman in the background, it would be mere waste of time to pursue the question. But if the inference which the handbill suggested was correct—if she was really alone, at that moment, in the city of York—where was she likely to be?

Not in the crowded thoroughfares, to begin with. Not viewing the
objects of interest in the Minster, for it was now past the hour at which
the cathedral could be seen. Was she in the waiting-room at the railway?
She would hardly run that risk. Was she in one of the hotels? Doubtful,
considering that she was entirely by herself. In a pastrycook's shop? Far
more likely. Driving about in a cab? Possible, certainly; but no more.
Loitering away the time in some quiet locality, out of doors? Likely
enough, again, on that fine autumn evening. The captain paused, weighed
the relative claims on his attention of the quiet locality and the pastrycook's shop; and decided for the first of the two. There was time enough
to find her at the pastrycook's, to inquire after her at the principal hotels,
or, finally, to intercept her in Mr. Huxtable's immediate neighbourhood,
from seven to eight. While the light lasted, the wise course was to use it
in looking for her out of doors. Where? The Esplanade was a quiet
locality; but she was not there—not on the lonely road beyond, which ran
back by the Abbey Wall. Where, next? The captain stopped, looked
across the river, brightened under the influence of a new idea, and suddenly
hastened back to the ferry.

"The Walk on the Walls," thought this judicious man, with a twinkle
of his parti-coloured eyes. "The quietest place in York: and the place
that every stranger goes to see."

In ten minutes more, Captain Wragge was exploring the new field of
search. He mounted to the walls (which enclose the whole western portion
of the city) by the North Street Postern, from which the walk winds
round, until it ends again at its southernly extremity, in the narrow
passage of Rosemary Lane. It was then twenty minutes to seven. The
sun had set more than half an hour since; the red light lay broad and
low in the cloudless western heaven; all visible objects were softening in
the tender twilight, but were not darkening yet. The first few lamps lit in
the street below, looked like faint little specks of yellow light, as the
captain started on his walk through one of the most striking scenes which
England can show.

On his right hand, as he set forth, stretched the open country beyond the
walls—the rich green meadows, the boundary trees dividing them, the
broad windings of the river in the distance, the scattered buildings nearer to
view; all wrapped in the evening stillness, all made beautiful by the
evening peace. On his left hand, the majestic west front of York Minster
soared over the city, and caught the last brightest light of heaven on the
summits of its lofty towers. Had this noble prospect tempted the lost girl
to linger and look at it? No; thus far, not a sign of her. The captain
looked round him attentively, and walked on.

He reached the spot where the iron course of the railroad strikes its way
through arches in the old wall. He paused at this place—where the central

activity of a great railway enterprise beats with all the pulses of its loud-clanging life, side by side with the dead majesty of the past, deep under the old historic stones which tell of fortified York and the sieges of two centuries since—he stood on this spot, and searched for her again, and searched in vain. Others were looking idly down at the desolate activity on the wilderness of the iron rails; but she was not among them. The captain glanced doubtfully at the darkening sky, and walked on.

He stopped again, where the postern of Micklegate still stands, and still strengthens the city wall as of old. Here, the paved walk descends a few steps, passes through the dark stone guard-room of the ancient gate, ascends again, and continues its course southward until the walls reach the river once more. He paused, and peered anxiously into the dim inner corners of the old guard-room. Was she waiting there for the darkness to come, and hide her from prying eyes? No: a solitary workman loitered through the stone chamber; but no other living creature stirred in the place. The captain mounted the steps which led out from the postern, and walked on.

He advanced some fifty or sixty yards along the paved footway; the outlying suburbs of York on one side of him, a rope-walk*and some patches of kitchen garden occupying a vacant strip of ground, on the other. He advanced with eager eyes and quickened step—for he saw before him the lonely figure of a woman, standing by the parapet of the wall, with her face set towards the westward view. He approached cautiously, to make sure of her before she turned and observed him. There was no mistaking that tall dark figure, as it rested against the parapet with a listless grace. There she stood, in her long black cloak and gown, the last dim light of evening falling tenderly on her pale resolute young face. There she stood —not three months since the spoilt darling of her parents; the priceless treasure of the household, never left unprotected, never trusted alone—there she stood in the lovely dawn of her womanhood, a castaway in a strange city, wrecked on the world!

Vagabond as he was, the first sight of her staggered even the dauntless assurance of Captain Wragge. As she slowly turned her face and looked at him, he raised his hat, with the nearest approach to respect which a long life of unblushing audacity had left him capable of making.

"I think I have the honour of addressing the younger Miss Vanstone?" he began. "Deeply gratified, I am sure—for more reasons than one."

She looked at him with a cold surprise. No recollection of the day when he had followed her sister and herself on their way home with Miss Garth, rose in her memory, while she now confronted him, with his altered manner and his altered dress.

"You are mistaken," she said, quietly. "You are a perfect stranger to me."

"Pardon me," replied the captain; "I am a species of relation. I had the pleasure of seeing you in the spring of the present year. I presented myself on that memorable occasion to an honoured preceptress in your late father's family. Permit me, under equally agreeable circumstances to present myself to *you*. My name is Wragge."

By this time he had recovered complete possession of his own impudence; his parti-coloured eyes twinkled cheerfully, and he accompanied his modest announcement of himself with a dancing-master's bow.

Magdalen frowned, and drew back a step. The captain was not a man to be daunted by a cold reception. He tucked his umbrella under his arm, and jocosely spelt his name for her further enlightenment. "w, r, a, double g, e—Wragge," said the captain, ticking off the letters persuasively on his fingers.

"I remember your name," said Magdalen. "Excuse me for leaving you abruptly. I have an engagement."

She tried to pass him, and walk on northwards towards the railway. He instantly met the attempt by raising both hands, and displaying a pair of darned black gloves outspread in polite protest.

"Not that way," he said; "not that way, Miss Vanstone, I beg and entreat!"

"Why not?" she asked haughtily.

"Because," answered the captain, "that is the way which leads to Mr. Huxtable's."

In the ungovernable astonishment of hearing his reply, she suddenly bent forward, and, for the first time, looked him close in the face. He sustained her suspicious scrutiny, with every appearance of feeling highly gratified by it. "h, u, x—Hux," said the captain, playfully turning to the old joke; "t, a—ta, Huxta; b, l, e—ble; Huxtable."

"What do you know about Mr. Huxtable?" she asked. "What do you mean by mentioning him to me?"

The captain's curly lip took a new twist upwards. He immediately replied, to the best practical purpose, by producing the handbill from his pocket.

"There is just light enough left," he said, "for young (and lovely) eyes to read by. Before I enter upon the personal statement which your flattering inquiry claims from me, pray bestow a moment's attention on this Document."

She took the handbill from him. By the last gleam of twilight, she read the lines which set a price on her recovery—which published the description of her in pitiless print, like the description of a strayed dog. No tender consideration had prepared her for the shock, no kind word softened it to her when it came. The vagabond whose cunning eyes watched her eagerly while she read, knew no more that the handbill which he had stolen, had only been prepared in anticipation of the worst, and was only to be publicly used in the event of all more considerate means of tracing her being tried in vain—than she knew it. The bill dropped from her hand; her face flushed deeply. She turned away from Captain Wragge, as if all idea of his existence had passed out of her mind.

"Oh, Norah, Norah!" she said to herself, sorrowfully. "After the letter I wrote you—after the hard struggle I had to go away! Oh, Norah, Norah!"

"How is Norah?" inquired the captain, with the utmost politeness.

She turned upon him with an angry brightness in her large grey eyes. "Is this thing shown publicly?" she asked, stamping her foot on it. "Is the mark on my neck described all over York?"

"Pray compose yourself," pleaded the persuasive Wragge. "At present I have every reason to believe that you have just perused the only copy in circulation. Allow me to pick it up."

Before he could touch the bill, she snatched it from the pavement, tore it into fragments, and threw them over the wall.

"Bravo!" cried the captain. "You remind me of your poor dear mother. The family spirit, Miss Vanstone. We all inherit our hot blood from my maternal grandfather."

"How did you come by it?" she asked suddenly.

"My dear creature, I have just told you," remonstrated the captain. "We all come by it from my maternal grandfather."

"How did you come by that handbill?" she repeated passionately.

"I beg ten thousand pardons! My head was running on the family spirit.—How did I come by it? Briefly thus." Here Captain Wragge entered on his personal statement; taking his customary vocal exercise through the longest words of the English language, with the highest elocutionary relish. Having on this rare occasion nothing to gain by concealment, he departed from his ordinary habits; and with the utmost amazement at the novelty of his own situation, permitted himself to tell the unmitigated truth.

The effect of the narrative on Magdalen by no means fulfilled Captain Wragge's anticipations in relating it. She was not startled; she was not irritated; she showed no disposition to cast herself on his mercy, and to seek his advice. She looked him steadily in the face; and all she said when he had neatly rounded his last sentence, was—"Go on."

"Go on?" repeated the captain. "Shocked to disappoint you, I am sure —but the fact is, I have done."

"No, you have not," she rejoined; "you have left out the end of your story. The end of it is:—You came here to look for me; and you mean to earn the fifty pounds reward."

Those plain words so completely staggered Captain Wragge, that for the moment he stood speechless. But he had faced awkward truths of all sorts far too often to be permanently disconcerted by them. Before Magdalen could pursue her advantage, the vagabond had recovered his balance: Wragge was himself again.

"Smart," said the captain, laughing indulgently, and drumming with his umbrella on the pavement. "Some men might take it seriously. I'm not easily offended. Try again."

Magdalen looked at him through the gathering darkness, in mute perplexity. All her little experience of society, had been experience among people who possessed a common sense of honour, and a common responsibility of social position. She had hitherto seen nothing but the successful human product from the great manufactory of Civilization. Here was one of the failures—and, with all her quickness, she was puzzled how to deal with it.

"Pardon me for returning to the subject," pursued the captain. "It has just occurred to my mind that you might actually have spoken in earnest. My poor child! how can I earn the fifty pounds before the reward is offered to me? Those handbills may not be publicly posted for a week to come. Precious as you are to all your relatives (myself included), take my word for it, the lawyers who are managing this case will not pay fifty pounds for you if they can possibly help it. Are you still persuaded that my needy pockets are gaping for the money? Very good. Button them up in spite of me, with your own fair fingers. There is a train to London at nine-forty-five to-night. Submit yourself to your friend's wishes; and go back by it."

"Never!" said Magdalen, firing at the bare suggestion, exactly as the captain had intended she should. "If my mind had not been made up before, that vile handbill would have decided me. I forgive Norah," she added, turning away, and speaking to herself, "but not Mr. Pendril, and not Miss Garth."

"Quite right!" observed Captain Wragge. "The family spirit. I should have done the same myself at your age. It runs in the blood. Hark! there goes the clock again—half-past seven. Miss Vanstone, pardon this seasonable abruptness! If you are to carry out your resolution—if you are to be your own mistress much longer, you must take a course of some kind before eight o'clock. You are young, you are inexperienced, you are in imminent danger. Here is a position of emergency on one side—and here am I, on the other, with an uncle's interest in you, full of advice. Tap me."

"Suppose I choose to depend on nobody, and to act for myself?" said Magdalen. "What then?"

"Then," replied the captain, "you will walk straight into one of the four traps which are set to catch you in the ancient and interesting city of York. Trap the first, at Mr. Huxtable's house; trap the second, at all the hotels; trap the third, at the railway station; trap the fourth, at the theatre. That man with the handbills has had an hour at his disposal. If he has not set those four traps (with the assistance of the local solicitor) by this time, he is not the competent lawyer's clerk I take him for. Come, come, my dear girl! if there is somebody else in the background, whose advice you prefer to mine——"

"You see that I am alone," she interposed proudly. "If you knew me better, you would know that I depend on nobody but myself."

Those words decided the only doubt which now remained in the captain's mind—the doubt whether the course was clear before him. The motive of her flight from home was evidently what the handbills assumed it to be— a reckless fancy for going on the stage. "One of two things," thought Wragge to himself in his logical way. "She's worth more than fifty pounds to me in her present situation, or she isn't. If she is, her friends may whistle for her. If she isn't, I have only to keep her till the bills are posted." Fortified by this simple plan of action, the captain returned to the charge; and politely placed Magdalen between the two inevitable alternatives of trusting herself to him, on the one hand, or of returning to her friends, on the other.

"I respect independence of character, wherever I find it," he said, with an air of virtuous severity. "In a young and lovely relative, I more than respect—I admire it. But (excuse the bold assertion), to walk on a way of your own, you must first have a way to walk on. Under existing circumstances, where is *your* way? Mr. Huxtable is out of the question, to begin with."

"Out of the question for to-night," said Magdalen; "but what hinders me from writing to Mr. Huxtable, and making my own private arrangements with him for to-morrow?"

"Granted with all my heart—a hit, a palpable hit.* Now, for my turn. To get to to-morrow (excuse the bold assertion, once more), you must first pass through to-night. Where are you to sleep?"

"Are there no hotels in York?"

"Excellent hotels, for large families; excellent hotels for single gentlemen. The very worst hotels in the world for handsome young ladies, who present themselves alone at the door, without male escort, without a maid in attendance, and without a single article of luggage. Dark as it is, I think I could see a lady's box, if there was anything of the sort in our immediate neighbourhood."

"My box is at the cloak-room. What is to prevent my sending the ticket for it?"

"Nothing—if you want to communicate your address by means of your box—nothing whatever. Think; pray think! Do you really suppose that the people who are looking for you, are such fools as not to have an eye on the cloak-room? Do you think they are such fools—when they find you don t come to Mr. Huxtable's at eight to-night—as not to inquire at all the hotels?" Do you think a young lady of your striking appearance (even if they consented to receive you) could take up her abode at an inn, without becoming the subject of universal curiosity and remark? Here is night coming on as fast as it can. Don't let me bore you; only let me ask once more—Where are you to sleep?"

There was no answer to that question : in Magdalen's position, there was literally no answer to it on her side. She was silent.

"Where are you to sleep?" repeated the captain. "The reply is obvious —under my roof. Mrs. Wragge will be charmed to see you. Look upon her as your aunt; pray look upon her as your aunt. The landlady is a widow, the house is close by, there are no other lodgers, and there is a bedroom to let. Can anything be more satisfactory, under all the circumstances? Pray observe, I say nothing about to-morrow—I leave to-morrow to you, and confine myself exclusively to the night. I may, or may not, command theatrical facilities, which I am in a position to offer you. Sympathy and admiration may, or may not, be strong within me, when I contemplate the dash and independence of your character. Hosts of examples of bright stars of the British drama, who have begun their apprenticeship to the stage as you are beginning yours, may, or may not, crowd on my memory. These are topics for the future. For the present, I confine myself within my strict range of duty. We are within five minutes' walk of my present address. Allow me to offer you my arm. No? You hesitate? You distrust me? Good Heavens! is it possible you can have heard anything to my disadvantage?"

"Quite possible," said Magdalen, without a moment's flinching from the answer.

"May I inquire the particulars?" asked the captain, with the politest composure. "Don't spare my feelings; oblige me by speaking out. In the plainest terms, now, what have you heard?"

She answered him with a woman's desperate disregard of consequences, when she is driven to bay—she answered him instantly :

"I have heard you are a Rogue."

"Have you, indeed?" said the impenetrable Wragge. "A Rogue? Well! I waive my privilege of setting you right on that point for a fitter time. For the sake of argument, let us say I am a Rogue. What is Mr. Huxtable?"

"A respectable man, or I should not have seen him in the house where we first met."

"Very good. Now observe! You talked of writing to Mr. Huxtable, a minute ago. What do you think a respectable man is likely to do with a young lady, who openly acknowledges that she has run away from her home and her friends to go on the stage? My dear girl, on your own showing, it's not a respectable man you want in your present predicament. It's a Rogue—like me."

Magdalen laughed bitterly.

"There is some truth in that," she said. "Thank you for recalling me to myself and my circumstances. I have my end to gain—and who am I, to pick and choose the way of getting to it? It is my turn to beg pardon now. I have been talking as if I was a young lady of family and position. Absurd! We know better than that, don't we, Captain Wragge? You are quite right. Nobody's child must sleep under Somebody's roof—and why not yours?"

"This way," said the captain, dexterously profiting by the sudden change in her humour, and cunningly refraining from exasperating it by saying more himself. "This way."

She followed him a few steps, and suddenly stopped.

"Suppose I am discovered?" she broke out abruptly. "Who has any authority over me? Who can take me back, if I don't choose to go? If they all find me to-morrow, what then? Can't I say No, to Mr. Pendril? Can't I trust my own courage with Miss Garth?"

"Can you trust your courage with your sister?" whispered the captain, who had not forgotten the references to Norah which had twice escaped her already.

Her head drooped. She shivered, as if the cold night air had struck her, and leaned back wearily against the parapet of the wall.

"Not with Norah," she said, sadly. "I could trust myself with the others. Not with Norah."

"This way," repeated Captain Wragge. She roused herself; looked up at the darkening heaven, looked round at the darkening view. "What must be, must," she said—and followed him.

The Minster clock struck the quarter to eight as they left the Walk on the Wall, and descended the steps into Rosemary Lane. Almost at the same moment, the lawyer's clerk from London gave the last instructions to his subordinates, and took up his own position, on the opposite side of the river, within easy view of Mr. Huxtable's door.

CHAPTER II.

CAPTAIN WRAGGE stopped nearly midway in the one little row of houses composing Rosemary Lane, and let himself and his guest in at the door of his lodgings, with his own key. As they entered the passage, a care-worn woman, in a widow's cap, made her appearance with a candle. "My niece," said the captain, presenting Magdalen; "my niece on a visit to York. She has kindly consented to occupy your empty bedroom. Consider it let, if you please, to my niece—and be very particular in airing the sheets? Is Mrs. Wragge upstairs? Very good. You may lend me your candle. My dear girl, Mrs. Wragge's boudoir is on the first floor; Mrs. Wragge is visible. Allow me to show you the way up."

As he ascended the stairs first, the care-worn widow whispered piteously to Magdalen: "I hope you'll pay me, miss. Your uncle doesn't."

The captain threw open the door of the front room on the first floor; and disclosed a female figure, arrayed in a gown of tarnished amber-coloured satin, seated solitary on a small chair, with dingy old gloves on its hands, with a tattered old book on its knees, and with one little bedroom candle by its side. The figure terminated at its upper extremity, in a large, smooth, white round face—like a moon—encircled by a cap and green ribbons; and dimly irradiated by eyes of mild and faded blue, which looked straightforward into vacancy, and took not the smallest notice of Magdalen's appearance, on the opening of the door.

"Mrs. Wragge!" cried the captain, shouting at her, as if she was fast asleep. "Mrs. Wragge!"

The lady of the faded blue eyes slowly rose, to an apparently interminable height. When she had at last attained an upright position, she towered to a stature of two or three inches over six feet. Giants of both sexes are, by a wise dispensation of Providence, created for the most part gentle. If Mrs. Wragge and a lamb had been placed side by side—comparison, under those circumstances, would have exposed the lamb as a rank impostor.

"Tea, captain?" inquired Mrs. Wragge, looking submissively down at her husband, whose head when he stood on tiptoe barely reached her shoulder.

"Miss Vanstone, the younger," said the captain, presenting Magdalen. "Our fair relative, whom I have met by a fortunate accident. Our guest for the night. Our guest!" reiterated the captain, shouting once more, as if the tall lady was still fast asleep, in spite of the plain testimony of her own eyes to the contrary.

A smile expressed itself (in faint outline) on the large vacant space of Mrs. Wragge's countenance. "Oh?" she said, interrogatively. "Oh, indeed? Please, miss, will you sit down? I'm sorry—no, I don't mean I'm sorry; I mean I'm glad——" She stopped, and consulted her husband by a helpless look.

"Glad, of course!" shouted the captain.

"Glad, of course," echoed the giantess of the amber satin, more meekly than ever.

"Mrs. Wragge is not deaf," explained the captain. "She's only a little slow. Constitutionally torpid—if I may use the expression. I am merely loud with her (and I beg you will honour me by being loud, too) as a necessary stimulant to her ideas. Shout at her—and her mind comes up to time. Speak to her—and she drifts miles away from you directly. Mrs. Wragge!"

Mrs. Wragge instantly acknowledged the stimulant. "Tea, captain?" she inquired, for the second time.

"Put your cap straight!" shouted her husband. "I beg ten thousand pardons," he resumed, again addressing himself to Magdalen. "The sad truth is, I am a martyr to my own sense of order. All untidiness, all want of system and regularity, causes me the acutest irritation. My attention is distracted, my composure is upset; I can't rest till things are set straight again. Externally speaking, Mrs. Wragge is, to my infinite regret, the crookedest woman I ever met with. More to the right!" shouted the captain, as Mrs. Wragge, like a well-trained child, presented herself with her revised head-dress for her husband's inspection.

Mrs. Wragge immediately pulled the cap to the left. Magdalen rose, and set it right for her. The moon-face of the giantess brightened for the first time. She looked admiringly at Magdalen's cloak and bonnet. "Do you like dress, miss?" she asked suddenly, in a confidential whisper. "I do."

"Show Miss Vanstone her room," said the captain, looking as if the whole house belonged to him. "The spare-room, the landlady's spare-room, on the third floor front. Offer Miss Vanstone all articles connected with the toilet of which she may stand in need. She has no luggage with her. Supply the deficiency; and then come back and make tea."

Mrs. Wragge acknowledged the receipt of these lofty directions by a look of placid bewilderment, and led the way out of the room; Magdalen following her, with a candle presented by the attentive captain. As soon as they were alone on the landing outside, Mrs. Wragge raised the tattered old book which she had been reading when Magdalen was first presented to her, and which she had never let out of her hand since; and slowly tapped herself on the forehead with it. "Oh, my poor head," said the tall lady, in meek soliloquy; "it's Buzzing again worse than ever!"

"Buzzing?" repeated Magdalen, in the utmost astonishment.

Mrs. Wragge ascended the stairs, without offering any explanation; stopped at one of the rooms on the second floor and led the way in.

"This is not the third floor," said Magdalen. "This is not my room, surely?"

"Wait a bit," pleaded Mrs. Wragge. "Wait a bit, miss, before we go up any higher. I've got the Buzzing in my head worse than ever. Please wait for me till I'm a little better again."

"Shall I ask for help?" inquired Magdalen. "Shall I call the land-lady?"

"Help?" echoed Mrs. Wragge. "Bless you, I don't want help! I'm used to it. I've had the Buzzing in my head, off and on—how many years?" She stopped, reflected, lost herself, and suddenly tried a question in despair. "Have you ever been at Darch's Dining-Rooms in London?" she asked, with an appearance of the deepest interest.

"No," replied Magdalen, wondering at the strange inquiry.

"That's where the Buzzing in my head first began," said Mrs. Wragge, following the new clue, with the deepest attention and anxiety. "I was employed to wait on the gentlemen at Darch's Dining-Rooms—I was. The gentlemen all came together; the gentlemen were all hungry together; the gentlemen all gave their orders together——" She stopped, and tapped her head again despondently, with the tattered old book.

"And you had to keep all their orders in your memory, separate one from the other?" suggested Magdalen, helping her out. "And the trying to do that, confused you?"

"That's it!" said Mrs. Wragge, becoming violently excited in a moment. "Boiled pork and greens and peas-pudding, for Number One. Stewed beef and carrots and gooseberry tart, for Number Two. Cut of mutton, and quick about it, well done, and plenty of fat, for Number Three. Codfish and parsnips, two chops to follow, hot-and-hot, or I'll be the death of you, for Number Four. Five, six, seven, eight, nine, ten. Carrots and goose-berry tart—peas-pudding and plenty of fat—pork and beef and mutton, and cut 'em all, and quick about it—stout for one, and ale for t'other—and stale bread here, and new bread there—and this gentleman likes cheese, and that gentleman doesn't—Matilda, Tilda, Tilda, Tilda, fifty times over, till I didn't know my own name again—oh lord! oh lord!! oh lord!!! all together, all at the same time, all out of temper, all buzzing in my poor head like forty thousand million bees—don't tell the captain! don't tell the captain!" The unfortunate creature dropped the tattered old book, and beat both her hands on her head, with a look of blank terror fixed on the door.

"Hush! hush!" said Magdalen. "The captain hasn't heard you. I know what is the matter with your head now. Let me cool it."

She dipped a towel in water, and pressed it on the hot and helpless head which Mrs. Wragge submitted to her with the docility of a sick child.

"What a pretty hand you've got," said the poor creature, feeling the relief of the coolness, and taking Magdalen's hand admiringly in her own. "How soft and white it is! I try to be a lady; I always keep my gloves on—but I can't get my hands like yours. I'm nicely dressed, though, aint I? I like dress; it's a comfort to me. I'm always happy when I'm looking at my things. I say—you won't be angry with me?—I should so like to try your bonnet on."

Magdalen humoured her, with the ready compassion of the young. She stood smiling and nodding at herself in the glass, with the bonnet perched on the top of her head. "I had one, as pretty as this, once," she said—"only it was white, not black. I wore it when the captain married me."

"Where did you meet with him?" asked Magdalen, putting the question as a chance means of increasing her scanty stock of information on the subject of Captain Wragge.

"At the Dining-Rooms," said Mrs. Wragge. "He was the hungriest and the loudest to wait upon of the lot of 'em. I made more mistakes with him, than I did with all the rest of them put together. He used to swear—oh, didn't he use to swear! When he left off swearing at me, he married me. There was others wanted me besides him. Bless you, I had my pick. Why not? When you have a trifle of money left you that you didn't expect, if that don't make a lady of you, what does? Isn't a lady to have her pick? I had my trifle of money, and I had my pick, and I picked the captain—I did. He was the smartest and the shortest of them all. He took care of me and my money. I'm here, the money's gone. Don't you put that towel down on the the table—he won't have that! Don't move his razors—don't please, or I shall forget which is which. I've got to remember which is which to-morrow morning. Bless you, the captain don't shave himself! He had me taught. I shave him. I do his hair, and cut his nails—he's awfully particular about his nails. So he is about his trousers. And his shoes. And his newspaper in the morning. And his breakfasts, and lunches, and dinners, and teas——" She stopped, struck by a sudden recollection, looked about her, observed the tattered old book on the floor, and clasped her hands in despair. "I've lost the place!" she exclaimed, helplessly. "Oh, mercy, what will become of me! I've lost the place."

"Never mind," said Magdalen; "I'll soon find the place for you again."

She picked up the book, looked into the pages, and found that the object of Mrs. Wragge's anxiety was nothing more important than an old-fashioned Treatise on the Art of Cookery, reduced under the usual heads of Fish, Flesh, and Fowl, and containing the customary series of receipts. Turning over the leaves, Magdalen came to one particular page, thickly studded with little drops of moisture, half dry. "Curious!" she said. "If this was anything but a cookery-book, I should say somebody had been crying over it."

"Somebody?" echoed Mrs. Wragge, with a stare of amazement. "It isn't somebody—it's Me. Thank you kindly, that's the place sure enough. Bless you, I'm used to crying over it. You'd cry too, if you had to get the captain's dinners out of it. As sure as ever I sit down to this book, the Buzzing in my head begins again. Who's to make it out? Sometimes, I think I've got it, and it all goes away from me. Sometimes, I think I haven't got it, and it all comes back in a heap. Look here! Here's what he's ordered for his breakfast to-morrow :—'Omelette with Herbs. Beat up two eggs with a little water or milk, salt, pepper, chives, and parsley. Mince small.'—There! mince small! How am I to mince small, when it's all mixed up and running? 'Put a piece of butter the size of your thumb into the frying-pan.'—Look at my thumb, and look at yours! whose size does she mean? 'Boil, but not brown.'—If it mustn't be brown, what colour must it be? She won't tell me; she expects me to know, and I don't. 'Pour in the omelette.'—There! I can do that. 'Allow it to set, raise it round the edge; when done, turn it over to double it.'—Oh, the numbers of 'times I turned it over and doubled it in my head, before you came in to-night! 'Keep it soft; put the dish on the frying-pan, and turn it over.' Which am I to turn over—oh mercy, try the cold towel again, and tell me which—the dish or the frying-pan?"

"Put the dish on the frying-pan," said Magdalen; "and then turn the frying-pan over. That is what it means, I think."

"Thank you kindly," said Mrs. Wragge, "I want to get it into my head; please say it again."

Magdalen said it again.

"And then turn the frying-pan over," repeated Mrs. Wragge, with a sudden burst of energy. "I've got it now! Oh, the lots of omelettes all frying together in my head; and all frying wrong. Much obliged, I'm sure. You've put me all right again: I'm only a little tired with talking. And then turn the frying-pan, then turn the frying-pan, then turn the frying-pan over. It sounds like poetry, don't it?"

Her voice sank, and she drowsily closed her eyes. At the same moment, the door of the room below opened, and the captain's mellifluous bass notes floated up stairs, charged with the customary stimulant to his wife's faculties.

"Mrs. Wragge!" cried the captain. "Mrs. Wragge!"

She started to her feet at that terrible summons. "Oh, what did he tell me to do?" she asked distractedly. "Lots of things, and I've forgotten them all!"

"Say you have done them, when he asks you," suggested Magdalen. "They were things for me—things I don't want. I remember all that is necessary. My room is the front room, on the third floor. Go down stairs, and say I am coming directly."

She took up the candle, and pushed Mrs. Wragge out on the landing. "Say I am coming directly," she whispered again—and went upstairs by herself to the third story.

The room was small, close, and very poorly furnished. In former days, Miss Garth would have hesitated to offer such a room to one of the servants, at Combe-Raven. But it was quiet; it gave her a few minutes alone; and it was endurable, even welcome, on that account. She locked herself in; and walked mechanically, with a woman's first impulse in a strange bed-

room, to the rickety little table, and the dingy little looking-glass. She
waited there for a moment, and then turned away with weary contempt.
"What does it matter how pale I am?" she thought to herself. "Frank
can't see me—what does it matter now!"

She laid aside her cloak and bonnet, and sat down to collect herself. But
the events of the day had worn her out. The past, when she tried to
remember it, only made her heart ache. The future, when she tried to
penetrate it, was a black void. She rose again, and stood by the uncur-
tained window—stood looking out, as if there was some hidden sympathy
for her own desolation in the desolate night.

"Norah!" she said to herself, tenderly; "I wonder if Norah is thinking
of me? Oh, if I could be as patient as she is! If I could only forget the
debt we owe to Michael Vanstone!"

Her face darkened with a vindictive despair, and she paced the little cage
of a room backwards and forwards, softly. "No: never till the debt is
paid!" Her thoughts veered back again to Frank. "Still at sea, poor
fellow; farther and farther away from me; sailing through the day, sailing
through the night. Oh, Frank, love me!"

Her eyes filled with tears. She dashed them away, made for the door,
and laughed with a desperate levity, as she unlocked it again.

"Any company is better than my own thoughts," she burst out recklessly, as she left the room. "I'm forgetting my ready-made relations—
my half-witted aunt, and my uncle the rogue." She descended the stairs
to the landing on the first floor, and paused there in momentary hesitation.
"How will it end?" she asked herself. "Where is my blindfolded journey
taking me to now? Who knows, and who cares?"

She entered the room.

Captain Wragge was presiding at the tea-tray, with the air of a prince in
his own banqueting-hall. At one side of the table sat Mrs. Wragge,
watching her husband's eye, like an animal waiting to be fed. At the
other side, was an empty chair, towards which the captain waved his
persuasive hand, when Magdalen came in. "How do you like your
room?" he inquired; "I trust Mrs. Wragge has made herself useful?
You take milk and sugar? Try the local bread, honour the York butter,
test the freshness of a new and neighbouring egg. I offer my little all.
A pauper's meal, my dear girl—seasoned with a gentleman's welcome."

"Seasoned with salt, pepper, chives, and parsley," murmured Mrs.
Wragge, catching instantly at a word in connection with cookery, and har-
nessing her head to the omelette for the rest of the evening.

"Sit straight at the table!" shouted the captain. "More to the left,
more still—that will do. During your absence upstairs," he continued,
addressing himself to Magdalen, "my mind has not been unemployed. I

have been considering your position, with a view exclusively to your own benefit. If you decide on being guided to-morrow by the light of my experience, that light is unreservedly at your service. You may naturally say, 'I know but little of you, captain, and that little is unfavourable.' Granted, on one condition—that you permit me to make myself and my character quite familiar to you, when tea is over. False shame is foreign to my nature. You see my wife, my house, my bread, my butter, and my eggs, all exactly as they are. See me, too, my dear girl, while you are about it."

When tea was over, Mrs. Wragge, at a signal from her husband, retired to a corner of the room, with the eternal cookery-book still in her hand. "Mince small," she whispered confidentially, as she passed Magdalen. "That's a teaser, isn't it?"

"Down at heel again!" shouted the captain, pointing to his wife's heavy flat feet as they shuffled across the room. "The right shoe. Pull it up at heel, Mrs. Wragge—pull it up at heel! Pray allow me," he continued, offering his arm to Magdalen, and escorting her to a dirty little horsehair sofa. "You want repose—after your long journey, you really want repose." He drew his chair to the sofa, and surveyed her with a bland look of investigation—as if he had been her medical attendant, with a diagnosis on his mind.

"Very pleasant! very pleasant!" said the captain, when he had seen his guest comfortable on the sofa. "I feel quite in the bosom of my family. Shall we return to our subject—the subject of my rascally self? No! no! No apologies, no protestations, pray. Don't mince the matter on your side —and depend on me not to mince it on mine. Now come to facts; pray come to facts. Who, and what, am I? Carry your mind back to our conversation on the Walls of this interesting city, and let us start once more from your point of view. I am a Rogue; and, in that capacity (as I have already pointed out), the most useful man you possibly could have met with. Now observe! There are many várieties of Rogue; let me tell you my variety to begin with. I am a Swindler."

His entire shamelessness was really superhuman. Not the vestige of a blush varied the sallow monotony of his complexion; the smile wreathed his curly lips, as pleasantly as ever; his parti-coloured eyes twinkled at Magdalen, with the self-enjoying frankness of a naturally harmless man. Had his wife heard him? Magdalen looked over his shoulder to the corner of the room in which she was sitting behind him. No: the self-taught student of cookery was absorbed in her subject. She had advanced her imaginary omelette to the critical stage at which the butter was to be thrown in—that vaguely measured morsel of butter, the size of your thumb. Mrs. Wragge sat lost in contemplation of one of her own thumbs, and shook her head over it, as if it failed to satisfy her.

"Don't be shocked," proceeded the captain; "don't be astonished.

Swindler is nothing but a word of two syllables. S, W, I, N, D—swind; L, E, R—ler; Swindler. Definition: A moral agriculturist; a man who cultivates the field of human sympathy. I am that moral agriculturist, that cultivating man. Narrow-minded mediocrity, envious of my success in my profession, calls me a Swindler. What of that? The same low tone of mind assails men in other professions in a similar manner—calls great writers, scribblers—great generals, butchers—and so on. It entirely depends on the point of view. Adopting your point, I announce myself intelligibly as a Swindler. Now return the obligation, and adopt mine. Hear what I have to say for myself, in the exercise of my profession.—Shall I continue to put it frankly?"

"Yes," said Magdalen; "and I'll tell you frankly afterwards what I think of it."

The captain cleared his throat; mentally assembled his entire army of words—horse, foot, artillery, and reserves; put himself at the head; and dashed into action, to carry the moral entrenchments of Society by a general charge.

"Now, observe," he began. "Here am I, a needy object. Very good. Without complicating the question by asking how I come to be in that condition, I will merely inquire whether it is, or is not, the duty of a Christian community to help the needy. If you say, No, you simply shock me; and there is an end of it. If you say, Yes—then I beg to ask, Why am I to blame for making a Christian community do its duty? You may say, Is a careful man who has saved money, bound to spend it again on a careless stranger who has saved none? Why of course he is! And on what ground, pray? Good Heavens! on the ground that he has *got* the money, to be sure. All the world over, the man who has not got the thing, obtains it, on one pretence or another, of the man who has—and in nine cases out of ten, the pretence is a false one. What! your pockets are full, and my pockets are empty; and you refuse to help me? Sordid wretch! do you think I will allow you to violate the sacred obligations of charity in my person? I won't allow you—I say distinctly, I won't allow you. Those are my principles as a moral agriculturist. Principles which admit of trickery? Certainly. Am I to blame if the field of human sympathy can't be cultivated in any other way? Consult my brother agriculturists in the mere farming line—do they get their crops for the asking? No! they must circumvent arid Nature, exactly as a I circumvent sordid man. They must plough, and sow, and top-dress, and bottom-dress, and deep-drain, and surface-drain, and all the rest of it. Why am I to be checked in the vast occupation of deep-draining mankind? Why am I to be persecuted for habitually exciting the noblest feelings of our common nature? Infamous!—I can characterize it by no other word—infamous! If I hadn't confidence in the future, I should despair of humanity—but I

have confidence in the future. Yes! one of these days (when I am dead
and gone), as ideas enlarge and enlightenment progresses, the abstract
merits of the profession now called swindling, will be recognized. When
that day comes, don't drag me out of my grave and give me a public
funeral; don't take advantage of my having no voice to raise in my own
defence, and insult me by a national statue. No! do me justice on my
tombstone; dash me off, in one masterly sentence, on my epitaph. Here
lies Wragge, Embalmed in the tardy recognition of his species: he ploughed,
sowed, and reaped his fellow-creatures; and enlightened posterity con-
gratulates him on the uniform excellence of his crops."

He stopped; not from want of confidence, not from want of words—
purely from want of breath. "I put it frankly, with a dash of humour,"
he said, pleasantly. "I don't shock you—do I?" Weary and heartsick
as she was—suspicious of others, doubtful of herself—the extravagant impudence of Captain Wragge's defence of swindling, touched Magdalen's
natural sense of humour, and forced a smile to her lips. "Is the Yorkshire
crop a particularly rich one, just at present?" she inquired, meeting him,
in her neatly feminine way, with his own weapons.

"A hit—a palpable hit," said the captain, jocosely exhibiting the tails
of his threadbare shooting-jacket, as a practical commentary on Magdalen's
remark. "My dear girl, here or elsewhere, the crop never fails—but one
man can't always gather it in. The assistance of intelligent co-operation is,
I regret to say, denied me. I have nothing in common with the clumsy
rank and file of my profession, who convict themselves before recorders and
magistrates, of the worst of all offences—incurable stupidity in the exercise
of their own vocation. Such as you see me, I stand entirely alone. After
years of successful self-dependence, the penalties of celebrity are beginning
to attach to me. On my way from the North, I pause at this interesting
city for the third time; I consult my Books for the customary references
to past local experience; I find under the heading, 'Personal position in
York,' the initials, T. W. K. signifying Too Well Known. I refer to my
Index, and turn to the surrounding neighbourhood. The same brief remarks meet my eye. 'Leeds. T. W. K.—Scarborough. T. W. K.—
Harrowgate. T. W. K.'—and so on. What is the inevitable consequence?
I suspend my proceedings; my resources evaporate; and my fair relative
finds me the pauper gentleman whom she now sees before her."

"Your books?" said Magdalen. "What books do you mean?"

"You shall see," replied the captain. "Trust me, or not, as you like—I
trust *you* implicitly. You shall see."

With those words he retired into the back room. While he was gone,
Magdalen stole another look at Mrs. Wragge. Was she still self-isolated
from her husband's deluge of words? Perfectly self-isolated. She had
advanced the imaginary omelette to the last stage of culinary progress; and

she was now rehearsing the final operation of turning it over—with the palm of her hand to represent the dish, and the cookery-book to impersonate the frying-pan. "I've got it," said Mrs. Wragge, nodding across the room at Magdalen. "First put the frying-pan on the dish, and then tumble both of them over."

Captain Wragge returned, carrying a neat black despatch-box, adorned with a bright brass lock. He produced from the box five or six plump little books, bound in commercial calf and vellum, and each fitted comfortably with its own little lock.

"Mind!" said the moral agriculturist: "I take no credit to myself for this : it is my nature to be orderly, and orderly I am. I must have everything down in black and white, or I should go mad! Here is my commercial library :—Day Book, Ledger, Book of Districts, Book of Letters, Book of Remarks, and so on. Kindly throw your eye over any one of them. I flatter myself there is no such thing as a blot or a careless entry in it from the first page to the last. Look at this room—is there a chair out of place? Not if I know it! Look at *me*. Am I dusty? am I dirty? am I half shaved? Am I, in brief, a speckless pauper, or am I not? Mind! I take no credit to myself; the nature of the man, my dear girl— the nature of the man!"

He opened one of the books. Magdalen was no judge of the admirable correctness with which the accounts inside were all kept; but she could estimate the neatness of the handwriting, the regularity in the rows of figures, the mathematical exactness of the ruled lines in red and black ink, the cleanly absence of blots, stains, or erasures. Although Captain Wragge's inborn sense of order was, in him—as it is in others—a sense too inveterately mechanical to exercise any elevating moral influence over his actions, it had produced its legitimate effect on his habits, and had reduced his rogueries as strictly to method and system as if they had been the commercial transactions of an honest man.

"In appearance, my system looks complicated?" pursued the captain. "In reality, it is simplicity itself. I merely avoid the errors of inferior practitioners. That is to say, I never plead for myself; and I never apply to rich people—both fatal mistakes which the inferior practitioner perpetually commits. People with small means sometimes have generous impulses in connection with money—rich people, *never*. My lord, with forty thousand a year ; Sir John, with property in half a dozen counties—those are the men who never forgive the genteel beggar for swindling them out of a sovereign; those are the men who send for the mendicity officers ; those are the men who take care of their money. Who are the people who lose shillings and sixpences, by sheer thoughtlessness ? Servants and small clerks, to whom shillings and sixpences are of consequence. Did you ever hear of Rothschild or Baring dropping a fourpenny-piece down a gutter-hole ?

Fourpence in Rothschild's pocket is safer than fourpence in the pocket of that woman who is crying stale shrimps in Skeldergate at this moment. Fortified by these sound principles, enlightened by the stores of written information in my commercial library, I have ranged through the population for years past, and have raised my charitable crops with the most cheering success. Here, in book Number One, are all my Districts mapped out, with the prevalent public feeling to appeal to in each:—Military District, Clerical District, Agricultural District; Etcetera, Etcetera. Here, in Number Two, are my cases that I plead :—Family of an officer who fell at Waterloo; Wife of a poor curate stricken down by nervous debility; Widow of a grazier in difficulties gored to death by a mad bull; Etcetera, Etcetera. Here, in Number Three, are the people who have heard of the officer's family, the curate's wife, the grazier's widow, and the people who haven't; the people who have said Yes, and the people who have said No; the people to try again, the people who want a fresh case to stir them up, the people who are doubtful, the people to beware of; Etcetera, Etcetera. Here, in Number Four, are my Adopted Handwritings of public characters; my testimonials to my own worth and integrity; my Heartrending Statements of the officer's family, the curate's wife, and the grazier's widow, stained with tears, blotted with emotion; Etcetera, Etcetera. Here, in Numbers Five and Six, are my own personal subscriptions to local charities, actually paid in remunerative neighbourhoods, on the principle of throwing a sprat to catch a herring; also, my diary of each day's proceedings, my personal reflections and remarks, my statement of existing difficulties (such as the difficulty of finding myself T. W. K., in this interesting city); my out-goings and in-comings; wind and weather; politics and public events; fluctuations in my own health; fluctuations in Mrs. Wragge's head; fluctuations in our means and meals, our payments, prospects, and principles; Etcetera, Etcetera. So, my dear girl, the Swindler's Mill goes. So you see me, exactly as I am. You knew, before I met you, that I lived on my wits. Well! have I, or have I not, shown you that I have wits to live on ?"

" I have no doubt you have done yourself full justice," said Magdalen, quietly.

" I am not at all exhausted," continued the captain. " I can go on, if necessary, for the rest of the evening.—However, if I have done myself full justice, perhaps I may leave the remaining points in my character to develop themselves at future opportunities. For the present, I withdraw myself from notice. Exit Wragge. And now to business! Permit me to inquire what effect I have produced on your own mind? Do you still believe that the Rogue who has trusted you with all his secrets, is a Rogue who is bent on taking a mean advantage of a fair relative ?"

" I will wait a little," Magdalen rejoined, " before I answer that question.

When I came down to tea, you told me you had been employing your mind for my benefit. May I ask how?"

"By all means," said Captain Wragge. "You shall have the net result of the whole mental process. Said process ranges over the present and future proceedings of your disconsolate friends, and of the lawyers who are helping them to find you. Their present proceedings are, in all probability, assuming the following form:—The lawyer's clerk has given you up at Mr. Huxtable's, and has also, by this time, given you up after careful inquiry at all the hotels. His last chance is, that you may send for your box to the cloak-room—you don't send for it—and there the clerk is to-night (thanks to Captain Wragge and Rosemary Lane) at the end of his resources. He will forthwith communicate that fact to his employers in London; and those employers (don't be alarmed!) will apply for help to the detective police. Allowing for inevitable delays, a professional spy, with all his wits about him, and with those handbills to help him privately in identifying you, will be here, certainly not later than the day after to-morrow—possibly earlier. If you remain in York, if you attempt to communicate with Mr. Huxtable, that spy will find you out. If, on the other hand, you leave the city before he comes (taking your departure by other means than the railway, of course), you put him in the same predicament as the clerk—you defy him to find a fresh trace of you. There is my brief abstract of your present position. What do you think of it?"

"I think it has one defect," said Magdalen. "It ends in nothing."

"Pardon me," retorted the captain. "It ends in an arrangement for your safe departure, and in a plan for the entire gratification of your wishes in the direction of the stage. Both drawn from the resources of my own experience; and both waiting a word from you, to be poured forth immediately, in the fullest detail."

"I think I know what that word is," replied Magdalen, looking at him attentively.

"Charmed to hear it, I am sure. You have only to say, 'Captain Wragge, take charge of me'—and my plans are yours from that moment."

"I will take to-night to consider your proposal," she said, after an instant's reflection. "You shall have my answer to-morrow morning."

Captain Wragge looked a little disappointed. He had not expected the reservation on his side to be met so composedly by a reservation on hers.

"Why not decide at once?" he remonstrated, in his most persuasive tones. "You have only to consider——"

"I have more to consider than you think for," she answered. "I have another object in view, besides the object you know of."

"May I ask——?"

"Excuse me, Captain Wragge—you may *not* ask. Allow me to thank you for your hospitality, and to wish you good night. I am worn out. I want rest."

Once more, the captain wisely adapted himself to her humour, with the ready self-control of an experienced man.

"Worn-out, of course!" he said, sympathetically. "Unpardonable on my part not to have thought of it before. We will resume our conversation to-morrow. Permit me to give you a candle. Mrs. Wragge!"

Prostrated by mental exertion, Mrs. Wragge was pursuing the course of the omelette in dreams. Her head was twisted one way, and her body the other. She snored meekly. At intervals, one of her hands raised itself in the air, shook an imaginary frying-pan, and dropped again with a faint thump on the cookery-book in her lap. At the sound of her husband's voice, she started to her feet; and confronted him with her mind fast asleep, and her eyes wide open.

"Assist Miss Vanstone," said the captain. "And the next time you forget yourself in your chair, fall asleep straight—don't annoy me by falling asleep crooked."

Mrs. Wragge opened her eyes a little wider, and looked at Magdalen in helpless amazement.

"Is the captain breakfasting by candlelight?" she inquired, meekly. "And haven't I done the omelette?"

Before her husband's corrective voice could apply a fresh stimulant, Magdalen took her compassionately by the arm, and led her out of the room.

"Another object besides the object I know of?" repeated Captain Wragge, when he was left by himself. "*Is* there a gentleman in the background, after all? Is there mischief brewing in the dark, that I don't bargain for?"

CHAPTER III.

TOWARDS six o'clock the next morning, the light pouring in on her face awoke Magdalen in the bedroom in Rosemary Lane.

She started from her deep dreamless repose of the past night, with that painful sense of bewilderment on first waking which is familiar to all sleepers in strange beds. "Norah!" she called out mechanically, when she opened her eyes. The next instant, her mind roused itself, and her senses told her the truth. She looked round the miserable room with a loathing recognition of it. The sordid contrast which the place presented to all that she had been accustomed to see in her own bedchamber—the practical abandonment implied in its scanty furniture, of those elegant purities of personal habit to which she had been accustomed from her childhood—shocked that sense of bodily self-respect in Magdalen, which is a refined woman's second nature. Contemptible as the influence seemed when compared with her situation at that moment, the bare sight of the jug and basin in a corner of the room, decided her first resolution when she woke. She determined, then and there, to leave Rosemary Lane.

How was she to leave it? With Captain Wragge, or without him?

She dressed herself, with a dainty shrinking from everything in the room which her hands or her clothes touched in the process; and then opened the window. The autumn air felt keen and sweet; and the little patch of sky that she could see, was warmly bright already with the new sunlight. Distant voices of bargemen on the river, and the chirping of birds among the weeds which topped the old city wall, were the only sounds that broke the morning silence. She sat down by the window; and searched her mind for the thoughts which she had lost, when weariness overcame her on the night before.

The first subject to which she returned, was the vagabond subject of Captain Wragge.

The " moral agriculturist" had failed to remove her personal distrust of him, cunningly as he had tried to plead against it by openly confessing the impostures that he had practised on others. He had raised her opinion of his abilities; he had amused her by his humour; he had astonished her by his assurance—but he had left her original conviction that he was a Rogue, exactly where it was when he first met with her. If the one design then in her mind had been the design of going on the stage, she would, at all hazards, have rejected the more than doubtful assistance of Captain Wragge, on the spot.

But the perilous journey on which she had now adventured herself, had another end in view—an end, dark and distant—an end, with pitfalls hidden on the way to it, far other than the shallow pitfalls on the way to the stage. In the mysterious stillness of the morning, her mind looked on to its second and its deeper design; and the despicable figure of the swindler rose before her in a new view.

She tried to shut him out—to feel above him and beyond him again, as she had felt up to this time.

After a little trifling with her dress, she took from her bosom the white silk bag which her own hands had made on the farewell night at Combe-Raven. It drew together at the mouth with delicate silken strings. The first thing she took out, on opening it, was a lock of Frank's hair, tied with a morsel of silver thread; the next was a sheet of paper containing the extracts which she had copied from her father's will and her father's letter; the last was a closely folded packet of bank-notes, to the value of nearly two hundred pounds—the produce (as Miss Garth had rightly conjectured) of the sale of her jewelry and her dresses, in which the servant at the boarding school had privately assisted her. She put back the notes at once, without a second glance at them; and then sat looking thoughtfully at the lock of hair, as it lay on her lap. "You are better than nothing," she said, speaking to it with a girl's fanciful tenderness. "I can sit and look at you sometimes, till I almost think I am looking at Frank. Oh, my darling! my darling!" Her voice faltered softly, and she put the lock of hair, with a languid gentleness, to her lips. It fell from her fingers into her bosom. A lovely tinge of colour rose on her cheeks, and spread downward to her neck, as if it followed the falling hair. She closed her eyes, and let her fair head droop softly. The world passed from her; and, for one enchanted moment, Love opened the gates of Paradise to the daughter of Eve.

The trivial noises in the neighbouring street, gathering in number as the morning advanced, forced her back to the hard realities of the passing time. She raised her head, with a heavy sigh, and opened her eyes once more on the mean and miserable little room.

The extracts from the will and the letter—those last memorials of her father, now so closely associated with the purpose which had possession of her mind—still lay before her. The transient colour faded from her face, as she spread the little manuscript open on her lap. The extracts from the will stood highest on the page; they were limited to those few touching words, in which the dead father begged his children's forgiveness for the stain on their birth, and implored them to remember the untiring love and care by which he had striven to atone for it. The extract from the letter to Mr. Pendril came next. She read the last melancholy sentences aloud to herself:—" For God's sake come on the day when you receive this— come and relieve me from the dreadful thought that my two darling girls are at this moment unprovided for. If anything happened to me, and if my desire to do their mother justice, ended (through my miserable ignorance of the law) in leaving Norah and Magdalen disinherited, I should not rest in my grave!" Under these lines again, and close at the bottom of the page, was written the terrible commentary on that letter which had fallen from Mr. Pendril's lips :—" Mr. Vanstone's daughters are Nobody's Children, and the law leaves them helpless at their uncle's mercy."

Helpless when those words were spoken—helpless still, after all that she had resolved, after all that she had sacrificed. The assertion of her natural rights, and her sister's, sanctioned by the direct expression of her father's last wishes; the recall of Frank from China; the justification of her desertion of Norah—all hung on her desperate purpose of recovering the lost inheritance, at any risk, from the man who had beggared and insulted his brother's children. And that man was still a shadow to her! So little did she know of him that she was even ignorant, at that moment, of his place of abode.

She rose and paced the room, with the noiseless, negligent grace of a wild creature of the forest in its cage. "How can I reach him, in the dark?" she said to herself. "How can I find out——?" She stopped suddenly. Before the question had shaped itself to an end in her thoughts, Captain Wragge was back in her mind again.

A man well used to working in the dark; a man with endless resources of audacity and cunning; a man who would hesitate at no mean employment that could be offered to him, if it was employment that filled his pockets—was this the instrument for which, in its present need, her hand was waiting? Two of the necessities to be met, before she could take a single step in advance, were plainly present to her—the necessity of knowing more of her father's brother than she knew now; and the necessity of throwing him off his guard by concealing herself personally, during the process of inquiry. Resolutely self-dependent as she was, the inevitable spy's work at the outset must be work delegated to another. In her position, was there any ready human creature within reach, but the vagabond downstairs? Not one. She thought of it anxiously, she thought of it long. Not one! There the choice was, steadily confronting her: the choice of taking the Rogue, or of turning her back on the Purpose.

She paused in the middle of the room. "What can he do at his worst?" she said to herself. "Cheat me. Well! if my money governs him for me, what then? Let him have my money! She returned mechanically to her place by the window. A moment more decided her. A moment more, and she took the first fatal step downwards—she determined to face the risk, and try Captain Wragge.

At nine o'clock the landlady knocked at Magdalen's door, and informed her (with the captain's kind compliments), that breakfast was ready.

She found Mrs. Wragge alone; attired in a voluminous brown holland wrapper, with a limp cape, and a trimming of dingy pink ribbon. The ex-waitress at Darch's Dining Rooms was absorbed in the contemplation of a large dish, containing a leathery-looking substance of a mottled yellow colour, profusely sprinkled with little black spots.

"There it is!" said Mrs. Wragge. "Omelette with herbs. The landlady helped me. And that's what we've made of it. Don't you ask the captain for any when he comes in—don't, there's a good soul. It isn't nice. We had some accidents with it. It's been under the grate. It's been spilt on the stairs. It's scalded the landlady's youngest boy—he went and sat on it. Bless you, it isn't half as nice as it looks! Don't you ask for any. Perhaps he won't notice if you say nothing about it. What do you think of my wrapper? I should so like to have a white one. Have you got a white one? How is it trimmed? Do tell me!"

The formidable entrance of the captain suspended the next question on her lips. Fortunately for Mrs. Wragge, her husband was far too anxious for the promised expression of Magdalen's decision, to pay his customary attention to questions of cookery. When breakfast was over, he dismissed Mrs. Wragge, and merely referred to the omelette by telling her that she had his full permission to "give it to the dog."

"How does my little proposal look by daylight?" he asked, placing chairs for Magdalen and himself. "Which is it to be: 'Captain Wragge, take charge of me?' or, 'Captain Wragge, good morning?'"

"You shall hear directly," replied Magdalen. "I have something to say first. I told you, last night, that I had another object in view, besides the object of earning my living on the stage——"

"I beg your pardon," interposed Captain Wragge. "Did you say, earning your living?"

"Certainly. Both my sister and myself must depend on our own exertions to gain our daily bread."

"What ! ! !" cried the captain, starting to his feet. "The daughters of my wealthy and lamented relative by marriage, reduced to earn their own living? Impossible—wildly, extravagantly impossible!" He sat down again, and looked at Magdalen as if she had inflicted a personal injury on him.

"You are not acquainted with the full extent of our misfortune," she said, quietly. "I will tell you what has happened before I go any farther." She told him at once, in the plainest terms she could find, and with as few details as possible.

Captain Wragge's profound bewilderment left him conscious of but one distinct result, produced by the narrative on his own mind. The lawyer's offer of Fifty Pounds Reward for the missing young lady, ascended instantly to a place in his estimation which it had never occupied until that moment.

"Do I understand," he inquired, "that you are entirely deprived of present resources?"

"I have sold my jewelry and my dresses," said Magdalen, impatient of his mean harping on the pecuniary string. "If my want of experience keeps me back in a theatre, I can afford to wait till the stage can afford to pay me."

Captain Wragge mentally appraised the rings, bracelets, and necklaces, the silks, satins, and laces of the daughter of a gentleman of fortune, at—say, a third of their real value. In a moment more, the Fifty Pounds Reward suddenly sank again to the lowest depths in the deep estimation of this judicious man.

"Just so," he said, in his most business-like manner. "There is not the least fear, my dear girl, of your being kept back in a theatre, if you possess present resources, and if you profit by my assistance."

"I must accept more assistance than you have already offered—or none," said Magdalen. "I have more serious difficulties before me than the difficulty of leaving York, and the difficulty of finding my way to the stage."

"You don't say so! I am all attention; pray explain yourself!"

She considered her next words carefully before they passed her lips.

"There are certain inquiries," she said, "which I am interested in making. If I undertook them myself, I should excite the suspicion of the person inquired after, and should learn little or nothing of what I wish to know. If the inquiries could be made by a stranger, without my being seen in the matter, a service would be rendered me of much greater importance than the service you offered last night."

Captain Wragge's vagabond face became gravely and deeply attentive.

"May I ask," he said, "what the nature of the inquiries is likely to be?"

Magdalen hesitated. She had necessarily mentioned Michael Vanstone's name, in informing the captain of the loss of her inheritance. She must inevitably mention it to him again, if she employed his services. He would doubtless discover it for himself, by a plain process of inference, before she said many words more, frame them as carefully as she might. Under these circumstances was there any intelligible reason for shrinking from direct reference to Michael Vanstone? No intelligible reason—and yet, she shrank.

"For instance," pursued Captain Wragge, "are they inquiries about a man or a woman; inquiries about an enemy or a friend——?"

"An enemy," she answered quickly.

Her reply might still have kept the captain in the dark—but her eyes enlightened him. "Michael Vanstone!" thought the wary Wragge. "She looks dangerous; I'll feel my way a little farther."

"With regard, now, to the person who is the object of these inquiries," he resumed. "Are you thoroughly clear, in your own mind, about what you want to know?"

"Perfectly clear," replied Magdalen. "I want to know where he lives, to begin with?"

"Yes? And after that?"

"I want to know about his habits; about who the people are whom he associates with; about what he does with his money——" She considered a little. "And one thing more," she said; "I want to know whether there is any woman about his house—a relation, or a housekeeper—who has an influence over him."

"Harmless enough, so far," said the captain. "What next?"

"Nothing. The rest is my secret."

The clouds on Captain Wragge's countenance began to clear away again. He reverted with his customary precision to his customary choice of alternatives. "These inquiries of hers," he thought, "mean one of two things —Mischief, or Money! If it's Mischief, I'll slip through her fingers. If it's Money, I'll make myself useful, with a view to the future."

Magdalen's vigilant eyes watched the progress of his reflections suspiciously. "Captain Wragge," she said, "if you want time to consider, say so plainly."

"I don't want a moment," replied the captain. "Place your departure from York, your dramatic career, and your private inquiries under my care. Here I am, unreservedly at your disposal. Say the word—do you take me?"

Her heart beat fast; her lips turned dry—but she said the word.

"I do."

There was a pause. Magdalen sat silent, struggling with the vague dread of the future which had been roused in her mind by her own reply. Captain Wragge, on his side, was apparently absorbed in the consideration of a new set of alternatives. His hands descended into his empty pockets, and prophetically tested their capacity as receptacles for gold and silver. The brightness of the precious metals was in his face, the smoothness of the precious metals was in his voice, as he provided himself with a new supply of words, and resumed the conversation.

"The next question," he said, "is the question of time. Do these confidential investigations of ours require immediate attention—or can they wait?"

"For the present they can wait," replied Magdalen. "I wish to secure my freedom from all interference on the part of my friends, before the inquiries are made."

"Very good. The first step towards accomplishing that object is to beat our retreat—excuse a professional metaphor from a military man—to beat our retreat from York to-morrow. I see my way plainly so far; but I am all abroad, as we used to say in the militia, about my marching orders afterwards. The next direction we take, ought to be chosen with an eye to advancing your dramatic views. I am all ready, when I know what your views are. How came you to think of the theatre at all? I see the sacred fire burning in you; tell me, who lit it?"

Magdalen could only answer him in one way. She could only look back at the days that were gone for ever; and tell him the story of her first step towards the stage at Evergreen Lodge. Captain Wragge listened with his usual politeness; but he evidently derived no satisfactory impression from what he heard. Audiences of friends, were audiences whom he privately declined to trust; and the opinion of the stage-manager, was the opinion of a man who spoke with his fee in his pocket, and his eye on a future engagement.

"Interesting, deeply interesting," he said, when Magdalen had done.

"But not conclusive to a practical man. A specimen of your abilities is necessary to enlighten me. I have been on the stage myself; the comedy of the Rivals is familiar to me from beginning to end. A sample is all I want, if you have not forgotten the words—a sample of 'Lucy,' and a sample of 'Julia.'"

"I have not forgotten the words," said Magdalen, sorrowfully; "and I have the little books with me, in which my dialogue was written out. I have never parted with them: they remind me of a time——" Her lip trembled; and a pang of the heartache silenced her.

"Nervous," remarked the captain, indulgently. "Not at all a bad sign. The greatest actresses on the stage are nervous. Follow their example, and get over it. Where are the parts? Oh, here they are! Very nicely written, and remarkably clean. I'll give you the cues—it will all be over (as the dentists say), in no time. Take the back drawing-room for the stage, and take me for the audience. Tingle goes the bell; up runs the curtain; order in the gallery, silence in the pit—enter Lucy!"

She tried hard to control herself; she forced back the sorrow—the innocent, natural, human sorrow for the absent and the dead—pleading hard with her for the tears that she refused. Resolutely, with cold clenched hands, she tried to begin. As the first familiar words passed her lips, Frank came back to her from the sea; and the face of her dead father looked at her with the smile of happy old times. The voices of her mother and her sister talked gently in the fragrant country stillness; and the garden-walks at Combe-Raven opened once more on her view. With a faint wailing cry, she dropped into a chair; her head fell forward on the table, and she burst passionately into tears.

Captain Wragge was on his feet in a moment. She shuddered as he came near her; and waved him back vehemently with her hand. "Leave me!" she said; "leave me a minute by myself!" The compliant Wragge retired to the front room; looked out of window; and whistled under his breath. "The family spirit again!" he said. "Complicated by hysterics."

After waiting a minute or two, he returned to make inquiries.

"Is there anything I can offer you?" he asked. "Cold water? burnt feathers? smelling salts? medical assistance? Shall I summon Mrs. Wragge? Shall we put it off till to-morrow?"

She started up, wild and flushed, with a desperate self-command in her face, with an angry resolution in her manner.

"No!" she said. "I must harden myself—and I will! Sit down again, and see me act."

"Bravo!" cried the captain. "Dash at it, my beauty—and it's done!"

She dashed at it, with a mad defiance of herself—with a raised voice, and a glow like fever in her cheeks. All the artless, girlish charm of the performance in happier and better days, was gone. The native dramatic capacity that was in her, came, hard and bold, to the surface, stripped of every softening allurement which had once adorned it. She would have saddened and disappointed a man with any delicacy of feeling. She absolutely electrified Captain Wragge. He forgot his politeness, he forgot his long words. The essential spirit of the man's whole vagabond life, burst out of him irresistibly in his first exclamation. "Who the devil would have thought it? She *can* act, after all!" The instant the words escaped his lips, he recovered himself, and glided off into his ordinary colloquial channels. Magdalen stopped him in the middle of his first compliment. "No," she said; "I have forced the truth out of you, for once. I want no more."

"Pardon me," replied the incorrigible Wragge. "You want a little instruction; and I am the man to give it you."

With that answer, he placed a chair for her, and proceeded to explain himself.

She sat down in silence. A sullen indifference began to show itself in her manner; her cheeks turned pale again; and her eyes looked wearily vacant at the wall before her. Captain Wragge noticed these signs of heart-sickness and discontent with herself, after the effort she had made, and saw the importance of rousing her by speaking, for once, plainly and directly to the point. She had set a new value on herself in his mercenary eyes. She had suggested to him a speculation in her youth, her beauty, and her marked ability for the stage, which had never entered his mind until he saw her act. The old militiaman was quick at his shifts. He and his plans had both turned right about together, when Magdalen sat down to hear what he had to say.

"Mr. Huxtable's opinion is my opinion," he began. "You are a born actress. But you must be trained before you can do anything on the stage. I am disengaged—I am competent—I have trained others—I can train you. Don't trust my word: trust my eye to my own interests. I'll make it my interest to take pains with you, and to be quick about it. You shall pay me for my instructions from your profits on the stage. Half your salary, for the first year; a third of your salary for the second year; and half the sum you clear by your first benefit in a London theatre.* What do you say to that? Have I made it my interest to push you, or have I not?"

So far as appearances went, and so far as the stage went, it was plain that he had linked his interests and Magdalen's together. She briefly told him so, and waited to hear more.

"A month or six weeks' study," continued the captain, "will give me a reasonable idea of what you can do best. All ability runs in grooves; and your groove remains to be found. We can't find it here—for we can't keep you a close prisoner for weeks together in Rosemary Lane. A quiet country place, secure from all interference and interruption, is the place we want for a month certain. Trust my knowledge of Yorkshire; and consider the place found. I see no difficulties anywhere, except the difficulty of beating our retreat to-morrow."

"I thought your arrangements were made last night?" said Magdalen.

"Quite right," rejoined the captain. "They were made last night; and here they are. We can't leave by railway, because the lawyer's clerk is sure to be on the look-out for you at the York terminus. Very good; we take to the road instead, and leave in our own carriage. Where the deuce do we get it? We get it from the landlady's brother, who has a horse and chaise which he lets out for hire. That chaise comes to the end of Rosemary Lane at an early hour to-morrow morning. I take my wife and my niece out to show them the beauties of the neighbourhood. We have a picnic hamper with us which marks our purpose in the public eye. You disfigure yourself in a shawl, bonnet, and veil of Mrs. Wragge's; we turn our backs on York; and away we drive on a pleasure trip for the day—you and I on the front seat, Mrs. Wragge and the hamper behind. Good again. Once on the high road what do we do? Drive to the first station beyond York, northward, southward, or eastward, as may be hereafter determined. No lawyer's clerk is waiting for you there. You and Mrs. Wragge get out—first opening the hamper at a convenient opportunity. Instead of containing chickens and champagne, it contains a carpet-bag with the things you want for the night. You take your tickets for a place previously determined on; and I take the chaise back to York. Arrived once more in this house, I collect the luggage left behind, and send for the woman downstairs. 'Ladies so charmed with such-and-such-a-place (wrong place of course) that they have determined to stop there. Pray accept the customary week's rent, in place of a week's warning. Good day.' Is the clerk looking for *me* at the York terminus? Not he. I take my ticket, under his very nose; I follow you with the luggage along your line of railway—and where is the trace left of your departure? Nowhere. The fairy has vanished; and the legal authorities are left in the lurch."

"Why do you talk of difficulties?" asked Magdalen. "The difficulties seem to be provided for."

"All but ONE," said Captain Wragge, with an ominous emphasis on the last word. "The Grand Difficulty of humanity from the cradle to the grave—Money." He slowly winked his green eye; sighed with deep feeling; and buried his insolvent hands in his unproductive pockets.

"What is the money wanted for?" inquired Magdalen.

"To pay my bills," replied the captain, with a touching simplicity. "Pray understand! I never was—and never shall be—personally desirous of paying a single farthing to any human creature on the habitable globe. I am speaking in your interests, not in mine."

" My interest ?"

" Certainly. You can't get safely away from York to-morrow, without the chaise. And I can't get the chaise without money. The landlady's brother will lend it, if he sees his sister's bill receipted, and if he gets his day's hire beforehand—not otherwise. Allow me to put the transaction in a business light. We have agreed that I am to be remunerated for my course of dramatic instruction out of your future earnings on the stage. Very good. I merely draw on my future prospects ; and you, on whom those prospects depend, are naturally my banker. For mere argument's sake, estimate my share in your first year's salary at the totally inadequate value of a hundred pounds. Halve that sum ; quarter that sum——"

" How much do you want ?" said Magdalen, impatiently.

Captain Wragge was sorely tempted to take the Reward at the top of the handbills as his basis of calculation. But he felt the vast future importance of present moderation ; and actually wanting some twelve or thirteen pounds, he merely doubled the amount, and said, " Five-and-twenty."

Magdalen took the little bag from her bosom, and gave him the money, with a contemptuous wonder at the number of words which he had wasted on her for the purpose of cheating on so small a scale. In the old days at Combe-Raven, five-and-twenty pounds flowed from a stroke of her father's pen into the hands of any one in the house who chose to ask for it.

Captain Wragge's eyes dwelt on the little bag, as the eyes of lovers dwell on their mistresses. " Happy bag !" he murmured, as she put it back in her bosom. He rose ; dived into a corner of the room ; produced his neat despatch-box ; and solemnly unlocked it on the table between Magdalen and himself.

" The nature of the man, my dear girl—the nature of the man," he said, opening one of his plump little books, bound in calf and vellum. " A transaction has taken place between us. I must have it down in black and white." He opened the book at a blank page, and wrote at the top, in a fine mercantile hand :—" *Miss Vanstone the Younger: In account with Horatio Wragge, late of the Royal Militia. D*ʳ.—C*ʳ. Sept. 24th, 1846. D*ʳ.: To estimated value of H. Wragge's interest in Miss V.'s first year's salary—say* £200. *C*ʳ. *By paid on account* £25." Having completed the entry—and having also shown, by doubling his original estimate on the Debtor side, that Magdalen's easy compliance with his demand on her had not been thrown away on him—the captain pressed his blotting-paper over the wet ink, and put away the book with the air of a man who had done a virtuous action, and who was above boasting about it.

" Excuse me for leaving you abruptly," he said. " Time is of importance ; I must make sure of the chaise. If Mrs. Wragge comes in, tell her nothing—she is not sharp enough to be trusted. If she presumes to ask questions, extinguish her immediately. You have only to be loud. Pray take my authority into your own hands, and be as loud with Mrs. Wragge as I am!" He snatched up his tall hat, bowed, smiled, and tripped out of the room.

Sensible of little else but of the relief of being alone; feeling no more distinct impression than the vague sense of some serious change having taken place in herself and her position, Magdalen let the events of the morning come and go like shadows on her mind, and waited wearily for what the day might bring forth. After the lapse of some time, the door opened softly. The giant figure of Mrs. Wragge stalked into the room; and stopped opposite Magdalen in solemn astonishment.

"Where are your Things?" asked Mrs. Wragge, with a burst of incontrollable anxiety. "I've been upstairs, looking in your drawers. Where are your night-gowns and night-caps? and your petticoats and stockings? and your hairpins and bear's grease, and all the rest of it?"

"My luggage is left at the railway-station," said Magdalen.

Mrs. Wragge's moon-face brightened dimly. The ineradicable female instinct of Curiosity tried to sparkle in her faded blue eyes—flickered piteously—and died out.

"How much luggage?" she asked, confidentially. "The captain's gone out. Let's go and get it!"

"Mrs. Wragge!" cried a terrible voice at the door.

For the first time in Magdalen's experience, Mrs. Wragge was deaf to the customary stimulant. She actually ventured on a feeble remonstrance, in the presence of her husband.

"Oh, do let her have her Things!" pleaded Mrs. Wragge. "Oh, poor soul, do let her have her Things!"

The captain's inexorable forefinger pointed to a corner of the room—dropped slowly as his wife retired before it—and suddenly stopped at the region of her shoes.

"Do I hear a clapping on the floor!" exclaimed Captain Wragge, with an expression of horror. "Yes; I do. Down at heel again! The left shoe, this time. Pull it up, Mrs. Wragge! pull it up! The chaise will be here to-morrow morning at nine o'clock," he continued, addressing Magdalen. "We can't possibly venture on claiming your box. There is note-paper. Write down a list of the necessaries you want. I will take it myself to the shop, pay the bill for you, and bring back the parcel. We must sacrifice the box—we must indeed."

While her husband was addressing Magdalen, Mrs. Wragge had stolen out again from her corner; and had ventured near enough to the captain to hear the words, "shop" and "parcel." She clapped her great hands together in ungovernable excitement, and lost all control over herself immediately.

"Oh, if it's shopping, let me do it!" cried Mrs. Wragge. "She's going

out to buy her Things! Oh, let me go with her—please let me go with
her!"

"Sit down!" shouted the captain. "Straight! more to the right—more
still. Stop where you are!"

Mrs. Wragge crossed her helpless hands on her lap, and melted meekly
into tears.

"I do so like shopping," pleaded the poor creature; "and I get so little
of it now!"

Magdalen completed her list; and Captain Wragge at once left the room
with it. "Don't let my wife bore you," he said pleasantly, as he went out.
"Cut her short, poor soul—cut her short!"

"Don't cry," said Magdalen, trying to comfort Mrs. Wragge by patting
her on the shoulder. "When the parcel comes back you shall open it."

"Thank you, my dear," said Mrs. Wragge, meekly drying her eyes;
"thank you kindly. Don't notice my handkerchief, please. It's such a
very little one! I had a nice lot of them once, with lace borders. They're
all gone now. Never mind! It will comfort me to unpack your Things.
You're very good to me. I like you. I say—you won't be angry, will
you? Give us a kiss."

Magdalen stooped over her with the frank grace and gentleness of past
days, and touched her faded cheek. "Let me do something harmless!"
she thought, with a pang at her heart—"Oh let me do something innocent
and kind, for the sake of old times!"

She felt her eyes moistening, and silently turned away.

That night no rest came to her. That night the roused forces of Good
and Evil fought their terrible fight for her soul—and left the strife between
them still in suspense when morning came. As the clock of York Minster
struck nine, she followed Mrs. Wragge to the chaise, and took her seat
by the captain's side. In a quarter of an hour more, York was in the
distance; and the high-road lay bright and open before them in the morning sunlight.

THE END OF THE SECOND SCENE.

BETWEEN THE SCENES.

CHRONICLE OF EVENTS : PRESERVED IN CAPTAIN WRAGGE'S DESPATCH BOX.

I.

CHRONICLE FOR OCTOBER, 1846.

I HAVE retired into the bosom of my family. We are residing in the secluded village of Ruswarp, on the banks of the Esk, about two miles inland from Whitby. Our lodgings are comfortable, and we possess the additional blessing of a tidy landlady. Mrs. Wragge and Miss Vanstone preceded me here, in accordance with the plan I laid down for effecting our retreat from York. On the next day I followed them alone, with the luggage. On leaving the terminus, I had the satisfaction of seeing the lawyer's clerk in close confabulation with the detective officer whose advent I had prophesied. I left him in peaceable possession of the city of York, and the whole surrounding neighbourhood. He has returned the compliment, and has left us in peaceable possession of the valley of the Esk, thirty miles away from him.

Remarkable results have followed my first efforts at the cultivation of Miss Vanstone's dramatic abilities.

I have discovered that she possesses extraordinary talent as a mimic. She has the flexible face, the manageable voice, and the dramatic knack which fit a woman for character-parts and disguises on the stage. All she now wants is teaching and practice to make her sure of her own resources. The experience of her, thus gained, has revived an idea in my mind, which originally occurred to me at one of the "At Homes" of the late inimitable Charles Mathews, comedian.* I was in the Wine Trade at the time, I remember. We imitated the Vintage-processes of Nature, in a back-kitchen at Brompton ; and produced a dinner-sherry, pale and curious, tonic in character, round in the mouth, a favourite with the Court of Spain, at nineteen and sixpence a dozen, bottles included — *Vide* Prospectus of the period. The profits of myself and partners were small ; we were in advance of the tastes of the age, and in debt to the bottle merchant. Being at my wits' end for want of money, and seeing what audiences Mathews drew, the idea occurred to me of starting an imitation of the great Imitator himself, in the shape of an "At Home," given by a woman. The one trifling obstacle in the way was the difficulty of finding the woman. From that time to this,

I have hitherto failed to overcome it. I have conquered it at last: I have found the woman now. Miss Vanstone possesses youth and beauty as well as talent. Train her in the art of dramatic disguise; provide her with appropriate dresses for different characters; develop her accomplishments in singing and playing; give her plenty of smart talk addressed to the audience; advertise her as A Young Lady at Home; astonish the public by a dramatic entertainment which depends from first to last on that young lady's own sole exertions; commit the entire management of the thing to my care—and what follows as a necessary consequence? Fame for my fair relative, and a fortune for myself.

I put these considerations, as frankly as usual, to Miss Vanstone; offering to write the Entertainment, to manage all the business, and to share the profits. I did not forget to strengthen my case by informing her of the jealousies she would encounter, and the obstacles she would meet, if she went on the stage. And I wound up by a neat reference to the private inquiries which she is interested in making, and to the personal independence which she is desirous of securing before she acts on her information. "If you go on the stage," I said, "your services will be bought by a manager, and he may insist on his claims just at the time when you want to get free from him. If, on the contrary, you adopt my views, you will be your own mistress and your own manager, and you can settle your course just as you like." This last consideration appeared to strike her. She took a day to consider it; and when the day was over, gave her consent.

I had the whole transaction down in black and white immediately. Our arrangement is eminently satisfactory, except in one particular. She shows a morbid distrust of writing her name at the bottom of any document which I present to her; and roundly declares she will sign nothing. As long as it is her interest to provide herself with pecuniary resources for the future, she verbally engages to go on. When it ceases to be her interest, she plainly threatens to leave off at a week's notice. A difficult girl to deal with: she has found out her own value to me already. One comfort is, I have the cooking of the accounts; and my fair relative shall not fill her pockets too suddenly, if I can help it.

My exertions in training Miss Vanstone for the coming experiment, have been varied by the writing of two anonymous letters, in that young lady's interests. Finding her too fidgety about arranging matters with her friends to pay proper attention to my instructions, I wrote anonymously to the lawyer who is conducting the inquiry after her; recommending him in a friendly way to give it up. The letter was enclosed to a friend of mine in London, with instructions to post it at Charing Cross. A week later, I sent a second letter, through the same channel, requesting the lawyer to inform me, in writing, whether he and his clients had or had not decided on taking my advice. I directed him, with jocose reference to the collision of interests between us, to address his letter:—" Tit for Tat, Post Office, West Strand."

In a few days the answer arrived—privately forwarded, of course, to Post Office, Whitby, by arrangement with my friend in London.

The lawyer's reply was short and surly: " Sir—If my advice had been followed, you and your anonymous letter would both be treated with the contempt which they deserve. But the wishes of Miss Magdalen Vanstone's eldest sister have claims on my consideration which I cannot dispute; and at her entreaty I inform you that all further proceedings on my part are withdrawn—on the express understanding that this concession is to open facilities for written communication at least, between the two sisters. A letter from the elder Miss Vanstone is enclosed in this. If I don't hear in a week's time, that it has been received, I shall place the matter once more in the hands of the police.—WILLIAM PENDRIL." A sour man, this William Pendril. I can only say of him, what an eminent nobleman once said of his sulky servant—" I wouldn't have such a temper as that fellow has got, for any earthly consideration that could be offered me !"

As a matter of course, I looked into the letter which the lawyer enclosed, before delivering it. Miss Vanstone, the elder, described herself as distracted at not hearing from her sister; as suited with a governess's situation in a private family; as going into the situation in a week's time; and as longing for a letter to comfort her, before she faced the trial of undertaking her new duties. After closing the envelope again, I accompanied the delivery of the letter to Miss Vanstone the younger, by a word of caution. " Are you more sure of your own courage now," I said, " than you were when I met you ?" She was ready with her answer. " Captain Wragge, when you met me on the Walls of York, I had not gone too far to go back. I have gone too far now."

If she really feels this—and I think she does—her corresponding with her sister can do no harm. She wrote at great length the same day; cried profusely over her own epistolary composition; and was remarkably ill-tempered and snappish towards me, when we met in the evening. She wants experience, poor girl—she sadly wants experience of the world. How consoling to know that I am just the man to give it her !

II.

CHRONICLE FOR NOVEMBER.

We are established at Derby. The Entertainment is written; and the rehearsals are in steady progress. All difficulties are provided for, but the one eternal difficulty of money. Miss Vanstone's resources stretch easily enough to the limits of our personal wants; including pianoforte hire for practice, and the purchase and making of the necessary dresses. But the expenses of starting the Entertainment are beyond the reach of any means we possess. A theatrical friend of mine here, whom I had hoped to interest in our undertaking, proves unhappily to be at a crisis in his career. The field of human sympathy, out of which I might have raised the needful pecuniary crop, is closed to me from want of time to cultivate it. I see no other resource left—if we are to be ready by Christmas—than to try one of the local music-sellers in this town, who is said to be a speculating man. A private rehearsal at these lodgings, and a bargain which will fill the pockets of a grasping stranger—such are the sacrifices which dire necessity imposes on me at starting. Well! there is only one consolation: I'll cheat the music-seller.

III.

CHRONICLE FOR DECEMBER. FIRST FORTNIGHT.

The music-seller extorts my unwilling respect. He is one of the very few human beings I have met with in the course of my life who is not to be cheated. He has taken a masterly advantage of our helplessness; and has imposed terms on us, for performances at Derby and Nottingham, with such a business-like disregard of all interests but his own, that—fond as I am of putting things down in black and white—I really cannot prevail upon myself to record the bargain. It is needless to say, I have yielded with my best grace; sharing with my fair relative the wretched pecuniary prospects offered to us. Our turn will come. In the mean time, I cordially regret not having known the local music-seller in early life.

Personally speaking, I have no cause to complain of Miss Vanstone. We have arranged that she shall regularly forward her address (at the post office) to her friends, as we move about from place to place. Besides communicating in this way with her sister, she also reports herself to a certain Mr. Clare, residing in Somersetshire, who is to forward all letters exchanged between herself and his son. Careful inquiry has informed me that this latter individual is now in China. Having suspected, from the first, that there was a gentleman in the background, it is highly satisfactory to know that he recedes into the remote perspective of Asia. Long may he remain there!

The trifling responsibility of finding a name for our talented Magdalen to perform under, has been cast on my shoulders. She feels no interest whatever in this part of the subject. "Give me any name you like," she said; "I have as much right to one as to another. Make it yourself." I have readily consented to gratify her wishes. The resources of my commercial library include a list of useful names to assume; and we can choose one at five minutes' notice, when the admirable man of business who now oppresses us is ready to issue his advertisements. On this point my mind is easy enough : all my anxieties centre in the fair performer. I have not the least doubt she will do wonders if she is only left to herself on the first night. But if the day's post is mischievous enough to upset her by a letter from her sister, I tremble for the consequences.

IV.

Chronicle for December. Second Fortnight.

My gifted relative has made her first appearance in public, and has laid the foundation of our future fortunes.

On the first night, the attendance was larger than I had ventured to hope. The novelty of an evening's entertainment, conducted from beginning to end by the unaided exertions of a young lady (see advertisement) roused the public curiosity, and the seats were moderately well filled. As good luck would have it, no letter addressed to Miss Vanstone came that day. She was in full possession of herself, until she got the first dress on, and heard the bell ring for the music. At that critical moment she suddenly broke down. I found her alone in the waiting room, sobbing, and talking like a child. "Oh, poor papa! poor papa! Oh, my God, if he saw me now!" My experience in such matters at once informed me that it was a case of sal-volatile, accompanied by sound advice. We strung her up, in no time, to concert pitch ; set her eyes in a blaze ; and made her outblush her own rouge. The curtain rose when we had got her at a red heat. She dashed at it, exactly as she dashed at it in the back drawing-room at Rosemary Lane. Her personal appearance settled the question of her reception before she opened her lips. She rushed full gallop through her changes of character, her songs, and her dialogue ; making mistakes by the dozen, and never stopping to set them right; carrying the people along with her in a perfect whirlwind, and never waiting for the applause. The whole thing was over twenty minutes sooner than the time we had calculated on. She carried it through to the end ; and fainted on the waiting-room sofa, a minute after the curtain was down. The music-seller having taken leave of his senses from sheer astonishment; and I having no evening costume to appear in—we sent the doctor to make the necessary apology to the public, who were calling for her till the place rang again. I prompted our medical orator with a neat speech from behind the curtain; and I never heard such applause, from such a comparatively small audience, before in my life. I felt the tribute—I felt it deeply. Fourteen years ago I scraped together the wretched means of existence, in this very town, by reading the newspaper (with explanatory comments) to the company at a public-house. And now, here I am at the top of the tree.

It is needless to say that my first proceeding was to bowl out the music-seller on the spot. He called the next morning, no doubt with a liberal proposal for extending the engagement beyond Derby and Nottingham. My niece was described as not well enough to see him; and, when he asked for me, he was told I was not up. I happened to be, at that moment, engaged in putting the case pathetically to our gifted Magdalen. Her answer was in the highest degree satisfactory. She would permanently engage herself to nobody—least of all to a man who had taken sordid advantage of her position and mine. She would be her own mistress, and share the profits with me, while she wanted money, and while it suited her to go on. So far so good. But the reason she added next, for her flattering preference of myself, was less to my taste. "The music-seller is not the man whom I employ to make my inquiries," she said. "You are the man." I don't like her steadily remembering those inquiries, in the first bewilderment of her success. It looks ill for the future; it looks infernally ill for the future.

V.

CHRONICLE FOR JANUARY, 1847.

She has shown the cloven foot already. I begin to be a little afraid of her.

On the conclusion of the Nottingham engagement (the results of which more than equalled the results at Derby), I proposed taking the entertainment next—now we had got it into our own hands—to Newark. Miss Vanstone raised no objection, until we came to the question of time, when she amazed me by stipulating for a week's delay, before we appeared in public again.

"For what possible purpose?" I asked.

"For the purpose of making the inquiries which I mentioned to you at York," she answered.

I instantly enlarged on the danger of delay; putting all the considerations before her in every imaginable form. She remained perfectly immovable. I tried to shake her on the question of expenses. She answered by handing me over her share of the proceeds at Derby and Nottingham—and there were my expenses paid, at the rate of nearly two guineas a day. I wonder who first picked out a mule as the type of obstinacy? How little knowledge that man must have had of women!

There was no help for it. I took down my instructions in black and white, as usual. My first exertions were to be directed to the discovery of Mr. Michael Vanstone's address: I was also expected to find out how long he was likely to live there, and whether he had sold Combe-Raven or not. My next inquiries were to inform me of his ordinary habits of life; of what he did with his money; of who his intimate friends were; and of the sort of terms on which his son, Mr. Noel Vanstone, was now living with him. Lastly, the investigations were to end in discovering whether there was any female relative, or any woman exercising domestic authority in the house, who was known to have an influence over either father or son.

If my long practice in cultivating the field of human sympathy had not accustomed me to private investigations into the affairs of other people, I might have found some of these queries rather difficult to deal with in the course of a week. As it was, I gave myself all the benefit of my own experience; and brought the answers back to Nottingham in a day less than the given time. Here they are, in regular order, for convenience of future reference :—

(1.) Mr. Michael Vanstone is now residing at German Place, Brighton, and likely to remain there; as he finds the air suit him. He reached London from Switzerland in September last; and sold the Combe-Raven property immediately on his arrival.

(2.) His ordinary habits of life are secret and retired; he seldom visits, or receives company. Part of his money is supposed to be in the funds, and part laid out in railway investments, which have survived the panic of eighteen hundred and forty-six, and are rapidly rising in value. He is said to be a bold speculator. Since his arrival in England he has invested with great judgment in house property. He has some houses in remote parts of London; and some houses in certain watering-places on the east coast, which are shown to be advancing in public repute. In all these cases he is reported to have made remarkably good bargains.

(3). It is not easy to discover who his intimate friends are. Two names only have been ascertained. The first is Admiral Bartram; supposed to have been under friendly obligations, in past years, to Mr. Michael Vanstone. The second is Mr. George Bartram, nephew of the Admiral, and now staying on a short visit in the house at German Place. Mr. George Bartram is the son of the late Mr. Andrew Vanstone's sister, also deceased. He is therefore a cousin of Mr. Noel Vanstone's. This last—viz., Mr. Noel Vanstone —is in delicate health, and is living on excellent terms with his father, in German Place.

(4.) There is no female relative in Mr. Michael Vanstone's family circle. But there is a housekeeper who has lived in his service ever since his wife's death, and who has acquired a strong influence over both father and son. She is a native of Switzerland, elderly, and a widow. Her name is Mrs. Lecount.

On placing these particulars in Miss Vanstone's hands, she made no remark, except to thank me. I endeavoured to invite her confidence. No results; nothing but a renewal of civility, and a sudden shifting to the subject of the Entertainment. Very good. If she won't give me the information I want, the conclusion is obvious—I must help myself.

Business considerations claim the remainder of this page. Let me return to business.

Financial Statement.	Third Week in January.
Place Visited. Newark.	Performances. Two.
Net Receipts. In black and white. £25	Net Receipts, Actually Realized. £32 10s.
Apparent Division of Profits. Miss V. . . . . £12 10 Self £12 10	Actual Division of Profits. Miss V. . . . . £12 10 Self £20 0

Private Surplus on the Week,
Or say,
Self-presented Testimonial.
£7 10s.

Audited, H. Wragge.	Passed correct, H. Wragge.

The next stronghold of British sympathy which we take by storm is Sheffield. We open the first week in February.

VI.

CHRONICLE FOR FEBRUARY.

Practice has now given my fair relative the confidence which I predicted would come with time. Her knack of disguising her own identity in the impersonation of different characters, so completely staggers her audiences, that the same people come twice over, to find out how she does it. It is the amiable defect of the English public never to know when they have had enough of a good thing. They actually try to encore one of her characters —an old north-country lady; modelled on that honoured preceptress in the late Mr. Vanstone's family, to whom I presented myself at Combe-Raven. This particular performance fairly amazes the people. I don't wonder at it. Such an extraordinary assumption of age by a girl of nineteen, has never been seen in public before, in the whole course of my theatrical experience.

I find myself writing in a lower tone than usual; I miss my own dash of humour. The fact is, I am depressed about the future. In the very height of our prosperity, my perverse pupil sticks to her trumpery family quarrel. I feel myself at the mercy of the first whim in the Vanstone direction which may come into her head—I, the architect of her fortunes. Too bad; upon my soul, too bad.

She has acted already on the inquiries which she forced me to make for her. She has written two letters to Mr. Michael Vanstone.

To the first letter no answer came. To the second a reply was received. Her infernal cleverness put an obstacle I had not expected in the way of my intercepting it. Later in the day, after she had herself opened and read the answer, I laid another trap for her. It just succeeded, and no more. I had half a minute to look into the envelope in her absence. It contained nothing but her own letter returned. She is not the girl to put up quietly with such an insult as this. Mischief will come of it—Mischief to Michael Vanstone—which is of no earthly consequence : mischief to Me—which is a truly serious matter.

VII.

CHRONICLE FOR MARCH.

After performing at Sheffield and Manchester, we have moved to Liverpool, Preston, and Lancaster. Another change in this weathercock of a girl. She has written no more letters to Michael Vanstone; and she has become as anxious to make money as I am myself. We are realizing large profits, and we are worked to death. I don't like this change in her : she has a purpose to answer, or she would not show such extraordinary eagerness to fill her purse. Nothing I can do—no cooking of accounts ; no self-presented testimonials—can keep that purse empty. The success of the Entertainment, and her own sharpness in looking after her interests, literally force me into a course of comparative honesty. She puts into her pocket more than a third of the profits, in defiance of my most arduous exertions to prevent her. And this at my age! this after my long and successful career as a moral agriculturist! Marks of admiration are very little things ; but they express my feelings, and I put them in freely.

VIII.

CHRONICLE FOR APRIL AND MAY.

We have visited seven more large towns, and are now at Birmingham. Consulting my books, I find that Miss Vanstone has realized by the Entertainment, up to this time, the enormous sum of nearly four hundred pounds. It is quite possible that my own profits may reach one or two miserable hundreds more. But I am the architect of her fortunes—the publisher, so to speak, of her book—and, if anything, I am underpaid.

I made the above discovery on the twenty-ninth of the month—anniversary of the Restoration of my royal predecessor in the field of human sympathy, Charles the Second. I had barely finished locking up my despatch box—when the ungrateful girl, whose reputation I have made, came into the room; and told me in so many words, that the business connection between us was for the present at an end.

I attempt no description of my own sensations: I merely record facts. She informed me, with an appearance of perfect composure, that she needed rest, and that she had "new objects in view." She might possibly want me to assist those objects; and she might possibly return to the Entertainment. In either case it would be enough if we exchanged addresses, at which we could write to each other, in case of need. Having no desire to leave me too abruptly, she would remain the next day (which was Sunday); and would take her departure on Monday morning. Such was her explanation, in so many words.

Remonstrance, as I knew by experience, would be thrown away. Authority I had none to exert. My one sensible course to take in this emergency was to find out which way my own interests pointed—and to go that way without a moment's unnecessary hesitation.

A very little reflection has since convinced me that she has a deep-laid scheme against Michael Vanstone in view. She is young, handsome, clever, and unscrupulous; she has made money to live on, and has time at her disposal to find out the weak side of an old man; and she is going to attack Mr. Michael Vanstone unawares with the legitimate weapons of her sex. Is she likely to want *me* for such a purpose as this? Doubtful. Is she merely anxious to get rid of me on easy terms? Probable. Am I the sort of man to be treated in this way by my own pupil? Decidedly not: I am the man to see my way through a neat succession of alternatives; and here they are:—

First alternative:—To announce my compliance with her proposal; to exchange addresses with her; and then to keep my eye privately on all her future movements. Second alternative:—To express fond anxiety in a paternal capacity; and to threaten giving the alarm to her sister and the lawyer, if she persists in her design. Third alternative:—To turn the information I already possess to the best account, by making it a marketable commodity between Mr. Michael Vanstone and myself. At present, I incline towards the last of these three courses. But my decision is far too important to be hurried. To-day is only the twenty-ninth. I will suspend my Chronicle of Events until Monday.

May 31st.—My alternatives and her plans are both overthrown together.

The newspaper came in, as usual, after breakfast. I looked it over, and discovered this memorable entry, among the obituary announcements of the day :—

"On the 29th inst., at Brighton, Michael Vanstone, Esq., formerly of Zurich, aged 77."

Miss Vanstone was present in the room, when I read those two startling lines. Her bonnet was on ; her boxes were packed ; she was waiting impatiently until it was time to go to the train. I handed the paper to her, without a word on my side. Without a word on hers, she looked where I pointed, and read the news of Michael Vanstone's death.

The paper dropped out of her hand ; and she suddenly pulled down her veil. I caught one glance at her face before she hid it from me. The effect on my mind was startling in the extreme. To put it with my customary dash of humour—her face informed me that the most sensible action which Michael Vanstone, Esq., formerly of Zurich, had ever achieved in his life, was the action he performed at Brighton, on the 29th instant.

Finding the dead silence in the room singularly unpleasant under existing circumstances, I thought I would make a remark. My regard for my own interests supplied me with a subject. I mentioned the Entertainment.

"After what has happened," I said, "I presume we go on with our performances as usual ?"

"No," she answered, behind the veil. "We go on with my inquiries."

"Inquiries after a dead man ?"

"Inquiries after the dead man's son."

"Mr. Noel Vanstone ?"

"Yes ; Mr. Noel Vanstone."

Not having a veil to let down over my own face, I stooped and picked up the newspaper. Her devilish determination quite upset me for the moment. I actually had to steady myself, before I could speak to her again.

"Are the new inquiries as harmless as the old ones ?" I asked.

"Quite as harmless."

"What am I expected to find out ?"

"I wish to know whether Mr. Noel Vanstone remains at Brighton after the funeral."

"And if not ?"

"If not, I shall want to know his new address, wherever it may be."

"Yes. And what next ?"

"I wish you to find out next, if all the father's money goes to the son."

I began to see her drift. The word money relieved me ; I felt quite on my own ground again.

"Anything more ?" I asked.

"Only one thing more," she answered. "Make sure, if you please, whether Mrs. Lecount, the housekeeper, remains or not in Mr. Noel Vanstone's service."

Her voice altered a little, as she mentioned Mrs. Lecount's name: she is evidently sharp enough to distrust the housekeeper already.

"My expenses are to be paid as usual?" I said.

"As usual."

"When am I expected to leave for Brighton?"

"As soon as you can."

She rose, and left the room. After a momentary doubt, I decided on executing the new commission. The more private inquiries I conduct for my fair relative, the harder she will find it to get rid of hers truly, Horatio Wragge.

There is nothing to prevent my starting for Brighton to-morrow. So to-morrow, I go. If Mr. Noel Vanstone succeeds to his father's property, he is the only human being possessed of pecuniary blessings, who fails to inspire me with a feeling of unmitigated envy.

IX.

CHRONICLE FOR JUNE.

9th.—I returned yesterday with my information. Here it is, privately noted down for convenience of future reference:

Mr. Noel Vanstone has left Brighton; and has removed, for the purpose of transacting business in London, to one of his late father's empty houses in Vauxhall Walk, Lambeth. This singularly mean selection of a place of residence, on the part of a gentleman of fortune, looks as if Mr. N. V. and his money were not easily parted.

Mr. Noel Vanstone has stepped into his father's shoes under the following circumstances. Mr. Michael Vanstone appears to have died, curiously enough, as Mr. Andrew Vanstone died—intestate. With this difference, however, in the two cases, that the younger brother left an informal will, and the elder brother left no will at all. The hardest men have their weaknesses; and Mr. Michael Vanstone's weakness seems to have been an insurmountable horror of contemplating the event of his own death. His son, his housekeeper, and his lawyer, had all three tried over and over again, to get him to make a will; and had never shaken his obstinate resolution to put off performing the only business-duty he was ever known to neglect. Two doctors attended him in his last illness; warned him that he was too old a man to hope to get over it; and warned him in vain. He announced his own positive determination not to die. His last words in this world (as I succeeded in discovering from the nurse, who assisted Mrs. Lecount) were, "I'm getting better every minute; send for the fly directly and take me out for a drive." The same night, Death proved to be the more obstinate of the two; and left his son (and only child) to take the property in due course of law. Nobody doubts that the result would have been the same if a will had been made. The father and son had every confidence in each other; and were known to have always lived together on the most friendly terms.

Mrs. Lecount remains with Mr. Noel Vanstone, in the same housekeeping capacity which she filled with his father; and has accompanied him to the new residence in Vauxhall Walk. She is acknowledged on all hands to have been a sufferer by the turn events have taken. If Mr. Michael Vanstone had made his will, there is no doubt she would have received a handsome legacy. She is now left dependent on Mr. Noel Vanstone's sense of gratitude; and she is not at all likely, I should imagine, to let that sense fall asleep for want of a little timely jogging. Whether my fair relative's future intentions in this quarter, point towards Mischief or Money, is more than I can yet say. In either case, I venture to predict that she will find an awkward obstacle in Mrs. Lecount.

So much for my information to the present date. The manner in which it was received by Miss Vanstone showed the most ungrateful distrust of me. She confided nothing to my private ear, but the expression of her best thanks. A sharp girl—a devilish sharp girl. But there *is* such a thing as bowling a man out once too often; especially when the name of that man happens to be Wragge.

Not a word more about the Entertainment; not a word more about moving from our present quarters. Very good. My right hand lays my left hand a wager. Ten to one, on her opening communications with the son, as she opened them with the father. Ten to one, on her writing to Noel Vanstone before the month is out.

21st.—She has written by to-day's post. A long letter apparently—for she put two stamps on the envelope. (Private memorandum, addressed to myself. Wait for the answer.)

22nd, 23rd, 24th.—(Private memorandum continued. Wait for the answer.)

25th.—The answer has come. As an ex-military man, I have naturally employed stratagem to get at it. The success which rewards all genuine perseverance has rewarded me—and I have got at it accordingly.

The letter is written, not by Mr. Noel Vanstone, but by Mrs. Lecount. She takes the highest moral ground, in a tone of spiteful politeness. Mr. Noel Vanstone's delicate health and recent bereavement, prevent him from writing himself. Any more letters from Miss Vanstone will be returned unopened. Any personal application will produce an immediate appeal to the protection of the law. Mr. Noel Vanstone, having been expressly cautioned against Miss Magdalen Vanstone, by his late lamented father, has not yet forgotten his father's advice. Considers it a reflection cast on the memory of the best of men, to suppose that his course of action towards the Miss Vanstones, can be other than the course of action which his father pursued. This is what he has himself instructed Mrs. Lecount to say. She has endeavoured to express herself in the most conciliatory language she could select; she has tried to avoid giving unnecessary pain, by addressing Miss Vanstone (as a matter of courtesy) by the family name; and she trusts these concessions, which speak for themselves, will not be thrown away.—Such is the substance of the letter,—and so it ends.

I draw two conclusions from this little document. First—that it will lead to serious results. Secondly—that Mrs. Lecount, with all her politeness, is a dangerous woman to deal with. I wish I saw my way safe before me. I don't see it yet.

29th.—Miss Vanstone has abandoned my protection; and the whole lucrative future of the dramatic entertainment has abandoned me with her. I am swindled—I, the last man under Heaven who could possibly have expected to write in those disgraceful terms of himself—I AM SWINDLED !

Let me chronicle the events. They exhibit me, for the time being, in a sadly helpless point of view. But the nature of the man prevails: I must have the events down in black and white.

The announcement of her approaching departure was intimated to me yesterday. After another civil speech about the information I had procured at Brighton, she hinted that there was a necessity for pushing our inquiries a little further. I immediately offered to undertake them, as before. " No," she said ; " they are not in your way this time. They are inquiries relating to a woman ; and I mean to make them myself !" Feeling privately convinced that this new resolution pointed straight at Mrs. Lecount, I tried a few innocent questions on the subject. She quietly declined to answer them. I asked next, when she proposed to leave. She would leave on the twenty-eighth. For what destination ? London. For long ? Probably not. By herself ? No. With me ? No. With whom then ? With Mrs. Wragge, if I had no objection. Good Heavens ! for what possible purpose ? For the purpose of getting a respectable lodging, which she could hardly expect to accomplish unless she was accompanied by an elderly female friend. And was I, in the capacity of elderly male friend, to be left out of the business altogether ? Impossible to say at present. Was I not even to forward any letters which might come for her at our present address ? No: she would make the arrangement herself at the post-office ; and she would ask me, at the same time, for an address, at which I could receive a letter from her, in case of necessity for future communication. Further inquiries, after this last answer, could lead to nothing but waste of time. I saved time by putting no more questions.

It was clear to me, that our present position towards each other was what our position had been, previously to the event of Michael Vanstone's death. I returned, as before, to my choice of alternatives. Which way did my private interests point? Towards trusting the chance of her wanting me again? Towards threatening her with the interference of her relatives and friends? Or towards making the information which I possessed a marketable commodity between the wealthy branch of the family and myself? The last of the three was the alternative I had chosen in the case of the father. I chose it once more in the case of the son.

The train started for London nearly four hours since, and took her away in it, accompanied by Mrs. Wragge.

My wife is too great a fool, poor soul, to be actively valuable in the present emergency; but she will be passively useful in keeping up Miss Vanstone's connection with me—and, in consideration of that circumstance, I consent to brush my own trousers, shave my own chin, and submit to the other inconveniences of waiting on myself for a limited period. Any faint glimmerings of sense which Mrs. Wragge may have formerly possessed, appear to have now finally taken their leave of her. On receiving permission to go to London, she favoured us immediately with two inquiries. Might she do some shopping? and might she leave the cookery-book behind her? Miss Vanstone said, Yes, to one question; and I said, Yes, to the other—and from that moment, Mrs. Wragge has existed in a state of perpetual laughter. I am still hoarse with vainly-repeated applications of vocal stimulant; and I left her in the railway carriage, to my inexpressible disgust, with *both* shoes down at heel.

Under ordinary circumstances, these absurd particulars would not have dwelt on my memory. But, as matters actually stand, my unfortunate wife's imbecility may, in her present position, lead to consequences which we none of us foresee. She is nothing more or less than a grown-up child; and I can plainly detect that Miss Vanstone trusts her, as she would not have trusted a sharper woman, on that very account. I know children little and big, rather better than my fair relative does; and I say—beware of all forms of human innocence, when it happens to be your interest to keep a secret to yourself.

Let me return to business. Here I am, at two o'clock on a fine summer's afternoon, left entirely alone, to consider the safest means of approaching Mr. Noel Vanstone, on my own account. My private suspicions of his miserly character, produce no discouraging effect on me. I have extracted cheering pecuniary results in my time from people quite as fond of their money as he can be. The real difficulty to contend with is the obstacle of Mrs. Lecount. If I am not mistaken, this lady merits a little serious consideration on my part. I will close my chronicle for to-day, and give Mrs. Lecount her due.

Three o'clock.—I open these pages again, to record a discovery which has taken me entirely by surprise.

After completing the last entry, a circumstance revived in my memory, which I had noticed on escorting the ladies this morning, to the railway. I then remarked that Miss Vanstone had only taken one of her three boxes with her—and it now occurred to me that a private investigation of the luggage she had left behind, might possibly be attended with beneficial results. Having, at certain periods of my life, been in the habit of cultivating friendly terms with strange locks, I found no difficulty in establishing myself on a familiar footing with Miss Vanstone's boxes. One of the two presented nothing to interest me. The other—devoted to the preservation of the costumes, articles of toilette, and other properties used in the dramatic Entertainment—proved to be better worth examining : for it led me straight to the discovery of one of its owner's secrets.

I found all the dresses in the box complete—with one remarkable exception. That exception was the dress of the old north-country lady ; the character which I have already mentioned as the best of all my pupil's disguises, and as modelled in voice and manner on her old governess, Miss Garth. The wig ; the eyebrows ; the bonnet and veil ; the cloak, padded inside to disfigure her back and shoulders ; the paints and cosmetics used to age her face and alter her complexion—were all gone. Nothing but the gown remained ; a gaudily flowered silk, useful enough for dramatic purposes, but too extravagant in colour and pattern to bear inspection by daylight. The other parts of the dress are sufficiently quiet to pass muster ; the bonnet and veil are only old-fashioned, and the cloak is of a sober grey colour. But one plain inference can be drawn from such a discovery as this. As certainly as I sit here, she is going to open the campaign against Noel Vanstone and Mrs. Lecount, in a character which neither of those two persons can have any possible reason for suspecting at the outset—the character of Miss Garth.

What course am I to take under these circumstances ? Having got her secret, what am I to do with it ? These are awkward considerations ; I am rather puzzled how to deal with them.

It is something more than the mere fact of her choosing to disguise herself to forward her own private ends, that causes my present perplexity. Hundreds of girls take fancies for disguising themselves ; and hundreds of instances of it are related year after year, in the public journals. But my ex-pupil is not to be confounded, for one moment, with the average adventuress of the newspapers. She is capable of going a long way beyond the limit of dressing herself like a man, and imitating a man's voice and manner. She has a natural gift for assuming characters, which I have never seen equalled by a woman ; and she has performed in public until she has felt her own power, and trained her talent for disguising herself to the highest pitch. A girl who takes the sharpest people unawares by using such a capacity as this to help her own objects in private life; and who sharpens that capacity by a determination to fight her way to her own purpose which has beaten down everything before it, up to this time—is a girl who tries an experiment in deception, new enough and dangerous enough to lead, one way or the other, to very serious results. This is my conviction, founded on a large experience in the art of imposing on my fellow-creatures. I say of my fair relative's enterprise what I never said or thought of it till I introduced myself to the inside of her box. The chances for and against her winning the fight for her lost fortune are now so evenly balanced, that I cannot for the life of me see on which side the scale inclines. All I can discern is, that it will, to a dead certainty, turn one way or the other, on the day when she passes Noel Vanstone's doors in disguise.

Which way do my interests point now? Upon my honour, I don't know.

Five o'clock.—I have effected a masterly compromise; I have decided on turning myself into a Jack-on-both-sides.

By to-day's post I have despatched to London an anonymous letter for Mr. Noel Vanstone. It will be forwarded to its destination by the same means which I successfully adopted to mystify Mr. Pendril; and it will reach Vauxhall Walk, Lambeth, by the afternoon of to-morrow at the latest.

The letter is short, and to the purpose. It warns Mr. Noel Vanstone, in the most alarming language, that he is destined to become the victim of a conspiracy; and that the prime mover of it is a young lady who has already held written communication with his father and himself. It offers him the information necessary to secure his own safety, on condition that he makes it worth the writer's while to run the serious personal risk which such a disclosure will entail on him. And it ends by stipulating that the answer shall be advertised in the Times; shall be addressed to "An Unknown Friend;" and shall state plainly what remuneration Mr. Noel Vanstone offers for the priceless service which it is proposed to render him.

Unless some unexpected complication occurs, this letter places me exactly in the position which it is my present interest to occupy. If the advertisement appears, and if the remuneration offered is large enough to justify me in going over to the camp of the enemy, over I go. If no advertisement appears, or if Mr Noel Vanstone rates my invaluable assistance at too low a figure, here I remain, biding my time till my fair relative wants me—or till I make her want me, which comes to the same thing. If the anonymous letter falls by any accident into her hands, she will find disparaging allusions in it to myself, purposely introduced to suggest that the writer must be one of the persons whom I addressed, while conducting her inquiries. If Mrs. Lecount takes the business in hand, and lays a trap for me—I decline her tempting invitation, by becoming totally ignorant of the whole affair the instant any second person appears in it. Let the end come as it may, here I am ready to profit by it: here I am, facing both ways, with perfect ease and security—a moral agriculturist, with his eye on two crops at once, and his swindler's sickle ready for any emergency.

For the next week to come, the newspaper will be more interesting to me than ever. I wonder which side I shall eventually belong to?

THE THIRD SCENE.

VAUXHALL WALK, LAMBETH.

CHAPTER I.

THE old Archiepiscopal Palace of Lambeth, on the southern bank of the Thames—with its Bishop's Walk and Garden, and its terrace fronting the river—is an architectural relic of the London of former times, precious to all lovers of the picturesque, in the utilitarian London of the present day. Southward of this venerable structure lies the street labyrinth of Lambeth : and nearly mid-way in that part of the maze of houses which is placed nearest to the river, runs the dingy double row of buildings, now, as in former days, known by the name of Vauxhall Walk.

The network of dismal streets stretching over the surrounding neighbourhood contains a population for the most part of the poorer order. In the thoroughfares where shops abound, the sordid struggle with poverty shows itself unreservedly on the filthy pavement; gathers its forces through the week; and, strengthening to a tumult on Saturday night, sees the Sunday morning dawn in murky gaslight. Miserable women, whose faces never smile, haunt the butchers' shops in such London localities as these, with relics of the men's wages saved from the public-house, clutched fast in their hands, with eyes that devour the meat they dare not buy, with eager fingers that touch it covetously, as the fingers of their richer sisters touch a precious stone. In this district, as in other districts remote from the wealthy quarters of the metropolis, the hideous London vagabond—with the filth of the street outmatched in his speech, with the mud of the street outdirtied in his clothes—lounges, lowering and brutal, at the street corner and the gin-shop door ; the public disgrace of his country, the unheeded warning of social troubles that are yet to come. Here, the loud self-assertion of Modern Progress—which has reformed so much in manners, and altered so little in men—meets the flat contradiction that scatters its pretensions to the winds. Here, while the national prosperity feasts, like another Belshazzar, on the spectacle of its own magnificence, is the Writing on the Wall,* which warns the monarch, Money, that his glory is weighed in the balance, and his power found wanting.

Situated in such a neighbourhood as this, Vauxhall Walk gains by comparison, and establishes claims to respectability which no impartial observation can fail to recognize. A large proportion of the Walk is still composed of private houses. In the scattered situations where shops appear, those shops are not besieged by the crowds of more populous thoroughfares. Commerce is not turbulent, nor is the public consumer besieged by loud invitations to "buy." Bird-fanciers have sought the congenial tranquillity of the scene; and pigeons coo, and canaries twitter, in Vauxhall Walk. Second-hand carts and cabs, bedsteads of a certain age, detached carriage wheels for those who may want one to make up a set, are all to be found here in the same repository. One tributary stream in the great flood of gas which illuminates London, tracks its parent source to Works established in this locality. Here, the followers of John Wesley have set up a temple, built before the period of Methodist conversion to the principles of architectural religion. And here—most striking object of all—on the site where thousands of lights once sparkled; where sweet sounds of music made night tuneful till morning dawned; where the beauty and fashion of London feasted and danced through the summer seasons of a century—spreads, at this day, an awful wilderness of mud and rubbish; the deserted dead body of Vauxhall Gardens*mouldering in the open air.

On the same day when Captain Wragge completed the last entry in his Chronicle of Events, a woman appeared at the window of one of the houses in Vauxhall Walk, and removed from the glass a printed paper which had been wafered to it, announcing that Apartments were to be let. The apartments consisted of two rooms on the first floor. They had just been taken for a week certain, by two ladies who had paid in advance—those two ladies being Magdalen and Mrs. Wragge.

As soon as the mistress of the house had left the room, Magdalen walked to the window, and cautiously looked out from it at the row of buildings opposite. They were of superior pretensions in size and appearance to the other houses in the Walk: the date at which they had been erected was inscribed on one of them, and was stated to be the year 1759. They stood back from the pavement, separated from it by little strips of garden-ground. This peculiarity of position, added to the breadth of the roadway interposing between them and the smaller houses opposite, made it impossible

for Magdalen to see the numbers on the doors, or to observe more of any
one who might come to the windows than the bare general outline of dress
and figure. Nevertheless, there she stood, anxiously fixing her eyes on
one house in the row, nearly opposite to her—the house she had looked for
before entering the lodgings ; the house inhabited at that moment by Noel
Vanstone and Mrs. Lecount.

After keeping watch at the window, in silence, for ten minutes or more,
she suddenly looked back into the room, to observe the effect which her
behaviour might have produced on her travelling companion.

Not the slightest cause appeared for any apprehension in that quarter.
Mrs. Wragge was seated at the table, absorbed in the arrangement of a
series of smart circulars and tempting price-lists, issued by advertising
tradespeople, and flung in at the cab-windows as they left the London
terminus. "I've often heard tell of light reading," said Mrs. Wragge,
restlessly shifting the positions of the circulars, as a child restlessly shifts
the position of a new set of toys. " Here's light reading, printed in pretty
colours. Here's all the Things I'm going to buy when I'm out shopping
to-morrow. Lend us a pencil, please—you won't be angry, will you?—I
do so want to mark 'em off." She looked up at Magdalen, chuckled joy-
fully over her own altered circumstances, and beat her great hands on the
table in irrepressible delight. " No cookery-book !" cried Mrs. Wragge.
" No Buzzing in my head ! no captain to shave to-morrow ! I'm all down
at heel ; my cap's on one side ; and nobody bawls at me. My heart alive,
here *is* a holiday and no mistake !" Her hands began to drum on the
table louder than ever, until Magdalen quieted them by presenting her
with a pencil. Mrs. Wragge instantly recovered her dignity, squared her
elbows on the table, and plunged into imaginary shopping for the rest of
the evening.

Magdalen returned to the window. She took a chair, seated herself behind
the curtain, and steadily fixed her eyes once more on the house opposite.

The blinds were down over the windows of the first floor and the second.
The window of the room on the ground floor was uncovered and partly
open, but no living creature came near it. Doors opened and people came
and went, in the houses on either side ; children by the dozen poured out
on the pavement to play, and invaded the little strips of garden-ground to
recover lost balls and shuttlecocks ; streams of people passed backwards
and forwards perpetually ; heavy waggons piled high with goods, lumbered
along the road on their way to, or their way from, the railway station near ;
all the daily life of the district stirred with its ceaseless activity in every
direction but one. The hours passed—and there was the house opposite,
still shut up, still void of any signs of human existence, inside or out.
The one object which had decided Magdalen on personally venturing
herself in Vauxhall Walk—the object of studying the looks, manners, and

habits of Mrs. Lecount and her master from a post of observation known only to herself—was, thus far, utterly defeated. After three hours' watching at the window, she had not even discovered enough to show her that the house was inhabited at all.

Shortly after six o'clock, the landlady disturbed Mrs. Wragge's studies by spreading the cloth for dinner. Magdalen placed herself at the table in a position which still enabled her to command the view from the window. Nothing happened. The dinner came to an end; Mrs. Wragge (lulled by the narcotic influences of annotating circulars and eating and drinking with an appetite sharpened by the captain's absence) withdrew to an arm-chair, and fell asleep in an attitude which would have caused her husband the acutest mental suffering; seven o'clock struck; the shadows of the summer evening lengthened stealthily on the grey pavement and the brown house-walls—and still the closed door opposite remained shut; still the one window open, showed nothing but the black blank of the room inside, lifeless and changeless as if that room had been a tomb.

Mrs. Wragge's meek snoring deepened in tone; the evening wore on drearily; it was close on eight o'clock—when an event happened at last. The street-door opposite opened for the first time, and a woman appeared on the threshold.

Was the woman Mrs. Lecount? No. As she came nearer, her dress showed her to be a servant. She had a large door-key in her hand, and was evidently going out to perform an errand. Roused, partly by curiosity—partly by the impulse of the moment, which urged her impetuous nature into action, after the passive endurance of many hours past—Magdalen snatched up her bonnet, and determined to follow the servant to her destination, wherever it might be.

The woman led her to the great thoroughfare of shops close at hand, called Lambeth Walk. After proceeding some little distance, and looking about her with the hesitation of a person not well acquainted with the neighbourhood, the servant crossed the road, and entered a stationer's shop. Magdalen crossed the road after her, and followed her in.

The inevitable delay in entering the shop under these circumstances, made Magdalen too late to hear what the woman asked for. The first words spoken, however, by the man behind the counter, reached her ears, and informed her that the servant's object was to buy a railway guide.

"Do you mean a Guide for this month? or a Guide for July?" asked the shopman, addressing his customer.

"Master didn't tell me which," answered the woman. "All I know is, he's going into the country the day after to-morrow."

"The day after to-morrow is the first of July," said the shopman. "The Guide your master wants, is the Guide for the new month. It won't be published till to-morrow."

Engaging to call again on the next day, the servant left the shop, and took the way that led back to Vauxhall Walk.

Magdalen purchased the first trifle she saw on the counter, and hastily returned in the same direction. The discovery she had just made was of very serious importance to her; and she felt the necessity of acting on it with as little delay as possible.

On entering the front room at the lodgings, she found Mrs. Wragge just awake, lost in drowsy bewilderment, with her cap fallen off on her shoulders, and with one of her shoes missing altogether. Magdalen endeavoured to persuade her that she was tired after her journey, and that her wisest proceeding would be to go to bed. Mrs. Wragge was perfectly willing to profit by this suggestion, provided she could find her shoe first. In looking for the shoe, she unfortunately discovered the circulars, put by on a side table; and forthwith recovered her recollection of the earlier proceedings of the evening.

"Give us the pencil," said Mrs. Wragge, shuffling the circulars in a violent hurry. "I can't go to bed yet—I haven't half done marking down the things I want. Let's see; where did I leave off? *Try Finch's feeding-bottle for Infants.* No! there's a cross against that: the cross means I don't want it. *Comfort in the Field. Buckler's Indestructible Hunting Breeches.* Oh, dear, dear! I've lost the place. No, I haven't. Here it is; here's my mark against it. *Elegant Cashmere Robes; strictly oriental, very grand; reduced to one pound, nineteen, and sixpence. Be in time. Only three left.* Only three! Oh, do lend us the money and let's go and get one!"

"Not to-night," said Magdalen. "Suppose you go to bed now, and finish the circulars to-morrow? I will put them by the bedside for you, and you can go on with them as soon as you wake, the first thing in the morning."

This suggestion met with Mrs. Wragge's immediate approval. Magdalen took her into the next room and put her to bed like a child—with her toys by her side. The room was so narrow, and the bed was so small; and Mrs. Wragge, arrayed in the white apparel proper for the occasion, with her moon face framed round by a spacious halo of night-cap—looked so hugely and disproportionately large, that Magdalen, anxious as she was, could not repress a smile on taking leave of her travelling companion for the night.

"Aha!" cried Mrs. Wragge, cheerfully; "we'll have that Cashmere Robe to-morrow. Come here! I want to whisper something to you. Just you look at me—I'm going to sleep crooked, and the captain's not here to bawl at me!"

The front room at the lodgings contained a sofa bedstead, which the landlady arranged betimes for the night. This done, and the candles brought in, Magdalen was left alone to shape her future course, as her own thoughts counselled her.

The questions and answers which had passed in her presence that evening, at the stationer's shop, led plainly to the conclusion that one day more would bring Noel Vanstone's present term of residence in Vauxhall Walk to an end. Her first cautious resolution to pass many days together in unsuspected observation of the house opposite, before she ventured herself inside, was entirely frustrated by the turn events had taken. She was placed in the dilemma of running all risks headlong on the next day—or of pausing for a future opportunity, which might never occur. There was no middle course open to her. Until she had seen Noel Vanstone with her own eyes, and had discovered the worst there was to fear from Mrs. Lecount—until she had achieved this double object, with the needful precaution of keeping her own identity carefully in the dark—not a step could she advance towards the accomplishment of the purpose which had brought her to London.

One after another, the minutes of the night passed away; one after another, the thronging thoughts followed each other over her mind—and still she reached no conclusion; still she faltered and doubted, with a hesitation new to her in her experience of herself. At last she crossed the room impatiently to seek the trivial relief of unlocking her trunk, and taking from it the few things that she wanted for the night. Captain Wragge's suspicions had not misled him. There, hidden between two dresses, were the articles of costume which he had missed from her box at Birmingham. She turned them over one by one, to satisfy herself that nothing she wanted had been forgotten, and returned once more to her post of observation by the window.

The house opposite was dark down to the parlour. There, the blind, previously raised, was now drawn over the window: the light burning behind it, showed her for the first time that the room was inhabited. Her eyes brightened, and her colour rose as she looked at it.

"There he is!" she said to herself, in a low angry whisper. "There he lives on our money, in the house that his father's warning has closed against me!" She dropped the blind which she had raised to look out; returned to her trunk; and took from it the grey wig which was part of her dramatic costume, in the character of the north-country lady. The wig had been crumpled in packing; she put it on, and went to the toilette table to comb it out. "His father has warned him against Magdalen Vanstone," she said, repeating the passage in Mrs. Lecount's letter, and laughing bitterly, as she looked at herself in the glass. "I wonder whether his father has warned him against Miss Garth? To-morrow is sooner than I bargained for. No matter: to-morrow shall show."

CHAPTER II.

THE early morning, when Magdalen rose and looked out, was cloudy and overcast. But as time advanced to the breakfast hour, the threatening of rain passed away; and she was free to provide, without hindrance from the weather, for the first necessity of the day—the necessity of securing the absence of her travelling companion from the house.

Mrs. Wragge was dressed, armed at all points with her collection of circulars, and eager to be away by ten o'clock. At an earlier hour Magdalen had provided for her being properly taken care of by the land-lady's eldest daughter,—a quiet, well-conducted girl, whose interest in the shopping expedition was readily secured by a little present of money for the purchase, on her own account, of a parasol and a muslin dress. Shortly after ten o'clock, Magdalen dismissed Mrs. Wragge and her attendant in a cab. She then joined the landlady—who was occupied in setting the rooms in order upstairs—with the object of ascertaining by a little well-timed gossip, what the daily habits might be of the inmates of the house.

She discovered that there were no other lodgers but Mrs. Wragge and herself. The landlady's husband was away all day, employed at a railway station. Her second daughter was charged with the care of the kitchen, in the elder sister's absence. The younger children were at school, and would be back at one o'clock to dinner. The landlady herself " got up fine linen for ladies," and expected to be occupied over her work all that morning, in a little room built out at the back of the premises. Thus, there was every facility for Magdalen's leaving the house in disguise, and leaving it un-observed; provided she went out before the children came back to dinner at one o'clock.

By eleven o'clock the apartments were set in order, and the landlady had retired to pursue her own employments. Magdalen softly locked the door of her room; drew the blind over the window, and entered at once on her preparations for the perilous experiment of the day.

The same quick perception of dangers to be avoided, and difficulties to be overcome, which had warned her to leave the extravagant part of her character costume in the box at Birmingham, now kept her mind fully alive to the vast difference between a disguise worn by gaslight, for the amusement of an audience, and a disguise assumed by daylight to deceive the searching eyes of two strangers. The first article of dress which she put on was an old gown of her own (made of the material called "alpaca"),* of a dark-brown colour, with a neat pattern of little star-shaped spots in white. A double flounce running round the bottom of this dress was the only milliner's ornament which it presented—an ornament not at all out of character with the costume appropriate to an elderly lady. The disguise of

her head and face was the next object of her attention. She fitted and
arranged the grey wig with the dexterity which constant practice had given
her; fixed the false eyebrows (made rather large, and of hair darker than
the wig) carefully in their position, with the gum she had with her for the
purpose, and stained her face, with the customary stage materials, so as to
change the transparent fairness of her complexion to the dull, faintly
opaque colour of a woman in ill-health. The lines and markings of age
followed next; and here the first obstacles presented themselves. The art
which succeeded by gaslight failed by day: the difficulty of hiding the
plainly artificial nature of the marks was almost insuperable. She turned
to her trunk; took from it two veils; and putting on her old-fashioned
bonnet, tried the effect of them in succession. One of the veils (of black
lace) was too thick to be worn over the face at that summer season, without exciting remark. The other, of plain net, allowed her features to be
seen through it, just indistinctly enough to permit the safe introduction of
certain lines (many fewer than she was accustomed to use in performing
the character) on the forehead and at the sides of the mouth. But the
obstacle thus set aside only opened the way to a new difficulty—the difficulty of keeping her veil down while she was speaking to other persons,
without any obvious reason for doing so. An instant's consideration, and
a chance look at her little china pallette of stage colours, suggested to her
ready invention the production of a visible excuse for wearing her veil.
She deliberately disfigured herself by artificially reddening the insides of
her eyelids, so as to produce an appearance of inflammation which no
human creature but a doctor—and that doctor at close quarters—could
have detected as false. She sprang to her feet, and looked triumphantly at
the hideous transformation of herself reflected in the glass. Who could
think it strange now if she wore her veil down, and if she begged Mrs.
Lecount's permission to sit with her back to the light?

Her last proceeding was to put on the quiet grey cloak, which she had
brought from Birmingham, and which had been padded inside by Captain
Wragge's own experienced hands, so as to hide the youthful grace and
beauty of her back and shoulders. Her costume being now complete, she
practised the walk which had been originally taught her as appropriate to
the character—a walk with a slight limp—and, returning to the glass, after
a minute's trial, exercised herself next in the disguise of her voice and
manner. This was the only part of the character in which it had been
possible, with her physical peculiarities, to produce an imitation of Miss
Garth; and here the resemblance was perfect. The harsh voice, the blunt
manner, the habit of accompanying certain phrases by an emphatic nod of
the head, the Northumbrian *burr* expressing itself in every word which
contained the letter "r"—all these personal peculiarities of the old north-
country governess were reproduced to the life. The personal transformation

thus completed, was literally what Captain Wragge had described it to be
—a triumph in the art of self-disguise. Excepting the one case of seeing
her face close, with a strong light on it, nobody who now looked at
Magdalen could have suspected for an instant that she was other than an
ailing, ill-made, unattractive woman of fifty years old at least.

Before unlocking the door she looked about her carefully, to make sure
that none of her stage materials were exposed to view, in case the landlady
entered the room in her absence. The only forgotten object belonging to
her that she discovered was a little packet of Norah's letters, which she
had been reading overnight, and which had been accidentally pushed
under the looking-glass while she was engaged in dressing herself. As she
took up the letters to put them away, the thought struck her for the first
time—"Would Norah know me now if we met each other in the street?"
She looked in the glass, and smiled sadly. "No," she said, "not even
Norah."

She unlocked the door, after first looking at her watch. It was close on
twelve o'clock. There was barely an hour left to try her desperate experiment, and to return to the lodging before the landlady's children came back
from school.

An instant's listening on the landing assured her that all was quiet in
the passage below. She noiselessly descended the stairs, and gained the
street without having met any living creature on her way out of the house.
In another minute she had crossed the road, and had knocked at Noel
Vanstone's door.

The door was opened by the same woman servant whom she had followed on the previous evening to the stationer's shop. With a momentary
tremor, which recalled the memorable first night of her appearance in
public, Magdalen inquired (in Miss Garth's voice, and with Miss Garth's
manner), for Mrs. Lecount.

"Mrs. Lecount has gone out, ma'am," said the servant.

"Is Mr. Vanstone at home?" asked Magdalen, her resolution asserting
itself at once against the first obstacle that opposed it.

"My master is not up yet, ma'am."

Another check! A weaker nature would have accepted the warning.
Magdalen's nature rose in revolt against it.

"What time will Mrs. Lecount be back?" she asked.

"About one o'clock, ma'am."

"Say, if you please, that I will call again, as soon after one o'clock as
possible. I particularly wish to see Mrs. Lecount. My name is Miss
Garth."

She turned and left the house. Going back to her own room was out of
the question. The servant (as Magdalen knew by not hearing the door
close), was looking after her; and, moreover, she would expose herself, if

she went indoors, to the risk of going out again exactly at the time when the landlady's children were sure to be about the house. She turned mechanically to the right; walked on until she reached Vauxhall Bridge; and waited there, looking out over the river.

The interval of unemployed time now before her was nearly an hour. How should she occupy it?

As she asked herself the question, the thought which had struck her when she put away the packet of Norah's letters, rose in her mind once more. A sudden impulse to test the miserable completeness of her disguise, mixed with the higher and purer feeling at her heart; and strengthened her natural longing to see her sister's face again, though she dare not discover herself and speak. Norah's later letters had described, in the fullest detail, her life as a governess—her hours for teaching, her hours of leisure, her hours for walking out with her pupils. There was just time, if she could find a vehicle at once, for Magdalen to drive to the house of Norah's employer, with the chance of getting there a few minutes before the hour when her sister would be going out. " One look at her will tell me more than a hundred letters !" With that thought in her heart : with the one object of following Norah on her daily walk, under protection of the disguise, Magdalen hastened over the bridge, and made for the northern bank of the river.

So, at the turning point of her life—so, in the interval before she took the irrevocable step, and passed the threshold of Noel Vanstone's door— the forces of Good triumphing in the strife for her over the forces of Evil, turned her back on the scene of her meditated deception, and hurried her mercifully farther and farther away from the fatal house.

She stopped the first empty cab that passed her; told the driver to go to New Street, Spring Gardens ; and promised to double his fare if he reached his destination by a given time. The man earned the money—more than earned it, as the event proved. Magdalen had not taken ten steps in advance along New Street, walking towards St. James's Park, before the door of a house beyond her opened, and a lady in mourning came out accompanied by two little girls. The lady also took the direction of the Park, without turning her head towards Magdalen, as she descended the house step. It mattered little ; Magdalen's heart looked through her eyes, and told her that she saw Norah.

She followed them into St. James's Park, and thence (along the Mall) into the Green Park, venturing closer and closer as they reached the grass and ascended the rising ground in the direction of Hyde Park Corner. Her eager eyes devoured every detail in Norah's dress, and detected the slightest change that had taken place in her figure and her bearing. She had become thinner since the autumn—her head drooped a little ; she walked wearily. Her mourning dress, worn with the modest grace and neatness which no misfortune could take from her, was suited to her altered station; her black gown was made of stuff; her black shawl and bonnet were of the plainest and cheapest kind. The two little girls, walking on either side of her, were dressed in silk. Magdalen instinctively hated them.

She made a wide circuit on the grass, so as to turn gradually and meet her sister, without exciting suspicion that the meeting was contrived. Her heart beat fast; a burning heat glowed in her as she thought of her false hair, her false colour, her false dress, and saw the dear familiar face coming nearer and nearer. They passed each other close. Norah's dark gentle eyes looked up, with a deeper light in them, with a sadder beauty, than of old—rested all unconscious of the truth on her sister's face—and looked away from it again, as from the face of a stranger. That glance of an instant struck Magdalen to the heart. She stood rooted to the ground, after Norah had passed by. A horror of the vile disguise that concealed her; a yearning to burst its trammels and hide her shameful painted face on Norah's bosom, took possession of her, body and soul. She turned and looked back.

Norah and the two children had reached the higher ground, and were close to one of the gates in the iron railing which fenced the Park from the street. Drawn by an irresistible fascination, Magdalen followed them again, gained on them as they reached the gate, and heard the voices of the two children raised in angry dispute which way they wanted to walk next. She saw Norah take them through the gate, and then stoop and speak to them, while waiting for an opportunity to cross the road. They only grew the louder and the angrier for what she said. The youngest—a girl of eight or nine years old—flew into a child's vehement passion, cried, screamed, and even kicked at the governess. The people in the street stopped and laughed; some of them jestingly advised a little wholesome correction; one woman asked Norah if she was the child's mother; another pitied her audibly for being the child's governess. Before Magdalen could push her way through the crowd—before her all-mastering anxiety to help her sister had blinded her to every other consideration, and had brought her, self-betrayed, to Norah's side—an open carriage passed the pavement slowly, hindered in its progress by the press of vehicles before it. An old lady seated inside heard the child's cries, recognized Norah, and called to her immediately. The footman parted the crowd, and the children were put into the carriage. "It's lucky I happened to pass this way," said the old lady, beckoning contemptuously to Norah to take her place on the front seat; "you never could manage my daughter's children, and you never will." The footman put up the steps—the carriage drove on with the children and the governess—the crowd dispersed—and Magdalen was alone again.

" So be it !" she thought bitterly. " I should only have distressed her. We should only have had the misery of parting to suffer again."

She mechanically retraced her steps; she returned, as in a dream, to the open space of the Park. Arming itself treacherously with the strength of her love for her sister, with the vehemence of the indignation that she felt for her sister's sake, the terrible temptation of her life fastened its hold on her more firmly than ever. Through all the paint and disfigurement of the disguise, the fierce despair of that strong and passionate nature lowered haggard and horrible. Norah made an object of public curiosity and amusement; Norah reprimanded in the open street; Norah the hired victim of an old woman's insolence, and a child's ill-temper—and the same man to thank for it who had sent Frank to China !—and that man's son to thank after him ! The thought of her sister, which had turned her from the scene of her meditated deception, which had made the consciousness of her own disguise hateful to her—was now the thought which sanctioned that means, or any means, to compass her end; the thought which set wings to her feet, and hurried her back nearer and nearer to the fatal house.

She left the Park again; and found herself in the streets without knowing where. Once more she hailed the first cab that passsed her—and told the man to drive to Vauxhall Walk.

The change from walking to riding quieted her. She felt her attention returning to herself and her dress. The necessity of making sure that no accident had happened to her disguise, in the interval since she had left her own room, impressed itself immediately on her mind. She stopped the driver at the first pastrycook's shop which he passed, and there obtained the means of consulting a looking-glass before she ventured back to Vauxhall Walk.

Her grey head-dress was disordered, and the old-fashioned bonnet was a little on one side. Nothing else had suffered. She set right the few defects in her costume, and returned to the cab. It was half-past one, when she approached the house, and knocked, for the second time, at Noel Vanstone's door. The woman-servant opened it, as before.

" Has Mrs. Lecount come back ?"

" Yes, ma'am. Step this way, if you please."

The servant preceded Magdalen along an empty passage ; and, leading her past an uncarpeted staircase, opened the door of a room at the back of the house. The room was lighted by one window looking out on a yard ; the walls were bare ; the boarded floor was uncovered. Two bedroom chairs stood against the wall, and a kitchen-table was placed under the window. On the table stood a glass tank filled with water ; and ornamented in the middle by a miniature pyramid of rock-work interlaced with weeds.

Snails clung to the sides of the tank; tadpoles and tiny fish swam swiftly in the green water; slippery efts and slimy frogs twined their noiseless way in and out of the weedy rock-work—and, on top of the pyramid, there sat solitary, cold as the stone, brown as the stone, motionless as the stone, a little bright-eyed toad. The art of keeping fish and reptiles as domestic pets had not at that time been popularized in England; and Magdalen, on entering the room, started back, in irrepressible astonishment and disgust, from the first specimen of an Aquarium that she had ever seen.

"Don't be alarmed," said a woman's voice behind her. "My pets hurt nobody."

Magdalen turned, and confronted Mrs. Lecount. She had expected—founding her anticipations on the letter which the housekeeper had written to her—to see a hard, wily, ill-favoured, insolent old woman. She found herself in the presence of a lady of mild ingratiating manners; whose dress was the perfection of neatness, taste, and matronly simplicity; whose personal appearance was little less than a triumph of physical resistance to the deteriorating influence of time. If Mrs. Lecount had struck some fifteen or sixteen years off her real age, and had asserted herself to be eight-and-thirty, there would not have been one man in a thousand, or one woman in a hundred, who would have hesitated to believe her. Her dark hair was just turning to grey, and no more. It was plainly parted under a spotless lace cap, sparingly ornamented with mourning ribbons. Not a wrinkle appeared on her smooth white forehead, or her plump white cheeks. Her double chin was dimpled, and her teeth were marvels of whiteness and regularity. Her lips might have been critically considered as too thin, if they had not been accustomed to make the best of their defects by means of a pleading and persuasive smile. Her large black eyes might have looked fierce if they had been set in the face of another woman: they were mild and melting in the face of Mrs. Lecount; they were tenderly interested in everything she looked at—in Magdalen, in the toad on the rock-work, in the back-yard view from the window; in her own plump fair hands, which she rubbed softly one over the other while she spoke; in her own pretty cambric chemisette, which she had a habit of looking at complacently while she listened to others. The elegant black gown in which she mourned the memory of Michael Vanstone was not a mere dress—it was a well-made compliment paid to Death. Her innocent white muslin apron was a little domestic poem in itself. Her jet earrings were so modest in their pretensions, that a Quaker might have looked at them, and committed no sin. The comely plumpness of her face was matched by the comely plumpness of her figure: it glided smoothly over the ground; it flowed in sedate undulations when she walked. There are not many men who could have observed Mrs. Lecount entirely from the Platonic point of view—lads in their teens would have found her irresistible—women only could have hardened their hearts against her, and mercilessly forced their way inwards through that fair and smiling surface. Magdalen's first glance at this Venus of the autumn period of female life, more than satisfied her that she had done well to feel her ground in disguise, before she ventured on matching herself against Mrs. Lecount.

"Have I the pleasure of addressing the lady who called this morning?" inquired the housekeeper. "Am I speaking to Miss Garth?"

Something in the expression of her eyes, as she asked that question, warned Magdalen to turn her face farther inwards from the window than she had turned it yet. The bare doubt whether the housekeeper might not have seen her already under too strong a light, shook her self-possession for the moment. She gave herself time to recover it, and merely answered by a bow.

"Accept my excuses, ma'am, for the place in which I am compelled to receive you," proceeded Mrs. Lecount, in fluent English, spoken with a foreign accent. "Mr. Vanstone is only here for a temporary purpose. We leave for the sea-side to-morrow afternoon; and it has not been thought worth while to set the house in proper order. Will you take a seat, and oblige me by mentioning the object of your visit?"

She glided imperceptibly a step or two nearer to Magdalen, and placed a chair for her exactly opposite the light from the window. "Pray sit down," said Mrs. Lecount, looking with the tenderest interest at the visitor's inflamed eyes, through the visitor's net veil.

"I am suffering, as you see, from a complaint in the eyes," replied Magdalen, steadily keeping her profile towards the window, and carefully pitching her voice to the tone of Miss Garth's. "I must beg your permission to wear my veil down and to sit away from the light." She said those words, feeling mistress of herself again. With perfect composure she drew the chair back into the corner of the room beyond the window; and seated herself, keeping the shadow of her bonnet well over her face. Mrs. Lecount's persuasive lips murmured a polite expression of sympathy; Mrs. Lecount's amiable black eyes looked more interested in the strange lady than ever. She placed a chair for herself exactly on a line with Magdalen's, and sat so close to the wall as to force her visitor either to turn her head a little further round towards the window, or to fail in politeness by not looking at the person whom she addressed. "Yes," said Mrs. Lecount, with a confidential little cough. "And to what circumstances am I indebted for the honour of this visit?"

"May I inquire, first, if my name happens to be familiar to you?" said Magdalen, turning towards her as a matter of necessity—but coolly holding up her handkerchief, at the same time, between her face and the light.

"No," answered Mrs. Lecount, with another little cough, rather harsher than the first. "The name of Miss Garth is not familiar to me."

"In that case," pursued Magdalen, "I shall best explain the object that causes me to intrude on you, by mentioning who I am. I lived for many years, as governess, in the family of the late Mr. Andrew Vanstone, of Combe-Raven ; and I come here in the interest of his orphan daughters."

Mrs. Lecount's hands, which had been smoothly sliding one over the other, up to this time, suddenly stopped ; and Mrs. Lecount's lips self-forgetfully shutting up, owned they were too thin at the very outset of the interview.

"I am surprised you can bear the light out of doors, without a green shade," she quietly remarked ; leaving the false Miss Garth's announcement of herself as completely unnoticed as if she had not spoken at all.

"I find a shade over my eyes keeps them too hot at this time of the year," rejoined Magdalen, steadily matching the housekeeper's composure. "May I ask whether you heard what I said just now on the subject of my errand in this house ?"

"May I inquire, on my side, ma'am, in what way that errand can possibly concern *me* ?" retorted Mrs. Lecount.

"Certainly," said Magdalen. "I come to you because Mr. Noel Vanstone's intentions towards the two young ladies, were made known to them in the form of a letter from yourself."

That plain answer had its effect. It warned Mrs. Lecount that the strange lady was better informed than she had at first suspected, and that it might hardly be wise, under the circumstances, to dismiss her unheard.

"Pray pardon me," said the housekeeper, "I scarcely understood before ; I perfectly understand now. You are mistaken, ma'am, in supposing that I am of any importance, or that I exercise any influence in this painful matter. I am the mouthpiece of Mr. Noel Vanstone ; the pen he holds, if you will excuse the expression—nothing more. He is an invalid ; and like other invalids, he has his bad days and his good. It was his bad day, when that answer was written to the young person——, shall I call her Miss Vanstone ? I will, with pleasure, poor girl ; for who am I to make distinctions, and what is it to me whether her parents were married or not? As I was saying, it was one of Mr. Noel Vanstone's bad days, when that answer was sent, and therefore I had to write it ; simply as his secretary, for want of a better. If you wish to speak on the subject of these young ladies——, shall I call them young ladies, as you did just now ? no, poor things, I will call them the Miss Vanstones.—If you wish to speak on the subject of these Miss Vanstones, I will mention your name, and your object in favouring me with this call, to Mr. Noel Vanstone. He is alone in the parlour, and this is one of his good days. I have the influence of an old servant over him ; and I will use that influence with pleasure in your behalf. Shall I go at once ?" asked Mrs. Lecount, rising with the friendliest anxiety to make herself useful.

"If you please," replied Magdalen; "and if I am not taking any undue advantage of your kindness."

"On the contrary," rejoined Mrs. Lecount, "you are laying me under an obligation—you are permitting me, in my very limited way, to assist the performance of a benevolent action." She bowed, smiled, and glided out of the room.

Left by herself, Magdalen allowed the anger which she had suppressed in Mrs. Lecount's presence to break free from her. For want of a nobler object of attack, it took the direction of the toad. The sight of the hideous little reptile sitting placid on his rock throne, with his bright eyes staring impenetrably into vacancy, irritated every nerve in her body. She looked at the creature with a shrinking intensity of hatred; she whispered at it maliciously through her set teeth. "I wonder whose blood runs coldest," she said, "yours, you little monster, or Mrs. Lecount's? I wonder which is the slimiest, her heart or your back? You hateful wretch, do you know what your mistress is? Your mistress is a devil!"

The speckled skin under the toad's mouth mysteriously wrinkled itself, then slowly expanded again, as if he had swallowed the words just addressed to him. Magdalen started back in disgust from the first perceptible movement in the creature's body, trifling as it was, and returned to her chair. She had not seated herself again a moment too soon. The door opened noiselessly, and Mrs. Lecount appeared once more.

"Mr. Vanstone will see you," she said, "if you will kindly wait a few minutes. He will ring the parlour bell when his present occupation is at an end, and he is ready to receive you. Be careful, ma'am, not to depress his spirits, or to agitate him in any way. His heart has been a cause of serious anxiety to those about him, from his earliest years. There is no positive disease; there is only a chronic feebleness—a fatty degeneration —a want of vital power in the organ itself. His heart will go on well enough if you don't give his heart too much to do—that is the advice of all the medical men who have seen him. You will not forget it, and you will keep a guard over your conversation accordingly. Talking of medical men, have you ever tried the Golden Ointment for that sad affliction in your eyes? It has been described to me as an excellent remedy."

"It has not succeeded in my case," replied Magdalen, sharply. "Before I see Mr. Noel Vanstone," she continued, "may I inquire——"

"I beg your pardon," interposed Mrs. Lecount. "Does your question refer in any way to those two poor girls?"

"It refers to the Miss Vanstones."

"Then I can't enter into it. Excuse me, I really can't discuss these poor girls (I am so glad to hear you call them the Miss Vanstones!) except in my master's presence, and by my master's express permission. Let us talk of something else while we are waiting here. Will you notice my glass Tank? I have every reason to believe that it is a perfect novelty in England."

"I looked at the Tank while you were out of the room," said Magdalen.

"Did you? You take no interest in the subject, I dare say? Quite natural. I took no interest either until I was married. My dear husband —dead many years since—formed my tastes, and elevated me to himself. You have heard of the late Professor Lecomte, the eminent Swiss naturalist? I am his widow. The English circle at Zurich (where I lived in my late master's service) Anglicised my name to Lecount. Your generous country people will have nothing foreign about them—not even a name, if they can help it. But I was speaking of my husband—my dear husband, who permitted me to assist him in his pursuits. I have had only one interest since his death—an interest in science. Eminent in many things, the Professor was great at reptiles. He left me his Subjects and his Tank. I had no other legacy. There is the Tank. All the Subjects died but this quiet little fellow—this nice little toad. Are you surprised at my liking him? There is nothing to be surprised at. The Professor lived long enough to elevate me above the common prejudice against the reptile creation. Properly understood, the reptile creation is beautiful. Properly dissected, the reptile creation is instructive in the last degree." She stretched out her little finger, and gently stroked the toad's back with the tip of it. "So refreshing to the touch," said Mrs. Lecount. "So nice and cool this summer weather!"

The bell from the parlour rang. Mrs. Lecount rose, bent fondly over the Aquarium, and chirruped to the toad at parting as if it had been a bird. "Mr. Vanstone is ready to receive you. Follow me, if you please, Miss Garth." With these words she opened the door, and led the way out of the room.

CHAPTER III.

"MISS GARTH, sir," said Mrs. Lecount, opening the parlour door, and announcing the visitor's appearance, with the tone and manner of a well-bred servant.

Magdalen found herself in a long, narrow room—consisting of a back parlour and a front parlour, which had been thrown into one by opening the folding-doors between them. Seated not far from the front window, with his back to the light, she saw a frail, flaxen-haired, self-satisfied little man, clothed in a fair white dressing-gown, many sizes too large for him, with a nosegay of violets drawn neatly through the button-hole over his breast. He looked from thirty to five-and-thirty years old. His complexion was as delicate as a young girl's, his eyes were of the lightest blue, his upper lip was adorned by a weak little white moustache, waxed and twisted at either end into a thin spiral curl. When any object specially attracted his attention, he half closed his eyelids to look at it. When he smiled, the skin at his temples crumpled itself up into a nest of wicked little wrinkles. He had a plate of strawberries on his lap, with a napkin under them to preserve the purity of his white dressing-gown. At his right hand stood a large round table, covered with a collection of foreign curiosities, which seemed to have been brought together from the four quarters of the globe. Stuffed birds from Africa, porcelain monsters from China, silver ornaments and utensils from India and Peru, mosaic work from Italy, and bronzes from France—were all heaped together, pell-mell, with the coarse deal boxes and dingy leather cases which served to pack them for travelling. The little man apologized, with a cheerful and simpering conceit, for his litter of curiosities, his dressing-gown, and his delicate health; and, waving his hand towards a chair, placed his attention, with pragmatical politeness, at the visitor's disposal. Magdalen looked at him with a momentary doubt whether Mrs. Lecount had not deceived her. Was this the man who mercilessly followed the path on which his merciless father had walked before him? She could hardly believe it. "Take a seat, Miss Garth," he repeated; observing her hesitation, and announcing his own name, in a high, thin, fretfully-consequential voice: "I am Mr. Noel Vanstone. You wished to see me—here I am!"

"May I be permitted to retire, sir?" inquired Mrs. Lecount.

"Certainly not!" replied her master. "Stay here, Lecount, and keep us company. Mrs. Lecount has my fullest confidence," he continued, addressing Magdalen. "Whatever you say to me, ma'am, you say to her. She is a domestic treasure. There is not another house in England has such a treasure as Mrs. Lecount."

The housekeeper listened to the praise of her domestic virtues with eyes immovably fixed on her elegant chemisette. But Magdalen's quick penetration had previously detected a look that passed between Mrs. Lecount and her master, which suggested that Noel Vanstone had been instructed beforehand, what to say and do in his visitor's presence. The suspicion of this—and the obstacles which the room presented to arranging her position in it so as to keep her face from the light—warned Magdalen to be on her guard.

She had taken her chair at first nearly midway in the room. An instant's after-reflection induced her to move her seat towards the left hand, so as to place herself just inside, and close against, the left post of the folding-door. In this position, she dexterously barred the only passage by which Mrs. Lecount could have skirted round the large table, and contrived to front Magdalen by taking a chair at her master's side. On the right hand of the table the empty space was well occupied by the fireplace and fender, by some travelling trunks, and a large packing-case. There was no alternative left for Mrs. Lecount but to place herself on a line with Magdalen, against the opposite post of the folding-door—or to push rudely past the visitor, with the obvious intention of getting in front of her. With an expressive little cough, and with one steady look at her master, the housekeeper conceded the point, and took her seat against the right-hand door-post. "Wait a little," thought Mrs. Lecount, "my turn next!"

"Mind what you are about, ma'am!" cried Noel Vanstone, as Magdalen accidentally approached the table, in moving her chair. "Mind the sleeve of your cloak! Excuse me, you nearly knocked down that silver candle-stick. Pray don't suppose it's a common candlestick. It's nothing of the sort—it's a Peruvian candlestick. There are only three of that pattern in the world. One is in the possession of the President of Peru; one is locked up in the Vatican; and one is on My table. It cost ten pounds; it's worth fifty. One of my father's bargains, ma'am. All these things are my father's bargains. There is not another house in England which has such curiosities as these. Sit down, Lecount; I beg you will make yourself comfortable. Mrs. Lecount is like the curiosities, Miss Garth—she is one of my father's bargains. You are one of my father's bargains, are you not, Lecount? My father was a remarkable man, ma'am. You will be re-minded of him here, at every turn. I have got his dressing-gown on at this moment. No such linen as this is made now—you can't get it for love or money. Would you like to feel the texture? Perhaps you're no judge of texture? Perhaps you would prefer talking to me about these two pupils of yours? They are two, are they not? Are they fine girls? Plump, fresh, full-blown English beauties?"

"Excuse me, sir," interposed Mrs. Lecount sorrowfully. "I must really beg permission to retire if you speak of the poor things in that way. I can't sit by, sir, and hear them turned into ridicule. Consider their position; consider Miss Garth."

"You good creature!" said Noel Vanstone, surveying the housekeeper through his half-closed eyelids. "You excellent Lecount! I assure you, ma'am, Mrs. Lecount is a worthy creature. You will observe that she pities the two girls. I don't go so far as that myself—but I can make allowances for them. I am a large-minded man. I can make allowances for them and for you." He smiled with the most cordial politeness, and helped himself to a strawberry from the dish on his lap.

"You shock Miss Garth; indeed, sir, without meaning it, you shock Miss Garth," remonstrated Mrs. Lecount. "She is not accustomed to you as I am. Consider Miss Garth, sir. As a favour to me, consider Miss Garth."

Thus far, Magdalen had resolutely kept silence. The burning anger which would have betrayed her in an instant if she had let it flash its way to the surface, throbbed fast and fiercely at her heart, and warned her, while Noel Vanstone was speaking, to close her lips. She would have allowed him to talk on uninterruptedly for some minutes more, if Mrs. Lecount had not interfered for the second time. The refined insolence of the housekeeper's pity, was a woman's insolence; and it stung her into instantly controlling herself. She had never more admirably imitated Miss Garth's voice and manner, than when she spoke her next words.

"You are very good," she said to Mrs. Lecount. "I make no claim to be treated with any extraordinary consideration. I am a governess, and I don't expect it. I have only one favour to ask. I beg Mr. Noel Vanstone, for his own sake, to hear what I have to say to him."

"You understand, sir?" observed Mrs. Lecount. "It appears that Miss Garth has some serious warning to give you. She says you are to hear her, for your own sake."

Mr. Noel Vanstone's fair complexion suddenly turned white. He put away the plate of strawberries among his father's bargains. His hand shook, and his little figure twisted itself uneasily in the chair. Magdalen observed him attentively. "One discovery already," she thought; "he is a coward!"

"What do you mean, ma'am?" asked Noel Vanstone with visible trepidation of look and manner. "What do you mean by telling me I must listen to you for my own sake? If you come here to intimidate me, you come to the wrong man. My strength of character was universally noticed in our circle at Zurich—wasn't it, Lecount?"

"Universally, sir," said Mrs. Lecount. "But let us hear Miss Garth. Perhaps I have misinterpreted her meaning."

"On the contrary," replied Magdalen, "you have exactly expressed my meaning. My object in coming here is to warn Mr. Noel Vanstone against the course which he is now taking."

"Don't!" pleaded Mrs. Lecount. "Oh, if you want to help these poor girls, don't talk in that way! Soften his resolution, ma'am, by entreaties; don't strengthen it by threats!" She a little overstrained the tone of humility in which she spoke those words—a little overacted the look of apprehension which accompanied them. If Magdalen had not seen plainly enough already that it was Mrs. Lecount's habitual practice to decide everything for her master in the first instance, and then to persuade him that he was not acting under his housekeeper's resolution, but under his own—she would have seen it now.

"You hear what Lecount has just said?" remarked Noel Vanstone. "You hear the unsolicited testimony of a person who has known me from childhood? Take care, Miss Garth—take care!" He complacently arranged the tails of his white dressing-gown over his knees, and took the plate of strawberries back on his lap.

"I have no wish to offend you," said Magdalen. "I am only anxious to open your eyes to the truth. You are not acquainted with the characters of the two sisters whose fortunes have fallen into your possession. I have known them from childhood; and I come to give you the benefit of my experience in their interests and in yours. You have nothing to dread from the elder of the two; she patiently accepts the hard lot which you, and your father before you, have forced on her. The younger sister's conduct is the very opposite of this. She has already declined to submit to your father's decision; and she now refuses to be silenced by Mrs. Lecount's letter. Take my word for it, she is capable of giving you serious trouble if you persist in making an enemy of her."

Noel Vanstone changed colour once more, and began to fidget again in his chair. "Serious trouble," he repeated, with a blank look. "If you mean writing letters, ma'am, she has given trouble enough already. She has written once to me, and twice to my father. One of the letters to my father was a threatening letter—wasn't it, Lecount?"

"She expressed her feelings, poor child," said Mrs. Lecount. "I thought it hard to send her back her letter, but your dear father knew best. What I said at the time was, Why not let her express her feelings? What are a few threatening words, after all? In her position, poor creature, they are words, and nothing more."

"I advise you not to be too sure of that," said Magdalen. "I know her better than you do."

She paused at those words—paused in a momentary terror. The sting of Mrs. Lecount's pity had nearly irritated her into forgetting her assumed character, and speaking in her own voice.

"You have referred to the letters written by my pupil," she resumed, addressing Noel Vanstone, as soon as she felt sure of herself again. "We will say nothing about what she has written to your father; we will only speak of what she has written to you. Is there anything unbecoming in her letter, anything said in it that is false? Is it not true that these two sisters have been cruelly deprived of the provision which their father made for them? His will to this day speaks for him and for them; and it only speaks to no purpose, because he was not aware that his marriage obliged him to make it again, and because he died before he could remedy the error. Can you deny that?"

Noel Vanstone smiled, and helped himself to a strawberry. "I don't attempt to deny it," he said. "Go on, Miss Garth."

"Is it not true," persisted Magdalen, "that the law which has taken the money from these sisters, whose father made no second will, has now given that very money to you, whose father made no will at all? Surely, explain it how you may, this is hard on those orphan girls?"

"Very hard," replied Noel Vanstone. "It strikes you in that light, too —doesn't it, Lecount?"

Mrs. Lecount shook her head, and closed her handsome black eyes.

"Harrowing," she said; "I can characterize it, Miss Garth, by no other word —harrowing. How the young person—no! how Miss Vanstone the younger —discovered that my late respected master made no will, I am at a loss to understand. Perhaps it was put in the papers? But I am interrupting you, Miss Garth. You have something more to say about your pupil's letter?" She noiselessly drew her chair forward as she said those words, a few inches beyond the line of the visitor's chair. The attempt was neatly made, but it proved useless. Magdalen only kept her head more to the left—and the packing-case on the floor prevented Mrs. Lecount from advancing any farther.

"I have only one more question to put," said Magdalen. "My pupil's letter addressed a proposal to Mr. Noel Vanstone. I beg him to inform me why he has refused to consider it."

"My good lady!" cried Noel Vanstone, arching his white eyebrows in satirical astonishment. "Are you really in earnest? Do you know what the proposal is? Have you seen the letter?"

"I am quite in earnest," said Magdalen, "and I have seen the letter. It entreats you to remember how Mr. Andrew Vanstone's fortune has come into your hands; it informs you that one-half of that fortune, divided between his daughters, was what his will intended them to have; and it asks of your sense of justice to do for his children, what he would have done for them himself if he had lived. In plainer words still, it asks you to give one-half of the money to the daughters, and it leaves you free to keep the other half yourself. That is the proposal. Why have you refused to consider it?"

"For the simplest possible reason, Miss Garth," said Noel Vanstone, in high good humour. "Allow me to remind you of a well-known proverb: A fool and his money are soon parted. Whatever else I may be, ma'am, I'm not a fool."

"Don't put it in that way, sir!" remonstrated Mrs. Lecount. "Be serious—pray be serious!"

"Quite impossible, Lecount," rejoined her master. "I can't be serious. My poor father, Miss Garth, took a high moral point of view in this matter. Lecount, there, takes a high moral point of view—don't you, Lecount? I do nothing of the sort. I have lived too long in the continental atmosphere to trouble myself about moral points of view. My course in this business is as plain as two and two make four. I have got the money, and I should be a born idiot if I parted with it. There is my point of view! Simple enough, isn't it? I don't stand on my dignity; I don't meet you with the law, which is all on my side; I don't blame your coming here, as a total stranger, to try and alter my resolution; I don't blame the two girls for wanting to dip their fingers into my purse. All I say is, I am not fool enough to open it. *Pas si bête*, as we used to say in the English

circle at Zurich. You understand French, Miss Garth? *Pas si bête!*"
He set aside his plate of strawberries once more, and daintily dried his
fingers on his fine white napkin.

Magdalen kept her temper. If she could have struck him dead by
lifting her hand at that moment—it is probable she would have lifted it.
But she kept her temper.

"Am I to understand," she asked, "that the last words you have to say
in this matter, are the words said for you in Mrs. Lecount's letter?"

"Precisely so," replied Noel Vanstone.

"You have inherited your own father's fortune, as well as the fortune of
Mr. Andrew Vanstone, and yet you feel no obligation to act from motives
of justice or generosity towards these two sisters? All you think it
necessary to say to them is—you have got the money, and you refuse to
part with a single farthing of it?"

"Most accurately stated! Miss Garth, you are a woman of business.
Lecount, Miss Garth is a woman of business."

"Don't appeal to me, sir," cried Mrs. Lecount, gracefully wringing her
plump white hands. "I can't bear it! I must interfere! Let me
suggest—oh, what do you call it in English?—a compromise. Dear Mr.
Noel, you are perversely refusing to do yourself justice; you have better
reasons than the reason you have given to Miss Garth. You follow your
honoured father's example; you feel it due to his memory to act in this
matter as he acted before you. That is his reason, Miss Garth—I implore
you on my knees, take that as his reason. He will do what his dear
father did; no more, no less. His dear father made a proposal, and
he himself will now make that proposal, over again. Yes, Mr. Noel, you
will remember what this poor girl says in her letter to you. Her sister
has been obliged to go out as a governess; and she herself, in losing her
fortune, has lost the hope of her marriage for years and years to come.
You will remember this—and you will give the hundred pounds to one,
and the hundred pounds to the other, which your admirable father offered
in the past time? If he does this, Miss Garth, will he do enough? If he
gives a hundred pounds each to these unfortunate sisters—— ?"

"He will repent the insult to the last hour of his life," said Magdalen.

The instant that answer passed her lips, she would have given worlds to
recall it. Mrs. Lecount had planted her sting in the right place at last.
Those rash words of Magdalen's had burst from her passionately, in her
own voice.

Nothing but the habit of public performance saved her from making the
serious error that she had committed more palpable still, by attempting to
set it right. Here, her past practice in the Entertainment came to her
rescue, and urged her to go on instantly, in Miss Garth's voice, as if nothing
had happened.

"You mean well, Mrs. Lecount," she continued, "but you are doing harm instead of good. My pupils will accept no such compromise as you propose. I am sorry to have spoken violently, just now; I beg you will excuse me." She looked hard for information in the housekeeper's face while she spoke those conciliatory words. Mrs. Lecount baffled the look, by putting her handkerchief to her eyes. Had she, or had she not, noticed the momentary change in Magdalen's voice from the tones that were assumed to the tones that were natural? Impossible to say.

"What more can I do!" murmured Mrs. Lecount behind her handkerchief. "Give me time to think—give me time to recover myself. May I retire, sir, for a moment? My nerves are shaken by this sad scene. I must have a glass of water, or I think I shall faint. Don't go yet, Miss Garth. I beg you will give us time to set this sad matter right, if we can—I beg you will remain until I come back."

There were two doors of entrance to the room. One, the door into the front parlour, close at Magdalen's left hand. The other, the door into the back parlour, situated behind her. Mrs. Lecount politely retired—through the open folding-doors—by this latter means of exit, so as not to disturb the visitor by passing in front of her. Magdalen waited until she heard the door open and close again behind her; and then resolved to make the most of the opportunity which left her alone with Noel Vanstone. The utter hopelessness of rousing a generous impulse in that base nature, had now been proved by her own experience. The last chance left was to treat him like the craven creature he was, and to influence him through his fears.

Before she could speak, Noel Vanstone himself broke the silence. Cunningly as he strove to hide it, he was half angry, half alarmed at his housekeeper's desertion of him. He looked doubtingly at his visitor; he showed a nervous anxiety to conciliate her, until Mrs Lecount's return.

"Pray remember, ma'am, I never denied that this case was a hard one," he began. "You said just now you had no wish to offend me—and I'm sure I don't want to offend you. May I offer you some strawberries? Would you like to look at my father's bargains? I assure you, ma'am, I am naturally a gallant man; and I feel for both these sisters—especially the younger one. Touch me on the subject of the tender passion, and you touch me on a weak place. Nothing would please me more than to hear that Miss Vanstone's lover (I'm sure I always call her Miss Vanstone, and so does Lecount)—I say, ma'am, nothing would please me more than to hear that Miss Vanstone's lover had come back, and married her. If a loan of money would be likely to bring him back, and if the security offered was good, and if my lawyer thought me justified——"

"Stop, Mr. Vanstone," said Magdalen. "You are entirely mistaken in your estimate of the person you have to deal with. You are seriously wrong in supposing that the marriage of the younger sister—if she could be married in a week's time—would make any difference in the convictions which induced her to write to your father and to you. I don't deny that she may act from a mixture of motives. I don't deny that she clings to the hope of hastening her marriage, and to the hope of rescuing her sister from a life of dependence. But, if both those objects were accomplished by other means, nothing would induce her to leave you in possession of the inheritance which her father meant his children to have. I know her, Mr. Vanstone! She is a nameless, homeless, friendless wretch. The law which takes care of you, the law which takes care of all legitimate children, casts her like carrion to the winds. It is your law—not hers. She only knows it as the instrument of a vile oppression, an insufferable wrong. The sense of that wrong haunts her, like a possession of the devil. The resolution to right that wrong burns in her like fire. If that miserable girl was married and rich with millions to-morrow, do you think she would move an inch from her purpose? I tell you she would resist, to the last breath in her body, the vile injustice which has struck at the helpless children, through the calamity of their father's death! I tell you she would shrink from no means which a desperate woman can employ, to force that closed hand of yours open, or die in the attempt!"

She stopped abruptly. Once more, her own indomitable earnestness had betrayed her. Once more, the inborn nobility of that perverted nature had risen superior to the deception which it had stooped to practise. The scheme of the moment vanished from her mind's view; and the resolution of her life burst its way outward in her own words, in her own tones, pouring hotly and more hotly from her heart. She saw the abject mannikin before her, cowering silent in his chair. Had his fears left him sense enough to perceive the change in her voice? No: *his* face spoke the truth —his fears had bewildered him. This time, the chance of the moment had befriended her. The door behind her chair had not opened again yet. "No ears but his have heard me," she thought, with a sense of unutterable relief. " I have escaped Mrs. Lecount."

She had done nothing of the kind. Mrs. Lecount had never left the room.

After opening the door and closing it again, without going out, the housekeeper had noiselessly knelt down behind Magdalen's chair. Steadying herself against the post of the folding-door, she took a pair of scissors from her pocket, waited until Noel Vanstone (from whose view she was entirely hidden) had attracted Magdalen's attention by speaking to her; and then bent forward with the scissors ready in her hand. The skirt of the false Miss Garth's gown—the brown alpaca dress, with the white spots on it—touched the floor, within the housekeeper's reach. Mrs. Lecount lifted the outer of the two flounces which ran round the bottom of the dress, one over the other; softly cut away a little irregular fragment of stuff from the inner flounce; and neatly smoothed the outer one over it again, so as to hide the gap. By the time she had put the scissors back in her pocket, and had risen to her feet (sheltering herself behind the post of the folding-door), Magdalen had spoken her last words. Mrs. Lecount quietly repeated the ceremony of opening and shutting the back parlour door; and returned to her place.

"What has happened, sir, in my absence?" she inquired, addressing her master with a look of alarm. "You are pale; you are agitated! Oh, Miss Garth, have you forgotten the caution I gave you in the other room?"

"Miss Garth has forgotten everything," cried Noel Vanstone, recovering his lost composure on the reappearance of Mrs. Lecount. "Miss Garth has threatened me in the most outrageous manner. I forbid you to pity either of those two girls any more, Lecount—especially the younger one. She is the most desperate wretch I ever heard of! If she can't get my money by fair means, she threatens to have it by foul. Miss Garth has told me that to my face. To my face!" he repeated, folding his arms and looking mortally insulted.

"Compose yourself, sir," said Mrs. Lecount. "Pray compose yourself, and leave me to speak to Miss Garth.—I regret to hear, ma'am, that you have forgotten what I said to you in the next room. You have agitated Mr. Noel; you have compromised the interests you came here to plead; and you have only repeated what we knew before. The language you have allowed yourself to use in my absence, is the same language which your pupil was foolish enough to employ when she wrote for the second time, to my late master. How can a lady of your years and experience seriously repeat such nonsense? This girl boasts and threatens. She will do this; she will do that. You have her confidence, ma'am. Tell me, if you please, in plain words, what can she do?"

Sharply as the taunt was pointed, it glanced off harmless. Mrs. Lecount had planted her sting once too often. Magdalen rose in complete possession of her assumed character, and composedly terminated the interview. Ignorant as she was of what had happened behind her chair, she saw a change in Mrs. Lecount's look and manner, which warned her to run no more risks, and to trust herself no longer in the house.

"I am not in my pupil's confidence," she said. "Her own acts will answer your question when the time comes. I can only tell you, from my own knowledge of her, that she is no boaster. What she wrote to Mr. Michael Vanstone, was what she was prepared to do—what, I have reason to think, she was actually on the point of doing, when her plans were overthrown by his death. Mr. Michael Vanstone's son has only to persist in following his father's course to find, before long, that I am not mistaken in my pupil, and that I have not come here to intimidate him by empty threats. My errand is done. I leave Mr. Noel Vanstone with two alternatives to choose from. I leave him to share Mr. Andrew Vanstone's fortune with Mr. Andrew Vanstone's daughters—or to persist in his present refusal and face the consequences." She bowed, and walked to the door.

Noel Vanstone started to his feet, with anger and alarm struggling which should express itself first in his blank white face. Before he could open his lips, Mrs. Lecount's plump hands descended on his shoulders; put him softly back in his chair; and restored the plate of strawberries to its former position on his lap.

"Refresh yourself, Mr. Noel, with a few more strawberries," she said; "and leave Miss Garth to me."

She followed Magdalen into the passage, and closed the door of the room after her.

"Are you residing in London, ma'am?" asked Mrs. Lecount.

"No," replied Magdalen. "I reside in the country."

"If I want to write to you, where can I address my letter?"

"To the post-office, Birmingham," said Magdalen, mentioning the place which she had last left, and at which all letters were still addressed to her.

Mrs. Lecount repeated the direction to fix it in her memory—advanced two steps in the passage—and quietly laid her right hand on Magdalen's arm.

"A word of advice, ma'am," she said; "one word at parting. You are a bold woman and a clever woman. Don't be too bold; don't be too clever. You are risking more than you think for." She suddenly raised herself on tiptoe, and whispered the next words in Magdalen's ear. "*I hold you in the hollow of my hand!*" said Mrs. Lecount, with a fierce hissing emphasis on every syllable. Her left hand clenched itself stealthily as she spoke. It was the hand in which she had concealed the fragment of stuff from Magdalen's gown—the hand which held it fast at that moment.

"What do you mean?" asked Magdalen, pushing her back.

Mrs. Lecount glided away politely to open the house-door.

"I mean nothing now," she said; "wait a little, and time may show. One last question, ma'am, before I bid you good-bye. When your pupil was a little innocent child, did she ever amuse herself by building a house of cards?"

Magdalen impatiently answered by a gesture in the affirmative.

"Did you ever see her build up the house higher and higher," proceeded Mrs. Lecount, "till it was quite a pagoda of cards? Did you ever see her open her little child's eyes wide, and look at it, and feel so proud of what she had done already, that she wanted to do more? Did you ever see her steady her pretty little hand, and hold her innocent breath, and put one other card on the top—and lay the whole house, the instant afterwards, a heap of ruins on the table? Ah, you have seen that. Give her, if you please, a friendly message from me. I venture to say she has built the house high enough already; and I recommend her to be careful before she puts on that other card."

"She shall have your message," said Magdalen, with Miss Garth's bluntness, and Miss Garth's emphatic nod of the head. "But I doubt her minding it. Her hand is rather steadier than you suppose; and I think she will put on the other card."

"And bring the house down," said Mrs. Lecount.

"And build it up again," rejoined Magdalen. "I wish you good morning."

"Good morning," said Mrs. Lecount, opening the door. "One last word, Miss Garth. Do think of what I said in the back room! Do try the Golden Ointment for that sad affliction in your eyes!"

As Magdalen crossed the threshold of the door, she was met by the postman, ascending the house steps, with a letter picked out from the bundle in his hand. "Noel Vanstone, Esquire?" she heard the man say interrogatively, as she made her way down the front garden to the street.

She passed through the garden gate, little thinking from what new difficulty and new danger her timely departure had saved her. The letter which the postman had just delivered into the housekeeper's hands, was no other than the anonymous letter addressed to Noel Vanstone by Captain Wragge.

CHAPTER IV.

MRS. LECOUNT returned to the parlour, with the fragment of Magdalen's dress in one hand, and with Captain Wragge's letter in the other.

"Have you got rid of her?" asked Noel Vanstone. "Have you shut the door at last on Miss Garth?"

"Don't call her Miss Garth, sir," said Mrs. Lecount, smiling contemptuously. "She is as much Miss Garth as you are. We have been favoured by the performance of a clever masquerade; and if we had taken the disguise off our visitor, I think we should have found under it, Miss Vanstone herself.—Here is a letter for you, sir, which the postman has just left."

She put the letter on the table within her master's reach. Noel Vanstone's amazement at the discovery just communicated to him, kept his whole attention concentrated on the housekeeper's face. He never so much as looked at the letter when she placed it before him.

"Take my word for it, sir," proceeded Mrs. Lecount, composedly taking a chair. "When our visitor gets home she will put her grey hair away in a box, and will cure that sad affliction in her eyes with warm water and a sponge. If she had painted the marks on her face, as well as she painted the inflammation in her eyes, the light would have shown me nothing, and I should certainly have been deceived. But I saw the marks; I saw a young woman's skin under that dirty complexion of hers; I heard, in this room, a true voice in a passion, as well as a false voice talking with an accent,—and I don't believe in one morsel of that lady's personal appearance from top to toe. The girl herself in my opinion, Mr. Noel—and a bold girl too."

"Why didn't you lock the door and send for the police?" asked Mr. Noel. "My father would have sent for the police. You know, as well as I do, Lecount, my father would have sent for the police."

"Pardon me, sir," said Mrs. Lecount, "I think your father would have waited until he had got something more for the police to do than we have got for them yet. We shall see this lady again, sir. Perhaps, she will come here next time, with her own face and her own voice. I am curious to see what her own face is like. I am curious to know whether what I have heard of her voice in a passion, is enough to make me recognize her voice when she is calm. I possess a little memorial of her visit of which she is not aware; and she will not escape me so easily as she thinks. If it turns out a useful memorial, you shall know what it is. If not, I will abstain from troubling you on so trifling a subject.—Allow me to remind you, sir, of the letter under your hand. You have not looked at it yet."

Noel Vanstone opened the letter. He started as his eye fell on the first lines—hesitated—and then hurriedly read it through. The paper dropped from his hand, and he sank back in his chair. Mrs. Lecount sprang to her feet with the alacrity of a young woman, and picked up the letter.

"What has happened, sir?" she asked. Her face altered as she put the question; and her large black eyes hardened fiercely, in genuine astonishment and alarm.

"Send for the police," exclaimed her master. "Lecount, I insist on being protected. Send for the police!"

"May I read the letter, sir?"

He feebly waved his hand. Mrs. Lecount read the letter attentively, and put it aside, on the table, without a word, when she had done.

"Have you nothing to say to me?" asked Noel Vanstone, staring at his housekeeper in blank dismay. "Lecount, I'm to be robbed! The scoundrel who wrote that letter knows all about it, and won't tell me anything unless I pay him. I'm to be robbed! Here's property on this table worth thousands of pounds—property that can never be replaced—property that all the crowned heads in Europe could not produce if they tried. Lock me in, Lecount—and send for the police!"

Instead of sending for the police, Mrs. Lecount took a large green-paper fan from the chimney-piece, and seated herself opposite her master.

"You are agitated, Mr. Noel," she said, "you are heated. Let me cool you."

With her face as hard as ever—with less tenderness of look and manner than most women would have shown if they had been rescuing a half-drowned fly from a milk-jug—she silently and patiently fanned him for five minutes or more. No practised eye observing the peculiar bluish pallor of his complexion, and the marked difficulty with which he drew his breath, could have failed to perceive that the great organ of life was, in this man, what the housekeeper had stated it to be, too weak for the function which it was called on to perform. The heart laboured over its work, as if it had been the heart of a worn-out old man.

"Are you relieved, sir?" asked Mrs. Lecount. "Can you think a little? Can you exercise your better judgment?"

She rose and put her hand over his heart, with as much mechanical attention and as little genuine interest, as if she had been feeling the plates at dinner to ascertain if they had been properly warmed. "Yes," she went on, seating herself again, and resuming the exercise of the fan; "you are getting better already, Mr. Noel.—Don't ask me about this anonymous letter, until you have thought for yourself, and have given your own opinion first." She went on with the fanning, and looked him hard in the face all the time. "Think," she said; "think, sir, without troubling yourself to express your thoughts. Trust to my intimate sympathy with you to read them. Yes, Mr. Noel, this letter is a paltry attempt to frighten you. What does it say? It says you are the object of a conspiracy, directed by Miss Vanstone. We know that already—the lady of the inflamed eyes has told us. We snap our fingers at the conspiracy. What does the letter say next? It says the writer has valuable information to give you if you will pay for it. What did you call this person yourself, just now, sir?"

"I called him a scoundrel," said Noel Vanstone, recovering his self-importance, and raising himself gradually in his chair.

"I agree with you in that, sir, as I agree in everything else," proceeded Mrs. Lecount. "He is a scoundrel who really has this information, and who means what he says—or, he is a mouthpiece of Miss Vanstone's; and she has caused this letter to be written for the purpose of puzzling us by another form of disguise. Whether the letter is true, or whether the letter is false—am I not reading your own wiser thoughts, now, Mr. Noel?—you know better than to put your enemies on their guard by employing the police in this matter, too soon. I quite agree with you—no police just yet. You will allow this anonymous man or anonymous woman, to suppose you are easily frightened; you will lay a trap for the information in return for the trap laid for your money; you will answer the letter and see what comes of the answer; and you will only pay the expense of employing the police, when you know the expense is necessary. I agree with you again —no expense, if we can help it. In every particular, Mr. Noel, my mind and your mind in this matter, are one."

"It strikes you in that light, Lecount—does it?" said Noel Vanstone.

"I think so, myself; I certainly think so. I won't pay the police a farthing if I can possibly help it." He took up the letter again, and became fretfully perplexed over a second reading of it. "But the man wants money!" he broke out, impatiently. "You seem to forget, Lecount, that the man wants money."

"Money which you offer him, sir," rejoined Mrs. Lecount; "but—as your thoughts have already anticipated—money which you don't give him. No! no! you say to this man, 'Hold out your hand, sir;' and when he has held it, you give him a smack for his pains, and put your own hand back in your pocket.—I am so glad to see you laughing, Mr. Noel! so glad to see you getting back your good spirits. We will answer the letter by advertisement, as the writer directs—advertisement is so cheap! Your poor hand is trembling a little—shall I hold the pen for you? I am not fit to do more; but I can always promise to hold the pen."

Without waiting for his reply, she went into the back parlour, and returned with pen, ink, and paper. Arranging a blotting-book on her knees, and looking a model of cheerful submission, she placed herself once more in front of her master's chair.

"Shall I write from your dictation, sir?" she inquired. "Or, shall I make a little sketch, and will you correct it afterwards? I will make a little sketch. Let me see the letter. We are to advertise in the Times, and we are to address, 'An Unknown Friend.' What shall I say, Mr. Noel? Stay; I will write it, and then you can see for yourself: 'An Unknown Friend is requested to mention (by advertisement) an address at which a letter can reach him. The receipt of the information which he offers will be acknowledged by a reward of——' What sum of money do you wish me to set down, sir?"

"Set down nothing," said Noel Vanstone, with a sudden outbreak of impatience. "Money-matters are my business—I say money-matters are *my* business, Lecount. Leave it to me."

"Certainly, sir," replied Mrs. Lecount, handing her master the blotting-book. "You will not forget to be liberal in offering money, when you know beforehand you don't mean to part with it?"

"Don't dictate, Lecount! I won't submit to dictation!" said Noel Vanstone, asserting his own independence more and more impatiently. "I mean to conduct this business for myself. I am master, Lecount!"

"You are master, sir."

"My father was master before me. And I am my father's son. I tell you, Lecount, I am my father's son!"

Mrs. Lecount bowed submissively.

"I mean to set down any sum of money I think right," pursued Noel Vanstone, nodding his little flaxen head vehemently. "I mean to send this advertisement myself. The servant shall take it to the stationer's to be put into the Times. When I ring the bell twice, send the servant. You understand, Lecount? Send the servant."

Mrs. Lecount bowed again and walked slowly to the door. She knew to a nicety when to lead her master, and when to let him go alone. Experience had taught her to govern him in all essential points, by giving way to him afterwards on all points of minor detail. It was a characteristic of his weak nature—as it is of all weak natures—to assert itself obstinately on trifles. The filling in of the blank in the advertisement, was the trifle in this case; and Mrs. Lecount quieted her master's suspicions that she was leading him, by instantly conceding it. "My mule has kicked," she thought to herself, in her own language, as she opened the door. "I can do no more with him to-day."

"Lecount!" cried her master, as she stepped into the passage. "Come back."

Mrs. Lecount came back.

"You're not offended with me, are you?" asked Noel Vanstone, uneasily.

"Certainly not, sir," replied Mrs. Lecount. "As you said just now—you are master."

"Good creature! Give me your hand." He kissed her hand, and smiled in high approval of his own affectionate proceeding. "Lecount, you are a worthy creature!"

"Thank you, sir," said Mrs. Lecount. She curtseyed and went out. "If he had any brains in that monkey-head of his," she said to herself in the passage, "what a rascal he would be!"

Left by himself, Noel Vanstone became absorbed in anxious reflection over the blank space in the advertisement. Mrs. Lecount's apparently superfluous hint to him, to be liberal in offering money when he knew he had no intention of parting with it, had been founded on an intimate knowledge of his character. He had inherited his father's sordid love of money, without inheriting his father's hard-headed capacity for seeing the uses to which money can be put. His one idea in connection with his wealth, was the idea of keeping it. He was such an inborn miser, that the bare prospect of being liberal in theory only, daunted him. He took up the pen; laid it down again; and read the anonymous letter for the third time, shaking his head over it suspiciously. "If I offer this man a large sum of money," he thought, on a sudden; "how do I know he may not find a means of actually making me pay it? Women are always in a hurry. Lecount is always in a hurry. I have got the afternoon before me—I'll take the afternoon to consider it."

He fretfully put away the blotting-book, and the sketch of the advertisement, on the chair which Mrs. Lecount had just left. As he returned to his own seat, he shook his little head solemnly, and arranged his white dressing-gown over his knees, with the air of a man absorbed in anxious thought.

Minute after minute passed away ; the quarters and the half-hours succeeded each other on the dial of Mrs. Lecount's watch—and still Noel Vanstone remained lost in doubt; still no summons for the servant disturbed the tranquillity of the parlour bell.

* * * * * *

Meanwhile, after parting with Mrs. Lecount, Magdalen had cautiously abstained from crossing the road to her lodgings, and had only ventured to return after making a circuit in the neighbourhood. When she found herself once more in Vauxhall Walk, the first object which attracted her attention, was a cab drawn up before the door of the lodgings. A few steps more in advance showed her the landlady's daughter, standing at the cabdoor, engaged in a dispute with the driver on the subject of his fare. Noticing that the girl's back was turned towards her, Magdalen instantly profited by that circumstance, and slipped unobserved into the house.

She glided along the passage; ascended the stairs; and found herself, on the first landing, face to face with her travelling companion ! There stood Mrs. Wragge, with a pile of small parcels hugged up in her arms, anxiously waiting the issue of the dispute with the cabman in the street. To return was impossible—the sound of the angry voices below, was advancing into the passage. To hesitate was worse than useless. But one choice was left —the choice of going on—and Magdalen desperately took it. She pushed by Mrs. Wragge, without a word; ran into her own room; tore off her cloak, bonnet, and wig ; and threw them down out of sight, in the blank space between the sofa-bedstead and the wall.

For the first few moments, astonishment bereft Mrs. Wragge of the power of speech and rooted her to the spot where she stood. Two out of the collection of parcels in her arms fell from them on the stairs. The sight of that catastrophe roused her. " Thieves !" cried Mrs. Wragge, suddenly struck by an idea. " Thieves !"

Magdalen heard her through the room door, which she had not had time to close completely. " Is that you, Mrs. Wragge ?" she called out in her own voice. " What is the matter ?" She snatched up a towel while she spoke ; dipped it in water ; and passed it rapidly over the lower part of her face. At the sound of the familiar voice, Mrs. Wragge turned round—dropped a third parcel—and, forgetting it in her astonishment, ascended the second flight of stairs. Magdalen stepped out on the first-floor landing, with the towel held over her forehead as if she was suffering from headache. Her false eyebrows required time for their removal, and a headache assumed for the occasion, suggested the most convenient pretext she could devise for hiding them as they were hidden now.

" What are you disturbing the house for ?" she asked. " Pray be quiet, I am half blind with the headache."

" Anything wrong, ma'am ?" inquired the landlady, from the passage.

" Nothing whatever," replied Magdalen. " My friend is timid ; and the dispute with the cabman has frightened her. Pay the man what he wants, and let him go."

" Where is She?" asked Mrs. Wragge, in a tremulous whisper. " Where's the woman who scuttled by me into your room ?"

" Pooh !" said Magdalen. " No woman scuttled by you—as you call it. Look in and see for yourself."

She threw open the door. Mrs. Wragge walked into the room—looked all over it—saw nobody—and indicated her astonishment at the result, by dropping a fourth parcel, and trembling helplessly from head to foot.

" I saw her go in here," said Mrs. Wragge, in awe-struck accents. " A woman in a grey cloak and a poke bonnet. A rude woman. She scuttled by me, on the stairs—she did. Here's the room, and no woman in it. Give us a Prayer-Book !" cried Mrs. Wragge, turning deadly pale, and letting her whole remaining collection of parcels fall about her in a little cascade of commodities. " I want to read something Good. I want to think of my latter end. I've seen a Ghost !"

" Nonsense !" said Magdalen. " You're dreaming; the shopping has been too much for you. Go into your own room, and take your bonnet off."

" I've heard tell of ghosts in nightgowns; ghosts in sheets ; and ghosts in chains," proceeded Mrs Wragge, standing petrified in her own magic circle of linen-drapers' parcels. " Here's a worse ghost than any of 'em—a ghost in a grey cloak and a poke bonnet. I know what it is," continued Mrs. Wragge, melting into penitent tears. " It's a judgment on me for being so happy away from the captain. It's a judgment on me for having been down at heel in half the shops in London, first with one shoe and then with the other, all the time I've been out. I'm a sinful creature. Don't let go of me—whatever you do, my dear, don't let go of me !" She caught Magdalen fast by the arm, and fell into another trembling fit at the bare idea of being left by herself.

The one remaining chance, in such an emergency as this, was to submit to circumstances. Magdalen took Mrs. Wragge to a chair ; having first placed it in such a position as might enable her to turn her back on her travelling-companion, while she removed the false eyebrows by the help of a little water. " Wait a minute there," she said ; " and try if you can compose yourself, while I bathe my head."

" Compose myself?" repeated Mrs. Wragge. " How am I to compose myself when my head feels off my shoulders ? The worst Buzzing I ever had with the Cookery-book, was nothing to the Buzzing I've got now with the Ghost. Here's a miserable end to a holiday ! You may take me back again, my dear, whenever you like—I've had enough of it already !"

Having at last succeeded in removing the eyebrows, Magdalen was free to combat the unfortunate impression produced on her companion's mind, by every weapon of persuasion which her ingenuity could employ.

The attempt proved useless. Mrs. Wragge persisted—on evidence which, it may be remarked in parenthesis, would have satisfied many wiser ghost-seers than herself—in believing that she had been supernaturally favoured by a visitor from the world of spirits. All that Magdalen could do was to ascertain by cautious investigation, that Mrs. Wragge had not been quick enough to identify the supposed ghost with the character of the old north-country lady in the Entertainment. Having satisfied herself on this point, she had no resource but to leave the rest to the natural incapability of retaining impressions—unless those impressions were perpetually renewed—which was one of the characteristic infirmities of her companion's weak mind. After fortifying Mrs. Wragge by reiterated assurances that one appearance (according to all the laws and regulations of ghosts) meant nothing, unless it was immediately followed by two more— after patiently leading back her attention to the parcels dropped on the floor, and on the stairs—and after promising to keep the door of communication ajar between the two rooms, if Mrs. Wragge would engage on her side to retire to her own chamber, and to say no more on the terrible subject of the ghost—Magdalen at last secured the privilege of reflecting uninterruptedly on the events of that memorable day.

Two serious consequences had followed her first step forward. Mrs. Lecount had entrapped her into speaking in her own voice ; and accident had confronted her with Mrs. Wragge, in disguise.

What advantage had she gained to set against these disasters? The advantage of knowing more of Noel Vanstone and of Mrs. Lecount, than she might have discovered in months, if she had trusted to inquiries made for her by others. One uncertainty which had hitherto perplexed her, was set at rest already. The scheme she had privately devised against Michael Vanstone—which Captain Wragge's sharp insight had partially penetrated, when she first warned him that their partnership must be dissolved—was a scheme which she could now plainly see must be abandoned as hopeless, in the case of Michael Vanstone's son. The father's habits of speculation had been the pivot on which the whole machinery of her meditated conspiracy had been constructed to turn. No such vantage ground was discoverable in the doubly sordid character of the son. Noel Vanstone was invulnerable on the very point which had presented itself in his father as open to attack.

Having reached this conclusion, how was she to shape her future course? What new means could she discover, which would lead her secretly to her end, in defiance of Mrs. Lecount's malicious vigilance, and Noel Vanstone's miserly distrust?

She was seated before the looking-glass, mechanically combing out her hair, while that all-important consideration occupied her mind. The agitation of the moment had raised a feverish colour in her cheeks, and had brightened the light in her large grey eyes. She was conscious of looking her best; conscious how her beauty gained by contrast, after the removal of the disguise. Her lovely light brown hair, looked thicker and softer than ever, now that it had escaped from its imprisonment under the grey wig. She twisted it this way and that, with quick dexterous fingers; she laid it in masses on her shoulders; she threw it back from them in a heap, and turned sideways to see how it fell—to see her back and shoulders, freed from the artificial deformities of the padded cloak. After a moment, she faced the looking-glass once more; plunged both hands deep in her hair; and, resting her elbows on the table, looked closer and closer at the reflection of herself, until her breath began to dim the glass. " I can twist any man alive round my finger," she thought, with a smile of superb triumph, " as long as I keep my looks! If that contemptible wretch saw me now——" She shrank from following that thought to its end, with a sudden horror of herself: she drew back from the glass, shuddering, and put her hands over her face. " Oh, Frank !" she murmured, " but for you, what a wretch I might be !" Her eager fingers snatched the little white silk bag from its hiding-place in her bosom; her lips devoured it with silent kisses. " My darling ! my angel ! Oh, Frank, how I love you !" The tears gushed into her eyes. She passionately dried them, restored the bag to its place, and turned her back on the looking-glass. " No more of myself," she thought; " no more of my mad, miserable self for to-day !"

Shrinking from all further contemplation of her next step in advance—shrinking from the fast darkening future, with which Noel Vanstone was now associated in her inmost thoughts—she looked impatiently about the room for some homely occupation which might take her out of herself. The disguise which she had flung down between the wall and the bed recurred to her memory. It was impossible to leave it there. Mrs. Wragge (now occupied in sorting her parcels) might weary of her employment, might come in again at a moment's notice, might pass near the bed and see the grey cloak. What was to be done ?

Her first thought was to put the disguise back in her trunk. But, after what had happened, there was danger in trusting it so near to herself, while she and Mrs. Wragge were together under the same roof. She resolved to be rid of it that evening, and boldly determined on sending it back to Birmingham. Her bonnet-box fitted into her trunk. She took the box out, thrust in the wig and cloak; and remorselessly flattened down the bonnet at the top. The gown (which she had not yet taken off) was her own; Mrs. Wragge had been accustomed to see her in it—there was no need to send the gown back. Before closing the box, she hastily traced these lines on a sheet of paper : " I took the enclosed things away by mistake. Please keep them for me with the rest of my luggage in your possession, until you hear from me again." Putting the paper on the top of the bonnet, she directed the box to Captain Wragge, at Birmingham ;

took it down stairs immediately; and sent the landlady's daughter away
with it to the nearest Receiving House. "That difficulty is disposed of,"
she thought, as she went back to her own room again.

Mrs. Wragge was still occupied in sorting her parcels, on her narrow
little bed. She turned round with a faint scream, when Magdalen looked
in at her. "I thought it was the ghost again," said Mrs. Wragge. "I'm
trying to take warning, my dear, by what's happened to me. I've put all
my parcels straight, just as the captain would like to see 'em. I'm up at
heel with both shoes. If I close my eyes to-night—which I don't think I
shall—I'll go to sleep as straight as my legs will let me. And I'll never
have another holiday as long as I live. I hope I shall be forgiven," said
Mrs. Wragge, mournfully shaking her head. "I humbly hope I shall be
forgiven."

"Forgiven!" repeated Magdalen. "If other women wanted as little
forgiving as you do——Well! well! Suppose you open some of these
parcels. Come! I want to see what you have been buying to-day."

Mrs. Wragge hesitated, sighed penitently, considered a little, stretched
out her hand timidly towards one of the parcels, thought of the supernatural warning, and shrank back from her own purchases with a desperate
exertion of self-control.

"Open this one," said Magdalen, to encourage her: "What is it?"

Mrs. Wragge's faded blue eyes began to brighten dimly, in spite of her
remorse; but she self-denyingly shook her head. The master passion
of shopping might claim his own again—but the ghost was not laid yet.

"Did you get it a bargain?" asked Magdalen, confidentially.

"Dirt cheap!" cried poor Mrs. Wragge, falling headlong into the snare,
and darting at the parcel as eagerly as if nothing had happened.

Magdalen kept her gossiping over her purchases, for an hour or more;
and then wisely determined to distract her attention from all ghostly
recollections, in another way, by taking her out for a walk.

As they left the lodgings, the door of Noel Vanstone's house opened, and
the woman-servant appeared, bent on another errand. She was apparently
charged with a letter on this occasion, which she carried carefully in her
hand. Conscious of having formed no plan yet, either for attack or
defence, Magdalen wondered, with a momentary dread, whether Mrs.
Lecount had decided already on opening fresh communications, and
whether the letter was directed to "Miss Garth."

The letter bore no such address. Noel Vanstone had solved his pecuniary problem at last. The blank space in the advertisement was filled
up; and Mrs. Lecount's acknowledgment of the captain's anonymous
warning, was now on its way to insertion in the Times.

THE END OF THE THIRD SCENE.

BETWEEN THE SCENES.

PROGRESS OF THE STORY THROUGH THE POST.

I.

EXTRACT FROM THE ADVERTISING COLUMNS OF THE TIMES :—

"AN UNKNOWN FRIEND is requested to mention (by advertisement) an address at which a letter can reach him. The receipt of the information which he offers, will be acknowledged by a reward of Five Pounds."

II.

FROM CAPTAIN WRAGGE TO MAGDALEN.

" Birmingham, July 2nd, 1847.

"MY DEAR GIRL,

" The box containing the articles of costume which you took away by mistake, has come safely to hand. Consider it under my special protection, until I hear from you again.

" I embrace this opportunity to assure you, once more, of my unalterable fidelity to your interests. Without attempting to intrude myself into your confidence, may I inquire whether Mr. Noel Vanstone has consented to do you justice? I greatly fear he has declined—in which case, I can lay my hand on my heart, and solemnly declare that his meanness revolts me. Why do I feel a foreboding that you have appealed to him in vain? Why do I find myself viewing this fellow in the light of a noxious insect? We are total strangers to each other; I have no sort of knowledge of him, except the knowledge I picked up in making your inquiries. Has my intense sympathy with your interests made my perceptions prophetic? or, to put it fancifully, is there really such a thing as a former state of existence? and has Mr. Noel Vanstone mortally insulted me—say, in some other planet?

" I write, my dear Magdalen, as you see, with my customary dash of humour. But I am serious in placing my services at your disposal. Don't let the question of terms cause you an instant's hesitation. I accept, beforehand, any terms you like to mention. If your present plans point that way—I am ready to squeeze Mr. Noel Vanstone, in your interests, till the gold oozes out of him at every pore. Pardon the coarseness of this metaphor. My anxiety to be of service to you rushes into words; lays my meaning, in the rough, at your feet; and leaves your taste to polish it with the choicest ornaments of the English language.

"How is my unfortunate wife? I am afraid you find it quite impossible to keep her up at heel, or to mould her personal appearance into harmony with the eternal laws of symmetry and order. Does she attempt to be too familiar with you? I have always been accustomed to check her, in this respect. She has never been permitted to call me anything but Captain; and on the rare occasions, since our union, when circumstances may have obliged her to address me by letter, her opening form of salutation has been rigidly restricted to 'Dear Sir.' Accept these trifling domestic particulars as suggesting hints which may be useful to you in managing Mrs. Wragge; and believe me, in anxious expectation of hearing from you again,

"Devotedly yours,
"HORATIO WRAGGE."

III.

FROM NORAH TO MAGDALEN.

Forwarded, with the Two Letters that follow it, from the Post Office, Birmingham.

"Westmoreland House, Kensington,
"July 1st.

"MY DEAREST MAGDALEN,

"When you write next (and pray write soon!) address your letter to me at Miss Garth's. I have left my situation; and some little time may elapse before I find another.

"Now it is all over, I may acknowledge to you, my darling, that I was not happy. I tried hard to win the affection of the two little girls I had to teach; but they seemed, I am sure I can't tell why, to dislike me from the first. Their mother I have no reason to complain of. But their grandmother, who was really the ruling power in the house, made my life very hard to me. My inexperience in teaching was a constant subject of remark with her; and my difficulties with the children were always visited on me as if they had been entirely of my own making. I tell you this, so that you may not suppose I regret having left my situation. Far from it, my love—I am glad to be out of the house.

"I have saved a little money, Magdalen; and I should so like to spend it in staying a few days with you. My heart aches for a sight of my sister; my ears are weary for the sound of her voice. A word from you, telling me where we can meet, is all I want. Think of it—pray think of it.

"Don't suppose I am discouraged by this first check. There are many kind people in the world; and some of them may employ me next time. The way to happiness is often very hard to find; harder, I almost think, for women than for men. But, if we only try patiently, and try long enough, we reach it at last—in Heaven, if not on earth. I think *my* way now, is the way which leads to seeing you again. Don't forget that, my love, the next time you think of

"NORAH."

IV.

FROM MISS GARTH TO MAGDALEN.

"Westmoreland House, July 1st.

"MY DEAR MAGDALEN,

"You have no useless remonstrances to apprehend, at the sight of my handwriting. My only object in this letter is to tell you something, which I know your sister will not tell you of her own accord. She is entirely ignorant that I am writing to you. Keep her in ignorance, if you wish to spare her unnecessary anxiety—and me unnecessary distress.

"Norah's letter, no doubt, tells you that she has left her situation. I feel it my painful duty to add, that she has left it on your account.

"The matter occurred in this manner. Messrs. Wyatt, Pendril, and Gwilt are the solicitors of the gentleman in whose family Norah was employed. The life which you have chosen for yourself was known, as long ago as December last, to all the partners. You were discovered performing in public at Derby by the person who had been employed to trace you at York; and that discovery was communicated by Mr. Wyatt to Norah's employer, a few days since, in reply to direct inquiries about you no that gentleman's part. His wife, and his mother (who lives with him) had expressly desired that he would make those inquiries; their doubts having been aroused by Norah's evasive answers when they questioned her about her sister. You know Norah too well to blame her for this. Evasion was the only escape your present life had left her from telling a downright falsehood.

"That same day, the two ladies of the family, the elder and the younger, sent for your sister; and told her they had discovered that you were a public performer, roaming from place to place in the country, under an assumed name. They were just enough not to blame Norah for this; they were just enough to acknowledge that her conduct had been as irreproachable, as I had guaranteed it should be when I got her the situation. But, at the same time, they made it a positive condition of her continuing in their employment, that she should never permit you to visit her at their house—or to meet her and walk out with her when she was in attendance on the children. Your sister—who has patiently born all hardships that

fell on herself—instantly resented the slur cast on *you*. She gave her
employers warning on the spot. High words followed; and she left the
house that evening.

"I have no wish to distress you by representing the loss of this situation
in the light of a disaster. Norah was not so happy in it, as I had hoped
and believed she would be. It was impossible for me to know beforehand,
that the children were sullen and intractable—or that the husband's mother
was accustomed to make her domineering disposition felt by every one in
the house. I will readily admit that Norah is well out of this situation.
But the harm does not stop here. For all you and I know to the contrary,
the harm may go on. What has happened in this situation, may happen
in another. Your way of life, however pure your conduct may be—and I
will do you the justice to believe it pure—is a suspicious way of life to all
respectable people. I have lived long enough in this world to know, that
the Sense of Propriety, in nine Englishwomen out of ten, makes no allowances and feels no pity. Norah's next employers may discover you ; and
Norah may throw up a situation next time, which we may never be able to
find for her again.

"I leave you to consider this. My child ! don't think I am hard on you.
I am jealous for your sister's tranquillity. If you will forget the past,
Magdalen, and come back—trust to your old governess to forget it too, and
to give you the home which your father and mother once gave her.

                    "Your friend, my dear, always,

                                        "HARRIET GARTH."

                                V.

                FROM FRANCIS CLARE, JUN., TO MAGDALEN.

                                        "Shanghai, China,
                                            "April 23rd, 1847.
"MY DEAR MAGDALEN,

"I have deferred answering your letter, in consequence of the distracted state of my mind, which made me unfit to write to you. I am still
unfit—but I feel I ought to delay no longer. My sense of honour fortifies
me ; and I undergo the pain of writing this letter.

"My prospects in China are all at an end. The Firm, to which I was
brutally consigned as if I was a bale of merchandise, has worn out my
patience by a series of petty insults ; and I have felt compelled from motives
of self-respect, to withdraw my services, which were undervalued from the
first. My returning to England, under these circumstances, is out of the
question. I have been too cruelly used in my own country to wish to go
back to it—even if I could. I propose embarking on board a private
trading vessel in these seas, in a mercantile capacity, to make my way, if I

can, for myself. How it will end, or what will happen to me next, is more than I can say. It matters little what becomes of me. I am a wanderer and an exile, entirely through the fault of others. The unfeeling desire at home to get rid of me, has accomplished its object. I am got rid of for good.

"There is only one more sacrifice left for me to make—the sacrifice of my heart's dearest feelings. With no prospects before me, with no chance of coming home, what hope can I feel of performing my engagement to yourself? None! A more selfish man than I am, might hold you to that engagement; a less considerate man than I am, might keep you waiting for years —and to no purpose after all. Cruelly as they have been trampled on, my feelings are too sensitive to allow me to do this. I write it with the tears in my eyes—you shall not link your fate to an outcast. Accept these heart-broken lines as releasing you from your promise. Our engagement is at an end.

"The one consolation which supports me, in bidding you farewell, is— that neither of us is to blame. You may have acted weakly, under my father's influence, but I am sure you acted for the best. Nobody knew what the fatal consequences of driving me out of England would be, but myself—and I was not listened to. I yielded to my father, I yielded to you; and this is the end of it!

"I am suffering too acutely to write more. May you never know what my withdrawal from our engagement has cost me! I beg you will not blame yourself. It is not your fault that I have had all my energies misdirected by others—it is not your fault that I have never had a fair chance of getting on in life. Forget the deserted wretch, who breathes his heartfelt prayers for your happiness, and who will ever remain your friend and well-wisher,

"FRANCIS CLARE, JUN."

VI.

FROM FRANCIS CLARE, SEN., TO MAGDALEN.
Enclosing the preceding Letter.

"I always told your poor father my son was a Fool; but I never knew he was a Scoundrel until the mail came in from China. I have every reason to believe that he has left his employers under the most disgraceful circumstances. Forget him from this time forth, as I do. When you and I last set eyes on each other, you behaved well to me in this business. All I can now say in return, I do say. My girl, I am sorry for you.

"F. C."

VII.

From Mrs. Wragge to her Husband.

"dear sir for mercy's sake come here and help us She had a dreadful letter I don't know what yesterday but she read it in bed and when I went in with her breakfast I found her dead and if the doctor had not been two doors off nobody else could have brought her to life again and she sits and looks dreadful and wont speak a word her eyes frighten me so I shake from head to foot oh please do come I keep things as tidy as I can and I do like her so and she used to be so kind to me and the landlord says he's afraid she'll destroy herself I wish I could write straight but I do shake so your dutiful wife matilda wragge excuse faults and beg you on my knees come and help us the Doctor good man will put some of his own writing into this for fear you can't make out mine and remain once more your dutiful wife matilda wragge."

Added by the Doctor.

"Sir,—I beg to inform you that I was yesterday called into a neighbour's, in Vauxhall Walk, to attend a young lady who had been suddenly taken ill. I recovered her with great difficulty from one of the most obstinate fainting fits I ever remember to have met with. Since that time she has had no relapse, but there is apparently some heavy distress weighing on her mind, which it has hitherto been found impossible to remove. She sits, as I am informed, perfectly silent, and perfectly unconscious of what goes on about her, for hours together, with a letter in her hand, which she will allow nobody to take from her. If this state of depression continues, very distressing mental consequences may follow; and I only do my duty in suggesting that some relative or friend should interfere who has influence enough to rouse her.

"Your obedient servant,
"Richard Jarvis, M.R.C.S."

VIII.

From Norah to Magdalen.

"July 5th.

"For God's sake, write me one line to say if you are still at Birmingham, and where I can find you there! I have just heard from old Mr. Clare. Oh, Magdalen, if you have no pity on yourself, have some pity on me! The thought of you alone among strangers, the thought of you heart-broken under this dreadful blow, never leaves me for an instant. No words can tell how I feel for you! My own love, remember the better days at home before that cowardly villain stole his way into your heart;

remember the happy time at Combe-Raven, when we were always together. Oh, don't, don't treat me like a stranger! We are alone in the world now —let me come and comfort you—let me be more than a sister to you, if J can. One line—only one line to tell me where I can find you!"

IX.

FROM MAGDALEN TO NORAH.

"July 7th.

"MY DEAREST NORAH,

"All that your love for me can wish, your letter has done. You, and you alone, have found your way to my heart. I could think again, I could feel again, after reading what you have written to me. Let this assurance quiet your anxieties. My mind lives and breathes once more— it was dead until I got your letter.

"The shock I have suffered has left a strange quietness in me. I feel as if I had parted from my former self—as if the hopes, once so dear to me, had all gone back to some past time, from which I am now far removed. I can look at the wreck of my life more calmly, Norah, than you could look at it, if we were both together again. I can trust myself, already, to write to Frank.

"My darling, I think no woman ever knows how utterly she has given herself up to the man she loves—until that man has ill-treated her. Can you pity my weakness if I confess to having felt a pang at my heart when I read that part of your letter which calls Frank a coward and a villain? Nobody can despise me for this, as I despise myself. I am like a dog who crawls back and licks the master's hand that has beaten him. But it is sc —I would confess it to nobody but you—indeed, indeed it is so. He has deceived and deserted me; he has written me a cruel farewell—but don't call him a villain! If he repented, and came back to me, I would die rather than marry him now—but it grates on me to see that word coward written against him in your hand! If he is weak of purpose, who tried his weakness beyond what it could bear? Do you think this would have happened if Michael Vanstone had not robbed us of our own, and forced Frank away from me to China? In a week from to-day, the year of waiting would have come to an end; and I should have been Frank's wife, if my marriage portion had not been taken from me.

"You will say—after what has happened, it is well that I have escaped. My love! there is something perverse in my heart, which answers—No! Better have been Frank's wretched wife than the free woman I am now.

"I have not written to him. He sends me no address at which I could write, even if I would. But I have not the wish. I will wait, before I send him *my* farewell. If a day ever comes when I have the fortune which my father once promised I should bring to him—do you know what I would do with it? I would send it all to Frank, as my revenge on him for his letter; as the last farewell word, on my side, to the man who has deserted me. Let me live.for that day! Let me live, Norah, in the hope of better times for *you*, which is all the hope I have left. When I think of your hard life, I can almost feel the tears once more in my weary eyes. I can almost think I have come back again to my former self.

"You will not think me hard-hearted and ungrateful, if I say that we must wait a little yet, before we meet? I want to be more fit to see you than I am now. I want to put Frank farther away from me, and to bring you nearer still. Are these good reasons? I don't know—don't ask me for reasons. Take the kiss I have put for you here, where the little circle is drawn on the paper; and let that bring us together for the present, till I write again. Good-bye, my love. My heart is true to you, Norah—but I dare not see you yet.

" MAGDALEN."

X.

FROM MAGDALEN TO MISS GARTH.

"MY DEAR MISS GARTH,

"I have been long in answering your letter; but you know what has happened, and you will forgive me.

"All that I have to say may be said in few words. You may depend on my never making the general Sense of Propriety my enemy again: I am getting knowledge enough of the world to make it my accomplice next time. Norah will never leave another situation on my account—my life, as a public performer, is at an end. It was harmless enough, God knows —I may live, and so may you, to mourn the day when I parted from it— but I shall never return to it again. It has left me, as Frank has left me, as all my better thoughts have left me—except my thoughts of Norah.

"Enough of myself! Shall I tell you some news to brighten this dull letter? Mr. Michael Vanstone is dead; and Mr. Noel Vanstone has succeeded to the possession of my fortune and Norah's. He is quite worthy of his inheritance. In his father's place, he would have ruined us as his father did.

"I have no more to say that you would care to know. Don't be distressed about me. I am trying to recover my spirits—I am trying to forget the poor deluded girl who was foolish enough to be fond of Frank, in the old days at Combe-Raven. Sometimes, a pang comes which tells me the girl won't be forgotten—but not often.

"It was very kind of you, when you wrote to such a lost creature as I am, to sign yourself—*always my friend*. 'Always' is a bold word, my dear old governess! I wonder whether you will ever want to recall it? It will make no difference, if you do, in the gratitude I shall always feel for the trouble you took with me, when I was a little girl. I have ill repaid that trouble—ill repaid your kindness to me in after life. I ask your pardon and your pity. The best thing you can do for both of us, is to forget me. Affectionately yours,

"MAGDALEN.

"P.S.—I open the envelope to add one line. For God's sake, don't show this letter to Norah!"

XI.

FROM MAGDALEN TO CAPTAIN WRAGGE.

"Vauxhall Walk, July 17th.

"If I am not mistaken, it was arranged that I should write to you at Birmingham, as soon as I felt myself composed enough to think of the future. My mind is settled at last; and I am now able to accept the services which you have unreservedly offered to me.

"I beg you will forgive the manner in which I received you, on your arrival in this house, after hearing the news of my sudden illness. I was quite incapable of controlling myself—I was suffering an agony of mind which for the time deprived me of my senses. It is only your due that I should now thank you for treating me with great forbearance, at a time when forbearance was mercy.

"I will mention what I wish you to do, as plainly and briefly as I can.

"In the first place, I request you to dispose (as privately as possible) of every article of costume used in the dramatic Entertainment. I have done with our performances for ever; and I wish to be set free from everything which might accidentally connect me with them in the future. The key of my box is enclosed in this letter.

"The other box, which contains my own dresses, you will be kind enough to forward to this house. I do not ask you to bring it yourself, because I have a far more important commission to intrust to you.

"Referring to the note which you left for me at your departure, I conclude that you have, by this time, traced Mr. Noel Vanstone from Vauxhall Walk to the residence which he is now occupying. If you have made the discovery—and if you are quite sure of not having drawn the attention either of Mrs. Lecount or her master to yourself—I wish you to arrange immediately for my residing (with you and Mrs. Wragge) in the same town or village in which Mr. Noel Vanstone has taken up his abode. I write this, it is hardly necessary to say, under the impression that, wherever he may now be living, he is settled in the place for some little time.

"If you can find a small furnished house for me on these conditions, which is to be let by the month, take it for a month certain to begin with. Say that it is for your wife, your niece, and yourself; and use any assumed name you please, as long as it is a name that can be trusted to defeat the most suspicious inquiries. I leave this to your experience in such matters. The secret of who we really are, must be kept as strictly as if it was a secret on which our lives depend.

"Any expenses to which you may be put in carrying out my wishes, I will immediately repay. If you easily find the sort of house I want, there is no need for your returning to London to fetch us. We can join you as soon as we know where to go. The house must be perfectly respectable, and must be reasonably near to Mr. Noel Vanstone's present residence, wherever that is.

"You must allow me to be silent in this letter as to the object which I have now in view. I am unwilling to risk an explanation in writing. When all our preparations are made, you shall hear what I propose to do from my own lips; and I shall expect you to tell me plainly in return, whether you will, or will not, give me the help I want, on the best terms which I am able to offer you.

"One word more before I seal up this letter.

"If any opportunity falls in your way, after you have taken the house, and before we join you, of exchanging a few civil words either with Mr. Noel Vanstone or Mrs. Lecount, take advantage of it. It is very important to my present object that we should become acquainted with each other—as the purely accidental result of our being near neighbours. I want you to smooth the way towards this end, if you can, before Mrs. Wragge and I come to you. Pray throw away no chance of observing Mrs. Lecount, in particular, very carefully. Whatever help you can give me at the outset, in blindfolding that woman's sharp eyes, will be the most precious help I have ever received at your hands.

"There is no need to answer this letter immediately—unless I have written it under a mistaken impression of what you have accomplished since leaving London. I have taken our lodgings on for another week; and I can wait to hear from you, until you are able to send me such news as I wish to receive. You may be quite sure of my patience for the future, under all possible circumstances. My caprices are at an end; and my violent temper has tried your forbearance for the last time.

"MAGDALEN."

XII.

From Captain Wragge to Magdalen.

"North Shingles Villa, Aldborough, Suffolk,
"July 22nd.

"My dear Girl,

"Your letter has charmed and touched me. Your excuses have gone straight to my heart; and your confidence in my humble abilities has followed in the same direction. The pulse of the old militiaman throbs with pride as he thinks of the trust you have placed in him, and vows to deserve it. Don't be surprised at this genial outburst. All enthusiastic natures must explode occasionally: and *my* form of explosion is—Words.

"Everything you wanted me to do, is done. The house is taken; the name is found; and I am personally acquainted with Mrs. Lecount. After reading this general statement, you will naturally be interested in possessing your mind next of the accompanying details. Here they are, at your service:

"The day after leaving you in London, I traced Mr. Noel Vanstone to this curious little sea-side snuggery. One of his father's innumerable bargains was a house at Aldborough—a rising watering-place, or Mr. Michael Vanstone would not have invested a farthing in it. In this house the despicable little miser who lived rent free in London, now lives rent free again, on the coast of Suffolk. He is settled in his present abode for the summer and autumn; and you and Mrs. Wragge have only to join me here, to be established five doors away from him in this elegant villa. I have got the whole house for three guineas a week, with the option of remaining through the autumn at the same price. In a fashionable watering-place, such a residence would have been cheap at double the money.

"Our new name has been chosen with a wary eye to your suggestions. My books—I hope you have not forgotten my Books?—contain, under the heading of *Skins To Jump Into*, a list of individuals retired from this mortal scene, with whose names, families, and circumstances, I am well acquainted. Into some of those Skins I have been compelled to Jump, in the exercise of my profession, at former periods of my career. Others are still in the condition of new dresses, and remain to be tried on. The Skin which will exactly fit us, originally clothed the bodies of a family named Bygrave. I am in Mr. Bygrave's skin at this moment—and it fits without a wrinkle. If you will oblige me by slipping into Miss Bygrave (Christian name, Susan); and if you will afterwards push Mrs. Wragge—anyhow; head foremost if you like—into Mrs. Bygrave (Christian name, Julia), the transformation will be complete. Permit me to inform you that I am your paternal uncle. My worthy brother was established twenty years ago, in the mahogany and logwood trade at Belize, Honduras. He died in that place; and is buried on the south-west side of the local cemetery, with a neat monument of native wood carved by a self-taught negro artist. Nineteen months afterwards, his widow died of apoplexy at a boarding-house in Cheltenham. She was supposed to be the most corpulent woman in England; and was accommodated on the ground floor of the house in consequence of the difficulty of getting her up and down stairs. You are her only child; you have been under my care since the sad event at Cheltenham; you are twenty-one years old on the second of August next; and, corpulence excepted, you are the living image of your mother. I trouble you with these specimens of my intimate knowledge of our new family Skin, to quiet your mind on the subject of future inquiries. Trust to me and my books to satisfy any amount of inquiry. In the mean time, write down our new name and address, and see how they strike you :— 'Mr. Bygrave, Mrs. Bygrave, Miss Bygrave.; North Shingles Villa, Ald-borough.' Upon my life, it reads remarkably well!

"The last detail I have to communicate refers to my acquaintance with Mrs. Lecount.

"We met yesterday, in the grocer's shop here. Keeping my ears open, I found that Mrs. Lecount wanted a particular kind of tea, which the man had not got, and which he believed could not be procured any nearer than Ipswich. I instantly saw my way to beginning an acquaintance, at the trifling expense of a journey to that flourishing city. ' I have business, to-day, in Ipswich,' I said, ' and I propose returning to Alborough (if I can get back in time) this evening. Pray allow me to take your order for the tea, and to bring it back with my own parcels.' Mrs. Lecount politely declined giving me the trouble—I politely insisted on taking it. We fell into conversation. There is no need to trouble you with our talk. The result of it on my mind is—that Mrs. Lecount's one weak point, if she has such a thing at all, is a taste for science, implanted by her deceased hus-band, the Professor. I think I see a chance here, of working my way into her good graces, and casting a little needful dust into those handsome black eyes of hers. Acting on this idea, when I purchased the lady's tea at Ips-wich, I also bought on my own account that far-famed pocket manual of knowledge, ' Joyce's Scientific Dialogues.'* Possessing, as I do, a quick memory and boundless confidence in myself, I propose privately inflating my new skin with as much ready-made science as it will hold, and present-ing Mr. Bygrave to Mrs. Lecount's notice in the character of the most highly informed man she has met with since the Professor's death. The necessity of blindfolding that woman (to use your own admirable expres-sion) is as clear to me as to you. If it is to be done in the way I propose, make your mind easy—Wragge, inflated by Joyce, is the man to do it.

" You now have my whole budget of news. Am I, or am I not, worthy of your confidence in me? I say nothing of my devouring anxiety to know what your objects really are—that anxiety will be satisfied when we meet. Never yet, my dear girl, did I long to administer a productive pecuniary Squeeze to any human creature, as I long to administer it to Mr. Noel Vanstone. I say no more. *Verbum sap.** Pardon the pedantry of a Latin quotation, and believe me,

> "Entirely yours,
> "HORATIO WRAGGE.

"P. S.—I await my instructions, as you requested. You have only to say whether I shall return to London for the purpose of escorting you to this place—or whether I shall wait here to receive you. The house is in perfect order—the weather is charming—and the sea is as smooth as Mrs. Lecount's apron. She has just passed the window; and we have exchanged bows. A sharp woman, my dear Magdalen—but Joyce and I together, may prove a trifle too much for her."

XIII.

Extract from the East Suffolk Argus.

"ALDBOROUGH.—We notice with pleasure the arrival of visitors to this healthful and far-famed watering-place, earlier in the season than usual during the present year. *Esto Perpetua**is all we have to say.

"VISITORS' LIST.—Arrivals since our last. North Shingles Villa—Mrs. Bygrave; Miss Bygrave."

THE FOURTH SCENE.

ALDBOROUGH, SUFFOLK.*

———

CHAPTER I.

THE most striking spectacle presented to a stranger by the shores of Suffolk, is the extraordinary defencelessness of the land against the encroachments of the sea.

At Aldborough, as elsewhere on this coast, local traditions are, for the most part, traditions which have been literally drowned. The site of the old town, once a populous and thriving port, has almost entirely disappeared in the sea. The German Ocean*has swallowed up streets, market-places, jetties, and public walks; and the merciless waters, consummating their work of devastation, closed, no longer than eighty years since, over the salt-master's cottage at Aldborough, now famous in memory only, as the birth-place of the poet CRABBE.*

Thrust back year after year by the advancing waves, the inhabitants have receded, in the present century, to the last morsel of land which is firm enough to be built on—a strip of ground hemmed in between a marsh on one side and the sea on the other. Here—trusting for their future security to certain sandhills which the capricious waves have thrown up to encourage them—the people of Aldborough have boldly established their quaint little watering-place. The first fragment of their earthly possessions, is a low natural dyke of shingle, surmounted by a public path which runs parallel with the sea. Bordering this path in a broken, uneven line are the villa residences of modern Aldborough—fanciful little houses, standing mostly in their own gardens, and possessing here and there, as horticultural ornaments, staring figure-heads of ships, doing duty for statues among the flowers. Viewed from the low level on which these villas stand, the sea, in certain conditions of the atmosphere, appears to be higher than the land : coasting vessels gliding by, assume gigantic proportions, and look alarmingly near the windows. Intermixed with the houses of the better sort, are buildings of other forms and periods. In one direction, the tiny Gothic town-hall of old Aldborough—once the centre of the vanished port and borough—now stands fronting the modern villas close on the margin of the sea. At another point, a wooden tower of observation, crowned by the figure-head of a wrecked Russian vessel, rises high above the neighbouring

houses ; and discloses through its scuttle-window, grave men in dark
clothing, seated on the topmost story, perpetually on the watch—the pilots
of Aldborough looking out from their tower, for ships in want of help.
Behind the row of buildings thus curiously intermingled, runs the one straggling street of the town, with its sturdy pilots' cottages, its mouldering
marine storehouses, and its composite shops. Towards the northern end,
this street is bounded by the one eminence visible over all the marshy flat
—a low wooded hill on which the church is built. At its opposite extremity, the street leads to a deserted martello tower, and to the forlorn outlying suburb of Slaughden, between the river Alde and the sea. Such are
the main characteristics of this curious little outpost on the shores of England, as it appears at the present time.

On a hot and cloudy July afternoon, and on the second day which had
elapsed since he had written to Magdalen, Captain Wragge sauntered through
the gate of North Shingles Villa, to meet the arrival of the coach, which
then connected Aldborough with the Eastern Counties Railway. He
reached the principal inn as the coach drove up ; and was ready at the door
to receive Magdalen and Mrs. Wragge, on their leaving the vehicle.

The captain's reception of his wife was not characterized by an instant's
unnecessary waste of time. He looked distrustfully at her shoes—raised
himself on tiptoe—set her bonnet straight for her with a sharp tug—said,
in a loud whisper, "hold your tongue "—and left her, for the time being,
without further notice. His welcome to Magdalen, beginning with the usual
flow of words, stopped suddenly in the middle of the first sentence. Captain Wragge's eye was a sharp one ; and it instantly showed him something
in the look and manner of his old pupil which denoted a serious change.

There was a settled composure on her face which, except when she spoke,
made it look as still and cold as marble. Her voice was softer and more
equable, her eyes were steadier, her step was slower than of old. When she
smiled, the smile came and went suddenly, and showed a little nervous con-
traction on one side of her mouth, never visible there before. She was
perfectly patient with Mrs. Wragge ; she treated the captain with a courtesy and consideration entirely new in his experience of her—but she was
interested in nothing. The curious little shops in the back street ; the high
impending sea ; the old town-hall on the beach ; the pilots, the fishermen,
the passing ships—she noticed all these objects as indifferently as if Aldborough had been familiar to her from her infancy. Even when the captain
drew up at the garden-gate of North Shingles, and introduced her triumphantly to the new house, she hardly looked at it. The first question she
asked related, not to her own residence, but to Noel Vanstone's.

"How near to us does he live ?" she inquired, with the only betrayal of
emotion which had escaped her yet.

Captain Wragge answered by pointing to the fifth villa from North Shingles, on the Slaughden side of Aldborough. Magdalen suddenly drew back from the garden-gate as he indicated the situation, and walked away by herself to obtain a nearer view of the house.

Captain Wragge looked after her, and shook his head discontentedly.

"May I speak now?" inquired a meek voice behind him, articulating respectfully ten inches above the top of his straw hat.

The captain turned round, and confronted his wife. The more than ordinary bewilderment visible in her face, at once suggested to him that Magdalen had failed to carry out the directions in his letter; and that Mrs. Wragge had arrived at Aldborough, without being properly aware of the total transformation to be accomplished in her identity and her name. The necessity of setting this doubt at rest was too serious to be trifled with; and Captain Wragge instituted the necessary inquiries without a moment's delay.

"Stand straight, and listen to me," he began. "I have a question to ask you. Do you know whose Skin you are in at this moment? Do you know that you are dead and buried in London; and that you have risen like a phœnix from the ashes of Mrs. Wragge? No! you evidently don't know it. This is perfectly disgraceful. What is your name?"

"Matilda," answered Mrs. Wragge, in a state of the densest bewilderment.

"Nothing of the sort!" cried the captain, fiercely. "How dare you tell me your name's Matilda? Your name is Julia. Who am I? Hold that basket of sandwiches straight, or I'll pitch it into the sea!—Who am I?"

"I don't know," said Mrs. Wragge, meekly taking refuge in the negative side of the question this time.

"Sit down!" said her husband, pointing to the low garden wall of North Shingles Villa. "More to the right! More still! That will do. You don't know?" repeated the captain, sternly confronting his wife, as soon as he had contrived, by seating her, to place her face on a level with his own. "Don't let me hear you say that a second time. Don't let me have a woman who doesn't know who I am, to operate on my beard to-morrow morning. Look at me! More to the left—more still—that will do. Who am I? I'm Mr. Bygrave—Christian name, Thomas. Who are you? You're Mrs. Bygrave—Christian name, Julia. Who is that young lady who travelled with you from London? That young lady is Miss Bygrave—Christian name, Susan. I'm her clever uncle Tom; and you're her addle-headed aunt Julia. Say it all over to me instantly, like the Catechism! What is your name?"

"Spare my poor head!" pleaded Mrs. Wragge. "Oh please spare my poor head till I've got the stage-coach out of it!"

"Don't distress her," said Magdalen, joining them at that moment. "She will learn it in time. Come into the house."

Captain Wragge shook his wary head once more. "We are beginning badly," he said, with less politeness than usual. "My wife's stupidity stands in our way already."

They went into the house. Magdalen was perfectly satisfied with all the captain's arrangements; she accepted the room which he had set apart for her; approved of the woman servant whom he had engaged; presented herself at tea-time the moment she was summoned—but still showed no interest whatever in the new scene around her. Soon after the table was cleared, although the daylight had not yet faded out, Mrs. Wragge's customary drowsiness after fatigue of any kind, overcame her; and she received her husband's orders to leave the room (taking care that she left it "up at heel"), and to betake herself (strictly in the character of Mrs. Bygrave) to bed. As soon as they were left alone, the captain looked hard at Magdalen, and waited to be spoken to. She said nothing. He ventured next on opening the conversation by a polite inquiry after the state of her health. "You look fatigued," he remarked, in his most insinuating manner. "I am afraid the journey has been too much for you."

"No," she replied, looking out listlessly through the window; "I am not more tired than usual. I am always weary now—weary at going to bed; weary at getting up. If you would like to hear what I have to say to you, to-night—I am willing and ready to say it. Can't we go out? It is very hot here; and the droning of those men's voices is beyond all endurance." She pointed through the window to a group of boatmen, idling, as only nautical men can idle, against the garden wall. "Is there no quiet walk in this wretched place?" she asked, impatiently. "Can't we breathe a little fresh air, and escape being annoyed by strangers?"

"There is perfect solitude within half-an-hour's walk of the house," replied the ready captain.

"Very well. Come out, then."

With a weary sigh, she took up her straw bonnet and her light muslin scarf from the side table upon which she had thrown them on coming in; and carelessly led the way to the door. Captain Wragge followed her to the garden-gate—then stopped, struck by a new idea.

"Excuse me," he whispered, confidentially. "In my wife's existing state of ignorance as to who she is, we had better not trust her alone in the house with a new servant. I'll privately turn the key on her, in case she wakes before we come back. Safe bind, safe find—you know the proverb!—I will be with you again in a moment."

He hastened back to the house; and Magdalen seated herself on the garden-wall to await his return.

She had hardly settled herself in that position, when two gentlemen walking together, whose approach along the public path she had not previously noticed, passed close by her.

The dress of one of the two strangers showed him to be a clergyman. His companion's station in life was less easily discernible to ordinary observation. Practised eyes would probably have seen enough in his look, his manner, and his walk, to show that he was a sailor. He was a man in the prime of life; tall, spare, and muscular; his face sunburnt to a deep brown; his black hair just turning grey; his eyes dark, deep, and firm—the eyes of a man with an iron resolution, and a habit of command. He was the nearest of the two to Magdalen, as he and his friend passed the place where she was sitting; and he looked at her with a sudden surprise at her beauty, with an open, hearty, undisguised admiration, which was too evidently sincere, too evidently beyond his own control to be justly resented as insolent—and yet, in her humour at that moment, Magdalen did resent it. She felt the man's resolute black eyes strike through her with an electric suddenness; and frowning at him impatiently, she turned away her head, and looked back at the house.

The next moment she glanced round again, to see if he had gone on. He had advanced a few yards—had then evidently stopped—and was now in the very act of turning to look at her once more. His companion, the clergyman, noticing that Magdalen appeared to be annoyed, took him familiarly by the arm; and, half in jest, half in earnest, forced him to walk on. The two disappeared round the corner of the next house. As they turned it, the sunburnt sailor twice stopped his companion again, and twice looked back.

"A friend of yours?" inquired Captain Wragge, joining Magdalen at that moment.

"Certainly not," she replied, "a perfect stranger. He stared at me in the most impertinent manner. Does he belong to this place?"

"I'll find out in a moment," said the compliant captain; joining the group of boatmen, and putting his questions right and left, with the easy familiarity which distinguished him. He returned in a few minutes with a complete budget of information. The clergyman was well known as the rector of a place situated some few miles inland. The dark man with him, was his wife's brother, commander of a ship in the merchant service. He was supposed to be staying with his relatives, as their guest for a short time only, preparatory to sailing on another voyage. The clergyman's name was Strickland, and the merchant captain's name was Kirke—and that was all the boatmen knew about either of them.

"It is of no consequence who they are," said Magdalen, carelessly. "The man's rudeness merely annoyed me for the moment. Let us have done with him. I have something else to think of—and so have you. Where is the solitary walk you mentioned just now? Which way do we go?"

The captain pointed southward, towards Slaughden, and offered his arm.

Magdalen hesitated before she took it. Her eyes wandered away inquiringly to Noel Vanstone's house. He was out in the garden; pacing backwards and forwards over the little lawn, with his head high in the air, and with Mrs. Lecount demurely in attendance on him, carrying her master's green fan. Seeing this, Magdalen at once took Captain Wragge's right arm, so as to place herself nearest to the garden when they passed it on their walk.

"The eyes of our neighbours are on us; and the least your niece can do is to take your arm," she said, with a bitter laugh. "Come! let us go on."

"They are looking this way," whispered the captain. "Shall I introduce you to Mrs. Lecount?"

"Not to-night," she answered. "Wait, and hear what I have to say to you first."

They passed the garden-wall. Captain Wragge took off his hat with a smart flourish, and received a gracious bow from Mrs. Lecount in return. Magdalen saw the housekeeper survey her face, her figure, and her dress, with that reluctant interest, that distrustful curiosity, which women feel in observing each other. As she walked on beyond the house, the sharp voice of Noel Vanstone reached her through the evening stillness. "A fine girl, Lecount," she heard him say. "You know I am a judge of that sort of thing—a fine girl!"

As those words were spoken, Captain Wragge looked round at his companion, in sudden surprise. Her hand was trembling violently on his arm, and her lips were fast closed with an expression of speechless pain.

Slowly and in silence the two walked on, until they reached the southern limit of the houses, and entered on a little wilderness of shingle and withered grass—the desolate end of Aldborough, the lonely beginning of Slaughden.

It was a dull airless evening. Eastward was the gray majesty of the sea, hushed in breathless calm ; the horizon line invisibly melting into the monotonous misty sky ; the idle ships shadowy and still on the idle water. Southward, the high ridge of the sea dyke, and the grim massive circle of a martello tower, reared high on its mound of grass, closed the view darkly on all that lay beyond. Westward, a lurid streak of sunset glowed red in the dreary heaven—blackened the fringing trees on the far borders of the great inland marsh—and turned its little gleaming water-pools to pools of blood. Nearer to the eye, the sullen flow of the tidal river Alde, ebbed noiselessly from the muddy banks ; and nearer still, lonely and unprosperous by the bleak waterside, lay the lost little port of Slaughden ; with its forlorn wharfs and warehouses of decaying wood, and its few scattered coasting vessels deserted on the oozy river-shore. No fall of waves was heard on the beach ; no trickling of waters bubbled audibly from the idle stream. Now and then, the cry of a sea-bird rose from the region of the marsh :

and, at intervals, from farm-houses far in the inland waste, the faint winding of horns to call the cattle home, travelled mournfully through the evening calm.

Magdalen drew her hand from the captain's arm, and led the way to the mound of the martello tower. "I am weary of walking," she said. "Let us stop and rest here."

She seated herself on the slope, and resting on her elbow, mechanically pulled up and scattered from her into the air the tufts of grass growing under her hand. After silently occupying herself in this way for some minutes, she turned suddenly on Captain Wragge. "Do I surprise you?" she asked with a startling abruptness. "Do you find me changed?"

The captain's ready tact warned him that the time had come to be plain with her, and to reserve his flowers of speech for a more appropriate occasion.

"If you ask the question, I must answer it," he replied. "Yes: I do find you changed."

She pulled up another tuft of grass. "I suppose you can guess the reason?" she said.

The captain was wisely silent. He only answered by a bow.

"I have lost all care for myself," she went on tearing faster and faster at the tufts of grass. "Saying that, is not saying much, perhaps—but it may help you to understand me. There are things I would have died sooner than do, at one time—things it would have turned me cold to think of. I don't care now, whether I do them or not. I am nothing to myself; I am no more interested in myself than I am in these handfuls of grass. I suppose I have lost something. What is it? Heart? Conscience? I don't know. Do you? What nonsense I am talking! Who cares what I have lost? It has gone: and there's an end of it. I suppose my outside is the best side of me—and that's left at any rate. I have not lost my good looks, have I? There! there! never mind answering; don't trouble yourself to pay me compliments. I have been admired enough to-day. First the sailor, and then Mr. Noel Vanstone—enough for any woman's vanity surely! Have I any right to call myself a woman? Perhaps not: I am only a girl in my teens. Oh me, I feel as if I was forty!" She scattered the last fragments of grass to the winds; and, turning her back on the captain, let her head droop till her cheek touched the turf bank. "It feels soft and friendly," she said, nestling to it with a hopeless tenderness horrible to see. "It doesn't cast me off. Mother Earth! The only mother I have left!"

Captain Wragge looked at her in silent surprise. Such experience of humanity as *he* possessed, was powerless to sound to its depths the terrible self-abandonment which had burst its way to the surface in her reckless words—which was now fast hurrying her to actions more reckless still. "Devilish odd!" he thought to himself uneasily. "Has the loss of her lover turned her brain?" He considered for a minute longer, and then spoke to her. "Leave it till to-morrow," suggested the captain confidentially. "You are a little tired to-night. No hurry, my dear girl—no hurry."

She raised her head instantly, and looked round at him, with the same angry resolution, with the same desperate defiance of herself, which he had seen in her face, on the memorable day at York when she had acted before him for the first time. "I came here to tell you what is in my mind," she said; "and, I *will* tell it!" She seated herself upright on the slope; and clasping her hands round her knees, looked out steadily, straight before her, at the slowly darkening view. In that strange position, she waited until she had composed herself; and then addressed the captain, without turning her head to look round at him, in these words:

"When you and I first met," she began abruptly, "I tried hard to keep my thoughts to myself. I know enough, by this time, to know that I failed. When I first told you at York that Michael Vanstone had ruined us, I believe you guessed for yourself that I, for one, was determined not to submit to it. Whether you guessed or not, it is so. I left my friends with that determination in my mind; and I feel it in me now, stronger, ten times stronger, than ever."

"Ten times stronger then ever," echoed the captain. "Exactly so—the natural result of firmness of character."

"No. The natural result of having nothing else to think of. I had something else to think of, before you found me ill in Vauxhall Walk. I have nothing else to think of now. Remember that—if you find me, for the future, always harping on the same string. One question first. Did you guess what I meant to do, on that morning when you showed me the newspaper, and when I read the account of Michael Vanstone's death?"

"Generally," replied Captain Wragge—"I guessed, generally, that you proposed dipping your hand into his purse, and taking from it (most properly) what was your own. I felt deeply hurt at the time by your not permitting me to assist you. Why is she so reserved with me? (I remarked to myself)—why is she so unreasonably reserved?"

"You shall have no reserve to complain of now," pursued Magdalen. "I tell you plainly—if events had not happened as they did, you *would* have assisted me. If Michael Vanstone had not died, I should have gone to Brighton, and have found my way safely to his acquaintance under an assumed name. I had money enough with me to live on respectably for many months together. I would have employed that time, I would have waited a whole year, if necessary, to destroy Mrs. Lecount's influence over him—and I would have ended by getting that influence on my own terms, into my own hands. I had the advantage of years, the advantage of novelty, the advantage of downright desperation, all on my side; and I should have succeeded. Before the year was out—before half the year was out—you should have seen Mrs. Lecount dismissed by her master; and you should have seen me taken into the house, in her place, as Michael Vanstone's adopted daughter—as the faithful friend who had saved him from an adventuress in his old age. Girls no older than I am have tried deceptions as hopeless in appearance as mine, and have carried them through to the end. I had my story ready; I had my plans all considered; I had the weak point in that old man to attack, in my way, which Mrs. Lecount had found out before me to attack in hers—and I tell you again I should have succeeded."

"I think you would," said the captain. "And what next?"

"Mr. Michael Vanstone would have changed his man of business, next. You would have succeeded to the place; and those clever speculations on which he was so fond of venturing, would have cost him the fortunes of which he had robbed my sister and myself. To the last farthing, Captain Wragge—as certainly as you sit there, to the last farthing! A bold conspiracy, a shocking deception—wasn't it? I don't care! Any conspiracy, any deception, is justified to my conscience by the vile law which has left us helpless. You talked of my reserve just now. Have I dropped it at last? Have I spoken out at the eleventh hour?"

The captain laid his hand solemnly on his heart, and launched himself once more on his broadest flow of language.

"You fill me with unavailing regret," he said. "If that old man had lived, what a crop I might have reaped from him! What enormous transactions in moral agriculture it might have been my privilege to carry on! *Ars longa,*" said Captain Wragge, pathetically drifting into Latin—"*vita brevis!*" Let us drop a tear on the lost opportunities of the past, and try what the present can do to console us. One conclusion is clear to my mind. The experiment you proposed to try with Mr. Michael Vanstone, is totally hopeless, my dear girl, in the case of his son. His son is impervious to all common forms of pecuniary temptation. You may trust my solemn assurance," continued the captain, speaking with an indignant recollection of the answer to his advertisement in the Times, "when I inform you that Mr. Noel Vanstone is, emphatically, the meanest of mankind."

"I can trust my own experience as well," said Magdalen. "I have seen him and spoken to him—I know him better than you do. Another disclosure, Captain Wragge, for your private ear! I sent you back certain articles of costume—when they had served the purpose for which I took them to London. That purpose was to find my way to Noel Vanstone, in disguise, and to judge for myself of Mrs. Lecount and her master. I gained my object; and I tell you again, I know the two people in that house yonder whom we have now to deal with, better than you do."

Captain Wragge expressed the profound astonishment, and asked the innocent questions appropriate to the mental condition of a person taken completely by surprise.

"Well," he resumed, when Madgalen had briefly answered him; "and what is the result on your own mind? There must be a result, or we should not be here. You see your way? Of course, my dear girl, you see your way?"

"Yes," she said quickly. "I see my way."

The captain drew a little nearer to her, with eager curiosity expressed in every line of his vagabond face.

"Go on," he said in an anxious whisper; "pray go on."

She looked out thoughtfully into the gathering darkness, without answering, without appearing to have heard him. Her lips closed; and her clasped hands tightened mechanically round her knees.

"There is no disguising the fact," said Captain Wragge, warily rousing her into speaking to him. "The son is harder to deal with than the father——"

"Not in my way," she interposed, suddenly.

"Indeed!" said the captain. "Well! they say there is a short cut to everything, if we only look long enough to find it. You have looked long enough, I suppose; and the natural result has followed—you have found it."

"I have not troubled myself to look; I have found it without looking."

"The deuce you have!" cried Captain Wragge in great perplexity. "My dear girl, is my view of your present position leading me altogether astray? As I understand it, here is Mr. Noel Vanstone in possession of your fortune and your sister's, as his father was—and determined to keep it, as his father was?"

"Yes."

"And here are you—quite helpless to get it by persuasion—quite helpless to get it by law—just as resolute in his case, as you were in his father's, to take it by stratagem in spite of him?"

"Just as resolute. Not for the sake of the fortune—mind that! For the sake of the right."

"Just so. And the means of coming at that right which were hard with the father—who was not a miser—are easy with the son, who is?"

"Perfectly easy."

"Write me down an Ass, for the first time in my life!" cried the captain, at the end of his patience. "Hang me if I know what you mean!"

She looked round at him for the first time—looked him straight and steadily in the face.

"I will tell you what I mean," she said. "I mean to marry him."

Captain Wragge started up on his knees; and stopped on them, petrified by astonishment.

"Remember what I told you," said Magdalen, looking away from him again. "I have lost all care for myself. I have only one end in life now; and the sooner I reach it—and die—the better. If——" She stopped; altered her position a little; and pointed with one hand to the fast-ebbing stream beneath her, gleaming dim in the darkening twilight—"if I had been what I once was, I would have thrown myself into that river sooner that do what I am going to do now. As it is, I trouble myself no longer; I weary my mind with no more schemes. The short way and the vile way, lies before me. I take it, Captain Wragge—and marry him."

"Keeping him in total ignorance of who you are?" said the captain, slowly rising to his feet, and slowly moving round, so as to see her face. "Marrying him, as my niece, Miss Bygrave?"

"As your niece, Miss Bygrave."

"And after the marriage——?" His voice faltered, as he began the question, and he left it unfinished.

"After the marriage," she said, "I shall stand in no further need of your assistance."

The captain stooped, as she gave him that answer—looked close at her—and suddenly drew back, without uttering a word. He walked away some paces, and sat down again doggedly on the grass. If Magdalen could have seen his face, in the dying light, his face would have startled her. For the first time, probably, since his boyhood, Captain Wragge had changed colour. He was deadly pale.

"Have you nothing to say to me?" she asked. "Perhaps you are waiting to hear what terms I have to offer? These are my terms. I pay all our expenses here; and when we part, on the day of the marriage, you take a farewell gift away with you of two hundred pounds. Do you promise me your assistance on those conditions?"

"What am I expected to do?" he asked, with a furtive look at her, and a sudden distrust in his voice.

"You are expected to preserve my assumed character and your own," she answered; "and you are to prevent any inquiries of Mrs. Lecount's from discovering who I really am. I ask no more. The rest is my responsibility—not yours."

"I have nothing to do with what happens—at any time, or in any place —after the marriage?"

"Nothing whatever."

"I may leave you at the church door, if I please?"

"At the church door—with your fee in your pocket."

"Paid from the money in your own possession?"

"Certainly! How else should I pay it?"

Captain Wragge took off his hat, and passed his handkerchief over his face with an air of relief.

" Give me a minute to consider it," he said.

" As many minutes as you like," she rejoined, reclining on tne bank in her former position, and returning to her former occupation of tearing up the tufts of grass and flinging them out into the air.

The captain's reflections were not complicated by any unnecessary divergences, from the contemplation of his own position to the contemplation of Magdalen's. Utterly incapable of appreciating the injury done her by Frank's infamous treachery to his engagement—an injury which had severed her, at one cruel blow, from the aspiration which, delusion though it was, had been the saving aspiration of her life—Captain Wragge accepted the simple fact of her despair, just as he found it; and then looked straight to the consequences of the proposal which she had made to him.

In the prospect *before* the marriage he saw nothing more serious involved than the practice of a deception, in no important degree different—except in the end to be attained by it—from the deceptions which his vagabond life had long since accustomed him to contemplate and to carry out. In the prospect *after* the marriage, he dimly discerned, through the ominous darkness of the future, the lurking phantoms of Terror and Crime, and the black gulfs behind them of Ruin and Death. A man of boundless audacity and resource, within his own mean limits; beyond those limits, the captain was as deferentially submissive to the majesty of the law as the most harmless man in existence; as cautious in looking after his own personal safety, as the veriest coward that ever walked the earth. But one serious question now filled his mind. Could he, on the terms proposed to him, join the conspiracy against Noel Vanstone up to the point of the marriage—and then withdraw from it, without risk of involving himself in the consequences which his experience told him must certainly ensue?

Strange as it may seem, his decision, in this emergency, was mainly influenced by no less a person than Noel Vanstone himself. The captain might have resisted the money-offer which Magdalen had made to him—for the profits of the Entertainment had filled his pockets with more than three times two hundred pounds. But the prospect of dealing a blow in the dark at the man who had estimated his information and himself at the value of a five-pound note, proved too much for his caution and his self-control. On the small neutral ground of self-importance, the best men and the worst meet on the same terms. Captain Wragge's indignation, when he saw the answer to his advertisement, stooped to no retrospective estimate of his own conduct : he was as deeply offended, as sincerely angry, as if he had made a perfectly honourable proposal, and had been rewarded for it by a personal insult. He had been too full of his own grievance, to keep it out of his first letter to Magdalen. He had more or less forgotten himself, on every subsequent occasion when Noel Vanstone's name was mentioned. And in now finally deciding the course he should take, it is not too much to say, that the motive of money receded, for the first time in his life, into the second place—and the motive of malice carried the day.

"I accept the terms," said Captain Wragge, getting briskly on his legs again. "Subject, of course, to the conditions agreed on between us. We part on the wedding-day. I don't ask where you go: you don't ask where I go. From that time forth we are strangers to each other."

Magdalen rose slowly from the mound. A hopeless depression, a sullen despair, showed itself in her look and manner. She refused the captain's offered hand; and her tones, when she answered him, were so low that he could hardly hear her.

"We understand each other," she said; "and we can now go back. You may introduce me to Mrs. Lecount to-morrow."

"I must ask a few questions first," said the captain, gravely. "There are more risks to be run in this matter, and more pitfalls in our way, than you seem to suppose. I must know the whole history of your morning call on Mrs. Lecount, before I put you and that woman on speaking terms with each other."

"Wait till to-morrow," she broke out impatiently. "Don't madden me by talking about it to-night."

The captain said no more. They turned their faces towards Aldborough, and walked slowly back.

By the time they reached the houses, night had overtaken them. Neither moon nor stars were visible. A faint noiseless breeze, blowing from the land, had come with the darkness. Magdalen paused on the lonely public walk to breathe the air more freely. After a while, she turned her face from the breeze, and looked out towards the sea. The immeasurable silence of the calm waters, lost in the black void of night, was awful. She stood looking into the darkness, as if its mystery had no secrets for her—she advanced towards it slowly, as if it drew her by some hidden attraction into itself.

"I am going down to the sea," she said to her companion. "Wait here, and I will come back."

He lost sight of her in an instant—it was as if the night had swallowed her up. He listened, and counted her footsteps by the crashing of them on the shingle in the deep stillness. They retreated slowly, farther and farther away into the night. Suddenly, the sound of them ceased. Had she paused on her course? or had she reached one of the strips of sand left bare by the ebbing tide?

He waited, and listened anxiously. The time passed and no sound reached him. He still listened with a growing distrust of the darkness.

Another moment, and there came a sound from the invisible shore. Far and faint from the beach below, a long cry moaned through the silence. Then, all was still once more.

In sudden alarm, he stepped forward to descend to the beach, and to call to her. Before he could cross the path, footsteps rapidly advancing, caught his ear. He waited an instant—and the figure of a man passed quickly along the walk, between him and the sea. It was too dark to discern anything of the stranger's face; it was only possible to see that he was a tall man—as tall as that officer in the merchant service, whose name was Kirke.

The figure passed on northward, and was instantly lost to view. Captain Wragge crossed the path; and advancing a few steps down the beach, stopped, and listened again. The crash of footsteps on the shingle caught his ear once more. Slowly, as the sound had left him, that sound now came back. He called, to guide her to him. She came on till he could just see her—a shadow ascending the shingly slope, and growing out of the blackness of the night.

"You alarmed me," he whispered nervously. "I was afraid something had happened. I heard you cry out, as if you were in pain."

"Did you?" she said carelessly. "I *was* in pain. It doesn't matter—it's over now."

Her hand mechanically swung something to and fro as she answered him. It was the little white silk bag, which she had always kept hidden in her bosom up to this time. One of the relics which it held—one of the relics which she had not had the heart to part with before—was gone from its keeping for ever. Alone on a strange shore, she had torn from her the fondest of her virgin memories, the dearest of her virgin hopes. Alone on a strange shore, she had taken the lock of Frank's hair from its once-treasured place, and had cast it away from her to the sea and the night.

CHAPTER II.

THE tall man who had passed Captain Wragge in the dark, proceeded rapidly along the public walk, struck off across a little waste patch of ground, and entered the open door of the Aldborough Hotel. The light in the passage, falling full on his face as he passed it, proved the truth of Captain Wragge's surmise, and showed the stranger to be Mr. Kirke, of the merchant service.

Meeting the landlord in the passage, Mr. Kirke nodded to him with the familiarity of an old customer. "Have you got the paper?" he asked, "I want to look at the visitors' list."

"I have got it in my room, sir," said the landlord, leading the way into a parlour at the back of the house. "Are there any friends of yours staying here, do you think?"

Without replying, the seaman turned to the list, as soon as the newspaper was placed in his hand, and ran his finger down it, name by name. The finger suddenly stopped at this line: "Sea-View Cottage; Mr. Noel Vanstone." Kirke of the merchant service, repeated the name to himself; and put down the paper thoughtfully.

"Have you found anybody you know, captain?" asked the landlord.

"I have found a name I know—a name my father used often to speak of in his time. Is this Mr. Vanstone a family man? Do you know if there is a young lady in the house?"

"I can't say, captain. My wife will be here directly: she is sure to know. It must have been some time ago, if your father knew this Mr. Vanstone?"

"It was some time ago. My father knew a subaltern officer of that name, when he was with his regiment in Canada. It would be curious if the person here turned out to be the same man—and if that young lady was his daughter."

"Excuse me, captain—but the young lady seems to hang a little on your mind," said the landlord, with a pleasant smile.

Mr. Kirke looked as if the form which his host's good-humour had just taken, was not quite to his mind. He returned abruptly to the subaltern officer and the regiment in Canada. "That poor fellow's story was as miserable a one as ever I heard," he said, looking back again absently at the visitors' list.

"Would there be any harm in telling it, sir?" asked the landlord. "Miserable or not—a story's a story, when you know it to be true."

Mr. Kirke hesitated. "I hardly think I should be doing right to tell it," he said. "If this man, or any relations of his are still alive, it is not a story they might like strangers to know. All I can tell you is, that my father was the salvation of that young officer, under very dreadful circumstances. They parted in Canada. My father remained with his regiment: the young officer sold out and returned to England—and from that moment they lost sight of each other. It would be curious if this Vanstone here was the same man. It would be curious——"

He suddenly checked himself, just as another reference to "the young lady" was on the point of passing his lips. At the same moment, the landlord's wife came in; and Mr. Kirke at once transferred his inquiries to the higher authority in the house.

"Do you know anything of this Mr. Vanstone who is down here on the visitors' list?" asked the sailor. "Is he an old man?"

"He's a miserable little creature to look at," replied the landlady—"but he's not old, captain!"

"Then he is not the man I mean. Perhaps, he is the man's son? Has he got any ladies with him?"

The landlady tossed her head, and pursed up her lips disparagingly.

"He has a housekeeper with him," she said. "A middle-aged person—not one of my sort. I dare say I'm wrong—but I don't like a dressy woman in her station of life."

Mr. Kirke began to look puzzled. "I must have made some mistake about the house," he said. "Surely there's a lawn cut octagon-shape at Sea-View Cottage, and a white flag-staff in the middle of the gravel walk?"

"That's not Sea-View, sir! It's North Shingles you're talking of. Mr. Bygrave's. His wife and his niece came here, by the coach, to-day. His wife's tall enough to be put in a show, and the worst dressed woman I ever set eyes on. But Miss Bygrave is worth looking at, if I may venture to say so. She's the finest girl, to my mind, we've had at Aldborough for many a long day. I wonder who they are! Do you know the name, captain?"

"No," said Mr. Kirke, with a shade of disappointment on his dark, weather-beaten face; "I never heard the name before."

After replying in those words, he rose to take his leave. The landlord vainly invited him to drink a parting glass; the landlady vainly pressed him to stay another ten minutes, and try a cup of tea. He only replied that his sister expected him, and that he must return to the parsonage immediately.

On leaving the hotel, Mr. Kirke set his face westward, and walked inland along the high road, as fast as the darkness would let him.

"Bygrave?" he thought to himself. "Now I know her name, how much am I the wiser for it! If it had been Vanstone, my father's son might have had a chance of making acquaintance with her." He stopped, and looked back in the direction of Aldborough. "What a fool I am!" he burst out suddenly, striking his stick on the ground. "I was forty last birthday." He turned, and went on again faster than ever—his head down; his resolute black eyes searching the darkness on the land as they had searched it many a time on the sea, from the deck of his ship.

After more than an hour's walking, he reached a village, with a primitive little church and parsonage nestled together in a hollow. He entered the house by the back way, and found his sister, the clergyman's wife, sitting alone over her work in the parlour.

"Where is your husband, Lizzie?" he asked, taking a chair in a corner.

"William has gone out to see a sick person. He had just time enough, before he went," she added, with a smile, "to tell me about the young lady; and he declares he will never trust himself at Aldborough with you again, until you are a steady married man." She stopped; and looked at her brother more attentively than she had looked at him yet. "Robert!" she said, laying aside her work, and suddenly crossing the room to him. "You look anxious, you look distressed. William only laughed about your meeting with the young lady. Is it serious? Tell me, what is she like?"

He turned his head away at the question.

She took a stool at his feet, and persisted in looking up at him. "Is it serious, Robert?" she repeated softly.

Kirke's weatherbeaten face was accustomed to no concealments — it answered for him before he spoke a word. "Don't tell your husband till I am gone," he said, with a roughness quite new in his sister's experience of him. "I know I only deserve to be laughed at—but it hurts me, for all that."

"Hurts you?" she repeated, in astonishment.

"You can't think me half such a fool, Lizzie, as I think myself," pursued Kirke, bitterly. "A man at my age ought to know better. I didn't set eyes on her for as much as a minute altogether; and there I have been, hanging about the place till after nightfall, on the chance of seeing her again—skulking, I should have called it, if I had found one of my men doing what I have been doing myself. I believe I'm bewitched. She's a mere girl, Lizzie,—I doubt if she's out of her teens—I'm old enough to be her father. It's all one; she stops in my mind in spite of me. I've had her face looking at me, through the pitch darkness, every step of the way to this house; and it's looking at me now—as plain as I see yours, and plainer."

He rose impatiently, and began to walk backwards and forwards in the room. His sister looked after him with surprise, as well as sympathy, expressed in her face. From his boyhood upwards, she had always been accustomed to see him master of himself. Years since, in the failing fortunes of the family, he had been their example and their support. She had heard of him, in the desperate emergencies of a life at sea, when hundreds of his fellow-creatures had looked to his steady self-possession for rescue from close-threatening death—and had not looked in vain. Never, in all her life before, had his sister seen the balance of that calm and equal mind lost, as she saw it lost now.

"How can you talk so unreasonably about your age and yourself?" she said. "There is not a woman alive, Robert, who is good enough for you. What is her name?"

"Bygrave. Do you know it?"

"No. But I might soon make acquaintance with her. If we only had a little time before us; if I could only get to Aldborough and see her—but you are going away to-morrow; your ship sails at the end of the week."

"Thank God for that!" said Kirke, fervently.

"Are you glad to be going away?" she asked, more and more amazed at him.

"Right glad, Lizzie, for my own sake. If I ever get to my senses again, I shall find my way back to them on the deck of my ship. This girl has got between me and my thoughts already: she sha'n't go a step further, and get between me and my duty. I'm determined on that. Fool as I am, I have sense enough left not to trust myself within easy hail of Aldborough to-morrow morning. I'm good for another twenty miles of walking—and I'll begin my journey back to-night."

His sister started up, and caught him fast by the arm. "Robert!" she exclaimed; "you're not serious? You don't mean to leave us on foot, alone in the dark?"

"It's only saying good-bye, my dear, the last thing at night, instead of the first thing in the morning," he answered, with a smile. "Try and make allowances for me, Lizzie. My life has been passed at sea; and I'm not used to having my mind upset in this way. Men ashore are used to it; men ashore can take it easy. I can't. If I stopped here, I shouldn't rest. If I waited till to-morrow, I should only be going back to have another look at her. I don't want to feel more ashamed of myself than I do already. I want to fight my way back to my duty and myself, without stopping to think twice about it. Darkness is nothing to me—I'm used to darkness. I have got the high road to walk on, and I can't lose my way. Let me go, Lizzie! The only sweetheart I have any business with, at my age, is my ship. Let me get back to her!"

His sister still kept her hold of his arm, and still pleaded with him to stay till the morning. He listened to her with perfect patience and kindness—but she never shook his determination for an instant.

"What am I to say to William?" she pleaded. "What will he think, when he comes back, and finds you gone?"

"Tell him I have taken the advice he gave us, in his sermon last Sunday. Say I have turned my back on the world, the flesh, and the devil."

"How can you talk so, Robert! And the boys too—you promised not to go without bidding the boys good-bye."

"That's true. I made my little nephews a promise; and I'll keep it." He kicked off his shoes, as he spoke, on the mat outside the door. "Light me up-stairs, Lizzie; I'll bid the two boys good-bye without waking them."

She saw the uselessness of resisting him any longer; and, taking the candle, went before him up-stairs.

The boys—both young children—were sleeping together in the same bed. The youngest was his uncle's favourite, and was called by his uncle's name. He lay peacefully asleep, with a rough little toy ship hugged fast in his arms. Kirke's eyes softened as he stole on tiptoe to the child's side, and kissed him with the gentleness of a woman. "Poor little man!" said the sailor, tenderly. "He is as fond of his ship as I was at his age. I'll cut him out a better one when I come back. Will you give me my nephew one of these days, Lizzie, and will you let me make a sailor of him?"

"O, Robert, if you were only married and happy, as I am!"

"The time has gone by, my dear. I must make the best of it as I am, with my little nephew there to help me."

He left the room. His sister's tears fell fast as she followed him into the parlour. "There is something so forlorn and dreadful in your leaving us like this," she said. "Shall I go to Aldborough to-morrow, Robert, and try if I can get acquainted with her, for your sake?"

"No!" he replied. "Let her be. If it's ordered that I am to see that girl again, I *shall* see her. Leave it to the future, and you leave it right." He put on his shoes, and took up his hat and stick. "I won't over-walk myself," he said, cheerfully. "If the coach doesn't overtake me on the road, I can wait for it where I stop to breakfast. Dry your eyes, my dear; and give me a kiss."

She was like her brother, in features and complexion; and she had a touch of her brother's spirit—she dashed away the tears, and took her leave of him bravely.

"I shall be back in a year's time," said Kirke, falling into his old sailor-like way, at the door. "I'll bring you a China shawl, Lizzie, and a chest of tea for your store-room. Don't let the boys forget me; and don't think I'm doing wrong to leave you in this way. I know I am doing right. God bless you and keep you, my dear—and your husband, and your children! Good-bye!"

He stooped, and kissed her. She ran to the door to look after him. A puff of air extinguished the candle—and the black night shut him out from her in an instant.

Three days afterwards the first-class merchantman, DELIVERANCE—Kirke, commander—sailed from London for the China Sea.

CHAPTER III.

THE threatening of storm and change passed away with the night. When morning rose over Aldborough, the sun was master in the blue heaven, and the waves were rippling gaily under the summer breeze.

At an hour when no other visitors to the watering-place were yet astir, the indefatigable Wragge appeared at the door of North Shingles Villa, and directed his steps northward, with a neatly-bound copy of Joyce's Scientific Dialogues in his hand. Arriving at the waste ground beyond the houses, he descended to the beach, and opened his book. The interview of the past night had sharpened his perception of the difficulties to be encountered in the coming enterprise. He was now doubly determined to try the characteristic experiment at which he had hinted in his letter to Magdalen: and to concentrate on himself—in the character of a remarkably well-informed man—the entire interest and attention of the formidable Mrs. Lecount.

Having taken his dose of ready-made science (to use his own expression) the first thing in the morning on an empty stomach, Captain Wragge joined his small family circle at breakfast-time, inflated with information for the day. He observed that Magdalen's face showed plain signs of a sleepless night. She made no complaint: her manner was composed, and her temper perfectly under control. Mrs. Wragge—refreshed by some thirteen consecutive hours of uninterrupted repose—was in excellent spirits, and up at heel (for a wonder) with both shoes. She brought with her into the room several large sheets of tissue paper, cut crisply into mysterious and many-varying forms, which immediately provoked from her husband the short and sharp question, "What have you got there?"

"Patterns, captain," said Mrs. Wragge, in timidly conciliating tones. "I went shopping in London, and bought an Oriental Cashmere Robe. It cost a deal of money; and I'm going to try and save, by making it myself. I've got my patterns, and my dress-making directions written out as plain as print. I'll be very tidy, captain; I'll keep in my own corner, if you'll please to give me one; and whether my head Buzzes, or whether it don't, I'll sit straight at my work all the same."

"You will do your work," said the captain, sternly, "when you know who you are, who I am, and who that young lady is—not before. Show me your shoes! Good. Show me your cap! Good. Make the breakfast."

When breakfast was over, Mrs. Wragge received her orders to retire to an adjoining room, and to wait there until her husband came to release her. As soon as her back was turned, Captain Wragge at once resumed the conversation which had been suspended, by Magdalen's own desire, on the preceding night. The questions he now put to her, all related to the subject of her visit in disguise to Noel Vanstone's house. They were the questions of a thoroughly clear-headed man—short, searching, and straight to the point. In less than half-an-hour's time, he had made himself acquainted with every incident that had happened in Vauxhall Walk.

The conclusions which the captain drew, after gaining his information, were clear and easily stated.

On the adverse side of the question, he expressed his conviction that Mrs. Lecount had certainly detected her visitor to be disguised; that she had never really left the room, though she might have opened and shut the door;

and that on both the occasions, therefore, when Magdalen had been betrayed into speaking in her own voice, Mrs. Lecount had heard her. On the favourable side of the question, he was perfectly satisfied that the painted face and eyelids, the wig, and the padded cloak had so effectually concealed Magdalen's identity, that she might, in her own person, defy the housekeeper's closest scrutiny, so far as the matter of appearance was concerned. The difficulty of deceiving Mrs. Lecount's ears, as well as her eyes, was, he readily admitted, not so easily to be disposed of. But looking to the fact that Magdalen, on both the occasions when she had forgotten herself, had spoken in the heat of anger, he was of opinion that her voice had every reasonable chance of escaping detection—if she carefully avoided all outbursts of temper for the future, and spoke in those more composed and ordinary tones, which Mrs. Lecount had not yet heard. Upon the whole, the captain was inclined to pronounce the prospect hopeful, if one serious obstacle were cleared away at the outset—that obstacle being nothing less than the presence on the scene of action of Mrs. Wragge.

To Magdalen's surprise, when the course of her narrative brought her to the story of the ghost, Captain Wragge listened with the air of a man who was more annoyed than amused by what he heard. When she had done, he plainly told her that her unlucky meeting on the stairs of the lodging-house with Mrs. Wragge was, in his opinion, the most serious of all the accidents that had happened in Vauxhall Walk.

"I can deal with the difficulty of my wife's stupidity," he said, "as I have often dealt with it before. I can hammer her new identity *into* her head, but I can't hammer the ghost *out* of it. We have no security that the woman in the grey cloak and poke bonnet may not come back to her recollection at the most critical time, and under the most awkward circumstances. In plain English, my dear girl, Mrs. Wragge is a pitfall under our feet at every step we take."

"If we are aware of the pitfall," said Magdalen, "we can take our measures for avoiding it. What do you propose?"

"I propose," replied the captain, "the temporary removal of Mrs. Wragge. Speaking purely in a pecuniary point of view, I can't afford a total separation from her. You have often read of very poor people being suddenly enriched by legacies reaching them from remote and unexpected quarters? Mrs. Wragge's case, when I married her, was one of these. An elderly female relative shared the favours of fortune, on that occasion, with my wife; and if I only keep up domestic appearances, I happen to know that Mrs. Wragge will prove a second time profitable to me, on that elderly relative's death. But for this circumstance, I should probably long since have transferred my wife to the care of society at large—in the agreeable conviction that if I didn't support her, somebody else would. Although I can't afford to take this course, I see no objection to having her comfortably boarded and lodged out of our way, for the time being—say, at a retired farm-house, in the character of a lady in infirm mental health. *You* would find the expense trifling; *I* should find the relief unutterable. What do you say? Shall I pack her up at once, and take her away by the next coach?"

"No!" replied Magdalen, firmly. "The poor creature's life is hard enough already; I won't help to make it harder. She was affectionately and truly kind to me when I was ill—and I won't allow her to be shut up among strangers while I can help it. The risk of keeping her here is only one risk more. I will face it, Captain Wragge—if you won't."

"Think twice," said the captain, gravely, "before you decide on keeping Mrs. Wragge."

"Once is enough," rejoined Magdalen. "I won't have her sent away."

"Very good," said the captain, resignedly. "I never interfere with questions of sentiment. But I have a word to say, on my own behalf. If my services are to be of any use to you, I can't have my hands tied at starting. This is serious. I won't trust my wife and Mrs. Lecount together. I'm afraid, if you're not—and I make it a condition that, if Mrs. Wragge stops here, she keeps her room. If you think her health requires it, you can take her for a walk early in the morning, or late in the evening—but you must never trust her out with the servant, and never trust her out by herself. I put the matter plainly, it is too important to be trifled with. What do you say—yes, or no?"

"I say, yes," replied Magdalen, after a moment's consideration. "On the understanding that I am to take her out walking as you propose."

Captain Wragge bowed, and recovered his suavity of manner. "What are our plans?" he inquired. "Shall we start our enterprise this afternoon? Are you ready for your introduction to Mrs. Lecount and her master?"

"Quite ready."

"Good, again. We will meet them on the Parade, at their usual hour for going out—two o'clock. It is not twelve yet. I have two hours before me—just time enough to fit my wife into her new Skin. The process is absolutely necessary, to prevent her compromising us with the servant. Don't be afraid about the results; Mrs. Wragge has had a copious selection of assumed names hammered into her head in the course of her matrimonial career. It is merely a question of hammering hard enough—nothing more. I think we have settled everything now. Is there anything I can do before two o'clock? Have you any employment for the morning?"

"No," said Magdalen. "I shall go back to my own room, and try to rest."

"You had a disturbed night, I am afraid?" said the captain, politely opening the door for her.

"I fell asleep once or twice," she answered, carelessly. "I suppose my nerves are a little shaken. The bold black eyes of that man who stared so rudely at me yesterday evening, seemed to be looking at me again in my dreams. If we see him to-day, and if he annoys me any more, I must trouble you to speak to him. We will meet here again at two o'clock. Don't be hard with Mrs. Wragge; teach her what she must learn as tenderly as you can."

With those words she left him, and went up-stairs.

She lay down on her bed, with a heavy sigh, and tried to sleep. It was useless. The dull weariness of herself which now possessed her, was not the weariness which finds its remedy in repose. She rose again, and sat by the window, looking out listlessly over the sea.

A weaker nature than hers would not have felt the shock of Frank's desertion as she had felt it—as she was feeling it still. A weaker nature would have found refuge in indignation and comfort in tears. The passionate strength of Magdalen's love clung desperately to the sinking wreck of its own delusion—clung, until she tore herself from it, by main force of will. All that her native pride, her keen sense of wrong could do, was to shame her from dwelling on the thoughts which still caught their breath of life from the undying devotion of the past; which still perversely ascribed Frank's heartless farewell to any cause but the inborn baseness of the man who had written it. The woman never lived yet who could cast a true love out of her heart, because the object of that love was unworthy of her. All she can do is to struggle against it in secret—to sink in the contest, if she is weak; to win her way through it, if she is strong, by a process of self-laceration, which is of all moral remedies applied to a woman's nature, the most dangerous and the most desperate; of all moral changes the change that is surest to mark her for life. Magdalen's strong nature had sustained her through the struggle; and the issue of it had left her—what she now was.

After sitting by the window for nearly an hour—her eyes looking mechanically at the view; her mind empty of all impressions, and conscious of no thoughts—she shook off the strange waking stupor that possessed her, and rose to prepare herself for the serious business of the day.

She went to the wardrobe, and took down from the pegs two bright, delicate muslin dresses, which had been made for summer wear at Combe-Raven, a year since, and which had been of too little value to be worth selling when she parted with her other possessions. After placing these dresses side by side on the bed, she looked into the wardrobe once more. It only contained one other summer dress—the plain alpaca gown which she had worn during her memorable interview with Noel Vanstone and Mrs. Lecount. This she left in its place; resolving not to wear it, less from any dread that the housekeeper might recognize a pattern too quiet to be noticed, and too common to be remembered, than from the conviction that it was neither gay enough nor becoming enough for her purpose. After taking a plain white muslin scarf, a pair of light grey kid gloves, and a garden hat of Tuscan straw, from the drawers of the wardrobe, she locked it, and put the key carefully in her pocket.

Instead of at once proceeding to dress herself, she sat idly looking at the two muslin gowns; careless which she wore, and yet inconsistently hesitating which to choose. " What does it matter !" she said to herself with a reckless laugh; "I am equally worthless in my own estimation, whichever I put on." She shuddered, as if the sound of her own laughter had startled her; and abruptly caught up the dress which lay nearest to her hand. Its colours were blue and white—the shade of blue which best suited her fair complexion. She hurriedly put on the gown, without going near her looking-glass. For the first time in her life, she shrank from meeting the reflection of herself—except for a moment, when she arranged her hair under her garden-hat, leaving the glass again immediately. She drew her scarf over her shoulders, and fitted on her gloves, with her back to the toilet-table. "Shall I paint ?" she asked herself, feeling instinctively that she was turning pale. " The rouge is still left in my box. It can't make my face more false than it is already." She looked round towards the glass, and again turned away from it. " No !" she said. " I have Mrs. Lecount to face, as well as her master. No paint." After consulting her watch, she left the room, and went down stairs again. It wanted ten minutes only of two o'clock.

Captain Wragge was waiting for her in the parlour—respectable in a frock-coat, a stiff summer cravat, and a high white hat; specklessly and cheerfully rural, in a buff waistcoat, grey trousers, and gaiters to match. His collars were higher than ever, and he carried a bran-new camp-stool in his hand. Any tradesman in England who had seen him at that moment, would have trusted him on the spot.

" Charming !" said the captain, paternally surveying Magdalen when she entered the room. " So fresh and cool ! A little too pale, my dear, and a great deal too serious. Otherwise perfect. Try if you can smile."

" When the time comes for smiling," said Magdalen, bitterly, " trust my dramatic training for any change of face that may be necessary. Where is Mrs. Wragge ?"

" Mrs. Wragge has learnt her lesson," replied the captain, " and is rewarded by my permission to sit at work in her own room. I sanction her new fancy for dressmaking, because it is sure to absorb all her attention, and to keep her at home. There is no fear of her finishing the Oriental Robe in a hurry—for there is no mistake in the process of making it which she is not certain to commit. She will sit incubating her gown—pardon the expression—like a hen over an addled egg. I assure you her new whim relieves me. Nothing could be more convenient under existing circumstances."

He strutted away to the window—looked out—and beckoned to Magdalen to join him. "There they are!" he said, and pointed to the Parade.

Noel Vanstone slowly walked by, as she looked, dressed in a complete suit of old-fashioned nankeen. It was apparently one of the days when the state of his health was at the worst. He leaned on Mrs. Lecount's arm, and was protected from the sun by a light umbrella which she held over him. The housekeeper—dressed to perfection, as usual, in a quiet, lavender-coloured summer gown, a black mantilla, an unassuming straw bonnet, and a crisp blue veil—escorted her invalid master with the tenderest attention; sometimes, directing his notice respectfully to the various objects of the sea view; sometimes, bending her head in graceful acknowledgment of the courtesy of passing strangers on the Parade, who stepped aside to let the invalid pass by. She produced a visible effect among the idlers on the beach. They looked after her, with unanimous interest; and exchanged confidential nods of approval, which said as plainly as words could have expressed it:—"A very domestic person! a truly superior woman!"

Captain Wragge's parti-coloured eyes followed Mrs. Lecount with a steady, distrustful attention. "Tough work for us *there*," he whispered in Magdalen's ear; "tougher work than you think, before we turn that woman out of her place."

"Wait," said Magdalen, quietly. "Wait, and see."

She walked to the door. The captain followed her without making any further remark. "I'll wait till you're married," he thought to himself—"not a moment longer, offer me what you may."

At the house door, Magdalen addressed him again.

"We will go that way," she said, pointing southward—"then turn, and meet them as they come back."

Captain Wragge signified his approval of the arrangement, and followed Magdalen to the garden gate. As she opened it to pass through, her attention was attracted by a lady, with a nursery-maid and two little boys behind her, loitering on the path outside the garden wall. The lady started, looked eagerly, and smiled to herself, as Magdalen came out. Curiosity had got the better of Kirke's sister—and she had come to Aldborough for the express purpose of seeing Miss Bygrave.

Something in the shape of the lady's face, something in the expression of her dark eyes, reminded Magdalen of the merchant-captain, whose uncontrolled admiration had annoyed her on the previous evening. She instantly returned the stranger's scrutiny by a frowning, ungracious look. The lady coloured, paid the look back with interest, and slowly walked on.

"A hard, bold, bad girl," thought Kirke's sister. "What could Robert be thinking of to admire her? I am almost glad he is gone. I hope and trust he will never set eyes on Miss Bygrave again."

"What boors the people are here!" said Magdalen to Captain Wragge. "That woman was even ruder than the man last night. She is like him in the face. I wonder who she is?"

"I'll find out directly," said the captain. "We can't be too cautious about strangers." He at once appealed to his friends, the boatmen. They were close at hand; and Magdalen heard the questions and answers plainly.

"How are you all, this morning?" said Captain Wragge, in his easy jocular way. "And how's the wind? Nor'-west and by west, is it? Very good. Who is that lady?"

"That's Mrs. Strickland, sir."

"Ay! ay! The clergyman's wife and the captain's sister. Where's the captain to-day?"

"On his way to London, I should think, sir. His ship sails for China, at the end of the week."

China! As that one word passed the man's lips, a pang of the old sorrow struck Magdalen to the heart. Stranger as he was, she began to hate the bare mention of the merchant-captain's name. He had troubled her dreams of the past night—and now, when she was most desperately and recklessly bent on forgetting her old home-existence, he had been indirectly the cause of recalling her mind to Frank.

"Come!" she said angrily to her companion. "What do we care about the man or his ship? Come away."

"By all means," said Captain Wragge. "As long as we don't find friends of the Bygraves, what do we care about anybody?"

They walked on, southwards, for ten minutes or more—then turned and walked back again to meet Noel Vanstone and Mrs. Lecount.

CHAPTER IV.

CAPTAIN WRAGGE and Magdalen retraced their steps until they were again within view of North Shingles Villa, before any signs appeared of Mrs. Lecount and her master. At that point, the housekeeper's lavender-coloured dress, the umbrella, and the feeble little figure in nankeen walking under it, became visible in the distance. The captain slackened his pace immediately; and issued his directions to Magdalen for her conduct at the coming interview, in these words:

"Don't forget your smile," he said. "In all other respects you will do. The walk has improved your complexion, and the hat becomes you. Look Mrs. Lecount steadily in the face; show no embarrassment when you speak; and if Mr. Noel Vanstone pays you pointed attention, don't take too

much notice of him while his housekeeper's eye is on you. Mind one
thing! I have been at Joyce's Scientific Dialogues all the morning; and I
am quite serious in meaning to give Mrs. Lecount the full benefit of my
studies. If I can't contrive to divert her attention from you and her
master, I won't give sixpence for our chance of success. Small-talk won't
succeed with that woman; compliments won't succeed; jokes won't succeed
—ready-made science may recall the deceased Professor, and ready-made
science may do. We must establish a code of signals to let you know
what I am about. Observe this camp-stool. When I shift it from my
left hand to my right, I am talking Joyce. When I shift it from my
right hand to my left, I am talking Wragge. In the first case, don't
interrupt me—I am leading up to my point. In the second case, say
anything you like; my remarks are not of the slightest consequence.
Would you like a rehearsal? Are you sure you understand? Very good
—take my arm, and look happy. Steady! here they are."

The meeting took place nearly midway between Sea View Cottage and
North Shingles. Captain Wragge took off his tall white hat, and opened
the interview immediately on the friendliest terms.

"Good morning, Mrs. Lecount," he said, with the frank and cheerful
politeness of a naturally sociable man. "Good morning, Mr. Vanstone; I
am sorry to see you suffering to-day. Mrs. Lecount, permit me to introduce my niece—my niece, Miss Bygrave. My dear girl, this is Mr. Noel
Vanstone, our neighbour at Sea View Cottage. We must positively be
sociable at Aldborough, Mrs. Lecount. There is only one walk in the
place (as my niece remarked to me just now, Mr. Vanstone); and on that
walk we must all meet every time we go out. And why not? Are we
formal people on either side? Nothing of the sort—we are just the reverse.
You possess the continental facility of manner, Mr. Vanstone—I match you,
with the blunt cordiality of an old-fashioned Englishman—the ladies
mingle together in harmonious variety, like flowers on the same bed—and
the result is a mutual interest in making our sojourn at the sea-side agreeable to each other. Pardon my flow of spirits; pardon my feeling so
cheerful and so young. The Iodine in the sea-air, Mrs. Lecount—the
notorious effect of the Iodine in the sea-air!"

"You arrived yesterday, Miss Bygrave, did you not?" said the housekeeper, as soon as the captain's deluge of language had come to an end.

She addressed those words to Magdalen with a gentle motherly interest
in her youth and beauty, chastened by the deferential amiability which
became her situation in Noel Vanstone's household. Not the faintest
token of suspicion or surprise betrayed itself in her face, her voice, or her
manner, while she and Madgalen now looked at each other. It was plain
at the outset that the true face and figure which she now saw, recalled
nothing to her mind of the false face and figure which she had seen in

Vauxhall Walk. The disguise had evidently been complete enough even to baffle the penetration of Mrs. Lecount.

"My aunt and I came here yesterday evening," said Magdalen. "We found the latter part of the journey very fatiguing. I dare say you found it so too?"

She designedly made her answer longer than was necessary, for the purpose of discovering, at the earliest opportunity, the effect which the sound of her voice produced on Mrs. Lecount.

The housekeeper's thin lips maintained their motherly smile; the housekeeper's amiable manner lost none of its modest deference—but the expression of her eyes suddenly changed, from a look of attention to a look of inquiry. Magdalen quietly said a few words more; and then waited again for results. The change spread gradually all over Mrs. Lecount's face; the motherly smile died away; and the amiable manner betrayed a slight touch of restraint. Still, no signs of positive recognition appeared; the housekeeper's expression remained what it had been from the first—an expression of inquiry, and nothing more.

"You complained of fatigue, sir, a few minutes since," she said, dropping all further conversation with Magdalen, and addressing her master. "Will you go in-doors and rest?"

The proprietor of Sea View Cottage had hitherto confined himself to bowing, simpering, and admiring Magdalen through his half-closed eyelids. There was no mistaking the sudden flutter and agitation in his manner, and the heightened colour in his wizen little face. Even the reptile temperament of Noel Vanstone warmed under the influence of the sex: he had an undeniably appreciative eye for a handsome woman, and Magdalen's grace and beauty were not thrown away on him.

"Will you go in-doors, sir, and rest?" asked the housekeeper, repeating her question.

"Not yet, Lecount," said her master. "I fancy I feel stronger; I fancy I can go on a little." He turned simpering to Magdalen, and added in a lower tone, "I have found a new interest in my walk, Miss Bygrave. Don't desert us, or you will take the interest away with you."

He smiled and smirked in the highest approval of the ingenuity of his own compliment—from which Captain Wragge dexterously diverted the housekeeper's attention, by ranging himself on her side of the path and speaking to her at the same moment. They all four walked on slowly. Mrs. Lecount said nothing more. She kept fast hold of her master's arm, and looked across him at Magdalen with the dangerous expression of inquiry more marked than ever in her handsome black eyes. That look was not lost on the wary Wragge. He shifted his indicative camp-stool from the left hand to the right, and opened his scientific batteries on the spot.

"A busy scene, Mrs. Lecount," said the captain, politely waving his camp-stool over the sea and the passing ships. "The greatness of England, ma'am—the true greatness of England. Pray observe how heavily some of those vessels are laden! I am often inclined to wonder whether the British sailor is at all aware, when he has got his cargo on board, of the Hydrostatic importance of the operation that he has performed. If I were suddenly transported to the deck of one of those ships (which Heaven forbid, for I suffer at sea); and if I said to a member of the crew, 'Jack! you have done wonders; you have grasped the Theory of Floating Vessels' —how the gallant fellow would stare! And yet, on that theory Jack's life depends. If he loads his vessel one-thirtieth part more than he ought, what happens? He sails past Aldborough, I grant you, in safety. He enters the Thames, I grant you again, in safety. He gets on into the fresh water, as far, let us say, as Greenwich; and—down he goes! Down, ma'am, to the bottom of the river, as a matter of scientific certainty!"

Here he paused; and left Mrs. Lecount no polite alternative but to request an explanation.

"With infinite pleasure, ma'am," said the captain, drowning in the deepest notes of his voice the feeble treble in which Noel Vanstone paid his compliments to Magdalen. "We will start, if you please, with a first principle. All bodies whatever that float on the surface of the water, displace as much fluid as is equal in weight to the weight of the bodies. Good! We have got our first principle. What do we deduce from it? Manifestly this: That in order to keep a vessel above water, it is necessary to take care that the vessel and its cargo shall be of less weight than the weight of a quantity of water—pray follow me here!—of a quantity of water equal in bulk to that part of the vessel which it will be safe to immerse in the water. Now, ma'am, salt water is specifically thirty times heavier than fresh or river water; and a vessel in the German Ocean will not sink so deep as a vessel in the Thames. Consequently, when we load our ship with a view to the London market, we have (Hydrostatically speaking) three alternatives. Either we load with one-thirtieth part less than we can carry at sea; or we take one-thirtieth part out at the mouth of the river; or we do neither the one nor the other, and, as I have already had the honour of remarking—down we go! Such," said the captain, shifting the camp-stool back again from his right hand to his left, in token that Joyce was done with for the time being; "such, my dear madam, is the Theory of Floating Vessels. Permit me to add, in conclusion—you are heartily welcome to it."

"Thank you, sir," said Mrs. Lecount. "You have unintentionally saddened me, but the information I have received is not the less precious on that account. It is long, long ago, Mr. Bygrave, since I have heard myself addressed in the language of science. My dear husband made me his companion—my dear husband improved my mind as you have been trying to improve it. Nobody has taken pains with my intellect since. Many thanks, sir. Your kind consideration for me is not thrown away."

She sighed with a plaintive humility; and privately opened her ears to the conversation on the other side of her.

A minute earlier, she would have heard her master expressing himself in the most flattering terms on the subject of Miss Bygrave's appearance in her sea-side costume. But Magdalen had seen Captain Wragge's signal with the camp-stool, and had at once diverted Noel Vanstone to the topic of himself and his possessions, by a neatly-timed question about his house at Aldborough.

"I don't wish to alarm you, Miss Bygrave," were the first words of Noel Vanstone's which caught Mrs. Lecount's attention—"but there is only one safe house in Aldborough—and that house is Mine. The sea may destroy all the other houses—it can't destroy Mine. My father took care of that; my father was a remarkable man. He had My house built on piles. I have reason to believe they are the strongest piles in England. Nothing can possibly knock them down—I don't care what the sea does—nothing can possibly knock them down."

"Then if the sea invades us," said Magdalen, "we must all run for refuge to you."

Noel Vanstone saw his way to another compliment; and, at the same moment, the wary captain saw his way to another burst of science.

"I could almost wish the invasion might happen," murmured one of the gentlemen, "to give me the happiness of offering the refuge."

"I could almost swear the wind had shifted again!" exclaimed the other. "Where is a man I can ask? Oh, there he is. Boatman! How's the wind, now? Nor'-west and by west still—hey? And south-east and by south yesterday evening—ha? Is there anything more remarkable, Mrs. Lecount, than the variableness of the wind in this·climate?" proceeded the captain, shifting the camp-stool to the scientific side of him. "Is there any natural phenomenon more bewildering to the scientific inquirer? You will tell me that the electric fluid which abounds in the air is the principal cause of this variableness. You will remind me of the experiment of that illustrious philosopher who measured the velocity of a great storm by a flight of small feathers. My dear madam, I grant all your propositions——"

"I beg your pardon, sir," said Mrs. Lecount; "you kindly attribute to me a knowledge that I don't possess. Propositions, I regret to say, are quite beyond me."

"Don't misunderstand me, ma'am," continued the captain, politely unconscious of the interruption. "My remarks apply to the temperate zone only. Place me on the coasts beyond the tropics—place me where the wind blows towards the shore in the daytime, and towards the sea by night —and I instantly advance towards conclusive experiments. For example, I know that the heat of the sun during the day, rarefies the air over the land, and so causes the wind. You challenge me to prove it. I escort you down the kitchen-stairs (with your kind permission); I take my largest pie-dish out of the cook's hands; I fill it with cold water. Good! that dish of cold water represents the ocean. I next provide myself with one of our most precious domestic conveniences—a hot-water plate—I fill it with hot water, and I put it in the middle of the pie-dish. Good again! the hot-water plate represents the land rarefying the air over it. Bear that in mind, and give me a lighted candle. I hold my lighted candle over the cold water, and blow it out. The smoke immediately moves from the dish to the plate. Before you have time to express your satisfaction, I light the candle once more, and reverse the whole proceeding. I fill the pie-dish with hot water, and the plate with cold; I blow the candle out again, and the smoke moves this time from the plate to the dish. The smell is disagreeable—but the experiment is conclusive."

He shifted the camp-stool back again, and looked at Mrs. Lecount with his ingratiating smile. "You don't find me long-winded, ma'am—do you?" he said, in his easy, cheerful way, just as the housekeeper was privately opening her ears once more to the conversation on the other side of her.

"I am amazed, sir, by the range of your information," replied Mrs. Lecount, observing the captain with some perplexity—but, thus far, with no distrust. She thought him eccentric, even for an Englishman, and possibly a little vain of his knowledge. But he had at least paid her the implied compliment of addressing that knowledge to herself; and she felt it the more sensibly, from having hitherto found her scientific sympathies with her deceased husband, treated with no great respect by the people with whom she came in contact. "Have you extended your inquiries, sir," she proceeded, after a momentary hesitation, "to my late husband's branch of science? I merely ask, Mr. Bygrave, because (though I am only a woman) I think I might exchange ideas with you, on the subject of the reptile creation."

Captain Wragge was far too sharp to risk his ready-made science on the enemy's ground. The old militiaman shook his wary head.

"Too vast a subject, ma'am," he said, "for a smatterer like me. The life and labours of such a philosopher as your husband, Mrs. Lecount, warn men of my intellectual calibre not to measure themselves with a giant. May I inquire," proceeded the captain, softly smoothing the way for future intercourse with Sea View Cottage, "whether you possess any scientific memorials of the late Professor?"

"I possess his Tank, sir," said Mrs. Lecount, modestly casting her eyes on the ground; "and one of his Subjects—a little foreign Toad."

"His Tank!" exclaimed the captain, in tones of mournful interest. "And his Toad! Pardon my blunt way of speaking my mind, ma'am. You possess an object of public interest; and, as one of the public, I acknowledge my curiosity to see it."

Mrs. Lecount's smooth cheeks coloured with pleasure. The one assailable place in that cold and secret nature, was the place occupied by the memory of the Professor. Her pride in his scientific achievements, and her mortification at finding them but little known out of his own country, were genuine feelings. Never had Captain Wragge burnt his adulterated incense on the flimsy altar of human vanity to better purpose than he was burning it now.

"You are very good, sir," said Mrs. Lecount. "In honouring my husband's memory, you honour *me*. But though you kindly treat me on a footing of equality, I must not forget that I fill a domestic situation. I shall feel it a privilege to show you my relics, if you will allow me to ask my master's permission first."

She turned to Noel Vanstone; her perfectly sincere intention of making the proposed request, mingling—in that strange complexity of motives which is found so much oftener in a woman's mind than in a man's—with her jealous distrust of the impression which Magdalen had produced on her master.

"May I make a request, sir?" asked Mrs. Lecount, after waiting a moment to catch any fragments of tenderly-personal talk that might reach her, and after being again neatly baffled by Magdalen—thanks to the camp-stool. "Mr. Bygrave is one of the few persons in England who appreciate my husband's scientific labours. He honours me by wishing to see my little world of reptiles. May I show it to him?"

"By all means, Lecount," said Noel Vanstone, graciously. "You are an excellent creature, and I like to oblige you. Lecount's Tank, Mr. Bygrave, is the only Tank in England—Lecount's Toad, is the oldest Toad in the world. Will you come and drink tea at seven o'clock to-night? And will you prevail on Miss Bygrave to accompany you? I want her to see my house. I don't think she has any idea what a strong house it is. Come and survey my premises, Miss Bygrave. You shall have a stick, and rap on the walls; you shall go upstairs and stamp on the floors—and then you shall hear what it all cost." His eyes wrinkled up cunningly at the corners, and he slipped another tender speech into Magdalen's ear, under cover of the all-predominating voice in which Captain Wragge thanked him for the invitation. "Come punctually at seven," he whispered, "and pray wear that charming hat!"

Mrs. Lecount's lips closed ominously. She set down the captain's niece as a very serious drawback to the intellectual luxury of the captain's society.

"You are fatiguing yourself, sir," she said to her master. "This is one of your bad days. Let me recommend you to be careful; let me beg you to walk back."

Having carried his point by inviting the new acquaintances to tea, Noel Vanstone proved to be unexpectedly docile. He acknowledged that he was a little fatigued, and turned back at once in obedience to the housekeeper's advice.

"Take my arm, sir—take my arm on the other side," said Captain Wragge, as they turned to retrace their steps. His parti-coloured eyes looked significantly at Magdalen while he spoke, and warned her not to stretch Mrs. Lecount's endurance too far at starting. She instantly understood him; and, in spite of Noel Vanstone's reiterated assertions that he stood in no need of the captain's arm, placed herself at once by the housekeeper's side. Mrs. Lecount recovered her good humour, and opened another conversation with Magdalen, by making the one inquiry of all others which, under existing circumstances, was the hardest to answer.

"I presume Mrs. Bygrave is too tired, after her journey, to come out to-day?" said Mrs. Lecount. "Shall we have the pleasure of seeing her to-morrow?"

"Probably not," replied Magdalen. "My aunt is in delicate health."

"A complicated case, my dear madam," added the captain; conscious that Mrs. Wragge's personal appearance (if she happened to be seen by accident) would offer the flattest of all possible contradictions to what Magdalen had just said of her. "There is some remote nervous mischief which doesn't express itself externally. You would think my wife the picture of health, if you looked at her—and yet, so delusive are appearances, I am obliged to forbid her all excitement. She sees no society—our medical attendant, I regret to say, absolutely prohibits it."

"Very sad," said Mrs. Lecount. "The poor lady must often feel lonely, sir, when you and your niece are away from her?"

"No," replied the captain. "Mrs. Bygrave is a naturally domestic woman. When she is able to employ herself, she finds unlimited resources in her needle and thread." Having reached this stage of the explanation—and having purposely skirted, as it were, round the confines of truth, in the event of the housekeeper's curiosity leading her to make any private inquiries on the subject of Mrs. Wragge—the captain wisely checked his fluent tongue from carrying him into any further details. "I have great hope from the air of this place," he remarked in conclusion. "The Iodine, as I have already observed, does wonders."

Mrs. Lecount acknowledged the virtues of Iodine in the briefest possible form of words, and withdrew into the innermost sanctuary of her own thoughts. "Some mystery here," said the housekeeper to herself. "A lady who looks the picture of health; a lady who suffers from a complicated nervous malady; and a lady whose hand is steady enough to use her needle and thread—is a living mass of contradictions I don't quite understand. Do you make a long stay at Aldborough, sir?" she added aloud; her eyes resting for a moment, in steady scrutiny, on the captain's face.

"It all depends, my dear madam, on Mrs. Bygrave. I trust we shall stay through the autumn. You are settled at Sea View Cottage, I presume, for the season?"

"You must ask my master, sir. It is for him to decide, not for me."

The answer was an unfortunate one. Noel Vanstone had been secretly annoyed by the change in the walking arrangements, which had separated him from Magdalen. He attributed that change to the meddling influence of Mrs. Lecount, and he now took the earliest opportunity of resenting it on the spot.

"I have nothing to do with our stay at Aldborough," he broke out peevishly. "You know as well as I do, Lecount, it all depends on *you*. Mrs. Lecount has a brother in Switzerland," he went on, addressing himself to the captain—"a brother who is seriously ill. If he gets worse, she will have to go there and see him. I can't accompany her, and I can't be left in the house by myself. I shall have to break up my establishment at Aldborough, and stay with some friends. It all depends on you, Lecount —or on your brother, which comes to the same thing. If it depended on *me*," continued Mr. Noel Vanstone, looking pointedly at Magdalen across the housekeeper, " I should stay at Aldborough all through the autumn with the greatest pleasure. With the greatest pleasure," he reiterated, repeating the words with a tender look for Magdalen, and a spiteful accent for Mrs. Lecount.

Thus far, Captain Wragge had remained silent; carefully noting in his mind the promising possibilities of a separation between Mrs. Lecount and her master, which Noel Vanstone's little fretful outbreak had just disclosed to him. An ominous trembling in the housekeeper's thin lips, as her master openly exposed her family affairs before strangers, and openly set her jealousy at defiance, now warned him to interfere. If the misunderstanding were permitted to proceed to extremities, there was a chance that the invitation for that evening to Sea View Cottage might be put off. Now, as ever, equal to the occasion, Captain Wragge called his useful information, once more to the rescue. Under the learned auspices of Joyce, he plunged, for the third time, into the ocean of science, and brought up another pearl. He was still haranguing (on Pneumatics this time), still improving Mrs. Lecount's mind with his politest perseverance and his smoothest flow of language—when the walking party stopped at Noel Vanstone's door.

"Bless my soul, here we are at your house, sir!" said the captain, interrupting himself in the middle of one of his graphic sentences. "I won't keep you standing a moment. Not a word of apology, Mrs. Lecount, I beg and pray! I will put that curious point in Pneumatics more clearly before you on a future occasion. In the mean time, I need only repeat, that you can perform the experiment I have just mentioned, to your own entire satisfaction, with a bladder, an exhausted receiver, and a square box. At seven o'clock this evening, sir—at seven o'clock, Mrs. Lecount. We have had a remarkably pleasant walk, and a most instructive interchange of ideas. Now, my dear girl! your aunt is waiting for us."

While Mrs. Lecount stepped aside to open the garden gate, Noel Vanstone seized his opportunity, and shot a last tender glance at Magdalen—under shelter of the umbrella, which he had taken into his own hands for that express purpose. "Don't forget," he said, with the sweetest smile; "don't forget, when you come this evening, to wear that charming hat!" Before he could add any last words, Mrs. Lecount glided back to her place; and the sheltering umbrella changed hands again immediately.

"An excellent morning's work!" said Captain Wragge, as he and Magdalen walked on together to North Shingles. "You and I and Joyce have all three done wonders. We have secured a friendly invitation at the first day's fishing for it."

He paused for an answer; and, receiving none, observed Magdalen more attentively than he had observed her yet. Her face had turned deadly pale again; her eyes looked out mechanically straight before her, in heedless reckless despair.

"What is the matter?" he asked with the greatest surprise. "Are you ill?"

She made no reply; she hardly seemed to hear him.

"Are you getting alarmed about Mrs. Lecount?" he inquired next. "There is not the least reason for alarm. She may fancy she has heard something like your voice before; but your face evidently bewilders her. Keep your temper, and you keep her in the dark. Keep her in the dark; and you will put that two hundred pounds into my hands before the autumn is over."

He waited again for an answer; and again she remained silent. The captain tried for the third time, in another direction.

"Did you get any letters this morning?" he went on. "Is there bad news again from home? Any fresh difficulties with your sister?"

"Say nothing about my sister!" she broke out passionately. "Neither you nor I are fit to speak of her."

She said those words at the garden gate, and hurried into the house by herself. He followed her, and heard the door of her own room violently shut to, violently locked and double-locked. Solacing his indignation by an oath, Captain Wragge sullenly went into one of the parlours on the ground floor to look after his wife. The room communicated with a smaller and darker room at the back of the house, by means of a quaint little door with a window in the upper half of it. Softly approaching this door, the captain lifted the white muslin curtain which hung over the window, and looked into the inner room.

There was Mrs. Wragge, with her cap on one side, and her shoes down at heel; with a row of pins between her teeth; with the Oriental Cashmere Robe slowly slipping off the table; with her scissors suspended uncertain in one hand, and her written directions for dressmaking held doubtfully in the other—so absorbed over the invincible difficulties of her employment, as to be perfectly unconscious that she was at that moment the object of her husband's superintending eye. Under other circumstances, she would have been soon brought to a sense of her situation by the sound of his voice. But Captain Wragge was too anxious about Magdalen to waste any time on his wife, after satisfying himself that she was safe in her seclusion, and that she might be trusted to remain there.

He left the parlour, and, after a little hesitation in the passage, stole upstairs, and listened anxiously outside Magdalen's door. A dull sound of sobbing—a sound stifled in her handkerchief, or stifled in the bed-clothes—was all that caught his ear. He returned at once to the ground floor, with some faint suspicion of the truth dawning on his mind at last.

"The devil take that sweetheart of hers!" thought the captain. "Mr. Noel Vanstone has raised the ghost of him at starting."

CHAPTER V.

WHEN Magdalen appeared in the parlour, shortly before seven o'clock, not a trace of discomposure was visible in her manner. She looked and spoke as quietly and unconcernedly as usual.

The lowering distrust on Captain Wragge's face cleared away at the sight of her. There had been moments during the afternoon, when he had seriously doubted whether the pleasure of satisfying the grudge he owed to Noel Vanstone, and the prospect of earning the sum of two hundred pounds, would not be dearly purchased, by running the risk of discovery to which Magdalen's uncertain temper might expose him at any hour of the day. The plain proof now before him of her powers of self-control, relieved his mind of a serious anxiety. It mattered little to the captain what she suffered in the privacy of her own chamber, as long as she came out of it with a face that would bear inspection, and a voice that betrayed nothing.

On the way to Sea View Cottage, Captain Wragge expressed his intention of asking the housekeeper a few sympathizing questions on the subject of her invalid brother in Switzerland. He was of opinion that the critical condition of this gentleman's health might exercise an important influence on the future progress of the conspiracy. Any chance of a separation, he remarked, between the housekeeper and her master was, under existing circumstances, a chance which merited the closest investigation. "If we can only get Mrs. Lecount out of the way at the right time," whispered the captain, as he opened his host's garden gate, "our man is caught!"

In a minute more, Magdalen was again under Noel Vanstone's roof; this time in the character of his own invited guest.

The proceedings of the evening were for the most part a repetition of the proceedings during the morning walk. Noel Vanstone vibrated between his admiration of Magdalen's beauty and his glorification of his own possessions. Captain Wragge's inexhaustible outbursts of information—relieved by delicately-indirect inquiries relating to Mrs. Lecount's brother—perpetually diverted the housekeeper's jealous vigilance from dwelling on the looks and language of her master. So the evening passed until ten o'clock. By that time, the captain's ready-made science was exhausted, and the housekeeper's temper was forcing its way to the surface. Once more, Captain Wragge warned Magdalen by a look, and, in spite of Noel Vanstone's hospitable protest, wisely rose to say good-night.

"I have got my information," remarked the captain, on the way back. "Mrs. Lecount's brother lives at Zurich. He is a bachelor; he possesses a little money; and his sister is his nearest relation. If he will only be so obliging as to break up altogether, he will save us a world of trouble with Mrs. Lecount."

It was a fine moonlight night. He looked round at Magdalen, as he said those words, to see if her intractable depression of spirits had seized on her again.

No! her variable humour had changed once more. She looked about her with a flaunting, feverish gaiety; she scoffed at the bare idea of any serious difficulty with Mrs. Lecount; she mimicked Noel Vanstone's high-pitched voice, and repeated Noel Vanstone's high-flown compliments, with a bitter enjoyment of turning him into ridicule. Instead of running into the house as before, she sauntered carelessly by her companion's side, humming little snatches of song, and kicking the loose pebbles right and left on the garden walk. Captain Wragge hailed the change in her as the best of good omens. He thought he saw plain signs that the family spirit was at last coming back again.

"Well," he said, as he lit her bedroom candle for her, "when we all meet on the Parade to-morrow, we shall see, as our nautical friends say, how the land lies. One thing I can tell you, my dear girl—I have used my eyes to very little purpose, if there is not a storm brewing to-night in Mr. Noel Vanstone's domestic atmosphere."

The captain's habitual penetration had not misled him. As soon as the door of Sea View Cottage was closed on the parting guests, Mrs. Lecount made an effort to assert the authority which Magdalen's influence was threatening already.

She employed every artifice of which she was mistress to ascertain Magdalen's true position in Noel Vanstone's estimation. She tried again and again to lure him into an unconscious confession of the pleasure which he felt already in the society of the beautiful Miss Bygrave; she twined herself in and out of every weakness in his character, as the frogs and efts twined themselves in and out of the rock-work of her Aquarium. But she made one serious mistake which very clever people in their intercourse with their intellectual inferiors are almost universally apt to commit—she trusted implicitly to the folly of a fool. She forgot that one of the lowest of human qualities —cunning—is exactly the capacity which is often most largely developed in the lowest of intellectual natures. If she had been honestly angry with her master she would probably have frightened him. If she had opened her mind plainly to his view, she would have astonished him by presenting a chain of ideas to his limited perceptions, which they were not strong enough to grasp; his curiosity would have led him to ask for an explanation; and by practising on that curiosity, she might have had him at her mercy. As it was, she set her cunning against his—and the fool proved a match for her. Noel Vanstone, to whom all large-minded motives under heaven were inscrutable mysteries, saw the small-minded motive at the bottom of his housekeeper's conduct, with as instantaneous a penetration as if he had been a man of the highest ability. Mrs. Lecount left him for the night, foiled, and knowing she was foiled—left him, with the tigerish side of her uppermost, and a low-lived longing in her elegant finger-nails to set them in her master's face.

She was not a woman to be beaten by one defeat or by a hundred. She was positively determined to think, and think again, until she had found a means of checking the growing intimacy with the Bygraves at once and for ever. In the solitude of her own room, she recovered her composure, and set herself, for the first time, to review the conclusions which she had gathered from the events of the day.

There was something vaguely familiar to her in the voice of this Miss Bygrave; and, at the same time, in unaccountable contradiction, something strange to her as well. The face and figure of the young lady were entirely new to her. It was a striking face, and a striking figure; and if she had seen either, at any former period, she would certainly have remembered it. Miss Bygrave was unquestionably a stranger; and yet——

She had got no farther than this during the day; she could get no farther now: the chain of thought broke. Her mind took up the fragments, and formed another chain which attached itself to the lady who was kept in seclusion—to the aunt, who looked well, and yet was nervous; who was nervous, and yet able to ply her needle and thread. An incomprehensible resemblance to some unremembered voice, in the niece; an unintelligible malady which kept the aunt secluded from public view; an extraordinary range of scientific cultivation in the uncle, associated with a coarseness and audacity of manner which by no means suggested the idea of a man engaged in studious pursuits—were the members of this small family of three, what they seemed on the surface of them?

With that question on her mind, she went to bed.

As soon as the candle was out, the darkness seemed to communicate some inexplicable perversity to her thoughts. They wandered back from present things to past, in spite of her. They brought her old master back to life again; they revived forgotten sayings and doings in the English circle at Zurich; they veered away to the old man's death-bed at Brighton; they moved from Brighton to London; they entered the bare, comfortless room at Vauxhall Walk; they set the Aquarium back in its place on the kitchen table, and put the false Miss Garth in the chair by the side of it, shading her inflamed eyes from the light; they placed the anonymous letter, the letter which glanced darkly at a conspiracy, in her hand again, and brought her with it into her master's presence; they recalled the discussion about filling in the blank space in the advertisement, and the quarrel that followed, when she told Noel Vanstone that the sum he had offered was preposterously small; they revived an old doubt which had not troubled her for weeks past—a doubt whether the threatened conspiracy had evaporated in mere words, or whether she and her master were likely to hear of it again. At this point her thoughts broke off once more, and there was a momentary blank. The next instant she started up in bed; her heart beating violently, her head whirling as if she had lost her senses. With electric suddenness, her mind pieced together its scattered multitude of thoughts, and put them before her plainly under one intelligible form. In the all-mastering agitation of the moment, she clapped her hands together, and cried out suddenly in the darkness:

"Miss Vanstone again! ! !"

She got out of bed and kindled the light once more. Steady as her nerves were, the shock of her own suspicion had shaken them. Her firm hand trembled as she opened her dressing-case, and took from it a little bottle of sal-volatile. In spite of her smooth cheeks and her well-preserved hair, she looked every year of her age, as she mixed the spirit with water, greedily drank it, and, wrapping her dressing-gown round her, sat down on the bedside to get possession again of her calmer self.

She was quite incapable of tracing the mental process which had led her to discovery. She could not get sufficiently far from herself to see that her half-formed conclusions on the subject of the Bygraves, had ended in making that family objects of suspicion to her; that the association of ideas had thereupon carried her mind back to that other object of suspicion which was represented by the conspiracy against her master; and that the two ideas of those two separate subjects of distrust, coming suddenly in contact, had struck the light. She was not able to reason back in this way from the effect to the cause. She could only feel that the suspicion had become more than a suspicion already: conviction itself could not have been more firmly rooted in her mind.

Looking back at Magdalen by the new light now thrown on her, Mrs. Lecount would fain have persuaded herself that she recognized some traces left of the false Miss Garth's face and figure, in the graceful and beautiful girl who had sat at her master's table hardly an hour since—that she found resemblances now, which she had never thought of before, between the angry voice she had heard in Vauxhall Walk, and the smooth well-bred tones which still hung on her ears, after the evening's experience down stairs. She would fain have persuaded herself that she had reached these results with no undue straining of the truth as she really knew it; but the effort was in vain.

Mrs. Lecount was not a woman to waste time and thought in trying to impose on herself. She accepted the inevitable conclusion that the guess-work of a moment had led her to discovery. And, more than that, she recognized the plain truth—unwelcome as it was—that the conviction now fixed in her own mind was, thus far, unsupported by a single fragment of producible evidence to justify it to the minds of others.

Under these circumstances, what was the safe course to take with her master?

If she candidly told him, when they met the next morning, what had passed through her mind that night, her knowledge of Noel Vanstone warned her that one of two results would certainly happen. Either he would be angry and disputatious; would ask for proofs; and, finding none forthcoming, would accuse her of alarming him without a cause, to serve her own jealous end of keeping Magdalen out of the house—or, he would be seriously startled, would clamour for the protection of the law, and would warn the Bygraves to stand on their defence at the outset. If Magdalen only had been concerned in the plot, this latter consequence would have assumed no great importance in the housekeeper's mind. But seeing the deception as she now saw it, she was far too clever a woman to fail in estimating the captain's inexhaustible fertility of resource at its true value. "If I can't meet this impudent villain with plain proofs to help me," thought Mrs. Lecount, "I may open my master's eyes to-morrow morning, and Mr. Bygrave will shut them up again before night. The rascal is playing with all his own cards under the table; and he will win the game to a certainty if he sees my hand at starting."

This policy of waiting was so manifestly the wise policy—the wily Mr. Bygrave was so sure to have provided himself, in case of emergency, with evidence to prove the identity which he and his niece had assumed for their purpose—that Mrs. Lecount at once decided to keep her own counsel the next morning, and to pause before attacking the conspiracy, until she could produce unanswerable facts to help her. Her master's acquaintance with the Bygraves was only an acquaintance of one day's standing. There was no fear of its developing into a dangerous intimacy if she merely allowed it to continue for a few days more, and if she permanently checked it, at the latest, in a week's time.

In that period, what measures could she take to remove the obstacles which now stood in her way, and to provide herself with the weapons which she now wanted?

Reflection showed her three different chances in her favour—three different ways of arriving at the necessary discovery.

The first chance was to cultivate friendly terms with Magdalen,—and then, taking her unawares, to entrap her into betraying herself in Noel Vanstone's presence. The second chance was to write to the elder Miss Vanstone, and to ask (with some alarming reason for putting the question) for information on the subject of her younger sister's whereabouts, and of any peculiarities in her personal appearance, which might enable a stranger to identify her. The third chance was to penetrate the mystery of Mrs. Bygrave's seclusion, and to ascertain at a personal interview whether the invalid lady's real complaint might not possibly be a defective capacity for keeping her husband's secrets. Resolving to try all three chances, in the order in which they are here enumerated, and to set her snares for Magdalen on the day that was now already at hand, Mrs. Lecount at last took off her dressing-gown and allowed her weaker nature to plead with her for a little sleep.

The dawn was breaking over the cold grey sea, as she lay down in her bed again. The last idea in her mind, before she fell asleep, was character-istic of the woman—it was an idea that threatened the captain. "He has trifled with the sacred memory of my husband," thought the Professor's widow. "On my life and honour, I will make him pay for it!"

Early the next morning, Magdalen began the day—according to her agreement with the captain—by taking Mrs. Wragge out for a little exer-cise, at an hour when there was no fear of her attracting the public attention. She pleaded hard to be left at home; having the Oriental Cashmere Robe still on her mind, and feeling it necessary to read her directions for dress-making, for the hundredth time at least, before (to use her own expression) she could "screw up her courage to put the scissors into the stuff." But her companion would take no denial, and she was forced to go out. The one guileless purpose of the life which Magdalen now led, was the resolution that poor Mrs. Wragge should not be made a prisoner on her account—and to that resolution she mechanically clung, as the last token left her by which she knew her better self.

They returned later than usual to breakfast. While Mrs. Wragge was up-stairs, straightening herself from head to foot to meet the morning inspection of her husband's orderly eye, and while Magdalen and the captain were waiting for her in the parlour, the servant came in with a note from Sea View Cottage. The messenger was waiting for an answer, and the note was addressed to Captain Wragge.

The captain opened the note, and read these lines:—

" DEAR SIR,

" Mr. Noel Vanstone desires me to write and tell you that he proposes enjoying this fine day by taking a long drive to a place on the coast here, called Dunwich. He is anxious to know if you will share the expense of a carriage, and give him the pleasure of your company, and Miss Bygrave's company, on this excursion. I am kindly permitted to be one of the party, and if I may say so without impropriety, I would venture to add that I shall feel as much pleasure as my master if you and your young lady will consent to join us. We propose leaving Aldborough punctually at eleven o'clock,

" Believe me, dear sir,
" Your humble servant,
" VIRGINIE LECOUNT."

" Who is the letter from ?" asked Magdalen, noticing a change in Captain Wragge's face, as he read it. " What do they want with us at Sea View Cottage ?"

" Pardon me," said the captain, gravely, " this requires consideration. Let me have a minute or two to think."

He took a few turns up and down the room—then suddenly stepped aside to a table in a corner, on which his writing materials were placed. " I was not born yesterday, ma'am !" said the captain, speaking jocosely to himself. He winked his brown eye, took up his pen, and wrote the answer.

" Can you speak now ?" inquired Magdalen, when the servant had left the room. " What does that letter say, and how have you answered it ?"

The captain placed the letter in her hand. " I have accepted the invitation," he replied, quietly.

Magdalen read the letter. " Hidden enmity yesterday," she said, " and open friendship to-day. What does it mean ?"

" It means," said Captain Wragge, " that Mrs. Lecount is even sharper than I thought her. She has found you out."

" Impossible," cried Magdalen. " Quite impossible in the time."

" I can't say *how* she has found you out," proceeded the captain, with perfect composure. "She may know more of your voice than we supposed she knew. Or, she may have thought us, on reflection, rather a suspicious family; and anything suspicious in which a woman was concerned, may have taken her mind back to that morning call of yours in Vauxhall Walk. Whichever way it may be, the meaning of this sudden change is clear enough. She has found you out; and she wants to put her discovery to the proof, by slipping in an awkward question or two, under cover of a little friendly talk. My experience of humanity has been a varied one; and Mrs. Lecount is not the first sharp practitioner in petticoats whom I have had to deal with. All the world's a stage, my dear girl—and one of the scenes on our little stage is shut in from this moment."

With those words, he took his copy of Joyce's Scientific Dialogues out of his pocket. "You're done with already, my friend!" said the captain, giving his useful information a farewell smack with his hand, and locking it up in the cupboard. "Such is human popularity!" continued the indomitable vagabond, putting the key cheerfully in his pocket. "Yesterday, Joyce was my all-in-all. To-day, I don't care that for him!" He snapped his fingers and sat down to breakfast.

"I don't understand you," said Magdalen, looking at him angrily. "Are you leaving me to my own resources for the future?"

"My dear girl!" cried Captain Wragge, "can't you accustom yourself to my dash of humour yet? I have done with my ready-made science, simply because I am quite sure that Mrs. Lecount has done believing in me. Haven't I accepted the invitation to Dunwich? Make your mind easy. The help I have given you already, counts for nothing compared with the help I am going to give you now. My honour is concerned in bowling out Mrs. Lecount. This last move of hers has made it a personal matter between us. *The woman actually thinks she can take me in!!!*" cried the captain, striking his knife-handle on the table in a transport of virtuous indignation. "By Heavens I never was so insulted before in my life! Draw your chair in to the table, my dear; and give me half a minute's attention to what I have to say next."

Magdalen obeyed him. Captain Wragge cautiously lowered his voice before he went on.

"I have told you all along," he said, "the one thing needful is never to let Mrs. Lecount catch you with your wits wool-gathering. I say the same after what has happened this morning. Let her suspect you! I defy her to find a fragment of foundation for her suspicions, unless we help her. We shall see to-day if she has been foolish enough to betray herself to her master before she has any facts to support her. I doubt it. If she has told him, we will rain down proofs of our identity with the Bygraves on his feeble little head, till it absolutely aches with conviction. You have two things to do on this excursion. First, to distrust every word Mrs. Lecount says to you. Secondly, to exert all your fascinations, and make sure of Mr. Noel Vanstone, dating from to-day. I will give you the opportunity, when we leave the carriage, and take our walk at Dunwich. Wear your hat, wear your smile; do your figure justice, lace tight; put on your neatest boots and brightest gloves; tie the miserable little wretch to your apron-string—tie him fast; and leave the whole management of the matter after that, to me. Steady! here is Mrs. Wragge: we must be doubly careful in looking after her now. Show me your cap, Mrs. Wragge! show me your shoes! What do I see on your apron? A spot? I won't have spots! Take it off after breakfast, and put on another. Pull your chair to the middle of the table—more to the left—more still. Make the breakfast."

At a quarter before eleven, Mrs. Wragge (with her own entire concurrence) was dismissed to the back room, to bewilder herself over the science of dressmaking for the rest of the day. Punctually as the clock struck the hour, Mrs. Lecount and her master drove up to the gate of North Shingles, and found Magdalen and Captain Wragge waiting for them in the garden.

On the way to Dunwich nothing occurred to disturb the enjoyment of the drive. Noel Vanstone was in excellent health and high good humour. Lecount had apologized for the little misunderstanding of the previous night; Lecount had petitioned for the excursion as a treat to herself. He thought of these concessions, and looked at Magdalen, and smirked and simpered without intermission. Mrs. Lecount acted her part to perfection. She was motherly with Magdalen, and tenderly attentive to Noel Vanstone. She was deeply interested in Captain Wragge's conversation, and meekly disappointed to find it turn on general subjects, to the exclusion of science. Not a word or look escaped her, which hinted in the remotest degree at her real purpose. She was dressed with her customary elegance and propriety; and she was the only one of the party, on that sultry summer's day, who was perfectly cool in the hottest part of the journey.

As they left the carriage on their arrival at Dunwich, the captain seized a moment, when Mrs. Lecount's eye was off him, and fortified Magdalen by a last warning word.

"'Ware the cat!" he whispered. "She will show her claws on the way back."

They left the village and walked to the ruins of a convent near at hand —the last relic of the once-populous city of Dunwich which has survived the destruction of the place, centuries since, by the all-devouring sea. After looking at the ruins, they sought the shade of a little wood, between the village and the low sand-hills which overlook the German Ocean. Here, Captain Wragge manœuvred so as to let Magdalen and Noel Vanstone advance some distance in front of Mrs. Lecount and himself—took the wrong path—and immediately lost his way with the most consummate dexterity. After a few minutes' wandering (in the wrong direction), he reached an open space near the sea; and politely opening his camp-stool for the housekeeper's accommodation, proposed waiting where they were, until the missing members of the party came that way and discovered them.

Mrs. Lecount accepted the proposal. She was perfectly well aware that her escort had lost himself on purpose; but that discovery exercised no disturbing influence on the smooth amiability of her manner. Her day of reckoning with the captain had not come yet—she merely added the new item to her list, and availed herself of the camp-stool. Captain Wragge stretched himself in a romantic attitude at her feet; and the two determined enemies (grouped like two lovers in a picture) fell into as easy and pleasant a conversation, as if they had been friends of twenty years' standing.

"I know you, ma'am!" thought the captain, while Mrs. Lecount was talking to him. "You would like to catch me tripping in my ready-made science; and you wouldn't object to drown me in the Professor's Tank!"

"You villain with the brown eye and the green!" thought Mrs. Lecount, as the captain caught the ball of conversation in his turn; "thick as your skin is, I'll sting you through it yet!"

In this frame of mind towards each other, they talked fluently on general subjects, on public affairs, on local scenery, on society in England and society in Switzerland, on health, climate, books, marriage, and money—talked, without a moment's pause, without a single misunderstanding on either side, for nearly an hour, before Magdalen and Noel Vanstone strayed that way, and made the party of four complete again.

When they reached the inn at which the carriage was waiting for them, Captain Wragge left Mrs. Lecount in undisturbed possession of her master, and signed to Magdalen to drop back for a moment and speak to him.

"Well?" asked the captain in a whisper; "is he fast to your apron-string?"

She shuddered from head to foot, as she answered.

"He has kissed my hand," she said. "Does that tell you enough? Don't let him sit next me on the way home! I have borne all I can bear —spare me for the rest of the day."

"I'll put you on the front seat of the carriage," replied the captain, "side by side with me."

On the journey back, Mrs. Lecount verified Captain Wragge's prediction. She showed her claws.

The time could not have been better chosen; the circumstances could hardly have favoured her more. Magdalen's spirits were depressed: she was weary in body and mind; and she sat exactly opposite the house-keeper—who had been compelled, by the new arrangement, to occupy the seat of honour next her master. With every facility for observing the slightest changes that passed over Magdalen's face, Mrs. Lecount tried her first experiment by leading the conversation to the subject of London, and to the relative advantages offered to residents by the various quarters of the metropolis on both sides of the river. The ever-ready Wragge penetrated her intention sooner than she had anticipated, and interposed immediately. "You're coming to Vauxhall Walk, ma'am," thought the captain; "I'll get there before you."

He entered at once into a purely fictitious description of the various quarters of London in which he had himself resided; and, adroitly mentioning Vauxhall Walk as one of them, saved Magdalen from the sudden question relating to that very locality, with which Mrs. Lecount had proposed startling her to begin with. From his residences, he passed smoothly to himself; and poured his whole family history (in the character of Mr. Bygrave) into the housekeeper's ears—not forgetting his brother's grave in Honduras, with the monument by the self-taught negro artist; and his brother's hugely corpulent widow, on the ground floor of the boarding-house at Cheltenham. As a means of giving Magdalen time to compose herself, this outburst of autobiographical information attained its object, but it answered no other purpose. Mrs. Lecount listened, without being imposed on by a single word the captain said to her. He merely confirmed her conviction of the hopelessness of taking Noel Vanstone into her confidence, before she had facts to help her against Captain Wragge's otherwise unassailable position in the identity which he had assumed. She quietly waited until he had done, and then returned to the charge.

"It is a coincidence that your uncle should once have resided in Vauxhall Walk," she said, addressing herself to Magdalen. "Mr. Noel has a house in the same place; and we lived there before we came to Aldborough. May I inquire, Miss Bygrave, whether you know anything of a lady named Miss Garth."

This time, she put the question before the captain could interfere. Magdalen ought to have been prepared for it by what had already passed in her presence—but her nerves had been shaken by the earlier events of the day; and she could only answer the question in the negative, after an instant's preliminary pause to control herself. Her hesitation was of too momentary a nature to attract the attention of any unsuspicious person. But it lasted long enough to confirm Mrs. Lecount's private convictions, and to encourage her to advance a little further.

"I only asked," she continued, steadily fixing her eyes on Magdalen, steadily disregarding the efforts which Captain Wragge made to join in the conversation, "because Miss Garth is a stranger to me; and I am curious to find out what I can about her. The day before we left town, Miss Bygrave, a person who presented herself under the name I have mentioned, paid us a visit under very extraordinary circumstances."

With a smooth, ingratiating manner; with a refinement of contempt which was little less than devilish in its ingenious assumption of the language of pity, she now boldly described Magdalen's appearance in disguise, in Magdalen's own presence. She slightingly referred to the master and mistress of Combe-Raven, as persons who had always annoyed the elder and more respectable branch of the family; she mourned over the children as following their parents' example, and attempting to take a mercenary advantage of Mr. Noel Vanstone, under the protection of a respectable person's character and a respectable person's name. Cleverly including her master in the conversation, so as to prevent the captain from effecting a diversion in that quarter; sparing no petty aggravation; striking at every tender place which the tongue of a spiteful woman can wound—she would, beyond all doubt, have carried her point, and tortured Magdalen into openly betraying herself, if Captain Wragge had not checked her in full career, by a loud exclamation of alarm, and a sudden clutch at Magdalen's wrist.

"Ten thousand pardons, my dear madam!" cried the captain. "I see in my niece's face, I feel in my niece's pulse, that one of her violent neuralgic attacks has come on again. My dear girl, why hesitate among friends to confess that you are in pain? What mistimed politeness! Her face shows she is suffering—doesn't it, Mrs. Lecount? Darting pains, Mr. Vanstone, darting pains on the left side of the head. Pull down your veil, my dear, and lean on me. Our friends will excuse you; our excellent friends will excuse you for the rest of the day."

Before Mrs. Lecount could throw an instant's doubt on the genuineness of the neuralgic attack, her master's fidgety sympathy declared itself, exactly as the captain had anticipated, in the most active manifestations. He stopped the carriage, and insisted on an immediate change in the arrangement of the places—the comfortable back seat for Miss Bygrave and her uncle; the front seat for Lecount and himself. Had Lecount got her smelling-bottle? Excellent creature! let her give it directly to Miss Bygrave, and let the coachman drive carefully. If the coachman shook Miss Bygrave he should not have a halfpenny for himself. Mesmerism was frequently useful in these cases.* Mr. Noel Vanstone's father had been the most powerful mesmerist in Europe; and Mr. Noel Vanstone was his father's son. Might he mesmerize? Might he order that infernal coachman to draw up in a shady place adapted for the purpose? Would medical help be preferred? Could medical help be found any nearer than Aldborough? That ass of a coachman didn't know. Stop every respectable man who passed in a gig, and ask him if he was a doctor! So Mr. Noel Vanstone ran on—with brief intervals for breathing-time—in a continually-ascending scale of sympathy and self-importance, throughout the drive home.

Mrs. Lecount accepted her defeat, without uttering a word. From the moment when Captain Wragge interrupted her, her thin lips closed, and opened no more for the remainder of the journey. The warmest expressions of her master's anxiety for the suffering young lady, provoked from her no outward manifestations of anger. She took as little notice of him as possible. She paid no attention whatever to the captain, whose exasperating consideration for his vanquished enemy, made him more polite to her than ever. The nearer and the nearer they got to Aldborough, the more and more fixedly Mrs. Lecount's hard black eyes looked at Magdalen reclining on the opposite seat, with her eyes closed and her veil down.

It was only when the carriage stopped at North Shingles, and when Captain Wragge was handing Magdalen out, that the housekeeper at last condescended to notice him. As he smiled and took off his hat at the carriage-door, the strong restraint she had laid on herself suddenly gave way; and she flashed one look at him, which scorched up the captain's politeness on the spot. He turned at once, with a hasty acknowledgment of Noel Vanstone's last sympathetic inquiries, and took Magdalen into the house.

"I told you she would show her claws," he said. "It is not my fault that she scratched you before I could stop her. She hasn't hurt you, has she ?"

"She has hurt me, to some purpose," said Magdalen—"she has given me the courage to go on. Say what must be done, to-morrow, and trust me to do it." She sighed heavily as she said those words, and went up to her room.

Captain Wragge walked meditatively into the parlour, and sat down to consider. He felt by no means so certain as he could have wished, of the next proceeding on the part of the enemy after the defeat of that day. The housekeeper's farewell look had plainly informed him that she was not at the end of her resources yet; and the old militiaman felt the full importance of preparing himself in good time to meet the next step which she took in advance. He lit a cigar, and bent his wary mind on the dangers of the future.

While Captain Wragge was considering in the parlour at North Shingles, Mrs. Lecount was meditating in her bedroom at Sea View. Her exasperation at the failure of her first attempt to expose the conspiracy, had not blinded her to the instant necessity of making a second effort, before Noel Vanstone's growing infatuation got beyond her control. The snare set for Magdalen having failed, the chance of entrapping Magdalen's sister was the next chance to try. Mrs. Lecount ordered a cup of tea; opened her writing-case; and began the rough draught of a letter to be sent to Miss Vanstone the elder by the morrow's post.

So the day's skirmish ended. The heat of the battle was yet to come.

CHAPTER VI.

ALL human penetration has its limits. Accurately as Captain Wragge had seen his way hitherto, even his sharp insight was now at fault. He finished his cigar with the mortifying conviction that he was totally unprepared for Mrs. Lecount's next proceeding.

In this emergency, his experience warned him that there was one safe course, and one only, which he could take. He resolved to try the confusing effect on the housekeeper of a complete change of tactics, before she had time to press her advantage, and attack him in the dark. With this view he sent the servant upstairs, to request that Miss Bygrave would come down and speak to him.

"I hope I don't disturb you," said the captain, when Magdalen entered the room. "Allow me to apologize for the smell of tobacco, and to say two words on the subject of our next proceedings. To put it with my customary frankness, Mrs. Lecount puzzles me, and I propose to return the compliment by puzzling her. The course of action which I have to suggest is a very simple one. I have had the honour of giving you a severe neuralgic attack already, and I beg your permission (when Mr. Noel Vanstone sends to inquire to-morrow morning) to take the further liberty of laying you up altogether. Question from Sea View Cottage: 'How is Miss Bygrave this morning?' Answer from North Shingles: 'Much worse: Miss Bygrave is confined to her room.' Question repeated every day, say for a fortnight: 'How is Miss Bygrave?' Answer repeated, if necessary, for the same time: 'No better.' Can you bear the imprisonment? I see no objection to your getting a breath of fresh air the first thing in the morning, or the last thing at night. But for the whole of the day, there is no disguising it, you must put yourself in the same category with Mrs. Wragge—you must keep your room."

"What is your object in wishing me to do this?" inquired Magdalen.

"My object is twofold," replied the captain. "I blush for my own stupidity; but the fact is I can't see my way plainly to Mrs. Lecount's next move. All I feel sure of is, that she means to make another attempt at opening her master's eyes to the truth. Whatever means she may employ to discover your identity, personal communication with you, *must* be necessary to the accomplishment of her object. Very good. If I stop that communication, I put an obstacle in her way at starting—or, as we say at cards, I force her hand. Do you see the point?"

Magdalen saw it plainly. The captain went on.

"My second reason for shutting you up," he said, "refers entirely to Mrs. Lecount's master. The growth of love, my dear girl, is, in one respect, unlike all other growths—it flourishes under adverse circumstances. Our first course of action is to make Mr. Noel Vanstone feel the charm of your society. Our next, is to drive him distracted by the loss of it. I should have proposed a few more meetings, with a view to furthering this end, but for our present critical position towards Mrs. Lecount. As it is, we must trust to the effect you produced yesterday, and try the experiment of a sudden separation rather sooner than I could have otherwise wished. I shall see Mr. Noel Vanstone, though you don't—and if there *is* a raw place established anywhere about the region of that gentleman's heart, trust me to hit him on it! You are now in full possession of my views. Take your time to consider, and give me your answer—Yes or No."

" Any change is for the better," said Magdalen, " which keeps me out of the company of Mrs. Lecount and her master! Let it be as you wish."

She had hitherto answered faintly and wearily ; but she spoke those last words with a heightened tone, and a rising colour—signs which warned Captain Wragge not to press her farther.

" Very good," said the captain. " As usual, we understand each other. I see you are tired ; and I won't detain you any longer."

He rose to open the door, stopped half-way to it, and came back again. " Leave me to arrange matters with the servant downstairs," he continued. " You can't absolutely keep your bed; and we must purchase the girl's discretion when she answers the door—without taking her into our confidence, of course. I will make her understand that she is to say you are ill, just as she might say you are not at home, as a way of keeping unwelcome acquaintances out of the house. Allow me to open the door for you. —I beg your pardon, you are going into Mrs. Wragge's work-room, instead of going to your own."

" I know I am," said Magdalen. " I wish to remove Mrs. Wragge from the miserable room she is in now, and to take her upstairs with me."

" For the evening ?"

" For the whole fortnight."

Captain Wragge followed her into the dining-room and wisely closed the door before he spoke again.

" Do you seriously mean to inflict my wife's society on yourself, for a fortnight ?" he asked, in great surprise.

" Your wife is the only innocent creature in this guilty house," she burst out vehemently. " I must and will have her with me !"

" Pray don't agitate yourself," said the captain. " Take Mrs. Wragge by all means. I don't want her." Having resigned the partner of his existence in those terms, he discreetly returned to the parlour. " The weakness of the sex !" thought the captain, tapping his sagacious head. " Lay a strain on the female intellect—and the female temper gives way directly."

The strain, to which the captain alluded, was not confined that evening, to the female intellect at North Shingles : it extended to the female intellect at Sea View. For nearly two hours, Mrs. Lecount sat at her desk, writing, correcting, and writing again, before she could produce a letter to Miss Vanstone the elder, which exactly accomplished the object she wanted to attain. At last, the rough draft was completed to her satisfaction; and she made a fair copy of it, forthwith, to be posted the next day.

Her letter thus produced, was a master-piece of ingenuity. After the first preliminary sentences, the housekeeper plainly informed Norah of the appearance of the visitor in disguise at Vauxhall Walk; of the conversation which passed at the interview; and of her own suspicion that the person claiming to be Miss Garth was, in all probability, the younger Miss Vanstone herself. Having told the truth, thus far, Mrs. Lecount next proceeded to say, that her master was in possession of evidence which would justify him in putting the law in force ; that he knew the conspiracy with which he was threatened to be then in process of direction against him at Aldborough ; and that he only hesitated to protect himself, in deference to family considerations, and in the hope that the] elder Miss Vanstone might so influence her sister, as to render it unnecessary to proceed to extremities.

Under these circumstances (the letter continued) it was plainly necessary that the disguised visitor to Vauxhall Walk should be properly identified— for if Mrs. Lecount's guess proved to be wrong, and if the person turned out to be a stranger, Mr. Noel Vanstone was positively resolved to prosecute in his own defence. Events at 'Aldborough, on which it was not necessary to dwell, would enable Mrs. Lecount in a few days to gain sight of the suspected person in her own character. But as the housekeeper was entirely unacquainted with the younger Miss Vanstone, it was obviously desirable that some better informed person should, in this particular, take the matter in hand. If the elder Miss Vanstone happened to be at liberty to 'come to Aldborough herself, would she kindly write and say so ?—and Mrs. Lecount would write back again to appoint a day. If, on the other hand, Miss Vanstone was prevented from taking the journey, Mrs. Lecount suggested that her reply should contain the fullest description of her sister's personal appearance—should mention any little peculiarities which might exist in the way of marks on her face or her hands—and should state (in case she had written lately) what the address was in her last letter, and failing that, what the post-mark was on the envelope. With this information to help her, Mrs. Lecount would, in the interest of the misguided young lady herself, accept the responsibility of privately identifying her ; and would write back immediately to acquaint the elder Miss Vanstone with the result.

The difficulty of sending this letter to the right address gave Mrs. Lecount very little trouble. Remembering the name of the lawyer who had pleaded the cause of the two sisters in Michael Vanstone's time, she directed her letter to "Miss Vanstone, care of —— Pendril, Esquire, London." This she enclosed in a second envelope, addressed to Mr. Noel Vanstone's solicitor, with a line inside, requesting that gentleman to send it at once to the office of Mr. Pendril.

"Now," thought Mrs. Lecount, as she locked the letter up in her desk, preparatory to posting it the next day, with her own hand; "now I have got her!"

The next morning, the servant from Sea View came, with her master's compliments, to make inquiries after Miss Bygrave's health. Captain Wragge's bulletin was duly announced—Miss Bygrave was so ill, as to be confined to her room.

On the reception of this intelligence, Noel Vanstone's anxiety led him to call at North Shingles himself, when he went out for his afternoon walk. Miss Bygrave was no better. He inquired if he could see Mr. Bygrave. The worthy captain was prepared to meet this emergency. He thought a little irritating suspense would do Noel Vanstone no harm; and he had carefully charged the servant, in case of necessity, with her answer:—" Mr. Bygrave begged to be excused; he was not able to see any one."

On the second day, inquiries were made as before, by message in the morning, and by Noel Vanstone himself in the afternoon. The morning answer (relating to Magdalen) was, "a shade better." The afternoon answer (relating to Captain Wragge) was, " Mr. Bygrave has just gone out." That evening, Noel Vanstone's temper was very uncertain; and Mrs. Lecount's patience and tact were sorely tried in the effort to avoid offending him.

On the third morning, the report of the suffering young lady was less favourable—" Miss Bygrave was still very poorly, and not able to leave her bed." The servant returning to Sea View with this message, met the postman, and took into the breakfast-room with her two letters addressed to Mrs. Lecount.

The first letter was in a handwriting familiar to the housekeeper. It was from the medical attendant on her invalid brother at Zurich; and it announced that the patient's malady had latterly altered in so marked a manner for the better, that there was every hope now of preserving his life.

The address on the second letter was in a strange handwriting. Mrs. Lecount, concluding that it was the answer from Miss Vanstone, waited to read it until breakfast was over, and she could retire to her own room.

She opened the letter, looked at once for the name at the end, and started a little as she read it. The signature was not "Norah Vanstone," but " Harriet Garth."

Miss Garth announced that the elder Miss Vanstone had, a week since, accepted an engagement as governess—subject to the condition of joining the family of her employer at their temporary residence in the south of France, and of returning with them when they came back to England, probably in a month or six weeks' time. During the interval of this necessary absence, Miss Vanstone had requested Miss Garth to open all her letters; her main object in making that arrangement being to provide for the speedy answering of any communication which might arrive for her from her sister. Miss Magdalen Vanstone had not written since the middle of July—on which occasion the post-mark on the letter showed that it must have been posted in London, in the district of Lambeth—and her elder sister had left England in a state of the most distressing anxiety on her account.

Having completed this explanation, Miss Garth then mentioned that family circumstances prevented her from travelling personally to Aldborough to assist Mrs. Lecount's object—but that she was provided with a substitute, in every way fitter for the purpose, in the person of Mr. Pendril. That gentleman was well acquainted with Miss Magdalen Vanstone; and his professional experience and discretion would render his assistance doubly valuable. He had kindly consented to travel to Aldborough whenever it might be thought necessary. But, as his time was very valuable, Miss Garth specially requested that he might not be sent for, until Mrs. Lecount was quite sure of the day on which his services might be required.

While proposing this arrangement, Miss Garth added that she thought it right to furnish her correspondent with a written description of the younger Miss Vanstone, as well. An emergency might happen which would allow Mrs. Lecount no time for securing Mr. Pendril's services; and the execution of Mr. Noel Vanstone's intentions towards the unhappy girl who was the object of his forbearance, might be fatally delayed by an unforeseen difficulty in establishing her identity. The personal description, transmitted under these circumstances, then followed. It omitted no personal peculiarity by which Magdalen could be recognized; and it included the "two little moles close together on the left side of the neck," which had been formerly mentioned in the printed handbills sent to York.

In conclusion, Miss Garth expressed her fears that Mrs. Lecount's suspicions were only too likely to be proved true. While, however, there was the faintest chance that the conspiracy might turn out to be directed by a stranger, Miss Garth felt bound in gratitude towards Mr. Noel Vanstone, to assist the legal proceedings which would, in that case, be instituted. She accordingly appended her own formal denial—which she would personally repeat, if necessary—of any identity between herself and the person in disguise who had made use of her name. She was the Miss Garth who had filled the situation of the late Mr. Andrew Vanstone's governess; and she had never in her life been in, or near, the neighbourhood of Vauxhall Walk.

With this disclaimer—and with the writer's fervent assurances that she would do all for Magdalen's advantage which her sister might have done, if her sister had been in England—the letter concluded. It was signed in full, and was dated with the business-like accuracy in such manners which had always distinguished Miss Garth's character.

This letter placed a formidable weapon in the housekeeper's hands.

It provided a means of establishing Magdalen's identity through the intervention of a lawyer by profession. It contained a personal description minute enough to be used to advantage, if necessary, before Mr. Pendril's appearance. It presented a signed exposure of the false Miss Garth, under the hand of the true Miss Garth; and it established the fact, that the last letter received by the elder Miss Vanstone from the younger, had been posted (and therefore probably written) in the neighbourhood of Vauxhall Walk. If any later letter had been received, with the Aldborough post-mark, the chain of evidence, so far as the question of localities was concerned, might doubtless have been more complete. But, as it was, there was testimony enough (aided as that testimony might be, by the fragment of the brown alpaca dress still in Mrs. Lecount's possession) to raise tho veil which hung over the conspiracy, and to place Mr. Noel Vanstone face to face with the plain and startling truth.

The one obstacle which now stood in the way of immediate action on the housekeeper's part, was the obstacle of Miss Bygrave's present seclusion within the limits of her own room. The question of gaining personal access to her, was a question which must be decided before any communication could be opened with Mr. Pendril. Mrs. Lecount put on her bonnet at once, and called at North Shingles to try what discoveries she could make for herself, before post-time.

On this occasion, Mr. Bygrave was at home; and she was admitted without the least difficulty.

Careful consideration that morning had decided Captain Wragge on advancing matters a little nearer to the crisis. The means by which he proposed achieving this result, made it necessary for him to see the house-keeper and her master separately, and to set them at variance by producing two totally opposite impressions relating to himself, on their minds. Mrs. Lecount's visit, therefore, instead of causing him any embarrassment, was the most welcome occurrence he could have wished for. He received her in the parlour, with a marked restraint of manner, for which she was quite unprepared. His ingratiating smile was gone, and an impenetrable solemnity of countenance appeared in its stead.

"I have ventured to intrude on you, sir," said Mrs. Lecount, "to express the regret with which both my master and I have heard of Miss Bygrave's illness. Is there no improvement ?"

"No, ma'am," replied the captain, as briefly as possible. "My niece is no better."

"I have had some experience, Mr. Bygrave, in nursing. If I could be of any use——"

"Thank you, Mrs. Lecount. There is no necessity for our taking advantage of your kindness."

This plain answer was followed by a moment's silence. The housekeeper felt some little perplexity. What had become of Mr. Bygrave's elaborate courtesy, and Mr. Bygrave's many words? Did he want to offend her? If he did, Mrs. Lecount then and there determined that he should not gain his object.

"May I inquire the nature of the illness?" she persisted. "It is not connected, I hope, with our excursion to Dunwich?"

"I regret to say, ma'am," replied the captain, "it began with that neuralgic attack in the carriage."

"So! so!" thought Mrs. Lecount. "He doesn't even *try* to make me think the illness a real one; he throws off the mask, at starting—Is it a nervous illness, sir?" she added, aloud.

The captain answered by a solemn affirmative inclination of the head.

"Then you have *two* nervous sufferers in the house, Mr. Bygrave?"

"Yes, ma'am—two. My wife and my niece."

"That is rather a strange coincidence of misfortunes."

"It is, ma'am. Very strange."

In spite of Mrs. Lecount's resolution not to be offended, Captain Wragge's exasperating insensibility to every stroke she aimed at him, began to ruffle her. She was conscious of some little difficulty in securing her self-possession, before she could say anything more.

"Is there no immediate hope," she resumed, "of Miss Bygrave being able to leave her room?"

"None whatever, ma'am."

"You are satisfied, I suppose, with the medical attendance?"

"I have no medical attendance," said the captain, composedly. "I watch the case myself."

The gathering venom in Mrs. Lecount swelled up at that reply, and overflowed at her lips.

"Your smattering of science, sir," she said, with a malicious smile, "includes, I presume, a smattering of medicine as well?"

"It does, ma'am," answered the captain, without the slightest disturbance of face or manner. "I know as much of one as I do of the other."

The tone in which he spoke those words, left Mrs. Lecount but one dignified alternative. She rose to terminate the interview. The temptation of the moment proved too much for her; and she could not resist casting the shadow of a threat over Captain Wragge at parting.

"I defer thanking you, sir, for the manner in which you have received me," she said, "until I can pay my debt of obligation to some purpose. In the mean time, I am glad to infer, from the absence of a medical attendant in the house, that Miss Bygrave's illness is much less serious than I had supposed it to be when I came here."

"I never contradict a lady, ma'am," rejoined the incorrigible captain. "If it is your pleasure, when we next meet, to think my niece quite well, I shall bow resignedly to the expression of your opinion." With those words he followed the housekeeper into the passage, and politely opened the door for her. "I mark the trick, ma'am!" he said to himself, as he closed it again. "The trump-card in your hand is a sight of my niece; and I'll take care you don't play it!"

He returned to the parlour, and composedly awaited the next event which was likely to happen—a visit from Mrs. Lecount's master. In less than an hour, results justified Captain Wragge's anticipations; and Noel Vanstone walked in.

"My dear sir!" cried the captain, cordially seizing his visitor's reluctant hand, "I know what you have come for. Mrs. Lecount has told you of her visit here, and has no doubt declared that my niece's illness is a mere subterfuge. You feel surprised, you feel hurt—you suspect me of trifling with your kind sympathies—in short, you require an explanation. That explanation you shall have. Take a seat, Mr. Vanstone. I am about to throw myself on your sense and judgment as a man of the world. I acknowledge that we are in a false position, sir; and I tell you plainly at the outset —your housekeeper is the cause of it."

For once in his life, Noel Vanstone opened his eyes. "Lecount!" he exclaimed, in the utmost bewilderment.

"The same, sir," replied Captain Wragge. "I am afraid I offended Mrs. Lecount, when she came here this morning, by a want of cordiality in my manner. I am a plain man; and I can't assume what I don't feel. Far be it from me to breathe a word against your housekeeper's character. She is, no doubt, a most excellent and trustworthy woman; but she has one serious failing common to persons at her time of life who occupy her situation—she is jealous of her influence over her master, although you may not have observed it."

"I beg your pardon," interposed Noel Vanstone; "my observation is remarkably quick. Nothing escapes me."

"In that case, sir," resumed the captain, "you cannot fail to have noticed that Mrs. Lecount has allowed her jealousy to affect her conduct towards my niece?"

Noel Vanstone thought of the domestic passage at arms between Mrs. Lecount and himself, when his guests of the evening had left Sea View, and failed to see his way to any direct reply. He expressed the utmost surprise and distress—he thought Lecount had done her best to be agreeable on the drive to Dunwich—he hoped and trusted there was some unfortunate mistake.

"Do you mean to say, sir," pursued the captain, severely, "that you have not noticed the circumstance yourself? As a man of honour, and a man of observation, you can't tell me that! Your housekeeper's superficial civility has not hidden your housekeeper's real feeling. My niece has seen it, and so have you, and so have I. My niece, Mr. Vanstone, is a sensitive, high-spirited girl; and she has positively declined to cultivate Mrs. Lecount's society, for the future. Don't misunderstand me! To my niece, as well as to myself, the attraction of *your* society, Mr. Vanstone, remains the same. Miss Bygrave simply declines to be an apple of discord (if you will permit the classical allusion) cast into your household. I think she is right, so far; and I frankly confess that I have exaggerated a nervous indisposition, from which she is really suffering, into a serious illness—purely and entirely to prevent these two ladies, for the present, from meeting every day on the Parade, and from carrying unpleasant impressions of each other into your domestic establishment and mine."

"I allow nothing unpleasant in *my* establishment," remarked Noel Vanstone. "I'm master—you must have noticed that already, Mr. Bygrave?—I'm master."

"No doubt of it, my dear sir. But to live morning, noon, and night, in the perpetual exercise of your authority, is more like the life of a governor of a prison than the life of a master of a household. The wear and tear—consider the wear and tear."

"It strikes you in that light, does it?" said Noel Vanstone, soothed by Captain Wragge's ready recognition of his authority. "I don't know that you're not right. But I must take some steps directly. I won't be made ridiculous—I'll send Lecount away altogether, sooner than be made ridiculous." His colour rose; and he folded his little arms fiercely. Captain Wragge's artfully-irritating explanation had awakened that dormant suspicion of his housekeeper's influence over him, which habitually lay hidden in his mind; and which Mrs. Lecount was now not present to charm back to repose as usual. "What must Miss Bygrave think of me!" he exclaimed, with a sudden outburst of vexation. "I'll send Lecount away. Damme, I'll send Lecount away on the spot!"

"No, no, no!" said the captain, whose interest it was to avoid driving Mrs. Lecount to any desperate extremities. "Why take strong measures, when mild measures will do? Mrs. Lecount is an old servant; Mrs. Lecount is attached and useful. She has this little drawback of jealousy—jealousy of her domestic position with her bachelor master. She sees you paying courteous attention to a handsome young lady; she sees that young lady properly sensible of your politeness—and, poor soul, she loses her temper! What is the obvious remedy? Humour her—make a manly concession to the weaker sex. If Mrs. Lecount is with you, the next time we meet on the Parade, walk the other way. If Mrs. Lecount is not with you, give us the pleasure of your company by all means. In short, my dear sir, try the *suaviter in modo* (as we classical men say), before you commit yourself to the *fortiter in re* !"*

There was one excellent reason why Noel Vanstone should take Captain Wragge's conciliatory advice. An open rupture with Mrs. Lecount—even if he could have summoned the courage to face it—would imply the recognition of her claims to a provision, in acknowledgment of the services she had rendered to his father and to himself. His sordid nature quailed within him at the bare prospect of expressing the emotion of gratitude in a pecuniary form; and, after first consulting appearances by a show of hesitation, he consented to adopt the captain's suggestion, and to humour Mrs. Lecount.

"But I must be considered in this matter," proceeded Noel Vanstone. "My concession to Lecount's weakness must not be misunderstood. Miss Bygrave must not be allowed to suppose I am afraid of my housekeeper."

The captain declared that no such idea ever had entered, or ever could enter, Miss Bygrave's mind. Noel Vanstone returned to the subject nevertheless, again and again, with his customary pertinacity. Would it be indiscreet if he asked leave to set himself right personally with Miss Bygrave? Was there any hope that he might have the happiness of seeing her on that day? or, if not, on the next day? or, if not, on the day after? Captain Wragge answered cautiously: he felt the importance of not rousing Noel Vanstone's distrust by too great an alacrity in complying with his wishes.

"An interview to-day, my dear sir, is out of the question," he said. "She is not well enough; she wants repose. To-morrow I propose taking her out, before the heat of the day begins—not merely to avoid embarrassment, after what has happened with Mrs. Lecount—but because the morning air, and the morning quiet, are essential in these nervous cases. We are early people here—we shall start at seven o'clock. If you are early too, and if you would like to join us, I need hardly say that we can feel no objection to your company on our morning walk. The hour, I am aware, is an unusual one—but, later in the day, my niece may be resting on the sofa, and may not be able to see visitors."

Having made this proposal, purely for the purpose of enabling Noel Vanstone to escape to North Shingles at an hour in the morning when his housekeeper would be probably in bed, Captain Wragge left him to take the hint, if he could, as indirectly as it had been given. He proved sharp enough (the case being one in which his own interests were concerned) to close with the proposal on the spot. Politely declaring that he was always an early man when the morning presented any special attraction to him, he accepted the appointment for seven o'clock; and rose soon afterwards to take his leave.

"One word at parting," said Captain Wragge. "This conversation is entirely between ourselves. Mrs. Lecount must know nothing of the impression she has produced on my niece. I have only mentioned it to you, to account for my apparently churlish conduct, and to satisfy your own mind. In confidence, Mr. Vanstone—strictly in confidence. Good morning!"

With these parting words, the captain bowed his visitor out. Unless some unexpected disaster occurred, he now saw his way safely to the end of the enterprise. He had gained two important steps in advance, that morning. He had sown the seeds of variance between the housekeeper and her master; and he had given Noel Vanstone a common interest with Magdalen and himself, in keeping a secret from Mrs. Lecount. "We have caught our man," thought Captain Wragge, cheerfully rubbing his hands —"We have caught our man at last!"

On leaving North Shingles, Noel Vanstone walked straight home; fully restored to his place in his own estimation, and sternly determined to carry matters with a high hand, if he found himself in collision with Mrs. Lecount.

The housekeeper received her master at the door with her mildest manner, and her gentlest smile. She addressed him with downcast eyes; she opposed to his contemplated assertion of independence a barrier of impenetrable respect.

"May I venture to ask, sir," she began, "if your visit to North Shingles has led you to form the same conclusion as mine on the subject of Miss Bygrave's illness?"

"Certainly not, Lecount. I consider your conclusion to have been both hasty and prejudiced."

"I am sorry to hear it, sir. I felt hurt by Mr. Bygrave's rude reception of me—but I was not aware that my judgment was prejudiced by it. Perhaps he received *you*, sir, with a warmer welcome?"

"He received me like a gentleman—that is all I think it necessary to say, Lecount—he received me like a gentleman."

This answer satisfied Mrs. Lecount on the one doubtful point that had perplexed her. Whatever Mr. Bygrave's sudden coolness towards herself might mean, his polite reception of her master implied that the risk of detection had not daunted him, and that the plot was still in full progress. The housekeeper's eyes brightened: she had expressly calculated on this result. After a moment's thinking, she addressed her master with another question:

"You will probably visit Mr. Bygrave again, sir?"

"Of course I shall visit him—if I please."

"And perhaps see Miss Bygrave, if she gets better?"

"Why not? I should be glad to know why not? Is it necessary to ask your leave first, Lecount?"

"By no means, sir. As you have often said (and as I have often agreed with you), you are master. It may surprise you to hear it, Mr. Noel—but I have a private reason for wishing that you should see Miss Bygrave again."

Mr. Noel started a little, and looked at his housekeeper with some curiosity.

"I have a strange fancy of my own, sir, about that young lady," proceeded Mrs. Lecount. "If you will excuse my fancy, and indulge it, you will do me a favour for which I shall be very grateful."

"A fancy?" repeated her master, in growing surprise. "What fancy?"

"Only this, sir," said Mrs. Lecount.

She took from one of the neat little pockets of her apron a morsel of note-paper, carefully folded into the smallest possible compass; and respectfully placed it in Noel Vanstone's hands.

"If you are willing to oblige an old and faithful servant, Mr. Noel," she said, in a very quiet and very impressive manner, "you will kindly put that morsel of paper into your waistcoat-pocket; you will open and read it, for the first time, *when you are next in Miss Bygrave's company*; and you will say nothing of what has now passed between us to any living creature, from this time to that. I promise to explain my strange request, sir, when you have done what I ask, and when your next interview with Miss Bygrave has come to an end."

She curtseyed with her best grace and quietly left the room.

Noel Vanstone looked from the folded paper to the door, and from the door back to the folded paper, in unutterable astonishment. A mystery in his own house! under his own nose! What did it mean?

It meant that Mrs. Lecount had not wasted her time that morning. While the captain was casting the net over his visitor at North Shingles, the housekeeper was steadily mining the ground under his feet. The folded paper contained nothing less than a carefully-written extract from the personal description of Magdalen in Miss Garth's letter. With a daring ingenuity which even Captain Wragge might have envied, Mrs. Lecount had found her instrument for exposing the conspiracy, in the unsuspecting person of the victim himself!

CHAPTER VII.

LATE that evening, when Magdalen and Mrs. Wragge came back from their walk in the dark, the captain stopped Magdalen on her way up-stairs, to inform her of the proceedings of the day. He added the expression of his opinion that the time had come for bringing Noel Vanstone, with the least possible delay, to the point of making a proposal. She merely answered that she understood him, and that she would do what was required of her. Captain Wragge requested her, in that case, to oblige him by joining a walking excursion in Mr. Noel Vanstone's company, at seven o'clock the next morning. "I will be ready," she replied. "Is there anything more?" There was nothing more. Magdalen bade him good night, and returned to her own room.

She had shown the same disinclination to remain any longer than was necessary in the captain's company, throughout the three days of her seclusion in the house.

During all that time, instead of appearing to weary of Mrs. Wragge's society, she had patiently, almost eagerly, associated herself with her companion's one absorbing pursuit. She who had often chafed and fretted in past days, under the monotony of her life in the freedom of Combe-Raven, now accepted without a murmur, the monotony of her life at Mrs. Wragge's work-table. She who had hated the sight of her needle and thread, in old times—who had never yet worn an article of dress of her own making—now toiled as anxiously over the making of Mrs. Wragge's gown, and bore as patiently with Mrs. Wragge's blunders, as if the sole object of her existence had been the successful completion of that one dress. Anything was welcome to her—the trivial difficulties of fitting a gown: the small ceaseless chatter of the poor half-witted creature who was so proud of her assistance, and so happy in her company—anything was welcome that shut her out from the coming future, from the destiny to which she stood self-condemned. That sorely-wounded nature was soothed by such a trifle now as the grasp of her companion's rough and friendly hand—that desolate heart was cheered, when night parted them, by Mrs. Wragge's kiss.

The captain's isolated position in the house, produced no depressing effect on the captain's easy and equal spirits. Instead of resenting Magdalen's systematic avoidance of his society, he looked to results, and highly approved of it. The more she neglected him for his wife, the more directly useful she became in the character of Mrs. Wragge's self-appointed guardian. He had more than once seriously contemplated revoking the concession which had been extorted from him, and removing his wife at his own sole responsibility, out of harm's way; and he had only abandoned the idea, on discovering that Magdalen's resolution to keep Mrs. Wragge in her own company was really serious. While the two were together, his main anxiety was set at rest. They kept their door locked by his own desire, while he was out of the house, and, whatever Mrs. Wragge might do, Magdalen was to be trusted not to open it until he came back. That night, Captain Wragge enjoyed his cigar with a mind at ease; and sipped his brandy and water in happy ignorance of the pitfall which Mrs. Lecount had prepared for him in the morning.

Punctually at seven o'clock, Noel Vanstone made his appearance. The moment he entered the room, Captain Wragge detected a change in his visitor's look and manner. "Something wrong!" thought the captain. "We have not done with Mrs. Lecount yet."

"How is Miss Bygrave this morning?" asked Noel Vanstone. "Well enough, I hope, for our early walk?" His half-closed eyes, weak and watery with the morning light and the morning air, looked about the room furtively, and he shifted his place in a restless manner from one chair to another, as he made those polite inquiries.

"My niece is better—she is dressing for the walk," replied the captain, steadily observing his restless little friend while he spoke. "Mr. Vanstone!" he added, on a sudden, "I am a plain Englishman—excuse my blunt way of speaking my mind. You don't meet me this morning as cordially as you met me yesterday. There is something unsettled in your face. I distrust that housekeeper of yours, sir! Has she been presuming on your forbearance? Has she been trying to poison your mind against me or my niece?"

If Noel Vanstone had obeyed Mrs. Lecount's injunctions, and had kept her little morsel of note-paper folded in his pocket until the time came to use it, Captain Wragge's designedly blunt appeal might not have found him unprepared with an answer. But curiosity had got the better of him —he had opened the note at night, and again in the morning—it had seriously perplexed and startled him—and it had left his mind far too disturbed to allow him the possession of his ordinary resources. He hesitated; and his answer, when he succeeded in making it, began with a prevarication.

Captain Wragge stopped him before he had got beyond his first sentence.

"Pardon me, sir," said the captain in his loftiest manner. "If you have secrets to keep, you have only to say so, and I have done. I intrude on no man's secrets. At the same time, Mr. Vanstone, you must allow me to recall to your memory that I met you yesterday without any reserves on my side. I admitted you to my frankest and fullest confidence, sir—and, highly as I prize the advantages of your society, I can't consent to cultivate your friendship on any other than equal terms." He threw open his respectable frock-coat, and surveyed his visitor with a manly and virtuous severity.

"I mean no offence!" cried Noel Vanstone, piteously. "Why do you interrupt me, Mr. Bygrave? Why don't you let me explain? I mean no offence."

"No offence is taken, sir," said the captain. "You have a perfect right to the exercise of your own discretion. I am not offended—I only claim for myself the same privilege which I accord to you." He rose with great dignity and rang the bell. "Tell Miss Bygrave," he said to the servant, "that our walk this morning is put off until another opportunity, and that I won't trouble her to come down stairs."

This strong proceeding had the desired effect. Noel Vanstone vehemently pleaded for a moment's private conversation before the message was delivered. Captain Wragge's severity partially relaxed. He sent the servant down stairs again; and, resuming his chair, waited confidently for results. In calculating the facilities for practising on his visitor's weakness, he had one great superiority over Mrs. Lecount. His judgment was not warped by latent female jealousies; and he avoided the error into which the housekeeper had fallen, self-deluded—the error of underrating the impression on Noel Vanstone that Magdalen had produced. One of the forces in this world which no middle-aged woman is capable of estimating at its full value, when it acts against her—is the force of beauty in a woman younger than herself.

"You are so hasty, Mr. Bygrave—you won't give me time—you won't wait and hear what I have to say!" cried Noel Vanstone, piteously, when the servant had closed the parlour door.

"My family failing, sir—the blood of the Bygraves. Accept my excuses. We are alone, as you wished; pray proceed."

Placed between the alternatives of losing Magdalen's society or betraying Mrs. Lecount—unenlightened by any suspicion of the housekeeper's ultimate object; cowed by the immovable scrutiny of Captain Wragge's inquiring eye—Noel Vanstone was not long in making his choice. He confusedly described his singular interview of the previous evening with Mrs. Lecount; and taking the folded paper from his pocket, placed it in the captain's hand.

A suspicion of the truth dawned on Captain Wragge's mind, the moment he saw the mysterious note. He withdrew to the window before he opened it. The first lines that attracted his attention were these:—"Oblige me, Mr. Noel, by comparing the young lady who is now in your company, with the personal description which follows these lines, and which has been communicated to me by a friend. You shall know the name of the person described—which I have left a blank—as soon as the evidence of your own eyes has forced you to believe, what you would refuse to credit on the unsupported testimony of Virginie Lecount."

That was enough for the captain. Before he had read a word of the description itself, he knew what Mrs. Lecount had done, and felt with a profound sense of humiliation, that his female enemy had taken him by surprise.

There was no time to think; the whole enterprise was threatened with irrevocable overthrow. The one resource, in Captain Wragge's present situation, was to act instantly on the first impulse of his own audacity. Line by line he read on—and still the ready inventiveness which had never deserted him yet, failed to answer the call made on it now. He came to the closing sentence—to the last words which mentioned the two little moles on Magdalen's neck. At that crowning point of the description, an idea crossed his mind—his parti-coloured eyes twinkled; his curly lips twisted up at the corners—Wragge was himself again.

He wheeled round suddenly from the window; and looked Noel Vanstone straight in the face, with a grimly-quiet suggestiveness of something serious to come.

"Pray, sir, do you happen to know anything of Mrs. Lecount's family?" he inquired.

"A respectable family," said Noel Vanstone—"that's all I know. Why do you ask?"

"I am not usually a betting man," pursued Captain Wragge. "But on this occasion, I will lay you any wager you like, there is madness in your housekeeper's family."

"Madness!" repeated Noel Vanstone, amazedly.

"Madness!" reiterated the captain, sternly tapping the note with his forefinger. "I see the cunning of insanity, the suspicion of insanity, the feline treachery of insanity in every line of this deplorable document. There is a far more alarming reason, sir, than I had supposed for Mrs. Lecount's behaviour to my niece. It is clear to me, that Miss Bygrave resembles some other lady who has seriously offended your housekeeper— who has been formerly connected, perhaps, with an outbreak of insanity in your housekeeper—and who is now evidently confused with my niece, in your housekeeper's wandering mind. That is my conviction, Mr. Vanstone. I may be right, or I may be wrong. All I say is this—neither you, nor any man, can assign a sane motive for the production of that incomprehensible document, and for the use which you are requested to make of it."

"I don't think Lecount's mad," said Noel Vanstone, with a very blank look, and a very discomposed manner. "It couldn't have escaped me— with my habits of observation—it couldn't possibly have escaped me if Lecount had been mad."

"Very good, my dear sir. In my opinion she is the subject of an insane delusion. In your opinion she is in possession of her senses, and has some mysterious motive which neither you nor I can fathom. Either way, there can be no harm in putting Mrs. Lecount's description to the test, not only as a matter of curiosity, but for our own private satisfaction on both sides. It is of course impossible to tell my niece that she is to be made the subject of such a preposterous experiment as that note of yours suggests. But you can use your own eyes, Mr. Vanstone; you can keep your own counsel; and—mad or not—you can at least tell your housekeeper, on the testimony of your own senses, that she is wrong. Let me look at the description again. The greater part of it is not worth two straws for any purpose of identification; hundreds of young ladies have tall figures, fair complexions, light brown hair, and light grey eyes. You will say, on the other hand, hundreds of young ladies have not got two little moles close together on the left side of the neck. Quite true. The moles supply us with what we scientific men call, a Crucial Test. When my niece comes down stairs, sir, you have my full permission to take the liberty of looking at her neck."

Noel Vanstone expressed his high approval of the Crucial Test, by smirking and simpering for the first time that morning.

"Of looking at her neck," repeated the captain; returning the note to his visitor, and then making for the door. "I will go up-stairs myself, Mr. Vanstone," he continued, "and inspect Miss Bygrave's walking dress. If she has innocently placed any obstacles in your way—if her hair is a little too low, or her frill is a little too high—I will exert my authority, on the first harmless pretext I can think of, to have those obstacles removed. All I ask is, that you will choose your opportunity discreetly, and that you will not allow my niece to suppose that her neck is the object of a gentleman's inspection."

The moment he was out of the parlour, Captain Wragge ascended the stairs at the top of his speed, and knocked at Magdalen's door. She opened it to him, in her walking dress—obedient to the signal agreed on between them which summoned her down-stairs.

"What have you done with your paints and powders?" asked the captain, without wasting a word in preliminary explanations. "They were not in the box of costumes which I sold for you at Birmingham. Where are they?"

"I have got them here," replied Magdalen. "What can you possibly mean by wanting them now?"

"Bring them instantly into my dressing-room—the whole collection, brushes, palette, and everything. Don't waste time in asking questions; I'll tell you what has happened as we go on. Every moment is precious to us. Follow me instantly!"

His face plainly showed that there was a serious reason for his strange proposal. Magdalen secured her collection of cosmetics, and followed him into the dressing-room. He locked the door, placed her on a chair close to the light, and then told her what had happened.

"We are on the brink of detection," proceeded the captain, carefully mixing his colours with liquid glue, and with a strong "drier" added from a bottle in his own possession. "There is only one chance for us (lift up your hair from the left side of your neck)—I have told Mr. Noel Vanstone to take a private opportunity of looking at you; and I am going to give the lie direct to that she-devil Lecount, by painting out your moles."

"They can't be painted out," said Magdalen. "No colour will stop on them."

"*My* colour will," remarked Captain Wragge. "I have tried a variety of professions in my time—the profession of painting among the rest. Did you ever hear of such a thing as a Black Eye? I lived some months once in the neighbourhood of Drury Lane, entirely on Black Eyes. My flesh-colour stood on bruises of all sorts, shades, and sizes—and it will stand, I promise you, on your moles."

With this assurance, the captain dipped his brush into a little lump of opaque colour, which he had mixed in a saucer, and which he had graduated, as nearly as the materials would permit, to the colour of Magdalen's skin. After first passing a cambric handkerchief with some white powder on it, over the part of her neck on which he designed to operate, he placed two layers of colour on the moles, with the tip of the brush. The process was performed in a few moments—and the moles, as if by magic, disappeared from view. Nothing but the closest inspection could have discovered the artifice by which they had been concealed: at the distance of two or three feet only, it was perfectly invisible.

"Wait here, five minutes," said Captain Wragge, "to let the paint dry —and then join us in the parlour. Mrs. Lecount herself would be puzzled, if she looked at you now."

"Stop!" said Magdalen. "There is one thing you have not told me yet. How did Mrs. Lecount get the description which you read downstairs? Whatever else she has seen of me, she has not seen the mark on my neck—it is too far back, and too high up; my hair hides it."

"Who knows of the mark?" asked Captain Wragge.

She turned deadly pale under the anguish of a sudden recollection of Frank.

"My sister knows it," she said faintly.

"Mrs. Lecount may have written to your sister," suggested the captain.

"Do you think my sister would tell a stranger what no stranger has a right to know? Never! never!"

"Is there nobody else who could tell Mrs. Lecount? The mark was mentioned in the handbills at York. Who put it there?"

"Not Norah! Perhaps Mr. Pendril. Perhaps Miss Garth."

"Then Mrs. Lecount has written to Mr. Pendril or Miss Garth—more likely to Miss Garth. The governess would be easier to deal with than the lawyer."

"What can she have said to Miss Garth?"

Captain Wragge considered a little.

"I can't say what Mrs. Lecount may have written," he said; "but I can tell you what I should have written in Mrs. Lecount's place. I should have frightened Miss Garth by false reports about you, to begin with—and then I should have asked for personal particulars, to help a benevolent stranger in restoring you to your friends."

The angry glitter flashed up instantly in Magdalen's eyes.

"What *you* would have done, is what Mrs. Lecount has done," she said indignantly. "Neither lawyer, nor governess, shall dispute my right to my own will, and my own way. If Miss Garth thinks she can control my actions by corresponding with Mrs. Lecount—I will show Miss Garth she is mistaken! It is high time, Captain Wragge, to have done with these wretched risks of discovery. We will take the short way to the end we have in view, sooner than Mrs. Lecount or Miss Garth think for. How long can you give me to wring an offer of marriage out of that creature down-stairs?"

"I dare not give you long," replied Captain Wragge. "Now your friends know where you are, they may come down on us at a day's notice. Could you manage it in a week?"

"I'll manage it in half the time," she said, with a hard, defiant laugh. "Leave us together this morning as you left us at Dunwich—and take Mrs. Wragge with you, as an excuse for parting company. Is the paint dry yet? Go down-stairs, and tell him I am coming directly."

So, for the second time, Miss Garth's well-meant efforts defeated their own end. So, the fatal force of circumstance turned the hand that would fain have held Magdalen back, into the hand that drove her on.

The captain returned to his visitor in the parlour—after first stopping on the way, to issue his orders for the walking excursion to Mrs. Wragge.

"I am shocked to have kept you waiting," he said, sitting down again confidentially by Noel Vanstone's side. "My only excuse is, that my niece had accidentally dressed her hair, so as to defeat our object. I have been persuading her to alter it—and young ladies are apt to be a little obstinate on questions relating to their toilette. Give her a chair on that side of you, when she comes in—and take your look at her neck comfortably, before we start for our walk."

Magdalen entered the room, as he said those words—and, after the first greetings were exchanged, took the chair presented to her with the most unsuspicious readiness. Noel Vanstone applied the Crucial Test on the spot—with the highest appreciation of the fair material which was the subject of experiment. Not the vestige of a mole was visible on any part of the smooth white surface of Miss Bygrave's neck. It mutely answered the blinking inquiry of Noel Vanstone's half-closed eyes, by the flattest practical contradiction of Mrs. Lecount. That one central incident in the events of the morning, was of all the incidents that had hitherto occurred, the most important in its results. That one discovery shook the house-keeper's hold on her master, as nothing had shaken it yet.

In a few minutes, Mrs. Wragge made her appearance, and excited as much surprise in Noel Vanstone's mind as he was capable of feeling, while absorbed in the enjoyment of Magdalen's society. The walking party left the house at once; directing their steps northward, so as not to pass the windows of Sea View Cottage. To Mrs. Wragge's unutterable astonish-ment, her husband, for the first time in the course of their married life, politely offered her his arm, and led her on, in advance of the young people, as if the privilege of walking alone with her presented some special attrac-tion to him! "Step out!" whispered the captain, fiercely. "Leave your niece and Mr. Vanstone alone! If I catch you looking back at them, I'll put the Oriental Cashmere Robe on the top of the kitchen fire! Turn your toes out, and keep step—confound you, keep step!" Mrs. Wragge kept step to the best of her limited ability. Her sturdy knees trembled under her. She firmly believed the captain was intoxicated.

The walk lasted for rather more than an hour. Before nine o'clock they were all back again at North Shingles. The ladies went at once into the house. Noel Vanstone remained with Captain Wragge in the garden.

"Well," said the captain, "what do you think now of Mrs. Lecount?"

"Damn Lecount!" replied Noel Vanstone, in great agitation. "I'm half inclined to agree with you. I'm half inclined to think my infernal house-keeper is mad."

He spoke fretfully and unwillingly, as if the merest allusion to Mrs. Lecount was distasteful to him. His colour came and went; his manner was absent and undecided; he fidgeted restlessly about the garden walk. It would have been plain to a far less acute observation than Captain Wragge's, that Magdalen had met his advances by an unexpected grace and readiness of encouragement, which had entirely overthrown his self-control.

"I never enjoyed a walk so much in my life!" he exclaimed, with a sudden outburst of enthusiasm. "I hope Miss Bygrave feels all the better for it. Do you go out at the same time to-morrow morning? May I join you again?"

"By all means, Mr. Vanstone," said the captain, cordially. "Excuse me for returning to the subject—but what do you propose saying to Mrs. Lecount?"

"I don't know. Lecount is a perfect nuisance! What would you do, Mr. Bygrave, if you were in my place?"

"Allow me to ask a question, my dear sir, before I tell you. What is your breakfast hour?"

"Half-past nine."

"Is Mrs. Lecount an early riser?"

"No. Lecount is lazy in the morning. I hate lazy women! If you were in my place, what should you say to her?"

"I should say nothing," replied Captain Wragge. "I should return at once by the back way; I should let Mrs. Lecount see me in the front garden, as if I was taking a turn before breakfast; and I should leave her to suppose that I was only just out of my room. If she asks you whether you mean to come here to-day, say No. Secure a quiet life, until circumstances force you to give her an answer. Then tell the plain truth—say that Mr. Bygrave's niece and Mrs. Lecount's description are at variance with each other in the most important particular; and beg that the subject may not be mentioned again. There is my advice. What do you think of it?"

If Noel Vanstone could have looked into his counsellor's mind, he might have thought the captain's advice excellently adapted to serve the captain's interests. As long as Mrs. Lecount could be kept in ignorance of her master's visits to North Shingles—so long she would wait until the opportunity came for trying her experiment; and so long she might be trusted not to endanger the conspiracy by any further proceedings. Necessarily incapable of viewing Captain Wragge's advice under this aspect, Noel Vanstone simply looked at it, as offering him a temporary means of escape from an explanation with his housekeeper. He eagerly declared that the course of action suggested to him should be followed to the letter, and returned to Sea View without further delay.

On this occasion, Captain Wragge's anticipations were in no respect falsified by Mrs. Lecount's conduct. She had no suspicion of her master's visit to North Shingles—she had made up her mind, if necessary, to wait patiently for his interview with Miss Bygrave, until the end of the week—and she did not embarrass him by any unexpected questions, when he announced his intention of holding no personal communication with the Bygraves on that day. All she said was, "Don't you feel well enough, Mr. Noel? or don't you feel inclined?" He answered, shortly, "I don't feel well enough;" and there the conversation ended.

The next day, the proceedings of the previous morning were exactly repeated. This time, Noel Vanstone went home rapturously with a keepsake in his breast-pocket—he had taken tender possession of one of Miss Bygrave's gloves. At intervals during the day, whenever he was alone, he took out the glove, and kissed it with a devotion which was almost passionate in its fervour. The miserable little creature luxuriated in his moments of stolen happiness, with a speechless and stealthy delight which was a new sensation to him. The few young girls whom he had met with, in his father's narrow circle at Zurich, had felt a mischievous pleasure in treating him like a quaint little plaything; the strongest impression he could make on their hearts was an impression in which their lap-dogs might have rivalled him; the deepest interest he could create in them, was the interest they might have felt in a new trinket or a new dress. The only women who had hitherto invited his admiration, and taken his compliments seriously, had been women whose charms were on the wane, and whose chances of marriage were fast failing them. For the first time in his life, he had now passed hours of happiness in the society of a beautiful girl, who had left him to think of her afterwards without a single humiliating remembrance to lower him in his own esteem.

Anxiously as he tried to hide it, the change produced in his look and manner by the new feeling awakened in him, was not a change which could be concealed from Mrs. Lecount. On the second day, she pointedly asked him whether he had not made an arrangement to call on the Bygraves. He denied it as before. "Perhaps you are going to-morrow, Mr. Noel?" persisted the housekeeper. He was at the end of his resources; he was impatient to be rid of her inquiries; he trusted to his friend at North Shingles to help him—and, this time, he answered, Yes. "If you see the young lady," proceeded Mrs. Lecount, "don't forget that note of mine, sir, which you have in your waistcoat-pocket." No more was said on either side—but by that night's post, the housekeeper wrote to Miss Garth. The letter merely acknowledged, with thanks, the receipt of Miss Garth's communication; and informed her that, in a few days, Mrs. Lecount hoped to be in a position to write again, and summon Mr. Pendril to Aldborough.

Late in the evening, when the parlour at North Shingles began to get dark, and when the captain rang the bell for candles, as usual, he was surprised by hearing Magdalen's voice in the passage, telling the servant to take the lights down-stairs again. She knocked at the door immediately afterwards; and glided into the obscurity of the room, like a ghost.

"I have a question to ask you about your plans for to-morrow," she said. "My eyes are very weak this evening, and I hope you will not object to dispense with the candles for a few minutes."

She spoke in low stifled tones, and felt her way noiselessly to a chair far removed from the captain in the darkest part of the room. Sitting near the window, he could just discern the dim outline of her dress, he could just hear the faint accents of her voice. For the last two days he had seen nothing of her, except during their morning walk. On that afternoon, he had found his wife crying in the little back room down-stairs. She could only tell him that Magdalen had frightened her—that Magdalen was going the way again which she had gone when the letter came from China in the terrible past time at Vauxhall Walk.

"I was sorry to hear that you were ill to-day, from Mrs. Wragge," said the captain, unconsciously dropping his voice almost to a whisper as he spoke.

"It doesn't matter," she answered quietly, out of the darkness. "I am strong enough to suffer, and live. Other girls, in my place, would have been happier—they would have suffered, and died. It doesn't matter; it will be all the same a hundred years hence. Is he coming again to-morrow morning, at seven o'clock?"

"He is coming, if you feel no objection to it?"

"I have no objection to make; I have done with objecting. But I should like to have the time altered. I don't look my best in the early morning—I have bad nights, and I rise haggard and worn. Write him a note this evening, and tell him to come at twelve o'clock."

"Twelve is rather late, under the circumstances, for you to be seen out walking."

"I have no intention of walking. Let him be shown into the parlour——"

Her voice died away in silence, before she ended the sentence.

"Yes?" said Captain Wragge.

"And leave me alone in the parlour to receive him."

"I understand," said the captain. "An admirable idea. I'll be out of the way, in the dining-room, while he is here—and you can come and tell me about it when he has gone."

There was another moment of silence.

"Is there no way but telling you?" she asked suddenly. "I can control myself while he is with me—but I can't answer for what I may say or do, afterwards. Is there no other way?"

"Plenty of ways," said the captain. "Here is the first that occurs to me. Leave the blind down over the window of your room up-stairs, before he comes. I will go out on the beach, and wait there within sight of the house. When I see him come out again, I will look at the window. If he has said nothing, leave the blind down. If he has made you an offer —draw the blind up. The signal is simplicity itself; we can't misunderstand each other. Look your best to-morrow! Make sure of him, my dear girl—make sure of him, if you possibly can."

He had spoken loud enough to feel certain that she had heard him—but no answering word came from her. The dead silence was only disturbed by the rustling of her dress, which told him she had risen from her chair. Her shadowy presence crossed the room again; the door shut softly—she was gone. He rang the bell hurriedly for the lights. The servant found him standing close at the window—looking less self-possessed than usual. He told her he felt a little poorly, and sent her to the cupboard for the brandy.

At a few minutes before twelve, the next day, Captain Wragge withdrew to his post of observation—concealing himself behind a fishing-boat drawn up on the beach. Punctually as the hour struck, he saw Noel Vanstone approach North Shingles, and open the garden gate. When the house door had closed on the visitor, Captain Wragge settled himself comfortably against the side of the boat, and lit his cigar.

He smoked for half an hour—for ten minutes over the half-hour, by his watch. He finished the cigar down to the last morsel of it that he could hold in his lips. Just as he had thrown away the end, the door opened again; and Noel Vanstone came out.

The captain looked up instantly at Magdalen's window. In the absorbing excitement of the moment, he counted the seconds. She might get from the parlour to her own room in less than a minute. He counted to thirty— and nothing happened. He counted to fifty—and nothing happened. He gave up counting, and left the boat impatiently, to return to the house.

As he took his first step forward he saw the signal.

The blind was drawn up.

Cautiously ascending the eminence of the beach, Captain Wragge looked towards Sea View Cottage, before he showed himself on the Parade. Noel Vanstone had reached home again : he was just entering his own door.

"If all your money was offered me to stand in your shoes," said the captain, looking after him—" rich as you are, I wouldn't take it !"

CHAPTER VIII.

On returning to the house, Captain Wragge received a significant message from the servant. "Mr. Noel Vanstone would call again at two o'clock, that afternoon : when he hoped to have the pleasure of finding Mr. Bygrave at home."

The captain's first inquiry, after hearing this message, referred to Magdalen. "Where was Miss Bygrave ?" "In her own room." "Where was Mrs. Bygrave ?" "In the back parlour." Captain Wragge turned his steps at once in the latter direction ; and found his wife, for the second time, in tears. She had been sent out of Magdalen's room, for the whole day ; and she was at her wits' end to know what she had done to deserve it. Shortening her lamentations without ceremony, her husband sent her up-stairs on the spot ; with instructions to knock at the door, and to inquire whether Magdalen could give five minutes' attention to a question of importance, which must be settled before two o'clock.

The answer returned was in the negative. Magdalen requested that the subject on which she was asked to decide might be mentioned to her in writing. She engaged to reply in the same way—on the understanding that Mrs. Wragge, and not the servant, should be employed to deliver the note, and to take back the answer.

Captain Wragge forthwith opened his paper-case, and wrote these lines: —"Accept my warmest congratulations on the result of your interview with Mr. N. V. He is coming again at two o'clock; no doubt to make his proposals in due form. The question to decide is, whether I shall press him or not on the subject of settlements.* The considerations for your own mind are two in number. First, whether the said pressure (without at all underrating your influence over him) may not squeeze for a long time, before it squeezes money out of Mr. N. V. Secondly, whether we are altogether justified—considering our present position towards a certain sharp practitioner in petticoats—in running the risk of delay. Consider these points, and let me have your decision as soon as convenient."

The answer returned to this note was written in crooked blotted characters, strangely unlike Magdalen's usually firm and clear handwriting. It only contained these words:—"Give yourself no trouble about settlements. Leave the use to which he is to put his money for the future, in my hands."

"Did you see her?" asked the captain, when his wife had delivered the answer.

"I tried," said Mrs. Wragge, with a fresh burst of tears—"but she only opened the door far enough to put out her hand. I took and gave it a little squeeze—and, oh poor soul, it felt so cold in mine!"

When Mrs. Lecount's master made his appearance at two o'clock, he stood alarmingly in need of an anodyne application from Mrs. Lecount's green fan. The agitation of making his avowal to Magdalen; the terror of finding himself discovered by the housekeeper; the tormenting suspicion of the hard pecuniary conditions which Magdalen's relative and guardian might impose on him—all these emotions, stirring in conflict together, had overpowered his feebly-working heart with a trial that strained it sorely. He gasped for breath, as he sat down in the parlour at North Shingles; and that ominous bluish pallor which always overspread his face in moments of agitation, now made its warning appearance again. Captain Wragge seized the brandy bottle, in genuine alarm; and forced his visitor to drink a wine-glassful of the spirit, before a word was said between them on either side.

Restored by the stimulant, and encouraged by the readiness with which the captain anticipated everything that he had to say, Noel Vanstone contrived to state the serious object of his visit, in tolerably plain terms. All the conventional preliminaries proper to the occasion were easily disposed of. The suitor's family was respectable; his position in life was undeniably satisfactory; his attachment, though hasty, was evidently disinterested and sincere. All that Captain Wragge had to do was to refer to these various considerations with a happy choice of language, in a voice that trembled with manly emotion—and this he did to perfection. For the first half-hour of the interview, no allusion whatever was made to the delicate and dangerous part of the subject. The captain waited, until he had composed his visitor; and when that result was achieved, came smoothly to the point in these terms:

"There is one little difficulty, Mr. Vanstone, which I think we have both overlooked. Your housekeeper's recent conduct inclines me to fear that she will view the approaching change in your life with anything but a friendly eye. Probably, you have not thought it necessary yet to inform her of the new tie which you propose to form?"

Noel Vanstone turned pale at the bare idea of explaining himself to Mrs. Lecount.

"I can't tell what I'm to do," he said, glancing aside nervously at the window, as if he expected to see the housekeeper peeping in. "I hate all awkward positions; and this is the most unpleasant position I ever was placed in. You don't know what a terrible woman Lecount is. I'm not afraid of her; pray don't suppose I'm afraid of her——"

At those words, his fears rose in his throat, and gave him the lie direct by stopping his utterance.

"Pray don't trouble yourself to explain," said Captain Wragge, coming to the rescue. "This is the common story, Mr. Vanstone. Here is a woman who has grown old in your service, and in your father's service before you; a woman who has contrived, in all sorts of small underhand ways, to presume systematically on her position for years and years past; a woman, in short, whom your inconsiderate but perfectly natural kindness, has allowed to claim a right of property in you——"

"Property!" cried Noel Vanstone, mistaking the captain, and letting the truth escape him through sheer inability to conceal his fears any longer. "I don't know what amount of property she won't claim. She'll make me pay for my father as well as for myself. Thousands, Mr. Bygrave—thousands of pounds sterling out of my pocket!!!" He clasped his hands in despair at the picture of pecuniary compulsion, which his fancy had conjured up—his own golden life-blood spouting from him in great jets of prodigality under the lancet of Mrs. Lecount!

"Gently, Mr. Vanstone—gently! The woman knows nothing so far, and the money is not gone yet."

"No, no; the money is not gone, as you say. I'm only nervous about it; I can't help being nervous. You were saying something just now; you were going to give me advice. I value your advice—you don't know how highly I value your advice." He said those words with a conciliatory smile, which was more than helpless: it was absolutely servile in its dependence on his judicious friend.

"I was only assuring you, my dear sir, that I understood your position," said the captain. "I see your difficulty as plainly as you can see it yourself. Tell a woman like Mrs. Lecount that she must come off her domestic throne, to make way for a young and beautiful successor, armed with the authority of a wife; and an unpleasant scene must be the inevitable result. An unpleasant scene, Mr. Vanstone, if your opinion of your housekeeper's sanity is well founded. Something far more serious, if my opinion that her intellect is unsettled, happens to turn out the right one."

"I don't say it isn't my opinion too," rejoined Noel Vanstone. "Especially after what has happened to-day."

Captain Wragge immediately begged to know what the event alluded to might be.

Noel Vanstone, thereupon, explained—with an infinite number of parentheses, all referring to himself—that Mrs. Lecount had put the dreaded question relating to the little note in her master's pocket, barely an hour since. He had answered her inquiry as Mr. Bygrave had advised him. On hearing that the accuracy of the personal description had been fairly put to the test, and had failed in the one important particular of the moles on the neck, Mrs. Lecount had considered a little, and had then asked him whether he had shown her note to Mr. Bygrave, before the experiment was tried. He had answered in the negative, as the only safe form of reply that he could think of, on the spur of the moment—and the housekeeper had then addressed him in these strange and startling words : " You are keeping the truth from me, Mr. Noel. You are trusting strangers, and doubting your old servant and your old friend. Every time you go to Mr. Bygrave's house, every time you see Miss Bygrave, you are drawing nearer and nearer to your destruction. They have got the bandage over your eyes in spite of me ; but I tell them, and tell you, before many days are over, I will take it off !" To this extraordinary outbreak—accompanied, as it was, by an expression in Mrs. Lecount's face which he had never seen there before—Noel Vanstone had made no reply. Mr. Bygrave's conviction that there was a lurking taint of insanity in the housekeeper's blood, had recurred to his memory, and he had left the room at the first opportunity.

Captain Wragge listened with the closest attention to the narrative thus presented to him. But one conclusion could be drawn from it—it was a plain warning to him to hasten the end.

"I am not surprised," he said, gravely, " to hear that you are inclining more favourably to my opinion. After what you have just told me, Mr. Vanstone, no sensible man could do otherwise. This is becoming serious. I hardly know what results may not be expected to follow the communication of your approaching change in life to Mrs. Lecount. My niece may be involved in those results. She is nervous ; she is sensitive in the highest degree ; she is the innocent object of this woman's unreasoning hatred and distrust. You alarm me, sir ! I am not easily thrown off my balance—

but I acknowledge you alarm me for the future." He frowned, shook his head, and looked at his visitor despondently.

Noel Vanstone began to feel uneasy. The change in Mr. Bygrave's manner seemed ominous of a reconsideration of his proposals from a new, and unfavourable point of view. He took counsel of his inborn cowardice, and his inborn cunning; and proposed a solution of the difficulty, discovered by himself.

"Why should we tell Lecount at all?" he asked. "What right has Lecount to know? Can't we be married, without letting her into the secret? And can't somebody tell her afterwards, when we are both out of her reach?"

Captain Wragge received this proposal with an expression of surprise, which did infinite credit to his power of control over his own countenance. His foremost object, throughout the interview, had been to conduct it to this point—or, in other words, to make the first idea of keeping the marriage a secret from Mrs. Lecount, emanate from Noel Vanstone instead of from himself. No one knew better than the captain that the only responsibilities which a weak man ever accepts, are responsibilities which can be perpetually pointed out to him as resting exclusively on his own shoulders.

"I am accustomed to set my face against clandestine proceedings of all kinds," said Captain Wragge. "But there are exceptions to the strictest rules; and I am bound to admit, Mr. Vanstone, that your position in this matter is an exceptional position if ever there was one yet. The course you have just proposed—however unbecoming I may think it; however distasteful it may be to myself—would not only spare you a very serious embarrassment (to say the least of it), but would also protect you from the personal assertion of those pecuniary claims on the part of your housekeeper, to which you have already adverted. These are both desirable results to achieve—to say nothing of the removal, on my side, of all apprehension of annoyance to my niece. On the other hand, however, a marriage solemnized with such privacy as you propose, must be a hasty marriage—for, as we are situated, the longer the delay, the greater will be the risk that our secret may escape our keeping. I am not against hasty marriages, where a mutual flame is fanned by an adequate income. My own was a love-match, contracted in a hurry. There are plenty of instances in the experience of every one, of short courtships and speedy marriages, which have turned up trumps—I beg your pardon—which have turned out well, after all. But if you and my niece, Mr. Vanstone, are to add one to the number of these cases, the usual preliminaries of marriage among the higher classes must be hastened by some means. You doubtless understand me, as now referring to the subject of settlements."

"I'll take another teaspoonful of brandy," said Noel Vanstone, holding out his glass with a trembling hand as the word "settlements" passed Captain Wragge's lips.

"I'll take a teaspoonful with you," said the captain, nimbly dismounting from the pedestal of his respectability, and sipping his brandy with the highest relish. Noel Vanstone, after nervously following his host's example, composed himself to meet the coming ordeal, with reclining head and grasping hands—in the position familiarly associated to all civilized humanity with a seat in a dentist's chair.

The captain put down his empty glass and got up again on his pedestal.

"We were talking of settlements," he resumed. "I have already mentioned, Mr. Vanstone, at an early period of our conversation, that my niece presents the man of her choice with no other dowry than the most inestimable of all gifts—the gift of herself. This circumstance, however (as you are no doubt aware), does not disentitle me to make the customary stipulations with her future husband. According to the usual course in this matter, my lawyer would see yours—consultations would take place—delays would occur—strangers would be in possession of your intentions—and Mrs. Lecount would, sooner or later, arrive at that knowledge of the truth, which you are anxious to keep from her. Do you agree with me, so far?"

Unutterable apprehension closed Noel Vanstone's lips. He could only reply by an inclination of the head.

"Very good," said the captain. "Now, sir, you may possibly have observed that I am a man of a very original turn of mind. If I have not hitherto struck you in that light, it may then be necessary to mention that there are some subjects on which I persist in thinking for myself. The subject of marriage settlements is one of them. What, let me ask you, does a parent or guardian in my present condition usually do? After having trusted the man whom he has chosen for his son-in-law with the sacred deposit of a woman's happiness—he turns round on that man, and declines to trust him with the infinitely inferior responsibility of providing for her pecuniary future. He fetters his son-in-law with the most binding document the law can produce; and employs with the husband of his own child, the same precautions which he would use if he were dealing with a stranger and a rogue. I call such conduct as this, inconsistent and unbecoming in the last degree. You will not find it my course of conduct, Mr. Vanstone—you will not find me preaching what I don't practise. If I trust you with my niece, I trust you with every inferior responsibility towards her and towards me. Give me your hand, sir—tell me on your word of honour that you will provide for your wife, as becomes her position and your means—and the question of settlements is decided between us from this moment, at once and for ever!" Having carried out Magdalen's instructions in this lofty tone, he threw open his respectable frock-coat, and sat with head erect, and hand extended, the model of parental feeling, and the picture of human integrity.

For one moment, Noel Vanstone remained literally petrified by astonishment. The next, he started from his chair and wrung the hand of his magnanimous friend, in a perfect transport of admiration. Never yet, throughout his long and varied career, had Captain Wragge felt such difficulty in keeping his countenance, as he felt now. Contempt for the outburst of miserly gratitude of which he was the object; triumph in the sense of successful conspiracy against a man who had rated the offer of his protection at five pounds; regret at the lost opportunity of effecting a fine stroke of moral agriculture, which his dread of involving himself in coming consequences had forced him to let slip—all these varied emotions agitated the captain's mind; all strove together to find their way to the surface, through the outlets of his face or his tongue. He allowed Noel Vanstone to keep possession of his hand, and to heap one series of shrill protestations and promises on another, until he had regained his usual mastery over himself. That result achieved, he put the little man back in his chair, and returned forthwith to the subject of Mrs. Lecount.

"Suppose we now revert to the difficulty which we have not conquered yet," said the captain. "Let us say that I do violence to my own habits and feelings; that I allow the considerations I have already mentioned to weigh with me; and that I sanction your wish to be united to my niece, without the knowledge of Mrs. Lecount. Allow me to inquire, in that case, what means you can suggest for the accomplishment of your end?"

"I can't suggest anything," replied Noel Vanstone, helplessly. "Would you object to suggest for me?"

"You are making a bolder request than you think, Mr. Vanstone. I never do things by halves. When I am acting with my customary candour, I am frank (as you know already) to the utmost verge of imprudence. When exceptional circumstances compel me to take an opposite course, there isn't a slyer fox alive than I am. If, at your express request, I take off my honest English coat here, and put on a Jesuit's gown—if, purely out of sympathy for your awkward position, I consent to keep your secret for you from Mrs. Lecount—I must have no unseasonable scruples to contend with on your part. If it is neck or nothing on my side, sir—it must be neck or nothing on yours also!"

"Neck or nothing by all means," said Noel Vanstone, briskly—"on the understanding that you go first. I have no scruples about keeping Lecount in the dark. But she is devilish cunning, Mr. Bygrave. How is it to be done?"

"You shall hear directly," replied the captain. "Before I develop my views, I should like to have your opinion on an abstract question of morality. What do you think, my dear sir, of pious frauds in general?"

Noel Vanstone looked a little embarrassed by the question.

"Shall I put it more plainly?" continued Captain Wragge. "What do you say to the universally-accepted maxim, that 'all stratagems are fair in love and war?'—Yes, or No?"

"Yes!" answered Noel Vanstone, with the utmost readiness.

"One more question, and I have done," said the captain.   "Do you see any particular objection to practising a pious fraud on Mrs. Lecount?"

Noel Vanstone's resolution began to falter a little.

"Is Lecount likely to find it out?" he asked cautiously.

"She can't possibly discover it until you are married, and out of her reach."

"You are sure of that?"

"Quite sure."

"Play any trick you like on Lecount," said Noel Vanstone, with an air of unutterable relief. "I have had my suspicions lately, that she is trying to domineer over me—I am beginning to feel that I have borne with Lecount long enough. I wish I was well rid of her."

"You shall have your wish," said Captain Wragge. "You shall be rid of her in a week or ten days."

Noel Vanstone rose eagerly and approached the captain's chair.

"You don't say so!" he exclaimed. "How do you mean to send her away?"

"I mean to send her on a journey," replied Captain Wragge.

"Where?"

"From your house at Aldborough, to her brother's bedside at Zurich."

Noel Vanstone started back at the answer, and returned suddenly to his chair.

"How can you do that?" he inquired, in the greatest perplexity. "Her brother (hang him!) is much better. She had another letter from Zurich to say so, this morning."

"Did you see the letter?"

"Yes. She always worries about her brother—she *would* show it to me."

"Who was it from? and what did it say?"

"It was from the doctor—he always writes to her. I don't care two straws about her brother; and I don't remember much of the letter, except that it was a short one. The fellow was much better; and if the doctor didn't write again, she might take it for granted that he was getting well. That was the substance of it."

"Did you notice where she put the letter, when you gave it her back again?"

"Yes. She put it in the drawer, where she keeps her account-books."

"Can you get at that drawer?"

"Of course I can. I have got a duplicate key—I always insist on a duplicate key of the place where she keeps her account-books. I never allow the account-books to be locked up from my inspection: it's a rule of the house."

"Be so good as to get that letter to-day, Mr. Vanstone, without your housekeeper's knowledge; and add to the favour by letting me have it here privately for an hour or two."

"What do you want it for?"

"I have some more questions to ask, before I can tell you. Have you any intimate friend at Zurich, whom you could trust to help you in playing a trick on Mrs Lecount?"

"What sort of help do you mean?" asked Noel Vanstone.

"Suppose," said the captain, "you were to send a letter addressed to Mrs. Lecount, at Aldborough, enclosed in another letter addressed to one of your friends abroad? And suppose you were to instruct that friend to help a harmless practical joke by posting Mrs. Lecount's letter at Zurich? Do you know any one who could be trusted to do that?"

"I know two people who could be trusted!" cried Noel Vanstone. "Both ladies—both spinsters—both bitter enemies of Lecount's. But what is your drift, Mr. Bygrave? Though I am not usually wanting in penetration, I don't altogether see your drift."

"You shall see it directly, Mr. Vanstone."

With those words he rose, withdrew to his desk in the corner of the room, and wrote a few lines on a sheet of note-paper. After first reading them carefully to himself, he beckoned to Noel Vanstone to come and read them too.

"A few minutes since," said the captain, pointing complacently to his own composition with the feather end of his pen, "I had the honour of suggesting a pious fraud on Mrs. Lecount. There it is!"

He resigned his chair at the writing-table to his visitor. Noel Vanstone sat down, and read these lines:

"MY DEAR MADAM,—Since I last wrote, I deeply regret to inform you that your brother has suffered a relapse. The symptoms are so serious, that it is my painful duty to summon you instantly to his bedside. I am making every effort to resist the renewed progress of the malady; and I have not yet lost all hope of success. But I cannot reconcile it to my conscience to leave you in ignorance of a serious change in my patient for the worse, which *may* be attended by fatal results. With much sympathy, I remain, &c. &c."

Captain Wragge waited with some anxiety for the effect which this letter might produce. Mean, selfish, and cowardly as he was, even Noel Vanstone might feel some compunction at practising such a deception as was here suggested, on a woman who stood towards him in the position of Mrs. Lecount. She had served him faithfully, however interested her motives might be —she had lived, since he was a lad, in the full possession of his father's confidence—she was living now under the protection of his own roof. Could he fail to remember this; and, remembering it, could he lend his aid without hesitation to the scheme which was now proposed to him? Captain Wragge unconsciously retained belief enough in human nature to doubt it.

To his surprise, and, it must be added, to his relief also, his apprehensions proved to be perfectly groundless. The only emotions aroused in Noel Vanstone's mind by a perusal of the letter, were a hearty admiration of his friend's idea, and a vainglorious anxiety to claim the credit to himself of being the person who carried it out. Examples may be found every day of a fool who is no coward ; examples may be found occasionally of a fool who is not cunning—but it may reasonably be doubted whether there is a producible instance anywhere of a fool who is not cruel.

" Perfect !" cried Noel Vanstone, clapping his hands. " Mr. Bygrave, you are as good as Figaro in the French comedy.* Talking of French, there is one serious mistake in this clever letter of yours—it is written in the wrong language. When the doctor writes to Lecount, he writes in French. Perhaps you meant me to translate it ? You can't manage without my help can you ? I write French as fluently as I write English. Just look at me ! I'll translate it, while I sit here, in two strokes of the pen."

He completed the translation almost as rapidly as Captain Wragge had produced the original. " Wait a minute !" he cried, in high critical triumph at discovering another defect in the composition of his ingenious friend. " The doctor always dates his letters. Here is no date to yours."

" I leave the date to you," said the captain, with a sardonic smile. " You have discovered the fault, my dear sir—pray correct it !"

Noel Vanstone mentally looked into the great gulf which separates the faculty that can discover a defect, from the faculty that can apply a remedy—and, following the example of many a wiser man, declined to cross over it.

" I couldn't think of taking the liberty," he said, politely. " Perhaps you had a motive for leaving the date out ?"

" Perhaps I had," replied Captan Wragge, with his easiest good humour. " The date must depend on the time a letter takes to get to Zurich. I have had no experience on that point—you must have had plenty of experience in your father's time. Give me the benefit of your information ; and we will add the date before you leave the writing-table."

Noel Vanstone's experience was, as Captain Wragge had anticipated, perfectly competent to settle the question of time. The railway resources of the Continent (in the year eighteen hundred and forty-seven) were but scanty ; and a letter sent, at that period, from England to Zurich, and from Zurich back again to England, occupied ten days in making the double journey by post.*

" Date the letter, in French, five days on from to-morrow," said the captain, when he had got his information. " Very good. The next thing is to let me have the doctor's note, as soon as you can. I may be obliged to practise some hours before I can copy your translation in an exact imitation of the doctor's handwriting. Have you got any foreign note-paper? Let me have a few sheets; and send, at the same time, an envelope addressed to one of those lady-friends of yours at Zurich, accompanied by the necessary request to post the enclosure. This is all I need trouble you to do, Mr. Vanstone. Don't let me seem inhospitable—but the sooner you can supply me with my materials, the better I shall be pleased. We entirely understand each other, I suppose? Having accepted your proposal for my niece's hand, I sanction a private marriage in consideration of the circumstances on your side. A little harmless stratagem is necessary to forward your views. I invent the stratagem, at your request—and you make use of it without the least hesitation. The result is, that in ten days from to-morrow, Mrs. Lecount will be on her way to Switzerland—in fifteen days from to-morrow, Mrs. Lecount will reach Zurich, and discover the trick we have played her—in twenty days from to-morrow, Mrs. Lecount will be back at Aldborough, and will find her master's wedding-cards on the table, and her master himself away on his honeymoon trip. I put it arithmetically, for the sake of putting it plain. God bless you. Good-morning!"

"I suppose I may have the happiness of seeing Miss Bygrave to-morrow?" said Noel Vanstone, turning round at the door.

"We must be careful," replied Captain Wragge. "I don't forbid to-morrow—but I make no promise beyond that. Permit me to remind you that we have got Mrs. Lecount to manage for the next ten days."

"I wish Lecount was at the bottom of the German Ocean!" exclaimed Noel Vanstone, fervently. "It's all very well for you to manage her—you don't live in the house. What am I to do?"

"I'll tell you to-morrow," said the captain. "Go out for your walk alone, and drop in here, as you dropped in to-day, at two o'clock. In the mean time, don't forget those things I want you to send me. Seal them up together in a large envelope. When you have done that, ask Mrs. Lecount to walk out with you as usual; and while she is up-stairs putting her bonnet on, send the servant across to me. You understand? Good-morning."

An hour afterwards, the sealed envelope, with its enclosures, reached Captain Wragge in perfect safety. The double task of exactly imitating a strange handwriting, and accurately copying words written in a language with which he was but slightly acquainted, presented more difficulties to be overcome than the captain had anticipated. It was eleven o'clock before the employment which he had undertaken was successfully completed, and the letter to Zurich ready for the post.

Before going to bed, he walked out on the deserted Parade, to breathe the cool night air. All the lights were extinguished in Sea View Cottage, when he looked that way—except the light in the housekeeper's window. Captain Wragge shook his head suspiciously. He had gained experience enough, by this time, to distrust the wakefulness of Mrs. Lecount.

CHAPTER IX

If Captain Wragge could have looked into Mrs. Lecount's room—while he stood on the Parade watching the light in her window—he would have seen the housekeeper sitting absorbed in meditation over a worthless little morsel of brown stuff, which lay on her toilet-table.

However exasperating to herself the conclusion might be, Mrs. Lecount could not fail to see that she had been thus far met and baffled successfully at every point. What was she to do next? If she sent for Mr. Pendril, when he came to Aldborough (with only a few hours spared from his business at her disposal)—what definite course would there be for him to follow? If she showed Noel Vanstone the original letter from which her note had been copied, he would apply instantly to the writer for an explanation; would expose the fabricated story by which Mrs. Lecount had succeeded in imposing on Miss Garth; and would, in any event, still declare, on the evidence of his own eyes, that the test by the marks on the neck had utterly failed. Miss Vanstone the elder, whose unexpected presence at Aldborough might have done wonders—whose voice in the hall at North Shingles, even if she had been admitted no farther, might have reached her sister's ears, and led to instant results—Miss Vanstone the elder, was out of the country, and was not likely to return for a month at least. Look as anxiously as Mrs. Lecount might along the course which she had hitherto followed, she failed to see her way through the accumulated obstacles which now barred her advance.

Other women, in this position, might have waited until circumstances altered, and helped them. Mrs. Lecount boldly retraced her steps, and determined to find her way to her end in a new direction. Resigning, for the present, all further attempt to prove that the false Miss Bygrave was the true Magdalen Vanstone—she resolved to narrow the range of her next efforts; to leave the actual question of Magdalen's identity untouched; and to rest satisfied with convincing her master of this simple fact—that the young lady who was charming him at North Shingles, and the disguised woman who had terrified him in Vauxhall Walk, were one and the same person.

The means of effecting this new object were, to all appearance, far less easy of attainment than the means of effecting the object which Mrs. Lecount had just resigned. Here, no help was to be expected from others—no ostensibly benevolent motives could be put forward as a blind—no appeal could be made to Mr. Pendril or to Miss Garth. Here, the housekeeper's only chance of success depended in the first place on her being able to effect a stolen entrance into Mr. Bygrave's house; and, in the second place, on her ability to discover whether that memorable alpaca dress from which she had secretly cut the fragment of stuff, happened to form part of Miss Bygrave's wardrobe.

Taking the difficulties now before her in their order as they occurred, Mrs. Lecount first resolved to devote the next few days to watching the habits of the inmates of North Shingles, from early in the morning to late at night; and to testing the capacity of the one servant in the house to resist the temptation of a bribe. Assuming that results proved successful, and that, either by money or by stratagem, she gained admission to North Shingles (without the knowledge of Mr. Bygrave or his niece), she turned next to the second difficulty of the two—the difficulty of obtaining access to Miss Bygrave's wardrobe.

If the servant proved corruptible, all obstacles in this direction might be considered as removed beforehand. But, if the servant proved honest, the new problem was no easy one to solve.

Long and careful consideration of the question led the housekeeper, at last, to the bold resolution of obtaining an interview—if the servant failed her—with Mrs. Bygrave herself. What was the true cause of this lady's mysterious seclusion? Was she a person of the strictest and the most inconvenient integrity? or a person who could not be depended on to preserve a secret? or a person who was as artful as Mr. Bygrave himself, and who was kept in reserve to forward the object of some new deception which was yet to come? In the first two cases, Mrs. Lecount could trust in her own powers of dissimulation, and in the results which they might achieve. In the last case (if no other end was gained), it might be of vital importance to her to discover an enemy hidden in the dark. In any event, she determined to run the risk. Of the three chances in her favour, on which she had reckoned at the outset of the struggle—the chance of entrapping Magdalen by word of mouth, the chance of entrapping her by the help of her friends, and the chance of entrapping her by means of Mrs. Bygrave—two had been tried, and two had failed. The third remained to be tested yet; and the third might succeed.

So, the captain's enemy plotted against him in the privacy of her own chamber, while the captain watched the light in her window from the beach outside.

Before breakfast the next morning, Captain Wragge posted the forged letter to Zurich with his own hand. He went back to North Shingles with his mind not quite decided on the course to take with Mrs. Lecount, during the all-important interval of the next ten days.

Greatly to his surprise, his doubts on this point were abruptly decided by Magdalen herself.

He found her waiting for him, in the room where the breakfast was laid. She was walking restlessly to and fro, with her head drooping on her bosom, and her hair hanging disordered over her shoulders. The moment she looked up on his entrance, the captain felt the fear which Mrs. Wragge had felt before him—the fear that her mind would be struck prostrate again, as it had been struck once already, when Frank's letter reached her in Vauxhall Walk.

"Is he coming again to day?" she asked, pushing away from her the chair which Captain Wragge offered, with such violence that she threw it on the floor.

"Yes," said the captain, wisely answering her in the fewest words. "He is coming at two o'clock."

"Take me away!" she exclaimed, tossing her hair back wildly from her face. "Take me away before he comes. I can't get over the horror of marrying him, while I am in this hateful place—take me somewhere where I can forget it, or I shall go mad! Give me two days' rest—two days out of sight of that horrible sea—two days out of prison in this horrible house—two days anywhere in the wide world, away from Aldborough. I'll come back with you! I'll go through with it to the end! Only give me two days' escape from that man and everything belonging to him! Do you hear, you villain?" she cried, seizing his arm and shaking it in a frenzy of passion—"I have been tortured enough—I can bear it no longer!"

There was but one way of quieting her, and the captain instantly took it. "If you will try to control yourself," he said, "you shall leave Aldborough in an hour's time."

She dropped his arm, and leaned back heavily against the wall behind her. "I'll try," she answered, struggling for breath, but looking at him less wildly. "You sha'n't complain of me, if I can help it." She attempted confusedly to take her handkerchief from her apron pocket, and failed to find it. The captain took it out for her. Her eyes softened, and she drew her breath more freely, as she received the handkerchief from him. "You are a kinder man than I thought you were," she said; "I am sorry I spoke so passionately to you just now—I am very, very sorry." The tears stole into her eyes, and she offered him her hand with the native grace and gentleness of happier days. "Be friends with me again," she said, pleadingly. "I'm only a girl, Captain Wragge—I'm only a girl!"

He took her hand in silence—patted it for a moment—and then opened the door for her to go back to her own room again. There was genuine regret in his face, as he showed her that trifling attention. He was a vagabond and a cheat; he had lived a mean, shuffling, degraded life—but he was human; and she had found her way to the lost sympathies in him which not even the self-profanation of a swindler's existence could wholly destroy. "Damn the breakfast!" he said, when the servant came in for her orders. "Go to the inn directly, and say I want a carriage and pair at the door in an hour's time." He went out into the passage, still chafing under a sense of mental disturbance which was new to him; and shouted to his wife more fiercely than ever. "Pack up what we want for a week's absence—and be ready in half an hour!" Having issued those directions, he returned to the breakfast-room, and looked at the half-spread table with an impatient wonder at his disinclination to do justice to his own meal. "She has rubbed off the edge of my appetite," he said to himself, with a forced laugh. "I'll try a cigar, and a turn in the fresh air."

If he had been twenty years younger, those remedies might have failed him. But where is the man to be found, whose internal policy succumbs to revolution, when that man is on the wrong side of fifty? Exercise and change of place gave the captain back into the possession of himself. He recovered the lost sense of the flavour of his cigar; and recalled his wandering attention to the question of his approaching absence from Aldborough. A few minutes' consideration satisfied his mind that Magdalen's outbreak had forced him to take the course of all others, which, on a fair review of existing emergencies, it was now most desirable to adopt.

Captain Wragge's inquiries, on the evening when he and Magdalen had drunk tea at Sea View, had certainly informed him that the housekeeper's brother possessed a modest competence; that his sister was his nearest living relative; and that there were some unscrupulous cousins on the spot, who were anxious to usurp the place in his will which properly belonged to Mrs. Lecount. Here were strong motives to take the housekeeper to Zurich, when the false report of her brother's relapse reached England. But, if any idea of Noel Vanstone's true position dawned on her, in the mean time—who could say whether she might not, at the eleventh hour, prefer asserting her large pecuniary interest in her master, to defending her small pecuniary interest at her brother's bedside? While that question remained undecided, the plain necessity of checking the growth of Noel Vanstone's intimacy with the family at North Shingles, did not admit of a doubt; and of all means of effecting that object, none could be less open to suspicion than the temporary removal of the household from their residence at Aldborough. Thoroughly satisfied with the soundness of this conclusion, Captain Wragge made straight for Sea View Cottage, to apologize and explain before the carriage came and the departure took place.

Noel Vanstone was easily accessible to visitors: he was walking in the garden before breakfast. His disappointment and vexation were freely expressed when he heard the news which his friend had to communicate. The captain's fluent tongue, however, soon impressed on him the necessity of resignation to present circumstances. The bare hint that the "pious fraud" might fail after all, if anything happened in the ten days' interval to enlighten Mrs. Lecount, had an instant effect in making Noel Vanstone as patient and as submissive as could be wished.

"I won't tell you where we are going, for two good reasons," said Captain Wragge, when his preliminary explanations were completed. "In the first place, I haven't made up my mind yet; and, in the second place, if you don't know what our destination is, Mrs. Lecount can't worm it out of you. I have not the least doubt she is watching us, at this moment, from behind her window-curtain. When she asks what I wanted with you this morning, tell her I came to say good-bye for a few days—finding my niece not so well again, and wishing to take her on a short visit to some friends, to try change of air. If you could produce an impression on Mrs. Lecount's mind (without overdoing it), that you are a little disappointed in me, and that you are rather inclined to doubt my heartiness in cultivating your acquaintance, you will greatly help our present object. You may depend on our return to North Shingles in four or five days at farthest. If anything strikes me in the mean while, the post is always at our service, and I won't fail to write to you."

"Won't Miss Bygrave write to me?" inquired Noel Vanstone piteously. "Did she know you were coming here? Did she send me no message?"

"Unpardonable on my part to have forgotten it!" cried the captain. "She sent you her love."

Noel Vanstone closed his eyes in silent ecstasy.

When he opened them again, Captain Wragge had passed through the garden gate and was on his way back to North Shingles. As soon as his own door had closed on him, Mrs. Lecount descended from the post of observation which the captain had rightly suspected her of occupying; and addressed the inquiry to her master which the captain had rightly foreseen would follow his departure. The reply she received produced but one impression on her mind. She at once set it down as a falsehood, and returned to her own window, to keep watch over North Shingles more vigilantly than ever.

To her utter astonishment, after a lapse of less than half an hour, she saw an empty carriage draw up at Mr. Bygrave's door. Luggage was brought out and packed on the vehicle. Miss Bygrave appeared, and took her seat in it. She was followed into the carriage by a lady of great size and stature, whom the housekeeper conjectured to be Mrs. Bygrave. The servant came next, and stood waiting on the path. The last person to appear was Mr. Bygrave. He locked the house-door, and took the key away with him to a cottage near at hand, which was the residence of the landlord of North Shingles. On his return, he nodded to the servant—who walked away by herself towards the humbler quarter of the little town—and joined the ladies in the carriage. The coachman mounted the box, and the vehicle disappeared.

Mrs. Lecount laid down the opera-glass, through which she had been closely investigating these proceedings, with a feeling of helpless perplexity which she was almost ashamed to acknowledge to herself. The secret of Mr. Bygrave's object in suddenly emptying his house at Aldborough of every living creature in it, was an impenetrable mystery to her.

Submitting herself to circumstances with a ready resignation which Captain Wragge had not shown, on his side, in a similar situation, Mrs. Lecount wasted neither time nor temper in unprofitable guess-work. She left the mystery to thicken or to clear, as the future might decide; and looked exclusively at the uses to which she might put the morning's event in her own interests. Whatever might have become of the family at North Shingles, the servant was left behind—and the servant was exactly the person whose assistance might now be of vital importance to the house-keeper's projects. Mrs. Lecount put on her bonnet, inspected the collection of loose silver in her purse, and set forth on the spot to make the servant's acquaintance.

She went first to the cottage, at which Mr. Bygrave had left the key of North Shingles, to discover the servant's present address from the landlord. So far as this object was concerned, her errand proved successful. The landlord knew that the girl had been allowed to go home for a few days to her friends, and knew in what part of Aldborough her friends lived. But here his sources of information suddenly dried up. He knew nothing of the destination to which Mr. Bygrave and his family had betaken themselves; and he was perfectly ignorant of the number of days over which their absence might be expected to extend. All he could say was, that he had not received a notice to quit from his tenant, and that he had been requested to keep the key of the house in his possession until Mr. Bygrave returned to claim it in his own person.

Baffled, but not discouraged, Mrs. Lecount turned her steps next towards the back street of Aldborough, and astonished the servant's relatives by conferring on them the honour of a morning call.

Easily imposed on, at starting, by Mrs. Lecount's pretence of calling to engage her, under the impression that she had left Mr. Bygrave's service— the servant did her best to answer the questions put to her. But she knew as little as the landlord of her master's plans. All she could say about them was, that she had not been dismissed, and that she was to await the receipt of a note recalling her when necessary to her situation at North Shingles. Not having expected to find her better informed on this part of the subject, Mrs. Lecount smoothly shifted her ground, and led the woman into talking generally of the advantages and defects of her situation in Mr. Bygrave's family.

Profiting by the knowledge gained, in this indirect manner, of the little secrets of the household, Mrs. Lecount made two discoveries. She found out, in the first place, that the servant (having enough to do in attending to the coarser part of the domestic work) was in no position to disclose the secrets of Miss Bygrave's wardrobe, which were known only to the young lady herself and to her aunt. In the second place, the housekeeper ascertained that the true reason of Mrs. Bygrave's rigid seclusion, was to be found in the simple fact that she was little better than an idiot, and that her husband was probably ashamed of allowing her to be seen in public. These apparently trivial discoveries enlightened Mrs. Lecount on a very important point which had been previously involved in doubt. She was now satisfied that the likeliest way to obtaining a private investigation of Magdalen's wardrobe, lay through deluding the imbecile lady and not through bribing the ignorant servant.

Having reached that conclusion—pregnant with coming assaults on the weakly-fortified discretion of poor Mrs. Wragge—the housekeeper cautiously abstained from exhibiting herself any longer under an inquisitive aspect. She changed the conversation to local topics; waited until she was sure of leaving an excellent impression behind her; and then took her leave.

Three days passed; and Mrs. Lecount and her master—each with their widely-different ends in view—watched with equal anxiety for the first signs of returning life in the direction of North Shingles. In that interval, no letter either from the uncle or the niece arrived for Noel Vanstone. His sincere feeling of irritation under this neglectful treatment, greatly assisted the effect of those feigned doubts on the subject of his absent friends, which the captain had recommended him to express in the housekeeper's presence. He confessed his apprehensions of having been mistaken, not in Mr. Bygrave only, but even in his niece as well, with such a genuine air of annoyance, that he actually contributed a new element of confusion to the existing perplexities of Mrs. Lecount.

On the morning of the fourth day, Noel Vanstone met the postman in the garden; and, to his great relief, discovered among the letters delivered to him, a note from Mr. Bygrave.

The date* of the note was "Woodbridge," and it contained a few lines only. Mr. Bygrave mentioned that his niece was better, and that she sent her love as before. He proposed returning to Aldborough on the next day—when he would have some new considerations, of a strictly private nature, to present to Mr. Noel Vanstone's mind. In the mean time he would beg Mr. Vanstone not to call at North Shingles, until he received a special invitation to do so—which invitation should certainly be given on the day when the family returned. The motive of this apparently strange request should be explained to Mr. Vanstone's perfect satisfaction, when he was once more united to his friends. Until that period arrived, the strictest caution was enjoined on him in all his communications with Mrs. Lecount—and the instant destruction of Mr. Bygrave's letter, after due perusal of it was (if the classical phrase might be pardoned) a *sine quâ non.*

The fifth day came. Noel Vanstone (after submitting himself to the *sine quâ non*, and destroying the letter) waited anxiously for results; while Mrs. Lecount, on her side, watched patiently for events. Towards three o'clock in the afternoon, the carriage appeared again at the gate of North Shingles. Mr. Bygrave got out and tripped away briskly to the landlord's cottage for the key. He returned with the servant at his heels. Miss Bygrave left the carriage; her giant-relative followed her example; the house-door was opened; the trunks were taken off; the carriage disappeared, and the Bygraves were at home again !

Four o'clock struck, five o'clock, six o'clock, and nothing happened. In half an hour more, Mr. Bygrave—spruce, speckless, and respectable as ever —appeared on the Parade, sauntering composedly in the direction of Sea View.

Instead of at once entering the house, he passed it; stopped, as if struck by a sudden recollection; and retracing his steps, asked for Mr. Vanstone at the door. Mr. Vanstone came out hospitably into the passage. Pitching his voice to a tone which could be easily heard by any listening individual, through any open door in the bedroom regions, Mr. Bygrave announced the object of his visit on the door-mat, in the fewest possible words. He had been staying with a distant relative. The distant relative possessed two pictures—Gems by the Old Masters—which he was willing to dispose of, and which he had intrusted for that purpose to Mr. Bygrave's care. If Mr. Noel Vanstone, as an amateur in such matters, wished to see the Gems, they would be visible in half an hour's time, when Mr. Bygrave would have returned to North Shingles.

Having delivered himself of this incomprehensible announcement, the arch-conspirator laid his significant forefinger along the side of his short Roman nose—said, " Fine weather, isn't it ? Good afternoon !"—and sauntered out inscrutably to continue his walk on the Parade.

On the expiration of the half-hour, Noel Vanstone presented himself at North Shingles—with the ardour of a lover burning inextinguishably in his bosom, through the superincumbent mental fog of a thoroughly bewildered man. To his inexpressible happiness, he found Magdalen alone in the parlour. Never yet had she looked so beautiful in his eyes. The rest and relief of her four days' absence from Aldborough had not failed to produce their results; she had more than recovered her composure. Vibrating perpetually from one violent extreme to another, she had now passed from the passionate despair of five days since, to a feverish exaltation of spirits, which defied all remorse and confronted all consequences. Her eyes sparkled ; her cheeks were bright with colour ; she talked incessantly, with a forlorn mockery of the girlish gaiety of past days—she laughed with a deplorable persistency in laughing—she imitated Mrs. Lecount's smooth voice, and Mrs. Lecount's insinuating graces of manner, with an overcharged resemblance to the original, which was but the coarse reflection of the delicately-accurate mimicry of former times. Noel Vanstone, who had never yet seen her as he saw her now, was enchanted; his weak head whirled with an intoxication of enjoyment; his wizen cheeks flushed as if they had caught the infection from hers. The half-hour during which he was alone with her, passed like five minutes to him. When that time had elapsed, and when she suddenly left him—to obey a previously-arranged summons to her aunt's presence—miser as he was, he would have paid, at that moment, five golden sovereigns out of his pocket, for five golden minutes more, passed in her society.

The door had hardly closed on Magdalen, before it opened again, and the captain walked in. He entered on the explanations which his visitor naturally expected from him, with the unceremonious abruptness of a man hard pressed for time, and determined to make the most of every moment at his disposal.

"Since we last saw each other," he began, "I have been reckoning up the chances for and against us, as we stand at present. The result on my own mind, is this:—If you are still at Aldborough, when that letter from Zurich reaches Mrs. Lecount, all the pains we have taken will have been pains thrown away. If your housekeeper had fifty brothers all dying together, she would throw the whole fifty over, sooner than leave you alone at Sea View, while we are your neighbours at North Shingles."

Noel Vanstone's flushed cheeks turned pale with dismay. His own knowledge of Mrs. Lecount told him that this view of the case was the right one.

"If we go away again," proceeded the captain, "nothing will be gained —for nothing would persuade your housekeeper, in that case, that we have not left you the means of following us. You must leave Aldborough, this time; and, what is more, you must go without leaving a single visible trace behind you for us to follow. If we accomplish this object, in the course of the next five days, Mrs. Lecount will take the journey to Zurich. If we fail, she will be a fixture at Sea View to a dead certainty. Don't ask questions! I have got your instructions ready for you; and I want your closest attention to them. Your marriage with my niece depends on your not forgetting a word of what I am now going to tell you.—One question first. Have you followed my advice? Have you told Mrs. Lecount you are beginning to think yourself mistaken in me?"

"I did worse than that," replied Noel Vanstone, penitently. "I committed an outrage on my own feelings. I disgraced myself by saying that I doubted Miss Bygrave!"

"Go on disgracing yourself, my dear sir! Doubt us both with all your might—and I'll help you. One question more. Did I speak loud enough this afternoon? Did Mrs. Lecount hear me?"

"Yes. ' Lecount opened her door; Lecount heard you. What made you give me that message? I see no pictures here. Is this another pious fraud, Mr. Bygrave?"

"Admirably guessed, Mr. Vanstone! You will see the object of my imaginary picture-dealing in the very next words which I am now about to address to you. When you get back to Sea View, this is what you are to say to Mrs. Lecount. Tell her that my relative's works of Art are two worthless pictures—copies from the Old Masters, which I have tried to sell you, as originals, at an exorbitant price. Say you suspect me of being little better than a plausible impostor; and pity my unfortunate niece, for being associated with such a rascal as I am. There is your text to speak from. Say in many words what I have just said in few. You can do that, can't you?"

"Of course I can do it," said Noel Vanstone. "But I can tell you one thing—Lecount won't believe me."

"Wait a little, Mr. Vanstone; I have not done with my instructions yet. You understand what I have just told you? Very good. We may get on from to-day to to-morrow. Go out to-morrow with Mrs. Lecount at your usual time. I will meet you on the Parade, and bow to you. Instead of returning my bow, look the other way. In plain English, cut me! That is easy enough to do, isn't it?"

"She won't believe me, Mr. Bygrave—she won't believe me?"

"Wait a little again, Mr. Vanstone. There are more instructions to come. You have got your directions for to-day, and you have got your directions for to-morrow. Now for the day after. The day after is the seventh day since we sent the letter to Zurich. On the seventh day, decline to go out walking as before, from dread of the annoyance of meeting me again. Grumble about the smallness of the place; complain of your health; wish you had never come to Aldborough, and never made acquaintance with the Bygraves; and when you have well worried Mrs. Lecount with your discontent, ask her on a sudden, if she can't suggest a change for the better. If you put that question to her naturally, do you think she can be depended on to answer it?"

"She won't want to be questioned at all," replied Noel Vanstone, irritably. "I have only got to say I am tired of Aldborough; and, if she believes me—which she won't; I'm quite positive, Mr. Bygrave, she won't!—she will have her suggestion ready before I can ask for it."

"Ay! ay!" said the captain eagerly. "There is some place, then, that Mrs. Lecount wants to go to, this autumn?"

"She wants to go there (hang her!) every autumn."

"To go where?"

"To Admiral Bartram's—you don't know him, do you?—at St. Crux-in-the-Marsh."

"Don't lose your patience, Mr. Vanstone! What you are now telling me, is of the most vital importance to the object we have in view. Who is Admiral Bartram?"

"An old friend of my father's. My father laid him under obligations—my father lent him money, when they were both young men. I am like one of the family at St. Crux; my room is always kept ready for me. Not that there's any family at the admiral's, except his nephew, George Bartram. George is my cousin; I'm as intimate with George as my father was with the admiral—and I've been sharper than my father, for I haven't lent my friend any money. Lecount always makes a show of liking George —I believe to annoy me. She likes the admiral, too: he flatters her vanity. He always invites her to come with me to St. Crux. He lets her have one of the best bed-rooms; and treats her as if she was a lady. She's as proud as Lucifer—she likes being treated like a lady—and she pesters me every autumn to go to St. Crux. What's the matter? What are you taking out your pocket-book for?"

"I want the admiral's address, Mr. Vanstone—for a purpose which I will explain immediately."

With those words, Captain Wragge opened his pocket-book, and wrote down the address from Noel Vanstone's dictation, as follows: "Admiral Bartram, St. Crux-in-the-Marsh, near Ossory, Essex."

"Good!" cried the captain, closing his pocket-book again. "The only difficulty that stood in our way, is now cleared out of it. Patience, Mr. Vanstone—patience! Let us take up my instructions again at the point where we dropped them. Give me five minutes more attention; and you will see your way to your marriage, as plainly as I see it. On the day after to-morrow, you declare you are tired of Aldborough; and Mrs. Lecount suggests St. Crux. You don't say yes or no on the spot—you take the next day to consider it—and you make up your mind the last thing at night to go to St. Crux the first thing in the morning. Are you in the habit of superintending your own packing up? or do you usually shift all the trouble of it on Mrs. Lecount's shoulders?"

"Lecount has all the trouble, of course; Lecount is paid for it! But I don't really go, do I?"

"You go as fast as horses can take you to the railway; without having held any previous communication with this house, either personally or by letter. You leave Mrs. Lecount behind to pack up your curiosities, to settle with the tradespeople, and to follow you to St. Crux the next morning. The next morning is the tenth morning. On the tenth morning she receives the letter from Zurich; and if you only carry out my instructions, Mr. Vanstone—as sure as you sit there, to Zurich she goes!"

Noel Vanstone's colour began to rise again, as the captain's stratagem dawned on him at last in its true light.

"And what am I to do at St. Crux?" he inquired.

"Wait there till I call for you," replied the captain. "As soon as

Mrs. Lecount's back is turned, I will go to the church here and give the necessary notice of the marriage. The same day or the next, I will travel to the address written down in my pocket-book—pick you up at the admiral's—and take you on to London with me to get the licence. With that document in our possession, we shall be on our way back to Aldborough, while Mrs. Lecount is on her way out to Zurich—and before she starts on her return journey, you and my niece will be man and wife! There are your future prospects for you. What do you think of them?"

"What a head you have got!" cried Noel Vanstone, in a sudden outburst of enthusiasm. "You're the most extraordinary man I ever met with. One would think you had done nothing all your life but take people in."

Captain Wragge received that unconscious tribute to his native genius, with the complacency of a man who felt that he thoroughly deserved it.

"I have told you already, my dear sir," he said, modestly, "that I never do things by halves. Pardon me for reminding you that we have no time for exchanging mutual civilities. Are you quite sure about your instructions? I dare not write them down, for fear of accidents. Try the system of artificial memory—count your instructions off, after me, on your thumb and your four fingers. To-day, you tell Mrs. Lecount I have tried to take you in with my relative's works of Art. To-morrow, you cut me on the Parade. The day after, you refuse to go out, you get tired of Aldborough, and you allow Mrs. Lecount to make her suggestion. The next day, you accept the suggestion. And the next day to that, you go to St. Crux. Once more, my dear sir! Thumb—works of Art. Forefinger—cut me on the Parade. Middle finger—tired of Aldborough. Third finger—take Lecount's advice. Little finger—off to St. Crux. Nothing can be clearer —nothing can be easier to do. Is there anything you don't understand? Anything that I can explain over again, before you go?"

"Only one thing," said Noel Vanstone. "Is it settled that I am not to come here again before I go to St. Crux?"

"Most decidedly!" answered the captain. "The whole success of the enterprise depends on your keeping away. Mrs. Lecount will try the credibility of everything you say to her by one test—the test of your communicating, or not, with this house. She will watch you, night and day! Don't call here, don't send messages, don't write letters—don't even go out by yourself. Let her see you start for St. Crux, on her suggestion; with the absolute certainty in her own mind that you have followed her advice without communicating it in any form whatever to me or to my niece. Do that, and she *must* believe you, on the best of all evidence for our interests, and the worst for hers—the evidence of her own senses."

With those last words of caution, he shook the little man warmly by the hand, and sent him home on the spot.*

CHAPTER X.

On returning to Sea View, Noel Vanstone executed the instructions which prescribed his line of conduct for the first of the five days with unimpeachable accuracy. A faint smile of contempt hovered about Mrs. Lecount's lips, while the story of Mr. Bygrave's attempt to pass off his spurious pictures as originals was in progress, but she did not trouble herself to utter a single word of remark when it had come to an end. "Just what I said!" thought Noel Vanstone, cunningly watching her face—"she doesn't believe a word of it!"

The next day the meeting occurred on the Parade. Mr. Bygrave took off his hat; and Noel Vanstone looked the other way. The captain's start of surprise and scowl of indignation, were executed to perfection—but they plainly failed to impose on Mrs. Lecount. "I am afraid, sir, you have offended Mr. Bygrave to-day," she ironically remarked. "Happily for you, he is an excellent Christian! and I venture to predict that he will forgive you to-morrow."

Noel Vanstone wisely refrained from committing himself to an answer. Once more, he privately applauded his own penetration; once more, he triumphed over his ingenious friend.

Thus far, the captain's instructions had been too clear and simple to be mistaken by any one. But they advanced in complication with the advance of time; and on the third day, Noel Vanstone fell confusedly into the commission of a slight error. After expressing the necessary weariness of Aldborough, and the consequent anxiety for change of scene, he was met (as he had anticipated) by an immediate suggestion from the housekeeper, recommending a visit to St. Crux. In giving his answer to the advice thus tendered, he made his first mistake. Instead of deferring his decision until the next day, he accepted Mrs. Lecount's suggestion on the day when it was offered to him.

The consequences of this error were of no great importance. The housekeeper merely set herself to watch her master, one day earlier than had been calculated on—a result which had been already provided for by the wise precautionary measure of forbidding Noel Vanstone all communication with North Shingles. Doubting, as Captain Wragge had foreseen, the sincerity of her master's desire to break off his connection with the Bygraves by going to St. Crux, Mrs. Lecount tested the truth or falsehood of the impression produced on her own mind, by vigilantly watching for signs of secret communication on one side or on the other. The close attention with which she had hitherto observed the out-goings and in-comings at North Shingles, was now entirely transferred to her master. For the rest of that third day, she never let him out of her sight; she never allowed any third person who came to the house, on any pretence whatever, a minute's chance of private communication with him. At intervals, through the night, she stole to the door of his room, to listen and assure herself that he was in bed; and before sunrise the next morning, the coastguardsman going his rounds was surprised to see a lady who had risen as early as himself, engaged over her work at one of the upper windows of Sea View.

On the fourth morning, Noel Vanstone came down to breakfast conscious of the mistake that he had committed on the previous day. The obvious course to take, for the purpose of gaining time, was to declare that his mind was still undecided. He made the assertion boldly, when the housekeeper asked him if he meant to move that day. Again, Mrs. Lecount offered no remark; and again the signs and tokens of incredulity showed themselves in her face. Vacillation of purpose was not at all unusual in her experience of her master. But, on this occasion, she believed that his caprice of conduct was assumed, for the purpose of gaining time to communicate with North Shingles; and she accordingly set her watch on him once more, with doubled and trebled vigilance.

No letters came that morning. Towards noon the weather changed for the worse, and all idea of walking out as usual was abandoned. Hour after hour, while her master sat in one of the parlours, Mrs. Lecount kept watch in the other—with the door into the passage open, and with a full view of North Shingles through the convenient side window at which she had established herself. Not a sign that was suspicious appeared; not a sound that was suspicious caught her ear. As the evening closed in, her master's hesitation came to an end. He was disgusted with the weather; he hated the place; he foresaw the annoyance of more meetings with Mr. Bygrave—and he was determined to go to St. Crux the first thing the next morning. Lecount could stay behind to pack up the curiosities and settle with the tradespeople, and could follow him to the admiral's on the next day. The housekeeper was a little staggered by the tone and manner in which he gave these orders. He had, to her own certain knowledge, effected no communication of any sort with North Shingles—and yet he seemed determined to leave Aldborough at the earliest possible opportunity. For the first time she hesitated in her adherence to her own conclusions. She remembered that her master had complained of the Bygraves, before they returned to Aldborough; and she was conscious that her own incredulity had once already misled her, when the appearance of the travelling carriage at the door had proved even Mr. Bygrave himself to be as good as his word.

Still, Mrs. Lecount determined to act with unrelenting caution to the last. That night, when the doors were closed, she privately removed the keys from the door in front and the door at the back. She then softly opened her bedroom window, and sat down by it, with her bonnet and cloak on, to prevent her taking cold. Noel Vanstone's window was on the same side of the house as her own. If any one came in the dark to speak to him from the garden beneath, they would speak to his housekeeper as well. Prepared at all points to intercept every form of clandestine communication which stratagem could invent, Mrs. Lecount watched through the quiet night. When morning came, she stole down-stairs before the servant was up, restored the keys to their places, and reoccupied her position in the parlour, until Noel Vanstone made his appearance at the breakfast-table. Had he altered his mind? No. He declined posting to the railway on account of the expense; but he was as firm as ever in his resolution to go to St. Crux. He desired that an inside place might be secured for him in the early coach. Suspicious to the last, Mrs. Lecount sent the baker's man to take the place. He was a public servant, and Mr. Bygrave would not suspect him of performing a private errand.

The coach called at Sea View. Mrs. Lecount saw her master established in his place, and ascertained that the other three inside seats were already occupied by strangers. She inquired of the coachman if the outside places (all of which were not yet filled up) had their full complement of passengers also. The man replied in the affirmative. He had two gentlemen to call for in the town, and the others would take their places at the inn. Mrs. Lecount forthwith turned her steps towards the inn, and took up her position on the Parade opposite, from a point of view which would enable her to see the last of the coach on its departure. In ten minutes more it rattled away, full outside and in ; and the housekeeper's own eyes assured her that neither Mr. Bygrave himself, nor any one belonging to North Shingles, was among the passengers.

There was only one more precaution to take, and Mrs. Lecount did not neglect it. Mr. Bygrave had doubtless seen the coach call at Sea View. He might hire a carriage and follow it to the railway, on pure speculation. Mrs. Lecount remained within view of the inn (the only place at which a carriage could be obtained) for nearly an hour longer, waiting for events. Nothing happened ; no carriage made its appearance ; no pursuit of Noel Vanstone was now within the range of human possibility. The long strain on Mrs. Lecount's mind relaxed at last. She left her seat on the Parade, and returned in higher spirits than usual, to perform the closing household ceremonies at Sea View.

She sat down alone in the parlour and drew a long breath of relief. Captain Wragge's calculations had not deceived him. The evidence of her own senses had at last conquered the housekeeper's incredulity, and had literally forced her into the opposite extreme of belief.

Estimating the events of the last three days from her own experience of them ; knowing (as she certainly knew) that the first idea of going to St.

Crux had been started by herself, and that her master had found no opportunity and shown no inclination to inform the family at North Shingles that he had accepted her proposal—Mrs. Lecount was fairly compelled to acknowledge that not a fragment of foundation remained to justify the continued suspicion of treachery in her own mind. Looking at the succession of circumstances under the new light thrown on them by results, she could see nothing unaccountable—nothing contradictory anywhere. The attempt to pass off the forged pictures as originals, was in perfect harmony with the character of such a man as Mr. Bygrave. Her master's indignation at the attempt to impose on him; his plainly-expressed suspicion that Miss Bygrave was privy to it; his disappointment in the niece; his contemptuous treatment of the uncle on the Parade, his weariness of the place which had been the scene of his rash intimacy with strangers, and his readiness to quit it that morning—all commended themselves as genuine realities to the housekeeper's mind, for one sufficient reason. Her own eyes had seen Noel Vanstone take his departure from Aldborough without leaving, or attempting to leave, a single trace behind him for the Bygraves to follow.

Thus far the housekeeper's conclusions led her—but no farther. She was too shrewd a woman to trust the future to chance and fortune. Her master's variable temper might relent. Accident might, at any time, give Mr. Bygrave an opportunity of repairing the error that he had committed, and of artfully regaining his lost place in Noel Vanstone's estimation. Admitting that circumstances had at last declared themselves unmistakably in her favour, Mrs. Lecount was not the less convinced that nothing would permanently assure her master's security for the future, but the plain exposure of the conspiracy which she had striven to accomplish from the first —which she was resolved to accomplish still.

"I always enjoy myself at St. Crux," thought Mrs. Lecount, opening her account-books, and sorting the tradesmen's bills. "The admiral is a gentleman, the house is noble, the table is excellent. No matter! Here, at Sea View, I stay by myself, till I have seen the inside of Miss Bygrave's wardrobe."

She packed her master's collection of curiosities in their various cases, settled the claims of the tradespeople, and superintended the covering of the furniture in the course of the day. Towards nightfall she went out, bent on investigation; and ventured into the garden at North Shingles, under cover of the darkness. She saw the light in the parlour window, and the lights in the windows of the rooms up-stairs, as usual. After an instant's hesitation she stole to the house-door, and noiselessly tried the handle from the outside. It turned the lock as she had expected, from her experience of houses at Aldborough and at other watering-places—but the door resisted her; the door was distrustfully bolted on the inside. After making that discovery, she went round to the back of the house, and ascertained that the door on that side was secured in the same manner. "Bolt your doors, Mr. Bygrave, as fast as you like," said the housekeeper, stealing back again to the Parade. "You can't bolt the entrance to your servant's pocket. The best lock you have may be opened by a golden key."

She went back to bed. The ceaseless watching, the unrelaxing excitement of the last two days, had worn her out.

The next morning she rose at seven o'clock. In half an hour more she saw the punctual Mr. Bygrave—as she had seen him on many previous mornings, at the same time—issue from the gate of North Shingles, with his towels under his arm, and make his way to a boat that was waiting for him on the beach. Swimming was one among the many personal accomplishments of which the captain was master. He was rowed out to sea every morning, and took his bath luxuriously in the deep blue water. Mrs. Lecount had already computed the time consumed in this recreation by her watch; and had discovered that a full hour usually elapsed, from the moment when he embarked on the beach to the moment when he returned.

During that period, she had never seen any other inhabitant of North Shingles leave the house. The servant was no doubt at her work in the kitchen; Mrs. Bygrave was probably still in her bed; and Miss Bygrave (if she was up at that early hour) had perhaps received directions not to venture out in her uncle's absence. The difficulty of meeting the obstacle of Magdalen's presence in the house, had been, for some days past, the one difficulty which all Mrs. Lecount's ingenuity had thus far proved unable to overcome.

She sat at the window for a quarter of an hour after the captain's boat had left the beach, with her mind hard at work, and her eyes fixed mechanically on North Shingles—she sat, considering what written excuse she could send to her master for delaying her departure from Aldborough for some days to come—when the door of the house she was watching suddenly opened; and Magdalen herself appeared in the garden. There was no mistaking her figure and her dress. She took a few steps hastily towards the gate, stopped, and pulled down the veil of her garden hat, as if she felt the clear morning light too much for her—then hurried out on the Parade, and walked away northward, in such haste, or in such preoccupation of mind, that she went through the garden-gate without closing it after her.

Mrs. Lecount started up from her chair, with a moment's doubt of the evidence of her own eyes. Had the opportunity which she had been vainly plotting to produce, actually offered itself to her, of its own accord? Had the chances declared themselves at last in her favour, after steadily acting against her for so long? There was no doubt of it: in the popular phrase, "her luck had turned." She snatched up her bonnet and mantilla; and made for North Shingles, without an instant's hesitation. Mr. Bygrave out at sea; Miss Bygrave away for a walk; Mrs. Bygrave and the servant both at home, and both easily dealt with—the opportunity was not to be lost; the risk was well worth running!

This time, the house-door was easily opened: no one had bolted it again, after Magdalen's departure. Mrs. Lecount closed the door softly; listened for a moment in the passage; and heard the servant noisily occupied in the kitchen with her pots and pans. "If my lucky star leads me straight into Miss Bygrave's room," thought the housekeeper, stealing noiselessly up the stairs, "I may find my way to her wardrobe without disturbing anybody."

She tried the door nearest to the front of the house, on the right-hand side of the landing. Capricious chance had deserted her already. The lock was turned. She tried the door opposite, on her left hand. The boots ranged symmetrically in a row, and the razors on the dressing-table, told her at once that she had not found the right room yet. She returned to the right-hand side of the landing, walked down a little passage, leading to the back of the house, and tried a third door. The door opened—and the two opposite extremes of female humanity, Mrs. Wragge and Mrs. Lecount, stood face to face in an instant!

"I beg ten thousand pardons!" said Mrs. Lecount, with the most consummate self-possession.

"Lord bless us and save us!" cried Mrs. Wragge, with the most helpless amazement.

The two exclamations were uttered in a moment; and, in that moment, Mrs. Lecount took the measure of her victim. Nothing of the least importance escaped her. She noticed the Oriental Cashmere Robe lying half made, and half unpicked again, on the table; she noticed the imbecile foot of Mrs. Wragge searching blindly in the neighbourhood of her chair for a lost shoe; she noticed that there was a second door in the room besides the door by which she had entered, and a second chair within easy reach, on which she might do well to seat herself in a friendly and confidential way. "Pray don't resent my intrusion," pleaded Mrs. Lecount, taking the chair. "Pray allow me to explain myself!"

Speaking in her softest voice; surveying Mrs. Wragge with a sweet smile on her insinuating lips, and a melting interest in her handsome black eyes, the housekeeper told her little introductory series of falsehoods, with an artless truthfulness of manner which the Father of Lies himself might have envied. She had heard from Mr. Bygrave that Mrs. Bygrave was a great invalid; she had constantly reproached herself, in her idle half-hours at Sea View (where she filled the situation of Mr. Noel Vanstone's housekeeper), for not having offered her friendly services to Mrs. Bygrave; she had been directed by her master (doubtless well known to Mrs. Bygrave, as one of her husband's friends, and, naturally, one of her charming niece's admirers) to join him that day at the residence to which he had removed from Aldborough; she was obliged to leave early, but she could not reconcile it to her conscience to go, without calling to apologize for her apparent want of neighbourly consideration; she had found nobody in the house, she had not been able to make the servant hear, she had presumed (not discovering that apartment down-stairs) that Mrs. Bygrave's boudoir might be on the upper story; she had thoughtlessly committed an intrusion of which she was sincerely ashamed, and she could now only trust to Mrs. Bygrave's indulgence to excuse and forgive her.

A less elaborate apology might have served Mrs. Lecount's purpose. As soon as Mrs. Wragge's struggling perceptions had grasped the fact that her unexpected visitor was a neighbour, well known to her by repute, her whole being became absorbed in admiration of Mrs. Lecount's lady-like manners, and Mrs. Lecount's perfectly-fitting gown! "What a noble way she has of talking!" thought poor Mrs. Wragge, as the housekeeper reached her closing sentence. "And, oh my heart alive, how nicely she's dressed!"

"I see I disturb you," pursued Mrs. Lecount, artfully availing herself of the Oriental Cashmere Robe, as a means ready at hand of reaching the end she had in view—"I see I disturb you, ma'am, over an occupation which, I know by experience, requires the closest attention. Dear, dear me, you are unpicking the dress again, I see, after it has been made! This is my own experience again, Mrs. Bygrave. Some dresses are so obstinate! Some dresses seem to say to one, in so many words, 'No! you may do what you like with me; I won't fit!'"

Mrs. Wragge was greatly struck by this happy remark. She burst out laughing, and clapped her great hands in hearty approval.

"That's what this gown has been saying to me, ever since I first put the scissors into it," she exclaimed cheerfully. "I know I've got an awful big back—but that's no reason. Why should a gown be weeks on hand, and then not meet behind you after all? It hangs over my Boasom like a sack—it does. Look here, ma'am, at the skirt. It won't come right. It draggles in front, and cocks up behind. It shows my heels—and, Lord knows, I get into scrapes enough about my heels, without showing them into the bargain!"

"May I ask a favour?" inquired Mrs. Lecount, confidentially. "May I try, Mrs. Bygrave, if I can make my experience of any use to you? I think our bosoms, ma'am, are our great difficulty. Now, this bosom of yours?—Shall I say in plain words what I think? This bosom of yours is an Enormous Mistake!"

"Don't, say that!" cried Mrs. Wragge, imploringly. "Don't please, there's a good soul! It's an awful big one, I know; but it's modelled, for all that. from one of Magdalen's own."

She was far too deeply interested on the subject of the dress to notice that she had forgotten herself already, and that she had referred to Magdalen by her own name. Mrs. Lecount's sharp ears detected the mistake the instant it was committed. "So! so!" she thought. "One discovery already. If I had ever doubted my own suspicions, here is an estimable lady who would now have set me right.—I beg your pardon," she proceeded, aloud, "did you say this was modelled from one of your niece's dresses?"

"Yes," said Mrs. Wragge. "It's as like as two peas."

"Then," replied Mrs. Lecount, adroitly, "there must be some serious mistake in the making of your niece's dress. Can you show it to me?"

"Bless your heart—yes!" cried Mrs. Wragge. "Step this way, ma'am; and bring the gown along with you, please. It keeps sliding off, out of pure aggravation, if you lay it out on the table. There's lots of room on the bed in here."

She opened the door of communication, and led the way eagerly into Magdalen's room. As Mrs. Lecount followed, she stole a look at her watch. Never before had time flown as it flew that morning! In twenty minutes more, Mr. Bygrave would be back from his bath.

"There!" said Mrs. Wragge, throwing open the wardrobe, and taking a dress down from one of the pegs. "Look there! There's plaits on her Boasom, and plaits on mine. Six of one, and half a dozen of the other; and mine are the biggest—that's all!"

Mrs. Lecount shook her head gravely, and entered forthwith into subtleties of disquisition on the art of dress-making, which had the desired effect of utterly bewildering the proprietor of the Oriental Cashmere Robe, in less than three minutes.

"Don't!" cried Mrs. Wragge, imploringly. "Don't go on like that! I'm miles behind you; and my head's Buzzing already. Tell us, like a good soul, what's to be done. You said something about the pattern just now. Perhaps I'm too big for the pattern? I can't help it, if I am. Many's the good cry I had, when I was a growing girl, over my own size! There's half too much of me, ma'am—measure me along or measure me across, I don't deny it—there's half too much of me, any way."

"My dear madam," protested Mrs. Lecount, "you do yourself a wrong! Permit me to assure you that you possess a commanding figure—a figure of Minerva. A majestic simplicity in the form of a woman, imperatively demands a majestic simplicity in the form of that woman's dress. The laws of costume are classical; the laws of costume must not be trifled with! Plaits for Venus — puffs for Juno—folds for Minerva. I venture to suggest a total change of pattern. Your niece has other dresses in her collection. Why may we not find a Minerva pattern among them?"

As she said those words, she led the way back to the wardrobe.

Mrs. Wragge followed, and took the dresses out, one by one, shaking her head despondently. Silk dresses appeared, muslin dresses appeared. The one dress which remained invisible, was the dress of which Mrs. Lecount was in search.

"There's the lot of 'em," said Mrs. Wragge. "They may do for Venus and the two other Ones (I've seen 'em in picters without a morsel of decent linen among the three)—but they won't do for Me."

"Surely there is another dress left?" said Mrs. Lecount, pointing to the wardrobe, but touching nothing in it. "Surely I see something hanging in the corner, behind that dark shawl?"

Mrs. Wragge removed the shawl; Mrs. Lecount opened the door of the wardrobe a little wider. There—hitched carelessly on the innermost peg— there, with its white spots, and its double flounce, was the brown Alpaca dress!

The suddenness and completeness of the discovery threw the house-keeper, practised dissembler as she was, completely off her guard. She started at the sight of the dress. The instant afterwards, her eyes turned uneasily towards Mrs. Wragge. Had the start been observed? It had passed entirely unnoticed. Mrs. Wragge's whole attention was fixed on the Alpaca dress: she was staring at it incomprehensibly, with an ex-pression of the utmost dismay.

"You seem alarmed, ma'am," said Mrs. Lecount. "What is there in the wardrobe to frighten you?"

"I'd have given a crown-piece out of my pocket," said Mrs. Wragge, "not to have set eyes on that gown. It had gone clean out of my head— and now it's come back again. Cover it up!" cried Mrs. Wragge, throwing the shawl over the dress in a sudden fit of desperation. "If I look at it much longer, I shall think I'm back again in Vauxhall Walk!"

Vauxhall Walk! Those two words told Mrs. Lecount she was on the brink of another discovery. She stole a second look at her watch. There was barely ten minutes to spare before the time when Mr. Bygrave might return; there was not one of those ten minutes which might not bring his niece back to the house. Caution counselled Mrs. Lecount to go, without running any more risks. Curiosity rooted her to the spot, and gave her the courage to stay at all hazards until the time was up. Her amiable smile began to harden a little, as she probed her way tenderly into Mrs. Wragge's feeble mind.

"You have some unpleasant remembrances of Vauxhall Walk?" she said, with the gentlest possible tone of inquiry in her voice. "Or, perhaps, I should say, unpleasant remembrances of that dress belonging to your niece?"

"The last time I saw her with that gown on," said Mrs. Wragge, dropping into a chair and beginning to tremble, "was the time when I came back from shopping, and saw the Ghost."

"The Ghost?" repeated Mrs. Lecount, clasping her hands in graceful astonishment. "Dear madam, pardon me! Is there such a thing in the world? Where did you see it? In Vauxhall Walk? Tell me—you are the first lady I ever met with who has seen a Ghost—pray tell me!"

Flattered by the position of importance which she had suddenly assumed in the housekeeper's eyes, Mrs. Wragge entered at full length into the narrative of her supernatural adventure. The breathless eagerness with which Mrs. Lecount listened to her description of the spectre's costume, the spectre's hurry on the stairs, and the spectre's disappearance in the bed-room; the extraordinary interest which Mrs. Lecount displayed on hearing that the dress in the wardrobe was the very dress in which Magdalen happened to be attired, at the awful moment when the ghost vanished—encouraged Mrs. Wragge to wade deeper and deeper into details, and to involve herself in a confusion of collateral circumstances, out of which there seemed to be no prospect of her emerging for hours to come. Faster and faster the inexorable minutes flew by; nearer and nearer came the fatal moment of Mr. Bygrave's return. Mrs. Lecount looked at her watch for the third time, without an attempt, on this occasion, to conceal the action from her companion's notice. There were literally two minutes left for her to get clear of North Shingles. Two minutes would be enough, if no accident happened. She had discovered the Alpaca dress; she had heard the whole story of the adventure in Vauxhall Walk; and, more than that, she had even informed herself of the number of the house—which Mrs. Wragge happened to remember, because it answered to the number of years in her own age. All that was necessary to her master's complete enlightenment, she had now accomplished. Even if there had been time to stay longer, there was nothing worth staying for. "I'll strike this worthy idiot dumb with a *coup d'état*," thought the housekeeper, "and vanish before she recovers herself."

"Horrible!" cried Mrs. Lecount, interrupting the ghostly narrative by a shrill little scream, and making for the door, to Mrs. Wragge's unutterable astonishment, without the least ceremony. "You freeze the very marrow off my bones. Good-morning!" She coolly tossed the Oriental Cashmere Robe into Mrs. Wragge's expansive lap, and left the room in an instant.

As she swiftly descended the stairs, she heard the door of the bed-room open.

"Where are your manners?" cried a voice from above, hailing her feebly over the banisters. "What do you mean by pitching my gown at me, in that way? You ought to be ashamed of yourself!" pursued Mrs. Wragge, turning from a lamb to a lioness, as she gradually realized the indignity offered to the Cashmere Robe. "You nasty foreigner, you ought to be ashamed of yourself!"

Pursued by this valedictory address, Mrs. Lecount reached the house-door, and opened it without interruption. She glided rapidly along the garden path; passed through the gate; and finding herself safe on the Parade, stopped, and looked towards the sea.

The first object which her eyes encountered, was the figure of Mr. Bygrave, standing motionless on the beach—a petrified bather, with his towels in his hand! One glance at him was enough to show that he had seen the housekeeper passing out through his garden-gate.

Rightly conjecturing that Mr. Bygrave's first impulse would lead him to make instant inquiries in his own house, Mrs. Lecount pursued her way back to Sea View as composedly as if nothing had happened. When she entered the parlour where her solitary breakfast was waiting for her, she was surprised to see a letter lying on the table. She approached to take it up, with an expression of impatience, thinking it might be some trades-man's bill which she had forgotten.

It was the forged letter from Zurich.

CHAPTER XI.

THE postmark and the handwriting on the address (admirably imitated from the original), warned Mrs. Lecount of the contents of the letter before she opened it.

After waiting a moment to compose herself, she read the announcement of her brother's relapse.

There was nothing in the handwriting, there was no expression in any part of the letter, which could suggest to her mind the faintest suspicion of foul play. Not the shadow of a doubt occurred to her that the summons to her brother's bedside was genuine. The hand that held the letter dropped heavily into her lap; she became pale, and old, and haggard, in a moment. Thoughts, far removed from her present aims and interests; remembrances that carried her back to other lands than England, to other times than the time of her life in service, prolonged their inner shadows to the surface, and showed the traces of their mysterious passage darkly on her face. The minutes followed each other; and still the servant below stairs waited vainly for the parlour bell. The minutes followed each other; and still she sat, tearless and quiet, dead to the present and the future, living in the past.

The entrance of the servant, uncalled, roused her. With a heavy sigh, the cold and secret woman folded the letter up again, and addressed herself to the interests and the duties of the passing time.

She decided the question of going or not going, to Zurich, after a very brief consideration of it. Before she had drawn her chair to the breakfast-table, she had resolved to go.

Admirably as Captain Wragge's stratagem had worked, it might have failed—unassisted by the occurrence of the morning—to achieve this result. The very accident against which it had been the captain's chief anxiety to guard—the accident which had just taken place in spite of him —was, of all the events that could have happened, the one event which falsified every previous calculation, by directly forwarding the main purpose of the conspiracy! If Mrs. Lecount had not obtained the information of which she was in search, before the receipt of the letter from Zurich, the letter might have addressed her in vain. She would have hesitated, before deciding to leave England; and that hesitation might have proved fatal to the captain's scheme.

As it was, with the plain proofs in her possession—with the gown discovered in Magdalen's wardrobe; with the piece cut out of it, in her own pocket-book; and with the knowledge, obtained from Mrs. Wragge, of the very house in which the disguise had been put on—Mrs. Lecount had now at her command, the means of warning Noel Vanstone, as she had never been able to warn him yet—or, in other words, the means of guarding against any dangerous tendencies towards reconciliation with the Bygraves, which might otherwise have entered his mind during her absence at Zurich. The only difficulty which now perplexed her, was the difficulty of deciding whether she should communicate with her master personally, or by writing, before her departure from England.

She looked again at the doctor's letter. The word "instantly," in the sentence which summoned her to her dying brother, was twice underlined. Admiral Bartram's house was at some distance from the railway; the time consumed in driving to St. Crux, and driving back again, might be time fatally lost on the journey to Zurich. Although she would infinitely have preferred a personal interview with Noel Vanstone, there was no choice on a matter of life and death, but to save the precious hours by writing to him.

After sending to secure a place at once in the early coach, she sat down to write to her master.

Her first thought was to tell him all that had happened at North Shingles that morning. On reflection, however, she rejected the idea. Once already (in copying the personal description from Miss Garth's letter) she had trusted her weapons in her master's hands, and Mr. Bygrave had contrived to turn them against her. She resolved this time to keep them strictly in her own possession. The secret of the missing fragment of the Alpaca dress was known to no living creature but herself; and, until her return to England, she determined to keep it to herself. The necessary impression might be produced on Noel Vanstone's mind without venturing into details. She knew, by experience, the form of letter which might be trusted to produce an effect on him, and she now wrote it in these words :

"DEAR MR. NOEL,

"Sad news has reached me from Switzerland. My beloved brother is dying, and his medical attendant summons me instantly to Zurich. The serious necessity of availing myself of the earliest means of conveyance to the Continent, leaves me but one alternative. I must profit by the permission to leave England, if necessary, which you kindly granted to me at the beginning of my brother's illness ; and I must avoid all delay, by going straight to London, instead of turning aside, as I should have liked, to see you first at St. Crux.

"Painfully as I am affected by the family calamity which has fallen on me, I cannot let this opportunity pass without adverting to another subject, which seriously concerns your welfare, and in which (on that account) your old housekeeper feels the deepest interest.

"I am going to surprise and shock you, Mr. Noel. Pray don't be agitated ! pray compose yourself!

"The impudent attempt to cheat you, which has happily opened your eyes to the true character of our neighbours at North Shingles, was not the only object which Mr. Bygrave had in forcing himself on your acquaintance. The infamous conspiracy with which you were threatened in London, has been in full progress against you, under Mr. Bygrave's direction, at Aldborough. Accident—I will tell you what accident when we meet—has put me in possession of information precious to your future security. I have discovered, to an absolute certainty, that the person calling herself Miss Bygrave, is no other than the woman who visited us in disguise at Vauxhall Walk.

"I suspected this, from the first; but I had no evidence to support my suspicions; I had no means of combating the false impression produced on you. My hands, I thank Heaven, are tied no longer. I possess absolute proof of the assertion that I have just made—proof that your own eyes can see ; proof that would satisfy you, if you were judge in a Court of Justice.

"Perhaps, even yet, Mr. Noel, you will refuse to believe me ? Be it so. Believe me or not, I have one last favour to ask, which your English sense of fair play will not deny me.

"This melancholy journey of mine will keep me away from England for a fortnight, or, at most, for three weeks. You will oblige me—and you will certainly not sacrifice your own convenience and pleasure—by staying through that interval with your friends at St. Crux. If, before my return, some unexpected circumstance throws you once more into the company of the Bygraves ; and if your natural kindness of heart inclines you to receive the excuses which they will, in that case, certainly address to you—place one trifling restraint on yourself, for your own sake, if not for mine. Suspend your flirtation with the young lady (I beg pardon of all other young ladies for calling her so!) until my return. If, when I come back, I fail to prove to you that Miss Bygrave is the woman who wore that disguise, and used those threatening words, in Vauxhall Walk, I will engage to leave your service at a day's notice; and I will atone for the sin of bearing false witness against my neighbour, by resigning every claim I have to your grateful remembrance, on your father's account as well as on your own. I make this engagement without reserves of any kind; and I promise to abide by it—if my proofs fail—on the faith of a good Catholic, and the word of an honest woman. Your faithful servant,

"VIRGINIE LECOUNT."

The closing sentences of this letter—as the housekeeper well knew when she wrote them—embodied the one appeal to Noel Vanstone, which could be certainly trusted to produce a deep and lasting effect. She might have staked her oath, her life, or her reputation on proving the assertion which she had made, and have failed to leave a permanent impression on his mind. But when she staked not only her position in his service, but her pecuniary claims on him as well, she at once absorbed the ruling passion of his life in expectation of the result. There was not a doubt of it, in the strongest of all his interests—the interest of saving his money—he would wait.

"Check-mate for Mr. Bygrave!" thought Mrs. Lecount, as she sealed and directed the letter. "The battle is over—the game is played out."

While Mrs. Lecount was providing for her master's future security at Sea View, events were in full progress at North Shingles.

As soon as Captain Wragge recovered his astonishment at the housekeeper's appearance on his own premises, he hurried into the house, and guided by his own forebodings of the disaster that had happened, made straight for his wife's room.

Never, in all her former experience, had poor Mrs. Wragge felt the full weight of the captain's indignation, as she felt it now. All the little intelligence she naturally possessed, vanished at once in the whirlwind of her husband's rage. The only plain facts which he could extract from her were two in number. In the first place, Magdalen's rash desertion of her post proved to have no better reason to excuse it than Magdalen's incorrigible impatience: she had passed a sleepless night; she had risen feverish and wretched; and she had gone out, reckless of all consequences, to cool her burning head in the fresh air. In the second place, Mrs. Wragge had, on her own confession, seen Mrs. Lecount, had talked with Mrs. Lecount, and had ended by telling Mrs. Lecount the story of the ghost. Having made these discoveries, Captain Wragge wasted no time in contending with his wife's terror and confusion. He withdrew at once to a window which commanded an uninterrupted prospect of Noel Vanstone's house; and there established himself, on the watch for events at Sea View, precisely as Mrs. Lecount had established herself, on the watch for events at North Shingles.

Not a word of comment on the disaster of the morning escaped him, when Magdalen returned, and found him at his post. His flow of language seemed at last to have run dry. "I told you what Mrs. Wragge would do," he said—"and Mrs. Wragge has done it." He sat unflinchingly at the window, with a patience which Mrs. Lecount herself could not have surpassed. The one active proceeding in which he seemed to think it necessary to engage, was performed by deputy. He sent the servant to the inn to hire a chaise and a fast horse, and to say that he would call himself, before noon that day, and tell the ostler when the vehicle would be wanted. Not a sign of impatience escaped him, until the time drew near for the departure of the early coach. Then the captain's curly lips began to twitch with anxiety, and the captain's restless fingers beat the devil's tattoo unremittingly on the window-pane.

The coach appeared at last, and drew up at Sea View. In a minute more, Captain Wragge's own observation informed him that one among the passengers who left Aldborough that morning, was—Mrs. Lecount.

The main uncertainty disposed of, a serious question—suggested by the events of the morning—still remained to be solved. Which was the destined end of Mrs. Lecount's journey—Zurich or St. Crux? That she would certainly inform her master of Mrs. Wragge's ghost story, and of every other disclosure in relation to names and places, which might have escaped Mrs. Wragge's lips, was beyond all doubt. But of the two ways at her disposal of doing the mischief—either personally, or by letter—it was vitally important to the captain to know which she had chosen. If she had gone to the admiral's, no choice would be left him but to follow the coach, to catch the train by which she travelled, and to outstrip her afterwards on the drive from the station in Essex to St. Crux. If, on the contrary, she had been contented with writing to her master, it would only be necessary to devise measures for intercepting the letter. The captain decided on going to the post-office, in the first place. Assuming that the housekeeper had written, she would not have left the letter at the mercy of the servant—she would have seen it safely in the letter-box before leaving Aldborough.

"Good morning," said the captain, cheerfully addressing the post-master. "I am Mr. Bygrave of North Shingles. I think you have a letter in the box, addressed to Mr.——?"

The post-master was a short man, and consequently a man with a proper idea of his own importance. He solemnly checked Captain Wragge in full career.

"When a letter is once posted, sir," he said, "nobody out of the office has any business with it, until it reaches its address."

The captain was not a man to be daunted, even by a post-master. A bright idea struck him. He took out his pocket-book, in which Admiral Bartram's address was written, and returned to the charge.

"Suppose a letter has been wrongly directed by mistake?" he began. "And suppose the writer wants to correct the error after the letter is put into the box?"

"When a letter is once posted, sir," reiterated the impenetrable local authority, "nobody out of the office touches it on any pretence whatever."

"Granted, with all my heart," persisted the captain. "I don't want to touch it—I only want to explain myself. A lady has posted a letter here, addressed to 'Noel Vanstone, Esq., Admiral Bartram's, St. Crux in the Marsh, Essex.' She wrote in a great hurry, and she is not quite certain whether she added the name of the post-town, 'Ossory.' It is of the last importance that the delivery of the letter should not be delayed. What is to hinder your facilitating the post-office work, and obliging a lady, by adding the name of the post-town (if it happens to be left out), with your own hand? I put it to you as a zealous officer—what possible objection can there be to granting my request?"

The post-master was compelled to acknowledge that there could be no objection—provided nothing but a necessary line was added to the address; provided nobody touched the letter but himself; and provided the precious time of the post-office was not suffered to run to waste. As there happened to be nothing particular to do at that moment, he would readily oblige the lady, at Mr. Bygrave's request.

Captain Wragge watched the post-master's hands, as they sorted the letters in the box, with breathless eagerness. Was the letter there? Would the hands of the zealous public servant suddenly stop? Yes! They stopped, and picked out a letter from the rest.

"'Noel Vanstone, Esquire,' did you say?" asked the post-master, keeping the letter in his own hand.

"'Noel Vanstone, Esquire,'" replied the captain, "'Admiral Bartram's, St. Crux in the Marsh.'"

"Ossory, Essex," chimed in the post-master, throwing the letter back into the box. "The lady has made no mistake, sir. The address is quite right."

Nothing but a timely consideration of the heavy debt he owed to appearances, prevented Captain Wragge from throwing his tall white hat up into the air, as soon as he found the street once more. All further doubt was now at an end. Mrs. Lecount had written to her master—therefore Mrs. Lecount was on her way to Zurich!

With his head higher than ever, with the tails of his respectable frock-coat floating behind him in the breeze, with his bosom's native impudence sitting lightly on its throne—the captain strutted to the inn and called for the railway time-table. After making certain calculations (in black and white, as a matter of course), he ordered his chaise to be ready in an hour —so as to reach the railway in time for the second train running to London—with which there happened to be no communication from Aldborough by coach.

His next proceeding was of a far more serious kind; his next proceeding implied a terrible certainty of success. The day of the week was Thursday. From the inn he went to the church; saw the clerk; and gave the necessary notice for a marriage by licence on the following Monday.

Bold as he was, his nerves were a little shaken by this last achievement; his hand trembled as it lifted the latch of the garden gate. He doctored his nerves with brandy and water, before he sent for Magdalen to inform her of the proceedings of the morning. Another outbreak might reasonably be expected, when she heard that the last irrevocable step had been taken, and that notice had been given of the wedding day.

The captain's watch warned him to lose no time in emptying his glass. In a few minutes, he sent the necessary message up-stairs. While waiting for Magdalen's appearance, he provided himself with certain materials which were now necessary to carry the enterprise to its crowning point. In the first place, he wrote his assumed name (by no means in so fine a hand as usual) on a blank visiting card; and added, underneath, these words: "Not a moment is to be lost. I am waiting for you at the door—come down to me directly." His next proceeding was to take some half-dozen envelopes out of the case, and to direct them all alike to the following address: "Thomas Bygrave, Esq., Mussared's Hotel, Salisbury Street, Strand, London." After carefully placing the envelopes and the card in his breast-pocket, he shut up the desk. As he rose from the writing-table, Magdalen came into the room.

The captain took a moment to decide on the best method of opening the interview; and determined, in his own phrase, to dash at it. In two words, he told Magdalen what had happened; and informed her that Monday was to be her wedding day.

He was prepared to quiet her if she burst into a frenzy of passion; to reason with her if she begged for time; to sympathize with her, if she melted into tears. To his inexpressible surprise, results falsified all his calculations. She heard him without uttering a word, without shedding a tear. When he had done, she dropped into a chair. Her large grey eyes stared at him vacantly. In one mysterious instant, all her beauty left her;

her face stiffened awfully, like the face of a corpse. For the first time in the captain's experience of her, fear—all-mastering fear—had taken possession of her, body and soul.

"You are not flinching," he said, trying to rouse her. "Surely you are not flinching at the last moment?"

No light of intelligence came into her eyes; no change passed over her face. But she heard him—for she moved a little in the chair, and slowly shook her head.

"You planned this marriage of your own free will," pursued the captain, with the furtive look and the faltering voice of a man ill at ease. "It was your own idea—not mine. I won't have the responsibility laid on my shoulders—no! not for twice two hundred pounds. If your resolution fails you; if you think better of it—— ?"

He stopped. Her face was changing; her lips were moving at last. She slowly raised her left hand, with the fingers outspread—she looked at it, as if it was a hand that was strange to her—she counted the days on it, the days before the marriage.

"Friday, one," she whispered to herself; "Saturday, two; Sunday, three; Monday——" Her hands dropped into her lap; her face stiffened again. The deadly fear fastened its paralyzing hold on her once more; and the next words died away on her lips.

Captain Wragge took out his handkerchief, and wiped his forehead.

"Damn the two hundred pounds!" he said. "Two thousand wouldn't pay me for this!"

He put the handkerchief back, took the envelopes which he had addressed to himself out of his pocket, and, approaching her closely for the first time, laid his hand on her arm.

"Rouse yourself," he said, "I have a last word to say to you. Can you listen?"

She struggled, and roused herself—a faint tinge of colour stole over her white cheeks—she bowed her head.

"Look at these," pursued Captain Wragge, holding up the envelopes. "If I turn these to the use for which they have been written, Mrs. Lecount's master will never receive Mrs. Lecount's letter. If I tear them up, he will know by to-morrow's post that you are the woman who visited him in Vauxhall Walk. Say the word! Shall I tear the envelopes up, or shall I put them back in my pocket?"

There was a pause of dead silence. The murmur of the summer waves on the shingle of the beach, and the voices of the summer idlers on the Parade, floated through the open window, and filled the empty stillness of the room.

She raised her head; she lifted her hand and pointed steadily to the envelopes.

"Put them back," she said.

"Do you mean it?" he asked.

"I mean it."

As she gave that answer, there was a sound of wheels on the road outside.

"You hear those wheels?" said Captain Wragge.

"I hear them."

"You see the chaise?" said the captain, pointing through the window, as the chaise which had been ordered from the inn made its appearance at the garden-gate.

"I see it."

"And, of your own free will, you tell me to go?"

"Yes.   Go!"

Without another word, he left her.   The servant was waiting at the door with his travelling-bag.   "Miss Bygrave is not well," he said.   "Tell your mistress to go to her in the parlour."

He stepped into the chaise, and started on the first stage of the journey to St. Crux.

CHAPTER XII

TOWARDS three o'clock in the afternoon, Captain Wragge stopped at the nearest station to Ossory which the railway passed in its course through Essex.   Inquiries made on the spot, informed him that he might drive to St. Crux, remain there for a quarter of an hour, and return to the station in time for an evening train to London.   In ten minutes more, the captain was on the road again, driving rapidly in the direction of the coast.

After proceeding some miles on the highway, the carriage turned off, and the coachman involved himself in an intricate network of cross-roads.

"Are we far from St. Crux?" asked the captain, growing impatient, after mile on mile had been passed, without a sign of reaching the journey's end.

"You'll see the house, sir, at the next turn in the road," said the man.

The next turn in the road brought them within view of the open country again.   Ahead of the carriage, Captain Wragge saw a long dark line against the sky—the line of the sea wall which protects the low coast of Essex from inundation.   The flat intermediate country was intersected by a labyrinth of tidal streams, winding up from the invisible sea in strange fantastic curves—rivers at high water, and channels of mud at low.   On his right hand, was a quaint little village, mostly composed of wooden houses, straggling down to the brink of one of the tidal streams.   On his left hand, farther away, rose the gloomy ruins of an Abbey, with a desolate pile of buildings, which covered two sides of a square attached to it.   One of the streams from the sea (called in Essex, "backwaters") curled almost entirely round the house. Another, from an opposite quarter, appeared to run straight through the grounds, and to separate one side of the shapeless mass of buildings, which was in moderate repair, from another, which was little better than a ruin. Bridges of wood, and bridges of brick, crossed the stream, and gave access to the house from all points of the compass. No human creature appeared in the neighbourhood, and no sound was heard but the hoarse barking of a house-dog from an invisible court-yard.

"Which door shall I drive to, sir?" asked the coachman. "The front, or the back?"

"The back," said Captain Wragge, feeling that the less notice he attracted in his present position, the safer that position might be.

The carriage twice crossed the stream before the coachman made his way through the grounds into a dreary enclosure of stone. At an open door on the inhabited side of the place, sat a weather-beaten old man, busily at work on a half-finished model of a ship. He rose and came to the carriage-door, lifting up his spectacles on his forehead, and looking disconcerted at the appearance of a stranger.

"Is Mr. Noel Vanstone staying here?" asked Captain Wragge.

"Yes, sir," replied the old man. "Mr. Noel came yesterday."

"Take that card to Mr. Vanstone, if you please," said the captain; "and say I am waiting here to see him."

In a few minutes, Noel Vanstone made his appearance, breathless and eager; absorbed in anxiety for news from Aldborough. Captain Wragge opened the carriage-door, seized his out-stretched hand, and pulled him in without ceremony.

"Your housekeeper has gone," whispered the captain, "and you are to be married on Monday. Don't agitate yourself, and don't express your feelings—there isn't time for it. Get the first active servant you can find in the house, to pack your bag in ten minutes—take leave of the admiral —and come back at once with me to the London train."

Noel Vanstone faintly attempted to ask a question. The captain declined to hear it.

"As much talk as you like on the road," he said. "Time is too precious for talking here. How do we know Lecount may not think better of it? How do we know she may not turn back, before she gets to Zurich?"

That startling consideration terrified Noel Vanstone into instant submission.

"What shall I say to the admiral?" he asked helplessly.

"Tell him you are going to be married, to be sure! What does it matter, now Lecount's back is turned? If he wonders you didn't tell him before, say it's a runaway match, and the bride is waiting for you. Stop! Any letters addressed to you, in your absence, will be sent to this place, of course? Give the admiral these envelopes, and tell him to forward your letters under cover to me. I am an old customer at the hotel we are going to; and if we find the place full, the landlord may be depended on to take care of any letters with my name on them. A safe address in London for your correspondence, may be of the greatest importance. How do we know Lecount may not write to you on her way to Zurich?"

"What a head you have got!" cried Noel Vanstone, eagerly taking the envelopes. "You think of everything."

He left the carriage in high excitement, and ran back into the house. In ten minutes more Captain Wragge had him in safe custody, and the horses started on their return journey.

The travellers reached London in good time that evening, and found accommodation at the hotel.

Knowing the restless, inquisitive nature of the man he had to deal with, Captain Wragge had anticipated some little difficulty and embarrassment in meeting the questions which Noel Vanstone might put to him on the way to London. To his great relief, a startling domestic discovery absorbed his travelling companion's whole attention at the outset of the journey. By some extraordinary oversight, Miss Bygrave had been left, on the eve of her marriage, unprovided with a maid. Noel Vanstone declared that he would take the whole responsibility of correcting this deficiency in the arrangements, on his own shoulders; he would not trouble Mr. Bygrave to give him any assistance; he would confer, when they got to their journey's end, with the landlady of the hotel, and would examine the candidates for the vacant office himself. All the way to London, he returned again and again to the same subject; all the evening, at the hotel, he was in and out of the landlady's sitting-room, until he fairly obliged her to lock the door. In every other proceeding which related to his marriage, he had been kept in the background; he had been compelled to follow in the footsteps of his ingenious friend. In the matter of the lady's maid he claimed his fitting position at last—he followed nobody; he took the lead!

The forenoon of the next day was devoted to obtaining the licence—the personal distinction of making the declaration on oath being eagerly accepted by Noel Vanstone, who swore, in perfect good faith (on information previously obtained from the captain) that the lady was of age. The document procured, the bridegroom returned to examine the characters and qualifications of the women-servants out of the place, whom the landlady had engaged to summon to the hotel—while Captain Wragge turned his steps, "on business personal to himself," towards the residence of a friend in a distant quarter of London.

The captain's friend was connected with the law, and the captain's business was of a twofold nature. His first object was to inform himself of the legal bearings of the approaching marriage on the future of the husband and the wife. His second object was to provide, beforehand, for destroying all traces of the destination to which he might betake himself, when he left Aldborough on the wedding-day. Having reached his end successfully, in both these cases, he returned to the hotel, and found Noel Vanstone nursing his offended dignity in the landlady's sitting-room. Three ladies'-maids had appeared to pass their examination, and had all, on coming to the question of wages, impudently declined accepting the place. A fourth candidate was expected to present herself on the next day ; and, until she made her appearance, Noel Vanstone positively declined removing from the metropolis. Captain Wragge showed his annoyance openly at the unnecessary delay thus occasioned in the return to Aldborough, but without producing any effect. Noel Vanstone shook his obstinate little head, and solemnly refused to trifle with his responsibilities.

The first event which occurred on Saturday morning, was the arrival of Mrs. Lecount's letter to her master, enclosed in one of the envelopes which the captain had addressed to himself. He received it (by previous arrangement with the waiter) in his bedroom—read it with the closest attention— and put it away carefully in his pocket-book. The letter was ominous of serious events to come, when the housekeeper returned to England ; and it was due to Magdalen—who was the person threatened—to place the warning of danger in her own possession.

Later in the day, the fourth candidate appeared for the maid's situation— a young woman of small expectations and subdued manners, who looked (as the landlady remarked) like a person overtaken by misfortune. She passed the ordeal of examination successfully, and accepted the wages offered without a murmur. The engagement having been ratified on both sides, fresh delays ensued, of which Noel Vanstone was once more the cause. He had not yet made up his mind whether he would, or would not, give more than a guinea for the wedding-ring ; and he wasted the rest of the day to such disastrous purpose in one jeweller's shop after another, that he and the captain, and the new lady's-maid (who travelled with them), were barely in time to catch the last train from London that evening.

It was late at night when they left the railway at the nearest station to Aldborough. Captain Wragge had been strangely silent all through the journey. His mind was ill at ease. He had left Magdalen, under very critical circumstances, with no fit person to control her ; and he was wholly ignorant of the progress of events, in his absence, at North Shingles.

CHAPTER XIII.

WHAT had happened at Aldborough, in Captain Wragge's absence?

Events had occurred which the captain's utmost dexterity might have found it hard to remedy.

As soon as the chaise had left North Shingles, Mrs. Wragge received the message which her husband had charged the servant to deliver. She hastened into the parlour, bewildered by her stormy interview with the captain, and penitently conscious that she had done wrong, without knowing what the wrong was. If Magdalen's mind had been unoccupied by the one idea of the marriage which now filled it—if she had possessed composure enough to listen to Mrs. Wragge's rambling narrative of what had happened during her interview with the housekeeper—Mrs. Lecount's visit to the wardrobe must, sooner or later, have formed part of the disclosure; and Magdalen, although she might never have guessed the truth, must at least have been warned that there was some element of danger lurking treacherously in the Alpaca dress. As it was, no such consequence as this followed Mrs. Wragge's appearance in the parlour; for no such consequence was now possible. .

Events which had happened earlier in the morning, events which had happened for days and weeks past, had vanished as completely from Magdalen's mind, as if they had never taken place. The horror of the coming Monday—the merciless certainty implied in the appointment of the day and hour—petrified all feeling in her, and annihilated all thought. Mrs. Wragge made three separate attempts to enter on the subject of the housekeeper's visit. The first time she might as well have addressed herself to the wind, or to the sea. The second attempt seemed likely to be more successful. Magdalen sighed, listened for a moment indifferently, and then dismissed the subject. "It doesn't matter," she said. "The end has come all the same. I'm not angry with you. Say no more." Later in the day, from not knowing what else to talk about, Mrs. Wragge tried again. This time, Magdalen turned on her impatiently. "For God's sake, don't worry me about trifles! I can't bear it." Mrs. Wragge closed her lips on the spot, and returned to the subject no more. Magdalen, who had been kind to her at all other times, had angrily forbidden it. The captain—utterly ignorant of Mrs. Lecount's interest in the secrets of the wardrobe—had never so much as approached it. All the information that he had extracted from his wife's mental confusion, he had extracted by putting direct questions, derived purely from the resources of his own knowledge. He had insisted on plain answers, without excuses of any kind; he had carried his point as usual; and his departure the same morning had left him no chance of re-opening the question, even if his irritation against his wife had permitted him to do so. There the Alpaca dress hung, neglected in the dark; the unnoticed, unsuspected centre of dangers that were still to come.

Towards the afternoon, Mrs. Wragge took courage to start a suggestion of her own—she pleaded for a little turn in the fresh air.

Magdalen passively put on her hat; passively accompanied her companion along the public walk, until they reached its northward extremity. Here the beach was left solitary, and here they sat down, side by side, on the shingle. It was a bright exhilarating day; pleasure-boats were sailing on the calm blue water; Aldborough was idling happily afloat and ashore. Mrs. Wragge recovered her spirits in the gaiety of the prospect—she amused herself, like a child, by tossing pebbles into the sea. From time to time she stole a questioning glance at Magdalen, and saw no encouragement in her manner, no change to cordiality in her face. She sat silent on the slope of the shingle, with her elbow on her knee, and her head resting on her hand, looking out over the sea—looking with rapt attention, and yet with eyes that seemed to notice nothing. Mrs. Wragge wearied of the pebbles, and lost her interest in looking at the pleasure-boats. Her great head began to nod heavily, and she dozed in the warm drowsy air. When she woke, the pleasure-boats were far off; their sails were white specks in the distance. The idlers on the beach were thinned in number; the sun was low in the heaven; the blue sea was darker, and rippled by a breeze. Changes on sky and earth and ocean told of the waning day; change was everywhere—except close at her side. There Magdalen sat, in the same position, with weary eyes that still looked over the sea, and still saw nothing

"Oh, do speak to me!" said Mrs. Wragge.

Magdalen started, and looked about her vacantly.

"It's late," she said, shivering under the first sensation that reached her of the rising breeze. "Come home; you want your tea."

They walked home in silence.

"Don't be angry with me for asking," said Mrs. Wragge, as they sat together at the tea-table. "Are you troubled, my dear, in your mind?"

"Yes," replied Magdalen. "Don't notice me. My trouble will soon be over."

She waited patiently until Mrs. Wragge had made an end of the meal, and then went up-stairs to her own room.

"Monday!" she said, as she sat down at her toilette-table. "Something may happen before Monday comes!"

Her fingers wandered mechanically among the brushes and combs, the tiny bottles and cases placed on the table. She set them in order, now in one way, and now in another—then on a sudden pushed them away from her in a heap. For a minute or two her hands remained idle. That interval passed, they grew restless again, and pulled the two little drawers backwards and forwards in their grooves. Among the objects laid in one of them was a Prayer-Book, which had belonged to her at Combe-Raven, and which she had saved with her other relics of the past, when she and her sister had taken their farewell of home. She opened the Prayer-Book after a long hesitation, at the Marriage Service—shut it again, before she had read a line—and put it back hurriedly in one of the drawers. After turning the key in the locks, she rose and walked to the window.

"The horrible sea!" she said, turning from it with a shudder of disgust. "The lonely, dreary, horrible sea!"

She went back to the drawer, and took the Prayer-Book out for the second time; half opened it again at the Marriage Service; and impatiently threw it back into the drawer. This time, after turning the lock, she took the key away—walked with it in her hand to the open window—and threw it violently from her into the garden. It fell on a bed thickly planted with flowers. It was invisible; it was lost. The sense of its loss seemed to relieve her.

"Something may happen on Friday; something may happen on Saturday; something may happen on Sunday. Three days still!"

She closed the green shutters outside the window, and drew the curtains, to darken the room still more. Her head felt heavy; her eyes were burning hot. She threw herself on her bed, with a sullen impulse to sleep away the time.

The quiet of the house helped her, the darkness of the room helped her; the stupor of mind into which she had fallen had its effect on her senses: she dropped into a broken sleep. Her restless hands moved incessantly; her head tossed from side to side of the pillow—but still she slept. Erelong, words fell by ones and twos from her lips; words whispered in her sleep, growing more and more continuous, more and more articulate, the longer the sleep lasted; words which seemed to calm her restlessness, and to hush her into deeper repose. She smiled; she was in the happy land of dreams—Frank's name escaped her. "Do you love me, Frank?" she whispered. "Oh, my darling, say it again! say it again!"

The time passed, the room grew darker; and still she slumbered and dreamed. Towards sunset—without any noise inside the house or out to account for it—she started up on the bed, awake again in an instant. The drowsy obscurity of the room struck her with terror. She ran to the window, pushed open the shutters, and leaned far out into the evening air and the evening light. Her eyes devoured the trivial sights on the beach; her ears drank in the welcome murmur of the sea. Anything to deliver her from the waking impression which her dreams had left! No more darkness; no more repose. Sleep that came mercifully to others, came treacherously to her. Sleep had only closed her eyes on the future, to open them on the past.

She went down again into the parlour, eager to talk—no matter how idly, no matter on what trifles. The room was empty. Perhaps Mrs. Wragge had gone to her work—perhaps, she was too tired to talk. Magdalen took her hat from the table, and went out. The sea that she had shrunk from, a few hours since, looked friendly now. How lovely it was in its cool evening blue! What a godlike joy in the happy multitude of waves, leaping up to the light of Heaven!

She stayed out, until the night fell and the stars appeared. The night steadied her.

By slow degrees, her mind recovered its balance, and she looked her position unflinchingly in the face. The vain hope that accident might defeat the very end for which, of her own free will, she had ceaselessly plotted and toiled, vanished and left her; self-dissipated in its own weakness. She knew the true alternative, and faced it. On one side, was the revolting ordeal of the marriage—on the other, the abandonment of her purpose. Was it too late to choose between the sacrifice of the purpose, and the sacrifice of herself? Yes! too late. The backward path had closed behind her. Time that no wish could change, Time that no prayers could recall, had made her purpose a part of herself: once she had governed it; now it governed her. The more she shrank, the harder she struggled, the more mercilessly it drove her on. No other feeling in her was strong enough to master it—not even the horror that was maddening her; the horror of her marriage.

Towards nine o'clock, she went back to the house.

"Walking again!" said Mrs. Wragge, meeting her at the door. "Come in and sit down, my dear. How tired you must be!"

Magdalen smiled, and patted Mrs. Wragge kindly on the shoulder.

"You forget how strong I am," she said. "Nothing hurts me."

She lit her candle, and went up-stairs again into her room. As she returned to the old place by her toilette table, the vain hope in the three days of delay, the vain hope of deliverance by accident, came back to her—this time, in a form more tangible than the form which it had hitherto worn.

"Friday, Saturday, Sunday. Something may happen to him; something may happen to me. Something serious; something fatal. One of us may die."

A sudden change came over her face. She shivered, though there was no cold in the air. She started, though there was no noise to alarm her.

"One of us may die. I may be the one."

She fell into deep thought—roused herself, after a while—and, opening the door, called to Mrs. Wragge to come and speak to her.

"You were right in thinking I should fatigue myself," she said. "My walk has been a little too much for me. I feel tired; and I am going to bed. Good-night." She kissed Mrs. Wragge, and softly closed the door again.

After a few turns backwards and forwards in the room, she abruptly opened her writing-case and began a letter to her sister. The letter grew and grew under her hands; she filled sheet after sheet of note-paper. Her heart was full of her subject: it was her own story addressed to Norah. She shed no tears; she was composed to a quiet sadness. Her pen ran smoothly on. After writing for more than two hours, she left off while the letter was still unfinished. There was no signature attached to it—there was a blank space reserved, to be filled up at some other time. After putting away the case, with the sheets of writing secured inside it, she walked to the window for air, and stood there looking out.

The moon was waning over the sea. The breeze of the earlier hours had died out. On earth and ocean, the spirit of the Night brooded in a deep and awful calm.

Her head drooped low on her bosom, and all the view waned before her eyes with the waning moon. She saw no sea, no sky. Death the Tempter, was busy at her heart. Death the Tempter, pointed homeward, to the grave of her dead parents in Combe-Raven churchyard.

"Nineteen last birthday," she thought. "Only nineteen!" She moved away from the window—hesitated—and then looked out again at the view. "The beautiful night!" she said gratefully. "Oh, the beautiful night!"

She left the window, and lay down on her bed. Sleep that had come treacherously before, came mercifully now; came deep and dreamless, the image of her last waking thought—the image of Death.

Early the next morning, Mrs. Wragge went into Magdalen's room, and found that she had risen betimes. She was sitting before the glass, drawing the comb slowly through and through her hair—thoughtful and quiet.

"How do you feel this morning, my dear?" asked Mrs. Wragge. "Quite well again?"

"Yes."

After replying in the affirmative, she stopped, considered for a moment, and suddenly contradicted herself. "No," she said, "not quite well. I am suffering a little from toothache." As she altered her first answer in those words, she gave a twist to her hair with the comb, so that it fell forward and hid her face.

At breakfast she was very silent; and she took nothing but a cup of tea.

"Let me go to the chemist's and get something," said Mrs. Wragge.

"No, thank you."

"Do let me!"

"No!"

She refused for the second time sharply and angrily. As usual, Mrs.

Wragge submitted, and let her have her own way. When breakfast was over she rose, without a word of explanation, and went out. Mrs. Wragge watched her from the window, and saw that she took the direction of the chemist's shop.

On reaching the chemist's door, she stopped—paused, before entering the shop, and looked in at the window—hesitated, and walked away a little—hesitated again—and took the first turning which led back to the beach.

Without looking about her, without caring what place she chose, she seated herself on the shingle. The only persons who were near to her, in the position she now occupied, were a nursemaid and two little boys. The youngest of the two had a tiny toy-ship in his hand. After looking at Magdalen for a little while, with the quaintest gravity and attention, the boy suddenly approached her; and opened the way to an acquaintance by putting his toy composedly on her lap.

"Look at my ship," said the child, crossing his hands on Magdalen's knee.

She was not usually patient with children. In happier days, she would not have met the boy's advance towards her, as she met it now. The hard despair in her eyes left them suddenly; her fast-closed lips parted, and trembled. She put the ship back into the child's hands, and lifted him on her lap.

"Will you give me a kiss?" she said, faintly.

The boy looked at his ship, as if he would rather have kissed the ship.

She repeated the question—repeated it, almost humbly. The child put his hand up to her neck, and kissed her.

"If I was your sister, would you love me?"

All the misery of her friendless position, all the wasted tenderness of her heart, poured from her in those words.

"Would you love me?" she repeated, hiding her face on the bosom of the child's frock.

"Yes," said the boy. "Look at my ship."

She looked at the ship through her gathering tears.

"What do you call it?" she asked, trying hard to find her way even to the interest of a child.

"I call it Uncle Kirke's ship," said the boy. "Uncle Kirke has gone away."

The name recalled nothing to her memory. No remembrances but old remembrances lived in her now. "Gone?" she repeated absently, thinking what she should say to her little friend next.

"Yes," said the boy. "Gone to China."

Even from the lips of a child, that word struck her to the heart. She put Kirke's little nephew off her lap, and instantly left the beach.

As she turned back to the house, the struggle of the past night renewed itself in her mind. But the sense of relief which the child had brought to her, the reviving tenderness which she had felt while he sat on her knee, influenced her still. She was conscious of a dawning hope, opening freshly on her thoughts, as the boy's innocent eyes had opened on her face when he came to her on the beach. Was it too late to turn back? Once more, she asked herself that question—and now, for the first time, she asked it in doubt.

She ran up to her own room with a lurking distrust in her changed self, which warned her to act, and not to think. Without waiting to remove her shawl or to take off her hat, she opened her writing-case, and addressed these lines to Captain Wragge, as fast as her pen could trace them.

"You will find the money I promised you, enclosed in this. My resolution has failed me. The horror of marrying him is more than I can face. I have left Aldborough. Pity my weakness, and forget me. Let us never meet again."

With throbbing heart, with eager, trembling fingers, she drew her little white silk bag from her bosom, and took out the bank-notes to enclose them in the letter. Her hand searched impetuously; her hand had lost its discrimination of touch. She grasped the whole contents of the bag in one handful of papers; and drew them out violently, tearing some and disarranging the folds of others. As she threw them down before her on the table, the first object that met her eye was her own handwriting, faded already with time. She looked closer, and saw the words she had copied from her dead father's letter—saw the lawyer's brief and terrible commentary on them, confronting her at the bottom of the page:

Mr. Vanstone's daughters are Nobody's Children, and the law leaves them helpless at their uncle's mercy.

Her throbbing heart stopped; her trembling hands grew icily quiet. All the Past rose before her in mute overwhelming reproach. She took up the lines which her own hand had written hardly a minute since, and looked at the ink still wet on the letters, with a vacant incredulity.

The colour that had risen on her cheeks faded from them once more. The hard despair looked out again, cold and glittering, in her tearless eyes. She folded the bank-notes carefully, and put them back in her bag. She pressed the copy of her father's letter to her lips, and returned it to its place, with the bank-notes. When the bag was in her bosom again, she waited a little, with her face hidden in her hands—then deliberately tore up the lines addressed to Captain Wragge. Before the ink was dry, the letter lay in fragments on the floor.

"No!" she said, as the last morsel of the torn paper dropped from her hand. "On the way I go, there is no turning back."

She rose composedly, and left the room. While descending the stairs she met Mrs. Wragge coming up. "Going out again, my dear?" asked Mrs. Wragge. "May I go with you?"

Magdalen's attention wandered. Instead of answering the question, she absently answered her own thoughts.

"Thousands of women marry for money," she said. "Why shouldn't I?"

The helpless perplexity of Mrs. Wragge's face, as she spoke those words, roused her to a sense of present things.

"My poor dear!" she said; "I puzzle you, don't I? Never mind what I say,—all girls talk nonsense; and I'm no better then the rest of them. Come! I'll give you a treat. You shall enjoy yourself while the captain is away. We will have a long drive by ourselves. Put on your smart bonnet, and come with me to the hotel. I'll tell the landlady to put a nice cold dinner into a basket. You shall have all the things you like—and I'll wait on you. When you are an old, old woman, you will remember me kindly, won't you? You will say, 'She wasn't a bad girl; hundreds worse then she was live and prosper, and nobody blames them.' There! there! go and put your bonnet on. Oh, my God, what is my heart made of! How it lives and lives, when other girls' hearts would have died in them long ago!"

In half an hour more, she and Mrs. Wragge were seated together in the carriage. One of the horses was restive at starting. "Flog him," she cried angrily to the driver. "What are you frightened about? Flog him! Suppose the carriage was upset," she said, turning suddenly to her companion; "and suppose I was thrown out, and killed on the spot? Nonsense! don't look at me in that way. I'm like your husband; I have a dash of humour, and I'm only joking."

They were out the whole day. When they reached home again, it was after dark. The long succession of hours passed in the fresh air, left them both with the same sense of fatigue. Again that night, Magdalen slept the deep dreamless sleep of the night before. And so the Friday closed.

Her last thought at night, had been the thought which had sustained her throughout the day. She had laid her head on the pillow, with the same reckless resolution to submit to the coming trial, which had already expressed itself in words, when she and Mrs. Wragge met by accident on the stairs. When she woke on the morning of Saturday, the resolution was gone. The Friday's thoughts—the Friday's events even—were blotted out of her mind. Once again, creeping chill through the flow of her young blood, she felt the slow and deadly prompting of despair, which had come to her in the waning moonlight, which had whispered to her in the awful calm.

"I saw the end, as the end must be," she said to herself, "on Thursday night. I have been wrong ever since."

When she and her companion met that morning, she reiterated her complaint of suffering from the toothache; she repeated her refusal to allow Mrs. Wragge to procure a remedy; she left the house after breakfast, in the direction of the chemist's shop, exactly as she had left it on the morning before.

This time she entered the shop without an instant's hesitation.

"I have got an attack of toothache," she said abruptly to an elderly man who stood behind the counter.

"May I look at the tooth, Miss?"

"There is no necessity to look. It is a hollow tooth. I think I have caught cold in it."

The chemist recommended various remedies, which were in vogue fifteen years since. She declined purchasing any of them.

"I have always found Laudanum relieve the pain better than anything else," she said, trifling with the bottles on the counter, and looking at them while she spoke, instead of looking at the chemist. "Let me have some Laudanum."

"Certainly, Miss. Excuse my asking the question—it is only a matter of form. You are staying at Aldborough, I think?"

"Yes. I am Miss Bygrave, of North Shingles."

The chemist bowed; and, turning to his shelves, filled an ordinary half-ounce bottle with laudanum, immediately. In ascertaining his customer's name and address beforehand, the owner of the shop had taken a precaution which was natural to a careful man—but which was by no means universal, under similar circumstances, in the state of the law at that time.

"Shall I put you up a little cotton wool with the laudanum?" he asked, after he had placed a label on the bottle, and had written a word on it in large letters.

"If you please. What have you just written on the bottle?" She put the question sharply, with something of distrust as well as curiosity in her manner.

The chemist answered the question by turning the label towards her. She saw written on it, in large letters—POISON.

"I like to be on the safe side, Miss," said the old man, smiling. "Very worthy people in other respects, are often sadly careless, where poisons are concerned."

She began trifling again with the bottles on the counter; and put another question, with an ill-concealed anxiety to hear the answer.

"Is there danger," she asked, "in such a little drop of Laudanum as that?"

"There is Death in it, Miss," replied the chemist quietly.

"Death to a child, or to a person in delicate health?"

"Death to the strongest man in England, let him be who he may."

With that answer, the chemist sealed up the bottle in its wrapping of white paper, and handed the laudanum to Magdalen across the counter. She laughed as she took it from him, and paid for it.

"There will be no fear of accidents at North Shingles," she said. "I shall keep the bottle locked up in my dressing-case. If it doesn't relieve the pain, I must come to you again, and try some other remedy. Good morning."

"Good morning, Miss."

She went straight back to the house, without once looking up, without noticing any one who passed her. She brushed by Mrs. Wragge in the passage, as she might have brushed by a piece of furniture. She ascended the stairs, and caught her foot twice in her dress, from sheer inattention to the common precaution of holding it up. The trivial daily interests of life had lost their hold on her already.

In the privacy of her own room, she took the bottle from its wrapping, and threw the paper and the cotton wool into the fireplace. At the moment when she did this there was a knock at the door. She hid the little bottle, and looked up impatiently. Mrs. Wragge came into the room.

"Have you got something for your toothache, my dear?"

"Yes."

"Can I do anything to help you?"

"No."

Mrs. Wragge still lingered uneasily near the door. Her manner showed plainly that she had something more to say.

"What is it?" asked Magdalen, sharply.

"Don't be angry," said Mrs. Wragge. "I'm not settled in my mind about the captain. He's a great writer—and he hasn't written. He's as quick as lightning—and he hasn't come back. Here's Saturday, and no signs of him. Has he run away, do you think? Has anything happened to him?"

"I should think not. Go down stairs; I'll come and speak to you about it directly."

As soon as she was alone again, Magdalen rose from her chair, advanced towards a cupboard in the room which locked, and paused for a moment, with her hand on the key, in doubt. Mrs. Wragge's appearance had disturbed the whole current of her thoughts. Mrs. Wragge's last question, trifling as it was, had checked her on the verge of the precipice—had roused the old vain hope in her once more of release by accident.

"Why not?" she said. "Why may something not have happened to one of them?"

She placed the laudanum in the cupboard, locked it, and put the key in her pocket. "Time enough still," she thought, "before Monday. I'll wait till the captain comes back."

After some consultation down-stairs, it was agreed that the servant should sit up that night, in expectation of her master's return. The day passed quietly, without events of any kind. Magdalen dreamed away the hours over a book. A weary patience of expectation was all she felt now —the poignant torment of thought was dulled and blunted at last. She passed the day and the evening in the parlour, vaguely conscious of a strange feeling of aversion to going back to her own room. As the night advanced, as the noises ceased indoors and out, her restlessness began to return. She endeavoured to quiet herself by reading. Books failed to fix her attention. The newspaper was lying in a corner of the room: she tried the newspaper next.

She looked mechanically at the headings of the articles; she listlessly turned over page after page, until her wandering attention was arrested by the narrative of an Execution in a distant part of England. There was nothing to strike her in the story of the crime; and yet she read it. It was a common, horribly common, act of bloodshed—the murder of a woman in farm-service, by a man in the same employment who was jealous of her. He had been convicted on no extraordinay evidence; he had been hanged under no unusual circumstances. He had made his confession, when he knew there was no hope for him, like other criminals of his class; and the newspaper had printed it at the end of the article, in these terms:—

"I kept company with the deceased for a year or thereabouts. I said I would marry her when I had money enough. She said I had money enough now. We had a quarrel. She refused to walk out with me any more; she wouldn't draw me my beer; she took up with my fellow-servant, David Crouch. I went to her on the Saturday, and said I would marry her as soon as we could be asked in church, if she would give up Crouch. She laughed at me. She turned me out of the washhouse, and the rest of them saw her turn me out. I was not easy in my mind. I went and sat on the gate—the gate in the meadow they call Pettit's Piece. I thought I would shoot her. I went and fetched my gun and loaded it. I went out into Pettit's Piece again. I was hard put to it, to make up my mind. I thought I would try my luck—I mean try whether to kill her or not—by throwing up the Spud of the plough into the air. I said to myself, if it falls flat, I'll spare her; if it falls point in the earth, I'll kill her. I took a good swing with it, and shied it up. It fell point in the earth. I went and shot her. It was a bad job, but I did it. I did it, as they said I did it at the trial. I hope the Lord will have mercy on me. I wish my mother to have my old clothes. I have no more to say."

In the happier days of her life, Magdalen would have passed over the narrative of the execution, and the printed confession which accompanied it, unread—the subject would have failed to attract her. She read the horrible story now—read it, with an interest unintelligible to herself.

Her attention, which had wandered over higher and better things, followed every sentence of the murderer's hideously direct confession, from beginning to end. If the man, or the woman, had been known to her—if the place had been familiar to her memory—she could hardly have followed the narrative more closely, or have felt a more distinct impression of it left on her mind. She laid down the paper, wondering at herself; she took it up once more, and tried to read some other portion of the contents. The effort was useless; her attention wandered again. She threw the paper away; and went out into the garden. The night was dark; the stars were few and faint. She could just see the gravel walk—she could just pace backwards and forwards between the house-door and the gate.

The confession in the newspaper had taken a fearful hold on her mind. As she paced the walk, the black night opened over the sea, and showed her the murderer in the field, hurling the Spud of the plough into the air. She ran, shuddering, back to the house. The murderer followed her into the parlour. She seized the candle, and went up into her room. The vision of her own distempered fancy followed her to the place where the laudanum was hidden—and vanished there.

It was midnight; and there was no sign yet of the captain's return.

She took from the writing-case the long letter which she had written to Norah, and slowly read it through. The letter quieted her. When she reached the blank space left at the end, she hurriedly turned back, and began it over again.

One o'clock struck from the church clock; and still the captain never appeared.

She read the letter for the second time; she turned back obstinately, despairingly; and began it for the third time. As she once more reached the last page, she looked at her watch. It was a quarter to two. She had just put the watch back in the belt of her dress, when there came to her— far off in the stillness of the morning—a sound of wheels.

She dropped the letter, and clasped her cold hands in her lap, and listened. The sound came on, faster and faster, nearer and nearer—the trivial sound to all other ears; the sound of Doom to hers. It passed the side of the house; it travelled a little further on; it stopped. She heard a loud knocking—then the opening of a window—then voices—then a long silence—then the wheels again, coming back—then the opening of the door below, and the sound of the captain's voice in the passage.

She could endure it no longer. She opened her door a little way, and called to him.

He ran up-stairs instantly, astonished that she was not in bed. She spoke to him through the narrow opening of the door; keeping herself hidden behind it, for she was afraid to let him see her face.

" Has anything gone wrong ?" she asked.

"Make your mind easy," he answered. "Nothing has gone wrong."

"Is no accident likely to happen between this and Monday?"

"None whatever. The marriage is a certainty."

"A certainty?"

"Yes."

"Good night."

She put her hand out through the door. He took it with some little surprise; it was not often in his experience that she gave him her hand of her own accord.

"You have sat up too long," he said, as he felt the clasp of her cold fingers. "I am afraid you will have a bad night—I'm afraid you will not sleep."

She softly closed the door.

"I shall sleep," she said, "sounder than you think for."

It was past two o'clock when she shut herself up alone in her room. Her chair stood in its customary place by the toilette table. She sat down for a few minutes thoughtfully—then opened her letter to Norah, and turned to the end, where the blank space was left. The last lines written above the space ran thus: . . . "I have laid my whole heart bare to you; I have hidden nothing. It has come to this. The end I have toiled for, at such terrible cost to myself, is an end which I must reach or die. It is wickedness, madness, what you will—but it is so. There are now two journeys before me to choose between. If I can marry him—the journey to the church. If the profanation of myself is more than I can bear—the journey to the grave!"

Under that last sentence, she wrote these lines:—

"My choice is made. If the cruel law will let you, lay me with my father and mother, in the churchyard at home. Farewell, my love! Be always innocent; be always happy. If Frank ever asks about me, say I died forgiving him. Don't grieve long for me, Norah—I am not worth it."

She sealed the letter, and addressed it to her sister. The tears gathered in her eyes as she laid it on the table. She waited until her sight was clear again, and then took the bank-notes once more from the little bag in her bosom. After wrapping them in a sheet of note-paper, she wrote Captain Wragge's name on the enclosure, and added these words below it: "Lock the door of my room, and leave me till my sister comes. The money I promised you is in this. You are not to blame; it is my fault, and mine only. If you have any friendly remembrance of me, be kind to your wife for my sake."

After placing the enclosure by the letter to Norah, she rose and looked round the room. Some few little things in it were not in their places. She set them in order, and drew the curtains on either side, at the head of her bed. Her own dress was the next object of her scrutiny. It was all as neat, as pure, as prettily arranged as ever. Nothing about her was disordered, but her hair. Some tresses had fallen loose on one side of her head; she carefully put them back in their places, with the help of her glass. "How pale I look!" she thought, with a faint smile. "Shall I be paler still, when they find me in the morning?"

She went straight to the place where the laudanum was hidden, and took it out. The bottle was so small, that it lay easily in the palm of her hand. She let it remain there for a little while, and stood looking at it.

"DEATH!" she said. "In this drop of brown drink—DEATH!"

As the words passed her lips, an agony of unutterable horror seized on her in an instant. She crossed the room unsteadily with a maddening confusion in her head, with a suffocating anguish at her heart. She caught at the table to support herself. The faint clink of the bottle, as it fell harmlessly from her loosened grasp, and rolled against some porcelain object on the table, struck through her brain like the stroke of a knife. The sound of her own voice, sunk to a whisper—her voice only uttering that one word, Death—rushed in her ears like the rushing of a wind. She dragged herself to the bedside, and rested her head against it, sitting on the floor. "O, my life! my life!" she thought; "what is my life worth, that I cling to it like this?"

An interval passed, and she felt her strength returning. She raised herself on her knees, and hid her face on the bed. She tried to pray—to pray to be forgiven for seeking the refuge of death. Frantic words burst from her lips—words which would have risen to cries, if she had not stifled them in the bed-clothes. She started to her feet; despair strengthened her with a headlong fury against herself. In one moment, she was back at the table; in another, the poison was once more in her hand.

She removed the cork, and lifted the bottle to her mouth.

At the first cold touch of the glass on her lips, her strong young life leapt up in her leaping blood, and fought with the whole frenzy of its loathing against the close terror of Death. Every active power in the exuberant vital force that was in her, rose in revolt against the destruction which her own will would fain have wreaked on her own life. She paused: for the second time, she paused in spite of herself. There, in the glorious perfection of her youth and health—there, trembling on the verge of human existence, she stood; with the kiss of the Destroyer close at her lips, and Nature, faithful to its sacred trust, fighting for the salvation of her to the last.

No word passed her lips. Her cheeks flushed deep; her breath came thick and fast. With the poison still in her hand, with the sense that she might faint in another moment, she made for the window, and threw back the curtain that covered it.

The new day had risen. The broad grey dawn flowed in on her, over the quiet eastern sea.

She saw the waters, heaving large and silent in the misty calm; she felt the fresh breath of the morning flutter cool on her face. Her strength returned; her mind cleared a little. At the sight of the sea, her memory recalled the walk in the garden, overnight, and the picture which her distempered fancy had painted on the black void. In thought, she saw the picture again—the murderer hurling the Spud*of the plough into the air, and setting the life or death of the woman who had deserted him, on the hazard of the falling point. The infection of that terrible superstition seized on her mind, as suddenly as the new day had burst on her view. The promise of release which she saw in it from the horror of her own hesitation, roused the last energies of her despair. She resolved to end the struggle, by setting her life or death on the hazard of a chance.

On what chance?

The sea showed it to her. Dimly distinguishable through the mist, she saw a little fleet of coasting vessels slowly drifting towards the house, all following the same direction with the favouring set of the tide. In half an hour—perhaps in less—the fleet would have passed her window. The hands of her watch pointed to four o'clock. She seated herself close at the side of the window, with her back towards the quarter from which the vessels were drifting down on her—with the poison placed on the window-sill, and the watch on her lap. For one half-hour to come, she determined to wait there, and count the vessels as they went by. If, in that time, an even number passed her—the sign given, should be a sign to live. If the uneven number prevailed—the end should be Death.

With that final resolution, she rested her head against the window, and waited for the ships to pass.

The first came; high, dark, and near in the mist; gliding silently over the silent sea. An interval—and the second followed, with the third close after it. Another interval, longer and longer drawn out—and nothing passed. She looked at her watch. Twelve minutes; and three ships. Three.

The fourth came; slower than the rest, larger than the rest, farther off in the mist than the rest. The interval followed; a long interval once more. Then the next vessel passed, darkest and nearest of all. Five. The next uneven number—Five.

She looked at her watch again. Nineteen minutes; and five ships. Twenty minutes. Twenty-one, two, three—and no sixth vessel. Twenty-four; and the sixth came by. Twenty-five, twenty-six, twenty-seven, twenty-eight; and the next uneven number—the fatal Seven—glided into view. Two minutes to the end of the half-hour. And seven ships.

Twenty-nine; and nothing followed in the wake of the seventh ship.

The minute-hand of the watch moved on half way to thirty—and still the white heaving sea was a misty blank. Without moving her head from the window, she took the poison in one hand, and raised the watch in the other. As the quick seconds counted each other out, her eyes, as quick as they, looked from the watch to the sea, from the sea to the watch—looked for the last time at the sea—and saw the EIGHTH ship.

She never moved; she never spoke. The death of thought, the death of feeling, seemed to have come to her already. She put back the poison mechanically on the ledge of the window; and watched, as in a dream, the ship gliding smoothly on its silent way—gliding till it melted dimly into shadow—gliding till it was lost in the mist.

The strain on her mind relaxed, when the Messenger of Life had passed from her sight.

"Providence?" she whispered faintly to herself. "Or chance?"

Her eyes closed, and her head fell back. When the sense of life returned to her, the morning sun was warm on her face—the blue heaven looked down on her—and the sea was a sea of gold.

She fell on her knees at the window, and burst into tears.

*   *   *   *   *   *

Towards noon that day, the captain, waiting below stairs, and hearing no movement in Magdalen's room, felt uneasy at the long silence. He desired the new maid to follow him up-stairs; and, pointing to the door, told her to go in softly, and see whether her mistress was awake.

The maid entered the room; remained there a moment; and came out again, closing the door gently.

"She looks beautiful, sir," said the girl; "and she's sleeping as quietly as a new-born child."

CHAPTER XIV.

THE morning of her husband's return to North Shingles was a morning memorable for ever in the domestic calendar of Mrs. Wragge. She dated from that occasion the first announcement which reached her of Magdalen's marriage.

It had been Mrs. Wragge's earthly lot to pass her life in a state of perpetual surprise. Never yet, however, had she wandered in such a maze of astonishment as the maze in which she lost herself when the captain coolly told her the truth. She had been sharp enough to suspect Mr. Noel Vanstone of coming to the house in the character of a sweetheart on approval; and she had dimly interpreted certain expressions of impatience which had fallen from Magdalen's lips, as boding ill for the success of his suit—but her utmost penetration had never reached as far as a suspicion of the impending marriage. She rose from one climax of amazement to another, as her husband proceeded with his disclosure. A wedding in the family at a day's notice! and that wedding Magdalen's! and not a single new dress ordered for anybody, the bride included! and the Oriental Cashmere Robe totally unavailable, on the occasion when she might have worn it to the greatest advantage! Mrs. Wragge dropped crookedly into a chair, and beat her disorderly hands on her unsymmetrical knees, in utter forgetfulness of the captain's presence, and the captain's terrible eye. It would not have surprised her to hear next, that the world had come to an end, and that the only mortal whom Destiny had overlooked in winding up the affairs of this earthly planet, was herself!

Leaving his wife to recover her composure by her own unaided efforts, Captain Wragge withdrew to wait for Magdalen's appearance in the lower regions of the house. It was close on one o'clock before the sound of footsteps in the room above, warned him that she was awake and stirring. He called at once for the maid (whose name he had ascertained to be Louisa), and sent her up-stairs to her mistress for the second time.

Magdalen was standing by her dressing-table, when a faint tap at the door suddenly roused her. The tap was followed by the sound of a meek voice, which announced itself as the voice of "her maid," and inquired if Miss Bygrave needed any assistance that morning.

"Not at present," said Magdalen, as soon as she had recovered the surprise of finding herself unexpectedly provided with an attendant. "I will ring when I want you."

After dismissing the woman with that answer, she accidentally looked from the door to the window. Any speculations on the subject of the new servant in which she might otherwise have engaged, were instantly suspended by the sight of the bottle of laudanum, still standing on the ledge of the window, where she had left it at sunrise. She took it once more in her hand, with a strange confusion of feeling—with a vague doubt even yet, whether the sight of it reminded her of a terrible reality or a terrible dream. Her first impulse was to rid herself of it on the spot. She raised the bottle to throw the contents out of the window—and paused, in sudden distrust of the impulse that had come to her. "I have accepted my new life," she thought. "How do I know what that life may have in store for me?" She turned from the window, and went back to the table. "I may be forced to drink it yet," she said—and put the laudanum into her dressing-case.

Her mind was not at ease when she had done this: there seemed to be some indefinable ingratitude in the act. Still she made no attempt to remove the bottle from its hiding-place. She hurried on her toilette; she hastened the time when she could ring for the maid, and forget herself and her waking thoughts in a new subject. After touching the bell, she took from the table her letter to Norah and her letter to the captain; put them both into her dressing-case with the laudanum; and locked it securely with the key which she kept attached to her watch-chain.

Magdalen's first impression of her attendant was not an agreeable one. She could not investigate the girl with the experienced eye of the landlady at the London hotel, who had characterized the stranger as a young person overtaken by misfortune; and who had showed plainly by her look and manner, of what nature she suspected that misfortune to be. But, with this drawback, Magdalen was perfectly competent to detect the tokens of sickness and sorrow, lurking under the surface of the new maid's activity and politeness. She suspected the girl was ill tempered; she disliked her name; and she was indisposed to welcome any servant who had been engaged by Noel Vanstone. But after the first few minutes, "Louisa" grew on her liking. She answered all the questions put to her, with perfect directness; she appeared to understand her duties thoroughly; and she never spoke until she was spoken to first. After making all the inquiries that occurred to her at the time, and after determining to give the maid a fair trial, Magdalen rose to leave the room. The very air in it was still heavy to her with the oppression of the past night.

"Have you anything more to say to me?" she asked, turning to the servant, with her hand on the door.

"I beg your pardon, Miss," said Louisa, very respectfully and very quietly. "I think my master told me that the marriage was to be to-morrow?"

Magdalen repressed the shudder that stole over her, at that reference to the marriage on the lips of a stranger, and answered in the affirmative.

"It's a very short time, Miss, to prepare in. If you would be so kind as to give me my orders about the packing before you go down stairs —— ?"

"There are no such preparations to make as you suppose," said Magdalen, hastily. "The few things I have here, can be all packed at once, if you like. I shall wear the same dress to-morrow which I have on to-day. Leave out the straw bonnet, and the light shawl, and put everything else into my boxes. I have no new dresses to pack—I have nothing ordered for the occasion, of any sort." She tried to add some commonplace phrases of explanation, accounting as probably as might be, for the absence of the usual wedding outfit, and wedding-dress. But no further reference to the marriage would pass her lips, and without another word she abruptly left the room.

The meek and melancholy Louisa stood lost in astonishment. "Something wrong here," she thought. "I'm half afraid of my new place already." She sighed resignedly—shook her head—and went to the wardrobe. She first examined the drawers underneath; took out the various articles of linen laid inside; and placed them on chairs. Opening the upper part of the wardrobe next, she ranged the dresses in it side by side on the bed. Her last proceeding was to push the empty boxes into the middle of the room, and to compare the space at her disposal with the articles of dress which she had to pack. She completed her preliminary calculations with the ready self-reliance of a woman who thoroughly understood her business, and began the packing forthwith. Just as she had placed the first article of linen in the smaller box, the door of the room opened; and the house-servant, eager for gossip, came in.

"What do you want?" asked Louisa, quietly.

"Did you ever hear of anything like this!" said the house-servant, entering on her subject immediately.

"Like what?"

"Like this marriage, to be sure. You're London bred, they tell me. Did you ever hear of a young lady being married, without a single new thing to her back? No wedding veil, and no wedding breakfast, and no wedding favours for the servants. It's flying in the face of Providence—that's what I say. I'm only a poor servant, I know. But it's wicked, downright wicked—and I don't care who hears me!"

Louisa went on with the packing.

"Look at her dresses!" persisted the house-servant, waving her hand indignantly at the bed. "I'm only a poor girl—but I wouldn't marry the best man alive without a new gown to my back. Look here! look at this dowdy brown thing here. Alpaca! You're not going to pack this Alpaca thing, are you? Why it's hardly fit for a servant! I don't know that I'd take a gift of it if it was offered me. It would do for me if I took it up in the skirt, and let it out in the waist—and it wouldn't look so bad with a bit of bright trimming, would it?"

"Let that dress alone, if you please," said Louisa, as quietly as ever.

"What did you say?" inquired the other, doubting whether her ears had not deceived her.

"I said—let that dress alone. It belongs to my mistress; and I have my mistress's orders to pack up everything in the room. You are not helping me by coming here—you are very much in my way."

"Well!" said the house-servant, "you may be London bred, as they say. But if these are your London manners—give me Suffolk!" She opened the door, with an angry snatch at the handle, shut it violently, opened it again, and looked in. "Give me Suffolk!" said the house-servant, with a parting nod of her head to point the edge of her sarcasm.

Louisa proceeded impenetrably with her packing up.

Having neatly disposed of the linen in the smaller box, she turned her attention to the dresses next. After passing them carefully in review, to ascertain which was the least valuable of the collection, and to place that one at the bottom of the trunk for the rest to lie on, she made her choice with very little difficulty. The first gown which she put into the box, was—the brown Alpaca dress.

Meanwhile, Magdalen had joined the captain down stairs. Although he could not fail to notice the languor in her face and the listlessness of all her movements, he was relieved to find that she met him with perfect composure. She was even self-possessed enough to ask him for news of his journey, with no other signs of agitation than a passing change of colour, and a little trembling of the lips.

"So much for the past," said Captain Wragge, when his narrative of the expedition to London, by way of St. Crux, had come to an end. "Now for the present. The bridegroom——"

"If it makes no difference," she interposed, "call him Mr. Noel Vanstone."

"With all my heart. Mr. Noel Vanstone is coming here this afternoon to dine and spend the evening. He will be tiresome in the last degree—but like all tiresome people, he is not to be got rid of on any terms. Before he comes, I have a last word or two of caution for your private ear. By this time to-morrow we shall have parted—without any certain knowledge, on either side, of our ever meeting again. I am anxious to serve your interests faithfully to the last—I am anxious you should feel that I have done all I could for your future security, when we say good-bye."

Magdalen looked at him in surprise. He spoke in altered tones. He was agitated; he was strangely in earnest. Something in his look and manner took her memory back to the first night at Aldborough, when she had opened her mind to him in the darkening solitude—when they two had sat together alone, on the slope of the martello tower.

"I have no reason to think otherwise than kindly of you," she said.

Captain Wragge suddenly left his chair, and took a turn backwards and forwards in the room. Magdalen's last words seemed to have produced some extraordinary disturbance in him.

"Damn it!" he broke out; "I can't let you say that. You have reason to think ill of me. I have cheated you. You never got your fair share of profit from the Entertainment, from first to last. There! now the murder's out!"

Magdalen smiled, and signed to him to come back to his chair.

"I know you cheated me," she said, quietly. "You were in the exercise of your profession, Captain Wragge. I expected it when I joined you. I made no complaint at the time; and I make none now. If the money you took is any recompense for all the trouble I have given you, you are heartily welcome to it."

"Will you shake hands on that?" asked the captain, with an awkwardness and hesitation, strongly at variance with his customary ease of manner.

Magdalen gave him her hand. He wrung it hard. "You are a strange girl," he said, trying to speak lightly. "You have laid a hold on me that I don't quite understand. I'm half uncomfortable at taking the money from you, now—and yet, you don't want it, do you?" He hesitated. "I almost wish," he said, "I had never met you on the walls of York."

"It is too late to wish that, Captain Wragge. Say no more. You only distress me—say no more. We have other subjects to talk about. What were those words of caution which you had for my private ear?"

The captain took another turn in the room, and struggled back again into his every-day character. He produced from his pocket-book Mrs. Lecount's letter to her master, and handed it to Magdalen.

"There is the letter that might have ruined us, if it had ever reached its address," he said. "Read it carefully. I have a question to ask you when you have done."

Magdalen read the letter. "What is this proof," she inquired, "which Mrs. Lecount relies on so confidently?"

"The very question I was going to ask you," said Captain Wragge. "Consult your memory of what happened, when you tried that experiment in Vauxhall Walk. Did Mrs. Lecount get no other chance against you, than the chances you have told me of already?"

"She discovered that my face was disguised, and she heard me speak in my own voice."

"And nothing more?"

"Nothing more."

"Very good. Then my interpretation of the letter is clearly the right one. The proof Mrs. Lecount relies on, is my wife's infernal ghost story—which is, in plain English, the story of Miss Bygrave having been seen in Miss Vanstone's disguise; the witness being the very person who is afterwards presented at Aldborough, in the character of Miss Bygrave's aunt. An excellent chance for Mrs. Lecount, if she can only lay her hand at the right time on Mrs. Wragge—and no chance at all, if she can't. Make your mind easy on that point. Mrs. Lecount and my wife have seen the last of each other. In the mean time, don't neglect the warning I give you, in giving you this letter. Tear it up, for fear of accidents—but don't forget it."

"Trust me to remember it," replied Magdalen, destroying the letter while she spoke. "Have you anything more to tell me?"

"I have some information to give you," said Captain Wragge, "which may be useful, because it relates to your future security. Mind, I want to know nothing about your proceedings when to-morrow is over—we settled that when we first discussed this matter. I ask no questions, and I make no guesses. All I want to do now, is to warn you of your legal position, after your marriage; and to leave you to make what use you please of your knowledge, at your own sole discretion. I took a lawyer's opinion on the point, when I was in London, thinking it might be useful to you."

"It is sure to be useful. What did the lawyer say?"

"To put it plainly, this is what he said. If Mr. Noel Vanstone ever discovers that you have knowingly married him under a false name, he can apply to the Ecclesiastical Court to have his marriage declared null and void. The issue of the application would rest with the Judges. But if he could prove that he had been intentionally deceived, the legal opinion is that his case would be a strong one."

"Suppose I chose to apply on my side?" said Magdalen, eagerly. "What then?"

"You might make the application," replied the captain. "But remember one thing—you would come into Court, with the acknowledgment of your own deception. I leave you to imagine what the Judges would think of that."

"Did the lawyer tell you anything else?"

"One thing besides," said Captain Wragge. "Whatever the law might do with the marriage in the lifetime of both the parties to it—on the death of either one of them, no application made by the survivor would avail; and, as to the case of that survivor, the marriage would remain valid. You understand? If he dies, or if you die—and if no application has been made to the Court—he the survivor, or you the survivor, would have no power of disputing the marriage. But, in the lifetime of both of you, if he claimed to have the marriage dissolved, the chances are all in favour of his carrying his point."

He looked at Magdalen with a furtive curiosity as he said those words. She turned her head aside, absently tying her watch-chain into a loop and untying it again; evidently thinking with the closest attention over what he had last said to her. Captain Wragge walked uneasily to the window, and looked out. The first object that caught his eye was Mr. Noel Vanstone approaching from Sea View. He returned instantly to his former place in the room, and addressed himself to Magdalen once more.

"Here is Mr. Noel Vanstone," he said. "One last caution before he comes in. Be on your guard with him about your age. He put the question to me before he got the Licence. I took the shortest way out of the difficulty, and told him you were Twenty-one—and he made the declaration accordingly. Never mind about *me*; after to-morrow, I am invisible. But, in your own interests, don't forget, if the subject turns up, that you were of age when you married. There is nothing more. You are provided with every necessary warning that I can give you. Whatever happens in the future—remember I have done my best."

He hurried to the door, without waiting for an answer, and went out into the garden to receive his guest.

Noel Vanstone made his appearance at the gate, solemnly carrying his bridal offering to North Shingles with both hands. The object in question was an ancient casket (one of his father's bargains); inside the casket reposed an old-fashioned carbuncle brooch, set in silver (another of his father's bargains)—bridal presents both, possessing the inestimable merit of leaving his money undisturbed in his pocket. He shook his head portentously when the captain inquired after his health and spirits. He had passed a wakeful night; ungovernable apprehensions of Lecount's sudden reappearance had beset him as soon as he found himself alone at Sea View. Sea View was redolent of Lecount: Sea View (though built on piles, and the strongest house in England) was henceforth odious to him. He had felt this all night; he had also felt his responsibilities. There was the lady's maid, to begin with. Now he had hired her, he began to think she wouldn't do. She might fall sick on his hands; she might have deceived him by a false character; she and the landlady of the hotel might have been in league together. Horrible! Really horrible to think of. Then there was the other responsibility—perhaps the heaviest of the two—the responsibility of deciding where he was to go and spend his honeymoon to-morrow. He would have preferred one of his father's empty houses. But, except at Vauxhall Walk (which he supposed would be objected to), and at Aldborough (which was of course out of the question), all the houses were let. He would put himself in Mr. Bygrave's hands. Where had Mr. Bygrave spent his own honeymoon? Given the British Islands to choose from, where would Mr. Bygrave pitch his tent, on a careful review of all the circumstances?

At this point, the bridegroom's questions suddenly came to an end, and the bridegroom's face exhibited an expression of ungovernable astonishment. His judicious friend whose advice had been at his disposal in every other emergency, suddenly turned round on him, in the emergency of the honeymoon, and flatly declined discussing the subject.

"No!" said the captain, as Noel Vanstone opened his lips to plead for a hearing, "you must really excuse me. My point of view, in this matter, is, as usual, a peculiar one. For some time past, I have been living in an atmosphere of deception, to suit your convenience. That atmosphere, my good sir, is getting close—my Moral Being requires ventilation. Settle the choice of a locality with my niece; and leave me, at my particular request, in total ignorance of the subject. Mrs. Lecount is certain to come here on her return from Zurich, and is certain to ask me where you are gone. You may think it strange, Mr. Vanstone—but when I tell her I don't know, I wish to enjoy the unaccustomed luxury of feeling, for once in a way, that I am speaking the truth!"

With those words, he opened the sitting-room door; introduced Noel Vanstone to Magdalen's presence; bowed himself out of the room again; and set forth alone to while away the rest of the afternoon by taking a walk. His face showed plain tokens of anxiety, and his parti-coloured eyes looked hither and thither distrustfully, as he sauntered along the shore. "The time hangs heavy on our hands," thought the captain. "I wish to-morrow was come and gone."

The day passed and nothing happened; the evening and the night followed, placidly and uneventfully. Monday came, a cloudless lovely day —Monday confirmed the captain's assertion that the marriage was a certainty. Towards ten o'clock, the clerk ascending the church steps, quoted the old proverb to the pew-opener, meeting him under the porch: "Happy the bride on whom the sun shines!"

In a quarter of an hour more, the wedding party was in the vestry, and the clergyman led the way to the altar. Carefully as the secret of the marriage had been kept, the opening of the church in the morning had been enough to betray it. A small congregation, almost entirely composed of women, was scattered here and there among the pews. Kirke's sister and her children were staying with a friend at Aldborough—and Kirke's sister was one of the congregation.

As the wedding party entered the church, the haunting terror of Mrs. Lecount spread from Noel Vanstone to the captain. For the first few minutes, the eyes of both of them looked among the women in the pews, with the same searching scrutiny; and looked away again with the same sense of relief. The clergyman noticed that look, and investigated the Licence more closely than usual. The clerk began to doubt privately whether the old proverb about the bride, was a proverb to be always depended on. The female members of the congregation murmured among themselves at the inexcusable disregard of appearances implied in the bride's dress. Kirke's sister whispered venomously in her friend's ear, "Thank God for to-day for Robert's sake." Mrs. Wragge cried silently, with the dread of some threatening calamity, she knew not what. The one person present who remained outwardly undisturbed was Magdalen herself. She stood with tearless resignation in her place before the altar—stood, as if all the sources of human emotion were frozen up within her.

The clergyman opened the Book.

*　　　*　　　*　　　*　　　*　　　*

It was done. The awful words which speak from earth to Heaven were pronounced. The children of the two dead brothers—inheritors of the implacable enmity which had parted their parents—were Man and Wife.

From that moment, events hurried with a headlong rapidity to the parting scene. They were back at the house, while the words of the Marriage Service seemed still ringing in their ears. Before they had been five minutes in-doors, the carriage drew up at the garden gate. In a minute more, the opportunity came for which Magdalen and the captain had been on the watch—the opportunity of speaking together in private for the last time. She still preserved her icy resignation—she seemed beyond all reach now of the fear that had once mastered her, of the remorse that had once tortured her to the soul. With a firm hand, she gave him the promised money. With a firm face, she looked her last at him. "I'm not to blame," he whispered eagerly; "I have only done what you asked me." She bowed her head—she bent it towards him kindly, and let him touch her forehead with his lips. "Take care!" he said. "My last words are—for God's sake take care when I'm gone!" She turned from him with a smile, and spoke her farewell words to his wife. Mrs. Wragge tried hard to face her loss bravely—the loss of the friend whose presence had fallen like light from Heaven over the dim pathway of her life. "You have been very good to me, my dear; I thank you kindly; I thank you with all my heart." She could say no more—she clung to Magdalen, in a passion of tears, as her mother might have clung to her, if her mother had lived to see that horrible day. "I'm frightened for you!" cried the poor creature in a wild wailing voice. "Oh, my darling, I'm frightened for you!" Magdalen desperately drew herself free—kissed her—and hurried out to the door. The expression of that artless gratitude, the cry of that guileless love, shook her as nothing else had shaken her that day. It was a refuge to get to the carriage—a refuge, though the man she had married stood there waiting for her at the door.

Mrs. Wragge tried to follow her into the garden. But the captain had seen Magdalen's face as she ran out; and he steadily held his wife back in the passage. From that distance, the last farewells were exchanged. As long as the carriage was in sight, Magdalen looked back at them—she waved her handkerchief, as she turned the corner. In a moment more, the last thread which bound her to them was broken; the familiar companionship of many months was a thing of the past already!.

Captain Wragge closed the house-door on the idlers who were looking in from the Parade. He led his wife back into the sitting-room, and spoke to her with a forbearance which she had never yet experienced from him.

"She has gone her way," he said, "and in another hour we shall have gone ours. Cry your cry out—I don't deny she's worth crying for."

Even then—even when the dread of Magdalen's future was at its darkest in his mind—the ruling habit of the man's life clung to him. Mechanically, he unlocked his despatch-box. Mechanically, he opened his Book of Accounts, and made the closing entry—the entry of his last transaction with Magdalen—in black and white. "By Rec^d from Miss Vanstone," wrote the captain, with a gloomy brow, "Two hundred pounds."

"You won't be angry with me?" said Mrs. Wragge, looking timidly at her husband through her tears. "I want a word of comfort, captain. Oh, do tell me—when shall I see her again?"

The captain closed the book, and answered in one inexorable word:
"Never!"

Between eleven and twelve o'clock that night, Mrs. Lecount drove into Zurich.

Her brother's house, when she stopped before it, was shut up. With some difficulty and delay the servant was aroused. She held up her hands in speechless amazement, when she opened the door, and saw who the visitor was.

"Is my brother alive?" asked Mrs. Lecount, entering the house.

"Alive!" echoed the servant. "He has gone holiday-making into the country, to finish his recovery in the fine fresh air."

The housekeeper staggered back against the wall of the passage. The coachman and the servant put her into a chair. Her face was livid, and her teeth chattered in her head.

"Send for my brother's doctor," she said, as soon as she could speak.

The doctor came. She handed him a letter, before he could say a word.

"Did you write that letter?"

He looked it over rapidly, and answered her without hesitation.

"Certainly not!"

"It is your handwriting."

"It is a forgery of my handwriting."

She rose from the chair, with a new strength in her.

"When does the return mail start for Paris?" she asked.

"In half an hour."

"Send instantly, and take me a place in it!"

The servant hesitated; the doctor protested. She turned a deaf ear to them both.

"Send!" she reiterated, "or I will go myself."

They obeyed. The servant went to take the place: the doctor remained, and held a conversation with Mrs. Lecount. When the half-hour had passed, he helped her into her place in the mail, and charged the conductor privately to take care of his passenger.

"She has travelled from England without stopping," said the doctor; "and she is travelling back again without rest. Be careful of her, or she will break down under the double journey."

The mail started. Before the first hour of the new day was at an end, Mrs. Lecount was on her way back to England.

THE END OF THE FOURTH SCENE.

BETWEEN THE SCENES.

PROGRESS OF THE STORY THROUGH THE POST.

———◆———

I.

FROM GEORGE BARTRAM TO NOEL VANSTONE.

"St. Crux, September 4th, 1847.

" MY DEAR NOEL,

"Here are two plain questions at starting. In the name of all that is mysterious, what are you hiding for? And why is everything relating to your marriage kept an impenetrable secret from your oldest friends?

"I have been to Aldborough to try if I could trace you from that place; and have come back as wise as I went. I have applied to your lawyer in London; and have been told in reply, that you have forbidden him to disclose the place of your retreat to any one, without first receiving your permission to do so. All I could prevail on him to say was, that he would forward any letter which might be sent to his care. I write accordingly— and, mind this, I expect an answer.

"You may ask, in your ill-tempered way, what business I have to meddle with affairs of yours, which it is you r pleasure to keep private. My dear Noel, there is a serious reason for our opening communications with you from this house. You don't know what events have taken place. at St. Crux, since you ran away to get married; and though I detest writing letters, I must lose an hour's shooting to-day in trying to enlighten you.

"On the twenty-third of last month, the admiral and I were disturbed over our wine after dinner, by the announcement that a visitor had unexpectedly arrived at St. Crux. Who do you think the visitor was? Mrs. Lecount!

"My uncle, with that old-fashioned bachelor gallantry of his, which pays equal respect to all wearers of petticoats, left the table directly to welcome Mrs. Lecount. While I was debating whether I should follow him or not, my meditations were suddenly brought to an end by a loud call from the admiral. I ran into the morning-room—and there was your unfortunate housekeeper, on the sofa, with all the women-servants about her, more dead than alive. She had travelled from England to Zurich, and from Zurich back again to England, without stopping; and she looked, seriously and literally, at death's door. I immediately agreed with my uncle, that the first thing to be done was to send for medical help. We despatched a groom on the spot; and at Mrs. Lecount's own request, sent all the servants, in a body, out of the room.

"As soon as we were alone, Mrs. Lecount surprised us by a singular question. She asked if you had received a letter which she had addressed to you before leaving England, at this house. When we told her that the letter had been forwarded, under cover to your friend Mr. Bygrave, by your own particular request, she turned as pale as ashes; and when we added that you had left us in company with this same Mr. Bygrave, she clasped her hands and stared at us as if she had taken leave of her senses. Her next question was, 'Where is Mr. Noel, now?' We could only give her one reply—Mr. Noel had not informed us. She looked perfectly thunderstruck at that answer. 'He has gone to his ruin?' she said. 'He has gone away in company with the greatest villain in England. I must find him! I tell you I must find Mr. Noel! If I don't find him at once, it will be too late. He will be married!' she burst out quite frantically. 'On my honour and my oath he will be married!' The admiral, incautiously perhaps, but with the best intentions, told her you were married already. She gave a scream that made the windows ring again, and dropped back on the sofa in a fainting fit. The doctor came, in the nick of time, and soon brought her to. But she was taken ill the same night—she has grown worse and worse ever since—and the last medical report is, that the fever from which she has been suffering is in a fair way to settle on her brain.

"Now, my dear Noel, neither my uncle nor I have any wish to intrude ourselves on your confidence. We are naturally astonished at the extraordinary mystery which hangs over you and your marriage; and we cannot be blind to the fact that your housekeeper has, apparently, some strong reason of her own for viewing Mrs. Noel Vanstone with an enmity and distrust, which we are quite ready to believe that lady has done nothing to deserve. Whatever strange misunderstanding there may have been in your household, is your business (if you choose to keep it to yourself), and not ours. All we have any right to do, is to tell you what the doctor says. His patient has been delirious; he declines to answer for her life if she goes on as she is going on now; and he thinks—finding that she is perpetually talking of her master—that your presence would be useful in quieting her, if you could come here at once, and exert your influence before it is too late.

"What do you say? Will you emerge from the darkness that surrounds you, and come to St. Crux? If this was the case of an ordinary servant, I could understand your hesitating to leave the delights of your honeymoon for any such object as is here proposed to you. But, my dear fellow, Mrs. Lecount is not an ordinary servant. You are under obligations to her fidelity and attachment, in your father's time, as well as in your own ; and if you *can* quiet the anxieties which seem to be driving this unfortunate woman mad, I really think you ought to come here and do so. Your leaving Mrs. Noel Vanstone is of course out of the question. There is no necessity for any such hard-hearted proceeding. The admiral desires me to remind you that he is your oldest friend living, and that his house is at your wife's disposal, as it has always been at yours. In this great rambling place she need dread no near association with the sick-room ; and, with all my uncle's oddities, I am sure she will not think the offer of his friendship an offer to be despised.

" Have I told you already that I went to Aldborough to try and find a clue to your whereabouts ? I can't be at the trouble of looking back to see ; so, if I have told you, I tell you again. The truth is, I made an acquaintance at Aldborough of whom you know something—at least, by report.

" After applying vainly at Sea View, I went to the hotel to inquire about you. The landlady could give me no information ; but the moment I mentioned your name, she asked if I was related to you—and when I told her I was your cousin, she said there was a young lady then at the hotel, whose name was Vanstone also ; who was in great distress about a missing relative ; and who might prove of some use to me—or I to her—if we knew of each other's errand at Aldborough. I had not the least idea who she was ; but I sent in my card at a venture ; and, in five minutes afterwards, I found myself in the presence of one of the most charming women these eyes ever looked on.

" Our first words of explanation informed me that my family name was known to her by repute. Who do you think she was ? The eldest daughter of my uncle and yours—Andrew Vanstone. I had often heard my poor mother, in past years, speak of her brother Andrew ; and I knew of that sad story at Combe-Raven. But our families, as you are aware, had always been estranged ; and I had never seen my charming cousin before. She has the dark eyes and hair, and the gentle retiring manners that I always admire in a woman. I don't want to renew our old disagreement about your father's conduct to those two sisters, or to deny that his brother Andrew may have behaved badly to him—I am willing to admit that the high moral position he took in the matter is quite unassailable by such a miserable sinner as I am—and I will not dispute that my own spendthrift habits incapacitate me from offering any opinion on the conduct of other people's pecuniary affairs. But, with all these allowances and drawbacks, I can tell you one thing, Noel. If you ever see the elder Miss Vanstone, I venture to prophesy that, for the first time in you life, you will doubt the propriety of following your father's example.

" She told me her little story, poor thing, most simply and unaffectedly. She is now occupying her second situation as a governess—and, as usual, I, who know everybody, know the family. They are friends of my uncle's, whom he has lost sight of latterly—the Tyrrels of Portland Place—and they treat Miss Vanstone with as much kindness and consideration as if she was a member of the family. One of their old servants accompanied her to Aldborough; her object in travelling to that place being what the landlady of the hotel had stated it to be. The family reverses have, it seems, had a serious effect on Miss Vanstone's younger sister, who has left her friends, and who has been missing from home for some time. She had been last heard of at Aldborough; and her elder sister, on her return from the Continent with the Tyrrels, had instantly set out to make inquiries at that place.

"This was all Miss Vanstone told me. She asked whether you had seen anything of her sister, or whether Mrs. Lecount knew anything of her sister—I suppose because she was aware you had been at Aldborough. Of course I could tell her nothing. She entered into no details on the subject, and I could not presume to ask her for any. All I did was to set to work with might and main to assist her inquiries. The attempt was an utter failure—nobody could give us any information. We tried personal description of course; and, strange to say, the only young lady formerly staying at Aldborough, who answered the description, was, of all the people in the world, the lady you have married! If she had not had an uncle and aunt (both of whom have left the place), I should have begun to suspect that you had married your cousin without knowing it! Is this the clue to the mystery? Don't be angry; I must have my little joke, and I can't help writing as carelessly as I talk. The end of it was, our inquiries were all baffled, and I travelled back with Miss Vanstone and her attendant, as far as our station here. I think I shall call on the Tyrrels, when I am next in London. I have certainly treated that family with the most inexcusable neglect.

"Here I am at the end of my third sheet of note paper! I don't often take the pen in hand; but when I do, you will agree with me, that I am in no hurry to lay it aside again. Treat the rest of my letter as you like—but consider what I have told you about Mrs. Lecount, and remember that time is of consequence.

"Ever yours,

"GEORGE BARTRAM."

II.

FROM NORAH VANSTONE TO MISS GARTH

"MY DEAR MISS GARTH,
"Portland Place.

"More sorrow, more disappointment! I have just returned from Aldborough, without making any discovery. Magdalen is still lost to us.

"I cannot attribute this new overthrow of my hopes to any want of perseverance or penetration in making the necessary inquiries. My inexperience in such matters was most kindly and unexpectedly assisted by Mr. George Bartram. By a strange coincidence, he happened to be at Aldborough, inquiring after Mr. Noel Vanstone, at the very time when I was there inquiring after Magdalen. He sent in his card, and knowing when I looked at the name, that he was my cousin—if I may call him so— I thought there would be no impropriety in my seeing him, and asking his advice. I abstained from entering into particulars, for Magdalen's sake; and I made no allusion to that letter of Mrs. Lecount's which you answered for me. I only told him Magdalen was missing, and had been last heard of at Aldborough. The kindness which he showed in devoting himself to my assistance, exceeds all description. He treated me, in my forlorn situation, with a delicacy and respect, which I shall remember gratefully, long after he has himself perhaps forgotten our meeting altogether. He is quite young—not more than thirty, I should think. In face and figure, he reminded me a little of the portrait of my father at Combe-Raven—I mean the portrait in the dining-room, of my father when he was a young man.

"Useless as our inquiries were, there is one result of them which has left a very strange and shocking impression on my mind.

"It appears that Mr. Noel Vanstone has lately married, under mysterious circumstances, a young lady whom he met with at Aldborough, named Bygrave. He has gone away with his wife, telling nobody but his lawyer where he has gone to. This I heard from Mr. George Bartram, who was endeavouring to trace him, for the purpose of communicating the news of his housekeeper's serious illness—the housekeeper being the same Mrs. Lecount whose letter you answered. So far, you may say, there is nothing which need particularly interest either of us. But I think you will be as much surprised as I was, when I tell you that the description given by the people at Aldborough of Miss Bygrave's appearance, is most startlingly and unaccountably like the description of Magdalen's appearance. This discovery, taken in connection with all the circumstances we know of, has had an effect on my mind, which I cannot describe to you—which I dare not realize to myself. Pray come and see me! I have never felt so wretched about Magdalen as I feel now. Suspense must have weakened my nerves in some strange way. I feel superstitious about the slightest things. This accidental resemblance of a total stranger to Magdalen, fills me, every now and then, with the most horrible misgivings—merely because Mr. Noel Vanstone's name happens to be mixed up with it. Once more, pray come to me—I have so much to say to you that I cannot, and dare not, say in writing.

"Gratefully and affectionately yours,

"NORAH."

III.

FROM MR. JOHN LOSCOMBE (SOLICITOR) TO GEORGE BARTRAM, ESQ.

"Lincoln's Inn, London.
"September 6th, 1847.

"SIR,

"I beg to acknowledge the receipt of your note, enclosing a letter addressed to my client, Mr. Noel Vanstone, and requesting that I will forward the same to Mr. Vanstone's present address.

"Since I last had the pleasure of communicating with you on this subject, my position towards my client is entirely altered. Three days ago, I received a letter from him which stated his intention of changing his place of residence on the next day then ensuing, but which left me entirely in ignorance on the subject of the locality to which it was his intention to remove. I have not heard from him since; and, as he had previously drawn on me for a larger sum of money than usual, there would be no present necessity for his writing to me again—assuming that it is his wish to keep his place of residence concealed from every one, myself included.

"Under these circumstances, I think it right to return you your letter, with the assurance that I will let you know, if I happen to be again placed in a position to forward it to its destination.

"Your obedient servant,
"JOHN LOSCOMBE."

IV.

FROM NORAH VANSTONE TO MISS GARTH.

"Portland Place.

"MY DEAR MISS GARTH,

"Forget the letter I wrote to you yesterday, and all the gloomy forebodings that it contains. This morning's post has brought new life to me. I have just received a letter, addressed to me at your house, and forwarded here, in your absence from home yesterday, by your sister. Can you guess who the writer is?—Magdalen!

"The letter is very short; it seems to have been written in a hurry. She says she has been dreaming of me for some nights past, and the dreams have made her fear that her long silence has caused me more distress, on her account, than she is worth. She writes therefore to assure me that she is safe and well—that she hopes to see me before long—and that she has something to tell me, when we meet, which will try my sisterly love for her as nothing has tried it yet. The letter is not dated; but the postmark is 'Allonby,' which I have found on referring to the Gazetteer, to be a little sea-side place in Cumberland. There is no hope of my being able to write back—for Magdalen expressly says that she is on the eve of departure from her present residence, and that she is not at liberty to say where she is going to next, or to leave instructions for forwarding any letters after her.

"In happier times, I should have thought this letter very far from being a satisfactory one—and I should have been seriously alarmed by that allusion to a future confidence on her part which will try my love for her as nothing has tried it yet. But, after all the suspense I have suffered, the happiness of seeing her handwriting again seems to fill my heart, and to keep all other feelings out of it. I don't send you her letter, because I know you are coming to me soon, and I want to have the pleasure of seeing you read it.

"Ever affectionately yours,
"NORAH.

"P.S. Mr. George Bartram called on Mrs. Tyrrel to-day. He insisted on being introduced to the children. When he was gone, Mrs. Tyrrel laughed in her good-humoured way, and said that his anxiety to see the children, looked to her mind, very much like an anxiety to see *me*. You may imagine how my spirits are improved, when I can occupy my pen in writing such nonsense as this!"

V.

FROM MRS. LECOUNT TO MR. DE BLERIOT, GENERAL AGENT, LONDON.

"St. Crux, October 23rd, 1847.

"DEAR SIR,

"I have been long in thanking you for the kind letter which promises me your assistance, in friendly remembrance of the commercial relations formerly existing between my brother and yourself. The truth is, I have overtasked my strength on my recovery from a long and dangerous illness; and for the last ten days I have been suffering under a relapse. I am now better again, and able to enter on the business which you so kindly offer to undertake for me.

"The person whose present place of abode it is of the utmost importance to me to discover, is Mr. Noel Vanstone. I have lived, for many years past, in this gentleman's service as housekeeper; and not having received my formal dismissal, I consider myself in his service still. During my absence on the Continent, he was privately married at Aldborough, in Suffolk, on the eighteenth of August last. He left Aldborough the same day; taking his wife with him to some place of retreat which was kept a secret from everybody, except his lawyer, Mr. Loscombe, of Lincoln's Inn. After a short time he again removed, on the 4th of September, without informing Mr. Loscombe, on this occasion, of his new place of abode. From that date to this, the lawyer has remained (or has pretended to remain) in total ignorance of where he now is. Application has been made to Mr. Loscombe, under the circumstances, to mention what that former place of residence was, of which Mr. Vanstone is known to have informed him. Mr. Loscombe has declined acceding to this request, for want of formal permission to disclose his client's proceedings after leaving Aldborough. I have all these latter particulars from Mr. Loscombe's correspondent—the nephew of the gentleman who owns this house, and whose charity has given me an asylum, during the heavy affliction of my sickness, under his own roof.

"I believe the reasons which have induced Mr. Noel Vanstone to keep himself and his wife in hiding, are reasons which relate entirely to myself. In the first place, he is aware that the circumstances under which he has married, are such as to give me the right of regarding him with a just indignation. In the second place, he knows that my faithful services, rendered through a period of twenty years, to his father and to himself, forbid him, in common decency, to cast me out helpless on the world, without a provision for the end of my life. He is the meanest of living men, and his wife is the vilest of living women. As long as he can avoid fulfilling his obligations to me, he will ; and his wife's encouragement may be trusted to fortify him in his ingratitude.

"My object in determining to find him out, is briefly this. His marriage has exposed him to consequences which a man of ten times his courage could not face without shrinking. Of those consequences he knows nothing. His wife knows, and keeps him in ignorance. I know, and can enlighten him. His security from the danger that threatens him, is in my hands alone ; and he shall pay the price of his rescue, to the last farthing of the debt that justice claims for me as my due—no more and no less.

"I have now laid my mind before you, as you told me, without reserve. You know why I want to find this man, and what I mean to do when I find him. I leave it to your sympathy for me, to answer the serious question that remains : How is the discovery to be made? If a first trace of them can be found, after their departure from Aldborough, I believe careful inquiry will suffice for the rest. The personal appearance of the wife, and the extraordinary contrast between her husband and herself, are certain to be remarked, and remembered, by every stranger who sees them.

"When you favour me with your answer, please address it to 'Care of Admiral Bartram, St. Crux-in-the-Marsh, near Ossory, Essex.'

"Your much obliged,

"VIRGINIE LECOUNT."

VI.

From Mr. de Bleriot to Mrs. Lecount.

"Private and Confidential.

"Dark's Buildings, Kingsland,
"October 25th, 1847.

"Dear Madam,

"I hasten to reply to your favour of Saturday's date. Circumstances have enabled me to forward your interests, by consulting a friend of mine, possessing great experience in the management of private inquiries of all sorts. I have placed your case before him (without mentioning names); and I am happy to inform you that my views and his views of the proper course to take, agree in every particular.

"Both myself and friend, then, are of opinion that little or nothing can be done towards tracing the parties you mention, until the place of their temporary residence after they left Aldborough, has been discovered first. If this can be done, the sooner it is done the better. Judging from your letter, some weeks must have passed since the lawyer received his information that they had shifted their quarters. As they are both remarkable-looking people, the strangers who may have assisted them on their travels have probably not forgotten them yet. Nevertheless, expedition is desirable.

"The question for you to consider is, whether they may not possibly have communicated the address of which we stand in need, to some other person besides the lawyer. The husband may have written to members of his family, or the wife may have written to members of her family. Both myself and friend are of opinion that the latter chance is the likeliest of the two. If you have any means of access in the direction of the wife's family, we strongly recommend you to make use of them. If not, please supply us with the names of any of her near relations or intimate female friends whom you know, and we will endeavour to get access for you.

"In any case, we request you will at once favour us with the most exact personal description that can be written of both the parties. We may require your assistance, in this important particular, at five minutes' notice. Favour us, therefore, with the description by return of post. In the mean time, we will endeavour to ascertain, on our side, whether any information is] to be privately obtained at Mr. Loscombe's office. The lawyer himself is probably altogether beyond our reach. But if any one of his clerks can be advantageously treated with, on such terms as may not overtax your pecuniary resources, accept my assurance that the opportunity shall be made the most of, by,

"Dear Madam,
'Your faithful servant,
"Alfred de Bleriot."

VII.

From Mr. Pendril to Norah Vanstone.

"Serle Street, October 27th, 1847.

"My dear Miss Vanstone,

"A lady, named Lecount (formerly attached to Mr. Noel Vanstone's service, in the capacity of housekeeper), has called at my office this morning, and has asked me to furnish her with your address. I have begged her to excuse my immediate compliance with her request, and to favour me with a call to-morrow morning, when I shall be prepared to meet her with a definite answer.

"My hesitation in this matter does not proceed from any distrust of Mrs. Lecount personally—for I know nothing whatever to her prejudice. But in making her request to me, she stated that the object of the desired interview was to speak to you privately on the subject of your sister. Forgive me for acknowledging that I determined to withhold the address, as soon as I heard this. You will make allowances for your old friend and your sincere well-wisher? You will not take it amiss, if I express my strong disapproval of your allowing yourself on any pretence whatever, to be mixed up for the future with your sister's proceedings.

"I will not distress you by saying more than this. But I feel too deep an interest in your welfare, and too sincere an admiration of the patience with which you have borne all your trials, to say less.

"If I cannot prevail on you to follow my advice, you have only to say so, and Mrs. Lecount shall have your address to-morrow. In this case (which I cannot contemplate without the greatest unwillingness), let me at least recommend you to stipulate that Miss Garth shall be present at the interview. In any matter with which your sister is concerned, you may want an old friend's advice and an old friend's protection against your own generous impulses. If I could have helped you in this way, I would—but Mrs. Lecount gave me indirectly to understand that the subject to be discussed was of too delicate a nature to permit of my presence. Whatever this objection may be really worth, it cannot apply to Miss Garth, who has brought you both up from childhood. I say, again, therefore, if you see Mrs. Lecount, see her in Miss Garth's company.

"Always most truly yours,

"William Pendril."

VIII.

FROM NORAH VANSTONE TO MR. PENDRIL.

"Portland Place, Wednesday.

"DEAR MR. PENDRIL,

"Pray don't think I am ungrateful for your kindness. Indeed, indeed I am not! But I must see Mrs. Lecount. You were not aware when you wrote to me, that I had received a few lines from Magdalen—not telling me where she is, but holding out the hope of our meeting before long. Perhaps Mrs. Lecount may have something to say to me, on this very subject? Even if it should not be so, my sister—do what she may—is still my sister. I can't desert her; I can't turn my back on any one who comes to me in her name. You know, dear Mr. Pendril, I have always been obstinate on this subject; and you have always borne with me. Let me owe another obligation to you which I can never return—and bear with me still!

"Need I say that I willingly accept that part of your advice which refers to Miss Garth? I have already written to beg that she will come here at four, to-morrow afternoon. When you see Mrs. Lecount, please inform her that Miss Garth will be with me, and that she will find us both ready to receive her here, to-morrow, at four o'clock.

"Gratefully yours,

"NORAH VANSTONE."

IX.

FROM MR. DE BLERIOT TO MRS. LECOUNT.

"Private.

"Dark's Buildings, October 28th.

"DEAR MADAM,

"One of Mr. Loscombe's clerks has proved amenable to a small pecuniary consideration, and has mentioned a circumstance which it may be of some importance to you to know.

"Nearly a month since, accident gave the clerk in question an opportunity of looking into one of the documents on his master's table, which had attracted his attention from a slight peculiarity in the form and colour of the paper. He had only time, during Mr. Loscombe's momentary absence, to satisfy his curiosity by looking at the beginning of the document, and at the end. At the beginning, he saw the customary form used in making a will. At the end, he discovered the signature of Mr. Noel Vanstone; with the names of two attesting witnesses, and the date (of which he is quite certain)—*the thirtieth of September last.*

"Before the clerk had time to make any further investigations, his master returned, sorted the papers on the table, and carefully locked up the will, in the strong box devoted to the custody of Mr. Noel Vanstone's documents. It has been ascertained that, at the close of September, Mr. Loscombe was absent from the office. If he was then employed in superintending the execution of his client's will—which is quite possible—it follows clearly that he was in the secret of Mr. Vanstone's address, after the removal of the 4th of September; and if you can do nothing on your side, it may be desirable to have the lawyer watched on ours. In any case, it is certainly ascertained that Mr. Noel Vanstone has made his will, since his marriage. I leave you to draw your own conclusions from that fact, and remain, in the hope of hearing from you shortly,

"Your faithful servant,

"ALFRED DE BLERIOT."

X.

FROM MISS GARTH TO MR. PENDRIL.

"Portland Place, October 28th.

"MY DEAR SIR,

"Mrs. Lecount has just left us. If it was not too late to wish, I should wish from the bottom of my heart, that Norah had taken your advice, and had refused to see her.

"I write in such distress of mind, that I cannot hope to give you a clear and complete account of the interview. I can only tell you briefly what Mrs. Lecount has done, and what our situation now is. The rest must be left until I am more composed, and until I can speak to you personally.

"You will remember my informing you of the letter which Mrs. Lecount addressed to Norah from Aldborough, and which I answered for her in her absence. When Mrs. Lecount made her appearance to-day, her first words announced to us that she had come to renew the subject. As well as I can remember it, this is what she said, addressing herself to Norah :

"'I wrote to you on the subject of your sister, Miss Vanstone, some little time since; and Miss Garth was so good as to answer the letter. What I feared at that time has come true. Your sister has defied all my efforts to check her; she has disappeared in company with my master, Mr. Noel Vanstone; and she is now in a position of danger, which may lead to her disgrace and ruin at a moment's notice. It is my interest to recover my master; it is your interest to save your sister. Tell me—for time is precious—have you any news of her?'

"Norah answered, as well as her terror and distress would allow her, 'I have had a letter, but there was no address on it.'

"Mrs. Lecount asked, 'Was there no post-mark on the envelope?'

"Norah said—'Yes; Allonby.'

"'Allonby is better than nothing,' said Mrs. Lecount. 'Allonby may help you to trace her. Where is Allonby?'

"Norah told her. It all passed in a minute. I had been too much confused and startled to interfere before ; but I composed myself sufficiently to interfere now.

"'You have entered into no particulars,' I said. 'You have only frightened us—you have told us nothing.'

"'You shall hear the particulars, ma'am,' said Mrs. Lecount; 'and you and Miss Vanstone shall judge for yourselves, if I have frightened you without a cause.'

"Upon this, she entered at once upon a long narrative, which I cannot —I might almost say, which I dare not—repeat. You will understand the horror we both felt, when I tell you the end. If Mrs. Lecount's statement is to be relied on, Magdalen has carried her mad resolution of recovering her father's fortune, to the last and most desperate extremity— she has married Michael Vanstone's son, under a false name. Her husband is at this moment still persuaded that her maiden name was Bygrave, and that she is really the niece of a scoundrel who assisted her imposture, and whom I recognize by the description of him to have been Captain Wragge.

"I spare you Mrs. Lecount's cool avowal, when she rose to leave us, of her own mercenary motives in wishing to discover her master and to enlighten him. I spare you the hints she dropped of Magdalen's purpose in contracting this infamous marriage. The one aim and object of my letter is, to implore you to assist me in quieting Norah's anguish of mind. The shock she has received at hearing this news of her sister, is not the worst result of what has happened. She has persuaded herself that the answers she innocently gave in her distress, to Mrs. Lecount's questions on the subject of her letter—the answers wrung from her under the sudden pressure of confusion and alarm—may be used to Magdalen's prejudice by the woman who purposely startled her into giving the information. I can only prevent her from taking some desperate step on her side—some step by which she may forfeit the friendship and protection of the excellent people with whom she is now living—by reminding her that if Mrs. Lecount traces her master by means of the post-mark on the letter, we may trace Magdalen at the same time, and by the same means. Whatever objection you may personally feel to renewing the efforts for the rescue of this miserable girl, which failed so lamentably at York, I entreat you, for Norah's sake, to take the same steps now which we took then. Send me the only assurance which will quiet her—the assurance, under your own hand, that the search on our side has begun. If you will do this, you may trust me when the time comes, to stand between these two sisters, and to defend Norah's peace, character, and future prosperity, at any price.

"Most sincerely yours,

"HARRIET GARTH.'

XI.

From Mrs. Lecount to Mr. de Bleriot.

"October 28th.

" Dear Sir,

"I have found the trace you wanted. Mrs. Noel Vanstone has written to her sister. The letter contains no address; but the post-mark is Allonby, in Cumberland. From Allonby, therefore, the inquiries must begin. You have already in your possession the personal description of both husband and wife. I urgently recommend you not to lose one unnecessary moment. If it is possible to send to Cumberland immediately on receipt of this letter, I beg you will do so.

"I have another word to say before I close my note—a word about the discovery in Mr. Loscombe's office.

"It is no surprise to me, to hear that Mr. Noel Vanstone has made his will since his marriage; and I am at no loss to guess in whose favour the will is made. If I succeed in finding my master—let that person get the money if that person can! A course to follow in this matter has presented itself to my mind, since I received your letter—but my ignorance of details of business and intricacies of law, leaves me still uncertain whether my idea is capable of ready and certain execution. I know no professional person whom I can trust in this delicate and dangerous business. Is your large experience in other matters, large enough to help me in this? I will call at your office to-morrow at two o'clock, for the purpose of consulting you on the subject. It is of the greatest importance, when I next see Mr. Noel Vanstone, that he should find me thoroughly prepared beforehand, in this matter of the will.

" Your much obliged servant,
" Virginie Lecount."

XII.

From Mr. Pendril to Miss Garth.

" Serle Street, October 29th.

" Dear Miss Garth,

"I have only a moment to assure you of the sorrow with which I have read your letter. The circumstances under which you urge your request, and the reasons you give for making it, are sufficient to silence any objection I might otherwise feel to the course you propose. A trustworthy person, whom I have myself instructed, will start for Allonby to-day; and as soon as I receive any news from him, you shall hear of it by special messenger. Tell Miss Vanstone this, and pray add the sincere expression of my sympathy and regard.

" Faithfully yours,
William Pendril."

XIII.

FROM MR. DE BLERIOT TO MRS. LECOUNT.

"Dark's Buildings, November 1st.

"DEAR MADAM,

"I have the pleasure of informing you that the discovery has been made, with far less trouble than I had anticipated.

"Mr. and Mrs. Noel Vanstone have been traced across the Solway Firth, to Dumfries; and thence to a cottage, a few miles from the town, on the banks of the Nith. The exact address is, Baliol Cottage, near Dumfries.

"This information, though easily hunted up, has nevertheless been obtained under rather singular circumstances.

"Before leaving Allonby, the persons in my employ discovered, to their surprise, that a stranger was in the place pursuing the same inquiry as themselves. In the absence of any instructions preparing them for such an occurrence as this, they took their own view of the circumstance. Considering the man as an intruder on their business, whose success might deprive them of the credit and reward of making the discovery, they took advantage of their superiority in numbers, and of their being first in the field, and carefully misled the stranger before they ventured any further with their own investigations. I am in possession of the details of their proceedings—with which I need not trouble you. The end is, that this person, whoever he may be, was cleverly turned back southward, on a false scent, before the men in my employment crossed the Firth.

"I mention the circumstance, as you may be better able than I am to find a clue to it, and as it may possibly be of a nature to induce you to hasten your journey.

"Your faithful servant,
"ALFRED DE BLERIOT."

XIV.

FROM MRS. LECOUNT TO MR. DE BLERIOT.

"November 1st.

"DEAR SIR,

"One line to say that your letter has just reached me at my lodging in London. I think I know who sent the strange man to inquire at Allonby. It matters little. Before he finds out his mistake, I shall be at Dumfries. My luggage is packed—and I start for the North by the next train.

"Your deeply obliged,
"VIRGINIE LECOUNT."

THE FIFTH SCENE.

BALIOL COTTAGE, DUMFRIES.

CHAPTER I.

TOWARDS eleven o'clock, on the morning of the third of November, the breakfast-table at Baliol Cottage presented that essentially comfortless appearance which is caused by a meal in a state of transition—that is to say, by a meal prepared for two persons, which has been already eaten by one, and which has not yet been approached by the other. It must be a hardy appetite which can contemplate without a momentary discouragement, the battered egg-shell, the fish half-stripped to a skeleton, the crumbs in the plate, and the dregs in the cup. There is surely a wise submission to those weaknesses in human nature which must be respected and not reproved, in the sympathising rapidity with which servants in places of public refreshment, clear away all signs of the customer in the past, from the eyes of the customer in the present. Although his predecessor may have been the wife of his bosom or the child of his loins, no man can find himself confronted at table by the traces of a vanished eater, without a passing sense of injury in connection with the idea of his own meal.

Some such impression as this found its way into the mind of Mr. Noel Vanstone, when he entered the lonely breakfast-parlour at Baliol Cottage, shortly after eleven o'clock. He looked at the table with a frown, and rang the bell with an expression of disgust.

"Clear away this mess," he said, when the servant appeared. "Has your mistress gone?"

"Yes, sir—nearly an hour ago."

"Is Louisa down-stairs?"

"Yes, sir."

"When you have put the table right, send Louisa up to me."

He walked away to the window. The momentary irritation passed away from his face; but it left an expression there which remained—an expression of pining discontent. Personally, his marriage had altered him for the worse. His wizen little cheeks were beginning to shrink into hollows; his frail little figure had already contracted a slight stoop. The former delicacy of his complexion had gone—the sickly paleness of it was all that remained. His thin flaxen moustachios were no longer pragmatically waxed and twisted into a curl: their weak feathery ends hung meekly pendent over the querulous corners of his mouth. If the ten or twelve weeks since his marriage had been counted by his looks, they might have reckoned as ten or twelve years. He stood, at the window mechanically picking leaves from a pot of heath placed in front of it, and drearily humming the forlorn fragment of a tune.

The prospect from the window overlooked the course of the Nith, at a bend of the river a few miles above Dumfries. Here and there, through wintry gaps in the wooded bank, broad tracts of the level cultivated valley met the eye. Boats passed on the river, and carts plodded along the high road on their way to Dumfries. The sky was clear; the November sun shone as pleasantly as if the year had been younger by two good months; and the view, noted in Scotland for its bright and peaceful charm, was presented at the best which its wintry aspect could assume. If it had been hidden in mist or drenched with rain, Mr. Noel Vanstone would, to all appearance, have found it as attractive as he found it now. He waited at the window until he heard Louisa's knock at the door—then turned back sullenly to the breakfast-table and told her to come in.

"Make the tea," he said. "I know nothing about it. I'm left here neglected. Nobody helps me."

The discreet Louisa silently and submissively obeyed.

"Did your mistress leave any message for me," he asked, "before she went away?"

"No message in particular, sir. My mistress only said she should be too late if she waited breakfast any longer."

"Did she say nothing else?"

"She told me at the carriage-door, sir, that she would most likely be back in a week."

"Was she in good spirits at the carriage-door?"

"No, sir. I thought my mistress seemed very anxious and uneasy. Is there anything more I can do, sir?"

"I don't know. Wait a minute."

He proceeded discontentedly with his breakfast. Louisa waited resignedly at the door.

"I think your mistress has been in bad spirits, lately," he resumed, with a sudden outbreak of petulance.

"My mistress has not been very cheerful, sir."

"What do you mean by not very cheerful? Do you mean to prevaricate? Am I nobody in the house? Am I to be kept in the dark about everything? Is your mistress to go away on her own affairs, and leave me at home like a child—and am I not even to ask a question about her? Am I to be prevaricated with by a servant? I won't be prevaricated with! Not very cheerful? What do you mean by not very cheerful?"

"I only meant that my mistress was not in good spirits, sir."

"Why couldn't you say it then? Don't you know the value of words? The most dreadful consequences sometimes happen from not knowing the value of words. Did your mistress tell you she was going to London?"

"Yes, sir."

"What did you think when your mistress told you she was going to London? Did you think it odd she was going without me?"

"I did not presume to think it odd, sir.—Is there anything more I can do for you, if you please, sir?"

"What sort of a morning is it out? Is it warm? Is the sun on the garden?"

"Yes, sir."

"Have you seen the sun yourself on the garden?"

"Yes, sir."

"Get me my great-coat; I'll take a little turn. Has the man brushed it? Did you see the man brush it yourself? What do you mean by saying he has brushed it, when you didn't see him? Let me look at the tails. If there's a speck of dust on the tails, I'll turn the man off!—Help me on with it."

Louisa helped him on with his coat, and gave him his hat. He went out irritably. The coat was a large one (it had belonged to his father); the hat was a large one (it was a misfit purchased as a bargain by himself). He was submerged in his hat and coat; he looked singularly small, and frail, and miserable, as he slowly wended his way, in the wintry sunlight, down the garden-walk. The path sloped gently from the back of the house to the water-side, from which it was parted by a low wooden fence. After pacing backwards and forwards slowly for some little time, he stopped at the lower extremity of the garden; and leaning on the fence, looked down listlessly at the smooth flow of the river.

His thoughts still ran on the subject of his first fretful question to Louisa—he was still brooding over the circumstances under which his wife had left the cottage that morning, and over the want of consideration towards himself, implied in the manner of her departure. The longer he thought of his grievance, the more acutely he resented it. He was capable of great tenderness of feeling, where any injury to his sense of his own importance was concerned. His head drooped little by little on his arms, as they rested on the fence; and, in the deep sincerity of his mortification, he sighed bitterly.

The sigh was answered by a voice close at his side.

"You were happier with *me*, sir," said the voice in accents of tender regret.

He looked up with a scream—literally with a scream—and confronted Mrs. Lecount.

Was it the spectre of the woman? or the woman herself? Her hair was white; her face had fallen away; her eyes looked out large, bright, and haggard over her hollow cheeks. She was withered and old. Her dress hung loose round her wasted figure; not a trace of its buxom autumnal beauty remained. The quietly impenetrable resolution, the smoothly insinuating voice—these were the only relics of the past which sickness and suffering had left in Mrs. Lecount.

"Compose yourself, Mr. Noel," she said, gently. "You have no cause to be alarmed at seeing me. Your servant, when I inquired, said you were in the garden; and I came here to find you. I have traced you out, sir, with no resentment against yourself, with no wish to distress you by so much as the shadow of a reproach. I come here, on what has been, and is still, the business of my life—your service."

He recovered himself a little; but he was still incapable of speech. He held fast by the fence, and stared at her.

"Try to possess your mind, sir, of what I say," proceeded Mrs. Lecount. "I have not come here as your enemy, but as your friend. I have been tried by sickness; I have been tried by distress. Nothing remains of me, but my heart. My heart forgives you; my heart, in your sore need—need which you have yet to feel—places me at your service. Take my arm, Mr. Noel. A little turn in the sun will help you to recover yourself."

She put his hand through her arm, and marched him slowly up the garden-walk. Before she had been five minutes in his company, she had resumed full possession of him, in her own right.

"Now down again, Mr. Noel," she said. "Gently down again, in this fine sunlight. I have much to say to you, sir, which you never expected to hear from me. Let me ask a little domestic question first. They told me, at the house door, Mrs. Noel Vanstone was gone away on a journey. Has she gone for long?"

Her master's hand trembled on her arm, as she put that question. Instead of answering it, he tried faintly to plead for himself. The first words that escaped him were prompted by his first returning sense—the sense that his housekeeper had taken him into custody. He tried to make his peace with Mrs. Lecount.

"I always meant to do something for you," he said, coaxingly. "You would have heard from me, before long. Upon my word and honour, Lecount, you would have heard from me, before long!"

"I don't doubt it, sir," replied Mrs. Lecount. "But for the present, never mind about Me. You, and your interests first."

"How did you come here?" he asked, looking at her in astonishment. "How came you to find me out?"

"It is a long story, sir; I will tell it you some other time. Let it be enough to say now, that I *have* found you. Will Mrs. Noel be back again at the house to-day? A little louder, sir; I can hardly hear you. So! so! Not back again for a week! And where has she gone? To London, did you say? And what for?—I am not inquisitive, Mr. Noel; I am asking serious questions, under serious necessity. Why has your wife left you here, and gone to London by herself?"

They were down at the fence again as she made that last inquiry; and they waited, leaning against it, while Noel Vanstone answered. Her reiterated assurances that she bore him no malice were producing their effect; he was beginning to recover himself. The old helpless habit of addressing all his complaints to his housekeeper, was returning already with the reappearance of Mrs. Lecount—returning insidiously, in company with that besetting anxiety to talk about his grievances, which had got the better of him at the breakfast-table, and which had shown the wound inflicted on his vanity to his wife's maid.

"I can't answer for Mrs. Noel Vanstone," he said, spitefully. "Mrs. Noel Vanstone has not treated me with the consideration which is my due. She has taken my permission for granted; and she has only thought proper to tell me that the object of her journey is to see her friends in London. She went away this morning, without bidding me good-bye. She takes her own way, as if I was nobody; she treats me like a child. You may not believe it, Lecount—but I don't even know who her friends are. I am left quite in the dark—I am left to guess for myself that her friends in London are her uncle and aunt."

Mrs. Lecount privately considered the question by the help of her own knowledge, obtained in London. She soon reached the obvious conclusion. After writing to her sister in the first instance, Magdalen had now in all probability, followed the letter in person. There was little doubt that the friends she had gone to visit in London, were her sister and Miss Garth.

"Not her uncle and aunt, sir," resumed Mrs. Lecount, composedly. "A secret for your private ear! She has no uncle and aunt. Another little turn before I explain myself—another little turn to compose your spirits."

She took him into custody once more; and marched him back towards the house.

"Mr. Noel!" she said, suddenly stopping in the middle of the walk. "Do you know what was the worst mischief you ever did yourself in your life? I will tell you. That worst mischief was sending me to Zurich."

His hand began to tremble on her arm once more.

"I didn't do it!" he cried, piteously. "It was all Mr. Bygrave."

"You acknowledge, sir, that Mr. Bygrave deceived *me*?" proceeded Mrs. Lecount. "I am glad to hear that. You will be all the readier to make the next discovery which is waiting for you—the discovery that Mr

Bygrave has deceived *you*. He is not here to slip through my fingers now; and I am not the helpless woman in this place that I was at Aldborough. Thank God!"

She uttered that devout exclamation through her set teeth. All her hatred of Captain Wragge hissed out of her lips in those two words.

"Oblige me, sir, by holding one side of my travelling-bag," she resumed, "while I open it and take something out."

The interior of the bag disclosed a series of neatly-folded papers, all laid together in order, and numbered outside. Mrs. Lecount took out one of the papers, and shut up the bag again with a loud snap of the spring that closed it.

"At Aldborough, Mr. Noel, I had only my own opinion to support me," she remarked. "My own opinion was nothing against Miss Bygrave's youth and beauty, and Mr. Bygrave's ready wit. I could only hope to attack your infatuation with proofs—and at that time I had not got them. I have got them now! I am armed at all points with proofs—I bristle from head to foot with proofs—I break my forced silence, and speak with the emphasis of my proofs. Do you know this writing, sir?"

He shrank back from the paper which she offered to him.

"I don't understand this," he said nervously. "I don't know what you want, or what you mean."

Mrs. Lecount forced the paper into his hand. "You shall know what I mean, sir, if you will give me a moment's attention," she said. "On the day after you went away to St. Crux, I obtained admission to Mr. Bygrave's house, and I had some talk in private with Mr. Bygrave's wife. That talk supplied me with the means to convince you which I had wanted to find for weeks and weeks past. I wrote you a letter to say so—I wrote to tell you, that I would forfeit my place in your service, and my expectations from your generosity, if I did not prove to you when I came back from Switzerland, that my own private suspicion of Miss Bygrave was the truth. I directed that letter to you at St. Crux, and I posted it myself. Now, Mr. Noel, read the paper which I have forced into your hand. It is Admiral Bartram's written affirmation, that my letter came to St. Crux, and that he enclosed it to you, under cover to Mr. Bygrave, at your own request. Did Mr. Bygrave ever give you that letter? Don't agitate yourself, sir! One word of reply will do—Yes? or No?"

He read the paper, and looked up at her with growing bewilderment and fear. She obstinately waited until he spoke. "No," he said faintly; "I never got the letter."

"First proof!" said Mrs. Lecount, taking the paper from him, and putting it back in the bag. "One more, with your kind permission, before we come to things more serious still. I gave you a written description, sir, at Aldborough, of a person not named; and I asked you to compare it with Miss Bygrave, the next time you were in her company. After having first shown the description to Mr. Bygrave—it is useless to deny it now, Mr. Noel; your friend at North Shingles is not here to help you!—after having first shown my note to Mr. Bygrave, you made the comparison; and you found it fail in the most important particular. There were two little moles placed close together on the left side of the neck, in my description of the unknown lady, and there were no little moles at all when you looked at Miss Bygrave's neck. I am old enough to be your mother, Mr. Noel. If the question is not indelicate—may I ask what the present state of your knowledge is, on the subject of your wife's neck?"

She looked at him with a merciless steadiness. He drew back a few steps, cowering under her eye. "I can't say," he stammered. "I don't know. What do you mean by these questions? I never thought about the moles afterwards; I never looked. She wears her hair low——"

"She has excellent reasons to wear it low, sir," remarked Mrs. Lecount. "We will try and lift that hair, before we have done with the subject. When I came out here to find you in the garden, I saw a neat young person, through the kitchen window, with her work in her hand, who looked to my eyes, like a lady's maid. Is this young person your wife's maid? I beg your pardon, sir, did you say yes? In that case, another question, if you please. Did you engage her, or did your wife?"

"I engaged her——"

"While I was away? While I was in total ignorance that you meant to have a wife, or a wife's maid?"

"Yes."

"Under those circumstances, Mr. Noel, you cannot possibly suspect me of conspiring to deceive you, with the maid for my instrument. Go into the house, sir, while I wait here. Ask the woman who dresses Mrs. Noel Vanstone's hair, morning and night, whether her mistress has a mark on the left side of her neck, and (if so) what that mark is?"

He walked a few steps towards the house, without uttering a word, then stopped, and looked back at Mrs. Lecount. His blinking eyes were steady, and his wizen face had become suddenly composed. Mrs. Lecount advanced a little and joined him. She saw the change; but, with all her experience of him, she failed to interpret the true meaning of it.

"Are you in want of a pretence, sir?" she asked. "Are you at a loss to account to your wife's maid for such a question as I wish you to put to her? Pretences are easily found, which will do for persons in her station of life. Say I have come here, with news of a legacy for Mrs. Noel Vanstone, and that there is a question of her identity to settle, before she can receive the money."

She pointed to the house. He paid no attention to the sign. His face grew paler and paler. Without moving or speaking, he stood and looked at her.

"Are you afraid?" asked Mrs. Lecount.

Those words roused him; those words lit a spark of the fire of manhood in him at last. He turned on her, like a sheep on a dog.

"I won't be questioned and ordered!" he broke out, trembling violently under the new sensation of his own courage. "I won't be threatened and mystified any longer! How did you find me out at this place? What do you mean by coming here with your hints and your mysteries? What have you got to say against my wife?"

Mrs. Lecount composedly opened the travelling-bag, and took out her smelling-bottle, in case of emergency.

"You have spoken to me in plain words," she said. "In plain words, sir, you shall have your answer. Are you too angry to listen?"

Her looks and tones alarmed him, in spite of himself. His courage began to sink again; and, desperately as he tried to steady it, his voice trembled when he answered her.

"Give me my answer," he said, "and give it at once."

"Your commands shall be obeyed, sir, to the letter," replied Mrs. Lecount. "I have come here with two objects. To open your eyes to your own situation; and to save your fortune—perhaps your life. Your situation is this. Miss Bygrave has married you, under a false character and a false name. Can you rouse your memory? Can you call to mind the disguised woman who threatened you in Vauxhall Walk? That woman—as certainly as I stand here—is now your wife."

He looked at her in breathless silence. His lips falling apart; his eyes fixed in vacant inquiry. The suddenness of the disclosure had over-reached its own end. It had stupefied him.

"My wife?" he repeated—and burst into an imbecile laugh.

"Your wife," reiterated Mrs. Lecount.

At the repetition of those two words, the strain on his faculties relaxed. A thought dawned on him for the first time. His eyes fixed on her with a furtive alarm, and he drew back hastily. "Mad!" he said to himself, with a sudden remembrance of what his friend Mr. Bygrave had told him at Aldborough; sharpened by his own sense of the haggard change that he saw in her face.

He spoke in a whisper—but Mrs. Lecount heard him. She was close at his side again, in an instant. For the first time, her self-possession failed her; and she caught him angrily by the arm.

"Will you put my madness to the proof, sir?" she asked.

He shook off her hold; he began to gather courage again, in the intense sincerity of his disbelief—courage to face the assertion which she persisted in forcing on him.

"Yes," he answered. "What must I do?"

"Do what I told you," said Mrs. Lecount. "Ask the maid that question about her mistress, on the spot And, if she tells you the mark is there, do one thing more. Take me up into your wife's room, and open her wardrobe in my presence, with your own hands."

"What do you want with her wardrobe?" he asked.

"You shall know when you open it."

"Very strange!" he said to himself, vacantly. "It's like a scene in a novel—it's like nothing in real life."

He went slowly into the house; and Mrs. Lecount waited for him in the garden.

After an absence of a few minutes only, he appeared again, on the top of the flight of steps which led into the garden from the house. He held by the iron rail, with one hand; while with the other he beckoned to Mrs. Lecount to join him on the steps.

"What does the maid say?" she asked as she approached him. "Is the mark there?"

He answered in a whisper, "Yes." What he had heard from the maid had produced a marked change in him. The horror of the coming discovery had laid its paralyzing hold on his mind. He moved mechanically; he looked and spoke like a man in a dream.

"Will you take my arm, sir?"

He shook his head; and, preceding her along the passage and up the stairs, led the way into his wife's room. When she joined him, and locked the door, he stood passively waiting for his directions, without making any remark, without showing any external appearance of surprise. He had not removed either his hat or coat. Mrs. Lecount took them off for him. "Thank you," he said, with the docility of a well-trained child. "It's like a scene in a novel—it's like nothing in real life."

The bed-chamber was not very large, and the furniture was heavy and old fashioned. But evidences of Magdalen's natural taste and refinement were visible everywhere, in the little embellishments that graced and enlivened the aspect of the room. The perfume of dried rose-leaves hung fragrant on the cool air. Mrs. Lecount sniffed the perfume with a disparaging frown, and threw the window up to its full height. "Pah!" she said, with a shudder of virtuous disgust—"the atmosphere of deceit!"

She seated herself near the window. The wardrobe stood against the wall opposite, and the bed was at the side of the room on her right hand. "Open the wardrobe, Mr. Noel," she said. "I don't go near it. I touch nothing in it, myself. Take out the dresses with your own hand, and put them on the bed. Take them out one by one, until I tell you to stop."

He obeyed her. "I'll do it as well as I can," he said. "My hands are cold, and my head feels half asleep."

The dresses to be removed were not many—for Magdalen had taken some of them away with her. After he had put two dresses on the bed, he was obliged to search in the inner recesses of the wardrobe, before he could find a third. When he produced it, Mrs. Lecount made a sign to him to stop. The end was reached already : he had found the brown alpaca dress.

"Lay it out on the bed, sir," said Mrs. Lecount. "You will see a double flounce running round the bottom of it. Lift up the outer flounce, and pass the inner one through your fingers, inch by inch. If you come to a place where there is a morsel of the stuff missing, stop, and look up at me."

He passed the flounce slowly through his fingers, for a minute or more—then stopped and looked up. Mrs. Lecount produced her pocket-book, and opened it.

"Every word I now speak, sir, is of serious consequence to you and to me," she said. "Listen with your closest attention. When the woman calling herself Miss Garth came to see us in Vauxhall Walk, I knelt down behind the chair in which she was sitting, and I cut a morsel of stuff from the dress she wore, which might help me to know that dress, if I ever saw it again. I did this, while the woman's whole attention was absorbed in talking to you. The morsel of stuff has been kept in my pocket-book, from that time to this. See for yourself, Mr. Noel, if it fits the gap in that dress, which your own hands have just taken from your wife's wardrobe."

She rose, and handed him the fragment of stuff across the bed. He put it into the vacant space in the flounce, as well as his trembling fingers would let him.

"Does it fit, sir?" asked Mrs. Lecount.

The dress dropped from his hands; and the deadly bluish pallor—which every doctor who attended him had warned his housekeeper to dread—overspread his face slowly. Mrs. Lecount had not reckoned on such an answer to her question as she now saw in his cheeks. She hurried round to him, with the smelling-bottle in her hand. He dropped to his knees, and caught at her dress with the grasp of a drowning man. "Save me !" he gasped, in a hoarse, breathless whisper. "Oh, Lecount, save me !"

"I promise to save you," said Mrs. Lecount; "I am here with the means and the resolution to save you. Come away from this place—come nearer to the air." She raised him as she spoke, and led him across the room to the window. "Do you feel the chill pain again on your left side?" she asked, with the first signs of alarm that she had shown yet. "Has your wife got any eau-de-cologne, any sal-volatile in her room. Don't exhaust yourself by speaking—point to the place !"

He pointed to a little triangular cupboard, of old worm-eaten walnut-wood, fixed high in a corner of the room. Mrs. Lecount tried the door—it was locked.

As she made that discovery, she saw his head sink back gradually on the easy-chair in which she had placed him. The warning of the doctors in past years—"If you ever let him faint, you let him die"—recurred to her memory, as if it had been spoken the day before. She looked at the cupboard again. In a recess under it, lay some ends of cord, placed there apparently for purposes of packing. Without an instant's hesitation, she snatched up a morsel of cord; tied one end fast round the knob of the cupboard door; and seizing the other end in both hands, pulled it suddenly with the exertion of her whole strength. The rotten wood gave way; the cupboard-doors flew open; and a heap of little trifles poured out noisily on the floor. Without stopping to notice the broken china and glass at her feet, she looked into the dark recesses of the cupboard, and saw the gleam of two glass bottles. One was put away at the extreme back of the shelf; the other was a little in advance, almost hiding it. She snatched them both out at once, and took them, one in each hand, to the window, where she could read their labels in the clearer light.

The bottle in her right hand was the first bottle she looked at. It was marked—*Sal-volatile*.

She instantly laid the other bottle aside on the table without looking at it. The other bottle lay there, waiting its turn. It held a dark liquid, and it was labelled—Poison.

CHAPTER II.

Mrs. Lecount mixed the sal-volatile with water, and administered it immediately. The stimulant had its effect. In a few minutes, Noel Vanstone was able to raise himself in the chair without assistance: his colour changed again for the better, and his breath came and went more freely.

"How do you feel now, sir?" asked Mrs. Lecount. "Are you warm again, on your left side?"

He paid no attention to that inquiry: his eyes, wandering about the room, turned by chance, towards the table. To Mrs. Lecount's surprise, instead of answering her, he bent forward in his chair, and looked with staring eyes and pointing hand at the second bottle which she had taken from the cupboard, and which she had hastily laid aside, without paying attention to it. Seeing that some new alarm possessed him, she advanced to the table, and looked where he looked. The labelled side of the bottle was full in view; and there, in the plain handwriting of the chemist at Aldborough, was the one startling word, confronting them both—"Poison."

Even Mrs. Lecount's self-possession was shaken by that discovery. She was not prepared to see her own darkest forebodings—the unacknowledged offspring of her hatred for Magdalen—realized as she saw them realized now. The suicide-despair in which the poison had been procured; the suicide-purpose for which, in distrust of the future, the poison had been kept, had brought with them their own retribution. There the bottle lay, in Magdalen's absence, a false witness of treason which had never entered her mind—treason against her husband's life!

With his hand still mechanically pointing at the table, Noel Vanstone raised his head, and looked up at Mrs. Lecount.

"I took it from the cupboard," she said, answering the look. "I took both bottles out together, not knowing which might be the bottle I wanted. I am as much shocked, as much frightened, as you are."

"Poison!" he said to himself, slowly. "Poison locked up by my wife, in the cupboard in her own room." He stopped, and looked at Mrs. Lecount once more. "For *me*?" he asked, in a vacant, inquiring tone.

"We will not talk of it, sir, until your mind is more at ease," said Mrs. Lecount. "In the mean time, the danger that lies waiting in this bottle, shall be instantly destroyed in your presence." She took out the cork, and threw the laudanum out of window, and the empty bottle after it. "Let us try to forget this dreadful discovery for the present," she resumed; "let us go down-stairs at once. All that I have now to say to you, can be said in another room."

She helped him to rise from the chair, and took his arm in her own. "It is well for him; it is well for me," she thought, as they went down-stairs together, "that I came when I did."

On crossing the passage, she stepped to the front door, where the carriage was waiting which had brought her from Dumfries, and instructed the coachman to put up his horses at the nearest inn, and to call again for her in two hours' time. This done, she accompanied Noel Vanstone into the sitting-room, stirred up the fire, and placed him before it comfortably in an easy-chair. He sat for a few minutes, warming his hands feebly like an old man, and staring straight into the flame. Then he spoke.

"When the woman came and threatened me in Vauxhall Walk," he began, still staring into the fire, "you came back to the parlour, after she was gone; and you told me——?" He stopped, shivered a little, and lost the thread of his recollections at that point.

"I told you, sir," said Mrs. Lecount, "that the woman was, in my opinion, Miss Vanstone herself. Don't start, Mr. Noel! Your wife is away, and I am here to take care of you. Say to yourself, if you feel frightened, 'Lecount is here; Lecount will take care of me.' The truth must be told, sir—however hard to bear the truth may be. Miss Magdalen Vanstone was the woman who came to you in disguise; and the woman who came to you in disguise, is the woman you have married. The conspiracy which she threatened you with in London, is the conspiracy which has made her your wife. That is the plain truth. You have seen the dress up-stairs. . If that dress had been no longer in existence, I should still have had my proofs to convince you. Thanks to my interview with Mrs. Bygrave, I have discovered the house your wife lodged at in London —it was opposite our house in Vauxhall Walk. I have laid my hand on one of the landlady's daughters, who watched your wife from an inner room, and saw her put on the disguise; who can speak to her identity, and to the identity of her companion, Mrs. Bygrave; and who has furnished me, at my own request, with a written statement of facts, which she is ready to affirm on oath, if any person ventures to contradict her. You shall read the statement, Mr. Noel, if you like, when you are fitter to understand it. You shall also read a letter in the handwriting of Miss Garth—who will repeat to you personally every word she has written to me—a letter formally denying that she was ever in Vauxhall Walk, and formally asserting that those moles on your wife's neck, are marks peculiar to Miss Magdalen Vanstone, whom she has known from childhood. I say it with a just pride—you will find no weak place anywhere in the evidence which I bring you. If Mr. Bygrave had not stolen my letter, you would have had your warning, before I was cruelly deceived into going to Zurich; and the proofs which I now bring you, after your marriage, I should then have offered to you before it. Don't hold me responsible, sir, for what has happened since I left England. Blame your uncle's bastard daughter, and blame that villain with the brown eye and the green!"

She spoke her last venomous words as slowly and distinctly as she had spoken all the rest. Noel Vanstone made no answer—he still sat cowering over the fire. She looked round into his face. He was crying silently. "I was so fond of her!" said the miserable little creature; "and I thought she was so fond of Me!"

Mrs. Lecount turned her back on him in disdainful silence. "Fond of her!" As she repeated those words to herself, her haggard face became almost handsome again in the magnificent intensity of its contempt.

She walked to a book-case at the lower end of the room, and began examining the volumes in it. Before she had been long engaged in this way, she was startled by the sound of his voice, affrightedly calling her back. The tears were gone from his face: it was blank again with terror when he now turned it towards her.

"Lecount!" he said, holding to her with both hands. "Can an egg be poisoned? I had an egg for breakfast this morning—and a little toast."

"Make your mind, easy, sir," said Mrs. Lecount. "The poison of your wife's deceit is the only poison you have taken yet. If she had resolved already on making you pay the price of your folly with your life, she would not be absent from the house while you were left living in it. Dismiss the thought from your mind. It is the middle of the day; you want refreshment. I have more to say to you, in the interests of your own safety—I have something for you to do, which must be done at once. Recruit your strength, and you will do it. I will set you the example of eating, if you still distrust the food in this house. Are you composed enough to give the servant her orders, if I ring the bell? It is necessary to the object I have in view for you, that nobody should think you ill in body, or troubled in mind. Try first with me before the servant comes in. Let us see how you look and speak when you say, ' Bring up the lunch.' "

After two rehearsals, Mrs. Lecount considered him fit to give the order, without betraying himself.

The bell was answered by Louisa—Louisa looked hard at Mrs. Lecount. The luncheon was brought up by the housemaid—the housemaid looked hard at Mrs. Lecount. When luncheon was over, the table was cleared by the cook—the cook looked hard at Mrs. Lecount. The three servants were plainly suspicious that something extraordinary was going on in the house. It was hardly possible to doubt that they had arranged to share among themselves the three opportunities which the service of the table afforded them of entering the room.

The curiosity of which she was the object did not escape the penetration of Mrs. Lecount. "I did well," she thought, "to arm myself in good time with the means of reaching my end. If I let the grass grow under my feet, one or other of those women might get in my way." Roused by this consideration, she produced her travelling-bag from a corner, as soon as the last of the servants had entered the room ;* and seating herself at the end of the table opposite Noel Vanstone, looked at him for a moment, with a steady investigating attention. She had carefully regulated the quantity of wine which he had taken at luncheon—she had let him drink exactly enough to fortify, without confusing him—and she now examined his face critically, like an artist examining his picture, at the end of the day's work. The result appeared to satisfy her ; and she opened the serious business of the interview on the spot.

" Will you look at the written evidence I have mentioned to you, Mr. Noel, before I say any more ?" she inquired. " Or are you sufficiently persuaded of the truth to proceed at once to the suggestion which I have now to make to you ?"

"Let me hear your suggestion," he said, sullenly resting his elbows on the table, and leaning his head on his hands.

Mrs. Lecount took from her travelling-bag the written evidence to which she had just alluded, and carefully placed the papers on one side of him, within easy reach, if he wished to refer to them. Far from being daunted, she was visibly encouraged by the ungraciousness of his manner. Her experience of him informed her that the sign was a promising one. On those rare occasions when the little resolution that he possessed was roused in him, it invariably asserted itself—like the resolution of most other weak men—aggressively. At such times, in proportion as he was outwardly sullen and discourteous to those about him, his resolution rose; and in proportion as he was considerate and polite, it fell. The tone of the answer he had just given, and the attitude he assumed at the table, convinced Mrs. Lecount that Spanish wine and Scotch mutton had done their duty, and had rallied his sinking courage.

"I will put the question to you for form's sake, sir, if you wish it," she proceeded. "But I am already certain, without any question at all, that you have made your will?"

He nodded his head without looking at her.

"You have made it in your wife's favour?"

He nodded again.

"You have left her everything you possess?"

"No."

Mrs. Lecount looked surprised.

"Did you exercise a reserve towards her, Mr. Noel, of your own accord?" she inquired, "or is it possible that your wife put her own limits to her interest in your will?"

He was uneasily silent—he was plainly ashamed to answer the question. Mrs. Lecount repeated it in a less direct form.

"How much have you left your widow, Mr. Noel, in the event of your death?"

"Eighty thousand pounds."

That reply answered the question. Eighty thousand pounds was exactly the fortune which Michael Vanstone had taken from his brother's orphan children, at his brother's death—exactly the fortune of which Michael Vanstone's son had kept possession, in his turn, as pitilessly as his father before him. Noel Vanstone's silence was eloquent of the confession which he was ashamed to make. His doting weakness had, beyond all doubt, placed his whole property at the feet of his wife. And this girl, whose vindictive daring had defied all restraints—this girl, who had not shrunk from her desperate determination even at the church-door—had, in the very hour of her triumph, taken part only from the man who would willingly have given all!—had rigorously exacted her father's fortune from him to the last farthing; and had then turned her back on the hand that was tempting her with tens of thousands more! For the moment, Mrs. Lecount was fairly silenced by her own surprise; Magdalen had forced the astonishment from her which is akin to admiration, the astonishment which her enmity would fain have refused. She hated Magdalen with a tenfold hatred from that time.

"I have no doubt, sir," she resumed, after a momentary silence, "that Mrs. Noel gave you excellent reasons why the provision for her at your death should be no more, and no less, than eighty thousand pounds. And,

on the other hand, I am equally sure that you, in your innocence of all
suspicion, found those reasons conclusive at the time. That time has now
gone by. Your eyes are opened, sir—and you will not fail to remark (as I
remark) that the Combe-Raven property happens to reach the same sum
exactly, as the legacy which your wife's own instructions directed you to
leave her. If you are still in any doubt of the motive for which she
married you, look in your own will—and there the motive is !"

He raised his head from his hands, and became closely attentive to what
she was saying to him, for the first time since they had faced each other at
the table. The Combe-Raven property had never been classed by itself in
his estimation. It had come to him merged in his father's other possessions,
at his father's death. The discovery which had now opened before him,
was one to which his ordinary habits of thought, as well as his innocence
of suspicion, had hitherto closed his eyes. He said nothing ; but he looked
less sullenly at Mrs. Lecount. His manner was more ingratiating ; the
high tide of his courage was already on the ebb.

"Your position, sir, must be as plain by this time to you as it is to me,"
said Mrs. Lecount. "There is only one obstacle now left, between this
woman and the attainment of her end. *That obstacle is your life.* After
the discovery we have made up-stairs, I leave you to consider for yourself
what your life is worth."

At those terrible words, the ebbing resolution in him ran out to the last
drop. "Don't frighten me !" he pleaded ; "I have been frightened enough
already." He rose, and dragged his chair after him round the table to Mrs.
Lecount's side. He sat down and caressingly kissed her hand. "You
good creature !" he said, in a sinking voice. "You excellent Lecount !
Tell me what to do. I'm full of resolution—I'll do anything to save my
life !"

"Have you got writing materials in the room, sir ?" asked Mrs. Lecount.
"Will you put them on the table, if you please ?"

While the writing materials were in process of collection, Mrs. Lecount
made a new demand on the resources of her travelling-bag. She took two
papers from it, each endorsed in the same neat commercial handwriting.
One was described as "Draft for proposed Will;" and the other, as "Draft
for proposed Letter." When she placed them before her on the table, her
hand shook a little ; and she applied the smelling-salts, which she had
brought with her in Noel Vanstone's interests, to her own nostrils.

"I had hoped, when I came here, Mr. Noel," she proceeded, "to have
given you more time for consideration, than it seems safe to give you now.
When you first told me of your wife's absence in London, I thought it
probable that the object of her journey was to see her sister and Miss
Garth. Since the horrible discovery we have made up-stairs, I am
inclined to alter that opinion. Your wife's determination not to tell you

who the friends are whom she has gone to see, fill me with alarm. She may have accomplices in London—accomplices, for anything we know to the contrary, in this house. All three of your servants, sir, have taken the opportunity in turn of coming into the room, and looking at me. I don't like their looks! Neither you nor I know what may happen from day to day—or even from hour to hour. If you take my advice, you will get the start at once of all possible accidents; and when the carriage comes back, you will leave this house with me!"

"Yes, yes!" he said eagerly; "I'll leave the house with you. I wouldn't stop here by myself for any sum of money that could be offered me. What do we want the pen and ink for? Are you to write, or am I?"

"You are to write, sir," said Mrs. Lecount. "The means taken for promoting your own safety are to be means set in motion, from beginning to end, by yourself. I suggest, Mr. Noel—and you decide. Recognise your own position, sir. What is your first and foremost necessity? It is plainly this. You must destroy your wife's interest in your death, by making another will."

He vehemently nodded his approval; his colour rose and his blinking eyes brightened in malicious triumph. "She sha'n't have a farthing," he said to himself, in a whisper—"she sha'n't have a farthing!"

"When your will is made, sir," proceeded Mrs. Lecount, "you must place it in the hands of a trustworthy person—not my hands, Mr. Noel; I am only your servant! Then, when the will is safe, and when you are safe, write to your wife at this house. Tell her, her infamous imposture is discovered—tell her you have made a new will, which leaves her penniless at your death—tell her, in your righteous indignation, that she enters your doors no more. Place yourself in that strong position, and it is no longer you who are at your wife's mercy, but your wife who is at yours. Assert your own power, sir, with the law to help you—and crush this woman into submission to any terms for the future that you please to impose."

He eagerly took up the pen. "Yes," he said, with a vindictive self-importance, "any terms I please to impose." He suddenly checked himself, and his face became dejected and perplexed. "How can I do it now?" he asked, throwing down the pen as quickly as he had taken it up.

"Do what, sir?" inquired Mrs. Lecount.

"How can I make my will, with Mr. Loscombe away in London, and no lawyer here to help me?"

Mrs. Lecount gently tapped the papers before her on the table with her forefinger.

"All the help you need, sir, is waiting for you here," she said. "I considered this matter carefully, before I came to you; and I provided myself with the confidential assistance of a friend, to guide me through those difficulties which I could not penetrate for myself. The friend to whom I refer, is a gentleman of Swiss extraction, but born and bred in England. He is not a lawyer by profession—but he has had his own sufficient experience of the law, nevertheless; and he has supplied me, not only with a model by which you may make your will, but with the written sketch of a letter which it is as important for us to have, as the model of the will itself. There is another necessity waiting for you, Mr. Noel, which I have not mentioned yet—but which is no less urgent in its way, than the necessity of the will."

" What is it ?" he asked, with roused curiosity.

" We will take it in its turn, sir," answered Mrs. Lecount. " Its turn has not come yet. The will, if you please, first. I will dictate from the model in my possession—and you will write."

Noel Vanstone looked at the draft for the Will and the draft for the Letter, with suspicious curiosity.

" I think I ought to see the papers myself, before you dictate," he said. " It would be more satisfactory to my own mind, Lecount."

" By all means, sir," rejoined Mrs. Lecount, handing him the papers immediately.

He read the draft for the Will first, pausing and knitting his brows distrustfully, wherever he found blank spaces left in the manuscript, to be filled in with the names of persons, and the enumeration of sums bequeathed to them. Two or three minutes of reading brought him to the end of the paper. He gave it back to Mrs. Lecount without making any objection to it.

The draft for the Letter was a much longer document. He obstinately read it through to the end, with an expression of perplexity and discontent which showed that it was utterly unintelligible to him. " I must have this explained," he said, with a touch of his old self-importance, " before I take any steps in the matter."

" It shall be explained, sir, as we go on," said Mrs. Lecount.

" Every word of it ?"

" Every word of it, Mr. Noel, when its turn comes. You have no objection to the will ? To the will, then, as I said before, let us devote ourselves first. You have seen for yourself that it is short enough and simple enough for a child to understand it. But if any doubts remain on your mind, by all means compose those doubts by showing your will to a lawyer by profession. In the mean time, let me not be considered intrusive, if I remind you that we are all mortal, and that the lost opportunity can never be recalled. While your time is your own, sir, and while your enemies are unsuspicious of you, make your will !"

She opened a sheet of note-paper, and smoothed it out before him; she dipped the pen in ink, and placed it in his hands. He took it from her without speaking—he was, to all appearance, suffering under some temporary uneasiness of mind. But the main point was gained. There he sat, with the paper before him, and the pen in his hand; ready at last, in right earnest, to make his will.

"The first question for you to decide, sir," said Mrs. Lecount, after a preliminary glance at her Draft, "is your choice of an executor. I have no desire to influence your decision; but I may, without impropriety, remind you that a wise choice means, in other words, the choice of an old and tried friend whom you know that you can trust."

"It means the admiral, I suppose?" said Noel Vanstone.

Mrs. Lecount bowed.

"Very well," he continued. "The admiral let it be."

There was plainly some oppression still weighing on his mind. Even under the trying circumstances in which he was placed, it was not in his nature to take Mrs. Lecount's perfectly sensible and disinterested advice without a word of cavil, as he had taken it now.

"Are you ready, sir?"

"Yes."

Mrs. Lecount dictated the first paragraph, from the Draft, as follows:—

"This is the last Will and Testament of me, Noel Vanstone, now living at Baliol Cottage, near Dumfries. I revoke, absolutely and in every particular, my former will executed on the thirtieth of September, eighteen hundred and forty-seven; and I hereby appoint Rear-Admiral Arthur Everard Bartram, of St. Crux-in-the-Marsh, Essex, sole executor of this my will."

"Have you written those words, sir?"

"Yes."

Mrs. Lecount laid down the Draft; Noel Vanstone laid down the pen. They neither of them looked at each other. There was a long silence.

"I am waiting, Mr. Noel," said Mrs. Lecount, at last, "to hear what your wishes are, in respect to the disposal of your fortune. Your *large* fortune," she added, with merciless emphasis.

He took up the pen again, and began picking the feathers from the quill in dead silence.

"Perhaps, your existing will may help you to instruct me, sir," pursued Mrs. Lecount. "May I inquire to whom you left all your surplus money, after leaving the eighty thousand pounds to your wife?"

If he had answered that question plainly, he must have said, "I have left the whole surplus to my cousin, George Bartram"—and the implied acknowledgment that Mrs. Lecount's name was not mentioned in the will, must then have followed in Mrs. Lecount's presence. A much bolder man, in his situation, might have felt the same oppression and the same embarrassment which he was feeling now. He picked the last morsel of feather from the quill; and, desperately leaping the pitfall under his feet, advanced to meet Mrs. Lecount's claims on him of his own accord.

"I would rather not talk of any will, but the will I am making now," he said uneasily. "The first thing, Lecount——" He hesitated—put the bare end of the quill into his mouth—gnawed at it thoughtfully—and said no more.

"Yes, sir?" persisted Mrs. Lecount.

"The first thing is——"

"Yes, sir?"

"The first thing is, to—to make some provision for You?"

He spoke the last words in a tone of plaintive interrogation—as if all hope of being met by a magnanimous refusal had not deserted him, even yet. Mrs. Lecount enlightened his mind on this point, without a moment's loss of time.

"Thank you, Mr. Noel," she said, with the tone and manner of a woman who was not acknowledging a favour, but receiving a right.

He took another bite at the quill. The perspiration began to appear on his face.

"The difficulty is," he remarked, "to say how much."

"Your lamented father, sir," rejoined Mrs. Lecount, "met that difficulty (if you remember) at the time of his last illness?"

"I don't remember," said Noel Vanstone, doggedly.

"You were on one side of his bed, sir; and I was on the other. We were vainly trying to persuade him to make his will. After telling us he would wait, and make his will when he was well again—he looked round at me, and said some kind and feeling words which my memory will treasure to my dying day. Have you forgotten those words, Mr. Noel?"

"Yes," said Mr. Noel, without hesitation.

"In my present situation, sir," retorted Mrs. Lecount, "delicacy forbids me to improve your memory."

She looked at her watch, and relapsed into silence. He clenched his hands, and writhed from side to side of his chair, in an agony of indecision. Mrs. Lecount passively refused to take the slightest notice of him.

"What should you say—?" he began, and suddenly stopped again.

"Yes, sir?"

"What should you say to—a thousand pounds?"

Mrs. Lecount rose from her chair, and looked him full in the face, with the majestic indignation of an outraged woman.

"After the service I have rendered you to-day, Mr. Noel," she said, "I have at least earned a claim on your respect—if I have earned nothing more. I wish you good morning."

" Two thousand !" cried Noel Vanstone, with the courage of despair.

Mrs. Lecount folded up her papers, and hung her travelling-bag over her arm in contemptuous silence.

" Three thousand !"

Mrs. Lecount moved with impenetrable dignity from the table to the door.

" Four thousand !"

Mrs. Lecount gathered her shawl round her with a shudder, and opened the door.

" Five thousand !"

He clasped his hands, and wrung them at her in a 'frenzy of rage and suspense. " Five thousand," was the death-cry of his pecuniary suicide.

Mrs. Lecount softly shut the door again, and came back a step.

" Free of legacy duty, sir ?" she inquired.

" No !"

Mrs. Lecount turned on her heel, and opened the door again.

" Yes !"

Mrs. Lecount came back, and resumed her place at the table, as if nothing had happened.

" Five thousand pounds, free of legacy duty, was the sum, sir, which your father's grateful regard promised me in his will," she said, quietly. " If you choose to exert your memory, as you have not chosen to exert it yet, your memory will tell you that I speak the truth. I accept your filial performance of your father's promise, Mr. Noel—and there I stop. I scorn to take a mean advantage of my position towards you ; I scorn to grasp anything from 'your fears. You are protected by my respect for myself, and for the Illustrious Name I bear. You are welcome to all that I have done, and to all that I have suffered in your service. The widow of Professor Lecompte, sir, takes what is justly hers—and takes no more !"

As she spoke those words, the traces of sickness seemed, for the moment, to disappear from her face ; her eyes shone with a steady inner light ; all the woman warmed and brightened in the radiance of her own triumph—the triumph, trebly won, of carrying her point, of vindicating her integrity, and of matching Magdalen's incorruptible self-denial on Magdalen's own ground.

" When you are yourself again, sir, we will proceed. Let us wait a little first."

She gave him time to compose himself ; and then, after first looking at her Draft, dictated the second paragraph of the will, in these terms :

" I give and bequeath to Madame Virginie Lecompte (widow of Professor Lecompte, late of Zurich) the sum of Five Thousand Pounds, free of Legacy Duty. And, in making this bequest, I wish to place it on record that I am not only expressing my own sense of Madame Lecompte's attachment and fidelity in the capacity of my housekeeper, but that I also believe myself to be executing the intentions of my deceased father, who, but for the circumstance of his dying intestate, would have left Madame Lecompte, in *his* will, the same token of grateful regard for her services, which I now leave her in mine."

"Have you written the last words, sir?"

"Yes."

Mrs. Lecount leaned across the table, and offered Noel Vanstone her hand.

"Thank you, Mr. Noel," she said. "The five thousand pounds is the acknowledgment on your father's side of what I have done for him. The words in the will are the acknowledgment on yours."

A faint smile flickered over his face for the first time. It comforted him, on reflection, to think that matters might have been worse. There was balm for his wounded spirit, in paying the debt of gratitude by a sentence not negotiable at his banker's. Whatever his father might have done—*he* had got Lecount a bargain, after all!

"A little more writing, sir," resumed Mrs. Lecount, "and your painful, but necessary, duty will be performed. The trifling matter of my legacy being settled, we may come to the important question that is left. The future direction of a large fortune is now waiting your word of command. To whom is it to go?"

He began to writhe again in his chair. Even under the all-powerful fascination of his wife, the parting with his money on paper had not been accomplished without a pang. He had endured the pang; he had resigned himself to the sacrifice. And now, here was the dreaded ordeal again, awaiting him mercilessly for the second time!

"Perhaps it may assist your decision, sir, if I repeat a question which I have put to you already," observed Mrs. Lecount. "In the will that you made under your wife's influence, to whom did you leave the surplus money which remained at your own disposal?"

There was no harm in answering the question, now. He acknowledged that he had left the money to his cousin George.

"You could have done nothing better, Mr. Noel—and you can do nothing better now," said Mrs. Lecount. "Mr. George and his two sisters are your only relations left. One of those sisters is an incurable invalid, with more than money enough already for all the wants which her affliction allows her to feel. The other is the wife of a man, even richer than yourself. To leave the money to these sisters is to waste it. To leave the money to their brother George, is to give your cousin exactly the assistance which he will want, when he one day inherits his uncle's dilapidated house, and his uncle's impoverished estate. A will which names the admiral your executor, and Mr. George your heir, is the right will for you to make. It does honour to the claims of friendship, and it does justice to the claims of blood."

She spoke warmly—for she spoke with a grateful remembrance of all that she herself owed to the hospitality of St. Crux. Noel Vanstone took up another pen, and began to strip the second quill of its feathers as he had stripped the first.

"Yes," he said, reluctantly; "I suppose George must have it—I suppose George has the principal claim on me." He hesitated: he looked at the door, he looked at the window, as if he longed to make his escape by one way or the other. "Oh, Lecount," he cried, piteously, "it's such a large fortune! Let me wait a little, before I leave it to anybody."

To his surprise, Mrs. Lecount at once complied with this characteristic request.

"I wish you to wait, sir," she replied. "I have something important to say, before you add another line to your will. A little while since, I told you there was a second necessity connected with your present situation, which had not been provided for yet—but which must be provided for, when the time came. The time has come now. You have a serious difficulty to meet and conquer, before you can leave your fortune to your cousin George."

"What difficulty?" he asked.

Mrs. Lecount rose from her chair, without answering—stole to the door—and suddenly threw it open. No one was listening outside; the passage was a solitude, from one end to the other.

"I distrust all servants," she said, returning to her place—"your servants particularly. Sit closer, Mr. Noel. What I have now to say to you, must be heard by no living creature but ourselves."

CHAPTER III.

THERE was a pause of a few minutes, while Mrs. Lecount opened the second of the two papers which lay before her on the table, and refreshed her memory by looking it rapidly through. This done, she once more addressed herself to Noel Vanstone; carefully lowering her voice, so as to render it inaudible to any one who might be listening in the passage outside.

"I must beg your permission, sir," she began, "to return to the subject of your wife. I do so most unwillingly; and I promise you that what I have now to say about her, shall be said, for your sake and for mine, in the fewest words. What do we know of this woman, Mr. Noel—judging her by her own confession when she came to us in the character of Miss Garth, and by her own acts afterwards at Aldborough? We know that, if death had not snatched your father out of her reach, she was ready with her plot to rob him of the Combe-Raven money. We know that when you inherited the money in your turn, she was ready with her plot to rob *you*. We know how she carried that plot through to the end; and we know that nothing but your death is wanted, at this moment, to crown her rapacity and her deception with success. We are sure of these things. We are sure that she is young, bold, and clever—that she has neither doubts, scruples, nor pity—and that she possesses the personal qualities which men in general (quite incomprehensibly to *me*!) are weak enough to admire. These are not fancies, Mr. Noel, but facts—you know them as well as I do."

He made a sign in the affirmative, and Mrs. Lecount went on:

"Keep in your mind what I have said of the past, sir, and now look with me to the future. I hope and trust you have a long life still before you; but let us, for the moment only, suppose the case of your death—your death leaving this will behind you, which gives your fortune to your cousin George. I am told there is an office in London, in which copies of all wills must be kept. Any curious stranger who chooses to pay a shilling for the privilege, may enter that office, and may read any will in the place, at his or her discretion. Do you see what I am coming to, Mr. Noel? Your disinherited widow pays her shilling, and reads your will. Your disinherited widow sees that the Combe-Raven money, which has gone from your father to you, goes next from you to Mr. George Bartram. What is the certain end of that discovery? The end is that you leave to your cousin and your friend, the legacy of this woman's vengeance and this woman's deceit—vengeance made more resolute, deceit made more devilish than ever, by her exasperation at her own failure. What is your cousin George? He is a generous, unsuspicious man; incapable of deceit himself, and fearing no deception in others. Leave him at the mercy of your wife's unscrupulous fascinations and your wife's unfathomable deceit—and I see the end, as certainly as I see you sitting there! She will blind his eyes, as she blinded yours; and, in spite of *you*, in spite of *me*, she will have the money!"

She stopped; and left her last words time to gain their hold on his mind. The circumstances had been stated so clearly, the conclusion from them had been so plainly drawn, that he seized her meaning without an effort, and seized it at once.

"I see!" he said, vindictively clenching his hands. "I understand, Lecount! She sha'n't have a farthing. What shall I do? Shall I leave the money to the admiral?" He paused, and considered a little. "No," he resumed; "there's the same danger in leaving it to the admiral that there is in leaving it to George."

"There is no danger, Mr. Noel, if you take my advice."

"What is your advice?"

"Follow your own idea, sir. Take the pen in hand again, and leave the money to Admiral Bartram."

He mechanically dipped the pen in the ink—and then hesitated.

"You shall know where I am leading you, sir," said Mrs. Lecount, "before you sign your will. In the mean time, let us gain every inch of ground we can, as we go on. I want the will to be all written out, before we advance a single step beyond it. Begin your third paragraph, Mr. Noel, under the lines which leave me my legacy of five thousand pounds."

She dictated the last momentous sentence of the will (from the rough draft in her own possession) in these words:

"The whole residue of my estate, after payment of my burial expenses and my lawful debts, I give and bequeath to Rear-Admiral Arthur Everard Bartram, my Executor aforesaid; to be by him applied to such uses as he may think fit.

"Signed, sealed, and delivered this third day of November, eighteen hundred and forty-seven, by Noel Vanstone, the within-named testator, as and for his last Will and Testament, in the presence of us——."

"Is that all?" asked Noel Vanstone, in astonishment.

"That is enough, sir, to bequeath your fortune to the admiral; and, therefore, that is all. Now let us go back to the case which we have supposed already. Your widow pays her shilling, and sees this will. There is the Combe-Raven money left to Admiral Bartram; with a declaration in plain words that it is his, to use as he likes. When she sees this, what does she do? She sets her trap for the admiral. He is a bachelor, and he is an old man. Who is to protect him against the arts of this desperate woman? Protect him yourself, sir, with a few more strokes of that pen which has done such wonders already. You have left him this legacy, in your will—which your wife sees. Take the legacy away again, in a letter—which is a dead secret between the admiral and you. Put the will and the letter under one cover, and place them in the admiral's possession, with your written directions to him to break the seal on the day of your death. Let the will say what it says now; and let the letter (which is your secret and his) tell him the truth. Say that in leaving him your fortune, you leave it with the request that he will take his legacy with one hand from you, and give it with the other to his nephew George. Tell him that your trust in this matter rests solely on your confidence in his honour, and on your belief in his affectionate remembrance of your father and yourself. You have known the admiral since you were a boy. He has his little whims and oddities—but he is a gentleman from the crown of his head to the sole of his foot; and he is utterly incapable of proving false to a trust in his honour, reposed by his dead friend. Meet the difficulty boldly, by such a stratagem as this; and you save these two helpless men from your wife's snares, one by means of the other. Here, on one side, is your will, which gives the fortune to the admiral, and sets her plotting accordingly. And there, on the other side, is your letter, which privately puts the money into the nephew's hands !"

The malicious dexterity of this combination was exactly the dexterity which Noel Vanstone was most fit to appreciate. He tried to express his approval and admiration in words. Mrs. Lecount held up her hand warningly, and closed his lips.

"Wait, sir, before you express your opinion," she went on. "Half the difficulty is all that we have conquered yet. Let us say, the admiral has made the use of your legacy which you have privately requested him to make of it. Sooner or later, however well the secret may be kept, your wife will discover the truth. What follows that discovery ? She lays siege to Mr. George. All you have done is to leave him the money by a roundabout way. There he is, after an interval of time, as much at her mercy as if you had openly mentioned him in your will. What is the remedy for this ? The remedy is to mislead her, if we can, for the second time—to set up an obstacle between her and the money, for the protection of your cousin George. Can you guess for yourself, Mr. Noel, what is the most promising obstacle we can put in her way ?"

He shook his head. Mrs. Lecount smiled, and startled him into close attention by laying her hand on his arm.

"Put a Woman in her way, sir !" she whispered in her wiliest tones. "We don't believe in that fascinating beauty of hers—whatever you may do. Our lips don't burn to kiss those smooth cheeks. Our arms don't long to be round that supple waist. We see through her smiles and her graces, and her stays and her padding—she can't fascinate us ! Put a woman in her way, Mr. Noel ! Not a woman in my helpless situation,. who is only a servant—but a woman with the authority and the jealousy of a Wife. Make it a condition, in your letter to the admiral, that if Mr. George is a bachelor at the time of your death, he shall marry within a certain time afterwards—or he shall not have the legacy. Suppose he remains single in spite of your condition—who is to have the money then ? Put a woman in your wife's way, sir, once more—and leave the fortune, in that case, to the married sister of your cousin George."

She paused. Noel Vanstone again attempted to express his opinion ; and again Mrs. Lecount's hand extinguished him in silence.

"If you approve, Mr. Noel," she said, "I will take your approval for granted. If you object, I will meet your objection before it is out of your mouth. You may say :—Suppose this condition is sufficient to answer the purpose, why hide it in a private letter to the admiral ? Why not openly write it down, with my cousin's name, in the will ? Only for one reason, sir. Only because the secret way is the sure way, with such a woman as your wife. The more secret you can keep your intentions, the more time you force her to waste in finding them out for herself. That time which she loses, is time gained from her treachery by the admiral—time gained by Mr. George (if he is still a bachelor) for his undisturbed choice of a lady— time gained, for her own security, by the object of his choice, who might otherwise be the first object of your wife's suspicion and your wife's hostility. Remember the bottle we have discovered upstairs; and keep this desperate woman ignorant, and therefore harmless, as long as you can. There is my advice, Mr. Noel, in the fewest and plainest words. What do you say, sir? Am I almost as clever in my way as your friend Mr. Bygrave? Can I, too, conspire a little, when the object of my conspiracy is to assist your wishes and to protect your friends?"

Permitted the use of his tongue at last, Noel Vanstone's admiration of Mrs. Lecount expressed itself in terms precisely similar to those which he had used on a former occasion, in paying his compliments to Captain Wragge. "What a head you have got!" were the grateful words which he had once spoken to Mrs. Lecount's bitterest enemy. "What a head you have got!" were the grateful words which he now spoke again to Mrs. Lecount herself. So do extremes meet; and such is sometimes the all-embracing capacity of the approval of a fool!

"Allow my head, sir, to deserve the compliment which you have paid to it," said Mrs. Lecount. "The letter to the admiral is not written yet. Your will there, is a body without a soul—an Adam without an Eve— until the letter is completed, and laid by its side. A little more dictation on my part, a little more writing on yours—and our work is done. Pardon me. The letter will be longer than the will—we must have larger paper than the note-paper this time."

The writing-case was searched, and some letter-paper was found in it of the size required. Mrs. Lecount resumed her dictation; and Noel Vanstone resumed his pen.

"Private.

"Baliol Cottage, Dumfries,
"November 3rd, 1847.

"DEAR ADMIRAL BARTRAM,

"When you open my Will (in which you are named my sole executor), you will find that I have bequeathed the whole residue of my estate—after payment of one legacy of five thousand pounds—to yourself. It is the purpose of my letter to tell you privately what the object is for which I have left you the fortune which is now placed in your hands.

"I beg you to consider this large legacy, as intended, under certain conditions, to be given by you to your nephew George. If your nephew is married at the time of my death, and if his wife is living, I request you to put him at once in possession of your legacy; accompanying it by the expression of my desire (which I am sure he will consider a sacred and binding obligation on him) that he will settle the money on his wife—and on his children, if he has any. If, on the other hand, he is unmarried at the time of my death, or if he is a widower—in either of those cases, I make it a condition of his receiving the legacy, that he shall be married within the period of——"

Mrs. Lecount laid down the Draft letter from which she had been dictating thus far, and informed Noel Vanstone by a sign that his pen might rest.

"We have come to the question of time, sir," she observed. "How long will you give your cousin to marry, if he is single, or a widower, at the time of your death?"

"Shall I give him a year?" inquired Noel Vanstone.

"If we had nothing to consider but the interests of Propriety," said Mrs. Lecount, "I should say a year too, sir—especially if Mr. George should happen to be a widower. But we have your wife to consider, as well as the interests of Propriety. A year of delay, between your death and your cousin's marriage, is a dangerously long time to leave the disposal of your fortune in suspense. Give a determined woman a year to plot and contrive in, and there is no saying what she may not do."

"Six months?" suggested Noel Vanstone.

"Six months, sir," rejoined Mrs. Lecount, "is the preferable time of the two. A six months' interval from the day of your death is enough for Mr. George.—You look discomposed, sir. What is the matter?"

"I wish you wouldn't talk so much about my death," he broke out petulantly. "I don't like it! I hate the very sound of the word!"

Mrs. Lecount smiled resignedly, and referred to her Draft.

"I see the word 'decease' written here," she remarked. "Perhaps, Mr. Noel, you would prefer it?"

"Yes," he said; "I prefer 'Decease.' It doesn't sound so dreadful as 'Death.'"

"Let us go on with the letter, sir."

She resumed her dictation as follows:

". . . . . . in either of those cases, I make it a condition of his receiving the legacy that he shall be married within the period of Six calendar months from the day of my decease; that the woman he marries shall *not* be a widow; and that his marriage shall be a marriage by Banns, publicly celebrated in the parish church of Ossory—where he has been known from his childhood, and where the family and circumstances of his future wife are likely to be the subject of public interest and inquiry."

"This," said Mrs. Lecount, quietly looking up from the Draft, "is to protect Mr. George, sir, in case the same trap is set for him, which was successfully set for you. She will not find her false character and her false name fit quite so easily, next time—no, not even with Mr. Bygrave to help her! Another dip of ink, Mr. Noel; let us write the next paragraph. Are you ready?"

"Yes."

Mrs. Lecount went on :

"If your nephew fails to comply with these conditions—that is to say, if, being either a bachelor or a widower at the time of my decease, he fails to marry in all respects as I have here instructed him to marry, within Six calendar months from that time—it is my desire that he shall not receive the legacy, or any part of it. I request you, in the case here supposed, to pass him over altogether; and to give the fortune left you in my will, to his married sister, Mrs. Girdlestone.

"Having now put you in possession of my motives and intentions, I come to the next question which it is necessary to consider. If, when you open this letter, your nephew is an unmarried man, it is clearly indispensable that he should know of the conditions here imposed on him, as soon, if possible, as you know of them yourself. Are you, under these circumstances, freely to communicate to him what I have here written to you? Or, are you to leave him under the impression that no such private expression of my wishes as this is in existence; and are you to state all the conditions relating to his marriage, as if they emanated entirely from yourself?

"If you will adopt this latter alternative, you will add one more to the many obligations under which your friendship has placed me.

"I have serious reason to believe that the possession of my money, and the discovery of any peculiar arrangements relating to the disposal of it, will be objects (after my decease) of the fraud and conspiracy of an unscrupulous person. I am therefore anxious—for your sake, in the first place—that no suspicion of the existence of this letter should be conveyed to the mind of the person to whom I allude. And I am equally desirous— for Mrs. Girdlestone's sake, in the second place—that this same person should be entirely ignorant that the legacy will pass into Mrs. Girdlestone's possession, if your nephew is not married in the given time. I know George's easy, pliable disposition; I dread the attempts that will be made to practise on it; and I feel sure that the prudent course will be, to abstain from trusting him with secrets, the rash revelation of which might be followed by serious, and even dangerous results.

"State the conditions, therefore, to your nephew, as if they were your own. Let him think they have been suggested to your mind by the new responsibilities imposed on you as a man of property, by your position in my will, and by your consequent anxiety to provide for the perpetuation of the family name. If these reasons are not sufficient to satisfy him, there can be no objection to your referring him, for any further explanations which he may desire, to his wedding-day.

"I have done. My last wishes are now confided to you, in implicit reliance on your honour, and on your tender regard for the memory of your friend. Of the miserable circumstances which compel me to write as I have written here, I say nothing. You will hear of them, if my life is spared, from my own lips—for you will be the first friend whom I shall consult in my difficulty and distress. Keep this letter strictly secret, and strictly in your own possession, until my requests are complied with. Let no human being but yourself know where it is, on any pretence whatever.

> "Believe me, dear Admiral Bartram,
>> "Affectionately yours,
>>> "Noel Vanstone."

"Have you signed, sir?" asked Mrs. Lecount. "Let me look the letter over, if you please, before we seal it up."

She read the letter carefully. In Noel Vanstone's close, cramped hand-writing, it filled two pages of letter-paper, and ended at the top of the third page. Instead of using an envelope, Mrs. Lecount folded it, neatly and securely, in the old-fashioned way. She lit the taper in the inkstand, and returned the letter to the writer.

"Seal it, Mr. Noel," she said, "with your own hand, and your own seal." She extinguished the taper, and handed him the pen again. "Address the letter, sir," she proceeded, "to *Admiral Bartram, St. Crux-in the-Marsh, Essex.* Now add these words, and sign them, above the address: *To be kept in your own possession, and to be opened by yourself only, on the day of my death*—or 'Decease,' if you prefer it—*Noel Vanstone.* Have you done? Let me look at it again. Quite right in every particular. Accept my congratulations, sir. If your wife has not plotted her last plot for the Combe-Raven money, it is not your fault, Mr. Noel—and not mine!"

Finding his attention released by the completion of the letter, Noel Vanstone reverted at once to purely personal considerations. "There is my packing-up to be thought of now," he said. "I can't go away without my warm things."

"Excuse me, sir," rejoined Mrs. Lecount, "there is the Will to be signed first; and there must be two persons found to witness your signature." She looked out of the front window, and saw the carriage waiting at the door. "The coachman will do for one of the witnesses," she said. "He is in respectable service at Dumfries, and he can be found if he happens to be wanted. We must have one of your own servants, I suppose, for the other witness. They are all detestable women; but the cook is the least ill-looking of the three. Send for the cook, sir, while I go out and call the coachman. When we have got our witnesses here, you have only to speak to them in these words :—' I have a document here to sign, and I wish you to write your names on it, as witnesses of my signature.' Nothing more, Mr. Noel! Say those few words, in your usual manner—and, when the signing is over, I will see myself to your packing-up, and your warm things."

She went to the front door, and summoned the coachman to the parlour. On her return, she found the cook already in the room. The cook looked mysteriously offended, and stared without intermission at Mrs. Lecount. In a minute more, the coachman—an elderly man—came in. He was preceded by a relishing odour of whisky—but his head was Scotch; and nothing but his odour betrayed him.

"I have a document here to sign," said Noel Vanstone, repeating his lesson; "and I wish you to write your names on it, as witnesses of my signature."

The coachman looked at the will. The cook never removed her eyes from Mrs. Lecount.

"Ye'll no object, sir," said the coachman, with the national caution showing itself in every wrinkle on his face—"ye'll no' object, sir, to tell me, first, what the Doecument may be ?"

Mrs. Lecount interposed before Noel Vanstone's indignation could express itself in words.

"You must tell the man, sir, that this is your Will," she said. "When he witnesses your signature, he can see as much for himself if he looks at the top of the page."

"Ay, ay," said the coachman, looking at the top of the page immediately. "His last Wull and Testament. Hech, sirs! there's a sair confronting of Death, in a Doecument like yon! A' flesh is grass," continued the coachman, exhaling an additional puff of whisky, and looking up devoutly at the ceiling. "Tak' those words in connection with that other Screepture :—Many are ca'ad but few are chosen. Tak' that again, in connection with Rev'lations, Chapter the First; verses, One to Feftecn. Lay the whole to heart—and what's your Walth, then ? Dross, sirs! And your body ? (Screepture again.) Clay for the potter! And your life ? (Screepture once more.) The Breeth o' your Nostrils !"

The cook listened as if the cook was at church—but she never removed her eyes from Mrs. Lecount.

"You had better sign, sir. This is apparently some custom prevalent in Dumfries during the transaction of business," said Mrs. Lecount resignedly. "The man means well, I dare say."

She added those last words in a soothing tone, for she saw that Noel

Vanstone's indignation was fast merging into alarm. The coachman's outburst of exhortation seemed to have inspired him with fear, as well as disgust.

He dipped the pen in the ink, and signed the Will without uttering a word. The coachman (descending instantly from Theology to Business) watched the signature with the most scrupulous attention; and signed his own name as witness, with an implied commentary on the proceeding, in the form of another puff of whisky, exhaled through the medium of a heavy sigh. The cook looked away from Mrs. Lecount with an effort—signed her name in a violent hurry—and looked back again with a start, as if she expected to see a loaded pistol (produced in the interval) in the housekeeper's hands. "Thank you," said Mrs. Lecount, in her friendliest manner. The cook shut up her lips aggressively and looked at her master. "You may go!" said her master. The cook coughed contemptuously—and went.

"We sha'n't keep you long," said Mrs. Lecount, dismissing the coachman. "In half an hour, or less, we shall be ready for the journey back."

The coachman's austere countenance relaxed for the first time. He smiled mysteriously, and approached Mrs. Lecount on tiptoe.

"Ye'll no forget one thing, my leddy," he said, with the most ingratiating politeness. "Ye'll no' forget the witnessing as weel as the driving, when ye pay me for my day's wark!" He laughed with guttural gravity; and, leaving his atmosphere behind him, stalked out of the room.

"Lecount," said Noel Vanstone, as soon as the coachman closed the door. "Did I hear you tell that man we should be ready in half an hour?"

"Yes, sir."

"Are you blind?"

He asked the question with an angry stamp of his foot. Mrs. Lecount looked at him in astonishment.

"Can't you see the brute is drunk?" he went on, more and more irritably. "Is my life nothing? Am I to be left at the mercy of a drunken coachman? I won't trust that man to drive me, for any consideration under heaven! I'm surprised you could think of it, Lecount."

"The man has been drinking, sir," said Mrs. Lecount. "It is easy to see, and to smell, that. But he is evidently used to drinking. If he is sober enough to walk quite straight—which he certainly does—and to sign his name in an excellent handwriting—which you may see for yourself on the Will—I venture to think he is sober enough to drive us to Dumfries."

"Nothing of the sort! You're a foreigner, Lecount; you don't understand these people. They drink whisky from morning to night. Whisky is the strongest spirit that's made; whisky is notorious for its effect on the brain. I tell you, I won't run the risk. I never was driven, and I never will be driven, by anybody but a sober man."

"Must I go back to Dumfries by myself, sir?"

"And leave me here? Leave me alone in this house after what has happened? How do I know my wife may not come back to-night? How do I know her journey is not a blind to mislead me? Have you no feeling, Lecount? Can you leave me in my miserable situation——?" He sank into a chair and burst out crying over his own idea, before he had completed the expression of it in words. "Too bad!" he said, with his handkerchief over his face—"too bad!"

It was impossible not to pity him. If ever mortal was pitiable, he was the man. He had broken down at last, under the conflict of violent emotions which had been roused in him, since the morning. The effort to follow Mrs. Lecount along the mazes of intricate combination through which she had steadily led the way, had upheld him while that effort lasted: the moment it was at an end, he dropped. The coachman had hastened a result—of which the coachman was far from being the cause.

"You surprise me, you distress me, sir," said Mrs. Lecount. "I entreat you to compose yourself. I will stay here, if you wish it, with pleasure—I will stay here to-night, for your sake. You want rest and quiet after this dreadful day. The coachman shall be instantly sent away, Mr. Noel. I will give him a note to the landlord of the hotel,—and the carriage shall come back for us to-morrow morning, with another man to drive it."

The prospect which those words presented, cheered him. He wiped his eyes, and kissed Mrs. Lecount's hand.

"Yes!" he said faintly; "send the coachman away—and you stop here. You good creature! You excellent Lecount! Send the drunken brute away, and come back directly. We will be comfortable by the fire, Lecount—and have a nice little dinner—and try to make it like old times." His weak voice faltered; he returned to the fireside, and melted into tears again under the pathetic influence of his own idea.

Mrs. Lecount left him for a minute to dismiss the coachman. When she returned to the parlour, she found him with his hand on the bell.

"What do you want, sir?" she asked.

"I want to tell the servants to get your room ready," he answered. "I wish to show you every attention, Lecount."

"You are all kindness, Mr. Noel—but wait one moment. It may be well to have these papers put out of the way, before the servant comes in again. If you will place the Will and the Sealed Letter together in one envelope—and if you will direct it to the admiral—I will take care that the enclosure so addressed is safely placed in his own hands. Will you come to the table, Mr. Noel, only for one minute more?"

No! He was obstinate; he refused to move from the fire; he was sick

and tired of writing; he wished he had never been born, and he loathed
the sight of pen and ink. All Mrs. Lecount's patience, and all Mrs.
Lecount's persuasion, were required to induce him to write the admiral's
address for the second time. She only succeeded by bringing the blank
envelope to him upon the paper-case, and putting it coaxingly on his lap.
He grumbled, he even swore, but he directed the envelope at last, in these
terms: "To Admiral Bartram, St. Crux-in-the-Marsh. Favoured by Mrs.
Lecount." With that final act of compliance, his docility came to end.
He refused, in the fiercest terms, to seal the envelope.

There was no need to press this proceeding on him. His seal lay ready
on the table; and it mattered nothing whether he used it, or whether a
person in his confidence used it for him. Mrs. Lecount sealed the envelope,
with its two important enclosures placed safely inside.

She opened her travelling-bag for the last time, and pausing for a moment before she put the sealed packet away, looked at it with a triumph
too deep for words. She smiled as she dropped it into the bag. Not the
shadow of a suspicion that the Will might contain superfluous phrases and
expressions which no practical lawyer would have used; not the vestige of
a doubt whether the Letter was quite as complete a document as a practical
lawyer might have made it, troubled her mind. In blind reliance—born
of her hatred for Magdalen and her hunger for revenge—in blind reliance
on her own abilities, and on her friend's law, she trusted the future implicitly to the promise of the morning's work.

As she locked her travelling-bag, Noel Vanstone rang the bell. On this
occasion, the summons was answered by Louisa.

"Get the spare room ready," said her master; "this lady will sleep here
to-night. And air my warm things; this lady and I are going away to-
morrow morning."

The civil and submissive Louisa received her orders in sullen silence—
darted an angry look at her master's impenetrable guest—and left the room.
The servants were evidently all attached to their mistress's interests, and
were all of one opinion on the subject of Mrs. Lecount.

"That's done!" said Noel Vanstone, with a sigh of infinite relief.
"Come and sit down, Lecount. Let's be comfortable—let's gossip over
the fire."

Mrs. Lecount accepted the invitation; and drew an easy-chair to his
side. He took her hand with a confidential tenderness, and held it in his,
while the talk went on. A stranger, looking in through the window,
would have taken them for mother and son; and would have thought to
himself, "What a happy home!"

The gossip, led by Noel Vanstone, consisted as usual of an endless string
of questions, and was devoted entirely to the subject of himself and his
future prospects. Where would Lecount take him to, when they went

away the next morning? Why to London? Why should he be left in London, while Lecount went on to St. Crux to give the admiral the Letter and the Will? Because his wife might follow him, if he went to the admiral's? Well, there was something in that. And because he ought to be safely concealed from her, in some comfortable lodging, near Mr. Loscombe? Why near Mr. Loscombe? Ah, yes, to be sure—to know what the law would do to help him. Would the law set him free from the Wretch who had deceived him? How tiresome of Lecount not to know! Would the law say he had gone and married himself a second time, because he had been living with the Wretch, like husband and wife, in Scotland? Anything that publicly assumed to be a marriage, was a marriage (he had heard) in Scotland.* How excessively tiresome of Lecount to sit there, and say she knew nothing about it! Was he to stay long in London, by himself, with nobody but Mr. Loscombe to speak to? Would Lecount come back to him, as soon as she had put those important papers in the admiral's own hands? Would Lecount consider herself still in his service? The good Lecount! the excellent Lecount! And after all the law-business was over—what then? Why not leave this horrid England, and go abroad again? Why not go to France, to some cheap place, near Paris? Say Versailles? say St. Germain? In a nice little French house—cheap? With a nice French *bonne* to cook—who wouldn't waste his substance in the grease-pot? With a nice little garden—where he could work himself, and get health, and save the expense of keeping a gardener? It wasn't a bad idea. And it seemed to promise well for the future—didn't it, Lecount?

So he ran on—the poor, weak creature! the abject, miserable little man!

As the darkness gathered, at the close of the short November day, he began to grow drowsy—his ceaseless questions came to an end at last—he fell asleep. The wind outside sang its mournful winter-song; the tramp of passing footsteps, the roll of passing wheels on the road, ceased in dreary silence. He slept on quietly. The fire-light rose and fell on his wizen little face, and his nerveless drooping hands. Mrs. Lecount had not pitied him yet. She began to pity him, now. Her point was gained; her interest in his will was secured; he had put his future life, of his own accord, under her fostering care—the fire was comfortable; the circumstances were favourable to the growth of Christian feeling. "Poor wretch!" said Mrs. Lecount, looking at him with a grave compassion—"Poor wretch!"

The dinner-hour roused him. He was cheerful at dinner; he reverted to the idea of the cheap little house in France; he smirked and simpered; and talked French to Mrs. Lecount, while the housemaid and Louisa waited, turn and turn about, under protest. When dinner was over he returned to his comfortable chair before the fire, and Mrs. Lecount followed him. He resumed the conversation—which meant, in his case, repeating his questions. But he was not so quick and ready with them, as he had been earlier in the day. They began to flag—they continued, at longer and longer intervals—they ceased altogether. Towards nine o'clock he fell asleep again.

It was not a quiet sleep this time. He muttered, and ground his teeth, and rolled his head from side to side of the chair. Mrs. Lecount purposely made noise enough to rouse him. He woke with a vacant eye, and a flushed check. He walked about the room restlessly, with a new idea in his mind—the idea of writing a terrible letter; a letter of eternal farewell to his wife. How was it to be written? In what language should he express his feelings? The powers of Shakespeare himself would be un-equal to the emergency! He had been the victim of an outrage entirely without parallel. A wretch had crept into his bosom! A viper had hidden herself at his fireside! Where could words be found to brand her with the infamy she deserved? He stopped, with a suffocating sense in him of his own impotent rage—he stopped, and shook his fist tremulously in the empty air.

Mrs. Lecount interfered with an energy and a resolution inspired by serious alarm. After the heavy strain that had been laid on his weakness already, such an outbreak of passionate agitation as was now bursting from him, might be the destruction of his rest that night, and of his strength to travel the next day. With infinite difficulty, with endless promises to return to the subject, and to advise him about it in the morning, she pre-vailed on him, at last, to go up-stairs and compose himself for the night. She gave him her arm to assist him. On the way up-stairs, his attention, to her great relief, became suddenly absorbed by a new fancy. He remem-bered a certain warm and comfortable mixture of wine, egg, sugar, and spices, which she had often been accustomed to make for him, in former times; and which he thought he should relish exceedingly, before he went to bed. Mrs. Lecount helped him on with his dressing-gown—then went down-stairs again, to make his warm drink for him at the parlour fire.

She rang the bell, and ordered the necessary ingredients for the mixture, in Noel Vanstone's name. The servants, with the small ingenious malice of their race, brought up the materials, one by one, and kept her waiting for each of them as long as possible. She had got the saucepan, and the spoon, and the tumbler, and the nutmeg-grater, and the wine—but not the egg, the sugar, or the spices—when she heard him above, walking back-wards and forwards noisily in his room; exciting himself on the old subject again, beyond all doubt.

She went up-stairs once more; but he was too quick for her—he heard her outside the door; and when she opened it, she found him in his chair, with his back cunningly turned towards her. Knowing him too well to attempt any remonstrance, she merely announced the speedy arrival of the warm drink, and turned to leave the room. On her way out, she noticed a table in a corner, with an inkstand and a paper-case on it, and tried, without attracting his attention, to take the writing materials away. He was too quick for her again. He asked angrily, if she doubted his promise. She put the writing materials back on the table, for fear of offending him, and left the room.

In half an hour more, the mixture was ready. She carried it up to him, foaming and fragrant, in a large tumbler. "He will sleep after this," she thought to herself, as she opened the door; "I have made it stronger than usual on purpose."

He had changed his place. He was sitting at the table in the corner—still with his back to her, writing. This time, his quick ears had not served him. This time, she had caught him in the fact.

"Oh, Mr. Noel! Mr. Noel!" she said, reproachfully, "what is your promise worth?"

He made no answer. He was sitting with his left elbow on the table, and with his head resting on his left hand. His right hand lay back on the paper, with the pen lying loose in it. "Your drink, Mr. Noel," she said in a kinder tone, feeling unwilling to offend him. He took no notice of her.

She went to the table to rouse him. Was he deep in thought?

He was dead.

THE END OF THE FIFTH SCENE.

BETWEEN THE SCENES.

PROGRESS OF THE STORY THROUGH THE POST.

————⋅————

I.

From Mrs. Noel Vanstone to Mr. Loscombe.

" Park Terrace, St. John's Wood,
" November 5th.

"Dear Sir,

"I came to London yesterday, for the purpose of seeing a relative, leaving Mr. Vanstone at Baliol Cottage, and proposing to return to him in the course of the week. I reached London late last night, and drove to these lodgings, having written to secure accommodation beforehand.

"This morning's post has brought me a letter from my own maid, whom I left at Baliol Cottage, with instructions to write to me if anything extraordinary took place in my absence. You will find the girl's letter enclosed in this. I have had some experience of her; and I believe she is to be strictly depended on to tell the truth.

"I purposely abstain from troubling you by any useless allusions to myself. When you have read my maid's letter, you will understand the shock which the news contained in it has caused me. I can only repeat, that I place implicit belief in her statement. I am firmly persuaded that my husband's former housekeeper has found him out, has practised on his weakness in my absence, and has prevailed on him to make another Will. From what I know of this woman, I feel no doubt that she has used her influence over Mr. Vanstone, to deprive me, if possible, of all future interest in my husband's fortune.

"Under such circumstances as these, it is in the last degree important—for more reasons than I need mention here—that I should see Mr. Vanstone, and come to an explanation with him, at the earliest possible opportunity. You will find that my maid thoughtfully kept her letter open, until the last moment before post-time—without, however, having any later news to give me than that Mrs. Lecount was to sleep at the cottage last night, and that she and Mr. Vanstone were to leave together this morning. But for that last piece of intelligence, I should have been on my way back to Scotland before now. As it is, I cannot decide for myself what I ought to do next. My going back to Dumfries, after Mr. Vanstone has left it, seems like taking a journey for nothing—and my staying in London appears to be almost equally useless.

"Will you kindly advise me, in this difficulty? I will come to you at Lincoln's Inn at any time this afternoon or to-morrow which you may appoint. My next few hours are engaged. As soon as this letter is despatched, I am going to Kensington, with the object of ascertaining whether certain doubts I feel about the means by which Mrs. Lecount may have accomplished her discovery, are well founded or not. If you will let me have your answer by return of post, I will not fail to get back to St. John's Wood in time to receive it.

"Believe me, dear Sir, yours sincerely,
"MAGDALEN VANSTONE."

II.

FROM MR. LOSCOMBE TO MRS. NOEL VANSTONE.

"Lincoln's Inn, Nov. 5th.

"DEAR MADAM,

"Your letter and its enclosure have caused me great concern and surprise. Pressure of business allows me no hope of being able to see you either to-day or to-morrow morning. But if three o'clock to-morrow afternoon will suit you, at that hour you will find me at your service.

"I cannot pretend to offer a positive opinion, until I know more of the particulars connected with this extraordinary business than I find communicated either in your letter, or in your maid's. But with this reserve, I venture to suggest that your remaining in London until to-morrow, may possibly lead to other results besides your consultation at my chambers. There is at least a chance, that you, or I, may hear something further in this strange matter by the morning's post.

"I remain, dear Madam, faithfully yours,
"JOHN LOSCOMBE."

III.

FROM MRS. NOEL VANSTONE TO MISS GARTH.

"November 5th, Two o'Clock.

"I have just returned from Westmoreland House—after purposely leaving it in secret, and purposely avoiding you under your own roof. You shall know why I came, and why I went away. It is due to my remembrance of old times not to treat you like a stranger, although I can never again treat you like a friend.

"I set forth on the third from the North to London. My only object in taking this long journey, was to see Norah. I had been suffering for

many weary weeks past, such remorse as only miserable women like me
can feel. Perhaps, the suffering weakened me; perhaps, it roused some
old forgotten tenderness—God knows!—I can't explain it; I can only tell
you that I began to think of Norah by day, and to dream of Norah by
night, till I was almost heart-broken. I have no better reason than this to
give for running all the risks which I ran, and coming to London to see
her. I don't wish to claim more for myself than I deserve; I don't wish
to tell you I was the reformed and repenting creature whom *you* might
have approved. I had only one feeling in me that I know of. I wanted to
put my arms round Norah's neck, and cry my heart out on Norah's bosom.
Childish enough, I dare say. Something might have come of it; nothing
might have come of it—who knows?

"I had no means of finding Norah without your assistance. However
you might disapprove of what I had done, I thought you would not refuse
to help me to find my sister. When I lay down, last night, in my strange
bed, I said to myself, 'I will ask Miss Garth, for my father's sake and my
mother's sake, to tell me.' You don't know what a comfort I felt in that
thought. How should you? What do good women like you, know of
miserable sinners like me? All you know is that you pray for us at church.

"Well, I fell asleep happily that night—for the first time since my marriage. When the morning came, I paid the penalty of daring to be happy,
only for one night. When the morning came, a letter came with it, which
told me that my bitterest enemy on earth (you have meddled sufficiently
with my affairs to know what enemy I mean) had revenged herself on me
in my absence. In following the impulse which led me to my sister, I had
gone to my ruin.

"The mischief was beyond all present remedy, when I received the news
of it. Whatever had happened, whatever might happen, I made up my
mind to persist in my resolution of seeing Norah, before I did anything
else. I suspected *you* of being concerned in the disaster which had overtaken me—because I felt positively certain at Aldborough, that you and
Mrs. Lecount had written to each other. But I never suspected Norah.
If I lay on my death-bed at this moment, I could say with a safe conscience
I never suspected Norah.

"So I went this morning to Westmoreland House to ask you for my
sister's address, and to acknowledge plainly that I suspected you of being
again in correspondence with Mrs. Lecount.

"When I inquired for you at the door, they told me you had gone out,
but that you were expected back before long. They asked me if I would
see your sister, who was then in the schoolroom. I desired that your sister
should on no account be disturbed: my business was not with her, but
with you. I begged to be allowed to wait in a room by myself, until you
returned.

"They showed me into the double room on the ground floor, divided by curtains—as it was when I last remember it. There was a fire in the outer division of the room, but none in the inner; and for that reason, I suppose, the curtains were drawn. The servant was very civil and attentive to me. I have learnt to be thankful for civility and attention, and I spoke to her as cheerfully as I could. I said to her, 'I shall see Miss Garth here, as she comes up to the door, and I can beckon her in, through the long window.' The servant said I could do so, if you came that way—but that you let yourself in sometimes, with your own key, by the back-garden gate; and if you did this, she would take care to let you know of my visit. I mention these trifles, to show you that there was no premeditated deceit in my mind when I came to the house.

"I waited a weary time, and you never came: I don't know whether my impatience made me think so, or whether the large fire burning made the room really as hot as I felt it to be—I only know that, after a while, I passed through the curtains into the inner room, to try the cooler atmosphere.

"I walked to the long window which leads into the back garden, to look out; and almost at the same time, I heard the door opened—the door of the room I had just left—and your voice and the voice of some other woman, a stranger to me, talking. The stranger was one of the parlour-boarders, I dare say. I gathered from the first words you exchanged together, that you had met in the passage—she, on her way down stairs, and you, on your way in from the back garden. Her next question and your next answer, informed me that this person was a friend of my sister's, who felt a strong interest in her, and who knew that you had just returned from a visit to Norah. So far, I only hesitated to show myself, because I shrank, in my painful situation, from facing a stranger. But when I heard my own name immediately afterwards on your lips and on hers—then, I purposely came nearer to the curtain between us, and purposely listened.

"A mean action, you will say? Call it mean, if you like. What better can you expect from such a woman as I am?

"You were always famous for your memory. There is no necessity for my repeating the words you spoke to your friend, and the words your friend spoke to you, hardly an hour since. When you read these lines, you will know, as well as I know, what those words told me. I ask for no particulars; I will take all your reasons and all your excuses for granted. It is enough for me to know that you and Mr. Pendril have been searching for me again, and that Norah is in the conspiracy this time, to reclaim me in spite of myself. It is enough for me to know, that my letter to my sister has been turned into a trap to catch me, and that Mrs. Lecount's revenge has accomplished its object by means of information received from Norah's lips.

"Shall I tell you what I suffered, when I heard these things? No: it would only be a waste of time to tell you. Whatever I suffer, I deserve it —don't I?

"I waited in that inner room—knowing my own violent temper, and not trusting myself to see you, after what I had heard—I waited in that inner room, trembling lest the servant should tell you of my visit, before I could find an opportunity of leaving the house. No such misfortune happened. The servant, no doubt, heard the voices up-stairs, and supposed that we had met each other in the passage. I don't know how long, or how short a time it was, before you left the room to go and take off your bonnet—you went and your friend went with you. I raised the long window softly, and stepped into the back garden. The way by which you returned to the house, was the way by which I left it. No blame attaches to the servant. As usual, where I am concerned, nobody is to blame but me.

"Time enough has passed now to quiet my mind a little. You know how strong I am? You remember how I used to fight against all my illnesses, when I was a child? Now I am a woman, I fight against my miseries in the same way. Don't pity me, Miss Garth! Don't pity me!

"I have no harsh feeling against Norah. The hope I had of seeing her, is a hope taken from me; the consolation I had in writing to her, is a consolation denied me for the future. I am cut to the heart—but I have no angry feeling towards my sister. She means well, poor soul—I dare say she means well. It would distress her, if she knew what has happened. Don't tell her. Conceal my visit, and burn my letter.

"A last word to yourself and I have done:—

"If I rightly understand my present situation, your spies are still searching for me to just as little purpose as they searched at York. Dismiss them —you are wasting your money to no purpose. If you discovered me to-morrow, what could you do? My position has altered. I am no longer the poor outcast girl, the vagabond public performer, whom you once hunted after. I have done, what I told you I would do—I have made the general sense of propriety my accomplice this time. Do you know who I am? I am a respectable married woman, accountable for my actions to nobody under heaven but my husband. I have got a place in the world, and a name in the world, at last. Even the law, which is the friend of all you respectable people, has recognized my existence, and has become *my* friend too! The Archbishop of Canterbury gave me his licence to be married, and the vicar of Aldborough performed the service. If I found your spies following me in the street, and if I chose to claim protection from them, the law would acknowledge my claim. You forget what wonders my wickedness has done for me. It has made Nobody's Child, Somebody's Wife.

"If you will give these considerations their due weight; if you will exert your excellent common sense, I have no fear of being obliged to appeal to my newly-found friend and protector—the law. You will feel, by this time, that you have meddled with me at last to some purpose. I am estranged from Norah—I am discovered by my husband—I am defeated by Mrs. Le-count. You have driven me to the last extremity; you have strengthened me to fight the battle of my life, with the resolution which only a lost and friendless woman can feel. Badly as your schemes have prospered, they have not proved totally useless after all!

"I have no more to say. If you ever speak about me to Norah, tell her that a day may come when she will see me again—the day when we two sisters have recovered our natural rights; the day when I put Norah's fortune into Norah's hand.

"Those are my last words. Remember them the next time you feel tempted to meddle with me again.

"MAGDALEN VANSTONE."

IV.

FROM MR. LOSCOMBE TO MRS. NOEL VANSTONE.

"Lincoln's Inn, November 6th.

"DEAR MADAM,

"This morning's post has doubtless brought you the same shocking news which it has brought to me. You must know, by this time, that a terrible affliction has befallen you—the affliction of your husband's sudden death.

"I am on the point of starting for the North, to make all needful inquiries, and to perform whatever duties I may with propriety undertake, as solicitor to the deceased gentleman. Let me earnestly recommend you not to follow me to Baliol Cottage, until I have had time to write to you first, and to give you such advice as I cannot, through ignorance of all the circumstances, pretend to offer now. You may rely on my writing after my arrival in Scotland, by the first post.

"I remain, dear Madam, faithfully yours,

"JOHN LOSCOMBE."

V.

FROM MR. PENDRIL TO MISS GARTH.

"Serle Street, Nov. 6th.

"DEAR MISS GARTH,

"I return you Mrs. Noel Vanstone's letter. I can understand your mortification at the tone in which it is written, and your distress at the manner in which this unhappy woman has interpreted the conversation that she overheard at your house. I cannot honestly add that I lament what has happened. My opinion has never altered since the Combe-Raven time. I believe Mrs. Noel Vanstone to be one of the most reckless, desperate, and perverted women living; and any circumstances that estrange her from her sister, are circumstances which I welcome, for her sister's sake.

"There cannot be a moment's doubt on the course you ought to follow in this matter. Even Mrs. Noel Vanstone herself acknowledges the propriety of sparing her sister additional, and unnecessary, distress. By all means, keep Miss Vanstone in ignorance of the visit to Kensington, and of the letter which has followed it. It would be not only unwise, but absolutely cruel, to enlighten her. If we had any remedy to apply, or even any hope to offer, we might feel some hesitation in keeping our secret. But there is no remedy, and no hope. Mrs. Noel Vanstone is perfectly justified in the view she takes of her own position. Neither you nor I can assert the smallest right to control her.

"I have already taken the necessary measures for putting an end to our useless inquiries. In a few days I will write to Miss Vanstone, and will do my best to tranquillize her mind on the subject of her sister. If I can find no sufficient excuse to satisfy her, it will be better she should think we have discovered nothing, than that she should know the truth.

"Believe me, most truly yours,

"WILLIAM PENDRIL."

VI.
FROM MR. LOSCOMBE TO MRS. NOEL VANSTONE.

"Private.   "Lincoln's Inn, Nov. 15th.
"DEAR MADAM,

"In compliance with your request, I now proceed to communicate to you in writing, what (but for the calamity which has so recently befallen you) I should have preferred communicating by word of mouth. Be pleased to consider this letter as strictly confidential between yourself and me.

"I enclose, as you desire, a copy of the Will executed by your late husband on the third of this month. There can be no question of the genuineness of the original document. I protested, as a matter of form, against Admiral Bartram's solicitor assuming a position of authority at Baliol Cottage. But he took the position, nevertheless; acting as legal representative of the sole Executor under the second Will. I am bound to say I should have done the same myself in his place.

"The serious question follows—what can we do for the best, in your interests? The Will executed under my professional superintendence, on the thirtieth of September last, is at present superseded and revoked by the second and later Will, executed on the third of November. Can we dispute this document?

"I doubt the possibility of disputing the new Will, on the face of it. It is no doubt irregularly expressed—but it is dated, signed, and witnessed as the law directs; and the perfectly simple and straightforward provisions that it contains, are in no respect, that I can see, technically open to attack.

"This being the case, can we dispute the Will, on the ground that it has been executed when the Testator was not in a fit state to dispose of his own property? or when the Testator was subjected to undue and improper influence?

"In the first of these cases, the medical evidence would put an obstacle in our way. We cannot assert that previous illness had weakened the Testator's mind. It is clear that he died suddenly, as the doctors had all along declared he would die, of disease of the heart. He was out walking in his garden, as usual, on the day of his death; he ate a hearty dinner; none of the persons in his service noticed any change in him; he was a little more irritable with them than usual, but that was all. It is impossible to attack the state of his faculties: there is no case to go into court with, so far.

"Can we declare that he acted under undue influence—or, in plainer terms, under the influence of Mrs. Lecount?

"There are serious difficulties, again, in the way of taking this course. We cannot assert, for example, that Mrs. Lecount has assumed a place in the will, which she has no fair claim to occupy. She has cunningly limited her own legacy, not only to what is fairly her due, but to what the late Mr. Michael Vanstone himself had the intention of leaving her. If I were examined on the subject, I should be compelled to acknowledge that I had heard him express this intention myself. It is only the truth to say, that I have heard him express it more than once. There is no point of attack in Mrs. Lecount's legacy; and there is no point of attack in your late husband's choice of an executor. He has made the wise choice, and the natural choice, of the oldest and trustiest friend he had in the world.

"One more consideration remains—the most important which I have yet approached, and therefore the consideration which I have reserved to the last. On the thirtieth of September, the Testator executes a will, leaving his widow sole executrix, with a legacy of eighty thousand pounds. On the third of November following, he expressly revokes this will, and leaves another in its stead, in which his widow is never once mentioned, and in which the whole residue of his estate, after payment of one comparatively trifling legacy, is left to a friend.

"It rests entirely with you to say, whether any valid reason can, or can not, be produced to explain such an extraordinary proceeding as this. If no reason can be assigned—and I know of none myself—I think we have a point here, which deserves our careful consideration; for it may be a point which is open to attack. Pray understand that I am now appealing to you solely as a lawyer, who is obliged to look all possible eventualities in the face. I have no wish to intrude on your private affairs; I have no wish to write a word which could be construed into any indirect reflection on yourself.

"If you tell me that so far as you know, your husband capriciously struck you out of his will, without assignable reason or motive for doing so, and without other obvious explanation of his conduct, than that he acted in this matter entirely under the influence of Mrs. Lecount—I will immediately take Counsel's opinion touching the propriety of disputing the will on this ground. If, on the other hand, you tell me that there are reasons (known to yourself though unknown to me) for not taking the course I propose, I will accept that intimation without troubling you, unless you wish it, to explain yourself further. In this latter event, I will write to you again—for I shall then have something more to say, which may greatly surprise you, on the subject of the Will.

"Faithfully yours,
"JOHN LOSCOMBE."

VII.

FROM MRS. NOEL VANSTONE TO MR. LOSCOMBE.

"Nov. 16th.
"DEAR SIR,
"Accept my best thanks for the kindness and consideration with which you have treated me—and let the anxieties under which I am now suffering plead my excuse, if I reply to your letter without ceremony, in the fewest possible words.

"I have my own reasons for not hesitating to answer your question in the negative. It is impossible for us to go to law, as you propose, on the subject of the Will.

"Believe me, dear Sir, yours gratefully,
"MAGDALEN VANSTONE."

VIII.

FROM MR. LOSCOMBE TO MRS. NOEL VANSTONE.

"Lincoln's Inn, November 17th.
"DEAR MADAM,
"I beg to acknowledge the receipt of your letter, answering my proposal in the negative, for reasons of your own. Under these circum-

stances—on which I offer no comment—I beg to perform my promise of again communicating with you, on the subject of your late husband's Will.

"Be so kind as to look at your copy of the document. You will find that the clause which devises the whole residue of your husband's estate to Admiral Bartram, ends in these terms: *to be by him applied to such uses as he may think fit.*

"Simple as they may seem to you, these are very remarkable words. In the first place, no practical lawyer would have used them, in drawing your husband's will. In the second place, they are utterly useless to serve any plain straightforward purpose. The legacy is left unconditionally to the admiral; and in the same breath he is told that he may do what he likes with it! The phrase points clearly to one of two conclusions. It has either dropped from the writer's pen in pure ignorance—or it has been carefully set where it appears, to serve the purpose of a snare. I am firmly persuaded that the latter explanation is the right one. The words are expressly intended to mislead some person—yourself in all probability— and the cunning which has put them to that use, is a cunning which (as constantly happens when uninstructed persons meddle with law) has over-reached itself. My thirty years' experience reads those words in a sense exactly opposite to the sense which they are intended to convey. I say that Admiral Bartram is *not* free to apply his legacy to such purposes as he may think fit—I believe he is privately controlled by a supplementary document in the shape of a Secret Trust.

"I can easily explain to you what I mean by a Secret Trust. It is usually contained in the form of a letter from a Testator to his Executors, privately informing them of testamentary intentions on his part, which he has not thought proper openly to acknowledge in his will. I leave you a hundred pounds; and I write a private letter, enjoining you, on taking the legacy, not to devote it to your own purposes, but to give it to some third person, whose name I have my own reasons for not mentioning in my will. That is a Secret Trust.

"If I am right in my own persuasion that such a document as I here describe is at this moment in Admiral Bartram's possession—a persuasion based, in the first instance, on the extraordinary words that I have quoted to you, and, in the second instance, on purely legal considerations with which it is needless to encumber my letter—if I am right in this opinion, the discovery of the Secret Trust would be, in all probability, a most important discovery to your interests. I will not trouble you with technical reasons, or with references to my experience in these matters, which only a professional man could understand. I will merely say that I don't give up your cause as utterly lost, until the conviction now impressed on my own mind is proved to be wrong.

"I can add no more, while this important question still remains involved in doubt; neither can I suggest any means of solving that doubt. If the existence of the Trust was proved, and if the nature of the stipulations contained in it was made known to me, I could then say positively what the legal chances were of your being able to set up a Case on the strength of it : and I could also tell you, whether I should or should not feel justified in personally undertaking that Case, under a private arrangement with yourself.

"As things are, I can make no arrangement, and offer no advice. I can only put you confidentially in possession of my private opinion; leaving you entirely free to draw your own inferences from it; and regretting that I cannot write more confidently and more definitely than I have written here. All that I could conscientiously say on this very difficult and delicate subject, I have said.

"Believe me, dear Madam, faithfully yours,

"JOHN LOSCOMBE.

"P.S.—I omitted one consideration in my last letter, which I may mention here, in order to show you that no point in connection with the case has escaped me. If it had been possible to show that Mr. Vanstone was *domiciled* in Scotland at the time of his death, we might have asserted your interests by means of the Scotch law—which does not allow a husband the power of absolutely disinheriting his wife. But it is impossible to assert that Mr. Vanstone was legally domiciled in Scotland. He came there as a visitor only; he occupied a furnished house for the season; and he never expressed, either by word or deed, the slightest intention of settling permanently in the North."*

IX.

FROM MRS. NOEL VANSTONE TO MR. LOSCOMBE.

"DEAR SIR,

"I have read your letter more than once, with the deepest interest and attention—and the oftener I read it, the more firmly I believe that there is really such a Letter as you mention in Admiral Bartram's hands.

"It is my interest that the discovery should be made—and I at once acknowledge to you, that I am determined to find the means of secretly and certainly making it. My resolution rests on other motives than the motives which you might naturally suppose would influence me. I only tell you this, in case you feel inclined to remonstrate. There is good reason for what I say, when I assure you that remonstrance will be useless.

"I ask for no assistance in this matter; I will trouble nobody for advice. You shall not be involved in any rash proceedings on my part. Whatever danger there may be, I will risk it. Whatever delays may happen, I will bear them patiently. I am lonely and friendless and sorely troubled in mind—but I am strong enough to win my way through worse trials than these. My spirits will rise again, and my time will come. If that Secret Trust is in Admiral Bartram's possession—when you next see me, you shall see me with it in my own hands.

"Yours gratefully,

"MAGDALEN VANSTONE."

THE SIXTH SCENE.

ST. JOHN'S WOOD.

CHAPTER I.

IT wanted little more than a fortnight to Christmas; but the weather showed no signs yet of the frost and snow, conventionally associated with the coming season. The atmosphere was unnaturally warm; and the old year was dying feebly in sapping rain and enervating mist.

Towards the close of the December afternoon, Magdalen sat alone in the lodging which she had occupied since her arrival in London. The fire burnt sluggishly in the narrow little grate; the view of the wet houses and soaking gardens opposite was darkening fast; and the bell of the suburban muffin-boy tinkled in the distance drearily. Sitting close over the fire, with a little money lying loose in her lap, Magdalen absently shifted the coins to and fro on the smooth surface of her dress; incessantly altering their positions towards each other, as if they were pieces of a "child's puzzle" which she was trying to put together. The dim firelight flaming up on her faintly from time to time, showed changes which would have told their own tale sadly to friends of former days. Her dress had become loose through the wasting of her figure; but she had not cared to alter it. The old restlessness in her movements, the old mobility in her expression, appeared no more. Her face passively maintained its haggard composure, its changeless unnatural calm. Mr. Pendril might have softened his hard sentence on her, if he had seen her now; and Mrs. Lecount, in the plenitude of her triumph, might have pitied her fallen enemy at last.

Hardly four months had passed, since the wedding-day at Aldborough; and the penalty for that day was paid already—paid in unavailing remorse, in hopeless isolation, in irremediable defeat! Let this be said for her; let the truth which has been told of the fault, be told of the expiation as well. Let it be recorded of her that she enjoyed no secret triumph on the day of her success. The horror of herself with which her own act had inspired her, had risen to its climax when the design of her marriage was achieved. She had never suffered in secret, as she suffered when the Combe-Raven money was left to her in her husband's will. She had never felt the means taken to accomplish her end so unutterably degrading to herself, as she felt them on the day when the end was reached. Out of that feeling had grown the remorse, which had hurried her to seek pardon and consolation in her sister's love. Never since it had first entered her heart, never since she had first felt it sacred to her at her father's grave, had the Purpose to which she had vowed herself, so nearly lost its hold on her as at this time. Never might Norah's influence have achieved such good, as on the day when that influence was lost—the day when the fatal words were overheard at Miss Garth's—the day when the fatal letter from Scotland told of Mrs. Lecount's revenge.

The harm was done ; the chance was gone. Time and Hope alike, had both passed her by.

Faintly and more faintly, the inner voices now pleaded with her to pause on the downward way. The discovery which had poisoned her heart with its first distrust of her sister ; the tidings which had followed it of her husband's death ; the sting of Mrs. Lecount's triumph, felt through all— had done their work. The remorse which had embittered her married life, was deadened now to a dull despair. It was too late to make the atonement of confession—too late to lay bare to the miserable husband, the deeper secrets that had once lurked in the heart of the miserable wife. Innocent of all thought of the hideous treachery which Mrs. Lecount had imputed to her—she was guilty of knowing how his health was broken when she married him ; guilty of knowing, when he left her the Combe-Raven money, that the accident of a moment, harmless to other men, might place his life in jeopardy, and effect her release. His death had told her this—had told her plainly, what she had shrunk, in his lifetime, from openly acknowledging to herself. From the dull torment of that reproach ; from the dreary wretchedness of doubting everybody, even to Norah herself ; from the bitter sense of her defeated schemes ; from the blank solitude of her friendless life—what refuge was left ? But one refuge now. She turned to the relentless Purpose which was hurrying her to her ruin, and cried to it with the daring of her despair—Drive me on !

For days and days together, she had bent her mind on the one object which occupied it, since she had received the lawyer's letter. For days and days together, she had toiled to meet the first necessity of her position—to find a means of discovering the Secret Trust. There was no hope, this time, of assistance from Captain Wragge. Long practice had made the old militiaman an adept in the art of vanishing. The plough of the moral agriculturist left no furrows—not a trace of him was to be found ! Mr.

Loscombe was too cautious to commit himself to an active course of any kind: he passively maintained his opinion, and left the rest to his client— he desired to know nothing, until the Trust was placed in his hands. Magdalen's interests were now in Magdalen's own sole care. Risk, or no risk, what she did next, she must do by herself.

The prospect had not daunted her. Alone, she had calculated the chances that might be tried. Alone, she was now determined to make the attempt.

"The time has come," she said to herself, as she sat over the fire. "I must sound Louisa first."

She collected the scattered coins in her lap, and placed them in a little heap on the table—then rose, and rang the bell. The landlady answered it.

"Is my servant down stairs?" inquired Magdalen.

"Yes, ma'am. She is having her tea."

"When she has done, say I want her up here. Wait a moment. You will find your money on the table—the money I owe you for last week. Can you find it? or would you like to have a candle?"

"It's rather dark, ma'am."

Magdalen lit a candle. "What notice must I give you," she asked, as she put the candle on the table, "before I leave?"

"A week is the usual notice, ma'am. I hope you have no objection to make to the house?"

"None whatever. I only ask the question, because I may be obliged to leave these lodgings rather sooner than I anticipated. Is the money right?"

"Quite right, ma'am. Here is your receipt."

"Thank you. Don't forget to send Louisa to me, as soon as she has done her tea."

The landlady withdrew. As soon as she was alone again, Magdalen extinguished the candle, and drew an empty chair close to her own chair, on the hearth. This done, she resumed her former place, and waited until Louisa appeared. There was doubt in her face, as she sat looking mechanically into the fire. "A poor chance," she thought to herself; "but, poor as it is, a chance that I must try."

In ten minutes more, Louisa's meek knock was softly audible outside. She was surprised on entering the room, to find no other light in it than the light of the fire.

"Will you have the candles, ma'am?" she inquired respectfully.

"We will have candles if you wish for them yourself," replied Magdalen; "not otherwise. I have something to say to you. When I have said it, you shall decide whether we sit together in the dark or in the light."

Louisa waited near the door, and listened to those strange words in silent astonishment.

"Come here," said Magdalen, pointing to the empty chair; "come here and sit down."

Louisa advanced, and timidly removed the chair from its position at her mistress's side. Magdalen instantly drew it back again. "No!" she said. "Come closer—come close by me." After a moment's hesitation, Louisa obeyed.

"I ask you to sit near me," pursued Magdalen, "because I wish to speak to you on equal terms. Whatever distinctions there might once have been between us, are now at an end. I am a lonely woman thrown helpless on my own resources, without rank or place in the world. I may or may not keep you as my friend. As mistress and maid, the connection between us must come to an end."

"Oh, ma'am, don't, don't say that!" pleaded Louisa, faintly.

Magdalen sorrowfully and steadily went on.

"When you first came to me," she resumed, "I thought I should not like you. I have learnt to like you—I have learnt to be grateful to you. From first to last you have been faithful and good to me. The least I can do in return, is not to stand in the way of your future prospects."

"Don't send me away, ma'am!" said Louisa, imploringly. "If you can only help me with a little money now and then, I'll wait for my wages—I will indeed."

Magdalen took her hand, and went on, as sorrowfully and as steadily as before.

"My future life is all darkness, all uncertainty," she said. "The next step I take may lead me to my prosperity or may lead me to my ruin. Can I ask you to share such a prospect as this? If your future was as uncertain as mine is—if you, too, were a friendless woman thrown on the world—my conscience might be easy in letting you cast your lot with mine. I might accept your attachment, for I might feel I was not wronging you. How can I feel this in your case? You have a future to look to. You are an excellent servant; you can get another place—a far better place than mine. You can refer to me; and if the character I give is not considered sufficient, you can refer to the mistress you served before me——"

At the instant when that reference to the girl's last employer escaped Magdalen's lips, Louisa snatched her hand away, and started up affrightedly from her chair. There was a moment's silence. Both mistress and maid were equally taken by surprise.

Magdalen was the first to recover herself.

"Is it getting too dark?" she asked, significantly. "Are you going to light the candles, after all?"

Louisa drew back into the dimmest corner of the room.

"You suspect me, ma'am!" she answered out of the darkness, in a breathless whisper. "Who has told you? How did you find out——?" She stopped, and burst into tears. "I deserve your suspicion," she said, struggling to compose herself. "I can't deny it to *you*. You have treated me so kindly; you have made me so fond of you! Forgive me, Mrs. Vanstone—I am a wretch; I have deceived you."

"Come here, and sit down by me again," said Magdalen. "Come—or I will get up myself, and bring you back."

Louisa slowly returned to her place. Dim as the firelight was, she seemed to fear it. She held her handkerchief over her face, and shrank from her mistress as she seated herself again in the chair.

"You are wrong in thinking that any one has betrayed you to me," said Magdalen. "All that I know of you is, what your own looks and ways have told me. You have had some secret trouble weighing on your mind ever since you have been in my service. I confess I have spoken with the wish to find out more of you and your past life than I have found out yet— not because I am curious, but because I have my secret troubles, too. Are you an unhappy woman, like me? If you are, I will take you into my confidence. If you have nothing to tell me—if you choose to keep your secret—I don't blame you; I only say, Let us part. I won't ask how you have deceived me. I will only remember that you have been an honest and faithful and competent servant, while I have employed you—and I will say as much in your favour to any new mistress you like to send to me."

She waited for the reply. For a moment, and only for a moment, Louisa hesitated. The girl's nature was weak, but not depraved. She was honestly attached to her mistress; and she spoke with a courage which Magdalen had not expected from her.

"If you send me away, ma'am," she said, "I won't take my character from you till I have told you the truth; I won't return your kindness by deceiving you a second time. Did my master ever tell you how he engaged me?"

"No. I never asked him, and he never told me."

"He engaged me, ma'am, with a written character——"

"Yes?"

"The character was a false one."

Magdalen drew back in amazement. The confession she heard, was not the confession she had anticipated.

"Did your mistress refuse to give you a character?" she asked. "Why?"

Louisa dropped on her knees, and hid her face in her mistress's lap. "Don't ask me!" she said. "I'm a miserable, degraded creature; I'm not fit to be in the same room with you!"

Magdalen bent over her, and whispered a question in her ear. Louisa whispered back the one sad word of reply.

"Has he deserted you?" asked Magdalen, after waiting a moment, and thinking first.

"No."

" Do you love him ?"

" Dearly."

The remembrance of her own loveless marriage stung Magdalen to the quick.

" For God's sake, don't kneel to *me*!" she cried, passionately. " If there is a degraded woman in this room, I am the woman—not you !"

She raised the girl by main force from her knees, and put her back in the chair. They both waited a little in silence. Keeping her hand on Louisa's shoulder, Magdalen seated herself again, and looked with unutterable bitterness of sorrow into the dying fire. " Oh," she thought, " what happy women there are in the world ! Wives who love their husbands ! Mothers who are not ashamed to own their children ! Are you quieter ?" she asked, gently addressing Louisa once more. " Can you answer me, if I ask you something else ? Where is the child ?"

" The child is out at nurse."

" Does the father help to support it ?"

" He does all he can, ma'am."

" What is he ? Is he in service ? Is he in a trade ?"

" His father is a master-carpenter—he works in his father's yard."

" If he has got work, why has he not married you ?"

" It is his father's fault, ma'am—not his. His father has no pity on us. He would be turned out of house and home, if he married me."

" Can he get no work elsewhere ?"

" It's hard to get good work in London, ma'am. There are so many in London—they take the bread out of each other's mouths. If we had only had the money to emigrate, he would have married me long since."

" Would he marry you, if you had the money now ?"

" I am sure he would, ma'am. He could get plenty of work in Australia, and double and treble the wages he gets here. He is trying hard, and I am trying hard, to save a little towards it—I put by all I can spare from my child. But it is so little ! If we live for years to come, there seems no hope for us. I know I have done wrong every way—I know I don't deserve to be happy. But how could I let my child suffer ?—I was obliged to go to service. My mistress was hard on me, and my health broke down in trying to live by my needle. I would never have deceived anybody by a false character, if there had been another chance for me. I was alone and helpless, ma'am ; and I can only ask you to forgive me."

" Ask better women than I am," said Magdalen, sadly. " I am only fit to feel for you ; and I do feel for you with all my heart. In your place I should have gone into service with a false character too. Say no more of the past—you don't know how you hurt me in speaking of it. Talk of the future. I think I can help you—and do you no harm. I think you can help me, and do me the greatest of all services, in return. Wait, and you shall hear what I mean. Suppose you were married—how much would it cost for you and your husband to emigrate?"

Louisa mentioned the cost of a steerage passage to Australia for a man and his wife. She spoke in low, hopeless tones. Moderate as the sum was, it looked like unattainable wealth in her eyes.

Magdalen started in her chair, and took the girl's hand once more.

"Louisa!" she said, earnestly. "If I gave you the money, what would you do for me in return?"

The proposal seemed to strike Louisa speechless with astonishment. She trembled violently, and said nothing. Magdalen repeated her words.

"Oh, ma'am, do you mean it?" said the girl. "Do you really mean it?"

"Yes," replied Magdalen; "I really mean it. What would you do for me in return?"

"Do?" repeated Louisa. "Oh, what is there I would *not* do!" She tried to kiss her mistress's hand; but Magdalen would not permit it. She resolutely, almost roughly, drew her hand away.

"I am laying you under no obligation," she said. "We are serving each other—that is all. Sit quiet, and let me think."

For the next ten minutes there was silence in the room. At the end of that time, Magdalen took out her watch, and held it close to the grate. There was just firelight enough to show her the hour. It was close on six o'clock.

"Are you composed enough to go down-stairs, and deliver a message?" she asked, rising from her chair as she spoke to Louisa again. "It is a very simple message—it is only to tell the boy that I want a cab, as soon as he can get me one. I must go out immediately. You shall know why, later in the evening. I have much more to say to you—but there is no time to say it now. When I am gone, bring your work up here, and wait for my return. I shall be back before bed-time."

Without another word of explanation, she hurriedly lit a candle, and withdrew into the bedroom to put on her bonnet and shawl.

CHAPTER II.

BETWEEN nine and ten o'clock the same evening, Louisa, waiting anxiously, heard the long-expected knock at the house door. She ran down-stairs at once, and let her mistress in.

Magdalen's face was flushed. She showed far more agitation on returning to the house than she had shown on leaving it. "Keep your place at the table," she said to Louisa, impatiently; "but lay aside your work. I want you to attend carefully to what I am going to say."

Louisa obeyed. Magdalen seated herself at the opposite side of the table, and moved the candles, so as to obtain a clear and uninterrupted view of her servant's face.

"Have you noticed a respectable elderly woman," she began abruptly, "who has been here once or twice, in the last fortnight, to pay me a visit?"

"Yes, ma'am : I think I let her in, the second time she came. An elderly person, named Mrs. Attwood?"

"That is the person I mean. Mrs. Attwood is Mr. Loscombe's house-keeper; not the housekeeper at his private residence, but the housekeeper at his offices in Lincoln's Inn. I promised to go and drink tea with her, some evening this week—and I have been to-night. It is strange of me, is it not, to be on these familiar terms with a woman in Mrs. Attwood's situation?"

Louisa made no answer in words. Her face spoke for her : she could hardly avoid thinking it strange.

"I had a motive for making friends with Mrs. Attwood," Magdalen went on. "She is a widow, with a large family of daughters. Her daughters are all in service. One of them is an under-housemaid, in the service of Admiral Bartram, at St. Crux-in-the-Marsh. I found that out from Mrs. Attwood's master : and as soon as I arrived at the discovery, I privately determined to make Mrs. Attwood's acquaintance. Stranger still, is it not?"

Louisa began to look a little uneasy. Her mistress's manner was at variance with her mistress's words—it was plainly suggestive of something startling to come.

"What attraction Mrs. Attwood finds in my society," Magdalen continued, "I cannot presume to say. I can only tell you, she has seen better days; she is an educated person; and she may like my society on that account. At any rate, she has readily met my advances towards her. What attraction I find in this good woman, on my side, is soon told. I have a great curiosity—an unaccountable curiosity, you will think—about the present course of household affairs at St. Crux-in-the-Marsh. Mrs. Attwood's daughter is a good girl, and constantly writes to her mother. Her mother is proud of the letters and proud of the girl, and is ready enough to talk about her daughter, and her daughter's place. That is Mrs. Attwood's attraction to *me*. You understand, so far?"

Yes—Louisa understood. Magdalen went on.

"Thanks to Mrs. Attwood, and Mrs. Attwood's daughter," she said, "I know some curious particulars already of the household at St. Crux. Servants' tongues and servants' letters—as I need not tell *you*—are oftener occupied with their masters and mistresses, than their masters and mistresses suppose. The only mistress at St. Crux is the housekeeper. But there is a master—Admiral Bartram. He appears to be a strange old man, whose whims and fancies amuse his servants as well as his friends. One of his fancies (the only one we need trouble ourselves to notice) is, that he had men enough about him, when he was living at sea, and that now he is living on shore, he will be waited on by women-servants alone. The one man in the house, is an old sailor, who has been all his life with his master—he is a kind of pensioner at St. Crux, and has little or nothing to do with the house-work. The other servants, in-doors, are all women; and instead of a footman to wait on him at dinner, the admiral has a parlour-maid. The parlour-maid now at St. Crux, is engaged to be married; and, as soon as her master can suit himself, she is going away. These discoveries I made some days since. But when I saw Mrs. Attwood to-night, she had received another letter from her daughter, in the interval; and that letter has helped me to find out something more. The housekeeper is at her wits' end to find a new servant. Her master insists on youth and good looks—he leaves everything else to the housekeeper—but he will have that. All the inquiries made in the neighbourhood have failed to produce the sort of parlour-maid whom the admiral wants. If nothing can be done in the next fortnight or three weeks, the housekeeper will advertise in the Times; and will come to London herself to see the applicants, and to make strict personal inquiry into their characters."

Louisa looked at her mistress, more attentively than ever. The expression of perplexity left her face, and a shade of disappointment appeared there in its stead.

"Bear in mind what I have said," pursued Magdalen; "and wait a minute more, while I ask you some questions. Don't think you understand me yet—I can assure you, you don't understand me. Have you always lived in service as lady's maid?"

"No, ma'am."

"Have you ever lived as parlour-maid?"

"Only in one place, ma'am—and not for long there."

"I suppose you lived long enough to learn your duties?"

"Yes, ma'am."

"What were your duties, besides waiting at table?"

"I had to show visitors in."

"Yes—and what else?"

"I had the plate, and the glass to look after—and the table-linen was all under my care. I had to answer all the bells, except in the bedrooms. There were other little odds and ends sometimes to do——"

"But your regular duties were the duties you have just mentioned?"

"Yes, ma'am."

"How long ago is it, since you lived in service as parlour-maid?"

"A little better than two years, ma'am."

"I suppose you have not forgotten how to wait at table, and clean plate, and the rest of it, in that time?"

At this question, Louisa's attention, which had been wandering more and more during the progress of Magdalen's inquiries, wandered away altogether. Her gathering anxieties got the better of her discretion, and even of her timidity. Instead of answering her mistress, she suddenly and confusedly ventured on a question of her own.

"I beg your pardon, ma'am," she said. "Did you mean me to offer for the parlour-maid's place at St. Crux?"

"You?" replied Magdalen. "Certainly not! Have you forgotten what I said to you in this room, before I went out? I mean you to be married, and to go to Australia with your husband and your child. You have not waited as I told you, to hear me explain myself. You have drawn your own conclusions; and you have drawn them wrong. I asked a question just now, which you have not answered—I asked if you had forgotten your parlour-maid's duties?"

"Oh no, ma'am!" Louisa had replied rather unwillingly, thus far. She answered readily and confidently, now.

"Could you teach the duties to another servant?" asked Magdalen.

"Yes, ma'am—easily, if she was quick and attentive."

"Could you teach the duties to Me?"

Louisa started and changed colour. "You, ma'am!" she exclaimed, half in incredulity, half in alarm.

"Yes," said Magdalen. "Could you qualify *me* to take the parlour-maid's place at St. Crux?"

Plain as those words were, the bewilderment which they produced in Louisa's mind, seemed to render her incapable of comprehending her mistress's proposal. "You, ma'am!" she repeated, vacantly.

"I shall perhaps help you to understand this extraordinary project of mine," said Magdalen, "if I tell you plainly what the object of it is. Do you remember what I said to you about Mr. Vanstone's will, when you came here from Scotland to join me?"

"Yes, ma'am. You told me you had been left out of the will altogether. I'm sure my fellow-servant would never have been one of the witnesses, if she had known——"

"Never mind that now. I don't blame your fellow-servant—I blame nobody but Mrs. Lecount. Let me go on with what I was saying. It is not at all certain that Mrs. Lecount can do me the mischief which Mrs. Lecount intended. There is a chance that my lawyer, Mr. Loscombe, may be able to gain me what is fairly my due, in spite of the will. The chance turns on my discovering a letter, which Mr. Loscombe believes, and which I believe, to be kept privately in Admiral Bartram's possession. I have not the least hope of getting at that letter, if I make the attempt in my own person. Mrs. Lecount has poisoned the admiral's mind against me, and Mr. Vanstone has given him a secret to keep from me. If I wrote to him, he would not answer my letter. If I went to his house, the door would be closed in my face. I must find my way into St. Crux as a stranger—I must be in a position to look about the house, unsuspected—I must be there with plenty of time on my hands. All the circumstances are in my favour, if I am received into the house as a servant; and as a servant I mean to go."

"But you are a lady, ma'am," objected Louisa, in the greatest perplexity. "The servants at St. Crux would find you out."

"I am not at all afraid of their finding me out," said Magdalen. "I know how to disguise myself in other people's characters more cleverly than you suppose. Leave me to face the chances of discovery—that is my risk. Let us talk of nothing now, but what concerns *you*. Don't decide yet whether you will, or will not, give me the help I want. Wait, and hear first what the help is. You are quick and clever at your needle. Can you make me the sort of gown which it is proper for a servant to wear—and can you alter one of my best silk dresses, so as to make it fit yourself—in a week's time?"

"I think I could get them done in a week, ma'am. But why am I to wear——?"

"Wait a little, and you will see. I shall give the landlady her week's notice to-morrow. In the interval, while you are making the dresses, I can be learning the parlour-maid's duties. When the house-servant here has brought up the dinner, and when you and I are alone in the room—instead of your waiting on me, as usual, I will wait on you. (I am quite serious; don't interrupt me!) Whatever I can learn besides, without hindering you, I will practise carefully at every opportunity. When the week is over, and the dresses are done, we will leave this place, and go into other lodgings—you as the mistress; and I as the maid."

"I should be found out, ma'am," interposed Louisa, trembling at the prospect before her. "I am not a lady."

"And I am," said Magdalen, bitterly. "Shall I tell you what a lady is? A lady is a woman who wears a silk gown, and has a sense of her own importance. I shall put the gown on your back, and the sense in your head. You speak good English—you are naturally quiet, and self-restrained—if you can only conquer your timidity, I have not the least fear of you. There will be time enough, in the new lodging, for you to practise your character, and for me to practise mine. There will be time enough to make some more dresses—another gown for me, and your wedding-dress (which I mean to give you) for yourself. I shall have the newspaper sent every day. When the advertisement appears I shall answer it—in any name I can take on the spur of the moment; in your name, if you like to lend it to me—and when the housekeeper asks me for my character I shall refer her to you. She will see you in the position of mistress, and me in

the position of maid—no suspicion can possibly enter her mind, unless you
put it there. If you only have the courage to follow my instructions, and
to say what I shall tell you to say, the interview will be over in ten
minutes."

"You frighten me, ma'am," said Louisa, still trembling. "You take
my breath away with surprise. Courage! Where shall I find courage?"

"Where I keep it for you," said Magdalen—"in the passage-money to
Australia. Look at the new prospect which gives you a husband, and
restores you to your child— and you will find your courage there."

Louisa's sad face brightened; Louisa's faint heart beat quick. A spark
of her mistress's spirit flew up into her eyes, as she thought of the golden
future.

"If you accept my proposal," pursued Magdalen, "you can be asked in
church at once, if you like. I promise you the money, on the day when the
advertisement appears in the newspaper. The risk of the housekeeper's
rejecting me, is my risk—not yours. My good looks are sadly gone off, I
know. But I think I can still hold my place against the other servants—I
think I can still *look* the parlour-maid whom Admiral Bartram wants.
There is nothing for you to fear in this matter; I should not have mentioned it if there had been. The only danger, is the danger of my being
discovered at St. Crux—and that falls entirely on me. By the time I am
in the admiral's house, you will be married, and the ship will be taking
you to your new life."

Louisa's face, now brightening with hope, now clouding again with fear,
showed plain signs of the struggle which it cost her to decide. She tried
to gain time; she attempted confusedly to speak a few words of gratitude
—but her mistress silenced her.

"You owe me no thanks," said Magdalen. "I tell you again, we are
only helping each other. I have very little money, but it is enough for
your purpose, and I give it you freely. I have led a wretched life; I have
made others wretched about me. I can't even make *you* happy, except by
tempting you to a new deceit. There! there! it's not your fault. Worse
women than you are will help me, if you refuse. Decide as you like—but
don't be afraid of taking the money. If I succeed, I shall not want it. If
I fail——"

She stopped; rose abruptly from her chair; and hid her face from
Louisa by walking away to the fireplace.

"If I fail," she resumed, warming her foot carelessly at the fender, "all
the money in the world will be of no use to me. Never mind why—never
mind Me—think of yourself. I won't take advantage of the confession you
have made to me; I won't influence you against your will. Do as you
yourself think best. But remember one thing—my mind is made up: nothing you can say or do will change it."

Her sudden removal from the table, the altered tones of her voice as she spoke the last words, appeared to renew Louisa's hesitation. She clasped her hands together in her lap, and wrung them hard. "This has come on me very suddenly, ma'am," said the girl. "I am sorely tempted to say, Yes. And yet, I'm almost afraid——"

"Take the night to consider it," interposed Magdalen, keeping her face persistently turned towards the fire; "and tell me what you have decided to do, when you come into my room to-morrow morning. I shall want no help to-night—I can undress myself. You are not so strong as I am; you are tired, I dare say. Don't sit up on my account. Good night, Louisa, and pleasant dreams!"

Her voice sank lower and lower, as she spoke those kind words. She sighed heavily; and, leaning her arm on the mantelpiece, laid her head on it with a reckless weariness miserable to see. Louisa had not left the room, as she supposed—Louisa came softly to her side, and kissed her hand. Magdalen started; but she made no attempt, this time, to draw her hand away. The sense of her own horrible isolation subdued her, at the touch of the servant's lips. Her proud heart melted; her eyes filled with burning tears. "Don't distress me!" she said, faintly. "The time for kindness has gone by; it only overpowers me now. Good-night!"

When the morning came, the affirmative answer which Magdalen had anticipated, was the answer given.

On that day, the landlady received her week's notice to quit; and Louisa's needle flew fast through the stitches of the parlour-maid's dress.

THE END OF THE SIXTH SCENE.

BETWEEN THE SCENES.

PROGRESS OF THE STORY THROUGH THE POST.

———◆———

I.

From Miss Garth to Mr. Pendril.

"Westmoreland House, Jan. 3rd, 1848.

" Dear Mr Pendril,

"I write, as you kindly requested, to report how Norah is going on, and to tell you what changes I see for the better in the state of her mind on the subject of her sister.

"I cannot say that she is becoming resigned to Magdalen's continued silence—I know her faithful nature too well to say it. I can only tell you that she is beginning to find relief from the heavy pressure of sorrow and suspense, in new thoughts and new hopes. I doubt if she has yet realized this in her own mind; but I see the result, although she is not conscious of it herself. I see her heart opening to the consolation of another interest and another love. She has not said a word to me on the subject—nor have I said a word to her. But as certainly as I know that Mr. George Bartram's visits have lately grown more and more frequent to the family at Portland Place—so certainly I can assure you that Norah is finding a relief under her suspense, which is not of my bringing, and a hope in the future, which I have not taught her to feel.

"It is needless for me to say that I tell you this, in the strictest confidence. God knows whether the happy prospect which seems to me to be just dawning, will grow brighter or not, as time goes on. The oftener I see Mr. George Bartram—and he has called on me more than once—the stronger my liking for him grows. To my poor judgment he seems to be a gentleman, in the highest and truest sense of the word. If I could live to see Norah his wife—I should almost feel that I had lived long enough. But who can discern the future? We have suffered so much that I am afraid to hope.

"Have you heard anything of Magdalen? I don't know why or how it is—but since I have known of her husband's death, my old tenderness for her seems to cling to me more obstinately than ever.

"Always yours truly,

" Harriet Garth."

II.

FROM MR. PENDRIL TO MISS GARTH.

"Serle Street, Jan. 4th, 1848.

"DEAR MISS GARTH,

"Of Mrs. Noel Vanstone herself I have heard nothing. But I have learnt, since I saw you, that the report of the position in which she is left by the death of her husband may be depended upon as the truth. No legacy of any kind is bequeathed to her. Her name is not once mentioned in her husband's will.

"Knowing what we know, it is not to be concealed that this circumstance threatens us with more embarrassment, and perhaps with more distress. Mrs. Noel Vanstone is not the woman to submit, without a desperate resistance, to the total overthrow of all her schemes and all her hopes. The mere fact that nothing whatever has been heard of her since her husband's death, is suggestive to my mind of serious mischief to come. In her situation, and with her temper, the quieter she is now, the more inveterately I, for one, distrust her in the future. It is impossible to say to what violent measures her present extremity may not drive her. It is impossible to feel sure, that she may not be the cause of some public scandal, this time, which may affect her innocent sister as well as herself.

"I know you will not misinterpret the motive which has led me to write these lines; I know you will not think that I am inconsiderate enough to cause you unnecessary alarm. My sincere anxiety to see that happy prospect realized to which your letter alludes, has caused me to write far less reservedly than I might otherwise have written. I strongly urge you to use your influence, on every occasion when you can fairly exert it, to strengthen that growing attachment, and to place it beyond the reach of any coming disasters, while you have the opportunity of doing so. When I tell you that the fortune of which Mrs. Noel Vanstone has been deprived, is entirely bequeathed to Admiral Bartram—and when I add that Mr. George Bartram is generally understood to be his uncle's heir —you will, I think, acknowledge that I am not warning you without a cause.

"Yours most truly,
"WILLIAM PENDRIL."

III.

FROM ADMIRAL BARTRAM TO MRS. DRAKE (HOUSEKEEPER AT ST. CRUX).

"St. Crux, Jan. 10th, 1848.

"MRS. DRAKE,

"I have received your letter from London, stating that you have found me a new parlour-maid at last, and that the girl is ready to return with you to St. Crux, when your other errands in town allow you to come back.

"This arrangement must be altered immediately, for a reason which I am heartily sorry to have to write.

"The illness of my niece, Mrs. Girdlestone—which appeared to be so slight as to alarm none of us, doctors included—has ended fatally. I received this morning the shocking news of her death. Her husband is said to be quite frantic with grief. Mr. George has already gone to his brother-in-law's, to superintend the last melancholy duties—and I must follow him, before the funeral takes place. We propose to take Mr. Girdlestone away afterwards, and to try the effect on him of change of place and new scenes. Under these sad circumstances, I may be absent from St. Crux a month or six weeks at least—the house will be shut up—and the new servant will not be wanted until my return.

"You will therefore tell the girl, on receiving this letter, that a death in the family has caused a temporary change in our arrangements. If she is willing to wait, you may safely engage her to come here in six weeks' time—I shall be back then, if Mr. George is not. If she refuses, pay her what compensation is right, and so have done with her.

"Yours,

"ARTHUR BARTRAM."

_____

IV.

FROM MRS. DRAKE TO ADMIRAL BARTRAM.

"Jan. 11th.

"HONOURED SIR,

"I hope to get my errands done, and to return to St. Crux to-morrow—but write to save you anxiety, in case of delay.

"The young woman whom I have engaged (Louisa by name) is willing to wait your time; and her present mistress, taking an interest in her welfare, will provide for her during the interval. She understands that she is to enter on her new service in six weeks from the present date—namely, on the twenty-fifth of February next.

"Begging you will accept my respectful sympathy under the sad bereavement which has befallen the family,

'I remain, Honoured Sir, your humble servant,

"SOPHIA DRAKE."

THE SEVENTH SCENE.

ST. CRUX-IN-THE-MARSH.

———•———

CHAPTER I.

" THIS is where you are to sleep. Put yourself tidy; and then come down again to my room. The admiral has returned, and you will have to begin by waiting on him at dinner to-day."

With those words Mrs. Drake, the housekeeper, closed the door; and the new parlour-maid was left alone in her bed-chamber at St. Crux.

That day was the eventful twenty-fifth of February. In barely four months from the time when Mrs. Lecount had placed her master's private Instructions in his Executor's hands, the one combination of circumstances against which it had been her first and foremost object to provide, was exactly the combination which had now taken place. Mr. Noel Vanstone's widow, and Admiral Bartram's Secret Trust were together in the same house.

Thus far, events had declared themselves, without an exception, in Magdalen's favour. Thus far, the path which had led her to St. Crux, had been a path without an obstacle. Louisa—whose name she had now taken—had sailed three days since for Australia with her husband and her child: she was the only living creature whom Magdalen had trusted with her secret, and she was by this time out of sight of the English land. The girl had been careful, reliable, and faithfully devoted to her mistress's interests to the last. She had passed the ordeal of her interview with the housekeeper, and had forgotten none of the instructions by which she had been prepared to meet it. She had herself proposed to turn the six weeks' delay, caused by the death in the admiral's family, to good account, by continuing the all-important practice of those domestic lessons, on the perfect acquirement of which her mistress's daring stratagem depended for its success. Thanks to the time thus gained, when Louisa's marriage was over, and the day of parting had come, Magdalen had learnt and mastered, in the nicest detail, everything that her former servant could teach her. On the day when she passed the doors of St. Crux, she entered on her desperate venture, strong in the ready presence of mind under emergencies which her later life had taught her—stronger still, in the trained capacity that she possessed for the assumption of a character not her own—strongest of all, in her two months' daily familiarity with the practical duties of the position which she had undertaken to fill.

As soon as Mrs. Drake's departure had left her alone, she unpacked her box, and dressed herself for the evening.

She put on a lavender-coloured stuff gown—half-mourning for Mrs. Girdlestone; ordered for all the servants, under the admiral's instructions—a white muslin apron, and a neat white cap and collar, with ribbons to match the gown. In this servant's costume—in the plain gown fastening high round her neck, in the neat little white cap at the back of her head—in this simple dress, to the eyes of all men, not linendrapers, at once the most modest and the most alluring that a woman can wear, the sad changes which mental suffering had wrought in her beauty almost disappeared from view. In the evening costume of a lady; with her bosom uncovered, with her figure armed, rather than dressed, in unpliable silk—the admiral might have passed her by without notice in his own drawing-room. In the evening costume of a servant, no admirer of beauty could have looked at her once, and not have turned again to look at her for the second time.

Descending the stairs, on her way to the housekeeper's room, she passed by the entrances to two long stone corridors, with rows of doors opening on them; one corridor situated on the second, and one on the first floor of the house. "Many rooms!" she thought, as she looked at the doors. "Weary work, searching here for what I have come to find!"

On reaching the ground floor she was met by a weather-beaten old man, who stopped and stared at her with an appearance of great interest. He was the same old man whom Captain Wragge had seen, in the back-yard at St. Crux, at work on the model of a ship. All round the neighbourhood he was known, far and wide, as "the admiral's coxswain."* His name was Mazey. Sixty years had written their story of hard work at sea, and hard drinking on shore, on the veteran's grim and wrinkled face. Sixty years had proved his fidelity, and had brought his battered old carcase, at the end of the voyage, into port in his master's house.

Seeing no one else of whom she could inquire, Magdalen requested the old man to show her the way that led to the housekeeper's room.

"I'll show you, my dear," said old Mazey, speaking in the high and hollow voice peculiar to the deaf. "You're the new maid—eh? And a fine-grown girl, too! His honour, the admiral, likes a parlour-maid with a clean run fore and aft. You'll do, my dear—you'll do."

"You must not mind what Mr. Mazey says to you," remarked the housekeeper, opening her door as the old sailor expressed his approval of Magdalen in these terms. "He is privileged to talk as he pleases; and he is very tiresome and slovenly in his habits—but he means no harm."

With that apology for the veteran, Mrs. Drake led Magdalen first to the pantry, and next to the linen-room; installing her, with all due formality, in her own domestic dominions. This ceremony completed, the new parlour-maid was taken up-stairs, and was shown the dining-room, which opened out of the corridor on the first floor. Here, she was directed to lay the cloth, and to prepare the table for one person only—Mr. George Bartram not having returned with his uncle to St. Crux. Mrs. Drake's sharp eyes watched Magdalen attentively, as she performed this introductory duty; and Mrs. Drake's private convictions, when the table was spread, forced her to acknowledge, so far, that the new servant thoroughly understood her work.

An hour later, the soup-tureen was placed on the table; and Magdalen stood alone behind the admiral's empty chair, waiting her master's first inspection of her, when he entered the dining-room.

A large bell rang in the lower regions—quick, shambling footsteps pattered on the stone corridor outside—the door opened suddenly—and a tall lean yellow old man, sharp as to his eyes, shrewd as to his lips, fussily restless as to all his movements, entered the room, with two huge Labrador dogs at his heels, and took his seat in a violent hurry. The dogs followed him, and placed themselves, with the utmost gravity and composure, one on each side of his chair. This was Admiral Bartram—and these were the companions of his solitary meal.

"Ay! ay! ay! here's the new parlour-maid to be sure!" he began, looking sharply, but not at all unkindly, at Magdalen. "What's your name, my good girl? Louisa, is it? I shall call you Lucy, if you don't mind. ᛫ Take off the cover, my dear—I'm a minute or two late to-day. Don't be unpunctual to-morrow on that account; I am as regular as clock-work generally. How are you after your journey? Did my spring-cart bump you about much in bringing you from the station? Capital soup this—hot as fire—reminds me of the soup we used to have in the West Indies in the year Three. Have you got your half-mourning on? Stand there, and let me see. Ah, yes, very neat, and nice, and tidy. Poor Mrs. Girdlestone! Oh, dear, dear, dear, poor Mrs. Girdlestone! You're not afraid of dogs are you, Lucy? Eh? What? You like dogs? That's right! Always be kind to dumb animals. These two dogs dine with me every day, except when there's company. The dog with the black nose is Brutus; and the dog with the white nose is Cassius. Did you ever hear who Brutus and Cassius*were? Ancient Romans? That's right—good girl. Mind your book and your needle; and we'll get you a good husband one of these days. Take away the soup, my dear, take away the soup!"

This was the man whose secret it was now the one interest of Magdalen's life to surprise! This was the man whose name had supplanted hers in Noel Vanstone's will!

The fish and the roast meat followed; and the admiral's talk rambled on

—now in soliloquy, now addressed to the parlour-maid, and now directed to the dogs — as familiarly and as disconnectedly as ever. Magdalen observed with some surprise, that the companions of the admiral's dinner had, thus far, received no scraps from their master's plate. The two magnificent brutes sat squatted on their haunches, with their great heads over the table, watching the progress of the meal with the profoundest attention, but apparently expecting no share in it. The roast meat was removed, the admiral's plate was changed, and Magdalen took the silver covers off the two made-dishes on either side of the table. As she handed the first of the savoury dishes to her master, the dogs suddenly exhibited a breathless personal interest in the proceedings. Brutus gluttonously watered at the mouth; and the tongue of Cassius, protruding in unutterable expectation, smoked again between his enormous jaws.

The admiral helped himself liberally from the dish; sent Magdalen to the side-table to get him some bread; and, when he thought her eye was off him, furtively tumbled the whole contents of his plate into Brutus's mouth. Cassius whined faintly as his fortunate comrade swallowed the savoury mess at a gulp. "Hush! you fool," whispered the admiral. "Your turn next!"

Magdalen presented the second dish. Once more, the old gentleman helped himself largely—once more he sent her away to the side-table— once more, he tumbled the entire contents of the plate down the dog's throat; selecting Cassius, this time, as became a considerate master and an impartial man. When the next course followed—consisting of a plain pudding and an unwholesome "cream"—Magdalen's suspicion of the function of the dogs at the dinner-table was confirmed. While the master took the simple pudding, the dogs swallowed the elaborate cream. The admiral was plainly afraid of offending his cook on the one hand, and of offending his digestion on the other—and Brutus and Cassius were the two trained accomplices who regularly helped him every day off the horns of his dilemma. "Very good! very good!" said the old gentleman, with the most transparent duplicity. "Tell the cook, my dear, a capital cream!"

Having placed the wine and dessert on the table, Magdalen was about to withdraw. Before she could leave the room, her master called her back. "Stop, stop!" said the admiral. "You don't know the ways of the house yet, Lucy. Put another wine-glass here, at my right hand—the largest you can find, my dear. I've got a third dog, who comes in at dessert—a drunken old sea-dog who has followed my fortunes afloat and ashore, for fifty years, and more. Yes, yes; that's the sort of glass we want. You're a good girl—you're a neat, handy girl. Steady, my dear! there's nothing to be frightened at!"

A sudden thump on the outside of the door, followed by one mighty bark from each of the dogs, had made Magdalen start. "Come in!"

shouted the admiral. The door opened ; the tails of Brutus and Cassius cheerfully thumped the floor ; and old Mazey marched straight up to the right-hand side of his master's chair. The veteran stood there, with his legs wide apart and his balance carefully adjusted, as if the dining-room had been a cabin, and the house a ship, pitching in a sea-way.

The admiral filled the large glass with port, filled his own glass with claret, and raised it to his lips.

" God bless the Queen, Mazey," said the admiral.

" God bless the Queen, your honour," said old Mazey, swallowing his port, as the dogs swallowed the made-dishes, at a gulp.

" How's the wind, Mazey ?"

" West and by Noathe, your honour."

" Any report to-night, Mazey ?"

" No report, your honour."

" Good evening, Mazey."

" Good evening, your honour."

The after-dinner ceremony thus completed, old Mazey made his bow, and walked out of the room again. Brutus and Cassius stretched themselves on the rug to digest mushrooms and made gravies in the lubricating heat of the fire. " For what we have received, the Lord make us truly thankful," said the admiral. " Go down-stairs, my good girl, and get your supper. A light meal, Lucy, if you take my advice—a light meal or you will have the nightmare. Early to bed, my dear, and early to rise, makes a parlour-maid healthy and wealthy and wise. That's the wisdom of your ancestors — you mustn't laugh at it. Good night." In those words Magdalen was dismissed; and so her first day's experience of Admiral Bartram came to an end.

After breakfast, the next morning, the admiral's directions to the new parlour-maid, included among them one particular order which, in Magdalen's situation, it was especially her interest to receive. In the old gentleman's absence from home that day, on local business which took him to Ossory, she was directed to make herself acquainted with the whole inhabited quarter of the house, and to learn the positions of the various rooms, so as to know where the bells called her when the bells rang. Mrs. Drake was charged with the duty of superintending the voyage of domestic discovery, unless she happened to be otherwise engaged—in which case, any one of the inferior servants would be equally competent to act as Magdalen's guide.

At noon the admiral left for Ossory, and Magdalen presented herself in Mrs. Drake's room, to be shown over the house. Mrs. Drake happened to be otherwise engaged ; and referred her to the head housemaid. The head housemaid happened on that particular morning to be in the same condition as Mrs. Drake ; and referred her to the under-housemaids. The under-housemaids declared they were all behindhand and had not a minute to spare—they suggested, not too civilly, that old Mazey had nothing on earth to do, and that he knew the house as well, or better than he knew his A B C. Magdalen took the hint, with a secret indignation and contempt which it cost her a hard struggle to conceal. She had suspected, on the previous night, and she was certain now, that the women-servants all incomprehensibly resented her presence among them, with the same sullen unanimity of distrust. Mrs. Drake, as she had seen for herself, was really engaged that morning over her accounts. But of all the servants under her who had made their excuses, not one had even affected to be more occupied than usual. Their looks said plainly, " We don't like you ; and we won't show you over the house."

She found her way to old Mazey, not by the scanty directions given her, but by the sound of the veteran's cracked and quavering voice, singing in some distant seclusion, a verse of the immortal sea-song—" Tom Bowling." Just as she stopped among the rambling stone passages on the basement story of the house, uncertain which way to turn next, she heard the tuneless old voice in the distance, singing these lines :

> " His form was of the manliest beau-u-u-uty,
>   His heart was ki-i-ind and soft ;
> Faithful below Tom did his duty,
>   But now he's gone alo-o-o-o-oft—
>   But now he's go-o-o-one aloft !"

Magdalen followed in the direction of the quavering voice, and found herself in a little room, looking out on the back yard. There sat old Mazey, with his spectacles low on his nose, and his knotty old hands blundering over the rigging of his model ship. There were Brutus and Cassius digesting before the fire again, and snoring as if they thoroughly enjoyed it. There was Lord Nelson on one wall, in flaming water-colours ; and there on the other was a portrait of Admiral Bartram's last flag-ship, in full sail on a sea of slate, with a salmon-coloured sky to complete the illusion.

" What, they won't show you over the house—won't they ?" said old Mazey. " I will, then ! That head housemaid's a sour one, my dear—if ever there was a sour one yet. You're too young and good-looking to please 'em—that's what you are." He rose, took off his spectacles, and feebly mended the fire. " She's as straight as a poplar," said old Mazey, considering Magdalen's figure in drowsy soliloquy. " I say she's as straight as a poplar ; and his honour the admiral says so too! Come along, my dear," he proceeded, addressing himself to Magdalen again. " I'll teach you your Pints of the Compass first. When you know your Pints, blow high, blow low, you'll find it plain sailing all over the house."

He led the way to the door—stopped, and suddenly bethinking himself of his miniature ship, went back to put his model away in an empty cupboard —led the way to the door again—stopped once more—remembered that some of the rooms were chilly—and pottered about, swearing and grumbling, and looking for his hat. Magdalen sat down patiently to wait for him. She gratefully contrasted his treatment of her with the treatment she had received from the women. Resist it as firmly, despise it as proudly as we may, all studied unkindness—no matter how contemptible it may be—has a stinging power in it which reaches to the quick. Magdalen only knew how she had felt the small malice of the female servants, by the effect which the rough kindness of the old sailor produced on her afterwards. The dumb welcome of the dogs, when the movements in the room had roused them from their sleep, touched her more acutely still. Brutus pushed his mighty muzzle companionably into her hand; and Cassius laid his friendly fore-paw on her lap. Her heart yearned over the two creatures as she patted and caressed them. It seemed only yesterday since she and the dogs at Combe-Raven had roamed the garden 'together, and had idled away the summer mornings luxuriously on the shady lawn.

Old Mazey found his hat at last; and they started on their exploring expedition, with the dogs after them.

Leaving the basement story of the house, which was entirely devoted to the servants' offices, they ascended to the first floor, and entered the long corridor, with which Magdalen's last night's experience had already made her acquainted. "Put your back agin this wall," said old Mazey, pointing to the long wall—pierced at irregular intervals with windows looking out over a court-yard and fish-pond—which formed the right-hand side of the corridor, as Magdalen now stood. "Put your back here," said the veteran; "and look straight afore you. What do you see ?"—"The opposite wall of the passage," said Magdalen.—"Ay! ay! what else ?"—"The doors leading into the rooms."—"What else?"—"I see nothing else." Old Mazey chuckled, winked, and shook his knotty forefinger at Magdalen impressively. "You see one of the Pints of the Compass, my dear. When you've got your back agin this wall, and when you look straight afore you —you look Noathe. If you ever get lost hereaway, put your back agin the wall, look out straight afore you, and say to yourself, 'I look Noathe!' You do that like a good girl, and you won't lose your bearings."

After administering this preliminary dose of instruction, old Mazey opened the first of the doors on the left-hand side of the passage. It led into the dining-room, with which Magdalen was already familiar. The second room was fitted up as a library ; and the third, as a morning-room. The fourth and fifth doors—both belonging to dismantled and uninhabited rooms, and both locked—brought them to the end of the North wing of the house, and to the opening of a second and shorter passage, placed at a right angle to the first. Here old Mazey, who had divided his time pretty equally, during the investigation of the rooms in talking of "his honour the Admiral," and whistling to the dogs—returned with all possible expedition to the points of the compass; and gravely directed Magdalen to repeat the ceremony of putting her back against the wall. She attempted to shorten the proceedings, by declaring (quite correctly) that in her present position she knew she was looking East. "Don't you talk about the East, my dear," said old Mazey, proceeding unmoved with his own system of instruction, "till you know the East first. Put your back agin this wall, and look straight afore you. What do you see?" The remainder of the catechism proceeded as before. When the end was reached, Magdalen's instructor was satisfied. He chuckled and winked at her once more. "Now you may talk about the East, my dear," said the veteran, "for now you know it."

The East passage, after leading them on for a few yards only, terminated in a vestibule, with a high door in it which faced them as they advanced. The door admitted them to a large and lofty drawing-room, decorated, like all the other apartments, with valuable old-fashioned furniture. Leading the way across this room, Magdalen's conductor pushed back a heavy sliding door, opposite the door of entrance. "Put your apron over your head," said old Mazey. "We are coming to the Banketing Hall, now. The floor's mortal cold, and the damp sticks to the place like cockroaches to a collier. His honour the admiral calls it the Arctic Passage. I've got my name for it, too. I call it, Freeze-your-Bones."

Magdalen passed through the doorway, and found herself in the ancient Banqueting-Hall of St. Crux.

On her left hand, she saw a row of lofty windows, set deep in embrasures, and extending over a frontage of more than a hundred feet in length. On her right hand, ranged in one long row from end to end of the opposite wall, hung a dismal collection of black begrimed old pictures, rotting from their frames, and representing battle-scenes by sea and land. Below the pictures, midway down the length of the wall, yawned a huge cavern of a fireplace, surmounted by a towering mantelpiece of black marble. The one object of furniture (if furniture it might be called) visible far or near in the vast emptiness of the place, was a gaunt ancient tripod of curiously chased metal, standing lonely in the middle of the hall, and supporting a wide circular pan, filled deep with ashes from an extinct charcoal fire. The high ceiling, once finely carved and gilt, was foul with dirt and cobwebs; the naked walls at either end of the room were stained with damp; and the cold of the marble floor struck through the narrow strip of matting laid down, parallel with the windows, as a footpath for passengers across the wilderness of the room. No better name for it could have been devised than the name which old Mazey had found. "Freeze-your-Bones" accurately described in three words, the Banqueting-Hall at St. Crux.

" Do you never light a fire in this dismal place ?" asked Magdalen.

"It all depends on which side of Freeze-your-Bones his honour the admiral lives," said old Mazey. "His honour likes to shift his quarters, sometimes to one side of the house, sometimes to the other. If he lives Noathe of Freeze-your-Bones—which is where you've just come from—we don't waste our coals here. If he lives South of Freeze-your-Bones—which is where we are going to next—we light the fire in the grate and the charcoal in the pan. Every night, when we do that, the damp gets the better of us : every morning, we turn to again, and get the better of the damp."

With this remarkable explanation, old Mazey led the way to the lower end of the Hall, opened more doors, and showed Magdalen through another suite of rooms, four in number ; all of moderate size, and all furnished in much the same manner as the rooms in the northern wing. She looked out of the windows, and saw the neglected gardens of St. Crux, overgrown with brambles and weeds. Here and there, at no great distance in the grounds, the smoothly curving line of one of the tidal streams peculiar to the locality, wound its way, gleaming in the sunlight, through gaps in the brambles and trees. The more distant view ranged over the flat eastward country beyond, speckled with its scattered little villages ; crossed and re-crossed by its network of " backwaters ;" and terminated abruptly by the long straight line of sea-wall which protects the defenceless coast of Essex from invasion by the sea.

"Have we more rooms still to see ?" asked Magdalen, turning from the view of the garden, and looking about her for another door.

" No more, my dear—we've run aground here, and we may as well wear round and put back again," said old Mazey. " There's another side to the house—due south of you as you stand now—which is all tumbling about our ears. You must go out into the garden, if you want to see it ; it's built off from us by a brick bulkhead, t'other side of this wall here. The monks lived due south of us, my dear, hundreds of years afore his honour the admiral was born or thought of ; and a fine time of it they had, as I've heard. They sang in the church all the morning, and drank grog in the orchard all the afternoon. They slept off their grog on the best of featherbeds ; and they fattened on the neighbourhood all the year round. Lucky beggars ! lucky beggars !"

Apostrophizing the monks in these terms, and evidently regretting that he had not lived himself in those good old times, the veteran led the way back through the rooms. On the return passage across "Freeze-your-Bones," Magdalen preceded him. " She's as straight as a poplar," mumbled old Mazey to himself, hobbling along after his youthful companion, and wagging his venerable head in cordial approval. " I never was particular what nation they belonged to—but I always *did* like 'em straight and fine grown, and I always *shall* like 'em straight and fine grown, to my dying day."

"Are there more rooms to see up-stairs, on the second floor?" asked Magdalen, when they had returned to the point from which they had started.

The naturally clear distinct tones of her voice, had hitherto reached the old sailor's imperfect sense of hearing easily enough. Rather to her surprise, he became stone-deaf, on a sudden, to her last question.

"Are you sure of your Pints of the Compass?" he inquired. "If you're not sure, put your back agin the wall, and we'll go all over 'em again, my dear, beginning with the Noathe."

Magdalen assured him that she felt quite familiar, by this time, with all the points, the "Noathe" included—and then repeated her question in louder tones. The veteran obstinately matched her, by becoming deafer than ever.

"Yes, my dear," he said; "you're right; it *is* chilly in these passages; and unless I go back to my fire, my fire'll go out—won't it? If you don't feel sure of your Pints of the Compass, come into me, and I'll put you right again." He winked benevolently, whistled to the dogs, and hobbled off. Magdalen heard him chuckle over his own success in balking her curiosity on the subject of the second floor. "I know how to deal with 'em!" said old Mazey to himself, in high triumph. "Tall and short, native and foreign, sweethearts and wives—*I* know how to deal with 'em!"

Left by herself, Magdalen exemplified the excellence of the old sailor's method of treatment, in her particular case, by ascending the stairs immediately, to make her own observations on the second floor. The stone passage here was exactly similar—except that more doors opened out of it—to the passage on the first floor. She opened the two nearest doors, one after another, at a venture, and discovered that both rooms were bed-chambers. The fear of being discovered by one of the women-servants, in a part of the house with which she had no concern, warned her not to push her investigations on the bed-room floor, too far at starting. She hurriedly walked down the passage to see where it ended; discovered that it came to its termination in a lumber-room, answering to the position of the vestibule down stairs; and retraced her steps immediately.

On her way back, she noticed an object which had previously escaped her attention. It was a low truckle-bed, placed parallel with the wall, and close to one of the doors, on the bedroom side. In spite of its strange and comfortless situation, the bed was apparently occupied at night, by a sleeper: the sheets were on it, and the end of a thick red fisherman's cap, peeped out from under the pillow. She ventured on opening the door near which the bed was placed; and found herself, as she conjectured from certain signs and tokens, in the admiral's sleeping chamber. A moment's observation of the room was all she dared risk; and, softly closing the door again, she returned to the kitchen regions.

The truckle-bed, and the strange position in which it was placed, dwelt on her mind all through the afternoon. Who could possibly sleep in it? The remembrance of the red fisherman's cap, and the knowledge she had already gained of Mazey's dog-like fidelity to his master, helped her to guess that the old sailor might be the occupant of the truckle-bed. But why, with bedrooms enough and to spare, should he occupy that cold and comfortless situation at night? Why should he sleep on guard outside his master's door? Was there some nocturnal danger in the house, of which the admiral was afraid? The question seemed absurd—and yet the position of the bed forced it irresistibly on her mind.

Stimulated by her own ungovernable curiosity on this subject, Magdalen ventured to question the housekeeper. She acknowledged having walked from end to end of the passage on the second floor, to see if it was as long as the passage on the first; and she mentioned having noticed with astonishment the position of the truckle-bed. Mrs. Drake answered her implied inquiry shortly and sharply. "I don't blame a young girl like you," said the old lady, "for being a little curious, when she first comes into such a strange house as this. But remember, for the future, that your business does not lie on the bedroom story. Mr. Mazey sleeps on that bed you noticed. It is his habit at night, to sleep outside his master's door." With that meagre explanation Mrs. Drake's lips closed, and opened no more.

Later in the day, Magdalen found an opportunity of applying to old Mazey himself. She discovered the veteran in high good humour, smoking his pipe, and warming a tin mug of ale at his own snug fire.

"Mr. Mazey," she asked boldly, "why do you put your bed in that cold passage?"

"What! you have been up-stairs, you young jade, have you?" said old Mazey, looking up from his mug with a leer.

Magdalen smiled and nodded. "Come! come! tell me," she said, coaxingly. "Why do you sleep outside the admiral's door?"

"Why do you part your hair in the middle, my dear?" asked old Mazey, with another leer.

"I suppose, because I am accustomed to do it," answered Magdalen.

"Ay! ay!" said the veteran. "That's why, is it? Well, my dear, the reason why you part your hair in the middle, is the reason why I sleep outside the admiral's door. I know how to deal with 'em!" chuckled old Mazey, lapsing into soliloquy, and stirring up his ale in high triumph. "Tall and short, native and foreign, sweethearts and wives—*I* know how to deal with 'em!"

Magdalen's third, and last, attempt at solving the mystery of the trucklebed, was made while she was waiting on the admiral at dinner. The old gentleman's questions gave her an opportunity of referring to the subject, without any appearance of presumption or disrespect—but he proved to be quite as impenetrable, in his way, as old Mazey and Mrs. Drake had been in theirs. "It doesn't concern you, my dear," said the admiral, bluntly. "Don't be curious. Look in your Old Testament when you go down-stairs, and see what happened in the Garden of Eden through curiosity. Be a good girl—and don't imitate your mother Eve."

Late at night, as Magdalen passed the end of the second-floor passage, proceeding alone on her way up to her own room, she stopped and listened. A screen was placed at the entrance of the corridor, so as to hide it from the view of persons passing on the stairs. The snoring she heard on the other side of the screen, encouraged her to slip round it, and to advance a few steps. Shading the light of her candle with her hand, she ventured close to the admiral's door, and saw to her surprise that the bed had been moved, since she had seen it in the daytime, so as to stand exactly across the door, and to bar the way entirely to any one who might attempt to enter the admiral's room. After this discovery, old Mazey himself, snoring lustily, with the red fisherman's cap pulled down to his eyebrows, and the blankets drawn up to his nose—became an object of secondary importance only, by comparison with his bed. That the veteran did actually sleep on guard before his master's door—and that he and the admiral and the housekeeper were in the secret of this unaccountable proceeding—was now beyond all doubt.

"A strange end," thought Magdalen, pondering over her discovery as she stole up-stairs to her own sleeping-room—"a strange end to a strange day!"

CHAPTER II.

The first week passed, the second week passed, and Magdalen was, to all appearance, no nearer to the discovery of the Secret Trust, than on the day when she first entered on her service at St. Crux.

But the fortnight, uneventful though it was, had not been a fortnight lost. Experience had already satisfied her on one important point—experience had shown that she could set the rooted distrust of the other servants safely at defiance. Time had accustomed the women to her presence in the house, without shaking the vague conviction which possessed them all alike, that the new comer was not one of themselves. All that Magdalen could do, in her own defence, was to keep the instinctive female suspicion of her, confined within those purely negative limits which it had occupied from the first—and this she accomplished.

Day after day, the women watched her, with the untiring vigilance of malice and distrust; and day after day, not the vestige of a discovery rewarded them for their pains. Silently, intelligently, and industriously—with an ever-present remembrance of herself and her place—the new parlour-maid did her work. Her only intervals of rest and relaxation were the intervals passed occasionally, in the day, with old Mazey and the dogs, and the precious interval of the night, during which she was secure from observation in the solitude of her room. Thanks to the superfluity of bed-chambers at St. Crux, each one of the servants had the choice, if she pleased, of sleeping in a room of her own. Alone in the night, Magdalen might dare to be herself again—might dream of the past, and wake from the dream, encountering no curious eyes to notice that she was in tears—might ponder over the future, and be roused by no whispering in corners, which tainted her with the suspicion of " having something on her mind."

Satisfied, thus far, of the perfect security of her position in the house, she profited next by a second chance in her favour, which—before the fortnight was at an end—relieved her mind of all doubt on the formidable subject of Mrs. Lecount.

Partly from the accidental gossip of the women, at the table in the servants' hall—partly from a marked paragraph in a Swiss newspaper, which she had found one morning lying open on the admiral's easy-chair—she gained the welcome assurance that no danger was to be dreaded, this time, from the housekeeper's presence on the scene. Mrs. Lecount had, as it appeared, passed a week or more at St. Crux, after the date of her master's death, and had then left England, to live on the interest of her legacy, in honourable and prosperous retirement, in her native place. The paragraph in the Swiss newspaper described the fulfilment of this laudable project. Mrs. Lecount had not only established herself at Zurich, but (wisely mindful of the uncertainty of life) had also settled the charitable uses to which her fortune was to be applied after her death. One half of it was to go to the founding of a "Lecompte Scholarship," for poor students, in the University of Geneva. The other half was to be employed by the municipal authorities of Zurich, in the maintenance and education of a certain number of orphan girls, natives of the city, who were to be trained for domestic service in later life. The Swiss journalist adverted to these philanthropic bequests in terms of extravagant eulogy. Zurich was congratulated on the possession of a Paragon of public virtue; and William Tell, in the character of benefactor to Switzerland, was compared disadvantageously with Mrs. Lecount.

The third week began; and Magdalen was now at liberty to take her first step forward on the way to the discovery of the Secret Trust.

She ascertained, from old Mazey, that it was his master's custom, during the winter and spring months, to occupy the rooms in the north wing; and during the summer and autumn, to cross the Arctic passage of "Freeze-your-Bones," and live in the eastward apartments which looked out on the garden. While the Banqueting-Hall remained—owing to the admiral's inadequate pecuniary resources—in its damp and dismantled state, and while the interior of St. Crux was thus comfortlessly divided into two separate résidences, no more convenient arrangement than this could well have been devised. Now and then (as Magdalen understood from her informant) there were days, both in winter and summer, when the admiral became anxious about the condition of the rooms which he was not occupying at the time; and when he insisted on investigating the state of the furniture, the pictures, and the books with his own eyes. On these occasions—in summer as in winter—a blazing fire was kindled for some days previously, in the large grate, and the charcoal was lit in the tripod pan, to keep the Banqueting-Hall as warm as circumstances would admit. As soon as the old gentleman's anxieties were set at rest, the rooms were shut up again ; and "Freeze-your-Bones" was once more abandoned for weeks and weeks together to damp, desolation, and decay. The last of these temporary migrations had taken place only a few days since; the admiral had satisfied himself that the rooms in the east wing were none the worse for the absence of their master—and he might now be safely reckoned on as settled in the north wing for weeks, and perhaps, if the season was cold, for months to come.

Trifling as they might be in themselves, these particulars were of serious importance to Magdalen—for they helped her to fix the limits of the field of search. Assuming that the admiral was likely to keep all his important documents within easy reach of his own hand, she might now feel certain that the Secret Trust was secured in one or other of the rooms in the north wing.

In which room? That question was not easy to answer.

Of the four inhabitable rooms which were all at the admiral's disposal during the day—that is to say, of the dining-room, the library, the morning-room, and the drawing-room opening out of the vestibule—the library appeared to be the apartment in which, if he had a preference, he passed the greater part of his time. There was a table in this room, with drawers that locked; there was a magnificent Italian cabinet with doors that locked; there were five cupboards under the bookcases, every one of which locked. There were receptacles similarly secured, in the other rooms; and in all or any of these, papers might be kept.

She had answered the bell, and had seen him locking and unlocking, now in one room now in another—but oftenest in the library. She had noticed occasionally that his expression was fretful and impatient, when he looked round at her from an open cabinet or cupboard, and gave his orders; and she inferred that something in connection with his papers and possessions—it might, or might not, be the Secret Trust—irritated and annoyed him from time to time. She had heard him, more than once, lock something up in one of the rooms—come out, and go into another room—wait there a few minutes—then return to the first room, with his keys in his hand—and sharply turn the locks, and turn them again. This fidgety anxiety about his keys and his cupboards might be the result of the inbred restlessness of his disposition, aggravated in a naturally active man, by the aimless indolence of a life in retirement—a life drifting backwards and forwards among trifles, with no regular employment to steady it at any given hour of the day. On the other hand, it was just as probable that these comings and goings, these lockings and unlockings, might be attributable to the existence of some private responsibility, which had unexpectedly intruded itself into the old man's easy existence, and which tormented him with a sense of oppression, new to the experience of his later years. Either one of these interpretations might explain his conduct as reasonably and as probably as the other. Which was the right interpretation of the two, it was, in Magdalen's position, impossible to say.

The one certain discovery at which she arrived, was made in her first day's observation of him. The admiral was a rigidly careful man with his keys.

All the smaller keys he kept on a ring, in the breast-pocket of his coat. The larger, he locked up together; generally, but not always, in one of the drawers of the library table. Sometimes, he left them secured in this way at night; sometimes, he took them up to the bed-room with him in a little basket. He had no regular times for leaving them, or for taking them away with him; he had no discoverable reason for now securing them in the library-table drawer, and now again locking them up in some other place. The inveterate wilfulness and caprice of his proceedings, in these particulars, defied every effort to reduce them to a system, and baffled all attempts at calculating on them beforehand.

The hope of gaining positive information to act on, by laying artful snares for him which he might fall into in his talk, proved, from the outset, to be utterly futile.

In Magdalen's situation, all experiments of this sort would have been in the last degree difficult and dangerous, with any man. With the admiral, they were simply impossible. His tendency to veer about from one subject to another; his habit of keeping his tongue perpetually going, so long as there was anybody, no matter whom, within reach of the sound of his voice; his comical want of all dignity and reserve with his servants, promised, in appearance, much; and performed, in reality—nothing. No matter how diffidently, or how respectfully, Magdalen might presume on her master's example, and on her master's evident liking for her—the old man instantly discovered the advance she was making from her proper position, and instantly put her back in it again, with a quaint good humour which inflicted no pain, but with a blunt straightforwardness of purpose which permitted no escape. Contradictory as it may sound, Admiral

Bartram was too familiar to be approached; he kept the distance between himself and his servant more effectually than if he had been the proudest man in England. The systematic reserve of a superior towards an inferior, may be occasionally overcome—the systematic familiarity, never.

Slowly the time dragged on. The fourth week came; and Magdalen had made no new discoveries. The prospect was depressing in the last degree. Even in the apparently hopeless event of her devising a means of getting at the admiral's keys, she could not count on retaining possession of them unsuspected more than a few hours—hours which might be utterly wasted through her not knowing in what direction to begin the search. The Trust might be locked up in any one of some twenty receptacles for papers, situated in four different rooms. And which room was the likeliest to look in, which receptacle was the most promising to begin with, which position among other heaps of papers the one paper needful might be expected to occupy, was more than she could say. Hemmed in by immeasurable uncertainties on every side—condemned, as it were, to wander blindfold on the very brink of success—she waited for the chance that never came, for the event that never happened, with a patience which was sinking already into the patience of despair.

Night after night, she looked back over the vanished days—and not an event rose on her memory to distinguish them one from the other. The only interruptions to the weary uniformity of the life at St. Crux, were caused by the characteristic delinquencies of old Mazey and the dogs.

At certain intervals, the original wildness broke out in the natures of Brutus and Cassius. The modest comforts of home, the savoury charms of made-dishes, the decorous joy of digestions accomplished on hearthrugs, lost all their attractions; and the dogs ungratefully left the house, to seek dissipation and adventure in the outer world. On these occasions, the established after-dinner formula of question and answer between old Mazey and his master, varied a little in one particular. "God bless the Queen, Mazey," and "How's the wind, Mazey?" were followed by a new inquiry: "Where are the dogs, Mazey?" "Out on the loose, your honour, and be damned to 'em," was the veteran's unvarying answer. The admiral always sighed and shook his head gravely at the news, as if Brutus and Cassius had been sons of his own, who treated him with a want of proper filial respect. In two or three days' time, the dogs always returned, lean, dirty, and heartily ashamed of themselves. For the whole of the next day they were invariably tied up in disgrace. On the day after, they were scrubbed clean, and were formally readmitted to the dining-room. There, Civilization, acting through the subtle medium of the Saucepan, recovered its hold on them; and the admiral's two prodigal sons, when they saw the covers removed, watered at the mouth as copiously as ever.

Old Mazey, in his way, proved to be just as disreputably inclined on certain occasions as the dogs. At intervals, the original wildness in *his* nature broke out: he, too, lost all relish for the comforts of home, and ungratefully left the house. He usually disappeared in the afternoon, and returned at night as drunk as liquor could make him. He was by many degrees too seasoned a vessel to meet with any disasters, on these occasions. His wicked old legs might take roundabout methods of pro-gression, but they never failed him; his wicked old eyes might see double, but they always showed him the way home. Try as hard as they might, the servants could never succeed in persuading him that he was drunk: he always scorned the imputation. He even declined to admit the idea privately into his mind, until he had first tested his con-dition by an infallible criterion of his own.

It was his habit in these cases of Bacchanalian emergency, to stagger obstinately into his room on the ground floor—to take the model ship out of the cupboard—and to try if he could proceed with the never-to-be-com-pleted employment of setting up the rigging. When he had smashed the tiny spars, and snapped asunder the delicate ropes—then, and not till then, the veteran admitted facts as they were, on the authority of practical evidence. "Ay! ay!" he used to say confidentially to himself. "The women are right. Drunk again, Mazey—drunk again!" Having reached this discovery, it was his habit to wait cunningly in the lower regions, until the admiral was safe in his room; and then to ascend in discreet list slippers, to his post. Too wary to attempt getting into the truckle-bed (which would have been only inviting the catastrophe of a fall against his master's door), he always walked himself sober, up and down the passage. More than once, Magdalen had peeped round the screen, and had seen the old sailor unsteadily keeping his watch, and fancying himself once more at his duty on board ship. "This is an uncommonly lively vessel in a sea-way," he used to mutter under his breath, when his legs took him down the passage in zigzag directions, or left him for the moment, studying the "Pints of the Compass," on his own system, with his back against the wall. "A nasty night, mind you," he would maunder on, taking another turn. "As dark as your pocket, and the wind heading us again from the old quarter." On the next day, old Mazey, like the dogs, was kept down-stairs in disgrace. On the day after, like the dogs again, he was reinstated in his privileges; and another change was introduced in the after-dinner formula. On entering the room, the old sailor stopped short, and made his excuses, in this brief, yet comprehensive form of words, with his back against the door:—" Please your honour, I'm ashamed of myself," So the apology began and ended. "This mustn't happen again, Mazey," the admiral used to answer. "It sha'n't happen again, your honour." "Very good. Come here, and drink your glass of wine. God bless the Queen, Mazey."—The veteran tossed off his port, and the dialogue ended as usual.

So the days passed, with no incidents more important than these to relieve their monotony, until the end of the fourth week was at hand.

On the last day, an event happened; on the last day, the long-deferred promise of the future unexpectedly began to dawn. While Magdalen was spreading the cloth in the dining-room, as usual, Mrs. Drake looked in, and instructed her on this occasion, for the first time, to lay the table for two persons. The admiral had received a letter from his nephew. Early that evening, Mr. George Bartram was expected to return to St. Crux.

CHAPTER III.

AFTER placing the second cover, Magdalen awaited the ringing of the dinner-bell, with an interest and impatience, which she found it no easy task to conceal. The return of Mr. Bartram would, in all probability, produce a change in the life of the house—and from change of any kind, no matter how trifling, something might be hoped. The nephew might be accessible to influences which had failed to reach the uncle. In any case, the two would talk of their affairs, over their dinner; and through that talk—proceeding day after day, in her presence—the way to discovery, now absolutely invisible, might, sooner or later, show itself.

At last, the bell rang; the door opened; and the two gentlemen entered the room together.

Magdalen was struck, as her sister had been struck, by George Bartram's resemblance to her father—judging by the portrait at Combe-Raven, which presented the likeness of Andrew Vanstone in his younger days. The light hair and florid complexion, the bright blue eyes and hardy upright figure, familiar to her in the picture, were all recalled to her memory, as the nephew followed the uncle across the room, and took his place at table. She was not prepared for this sudden revival of the lost associations of home. Her attention wandered as she tried to conceal its effect on her; and she made a blunder in waiting at table, for the first time since she had entered the house.

A quaint reprimand from the admiral, half in jest, half in earnest, gave her time to recover herself. She ventured another look at George Bartram. The impression which he produced on her, this time, roused her curiosity immediately. His face and manner plainly expressed anxiety and pre-occupation of mind. He looked oftener at his plate than at his uncle—and at Magdalen herself (except one passing inspection of the new parlour-maid, when the admiral spoke to her) he never looked at all. Some uncertainty was evidently troubling his thoughts; some oppression was weighing on his natural freedom of manner. What uncertainty? what oppression? Would any personal revelations come out, little by little, in the course of conversation at the dinner-table?

No. One set of dishes followed another set of dishes—and nothing in the shape of a personal revelation took place. The conversation halted on irregularly, between public affairs on one side and trifling private topics on the other. Politics, home and foreign, took their turn with the small household history of St. Crux: the leaders of the revolution which expelled Louis Philippe from the throne of France,* marched side by side, in the dinner-table review, with old Mazey and the dogs. The dessert was put on the table—the old sailor came in—drank his loyal toast—paid his respects to "Master George"—and went out again. Magdalen followed him, on her way back to the servants' offices, having heard nothing in the conversation of the slightest importance to the furtherance of her own design, from the first word of it to the last. She struggled hard not to lose heart and hope on the first day. They could hardly talk again to-morrow, they could hardly talk again the next day, of the French Revolution and the dogs. Time might do wonders yet; and time was all her own.

Left together over their wine, the uncle and nephew drew their easy-chairs on either side of the fire; and, in Magdalen's absence, began the very conversation which it was Magdalen's interest to hear.

"Claret, George?" said the admiral, pushing the bottle across the table. "You look out of spirits."

"I am a little anxious, sir," replied George, leaving his glass empty, and looking straight into the fire.

"I am glad to hear it," rejoined the admiral. "I am more than a little anxious myself, I can tell you. Here we are at the last days of March—and nothing done! Your time comes to an end on the third of May; and there you sit, as if you had years still before you to turn round in."

George smiled, and resignedly helped himself to some wine.

"Am I really to understand, sir," he asked, "that you are serious in what you said to me last November? Are you actually resolved to bind me to that incomprehensible condition?"

"I don't call it incomprehensible," said the admiral, irritably.

"Don't you, sir? I am to inherit your estate, unconditionally—as you have generously settled it from the first. But I am not to touch a farthing of the fortune poor Noel left you, unless I am married within a certain time. The house and lands are to be mine (thanks to your kindness), under any circumstances. But the money with which I might improve them both, is to be arbitrarily taken away from me, if I am not a married man on the third of May. I am sadly wanting in intelligence, I dare say—but a more incomprehensible proceeding I never heard of!"

"No snapping and snarling, George! Say your say out. We don't understand sneering in Her Majesty's Navy!"

"I mean no offence, sir. But I think it's a little hard to astonish me by a change of proceeding on your part, entirely foreign to my experience of your character—and then, when I naturally ask for an explanation, to turn round coolly, and leave me in the dark. If you and Noel came to some private arrangement together, before he made his will—why not tell me? Why set up a mystery between us, where no mystery need be?"

"I won't have it, George!" cried the admiral, angrily drumming on the table with the nut-crackers. "You are trying to draw me like a badger—but I won't be drawn! I'll make any conditions I please; and I'll be accountable to nobody for them, unless I like. It's quite bad enough to have worries and responsibilities laid on my unlucky shoulders that I never bargained for—never mind what worries: they're not yours, they're mine—without being questioned and cross-questioned as if I was a witness in a box. Here's a pretty fellow!" continued the admiral, apostrophizing his nephew in red-hot irritation, and addressing himself to the dogs on the hearth-rug for want of a better audience. "Here's a pretty fellow! He is asked to help himself to two uncommonly comfortable things in their way—a fortune and a wife—he is allowed six months to get the wife in (we should have got her, in the Navy, bag and baggage, in six days)—he has a round dozen of nice girls, to my certain knowledge, in one part of the country and another, all at his disposal to choose from—and what does he do? He sits month after month, with his lazy legs crossed before him; he leaves the girls to pine on the stem; and he bothers his uncle to know the reason why! I pity the poor unfortunate women. Men were made of flesh and blood—and plenty of it, too—in my time. They're made of machinery now."

"I can only repeat, sir, I am sorry to have offended you," said George.

"Pooh! pooh! you needn't look at me in that languishing way, if you are," retorted the admiral. "Stick to your wine; and I'll forgive you. Your good health, George. I'm glad to see you again at St. Crux. Look at that plateful of sponge-cakes! The cook has sent them up in honour of your return. We can't hurt her feelings, and we can't spoil our wine. Here!"—The admiral tossed four sponge-cakes in quick succession down the accommodating throats of the dogs. "I am sorry, George," the old gentleman gravely proceeded; "I am really sorry, you haven't got your eye on one of those nice girls. You don't know what a loss you're inflicting on yourself—you don't know what trouble and mortification you're causing me—by this shilly-shally conduct of yours."

"If you would only allow me to explain myself, sir, you would view my conduct in a totally different light. I am ready to marry to-morrow, if the lady will have me."

"The devil you are! So you have got a lady in your eye, after all? Why in Heaven's name, couldn't you tell me so before? Never mind—I'll forgive you everything now I know you have laid your hand on a wife.

Fill your glass again. Here's her health in a bumper. By-the-by, who is she?"

"I'll tell you directly, admiral. When we began this conversation, I mentioned that I was a little anxious——"

"She's not one of my round dozen of nice girls—aha, Master George, I see that in your face already! Why are you anxious?"

"I am afraid you will disapprove of my choice, sir."

"Don't beat about the bush! How the deuce can I say whether I disapprove or not, if you won't tell me who she is?"

"She is the eldest daughter of Andrew Vanstone of Combe-Raven."

"Who!!!"

"Miss Vanstone, sir."

The admiral put down his glass of wine untasted.

"You're right, George," he said. "I do disapprove of your choice—strongly disapprove of it."

"Is it the misfortune of her birth, sir, that you object to?"

"God forbid! the misfortune of her birth is not her fault, poor thing. You know, as well as I do, George, what I object to."

"You object to her sister?"

"Certainly! The most liberal man alive might object to her sister, I think."

"It's hard, sir, to make Miss Vanstone suffer for her sister's faults."

"*Faults*, do you call them? You have a mighty convenient memory, George, where your own interests are concerned."

"Call them crimes, if you like, sir—I say again, it's hard on Miss Vanstone. Miss Vanstone's life is pure of all reproach. From first to last, she has borne her hard lot with such patience, and sweetness, and courage, as not one woman in a thousand would have shown in her place. Ask Miss Garth, who has known her from childhood. Ask Mrs. Tyrrel, who blesses the day when she came into the house——"

"Ask a fiddlestick's end! I beg your pardon, George—but you are enough to try the patience of a saint. My good fellow, I don't deny Miss Vanstone's virtues. I'll admit, if you like, she's the best woman that ever put on a petticoat. That is not the question——"

"Excuse me, admiral—it *is* the question, if she is to be my wife."

"Hear me out, George; look at it from my point of view, as well as your own. What did your cousin Noel do? Your cousin Noel fell a victim, poor fellow, to one of the vilest conspiracies I ever heard of—and the prime mover of that conspiracy was Miss Vanstone's damnable sister. She deceived him in the most infamous manner; and as soon as she was down for a handsome legacy in his will, she had the poison ready to take his life. This is the truth—we know it from Mrs. Lecount, who found the bottle locked up in her own room. If you marry Miss Vanstone, you make this wretch your sister-in-law. She becomes a member of our family. All the disgrace of what she has done; all the disgrace of what she *may* do—and the Devil who possesses her, only knows what lengths she may go to next—becomes *our* disgrace. Good Heavens, George, consider what a position that is! Consider what pitch you touch, if you make this woman your sister-in-law."

"You have put your side of the question, admiral," said George resolutely; "now let me put mine. A certain impression is produced on me by a young lady, whom I meet with under very interesting circumstances. I don't act headlong on that impression, as I might have done if I had been some years younger—I wait, and put it to the trial. Every time I see this young lady, the impression strengthens; her beauty grows on me, her character grows on me; when I am away from her I am restless and dissatisfied; when I am with her I am the happiest man alive. All I hear of her conduct from those who know her best, more than confirms the high opinion I have formed of her. The one drawback I can discover, is caused by a misfortune for which she is not responsible—the misfortune of having a sister who is utterly unworthy of her. Does this discovery—an unpleasant discovery, I grant you—destroy all those good qualities in Miss Vanstone for which I love and admire her? Nothing of the sort—it only makes her good qualities all the more precious to me by contrast. If I am to have a drawback to contend with—and who expects anything else in this world?—I would infinitely rather have the drawback attached to my wife's sister, than to my wife. My wife's sister is not essential to my happiness, but my wife is. In my opinion, sir, Mrs. Noel Vanstone has done mischief enough already—I don't see the necessity of letting her do more mischief, by depriving me of a good wife. Right or wrong, that is my point of view. I don't wish to trouble you with any questions of sentiment. All I wish to say is, that I am old enough, by this time, to know my own mind—and that my mind is made up. If my marriage is essential to the execution of your intentions on my behalf, there is only one woman in the world whom I *can* marry—and that woman is Miss Vanstone."

There was no resisting this plain declaration. Admiral Bartram rose from his chair without making any reply, and walked perturbedly up and down the room.

The situation was emphatically a serious one. Mrs. Girdlestone's death had already produced the failure of one of the two objects contemplated by the Secret Trust. If the third of May arrived, and found George a single man, the second (and last) of the objects would then have failed in its turn. In little more than a fortnight, at the very latest, the Banns must be published in Ossory church—or the time would fail for compliance with one of the stipulations insisted on in the Trust. Obstinate as the admiral was by nature, strongly as he felt the objections which attached to his nephew's contemplated alliance, he recoiled in spite of himself, as he paced the room and saw the facts on either side, immovably staring him in the face.

"Are you engaged to Miss Vanstone?" he asked, suddenly.

"No, sir," replied George. "I thought it due to your uniform kindness to me, to speak to you on the subject first."

"Much obliged, I'm sure. And you have put off speaking to me to the last moment, just as you put off everything else. Do you think Miss Vanstone will say Yes, when you ask her?"

George hesitated.

"The devil take your modesty!" shouted the admiral. "That is not a time for modesty—this is a time for speaking out. Will she or won't she?"

"I think she will, sir."

The admiral laughed sardonically, and took another turn in the room. He suddenly stopped; put his hands in his pockets; and stood still in a corner, deep in thought. After an interval of a few minutes, his face cleared a little; it brightened with the dawning of a new idea. He walked round briskly to George's side of the fire, and laid his hand kindly on his nephew's shoulder.

"You're wrong, George," he said—"but it is too late now to set you right. On the sixteenth of next month, the Banns must be put up in Ossory church, or you will lose the money. Have you told Miss Vanstone the position you stand in? Or have you put that off to the eleventh hour, like everything else?"

"The position is so extraordinary, sir, and it might lead to so much mis-apprehension of my motives, that I have felt unwilling to allude to it. I hardly know how I can tell her of it all."

"Try the experiment of telling her friends. Let them know it's a question of money; and they will overcome her scruples, if you can't. But that is not what I had to say to you. How long do you propose stopping here, this time?"

"I thought of staying a few days, and then——"

"And then of going back to London, and making your offer, I suppose? Will a week give you time enough to pick your opportunity with Miss Vanstone—a week out of the fortnight or so that you have to spare?"

"I will stay here a week, admiral, with pleasure, if you wish it."

"I don't wish it. I want you to pack up your traps, and be off to-morrow."

George looked at his uncle, in silent astonishment.

"You found some letters waiting for you, when you got here," proceeded the admiral. "Was one of those letters from my old friend, Sir Franklin Brock?"

"Yes, sir."

" Was it an invitation to you to go and stay at the Grange ?"

" Yes, sir."

" To go at once ?"

" At once, if I could manage it."

" Very good. I want you to manage it. I want you to start for the Grange to-morrow."

George looked back at the fire, and sighed impatiently.

" I understand you now, admiral," he said. " You are entirely mistaken in me. My attachment to Miss Vanstone is not to be shaken in *that* manner."

Admiral Bartram took his quarter-deck walk again, up and down the room.

" One good turn deserves another, George," said the old gentleman. " If I am willing to make concessions on my side, the least you can do is to meet me half-way, and make concessions on yours."

" I don't deny it, sir."

" Very well. Now listen to my proposal. Give me a fair hearing, George—a fair hearing is every man's privilege. I will be perfectly just to begin with. I won't attempt to deny that you honestly believe Miss Vanstone is the only woman in the world who can make you happy. I don't question that. What I do question is, whether you really know your own mind in this matter, quite so well as you think you know it yourself. You can't deny, George, that you have been in love with a good many women in your time ? Among the rest of them, you have been in love with Miss Brock. No longer ago than this time last year, there was a sneaking kindness between you and that young lady, to say the least of it. And quite right, too ! Miss Brock is one of that round dozen of darlings I mentioned over our first glass of wine."

" You are confusing an idle flirtation, sir, with a serious attachment," said George. " You are altogether mistaken—you are indeed."

" Likely enough ; I don't pretend to be infallible—I leave that to my juniors. But I happen to have known you, George, since you were the height of my old telescope; and I want to have this serious attachment of yours put to the test. If you can satisfy me that your whole heart and soul are as strongly set on Miss Vanstone, as you suppose them to be—I must knock under to necessity, and keep my objections to myself. But I *must* be satisfied first. Go to the Grange to-morrow, and stay there a week in Miss Brock's society. Give that charming girl a fair chance of lighting up the old flame again, if she can—and then come back to St. Crux, and let me hear the result. If you tell me, as an honest man, that your attachment to Miss Vanstone still remains unshaken, you will have heard the last of my objections from that moment. Whatever misgivings I may feel in my own mind, I will say nothing, and do nothing, adverse to your wishes. There is my proposal. I dare say it looks like an old man's folly, in your eyes. But the old man won't trouble you much longer, George—and it may be a pleasant reflection when you have got sons of your own, to remember that you humoured him in his last days."

He came back to the fireplace, as he said those words, and laid his hand once more on his nephew's shoulder. George took the hand and pressed it affectionately. In the tenderest and best sense of the word, his uncle had been a father to him.

"I will do what you ask me, sir," he replied, "if you seriously wish it. But it is only right to tell you that the experiment will be perfectly useless. However, if you prefer my passing a week at the Grange, to my passing it here—to the Grange I will go."

"Thank you, George," said the admiral, bluntly. "I expected as much from you, and you have not disappointed me. If Miss Brock doesn't get us out of this mess," thought the wily old gentleman, as he resumed his place at the table, "my nephew's weathercock of a head has turned steady with a vengeance! We'll consider the question settled for to-night, George," he continued aloud, "and call another subject. These family anxieties don't improve the flavour of my old claret. The bottle stands with you. What are they doing at the theatres in London? We always patronized the theatres, in my time, in the Navy. We used to like a good tragedy to begin with, and a hornpipe to cheer us up at the end of the entertainment."

For the rest of the evening, the talk flowed in the ordinary channels. Admiral Bartram only returned to the forbidden subject, when he and his nephew parted for the night.

"You won't forget to-morrow, George?"

"Certainly not, sir. I'll take the dog-cart, and drive myself over after breakfast."

Before noon the next day, Mr. George Bartram had left the house, and the last chance in Magdalen's favour had left it with him.

CHAPTER IV.

WHEN the servants' dinner-bell at St. Crux rang as usual on the day of George Bartram's departure, it was remarked that the new parlour-maid's place at table remained empty. One of the inferior servants was sent to her room to make inquiries, and returned with the information that "Louisa" felt a little faint, and begged that her attendance at table might be excused for that day. Upon this, the superior authority of the house-keeper was invoked; and Mrs. Drake went up-stairs immediately to ascertain the truth for herself. Her first look of inquiry satisfied her that the parlour-maid's indisposition, whatever the cause of it might be, was certainly not assumed to serve any idle or sullen purpose of her own. She respectfully declined taking any of the remedies which the housekeeper offered, and merely requested permission to try the efficacy of a walk in the fresh air.

"I have been accustomed to more exercise, ma'am, than I take here," she said. "Might I go into the garden, and try what the air will do for me?"

"Certainly. Can you walk by yourself? or shall I send some one with you?"

"I will go by myself, if you please, ma'am."

"Very well. Put on your bonnet and shawl—and, when you get out, keep in the east garden. The admiral sometimes walks in the north garden, and he might feel surprised at seeing you there. Come to my room, when you have had air and exercise enough, and let me see how you are."

In a few minutes more, Magdalen was out in the east garden. The sky was clear and sunny; but the cold shadow of the house rested on the garden walk, and chilled the midday air. She walked towards the ruins of the old monastery, situated on the south side of the more modern range of buildings. Here, there were lonely open spaces to breathe in freely; here, the pale March sunshine stole through the gaps of desolation and decay, and met her invitingly with the genial promise of spring.

She ascended three or four riven stone steps, and seated herself on some ruined fragments beyond them, full in the sunshine. The place she had chosen had once been the entrance to the church. In centuries long gone by, the stream of human sin and human suffering had flowed, day after day, to the confessional, over the place where she now sat. Of all the miserable women who had trodden those old stones in the bygone time, no more miserable creature had touched them, than the woman whose feet rested on them now.

Her hands trembled as she placed them on either side of 'her, to support herself on the stone seat. She laid them on her lap—they trembled there. She held them out, and looked at them wonderingly—they trembled as she looked. "Like an old woman!" she said faintly—and let them drop again at her side.

For the first time, that morning, the cruel discovery had forced itself on her mind—the discovery that her strength was failing her, at the time when she had most confidently trusted to it, at the time when she wanted it most. She had felt the surprise of Mr. Bartram's unexpected departure, as if it had been the shock of the severest calamity that could have befallen her. That one check to her hopes—a check which, at other times, would only have roused the resisting power in her to new efforts—had struck her with as suffocating a terror, had prostrated her with as all-mastering a despair, as if she had been overwhelmed by the crowning disaster of expulsion from St. Crux. But one warning could be read, in such a change as this. Into the space of little more than a year, she had crowded the wearing and wasting emotions of a life. The bountiful gifts of health and strength, so prodigally heaped on her by Nature, so long abused with impunity, were failing her at last.

She looked up at the far faint blue of the sky. She heard the joyous singing of birds among the ivy that clothed the ruins. Oh, the cold distance of the heavens! Oh, the pitiless happiness of the birds! Oh, the lonely horror of sitting there, and feeling old and weak and worn, in the heyday of her youth! She rose with a last effort of resolution, and tried to keep back the hysterical passion swelling at her heart, by moving and looking about her. Rapidly and more rapidly, she walked to and fro in the sunshine. The exercise helped her, through the very fatigue that she felt from it. She forced the rising tears desperately back to their sources—she fought with the clinging pain, and wrenched it from its hold. Little by little, her mind began to clear again: the despairing fear of herself, grew less vividly present to her thoughts. There were reserves of youth and strength in her, still to be wasted—there was a spirit, sorely wounded, but not yet subdued.

She gradually extended the limits of her walk ; she gradually recovered the exercise of her observation.

At the western extremity, the remains of the monastery were in a less ruinous condition than at the eastern. In certain places, where the stout old walls still stood, repairs had been made at some former time. Roofs of red tile had been laid roughly over four of the ancient cells ; wooden doors had been added ; and the old monastic chambers had been used as sheds to hold the multifarious lumber of St. Crux. No padlocks guarded any of the doors. Magdalen had only to push them, to let the daylight in on the litter inside. She resolved to investigate the sheds, one after the other— not from curiosity ; not with the idea of making discoveries of any sort. Her only object was to fill up the vacant time, and to keep the thoughts that unnerved her from returning to her mind.

The first shed she opened, contained the gardener's utensils, large and small. The second was littered with fragments of broken furniture, empty picture-frames of worm-eaten wood, shattered vases, boxes without covers, and books torn from their bindings. As Magdalen turned to leave the shed, after one careless glance round her at the lumber that it contained, her foot struck something on the ground which tinkled against a fragment of china lying near it. She stooped, and discovered that the tinkling substance was a rusty key.

N.N.—24

She picked up the key, and looked at it. She walked out into the air, and considered a little. More old forgotten keys were probably lying about among the lumber in the sheds. What, if she collected all she could find, and tried them, one after another, in the locks of the cabinets and cupboards now closed against her? Was there chance enough that any one of them might fit, to justify her in venturing on the experiment? If the locks at St. Crux were as old-fashioned as the furniture—if there were no protective niceties of modern invention to contend against—there was chance enough beyond all question. Who could say whether the very key in her hand, might not be the lost duplicate of one of the keys on the admiral's bunch? In the dearth of all other means of finding the way to her end, the risk was worth running. A flash of the old spirit sparkled in her weary eyes, as she turned, and re-entered the shed.

Half an hour more brought her to the limits of the time which she could venture to allow herself in the open air. In that interval, she had searched the sheds from first to last, and had found five more keys. "Five more chances!" she thought to herself, as she hid the keys, and hastily returned to the house.

After first reporting herself in the housekeeper's room, she went upstairs to remove her bonnet and shawl; taking that opportunity to hide the keys in her bedchamber, until night came. They were crusted thick with rust and dirt; but she dared not attempt to clean them, until bedtime secluded her from the prying eyes of the servants, in the solitude of her room.

When the dinner hour brought her, as usual, into personal contact with the admiral, she was at once struck by a change in him. For the first time in her experience, the old gentleman was silent and depressed. He ate less than usual, and he hardly said five words to her, from the beginning of the meal to the end. Some unwelcome subject of reflection had evidently fixed itself on his mind, and remained there persistently, in spite of his efforts to shake it off. At intervals through the evening, she wondered with an ever-growing perplexity what the subject could be.

At last, the lagging hours reached their end, and bedtime came. Before she slept that night, Magdalen had cleaned the keys from all impurities, and had oiled the wards, to help them smoothly into the locks. The last difficulty that remained, was the difficulty of choosing the time when the experiment might be tried, with the least risk of interruption and discovery. After carefully considering the question overnight, Magdalen could only resolve to wait and be guided by the events of the next day.

The morning came; and, for the first time at St. Crux, events justified the trust she had placed in them. The morning came—and the one remaining difficulty that perplexed her, was unexpectedly smoothed away by no less a person than the admiral himself! To the surprise of every one in the house, he announced at breakfast, that he had arranged to start for London in an hour ; that he should pass the night in town ; and that he might be expected to return to St. Crux in time for dinner on the next day. He volunteered no further explanations, to the housekeeper, or to any one else— but it was easy to see that his errand to London was of no ordinary import-ance in his own estimation. He swallowed his breakfast in a violent hurry ; and he was impatiently ready for the carriage before it came to the door.

Experience had taught Magdalen to be cautious. She waited a little, after Admiral Bartram's departure, before she ventured on trying her ex-periment with the keys. It was well she did so. Mrs. Drake took advantage of the admiral's absence to review the condition of the apart-ments on the first floor. The results of the investigation by no means satisfied her ; brooms and dusters were set to work ; and the housemaids were in and out of the rooms perpetually, as long as the daylight lasted.

The evening passed ; and still the safe opportunity for which Magdalen was on the watch never presented itself. Bedtime came again ; and found her placed between the two alternatives of trusting to the doubtful chances of the next morning—or of trying the keys boldly in the dead of night. In former times, she would have made her choice without hesitation. She hesitated now—but the wreck of her old courage still sustained her, and she determined to make the venture at night.

They kept early hours at St. Crux. If she waited in her room until half-past eleven, she would wait long enough. At that time, she stole out on to the staircase, with the keys in her pocket, and the candle in her hand.

On passing the entrance to the corridor on the bedroom floor, she stopped and listened. No sound of snoring, no shuffling of infirm footsteps, was to be heard on the other side of the screen. She looked round it distrustfully. The stone passage was a solitude, and the truckle-bed was empty. Her own eyes had shown her old Mazey on his way to the upper regions, more than an hour since, with a candle in his hand. Had he taken advantage of his master's absence, to enjoy the unaccustomed luxury of sleeping in a room? As the thought occurred to her, a sound from the farther end of the corridor just caught her ear. She softly advanced towards it ; and heard through the door of the last and remotest of the spare bed-chambers, the veteran's lusty snoring in the room inside. The discovery was start-ling, in more senses than one. It deepened the impenetrable mystery of the truckle-bed ; for it showed plainly that old Mazey had no barbarous preference of his own for passing his nights in the corridor—he occupied that strange and comfortless sleeping-place, purely and entirely on his master's account.

It was no time for dwelling on the reflections which this conclusion might suggest. Magdalen retraced her steps along the passage, and descended to the first floor. Passing the doors nearest to her, she tried the library first. On the staircase, and in the corridors, she had felt her heart throbbing fast with an unutterable fear—but a sense of security returned to her when she found herself within the four walls of the room, and when she had closed the door on the ghostly quiet outside.

The first lock she tried was the lock of the table-drawer. None of the keys fitted it. Her next experiment was made on the cabinet. Would the second attempt fail, like the first?

No! One of the keys fitted; one of the keys, with a little patient management, turned the lock. She looked in eagerly. There were open shelves above, and one long drawer under them. The shelves were devoted to specimens of curious minerals, neatly labelled and arranged. The drawer was divided into compartments. Two of the compartments contained papers. In the first, she discovered nothing but a collection of receipted bills. In the second, she found a heap of business-documents— but the writing, yellow with age, was enough of itself to warn her that the Trust was not there. She shut the doors of the cabinet; and, after locking them again with some little difficulty, proceeded to try the keys in the book-case cupboards next, before she continued her investigations in the other rooms.

The book-case cupboards were unassailable; the drawers and cupboards in all the other rooms were unassailable. One after another, she tried them patiently in regular succession. It was useless. The chance which the cabinet in the library had offered in her favour, was the first chance and the last.

She went back to her room; seeing nothing but her own gliding shadow; hearing nothing but her own stealthy footfall in the midnight stillness of the house. After mechanically putting the keys away in their former hiding-place, she looked towards her bed—and turned away from it, shuddering. The warning remembrance of what she had suffered that morning in the garden, was vividly present to her mind. "Another chance tried," she thought to herself, "and another chance lost! I shall break down again if I think of it—and I shall think of it, if I lie awake in the dark." She had brought a work-box with her to St. Crux, as one of the many little things which in her character of a servant it was desirable to possess; and she now opened the box, and applied herself resolutely to work. Her want of dexterity with her needle, assisted the object she had in view; it obliged her to pay the closest attention to her employment; it forced her thoughts away from the two subjects of all others which she now dreaded most—herself and the future.

The next day, as he had arranged, the admiral returned. His visit to London had not improved his spirits. The shadow of some unconquerable doubt still clouded his face : his restless tongue was strangely quiet, while

Magdalen waited on him at his solitary meal. That night, the snoring resounded once more on the inner side of the screen, and old Mazey was back again in the comfortless truckle-bed.

Three more days passed—April came. On the second of the month—returning as unexpectedly as he had departed a week before—Mr. George Bartram reappeared at St. Crux.

He came back early in the afternoon; and had an interview with his uncle in the library. The interview over, he left the house again; and was driven to the railway by the groom, in time to catch the last train to London that night. The groom noticed, on the road, that "Mr. George seemed to be rather pleased than otherwise at leaving St. Crux." He also remarked, on his return, that the admiral swore at him for over-driving the horses—an indication of ill-temper, on the part of his master, which he described as being entirely without precedent, in all his former experience. Magdalen, in her department of service, had suffered in like manner under the old man's irritable humour: he had been dissatisfied with everything she did in the dining-room; and he had found fault with all the dishes, one after another, from the mutton broth to the toasted cheese.

The next two days passed as usual. On the third day an event happened. In appearance, it was nothing more important than a ring at the drawing-room bell. In reality, it was the forerunner of approaching catastrophe—the formidable herald of the end.

It was Magdalen's business to answer the bell. On reaching the drawing-room door, she knocked as usual. There was no reply. After again knocking, and again receiving no answer, she ventured into the room—and was instantly met by a current of cold air flowing full on her face. The heavy sliding-door in the opposite wall was pushed back, and the Arctic atmosphere of Freeze-your-Bones was pouring unhindered into the empty room.

She waited near the door, doubtful what to do next; it was certainly the drawing-room bell that had rung, and no other. She waited, looking through the open doorway opposite, down the wilderness of the dismantled Hall.

A little consideration satisfied her that it would be best to go down-stairs again, and wait there for a second summons from the bell. On turning to leave the room, she happened to look back once more; and exactly at that moment, she saw the door open at the opposite extremity of the Banqueting-Hall—the door leading into the first of the apartments in the east wing. A tall man came out, wearing his greatcoat and his hat, and rapidly approached the drawing-room. His gait betrayed him, while he was still too far off for his features to be seen. Before he was quite half-way across the Hall, Magdalen had recognized—the admiral.

He looked, not irritated only, but surprised as well, at finding his parlour-maid waiting for him in the drawing-room, and inquired, sharply and suspiciously—what she wanted there? Magdalen replied that she had come there to answer the bell. His face cleared a little, when he heard the explanation. "Yes, yes; to be sure," he said. "I did ring, and then I forgot it." He pulled the sliding-door back into its place as he spoke. "Coals," he resumed, impatiently, pointing to the empty scuttle. "I rang for coals."

Magdalen went back to the kitchen regions. After communicating the admiral's order to the servant whose special duty it was to attend to the fires, she returned to the pantry; and gently closing the door, sat down alone to think.

It had been her impression in the drawing-room—and it was her impression still—that she had accidentally surprised Admiral Bartram on a visit to the east rooms, which, for some urgent reason of his own, he wished to keep a secret. Haunted day and night by the one dominant idea that now possessed her, she leapt all logical difficulties at a bound; and at once associated the suspicion of a secret proceeding on the admiral's part, with the kindred suspicion which pointed to him as the depositary of the Secret Trust. Up to this time, it had been her settled belief that he kept all his important documents in one or other of the suite of rooms which he happened to be occupying for the time being. Why—she now asked herself, with a sudden distrust of the conclusion which had hitherto satisfied her mind—why might he not lock some of them up in the other rooms as well? The remembrance of the keys still concealed in their hiding-place in her room, sharpened her sense of the reasonableness of this new view. With one unimportant exception, those keys had all failed when she tried them in the rooms on the north side of the house. Might they not succeed with the cabinets and cupboards in the east rooms, on which she had never tried them or thought of trying them, yet? If there was a chance, however small, of turning them to better account than she had turned them thus far, it was a chance to be tried. If there was a possibility, however remote, that the Trust might be hidden in any one of the locked repositories in the east wing, it was a possibility to be put to the test. When? Her own experience answered the question. At the time when no prying eyes were open, and no accidents were to be feared—when the house was quiet—in the dead of night.

She knew enough of her changed self to dread the enervating influence of delay. She determined to run the risk, headlong, that night.

More blunders escaped her, when dinner-time came; the admiral's criticisms on her waiting at table were sharper than ever. His hardest words inflicted no pain on her; she scarcely heard him—her mind was dull to every sense but the sense of the coming trial. The evening which had passed slowly to her on the night of her first experiment with the keys, passed quickly now. When bedtime came, bedtime took her by surprise.

She waited longer, on this occasion, than she had waited before. The admiral was at home; he might alter his mind and go down-stairs again, after he had gone up to his room; he might have forgotten something in the library, and might return to fetch it. Midnight struck from the clock in the servants' hall, before she ventured out of her room, with the keys again in her pocket, with the candle again in her hand.

At the first of the stairs on which she set her foot to descend, an all-mastering hesitation, an unintelligible shrinking from some peril unknown, seized her on a sudden. She waited, and reasoned with herself. She had recoiled from no sacrifices, she had yielded to no fears, in carrying out the stratagem by which she had gained admission to St. Crux; and now, when the long array of difficulties at the outset had been patiently conquered,— now, when by sheer force of resolution the starting-point was gained, she hesitated to advance. "I shrank from nothing to get here," she said to herself. "What madness possesses me that I shrink now?"

Every pulse in her quickened at the thought, with an animating shame that nerved her to go on. She descended the stairs, from the third floor to the second, from the second to the first, without trusting herself to pause again within easy reach of her own room. In another minute, she had reached the end of the corridor, had crossed the vestibule, and had entered the drawing-room. It was only when her grasp was on the heavy brass handle of the sliding-door—it was only at the moment before she pushed the door back—that she waited to take breath. The Banqueting-Hall was close on the other side of the wooden partition against which she stood ; her excited imagination felt the death-like chill of it flowing over her already.

She pushed back the sliding-door a few inches—and stopped in momentary alarm. When the admiral had closed it in her presence that day, she had heard no noise. When old Mazey had opened it to show her the rooms in the east wing, she had heard no noise. Now, in the night silence, she noticed for the first time, that the door made a sound—a dull, rushing sound, like the wind.

She roused herself, and pushed it farther back—pushed it half way into the hollow chamber in the wall constructed to receive it. She advanced boldly into the gap, and met the night-view of the Banqueting-Hall face to face.

The moon was rounding the southern side of the house. Her paling beams streamed through the nearer windows, and lay in long strips of slanting light on the marble pavement of the Hall. The black shadows of the pediments between each window, alternating with the strips of light, heightened the wan glare of the moonshine on the floor. Towards its lower end, the Hall melted mysteriously into darkness. The ceiling was lost to view ; the yawning fireplace, the overhanging mantelpiece, the long row of battle-pictures above, were all swallowed up in night. But one visible object was discernible, besides the gleaming windows and the moon-striped floor. Midway in the last and farthest of the strips of light, the tripod rose erect on its gaunt black legs, like a monster called to life by the moon—a monster rising through the light, and melting invisibly into the upper shadows of the Hall. Far and near, all sound lay dead, drowned in the stagnant cold. The soothing hush of night was awful here. The deep abysses of darkness hid abysses of silence more immeasurable still.

She stood motionless in the doorway, with straining eyes, with straining ears. She looked for some moving thing, she listened for some rising sound—and looked and listened in vain. A quick ceaseless shivering ran through her from head to foot. The shivering of fear? or the shivering of cold? The bare doubt roused her resolute will. "Now," she thought, advancing a step through the doorway—"or never! I'll count the strips of moonlight three times over—and cross the Hall."

"One, two, three, four, five. One, two, three, four, five. One, two, three, four, five."

As the final number passed her lips at the third time of counting, she crossed the Hall. Looking for nothing, listening for nothing, one hand holding the candle, the other mechanically grasping the folds of her dress—she sped ghostlike down the length of the ghostly place. She reached the door of the first of the eastern rooms—opened it—and ran in. The sudden relief of attaining a refuge, the sudden entrance into a new atmosphere, overpowered her for the moment. She had just time to put the candle safely on a table, before she dropped giddy and breathless into the nearest chair.

Little by little, she felt the rest quieting her. In a few minutes, she became conscious of the triumph of having won her way to the east rooms. In a few minutes, she was strong enough to rise from the chair, to take the keys from her pocket, and to look round her.

The first objects of furniture in the room which attracted her attention, were an old bureau of carved oak, and a heavy buhl table with a cabinet attached. She tried the bureau first: it looked the likeliest receptacle for papers of the two. Three of the keys proved to be of a size to enter the lock—but none of them would turn it. The bureau was unassailable. She left it, and paused to trim the wick of the candle before she tried the buhl cabinet next.

At the moment when she raised her hand to the candle, she heard the stillness of the Banqueting-Hall shudder with the terror of a sound—a sound, faint and momentary, like the distant rushing of the wind.

The sliding-door in the drawing-room had moved.

Which way had it moved? Had an unknown hand pushed it back in its socket, farther than she had pushed it—or pulled it to again, and closed it? The horror of being shut out all night, by some undiscoverable agency, from the life of the house, was stronger in her than the horror of looking across the Banqueting-Hall. She made desperately for the door of the room.

It had fallen to silently after her, when she had come in, but it was not closed. She pulled it open—and looked.

The sight that met her eyes, rooted her panic-stricken to the spot.

Close to the first of the row of windows, counting from the drawing-room, and full in the gleam of it, she saw a solitary figure. It stood motionless, rising out of the farthest strip of moonlight on the floor. As she looked, it suddenly disappeared. In another instant, she saw it again, in the second strip of moonlight—lost it again—saw it in the third strip—lost it once more—and saw it in the fourth. Moment by moment, it advanced, now mysteriously lost in the shadow, now suddenly visible again in the light, until it reached the fifth and nearest strip of moonlight. There it paused, and strayed aside slowly to the middle of the Hall. It stopped at the tripod, and stood, shivering audibly in the silence, with its hands raised over the dead ashes, in the action of warming them at a fire. It turned back again, moving down the path of the moonlight—stopped at the fifth window—turned once more—and came on softly through the shadow, straight to the place where Magdalen stood.

Her voice was dumb, her will was helpless. Every sense in her but the seeing-sense, was paralysed. The seeing-sense—held fast in the fetters of its own terror—looked unchangeably straightforward, as it had looked from the first. There she stood in the doorway, full in the path of the figure advancing on her through the shadow, nearer and nearer, step by step.

It came close.

The bonds of horror that held her, burst asunder when it was within arm's length. She started back. The light of the candle on the table fell full on its face, and showed her—Admiral Bartram.

A long grey dressing-gown was wrapped round him. His head was uncovered; his feet were bare. In his left hand he carried his little basket of keys. He passed Magdalen slowly; his lips whispering without intermission; his open eyes staring straight before him, with the glassy stare of death. His eyes revealed to her the terrifying truth. He was walking in his sleep.

The terror of seeing him, as she saw him now, was not the terror she had felt when her eyes first lighted on him—an apparition in the moonlight, a spectre in the ghostly Hall. This time, she could struggle against the shock; she could feel the depth of her own fear.

He passed her, and stopped in the middle of the room. Magdalen ventured near enough to him to be within reach of his voice, as he muttered to himself. She ventured nearer still, and heard the name of her dead husband fall distinctly from the sleep-walker's lips.

"Noel!" he said, in the low monotonous tones of a dreamer talking in his sleep. "My good fellow, Noel, take it back again! It worries me day and night. I don't know where it's safe; I don't know where to put it. Take it back, Noel—take it back!"

As those words escaped him, he walked to the buhl cabinet. He sat down in the chair placed before it, and searched in the basket among his keys. Magdalen softly followed him, and stood behind his chair, waiting with the candle in her hand. He found the key, and unlocked the cabinet. Without an instant's hesitation, he drew out a drawer, the second of a row. The one thing in the drawer, was a folded letter. He removed it, and put it down before him on the table. "Take it back, Noel!" he repeated, mechanically; "take it back!"

Magdalen looked over his shoulder, and read these lines, traced in her husband's handwriting, at the top of the letter:— *To be kept in your own possession, and to be opened by yourself only, on the day of my decease. Noel Vanstone.* She saw the words plainly, with the admiral's name and the admiral's address written under them.

The Trust within reach of her hand! The Trust traced to its hiding-place at last!

She took one step forward, to steal round his chair and to snatch the letter from the table. At the instant when she moved, he took it up once more; locked the cabinet, and, rising, turned and faced her.

In the impulse of the moment, she stretched out her hand towards the hand in which he held the letter. The yellow candlelight fell full on him. The awful death-in-life of his face—the mystery of the sleeping body, moving in unconscious obedience to the dreaming mind—daunted her. Her hand trembled, and dropped again at her side.

He put the key of the cabinet back in the basket; and crossed the room to the bureau, with the basket in one hand, and the letter in the other. Magdalen set the candle on the table again, and watched him. As he had opened the cabinet, so he now opened the bureau. Once more, Magdalen stretched out her hand; and once more she recoiled before the mystery and the terror of his sleep. He put the letter in a drawer, at the back of the bureau, and closed the heavy oaken lid again. "Yes," he said. "Safer there, as you say, Noel—safer there." So he spoke. So, time after time, the words that betrayed him, revealed the dead man living and speaking again in the dream.

Had he locked the bureau? Magdalen had not heard the lock turn. As he slowly moved away, walking back once more towards the middle of the room, she tried the lid. It was locked. That discovery made, she looked to see what he was doing next. He was leaving the room again, with his basket of keys in his hand. When her first glance overtook him, he was crossing the threshold of the door.

Some inscrutable fascination possessed her; some mysterious attraction drew her after him, in spite of herself. She took up the candle, and followed him mechanically, as if she too were walking in her sleep. One behind the other, in slow and noiseless progress, they crossed the Banqueting-

Hall. One behind the other, they passed through the drawing-room, and along the corridor, and up the stairs. She followed him to his own door. He went in, and shut it behind him softly. She stopped, and looked towards the truckle-bed. It was pushed aside at the foot, some little distance away from the bedroom door. Who had moved it? She held the candle close, and looked towards the pillow, with a sudden curiosity and a sudden doubt.

The truckle-bed was empty.

The discovery startled her for the moment, and for the moment only. Plain as the inferences were to be drawn from it, she never drew them. Her mind slowly recovering the exercise of its faculties, was still under the influence of the earlier and the deeper impressions produced on it. Her mind followed the admiral into his room, as her [body had followed him across the Banqueting-Hall.

Had he lain down again in his bed? Was he still asleep? She listened at the door. Not a sound was audible in the room. She tried the door; and, finding it not locked, softly opened it a few inches, and listened again. The rise and fall of his low, regular breathing instantly caught her ear. He was still asleep.

She went into the room, and, shading the candlelight with her hand, approached the bed-side to look at him. The dream was past; the old man's sleep was deep and peaceful—his lips were still; his quiet hand was laid over the coverlet, in motionless repose. He lay with his face turned towards the right-hand side of the bed. A little table stood there, within reach of his hand. Four objects were placed on it: his candle; his matches; his customary night-drink of lemonade—and his basket of keys.

The idea of possessing herself of his keys that night (if an opportunity offered when the basket was not in his hand), had first crossed her mind when she saw him go into his room. She had lost it again, for the moment, in the surprise of discovering the empty truckle-bed. She now recovered it, the instant the table attracted her attention. It was useless to waste time in trying to choose the one key wanted from the rest—the one key was not well enough known to her to be readily identified. She took all the keys from the table, in the basket as they lay, and noiselessly closed the door behind her, on leaving the room.

The truckle-bed, as she passed it, obtruded itself again on her attention; and forced her to think of it. After a moment's consideration, she moved the foot of the bed back to its customary position across the door. Whether he was in the house or out of it, the veteran might return to his deserted post at any moment. If he saw the bed moved from its usual place, he might suspect something wrong—he might rouse his master—and the loss of the keys might be discovered.

Nothing happened as she descended the stairs; nothing happened as she passed along the corridor—the house was as silent and as solitary as ever. She crossed the Banqueting-Hall, this time, without hesitation; the events of the night had hardened her mind against all imaginary terrors. "Now I have got it!" she whispered to herself, in an irrepressible outburst of exultation, as she entered the first of the east rooms, and put her candle on the top of the old bureau.

Even yet, there was a trial in store for her patience. Some minutes elapsed, minutes that seemed hours, before she found the right key, and raised the lid of the bureau. At last, she drew out the inner drawer! At last, she had the letter in her hand!

It had been sealed, but the seal was broken. She opened it on the spot, to make sure that she had actually possessed herself of the Trust, before leaving the room. The end of the letter was the first part of it she turned to. It came to its conclusion high on the third page, and it was signed by Noel Vanstone. Below the name, these lines were added in the admiral's handwriting :—

"This letter was received by me, at the same time with the will of my friend, Noel Vanstone. In the event of my death, without leaving any other directions respecting it, I beg my nephew and my executors to understand that I consider the requests made in this document as absolutely binding on me.—ARTHUR EVERARD BARTRAM."

She left those lines unread. She just noticed that they were not in Noel Vanstone's handwriting; and, passing over them instantly, as immaterial to the object in view, turned the leaves of the letter, and transferred her attention to the opening sentences on the first page.

She read these words :—

"DEAR ADMIRAL BARTRAM,

"When you open my Will (in which you are named my sole executor), you will find that I have bequeathed the whole residue of my estate—after payment of one legacy of five thousand pounds—to yourself. It is the purpose of my letter to tell you privately what the object is for which I have left you the fortune which is now placed in your hands.

"I beg you to consider this large legacy as intended——"

She had proceeded thus far with breathless curiosity and interest—when her attention suddenly failed her. Something—she was too deeply absorbed to know what—had got between her and the letter. Was it a sound in the Banqueting-Hall again? She looked over her shoulder at the door behind her, and listened. Nothing was to be heard; nothing was to be seen. She returned to the letter.

The writing was cramped and close. In her impatient curiosity to read more, she failed to find the lost place again. Her eyes, attracted by a blot, lighted on a sentence lower in the page than the sentence at which she had left off. The first three words she saw, riveted her attention anew—they were the first words she had met with in the letter which directly referred to George Bartram. In the sudden excitement of that discovery, she read the rest of the sentence eagerly, before she made any second attempt to return to the lost place :—

"If your nephew fails to comply with these conditions—that is to say, if being either a bachelor or a widower at the time of my decease, he fails to marry in all respects as I have here instructed him to marry, within Six calendar months from that time—it is my desire that he shall not receive——"

She had read to that point, to that last word and no farther—when a Hand passed suddenly from behind her, between the letter and her eye, and gripped her fast by the wrist in an instant.

She turned with a shriek of terror; and found herself face to face with old Mazey.

The veteran's eyes were bloodshot; his hand was heavy; his list slippers* were twisted crookedly on his feet; and his body swayed to and fro on his widely-parted legs. If he had tested his condition, that night, by the unfailing criterion of the model ship, he must have inevitably pronounced sentence on himself in the usual form :—"Drunk again, Mazey; drunk again."

"You young Jezabel!"*said the old sailor, with a leer on one side of his face, and a frown on the other. "The next time you take to night-walking in the neighbourhood of Freeze-your-Bones, use those sharp eyes of yours first, and make sure there's nobody else night-walking in the garden outside. Drop it, Jezabel!—drop it!"

Keeping fast hold of Magdalen's arm with one hand, he took the letter from her with the other, put it back into the open drawer, and locked the bureau. She never struggled with him, she never spoke. Her energy was gone; her powers of resistance were crushed. The terrors of that horrible night, following one close on the other in reiterated shocks, had struck her down at last. She yielded as submissively, she trembled as helplessly, as the weakest woman living.

Old Mazey dropped her arm, and pointed with drunken solemnity to a chair in an inner corner of the room. She sat down, still without uttering a word. The veteran (breathing very hard over it) steadied himself on both elbows against the slanting top of the bureau, and from that commanding position, addressed Magdalen once more.

"Come and be locked up!" said old Mazey, wagging his venerable head with judicial severity. "There'll be a court of inquiry to-morrow morning; and I'm witness—worse luck!—I'm witness. You young jade, you've committed burglary—that's what you've done. His honour the admiral's keys stolen; his honour the admiral's desk ramsacked; and his honour the admiral's private letters broke open. Burglary! Burglary! Come and be locked up!" He slowly recovered an upright position, with the assistance of his hands, backed by the solid resisting power of the bureau; and lapsed into lachrymose soliloquy. "Who'd have thought it?" said old Mazey, paternally watering at the eyes. "Take the outside of her, and she's as straight as a poplar; take the inside of her, and she's as crooked as Sin. Such a fine-grown girl, too. What a pity! what a pity!"

"Don't hurt me!" said Magdalen faintly, as old Mazey staggered up to the chair, and took her by the wrist again. "I'm frightened, Mr. Mazey—I'm dreadfully frightened."

"Hurt you?" repeated the veteran. "I'm a deal too fond of you—and more shame for me at my age!—to hurt you. If I let go of your wrist, will you walk straight before me, where I can see you all the way? Will you be a good girl, and walk straight up to your own door?"

Magdalen gave the promise required of her—gave it with an eager longing to reach the refuge of her room. She rose, and tried to take the candle from the bureau—but old Mazey's cunning hand was too quick for her. "Let the candle be," said the veteran, winking in momentary forgetfulness of his responsible position. "You're a trifle quicker on your legs than I am, my dear—and you might leave me in the lurch, if I don't carry the light."

They returned to the inhabited side of the house. Staggering after Magdalen, with the basket of keys in one hand, and the candle in the other, old Mazey sorrowfully compared her figure with the straightness of the poplar, and her disposition with the crookedness of Sin, all the way across "Freeze-your-Bones," and all the way up-stairs to her own door. Arrived at that destination, he peremptorily refused to give her the candle, until he had first seen her safely inside the room. The conditions being complied with, he resigned the light with one hand, and made a dash with the other at the key—drew it from the inside of the lock—and instantly closed the door. Magdalen heard him outside, chuckling over his own dexterity, and fitting the key into the lock again, with infinite difficulty. At last he secured the door, with a deep grunt of relief. "There she is safe!" Magdalen heard him say, in regretful soliloquy. "As fine a girl as ever I set eyes on. What a pity! what a pity!"

The last sounds of his voice died out in the distance; and she was left alone in her room.

Holding fast by the banister, old Mazey made his way down to the corridor on the second floor, in which a night-light was always burning. He advanced to the truckle-bed; and, steadying himself against the oppo-

site wall, looked at it attentively. Prolonged contemplation of his own
resting-place for the night, apparently failed to satisfy him. He shook his
head ominously; and, taking from the side-pocket of his great-coat a pair
of old patched slippers, surveyed them with an aspect of illimitable doubt.
"I'm all abroad to-night," he mumbled to himself. "Troubled in my
mind—that's what it is—troubled in my mind."

The old patched slippers and the veteran's existing perplexities, happened to be intimately associated, one with the other, in the relation of
cause and effect. The slippers belonged to the admiral, who had taken
one of his unreasonable fancies to this particular pair, and who still persisted in wearing them, long after they were unfit for his service. Early
that afternoon, old Mazey had taken the slippers to the village cobbler to
get them repaired on the spot, before his master called for them the next
morning. He sat superintending the progress and completion of the work,
until evening came; when he and the cobbler betook themselves to the
village inn to drink each other's healths at parting. They had prolonged
this social ceremony till far into the night; and they had parted, as a
necessary consequence, in a finished and perfect state of intoxication on
either side.

If the drinking-bout had led to no other result than those night wander-
ings in the grounds of St. Crux, which had shown old Mazey the light in
the east windows, his memory would unquestionably have presented it to
him the next morning, in the aspect of one of the praiseworthy achievements of his life. But another consequence had sprung from it, which the
old sailor now saw dimly, through the interposing bewilderment left in his
brain by the drink. He had committed a breach of discipline, and a breach
of trust. In plainer words, he had deserted his post.

The one safeguard against Admiral Bartram's constitutional tendency to
somnambulism, was the watch and ward which his faithful old servant
kept outside his door. No entreaties had ever prevailed on him to submit
to the usual precaution taken in such cases. He peremptorily declined to
be locked into his room; he even ignored his own liability, whenever a
dream disturbed him, to walk in his sleep. Over and over again, old
Mazey had been roused by the admiral's attempts to push past the truckle-
bed, or to step over it, in his sleep; and over and over again, when the
veteran had reported the fact the next morning, his master had declined to
believe him. As the old sailor now stood, staring in vacant inquiry at the
bedchamber door, these incidents of the past rose confusedly on his memory,
and forced on him the serious question, whether the admiral had left his
room during the earlier hours of the night? If by any mischance the
sleep-walking fit had seized him, the slippers in old Mazey's hand pointed
straight to the conclusion that followed—his master must have passed
barefoot in the cold night, over the stone stairs and passages of St. Crux,

"Lord send he's been quiet!" muttered old Mazey, daunted, bold as he was and drunk as he was, by the bare contemplation of that prospect. "If his honour's been walking to-night, it will be the death of him!"

He roused himself for the moment, by main force—strong in his dog-like fidelity to the admiral, though strong in nothing else—and fought off the stupor of the drink. He looked at the bed, with steadier eyes, and a clearer mind. Magdalen's precaution in returning it to its customary position, presented it to him necessarily in the aspect of a bed which had never been moved from its place. He next examined the counterpane carefully. Not the faintest vestige appeared of the indentation which must have been left by footsteps passing over it. There was the plain evidence before him—the evidence recognizable at last by his own bewildered eyes—that the admiral had never moved from his room. "I'll take the Pledge to-morrow!" mumbled old Mazey, in an outburst of grateful relief. The next moment the fumes of the liquor flowed back insidiously over his brain; and the veteran, returning to his customary remedy, paced the passage in zigzag as usual, and kept watch on the deck of an imaginary ship.

Soon after sunrise, Magdalen suddenly heard the grating of the key from outside, in the lock of the door. The door opened, and old Mazey reappeared on the threshold. The first fever of his intoxication had cooled, with time, into a mild penitential glow. He breathed harder than ever, in a succession of low growls, and wagged his venerable head at his own delinquencies, without intermission.

"How are you now, you young land-shark in petticoats?" inquired the old sailor. "Has your conscience been quiet enough to let you go to sleep?"

"I have not slept," said Magdalen, drawing back from him in doubt of what he might do next. "I have no remembrance of what happened after you locked the door—I think I must have fainted. Don't frighten me again, Mr. Mazey! I feel miserably weak and ill. What do you want?"

"I want to say something serious," replied old Mazey, with impenetrable solemnity. "It's been on my mind to come here, and make a clean breast of it, for the last hour or more. Mark my words, young woman. I'm going to disgrace myself."

Magdalen drew further and further back, and looked at him in rising alarm.

"I know my duty to his honour the admiral," proceeded old Mazey, waving his hand drearily in the direction of his master's door. "But, try as hard as I may, I can't find it in my heart, you young jade, to be witness against you. I liked the make of you (specially about the waist) when you first came into the house, and I can't help liking the make of you still —though you *have* committed burglary, and though you *are* as crooked as

Sin. I've cast the eyes of indulgence on fine-grown girls all my life—and it's too late in the day to cast the eyes of severity on 'em now. I'm seventy-seven, or seventy-eight, I don't rightly know which. I'm a battered old hulk, with my seams opening, and my pumps choked, and the waters of Death powering in on me as fast as they can. I'm as miserable a sinner as you'll meet with anywhere in these parts—Thomas Nagle, the cobbler, only excepted; and he's worse than I am, for he's the youngest of the two, and he ought to know better. But the long and the short of it is, I shall go down to my grave, with an eye of indulgence for a fine-grown girl. More shame for me, you young Jezabel—more shame for me!"

The veteran's unmanageable eyes began to leer again in spite of him, as he concluded his harangue in these terms: the last reserves of austerity left in his face, entrenched themselves dismally round the corners of his mouth. Magdalen approached him again, and tried to speak. He solemnly motioned her back, with another dreary wave of his hand.

"No carneying!"*said old Mazey; "I'm bad enough already, without that. It's my duty to make my report to his honour the admiral; and I *will* make it. But if you like to give the house the slip, before the burglary's reported, and the court of inquiry begins—I'll disgrace myself by letting you go. It's market morning at Ossory; and Dawkes will be driving the light cart over, in a quarter of an hour's time. Dawkes will take you, if I ask him. I know my duty—my duty is to turn the key on you, and see Dawkes damned first. But I can't find it in my heart to be hard on a fine girl like you. It's bred in the bone, and it wunt come out of the flesh. More shame for me, I tell you again—more shame for me!"

The proposal thus strangely and suddenly presented to her, took Magdalen completely by surprise. She had been far too seriously shaken by the events of the night, to be capable of deciding on any subject at a moment's notice. "You are very good to me, Mr. Mazey," she said. "May I have a minute by myself to think?"

"Yes, you may," replied the veteran, facing about forthwith, and leaving the room. "They're all alike," proceeded old Mazey, with his head still running on the sex. "Whatever you offer 'em, they always want something more. Tall and short, native and foreign, sweethearts and wives—they're all alike!"

Left by herself, Magdalen reached her decision, with far less difficulty than she had anticipated.

If she remained in the house, there were only two courses before her—to charge old Mazey with speaking under the influence of a drunken delusion, or to submit to circumstances. Though she owed to the old sailor her defeat in the very hour of success, his consideration for her at that moment, forbade the idea of defending herself at his expense—even supposing, what was in the last degree improbable, that the defence would be credited. In the second of the two cases (the case of submission to circumstances), but one result could be expected—instant dismissal; and perhaps, discovery as well. What object was to be gained by braving that degradation—by leaving the house, publicly disgraced in the eyes of the servants who had hated and distrusted her from the first? The accident which had literally snatched the Trust from her possession when she had it in her hand, was irreparable. The one apparent compensation under the disaster—in other words, the discovery that the Trust actually existed, and that George Bartram's marriage within a given time, was one of the objects contained in it—was a compensation which could only be estimated at its true value, by placing it under the light of Mr. Loscombe's experience. Every motive of which she was conscious, was a motive which urged her to leave the house secretly, while the chance was at her disposal. She looked out into the passage, and called softly to old Mazey to come back.

"I accept your offer thankfully, Mr. Mazey," she said. "You don't know what hard measure you dealt out to me, when you took that letter from my hand. But you did your duty—and I can be grateful to you for sparing me this morning, hard as you were upon me last night. I am not such a bad girl as you think me—I am not indeed."

Old Mazey dismissed the subject, with another dreary wave of his hand.

"Let it be," said the veteran; "let it be! It makes no difference, my girl, to such an old rascal as I am. If you were fifty times worse than you are, I should let you go all the same. Put on your bonnet and shawl, and come along. I'm a disgrace to myself and a warning to others—that's what I am. No luggage, mind! Leave all your rattle-traps behind you : to be overhauled, if necessary, at his honour the admiral's discretion. I can be hard enough on your boxes, you young Jezabel ; if I can't be hard on *you*."

With those words, old Mazey led the way out of the room. "The less I see of her the better—especially about the waist," he said to himself, as he hobbled down-stairs with the help of the banisters.

The cart was standing in the back-yard, when they reached the lower regions of the house ; and Dawkes (otherwise the farm-bailiff's man) was fastening the last buckle of the horse's harness. The hoar frost of the morning was still white in the shade. The sparkling points of it glistened brightly on the shaggy coats of Brutus and Cassius, as they idled about the yard, waiting, with steaming mouths and slowly-wagging tails, to see the cart drive off. Old Mazey went out alone, and used his influence with Dawkes, who, staring in stolid amazement, put a leather-cushion on the cart-seat for his fellow-traveller. Shivering in the sharp morning air, Magdalen waited, while the preliminaries of departure were in progress, conscious of nothing but a giddy bewilderment of thought, and a helpless suspension of feeling. The events of the night confused themselves hideously, with the trivial circumstances passing before her eyes in the court-yard. She started with the sudden terror of the night, when old Mazey reappeared to summon her out to the cart. She trembled with the helpless confusion of the night, when the veteran cast the eyes of indulgence on her for the last time, and gave her a kiss on the cheek at parting. The next minute, she felt him help her into the cart, and pat her on the back. The next, she heard him tell her in a confidential whisper that, sitting or standing, she was as straight as a poplar, either way. Then there was a pause, in which nothing was said, and nothing done; and then the driver took the reins in hand, and mounted to his place.

She roused herself at the parting moment, and looked back. The last sight she saw at St. Crux, was old Mazey wagging his head in the court-yard, with his fellow-profligates, the dogs, keeping time to him with their tails. The last words she heard, were the words in which the veteran paid his farewell tribute to her charms:—

"Burglary, or no burglary," said old Mazey, "she's a fine-grown girl, if ever there was a fine one yet. What a pity! what a pity!"

THE END OF THE SEVENTH SCENE.

BETWEEN THE SCENES.

PROGRESS OF THE STORY THROUGH THE POST.

———

I.

FROM GEORGE BARTRAM TO ADMIRAL BARTRAM.

"London, April 3rd, 1848.

"MY DEAR UNCLE,

"One hasty line, to inform you of a temporary obstacle, which we neither of us anticipated when we took leave of each other at St. Crux. While I was wasting the last days of the week at the Grange, the Tyrrels must have been making their arrangements for leaving London. I have just come from Portland Place. The house is shut up; and the family (Miss Vanstone, of course, included) left England yesterday, to pass the season in Paris.

"Pray don't let yourself be annoyed by this little check at starting. It is of no serious importance whatever. I have got the address at which the Tyrrels are living; and I mean to cross the Channel, after them, by the mail to-night. I shall find my opportunity in Paris, just as soon as I could have found it in London. The grass shall not grow under my feet, I promise you. For once in my life, I will take Time as fiercely by the fore-lock, as if I was the most impetuous man in England—and, rely on it, the moment I know the result, you shall know the result too.

"Affectionately yours,

"GEORGE BARTRAM."

II.

FROM GEORGE BARTRAM TO MISS GARTH.

"DEAR MISS GARTH,   "Paris, April 13th.

"I have just written, with a heavy heart, to my uncle; and I think I owe it to your kind interest in me, not to omit writing next to you.

"You will feel for my disappointment, I am sure, when I tell you, in the fewest and plainest words, that Miss Vanstone has refused me.

"My vanity may have grievously misled me; but I confess I expected a very different result. My vanity may be misleading me still—for I must acknowledge to you privately, that I think Miss Vanstone was sorry to refuse me. The reason she gave for her decision—no doubt a sufficient reason in her estimation—did not at the time, and does not now, seem sufficient to *me*. She spoke in the sweetest and kindest manner; but she firmly declared that 'her family misfortunes' left her no honourable alternative, but to think of my own interests, as I had not thought of them myself—and gratefully to decline accepting my offer.

"She was so painfully agitated that I could not venture to plead my own cause, as I might otherwise have pleaded it. At the first attempt I made to touch the personal question, she entreated me to spare her, and abruptly left the room. I am still ignorant whether I am to interpret the 'family misfortunes' which have set up this barrier between us, as meaning the misfortune for which her parents alone are to blame—or the misfortune of her having such a woman as Mrs. Noel Vanstone for her sister. In whichever of these circumstances the obstacle lies, it is no obstacle in my estimation. Can nothing remove it? Is there no hope? Forgive me for asking these questions. I cannot bear up against my bitter disappointment. Neither she, nor you, nor any one but myself, can know how I love her.

"Ever most truly yours,

"GEORGE BARTRAM.

"P.S.—I shall leave for England in a day or two, passing through London, on my way to St. Crux. There are family reasons, connected with the hateful subject of money, which make me look forward, with anything but pleasure, to my next interview with my uncle. If you address your letter to Long's Hotel, it will be sure to reach me."

III.

FROM MISS GARTH TO GEORGE BARTRAM.

"Westmoreland House, April 16th.

"DEAR MR. BARTRAM,

"You only did me justice in supposing that your letter would distress me. If you had supposed that it would make me excessively angry as well, you would not have been far wrong. I have no patience with the pride and perversity of the young women of the present day.

"I have heard from Norah. It is a long letter, stating the particulars in full detail. I am now going to put all the confidence in your honour and your discretion which I really feel. For your sake, and for Norah's, I am going to let you know what the scruple really is, which has misled her into the pride and folly of refusing you. I am old enough to speak out ; and I can tell you, if she had only been wise enough to let her own wishes guide her, she would have said, Yes—and gladly too.

"The original cause of all the mischief, is no less a person than your worthy uncle—Admiral Bartram.

"It seems that the admiral took it into his head (I suppose during your absence) to go to London by himself; and to satisfy some curiosity of his own about Norah, by calling in Portland Place, under pretence of renewing his old friendship with the Tyrrels. He came at luncheon-time, and saw Norah ; and, from all I can hear, was apparently better pleased with her than he expected or wished to be when he came into the house.

"So far, this is mere guess-work—but it is unluckily certain that he and Mrs. Tyrrel had some talk together alone when luncheon was over. Your name was not mentioned ; but when their conversation fell on Norah, you were in both their minds, of course. The admiral (doing her full justice personally) declared himself smitten with pity for her hard lot in life. The scandalous conduct of her sister must always stand (he feared) in the way of her future advantage. Who could marry her, without first making it a condition that she and her sister were to be absolute strangers to each other ? And even then, the objection would remain—the serious objection to the husband's family—of being connected by marriage with such a woman as Mrs. Noel Vanstone. It was very sad ; it was not the poor girl's fault— but it was none the less true that her sister was her rock ahead in life. So he ran on, with no real ill-feeling towards Norah, but with an obstinate belief in his own prejudices, which bore the aspect of ill-feeling, and which people with more temper than judgment would be but too readily disposed to resent accordingly.

"Unfortunately, Mrs. Tyrrel is one of those people. She is an excellent, warm-hearted woman, with a quick temper and very little judgment ; strongly attached to Norah, and heartily interested in Norah's welfare.

From all I can learn, she first resented the expression of the admiral's opinion, in his presence, as worldly and selfish in the last degree ; and then interpreted it behind his back, as a hint to discourage his nephew's visits, which was a downright insult offered to a lady in her own house. This was foolish enough so far—but worse folly was to come.

"As soon as your uncle was gone, Mrs. Tyrrel, most unwisely and improperly, sent for Norah ; and repeating the conversation that had taken place, warned her of the reception she might expect from the man who stood towards you in the position of a father, if she accepted an offer of marriage on your part. When I tell you that Norah's faithful attachment to her sister still remains unshaken, and that there lies hidden under her noble submission to the unhappy circumstances of her life, a proud susceptibility to slights of all kinds, which is deeply seated in her nature—you will understand the true motive of the refusal which has so naturally and so justly disappointed you. They are all three equally to blame in this matter. Your uncle was wrong to state his objections so roundly and inconsiderately as he did. Mrs. Tyrrel was wrong to let her temper get the better of her, and to suppose herself insulted where no insult was intended. And Norah was wrong to place a scruple of pride, and a hopeless belief in her sister which no strangers can be expected to share, above the higher claims of an attachment which might have secured the happiness and the prosperity of her future life.

"But the mischief has been done. The next question is—can the harm be remedied ?

"I hope and believe it can. My advice is this :—Don't take No for an answer. Give her time enough to reflect on what she has done, and to regret it (as I believe [she will regret it) in secret—trust to my influence over her to plead your cause for you at every opportunity I can find—wait patiently for the right moment—and ask her again. Men, being accustomed to act on reflection themselves, are a great deal too apt to believe that women act on reflection too. Women do nothing of the sort. They act on impulse—and, in nine cases out of ten, they are heartily sorry for it afterwards.

"In the mean while, you must help your own interests, by inducing your uncle to alter his opinion—or at least to make the concession of keeping his opinion to himself. Mrs. Tyrrel has rushed to the conclusion, that the harm he has done, he did intentionally—which is as much as to say, in so many words, that he had a prophetic conviction, when he came into the house, of what she would do when he left it. My explanation of the matter is a much simpler one. I believe that the knowledge of your attachment naturally aroused his curiosity to see the object of it, and that Mrs. Tyrrel's injudicious praises of Norah irritated his objections into openly declaring themselves. Any way, your course lies equally plain before you. Use your influence over your uncle to persuade him into setting matters right again; trust my settled resolution to see Norah your wife, before six months more are over our heads; and believe me, your friend and well-wisher,

"HARRIET GARTH."

IV.

From Mrs. Drake to George Bartram.

"St. Crux, April 17th.

" SIR,

" I direct these lines to the hotel you usually stay at in London; hoping that you may return soon enough from foreign parts to receive my letter without delay.

" I am sorry to say that some unpleasant events have taken place at St. Crux, since you left it, and that my honoured master, the admiral, is far from enjoying his usual good health. On both these accounts, I venture to write to you, on my own responsibility—for I think your presence is needed in the house.

" Early in the month, a most regretable circumstance took place. Our new parlour-maid was discovered by Mr. Mazey, at a late hour of the night (with her master's basket of keys in her possession), prying into the private documents kept in the east library. The girl removed herself from the house, the next morning, before we were any of us astir, and she has not been heard of since. This event has annoyed and alarmed my master very seriously; and to make matters worse, on the day when the girl's treacherous conduct was discovered, the admiral was seized with the first symptoms of a severe inflammatory cold. He was not himself aware, nor was any one else, how he had caught the chill. The doctor was sent for, and kept the inflammation down until the day before yesterday—when it broke out again, under circumstances which I am sure you will be sorry to hear, as I am truly sorry to write of them.

" On the date I have just mentioned—I mean the fifteenth of the month —my master himself informed me that he had been dreadfully disappointed by a letter received from you, which had come in the morning from foreign parts, and had brought him bad news. He did not tell me what the news was —but I have never, in all the years I have passed in the admiral's service, seen him so distressingly upset, and so unlike himself, as he was on that day. At night his uneasiness seemed to increase. He was in such a state of irritation, that he could not bear the sound of Mr. Mazey's hard breathing outside his door; and he laid his positive orders on the old man to go into one of the bedrooms for that night. Mr. Mazey, to his own great regret, was of course obliged to obey.

" Our only means of preventing the admiral from leaving his room in his sleep, if the fit unfortunately took him, being now removed, Mr. Mazey and I agreed to keep watch by turns through the night—sitting with the door ajar, in one of the empty rooms near our master's bed-chamber. We could think of nothing better to do than this—knowing he would not allow us to lock him in; and not having the door-key in our possession, even if we could have ventured to secure him in his room without his permission. I kept watch for the first two hours, and then Mr. Mazey took my place. After having been some little time in my own room, it occurred to me that the old man was hard of hearing, and that if his eyes grew at all heavy in the night, his ears were not to be trusted to warn him, if anything happened. I slipped on my clothes again, and went back to Mr. Mazey. He was neither asleep nor awake—he was between the two. My mind misgave me, and I went on to the admiral's room. The door was open, and the bed was empty.

" Mr. Mazey and I went down-stairs instantly. We looked in all the north rooms, one after another, and found no traces of him. I thought of the drawing-room next, and, being the most active of the two, went first to examine it. The moment I turned the sharp corner of the passage, I saw my master coming towards me through the open drawing-room door, asleep and dreaming, with his keys in his hands. The sliding-door behind him was open also; and the fear came to me then, and has remained with me ever since, that his dream had led him through the Banqueting-Hall, into the east rooms. We abstained from waking him, and followed his steps, until he returned of his own accord to his bed-chamber. The next morning, I grieve to say, all the bad symptoms came back; and none of the remedies employed have succeeded in getting the better of them yet. By the doctor's advice, we refrained from telling the admiral what had happened. He is still under the impression that he passed the night as usual in his own room.

" I have been careful to enter into all the particulars of this unfortunate accident, because neither Mr. Mazey nor myself desire to screen ourselves from blame, if blame we have deserved. We both acted for the best, and we both beg and pray you will consider our responsible situation, and come as soon as possible to St. Crux. Our honoured master is very hard to manage; and the doctor thinks, as we do, that your presence is wanted in the house.

" I remain, sir, with Mr. Mazey's respects and my own, your humble servant,

　　　　　　　　　　　　　　　　　　" SOPHIA DRAKE."

V.

FROM GEORGE BARTRAM TO MISS GARTH.

"St. Crux, April 22nd.

"DEAR MISS GARTH,

"Pray excuse my not thanking you sooner for your kind and consoling letter. We are in sad trouble at St. Crux. Any little irritation I might have felt at my poor uncle's unlucky interference in Portland Place, is all forgotten in the misfortune of his serious illness. He is suffering from internal inflammation, produced by cold; and symptoms have shown themselves which are dangerous at his age. A physician from London is now in the house. You shall hear more in a few days. Meantime, believe me, with sincere gratitude,

"Yours most truly,
"GEORGE BARTRAM."

VI.

FROM MR. LOSCOMBE TO MRS. NOEL VANSTONE.

"Lincoln's Inn Fields, May 6th.

"DEAR MADAM,

"I have unexpectedly received some information which is of the most vital importance to your interests. The news of Admiral Bartram's death has reached me this morning. He expired at his own house, on the fourth of the present month.

"This event at once disposes of the considerations which I had previously endeavoured to impress on you, in relation to your discovery at St. Crux. The wisest course we can now follow, is to open communications at once with the executors of the deceased gentleman; addressing them through the medium of the admiral's legal adviser, in the first instance.

"I have despatched a letter this day to the solicitor in question. It simply warns him that we have lately become aware of the existence of a private Document, controlling the deceased gentleman in his use of the legacy devised to him by Mr. Noel Vanstone's will. My letter assumes that the document will be easily found among the admiral's papers; and it mentions that I am the solicitor appointed by Mrs. Noel Vanstone to receive communications on her behalf. My object in taking this step, is to cause a search to be instituted for the Trust—in the very probable event of the executors not having met with it yet—before the usual measures are adopted for the administration of the admiral's estate. We will threaten legal proceedings, if we find that the object does not succeed. But I anticipate no such necessity. Admiral Bartram's executors must be men of high standing and position; and they will do justice to you and to themselves in this matter, by looking for the Trust.

"Under these circumstances, you will naturally ask—'What are our prospects when the document is found?' Our prospects have a bright side, and a dark side. Let us take the bright side to begin with.

"What do we actually know?

"We know, first, that the Trust does really exist. Secondly, that there is a provision in it, relating to the marriage of Mr. George Bartram in a given time. Thirdly, that the time (six months from the date of your husband's death) expired on the third of this month. Fourthly, that Mr. George Bartram (as I have found out by inquiry, in the absence of any positive information on the subject possessed by yourself) is, at the present moment, a single man. The conclusion naturally follows, that the object contemplated by the Trust, in this case, is an object that has failed.

"If no other provisions have been inserted in the document—or if, being inserted, those other provisions should be discovered to have failed also—I believe it to be impossible (especially if evidence can be found that the admiral himself considered the Trust binding on him) for the executors to deal with your husband's fortune as legally forming part of Admiral Bartram's estate. The legacy is expressly declared to have been left to him, on the understanding that he applies it to certain stated objects—and those objects have failed. What is to be done with the money? It was not left to the admiral himself, on the testator's own showing; and the purposes for which it *was* left, have not been, and cannot be, carried out. I believe (if the case here supposed really happens), that the money must revert to the testator's estate. In that event, the Law, dealing with it as a matter of necessity, divides it into two equal portions. One half goes to Mr. Noel Vanstone's childless widow; and the other half is divided among Mr. Noel Vanstone's next-of-kin.

"You will no doubt discover the obvious objection to the case in our favour, as I have here put it. You will see that it depends for its practical realization, not on one contingency, but on a series of contingencies, which must all happen exactly as we wish them to happen. I admit the force of the objection—but I can tell you, at the same time, that these said contingencies are by no means so improbable as they may look on the face of them.

"We have every reason to believe that the Trust, like the Will, was *not* drawn by a lawyer. That is one circumstance in our favour—that is enough of itself to cast a doubt on the soundness of all, or any, of the remaining provisions which we may not be acquainted with. Another chance which we may count on, is to be found, as I think, in that strange handwriting, placed under the signature on the third page of the Letter, which you saw, but which you unhappily omitted to read. All the probabilities point to those lines as written by Admiral Bartram; and the position which they occupy is certainly consistent with the theory that they touch the important subject of his own sense of obligation under the Trust.

"I wish to raise no false hopes in your mind. I only desire to satisfy you that we have a case worth trying.

"As for the dark side of the prospect, I need not enlarge on it. After what I have already written, you will understand that the existence of a sound provision, unknown to us, in the Trust, which has been properly carried out by the admiral—or which can be properly carried out by his representatives—would be necessarily fatal to our hopes. The legacy would be, in this case, devoted to the purpose or purposes contemplated by your husband—and, from that moment, you would have no claim.

"I have only to add, that as soon as I hear from the late admiral's man of business, you shall know the result.

"Believe me, dear madam,

"Faithfully yours,

"JOHN LOSCOMBE."

VII.

FROM GEORGE BARTRAM TO MISS GARTH.

"St. Crux, May 15th.

"DEAR MISS GARTH,

"I trouble you with 'another letter: partly to thank you for your kind expression of sympathy with me, under the loss that I have sustained; and partly to tell you of an extraordinary application made to my uncle's executors, in which you and Miss Vanstone may both feel interested, as Mrs. Noel Vanstone is directly concerned in it.

"Knowing my own ignorance of legal technicalities, I enclose a copy of the application, instead of trying to describe it. You will notice, as suspicious, that no explanation is given of the manner in which the alleged discovery of one of my uncle's secrets was made, by persons who are total strangers to him.

"On being made acquainted with the circumstances, the executors at once applied to me. I could give them no positive information—for my uncle never consulted me on matters of business. But I felt in honour bound to tell them, that during the last six months of his life, the admiral had occasionally let fall expressions of impatience in my hearing, which led to the conclusion that he was annoyed by a private responsibility of some kind. I also mentioned that he had imposed a very strange condition on me—a condition which, in spite of his own assurances to the contrary, I was persuaded could not have emanated from himself—of marrying within a given time (which time has now expired), or of not receiving from him a certain sum of money, which I believed to be the same in amount as the sum bequeathed to him in my cousin's will. The executors agreed with me that these circumstances gave a colour of probability to an otherwise incredible story; and they decided that a search should be instituted for the Secret Trust—nothing in the slightest degree resembling this same Trust having been discovered, up to that time, among the admiral's papers.

"The search (no trifle in such a house as this) has now been in full progress for a week. It is superintended by both the executors, and by my uncle's lawyer—who is personally, as well as professionally, known to Mr. Loscombe (Mrs. Noel Vanstone's solicitor), and who has been included in the proceedings at the express request of Mr. Loscombe himself. Up to this time, nothing whatever has been found. Thousands and thousands of letters have been examined—and not one of them bears the remotest resemblance to the letter we are looking for.

"Another week will bring the search to an end. It is only at my express request that it will be persevered with so long. But as the admiral's generosity has made me sole heir to everything he possessed, I feel bound to do the fullest justice to the interests of others, however hostile to myself those interests may be.

"With this view, I have not hesitated to reveal to the lawyer, a constitutional peculiarity of my poor uncle's, which was always kept a secret among us at his own request—I mean his tendency to somnambulism. I mentioned that he had been discovered (by the housekeeper and his old servant), walking in his sleep, about three weeks before his death, and that the part of the house in which he had been seen, and the basket of keys which he was carrying in his hand, suggested the inference that he had come from one of the rooms in the east wing, and that he might have opened some of the pieces of furniture in one of them. I surprised the lawyer (who seemed to be quite ignorant of the extraordinary actions constantly performed by somnambulists), by informing him that my uncle could find his way about the house, lock and unlock doors, and remove objects of all kinds from one place to another, as easily in his sleep, as in his waking hours. And I declared that, while I felt the faintest doubt in my own mind whether he might not have been dreaming of the Trust on the night in question, and putting the dream in action in his sleep, I should not feel satisfied unless the rooms in the east wing were searched again.

"It is only right to add that there is not the least foundation in fact for this idea of mine. During the latter part of his fatal illness, my poor uncle was quite incapable of speaking on any subject whatever. From the time of my arrival at St. Crux, in the middle of last month, to the time of his death, not a word dropped from him which referred in the remotest way to the Secret Trust.

"Here then, for the present, the matter rests. If you think it right to communicate the contents of this letter to Miss Vanstone, pray tell her that it will not be my fault if her sister's assertion (however preposterous it may seem to my uncle's executors) is not fairly put to the proof.

"Believe me, dear Miss Garth,

"Always truly yours,

"GEORGE BARTRAM.

"P.S.—As soon as all business matters are settled, I am going abroad for some months, to try the relief of change of scene. The house will be shut up, and left under the charge of Mrs. Drake. I have not forgotten your once telling me that you should like to see St. Crux, if you ever found yourself in this neighbourhood. If you are at all likely to be in Essex, during the time when I am abroad, I have provided against the chance of your being disappointed, by leaving instructions with Mrs. Drake to give you, and any friends of yours, the freest admission to the house and grounds."

VIII.

FROM MR. LOSCOMBE TO MRS. NOEL VANSTONE.

"Lincoln's Inn Fields, May 24th.

"DEAR MADAM,

"After a whole fortnight's search—conducted, I am bound to admit, with the most conscientious and unrelaxing care—no such document as the Secret Trust has been found among the papers left at St. Crux by the late Admiral Bartram.

"Under these circumstances, the executors have decided on acting under the only recognizable authority which they have to guide them—the admiral's own will. This document (executed some years since) bequeaths the whole of his estate, both real and personal (that is to say, all the lands he possesses, and all the money he possesses, at the time of his death), to his nephew. The will is plain, and the result is inevitable. Your husband's fortune is lost to you from this moment. Mr. George Bartram legally inherits it, as he legally inherits the house and estate of St. Crux.

"I make no comment upon this extraordinary close to the proceedings. The Trust may have been destroyed, or the Trust may be hidden in some place of concealment, inaccessible to discovery. Either way, it is, in my opinion, impossible to found any valid legal declaration on a knowledge of the document, so fragmentary and so incomplete, as the knowledge which you possess. If other lawyers differ from me on this point, by all means consult them. I have devoted money enough and time enough to the unfortunate attempt to assert your interests; and my connection with the matter, must, from this moment, be considered at an end.

"Your obedient servant,

"JOHN LOSCOMBE."

IX.

FROM MRS. RUDDOCK (LODGING-HOUSE KEEPER) TO MR. LOSCOMBE.

"Park Terrace, St. John's Wood,

"SIR,   "June 2nd.

"Having, by Mrs. Noel Vanstone's directions, taken letters for her to the post, addressed to you—and knowing no one else to apply to—I beg to inquire whether you are acquainted with any of her friends; for I think it right that they should be stirred up to take some steps about her.

"Mrs. Vanstone first came to me in November last, when she and her maid occupied my apartments. On that occasion, and again on this, she has given me no cause to complain of her. She has behaved like a lady, and paid me my due. I am writing, as a mother of a family, under a sense of responsibility—I am not writing with an interested motive.

"After proper warning given, Mrs. Vanstone (who is now quite alone) leaves me to-morrow. She has not concealed from me that her circumstances are fallen very low, and that she cannot afford to remain in my house. This is all she has told me—I know nothing of where she is going, or what she means to do next. But I have every reason to believe she desires to destroy all traces by which she might be found, after leaving this place—for I discovered her in tears yesterday, burning letters which were doubtless letters from her friends. In looks and conduct she has altered most shockingly in the last week. I believe there is some dreadful trouble on her mind—and I am afraid, from what I see of her, that she is on the eve of a serious illness. It is very sad to see such a young woman, so utterly deserted and friendless as she is now.

"Excuse my troubling you with this letter; it is on my conscience to write it. If you know any of her relations, please warn them that time is not to be wasted. If they lose to-morrow, they may lose the last chance of finding her.

"Your humble servant,

"CATHERINE RUDDOCK."

X.

FROM MR. LOSCOMBE TO MRS. RUDDOCK.

"MADAM,   "Lincoln's Inn Fields, June 2nd.

"My only connection with Mrs. Noel Vanstone was a professional one—and that connection is now at an end. I am not acquainted with any of her friends; and I cannot undertake to interfere personally, either with her present or future proceedings.

"Regretting my inability to afford you any assistance, I remain, your obedient servant,

"JOHN LOSCOMBE."

THE LAST SCENE.

AARON'S BUILDINGS.*

CHAPTER I.

On the seventh of June, the owners of the merchantman, DELIVERANCE, received news that the ship had touched at Plymouth to land passengers, and had then continued her homeward voyage to the Port of London. Five days later, the vessel was in the river, and was towed into the East India Docks.

Having transacted the business on shore for which he was personally responsible, Captain Kirke made the necessary arrangements by letter, for visiting his brother-in-law's parsonage in Suffolk, on the seventeenth of the month. As usual, in such cases, he received a list of commissions to execute for his sister on the day before he left London. One of these commissions took him into the neighbourhood of Camden Town. He drove to his destination from the Docks; and then, dismissing the vehicle, set forth to walk back southward, towards the New Road.

He was not well acquainted with the district; and his attention wandered, farther and farther away from the scene around him, as he went on. His thoughts, roused by the prospect of seeing his sister again, had led his memory back to the night when he had parted from her, leaving the house on foot. The spell so strangely laid on him, in that past time, had kept its hold through all after-events. The face that had haunted him on the lonely road, had haunted him again on the lonely sea. The woman who had followed him, as in a dream, to his sister's door, had followed him—thought of his thought, and spirit of his spirit—to the deck of his ship. Through storm and calm on the voyage out, through storm and calm on the voyage home, she had been with him. In the ceaseless turmoil of the London streets, she was with him now. He knew what the first question on his lips would be, when he had seen his sister and her boys. "I shall try to talk of something else," he thought; "but when Lizzie and I are alone, it will come out in spite of me."

The necessity of waiting to let a string of carts pass at a turning, before he crossed, awakened him to present things. He looked about in a momentary confusion. The street was strange to him; he had lost his way.

The first foot-passenger of whom he inquired, appeared to have no time to waste in giving information. Hurriedly directing him to cross to the other side of the road, to turn down the first street he came to on his right hand, and then to ask again, the stranger unceremoniously hastened on without waiting to be thanked.

Kirke followed his directions, and took the turning on his right. The street was short and narrow, and the houses on either side were of the poorer order. He looked up as he passed the corner, to see what the name of the place might be. It was called " Aaron's Buildings."

Low down on the side of the " Buildings " along which he was walking, a little crowd of idlers was assembled round two cabs, both drawn up before the door of the same house. Kirke advanced to the crowd, to ask his way of any civil stranger among them, who might *not* be in a hurry this time. On approaching the cabs, he found a woman disputing with the drivers; and heard enough to inform him that two vehicles had been sent for by mistake, where one only was wanted.

The house-door was open ; and when he turned that way next, he looked easily into the passage, over the heads of the people in front of him.

The sight that met his eyes should have been shielded in pity from the observation of the street. He saw a slatternly girl, with a frightened face, standing by an old chair placed in the middle of the passage, and holding a woman on the chair, too weak and helpless to support herself—a woman apparently in the last stage of illness, who was about to be removed, when the dispute outside was ended, in one of the cabs. Her head was drooping, when he first saw her, and an old shawl which covered it, had fallen forward so as to hide the upper part of her face.

Before he could look away again, the girl in charge of her, raised her head, and restored the shawl to its place. The action disclosed her face to view, for an instant only, before her head drooped once more on her bosom. In that instant, he saw the woman whose beauty was the haunting remembrance of his life—whose image had been vivid in his mind, not five minutes since.

The shock of the double recognition—the recognition, at the same moment, of the face, and of the dreadful change in it—struck him speechless and helpless. The steady presence of mind in all emergencies which had become a habit of his life, failed him for the first time. The poverty-stricken street, the squalid mob round the door, swam before his eyes. He staggered back, and caught at the iron-railings of the house behind him.

" Where are they taking her to ?" he heard a woman ask, close at his side.

"To the hospital, if they will have her," was the reply. " And to the workhouse, if they won't."

That horrible answer roused him. He pushed his way through the crowd, and entered the house.

The misunderstanding on the pavement had been set right; and one of the cabs had driven off. As he crossed the threshold of the door, he confronted the people of the house at the moment when they were moving her. The cabman who had remained, was on one side of the chair, and the woman who had been disputing with the two drivers was on the other. They were just lifting her, when Kirke's tall figure darkened the door.

"What are you doing with that lady?" he asked.

The cabman looked up with the insolence of his reply visible in his eyes, before his lips could utter it. But the woman, quicker than he, saw the suppressed agitation in Kirke's face, and dropped her hold of the chair in an instant.

"Do you know her, sir?" asked the woman, eagerly. "Are you one of her friends?"

"Yes," said Kirke, without hesitation.

"It's not my fault, sir," pleaded the woman, shrinking under the look he fixed on her. "I would have waited patiently till her friends found her— I would indeed!"

Kirke made no reply. He turned, and spoke to the cabman.

"Go out," he said, "and close the door after you. I'll send you down your money directly. What room in the house did you take her from, when you brought her here?" he resumed, addressing himself to the woman again.

"The first floor back, sir."

"Show me the way to it."

He stooped, and lifted Magdalen in his arms. Her head rested gently on the sailor's breast; her eyes looked up wonderingly into the sailor's face. She smiled and whispered to him vacantly. Her mind had wandered back to old days at home; and her few broken words showed that she fancied herself a child again in her father's arms. "Poor papa!" she said softly. "Why do you look so sorry? Poor papa!"

The woman led the way into the back room on the first floor. It was very small; it was miserably furnished. But the little bed was clean, and the few things in the room were neatly kept. Kirke laid her tenderly on the bed. She caught one of his hands in her burning fingers. "Don't distress mamma about me," she said. "Send for Norah." Kirke tried gently to release his hand; but she only clasped it the more eagerly. He sat down by the bedside to wait until it pleased her to release him. The woman stood looking at them and crying, in a corner of the room. Kirke observed her attentively. "Speak," he said, after an interval, in low quiet tones. "Speak, in her presence; and tell me the truth."

With many words, with many tears, the woman spoke.

She had let her first floor to the lady, a fortnight since. The lady had paid a week's rent, and had given the name of Gray. She had been out from morning till night, for the first three days, and had come home again, on every occasion, with a wretchedly weary, disappointed look. The woman of the house had suspected that she was in hiding from her friends, under a false name; and that she had been vainly trying to raise money, or to get some employment, on the three days when she was out for so long, and when she looked so disappointed on coming home. However that might be, on the fourth day she had fallen ill, with shivering fits and hot fits, turn and turn about. On the fifth day, she was worse; and on the sixth, she was too sleepy at one time, and too light-headed at another, to be spoken to. The chemist (who did the doctoring in those parts) had come and looked at her, and had said he thought it was a bad fever. He had left a "saline draught," which the woman of the house had paid for out of her own pocket, and had administered without effect. She had ventured on searching the only box which the lady had brought with her; and had found nothing in it but a few necessary articles of linen—no dresses, no ornaments, not so much as the fragment of a letter which might help in discovering her friends. Between the risk of keeping her under these circumstances, and the barbarity of turning a sick woman into the street, the landlady herself had not hesitated. She would willingly have kept her tenant, on the chance of the lady's recovery, and on the chance of friends turning up. But not half an hour since, her husband—who never came near the house, except to take her money—had come to rob her of her little earnings, as usual. She had been obliged to tell him that no rent was in hand for the first floor, and that none was likely to be in hand until the lady recovered, or her friends found her. On hearing this, he had mercilessly insisted—well or ill—that the lady should go. There was the hospital to take her to; and if the hospital shut its doors, there was the workhouse to try next. If she was not out of the place in an hour's time, he threatened to come back, and take her out himself. His wife knew, but too well, that he was brute enough to be as good as his word; and no other choice had been left her, but to do as she had done, for the sake of the lady herself.

The woman told her shocking story, with every appearance of being honestly ashamed of it. Towards the end, Kirke felt the clasp of the burning fingers slackening round his hand. He looked back at the bed again. Her weary eyes were closing; and, with her face still turned towards the sailor, she was sinking into sleep.

"Is there any one in the front room?" said Kirke, in a whisper. "Come in there; I have something to say to you."

The woman followed him, through the door of communication between the rooms.

"How much does she owe you?" he asked.

The landlady mentioned the sum. Kirke put it down before her on the table.

" Where is your husband?" was his next question.

" Waiting at the public-house, sir, till the hour is up."

" You can take him the money, or not, as you think right," said Kirke quietly. " I have only one thing to tell you, so far as your husband is concerned. If you want to see every bone in his skin broken, let him come to the house while I am in it. Stop! I have something more to say. Do you know of any doctor in the neighbourhood, who can be depended on?"

" Not in our neighbourhood, sir. But I know of one within half an hour's walk of us."

" Take the cab at the door; and, if you find him at home, bring him back in it. Say I am waiting here for his opinion, on a very serious case. He shall be well paid, and you shall be well paid. Make haste!"

The woman left the room.

Kirke sat down alone, to wait for her return. He hid his face in his hands; and tried to realize the strange and touching situation in which the accident of a moment had placed him.

Hidden in the squalid by-ways of London, under a false name; cast, friendless and helpless, on the mercy of strangers, by illness which had struck her prostrate, mind and body alike—so he met her again, the woman who had opened a new world of beauty to his mind; the woman who had called Love to life in him by a look! What horrible misfortune had struck her so cruelly, and struck her so low? What mysterious destiny had guided him to the last refuge of her poverty and despair, in the hour of her sorest need? " If it is ordered that I am to see her again, I *shall* see her." Those words came back to him now—the memorable words that he had spoken to his sister at parting. With that thought in his heart, he had gone where his duty called him. Months and months had passed; thousands and thousands of miles, protracting their desolate length on the unresting waters, had rolled between them. And through the lapse of time, and over the waste of oceans—day after day, and night after night, as the winds of heaven blew, and the good ship toiled on before them—he had advanced, nearer and nearer to the end that was waiting for him; he had journeyed blindfold to the meeting on the threshold of that miserable door. " What has brought me here?" he said to himself in a whisper. " The mercy of chance? No! The mercy of God."

He waited, unregardful of the place, unconscious of the time, until the sound of footsteps on the stairs came suddenly between him and his thoughts. The door opened, and the doctor was shown into the room.

" Dr. Merrick," said the landlady, placing a chair for him.

" *Mr.* Merrick," said the visitor, smiling quietly as he took the chair. " I am not a physician—I am a surgeon in general practice."*

Physician or surgeon, there was something in his face and manner which told Kirke, at a glance, that he was a man to be relied on.

After a few preliminary words on either side, Mr. Merrick sent the land-lady into the bedroom to see if his patient was awake or asleep. The woman returned, and said she was "betwixt the two, light in the head again, and burning hot." The doctor went at once into the bedroom, tell-ing the landlady to follow him, and to close the door behind her.

A weary time passed before he came back into the front room. When he reappeared, his face spoke for him, before any question could be asked.

"Is it a serious illness?" said Kirke, his voice sinking low, his eyes anxiously fixed on the doctor's face.

"It is a *dangerous* illness," said Mr. Merrick, with an emphasis on the word.

He drew his chair nearer to Kirke, and looked at him attentively.

"May I ask you some questions, which are not strictly medical?" he inquired.

Kirke bowed.

"Can you tell me what her life has been, before she came into this house, and before she fell ill?"

"I have no means of knowing. I have just returned to England, after a ong absence."

"Did you know of her coming here?"

"I only discovered it by accident."

"Has she no female relations? No mother? no sister? no one to take care of her but yourself?"

"No one—unless I can succeed in tracing her relations. No one but myself."

Mr. Merrick was silent. He looked at Kirke more attentively than ever. "Strange!" thought the doctor. "He is here, in sole charge of her—and is this all he knows?"

Kirke saw the doubt in his face; and addressed himself straight to that doubt, before another word passed between them.

"I see my position here surprises you," he said simply. "Will you consider it the position of a relation—the position of her brother or her father—until her friends can be found?" His voice faltered, and he laid his hand earnestly on the doctor's arm. "I have taken this trust on myself," he said: "and, as God shall judge me, I will not be unworthy of it!"

The poor weary head lay on his breast again, the poor fevered fingers clasped his hand once more, as he spoke those words.

"I believe you," said the doctor warmly. "I believe you are an honest man.—Pardon me if I have seemed to intrude myself on your confidence. I respect your reserve—from this moment, it is sacred to me. In justice to both of us, let me say that the questions I have asked, were not prompted by mere curiosity. No common cause will account for the illness which has laid my patient on that bed. She has suffered some long-continued mental trial, some wearing and terrible suspense—and she has broken down under it. It might have helped me, if I could have known what the nature of the trial was, and how long or how short a time elapsed before she sank under it. In that hope, I spoke."

"When you told me she was dangerously ill," said Kirke, "did you mean danger to her reason, or to her life?"

"To both," replied Mr. Merrick. "Her whole nervous system has given way; all the ordinary functions of her brain are in a state of collapse. I can give you no plainer explanation than that of the nature of the malady. The fever which frightens the people of the house, is merely the effect. The cause is what I have told you. She may lie on that bed for weeks to come; passing alternately, without a gleam of consciousness, from a state of delirium to a state of repose. You must not be alarmed if you find her sleep lasting far beyond the natural time. That sleep is a better remedy than any I can give, and nothing must disturb it. All our art can accomplish is to watch her—to help her with stimulants from time to time—and to wait for what Nature will do."

"Must she remain here? Is there no hope of our being able to remove her to a better place?"

"No hope whatever, for the present. She has already been disturbed, as I understand—and she is seriously the worse for it. Even if she gets better, even if she comes to herself again, it would still be a dangerous experiment to move her too soon—the least excitement or alarm would be fatal to her. You must make the best of this place as it is. The landlady has my directions; and I will send a good nurse to help her. There is nothing more to be done. So far as her life can be said to be in any human hands, it is as much in your hands now, as in mine. Everything depends on the care that is taken of her, under your direction, in this house." With those farewell words he rose, and quitted the room.

Left by himself, Kirke walked to the door of communication; and knocking at it softly, told the landlady he wished to speak with her.

He was far more composed, far more like his own resolute self, after his interview with the doctor, than he had been before it. A man living in the artificial social atmosphere which *this* man had never breathed, would have felt painfully the worldly side of the situation—its novelty and strangeness; the serious present difficulty in which it placed him; the numberless misinterpretations in the future, to which it might lead. Kirke never gave the situation a thought. He saw nothing but the duty it claimed from him—a duty which the doctor's farewell words had put plainly before his mind. Everything depended on the care taken of her, under his direction, in that house. There was his responsibility—and he unconsciously acted under it, exactly as he would have acted in a case of emergency with women and children, on board his own ship. He questioned the landlady in short, sharp sentences: the only change in him, was in the lowered tone of his voice, and in the anxious looks which he cast, from time to time, at the room where she lay.

"Do you understand what the doctor has told you?"

"Yes, sir."

"The house must be kept quiet. Who lives in the house?"

"Only me and my daughter, sir; we live in the parlours. Times have gone badly with us, since Lady Day.* Both the rooms above this are to let."

"I will take them both, and the two rooms down here as well. Do you know of any active trustworthy man, who can run on errands for me?"

"Yes, sir. Shall I go——?"

"No. Let your daughter go. You must not leave the house until the nurse comes. Don't send the messenger up here. Men of that sort tread heavily—I'll go down, and speak to him at the door."

He went down when the messenger came, and sent him first to purchase pen, ink, and paper. The man's next errand despatched him to make inquiries for a person who could provide for deadening the sound of passing wheels in the street, by laying down tan before the house in the usual way. This object accomplished, the messenger received two letters to post. The first was addressed to Kirke's brother-in-law. It told him, in few, and plain words, what had happened; and left him to break the news to his wife, as he thought best. The second letter was directed to the landlord of the Aldborough Hotel. Magdalen's assumed name at North Shingles, was the only name by which Kirke knew her; and the one chance of tracing her relatives that he could discern, was the chance of discovering her reputed uncle and aunt, by means of inquiries starting from Aldborough.

Towards the close of the afternoon, a decent middle-aged woman came to the house, with a letter from Mr. Merrick. She was well known to the doctor, as a trustworthy and careful person, who had nursed his own wife; and she would be assisted, from time to time, by a lady, who was a member of a religious Sisterhood in the district, and whose compassionate interest had been warmly aroused in the case. Towards eight o'clock, that evening, the doctor himself would call and see that his patient wanted for nothing.

The arrival of the nurse, and the relief of knowing that she was to be trusted, left Kirke free to think of himself. His luggage was ready packed for his contemplated journey to Suffolk, the next day. It was merely necessary to transport it from the hotel to the house in Aaron's Buildings.

He stopped once only on his way to the hotel, to look at a toy-shop in one of the great thoroughfares. The miniature ships in the window reminded him of his nephew. "My little namesake will be sadly disappointed at not seeing me to-morrow," he thought. "I must make it up to the boy, by sending him something from his uncle." He went into the shop, and bought one of the ships. It was secured in a box, and packed and directed in his presence. He put a card on the deck of the miniature vessel before the cover of the box was nailed on, bearing this inscription :— "A ship for the little sailor, with the big sailor's love."—"Children like to be written to, ma'am," he said, apologetically, to the woman behind the counter. "Send the box as soon as you can—I am anxious the boy should get it to-morrow."

Towards the dusk of the evening, he returned with his luggage to Aaron's Buildings. He took off his boots in the passage, and carried his trunk up-stairs himself; stopping, as he passed the first floor, to make his inquiries. Mr. Merrick was present to answer them.

"She was awake and wandering," said the doctor, "a few minutes since. But we have succeeded in composing her, and she is sleeping now."

"Have no words escaped her, sir, which might help us to find her friends ?"

Mr. Merrick shook his head.

"Weeks and weeks may pass yet," he said, "and that poor girl's story may still be a sealed secret to all of us. We can only wait."

So the day ended—the first of many days that were to come.

CHAPTER II.

THE warm sunlight of July shining softly through a green blind ; an open window with fresh flowers set on the sill ; a strange bed, in a strange room ; a giant figure of the female sex (like a dream of Mrs. Wragge) towering aloft on one side of the bed, and trying to clap its hands ; another woman (quickly) stopping the hands before they could make any noise ; a mild expostulating voice (like a dream of Mrs. Wragge again) breaking the silence in these words, " She knows me, ma'am, she knows me ; if I mustn't be happy, it will be the death of me !"—such were the first sights, such were the first sounds, to which, after six weeks of oblivion, Magdalen suddenly and strangely awoke.

After a little, the sights grew dim again, and the sounds sank into silence. Sleep, the merciful, took her once more, and hushed her back to repose.

Another day—and the sights were clearer, the sounds were louder. Another—and she heard a man's voice, through the door, asking for news from the sick-room. The voice was strange to her ; it was always cautiously lowered to the same quiet tone. It inquired after her, in the morning, when she woke—at noon, when she took her refreshment—in the evening, before she dropped to sleep again. "Who is so anxious about me?" That was the first thought her mind was strong enough to form :— "Who is so anxious about me?"

More days—and she could speak to the nurse at her bedside ; she could answer the questions of an elderly man, who knew far more about her than she knew about herself, and who told her he was Mr. Merrick, the doctor ; she could sit up in bed, supported by pillows, wondering what had happened to her, and where she was ; she could feel a growing curiosity about that quiet voice, which still asked after her, morning, noon, and night, on the other side of the door.

Another day's delay—and Mr. Merrick asked her if she was strong enough to see an old friend. A meek voice, behind him, articulating high in the air, said, "It's only me." The voice was followed by the prodigious bodily apparition of Mrs. Wragge, with her cap all awry, and one of her shoes in the next room. "Oh, look at her ! look at her !" cried Mrs. Wragge, in an ecstacy, dropping on her knees at Magdalen's bedside, with a thump that shook the house. "Bless her heart, she's well enough to laugh at me already. 'Cheer, boys, cheer—!' I beg your pardon, doctor, my conduct isn't ladylike, I know. It's my head, sir ; it isn't *me*. I must get vent somehow—or my head will burst !" No coherent sentence, in answer to any sort of question put to her, could be extracted that morning from Mrs. Wragge. She rose from one climax of verbal confusion to another—and finished her visit under the bed, groping inscrutably for the second shoe.

The morrow came—and Mr. Merrick promised that she should see another old friend on the next day. In the evening, when the inquiring voice asked after her, as usual, and when the door was opened a few inches to give the reply, she answered faintly for herself :—"I am better, thank you." There was a moment of silence—and then, just as the door was shut again, the voice sank to a whisper, and said fervently, "Thank God !" Who was he? She had asked them all, and no one would tell her. Who was he ?

The next day came ; and she heard her door opened softly. Brisk foot-steps tripped into the room ; a lithe little figure advanced to the bed-side. Was it a dream again ? No ! There he was in his own evergreen reality, with the copious flow of language pouring smoothly from his lips ; with the lambent dash of humour twinkling in his parti-coloured eyes—there he was, more audacious, more persuasive, more respectable than ever, in a suit of glossy black, with a speckless white cravat, and a rampant shirt-frill—the unblushing, the invincible, unchangeable, Wragge !

"Not a word, my dear girl !" said the captain, seating himself comfortably at the bedside, in his old confidential way. "I am to do all the talking ; and I think you will own, a more competent man for the purpose could not possibly have been found. I am really delighted—honestly delighted, if I may use such an apparently inappropriate word—to see you again, and to see you getting well. I have often thought of you; I have often missed you; I have often said to myself—never mind what ! Clear the stage, and drop the curtain on the past. *Dum vivimus, vivamus!* Pardon the pedantry of a Latin quotation, my dear, and tell me how I look. Am I, or am I not, the picture of a prosperous man ?"

Magdalen attempted to answer him. The captain's deluge of words flowed over her again in a moment.

"Don't exert yourself," he said. "I'll put all your questions for you. What have I been about? Why do I look so remarkably well off? And how in the world did I find my way to this house? My dear girl, I have been occupied, since we last saw each other, in slightly modifying my old professional habits. I have shifted from Moral Agriculture to Medical Agriculture. Formerly, I preyed on the public sympathy ; now, I prey on the public stomach. Stomach and sympathy, sympathy and stomach—look them both fairly in the face, when you reach the wrong side of fifty, and you will agree with me that they come to much the same thing. However that may be, here I am—incredible as it may appear—a man with an income, at last. The founders of my fortune are three in number. Their names are Aloes, Scammony, and Gamboge.* In plainer words, I am now living—on a Pill. I made a little money (if you remember) by my friendly connection with you. I made a little more, by the happy decease (*Requiescat in Pace !*) of that female relative of Mrs. Wragge's, from whom, as I told you, my wife had expectations. Very good. What do you think I did ? I invested the whole of my capital, at one fell swoop, in advertisements—and purchased my drugs and my pill-boxes on credit. The result is now before you. Here I am, a Grand Financial Fact. Here I am with my clothes positively paid for ; with a balance at my banker's ; with my servant in livery, and my gig at the door; solvent, flourishing, popular—and all on a Pill."

Magdalen smiled. The captain's face assumed an expression of mock gravity : he looked as if there was a serious side to the question, and as if he meant to put it next.

"It's no laughing matter to the public, my dear," he said. "They can't get rid of me and my Pill—they must take us. There is not a single form of appeal in the whole range of human advertisement, which I am not making to the unfortunate public at this moment. Hire the last new novel—there I am, inside the boards of the book. Send for the last new Song—the instant you open the leaves, I drop out of it. Take a cab—I fly in at the window, in red. Buy a box of tooth-powder at the chemist's —I wrap it up for you, in blue. Show yourself at the theatre—I flutter down on you, in yellow. The mere titles of my advertisements are quite irresistible. Let me quote a few from last week's issue. Proverbial Title:

—' A Pill in Time, saves Nine.' Familiar Title :—' Excuse me, how is your Stomach?' Patriotic Title :—' What are the three characteristics of a true-born Englishman? His Hearth, his Home, and his Pill.' Title in the form of a nursery dialogue :—' Mamma, I am not well.' ' What is the matter, my pet?' ' I want a little Pill.' Title in the form of an Historical Anecdote :—' New Discovery in the Mine of English History. When the Princes were smothered in the Tower, their faithful attendant collected all the little possessions left behind them. Among the touching trifles dear to the poor boys, he found a tiny Box. It contained the Pill of the Period. Is it necessary to say, how inferior that Pill was to its Successor, which prince and peasant alike may now obtain '—Et cætera, Et cætera. The place in which my Pill is made, is an advertisement in itself. I have got one of the largest shops in London. Behind one counter (visible to the public through the lucid medium of plate-glass), are four-and-twenty young men, in white aprons, making the Pill. Behind another counter, are four-and-twenty young men, in white cravats, making the boxes. At the bottom of the shop are three elderly accountants, posting the vast financial transactions accruing from the Pill, in three enormous ledgers. Over the door are my name, portrait, and autograph, expanded to colossal proportions, and surrounded, in flowing letters, by the motto of the establishment :—' Down with the Doctors !' Even Mrs. Wragge contributes her quota to this prodigious enterprise. She is the celebrated woman whom I have cured of indescribable agonies from every complaint under the sun. Her portrait is engraved on all the wrappers, with the following inscription beneath it :—' Before she took the Pill, you might have blown this patient away with a feather. Look at her now ! ! !' Last, not least, my dear girl, the Pill is the cause of my finding my way to this house. My department in the prodigious Enterprise already mentioned, is to scour the United Kingdom in a gig, establishing Agencies everywhere. While founding one of those Agencies, I heard of a certain friend of mine, who had lately landed in England, after a long sea voyage. I got his address in London—he was a lodger in this house. I called on him forthwith—and was stunned by the news of your illness. Such, in brief, is the history of my existing connection with British Medicine ; and so it happens that you see me at the present moment, sitting in the present chair, now as ever, yours truly, Horatio Wragge."

In these terms the captain brought his personal statement to a close. He looked more and more attentively at Magdalen, the nearer he got to the conclusion. Was there some latent importance attaching to his last words, which did not appear on the face of them ? There was. His visit to the sick-room had a serious object ; and that object he had now approached.

In describing the circumstances, under which he had become acquainted with Magdalen's present position, Captain Wragge had skirted with his customary dexterity round the remote boundaries of truth. Emboldened by the absence of any public scandal in connection with Noel Vanstone's marriage, or with the event of his death as announced in the newspaper obituary, the captain, roaming the eastern circuit, had ventured back to Aldborough, a fortnight since, to establish an agency there for the sale of his wonderful Pill. No one had recognised him but the landlady of the hotel, who at once insisted on his entering the house, and reading Kirke's letter to her husband. The same night, Captain Wragge was in London, and was closeted with the sailor, in the second-floor room at Aaron's Buildings.

The serious nature of the situation, the indisputable certainty that Kirke must fail in tracing Magdalen's friends, unless he first knew who she really was, had decided the captain on disclosing part, at least, of the truth. Declining to enter into any particulars—for family reasons, which Magdalen might explain on her recovery, if she pleased—he astounded Kirke by telling him that the friendless woman whom he had rescued, and whom he had only known, up to that moment, as Miss Bygrave—was no other than the youngest daughter of Andrew Vanstone. The disclosure, on Kirke's side, of his father's connection with the young officer in Canada, had followed naturally, on the revelation of Magdalen's real name. Captain Wragge had expressed his surprise, but had made no further remark at the time. A fortnight later, however, when the patient's recovery forced the serious difficulty on the doctor, of meeting the questions which Magdalen was sure to ask, the captain's ingenuity had come, as usual, to the rescue.

"You can't tell her the truth," he said, "without awakening painful recollections of her stay at Aldborough, into which I am not at liberty to enter. Don't acknowledge, just yet, that Mr. Kirke only knew her as Miss Bygrave of North Shingles, when he found her in this house. Tell her boldly that he knew who she was, and that he felt (what she must feel) that he had an hereditary right to help and protect her as his father's son. I am, as I have already told you," continued the captain, sticking fast to his old assertion, "a distant relative of the Combe-Raven family; and, if there is nobody else at hand to help you through this difficulty, my services are freely at your disposal."

No one else was at hand; and the emergency was a serious one. Strangers undertaking the responsibility might ignorantly jar on past recollections, which it would, perhaps, be the death of her to revive too soon. Near relatives might, by their premature appearance at the bedside, produce the same deplorable result. The alternative lay between irritating and alarming her by leaving her inquiries unanswered—or trusting Captain Wragge. In the doctor's opinion, the second risk was the least serious risk of the two—and the captain was now seated at Magdalen's bedside in discharge of the trust confided to him.

Would she ask the question which it had been the private object of all Captain Wragge's preliminary talk, lightly and pleasantly to provoke. Yes: as soon as his silence gave her the opportunity, she asked it :—Who was that friend of his living in the house?

"You ought by rights to know him as well as I do," said the captain. "He is the son of one of your father's old military friends—when your father was quartered with his regiment in Canada. Your cheeks mustn't flush up! If they do I shall go away."

She was astonished, but not agitated. Captain Wragge had begun by interesting her in the remote past, which she only knew by hearsay, before he ventured on the delicate ground of her own experience.

In a moment more, she advanced to her next question :—What was his name?

"Kirke," proceeded the captain. "Did you never hear of his father, Major Kirke—commanding officer of the regiment in Canada? Did you never hear that the major helped your father through a great difficulty, like the best of good fellows and good friends?"

Yes: she faintly fancied she had heard something about her father, and an officer who had once been very good to him when he was a young man. But she could not look back so long.—Was Mr. Kirke poor?

Even Captain Wragge's penetration was puzzled by that question. He gave the true answer at hazard. "No," he said, "not poor."

Her next inquiry showed what she had been thinking of.—If Mr. Kirke was not poor, why did he come to live in that house?

"She has caught me !" thought the captain. "There is only one way out of it—I must administer another dose of truth. Mr. Kirke discovered you here by chance," he proceeded aloud ; "very ill, and not nicely attended to. Somebody was wanted to take care of you, while you were not able to take care of yourself. Why not Mr. Kirke? He was the son of your father's old friend—which is the next thing to being *your* old friend. Who had a better claim to send for the right doctor, and get the right nurse—when I was not here to cure you with my wonderful Pill? Gently! gently! you mustn't take hold of my superfine black coat-sleeve in that unceremonious manner."

He put her hand back on the bed, but she was not to be checked in that way. She persisted in asking another question.—How came Mr. Kirke to know her? She had never seen him ; she had never heard of him in her life.

"Very likely," said Captain Wragge. "But your never having seen *him*, is no reason why he should not have seen *you*."

"When did he see me?"

The Captain corked up his doses of truth on the spot, without a moment's hesitation.

"Some time ago, my dear. I can't exactly say when."

" Only once ?"

Captain Wragge suddenly saw his way to the administration of another dose. " Yes," he said, " only once."

She reflected a little. The next question involved the simultaneous expression of two ideas—and the next question cost her an effort.

" He only saw me once," she said ; " and he only saw me some time ago. How came he to remember me, when he found me here ?"

" Aha !" said the captain. " Now you have hit the right nail on the head at last. You can't possibly be more surprised at his remembering you than I am. A word of advice, my dear. When you are well enough to get up and see Mr. Kirke, try how that sharp question of yours sounds in *his* ears—and insist on his answering it himself." Slipping out of the dilemma in that characteristically adroit manner, Captain Wragge got briskly on his legs again, and took up his hat.

" Wait !" she pleaded. " I want to ask you——"

" Not another word," said the captain. " I have given you quite enough to think of for one day. My time is up, and my gig is waiting for me. I am off, to scour the country as usual. I am off, to cultivate the field of public indigestion with the triple ploughshare of aloes, scammony, and gamboge." He stopped and turned round at the door. " By-the-by, a message from my unfortunate wife. If you will allow her to come and see you again, Mrs. Wragge solemnly promises *not* to lose her shoe next time. *I* don't believe her. What do you say ? May she come ?"

" Yes ; whenever she likes," said Magdalen. " If I ever get well again, may poor Mrs. Wragge come and stay with me ?"

" Certainly, my dear. If you have no objection, I will provide her, beforehand, with a few thousand impressions in red, blue, and yellow, of her own portrait (' You might have blown this patient away with a feather, before she took the Pill. Look at her now !'). She is sure to drop herself about perpetually wherever she goes, and the most gratifying results, in an advertising point of view, must inevitably follow. Don't think me mercenary—I merely understand the age I live in." He stopped on his way out, for the second time, and turned round once more at the door. " You have been a remarkably good girl," he said, " and you deserve to be rewarded for it. I'll give you a last piece of information before I go. Have you heard anybody inquiring after you, for the last day or two, outside your door ? Ah, I see you have. A word in your ear, my dear. That's Mr. Kirke.' He tripped away from the bedside, as briskly as ever. Magdalen heard him advertising himself to the nurse, before he closed the door. " If you are ever asked about it," he said, in a confidential whisper, " the name is Wragge, and the Pill is to be had in neat boxes, price thirteen pence half-penny, government stamp included. Take a few copies of the portrait of a female-patient, whom you might have blown away with a feather before she took the Pill, and whom you are simply requested to contemplate now. Many thanks. *Good* morning."

The door closed, and Magdalen was alone again. She felt no sense of solitude; Captain Wragge had left her with something new to think of. Hour after hour, her mind dwelt wonderingly on Mr. Kirke, until the evening came, and she heard his voice again, through the half-opened door.

"I am very grateful," she said to him, before the nurse could answer his inquiries—"very, very grateful for all your goodness to me."

"Try to get well," he replied kindly. "You will more than reward me, if you try to get well."

The next morning, Mr. Merrick found her impatient to leave her bed, and be moved to the sofa in the front room. The doctor said he supposed she wanted a change. "Yes," she replied; "I want to see Mr. Kirke." The doctor consented to move her on the next day, but he positively forbade the additional excitement of seeing anybody, until the day after. She attempted a remonstrance—Mr. Merrick was impenetrable. She tried, when he was gone, to win the nurse by persuasion—the nurse was impenetrable too.

On the next day, they wrapped her in shawls, and carried her in to the sofa, and made her a little bed on it. On the table near at hand, were some flowers and a number of an illustrated newspaper. She immediately asked who had put them there. The nurse (failing to notice a warning look from the doctor) said Mr. Kirke had thought that she might like the flowers, and that the pictures in the paper might amuse her. After that reply, her anxiety to see Mr. Kirke became too ungovernable to be trifled with. The doctor left the room at once to fetch him.

She looked eagerly at the opening door. Her first glance at him, as he came in, raised a doubt in her mind, whether she now saw that tall figure, and that open sunburnt face for the first time. But she was too weak and too agitated to follow her recollections as far back as Aldborough. She resigned the attempt, and only looked at him. He stopped at the foot of the sofa, and said a few cheering words. She beckoned to him to come nearer, and offered him her wasted hand. He tenderly took it in his, and sat down by her. They were both silent. His face told her of the sorrow and the sympathy which his silence would fain have concealed. She still held his hand—consciously now—as persistently as she had held it on the day when he found her. Her eyes closed, after a vain effort to speak to him, and the tears rolled slowly over her wan white cheeks.

The doctor signed to Kirke, to wait and give her time. She recovered a little and looked at him :—"How kind you have been to me!" she murmured. "And how little I have deserved it!"

"Hush! hush!" he said. "You don't know what a happiness it was to me to help you."

The sound of his voice seemed to strengthen her, and to give her courage. She lay looking at him with an eager interest, with a gratitude which artlessly ignored all the conventional restraints that interpose between a woman and a man. "Where did you see me," she said suddenly, "before you found me here?"

Kirke hesitated. Mr. Merrick came to his assistance.

"I forbid you to say a word about the past, to Mr. Kirke," interposed the doctor; "and I forbid Mr. Kirke to say a word about it to *you*. You are beginning a new life to-day—and the only recollections I sanction, are recollections five minutes old."

She looked at the doctor, and smiled. "I must ask him one question," she said—and turned back again to Kirke. "Is it true that you had only seen me once, before you came to this house?"

"Quite true!" He made the reply with a sudden change of colour which she instantly detected. Her brightening eyes looked at him more earnestly than ever, as she put her next question.

"How came you to remember me, after only seeing me once?"

His hand unconsciously closed on hers, and pressed it for the first time. He attempted to answer, and hesitated at the first word. "I have a good memory," he said at last—and suddenly looked away from her with a confusion so strangely unlike his customary self-possession of manner, that the doctor and the nurse both noticed it.

Every nerve in her body felt that momentary pressure of his hand, with the exquisite susceptibility, which accompanies the first faltering advance on the way to health. She looked at his changing colour, she listened to his hesitating words, with every sensitive perception of her sex and age, quickened to seize intuitively on the truth. In the moment when he looked away from her, she gently took her hand from him, and turned her head aside on the pillow. "*Can* it be?" she thought, with a flutter of delicious fear at her heart, with a glow of delicious confusion burning on her cheeks. " *Can* it be?"

The doctor made another sign to Kirke. He understood it, and rose immediately. The momentary discomposure in his face and manner had both disappeared. He was satisfied in his own mind that he had successfully kept his secret, and in the relief of feeling that conviction, he had become himself again.

"Good-bye; till to-morrow," he said, as he left the room.

"Good-bye," she answered, softly, without looking at him.

Mr. Merrick took the chair which Kirke had resigned, and laid his hand on her pulse. "Just what I feared," remarked the doctor: "too quick by half."

She petulantly snatched away her wrist. "Don't!" she said, shrinking from him. " Pray don't touch me !"

Mr. Merrick good-humouredly gave up his place to the nurse. " I'll return in half an hour," he whispered ; " and carry her back to bed. Don't let her talk. Show her the pictures in the newspaper, and keep her quiet in that way."

When the doctor returned, the nurse reported that the newspaper had not been wanted. The patient's conduct had been exemplary. She had not been at all restless, and she had never spoken a word.

The days passed ; and the time grew longer and longer which the doctor allowed her to spend in the front room. She was soon able to dispense with the bed on the sofa—she could be dressed, and could sit up, supported by pillows, in an arm-chair. Her hours of emancipation from the bed-room represented the great daily event of her life. They were the hours she passed in Kirke's society.

She had a double interest in him now—her interest in the man whose protecting care had saved her reason and her life ; her interest in the man whose heart's dearest and deepest secret she had surprised. Little by little, they grew as easy and familiar with each other as old friends ; little by little, she presumed on all her privileges, and wound her way unsuspected into the most intimate knowledge of his nature.

Her questions were endless. Everything that he could tell her of himself and his life, she drew from him delicately and insensibly : he, the least self-conscious of mankind, became an egotist in her dexterous hands. She found out his pride in his ship, and practised on it without remorse. She drew him into talking of the fine qualities of the vessel, of the great things the vessel had done in emergencies, as he had never in his life talked yet to any living creature on shore. She found him out in private seafaring anxieties and unutterable seafaring exultations, which he had kept a secret from his own mate. She watched his kindling face with a delicious sense of triumph in adding fuel to the fire ; she trapped him into forgetting all considerations of time and place, and striking as hearty a stroke on the rickety little lodging-house table, in the fervour of his talk, as if his hand had descended on the solid bulwark of his ship. His confusion at the discovery of his own forgetfulness, secretly delighted her ; she could have cried with pleasure, when he penitently wondered what he could possibly have been thinking of.

At other times, she drew him from dwelling on the pleasures of his life, and led him into talking of its perils—the perils of that jealous mistress the sea, which had absorbed so much of his existence, which had kept him so strangely innocent and ignorant of the world on shore. Twice he had been shipwrecked. Times innumerable, he and all with him had been threatened with death, and had escaped their doom by the narrowness of a hair's breadth. He was always unwilling at the outset to speak of this dark and dreadful side of his life: it was only by adroitly tempting him, by laying little snares for him in his talk, that she lured him into telling her of the terrors of the great deep. She sat listening to him with a breathless interest, looking at him with a breathless wonder, as those fearful stories—made doubly vivid by the simple language in which he told them—fell, one by one, from his lips. His noble unconsciousness of his own heroism—the artless modesty with which he described his own acts of dauntless endurance and devoted courage, without an idea that they were anything more than plain acts of duty to which he was bound by the vocation that he followed—raised him to a place in her estimation so hopelessly high above her, that she became uneasy and impatient until she had pulled down the idol again, which she herself had set up. It was on these occasions that she most rigidly exacted from him all those little familiar attentions so precious to women in their intercourse with men. "This hand," she thought, with an exquisite delight in secretly following the idea while he was close to her—"this hand that has rescued the drowning from death—is shifting my pillows so tenderly that I hardly know when they are moved. This hand that has seized men mad with mutiny, and driven them back to their duty by main force—is mixing my lemonade and peeling my fruit, more delicately and more neatly than I could do it for myself. Oh, if I could be a man, how I should like to be such a man as this!"

She never allowed her thoughts, while she was in his presence, to lead her beyond that point. It was only when the night had separated them, that she ventured to let her mind dwell on the self-sacrificing devotion which had so mercifully rescued her. Kirke little knew how she thought of him, in the secrecy of her own chamber, during the quiet hours that elapsed before she sunk to sleep. No suspicion crossed his mind of the influence which he was exerting over her—of the new spirit which he was breathing into that new life, so sensitively open to impression in the first freshness of its recovered sense! "She has nobody else to amuse her, poor thing," he used to think sadly, sitting alone in his small second-floor room. "If a rough fellow like me can beguile the weary hours, till her friends come here, she is heartily welcome to all that I can tell her."

He was out of spirits and restless now, whenever he was by himself. Little by little, he fell into a habit of taking long lonely walks at night, when Magdalen thought he was sleeping upstairs. Once, he went away abruptly in the daytime—on business, as he said. Something had passed between Magdalen and himself the evening before, which had led her into telling him her age. "Twenty, last birthday," he thought. "Take twenty from forty-one. An easy sum in subtraction—as easy a sum as my little nephew could wish for." He walked to the Docks, and looked bitterly at the shipping. "I mustn't forget how a ship is made," he said. "It won't be long before I am back at the old work again." On leaving the Docks, he paid a visit to a brother-sailor—a married man. In the course of conversation, he asked how much older his friend might be than his friend's wife. There was six years' difference between them. "I suppose that's difference enough?" said Kirke. "Yes," said his friend. "Quite enough. Are you looking out for a wife at last? Try a seasoned woman of thirty-five—that's your mark, Kirke, as near as I can calculate."

The time passed smoothly and quickly—the present time, in which *she* was recovering so happily—the present time, which *he* was beginning to distrust already.

Early one morning, Mr. Merrick surprised Kirke, by a visit in his little room on the second floor.

"I came to the conclusion yesterday," said the doctor, entering abruptly on his business, "that our patient was strong enough to justify us, at last, in running all risks, and communicating with her friends; and I have accordingly followed the clue which that queer fellow, Captain Wragge, put into our hands. You remember he advised us to apply to Mr. Pendril, the lawyer? I saw Mr. Pendril two days ago, and was referred by him—not over-willingly as I thought—to a lady named Miss Garth. I heard enough from her, to satisfy me that we have exercised a wise caution in acting as we have done. It is a very, very sad story—and I am bound to say that I, for one, make great allowances for the poor girl down-stairs. Her only relation in the world is her elder sister. I have suggested that the sister shall write to her in the first instance—and then, if the letter does her no harm, follow it personally in a day or two. I have not given the address, by way of preventing any visits from being paid here, without my permission. All I have done is to undertake to forward the letter; and I shall probably find it at my house when I get back. Can you stop at home until I send my man with it? There is not the least hope of my being able to bring it myself. All you need do, is to watch for an opportunity when she is not in the front room, and to put the letter where she can see it when she comes in. The handwriting on the address will break the news, before she opens the letter. Say nothing to her about it—take care that the landlady is within call—and leave her to herself. I know I can trust *you* to follow my directions; and that is why I ask you to do us this service. You look out of spirits this morning. Natural enough. You're used to plenty of fresh air, captain, and you're beginning to pine in this close place."

"May I ask a question, doctor? Is *she* pining in this close place, too? When her sister comes, will her sister take her away?"

"Decidedly—if my advice is followed. She will be well enough to be moved, in a week or less. Good day. You are certainly out of spirits, and your hand feels feverish. Pining for the blue water, captain—pining for the blue water!" With that expression of opinion, the doctor cheerfully went out.

In an hour, the letter arrived. Kirke took it from the landlady reluctantly, and almost roughly, without looking at it. Having ascertained that Magdalen was still engaged at her toilet, and having explained to the landlady the necessity of remaining within call, he went down-stairs immediately, and put the letter on the table in the front room.

Magdalen heard the sound of the familiar step on the floor. "I shall soon be ready," she called to him through the door.

He made no reply—he took his hat, and went out. After a momentary hesitation, he turned his face eastward, and called on the shipowners who employed him, at their office in Cornhill.

CHAPTER III.

MAGDALEN'S first glance round the empty room, showed her the letter on the table. The address, as the doctor had predicted, broke the news the moment she looked at it.

Not a word escaped her. She sat down by the table, pale and silent, with the letter in her lap. Twice she attempted to open it, and twice she put it back again. The bygone time was not alone in her mind, as she looked at her sister's handwriting—the fear of Kirke was there with it. "My past life!" she thought. "What will he think of me, when he knows my past life?"

She made another effort, and broke the seal. A second letter dropped out of the enclosure, addressed to her in a handwriting with which she was not familiar. She put the second letter aside, and read the lines which Norah had written.

"Ventnor, Isle of Wight, August 24th.

"MY DEAREST MAGDALEN,

"When you read this letter, try to think we have only been parted since yesterday; and dismiss from your mind (as I have dismissed from mine) the past and all that belongs to it.

"I am strictly forbidden to agitate you, or to weary you by writing a long letter. Is it wrong to tell you that I am the happiest woman living? I hope not, for I can't keep the secret to myself.

"My darling, prepare yourself for the greatest surprise I have ever caused you. I am married. It is only a week to-day, since I parted with my old name—it is only a week, since I have been the happy wife of George Bartram, of St. Crux.

"There were difficulties at first, in the way of our marriage; some of them, I am afraid, of my making. Happily for me, my husband knew from the beginning, that I really loved him—he gave me a second chance of telling him so, after I had lost the first—and as you see, I was wise enough to take it. You ought to be especially interested, my love, in this marriage; for you are the cause of it. If I had not gone to Aldborough to search for the lost trace of you—if George had not been brought there, at the same time, by circumstances in which you were concerned—my husband and I might never have met. When we look back to our first impressions of each other, we look back to *you*.

"I must keep my promise not to weary you; I must bring this letter (sorely against my will) to an end. Patience! patience!—I shall see you soon. George and I are both coming to London to take you back with us to Ventnor. This is my husband's invitation, mind, as well as mine. Don't suppose I married him, Magdalen, until I had taught him to think of you as I think—to wish with my wishes, and to hope with my hopes. I could say so much more about this, so much more about George, if I might only give my thoughts and my pen their own way. But I must leave Miss Garth (at her own special request) a blank space to fill up on the last page of this letter; and I must only add one word more, before I say good-bye—a word to warn you that I have another surprise in store, which I am keeping in reserve until we meet. Don't attempt to guess what it is. You might guess for ages, and be no nearer than you are now to a discovery of the truth.

"Your affectionate sister,

"NORAH BARTRAM."

(ADDED BY MISS GARTH.)

"MY DEAR CHILD,

"If I had ever lost my old loving recollection of you, I should feel it in my heart again now, when I know that it has pleased God to restore you to us, from the brink of the grave. I add these lines to your sister's letter, because I am not sure that you are are quite so fit yet, as she thinks you, to accept her proposal. She has not said a word of her husband, or herself, which is not true. But Mr. Bartram is a stranger to you—and if you think you can recover more easily and more pleasantly to yourself, under the wing of your old governess, than under the protection of your new brother-in-law, come to me first, and trust to my reconciling Norah to the change of plans. I have secured the refusal of a little cottage at Shanklin—near enough to your sister to allow of your seeing each other whenever you like, and far enough away, at the same time, to secure you the privilege, when you wish it, of being alone. Send me one line, before we meet, to say Yes or No—and I will write to Shanklin by the next post.

"Always yours affectionately,

"HARRIET GARTH."

The letter dropped from Magdalen's hand. Thoughts which had never risen in her mind yet, rose in it now.

Norah, whose courage under undeserved calamity, had been the courage of resignation—Norah, who had patiently accepted her hard lot; who, from first to last, had meditated no vengeance, and stooped to no deceit—Norah had reached the end which all her sister's ingenuity, all her sister's resolution, and all her sister's daring, had failed to achieve. Openly and honourably, with love on one side and love on the other, Norah had married the man who possessed the Combe-Raven money—and Magdalen's own scheme to recover it, had opened the way to the event which had brought husband and wife together!

As the light of that overwhelming discovery broke on her mind, the old strife was renewed; and Good and Evil struggled once more which should win her—but with added forces this time; with the new spirit that had been breathed into her new life; with the nobler sense that had grown with the growth of her gratitude to the man who had saved her, fighting on the better side. All the higher impulses of her nature, which had never, from first to last, let her err with impunity—which had tortured her, before her marriage and after it, with the remorse that no woman inherently heartless and inherently wicked can feel—all the nobler elements in her character gathered their forces for the crowning struggle, and strengthened her to meet, with no unworthy shrinking, the revelation that had opened on her view. Clearer and clearer, in the light of its own immortal life, the truth rose before her from the ashes of her dead passions, from the grave of her buried hopes. When she looked at the letter again—when she read the words once more, which told her that the recovery of the lost fortune was her sister's triumph, not hers—she had victoriously trampled down all little jealousies and all mean regrets; she could say in her heart of hearts, "Norah has deserved it!"

The day wore on. She sat absorbed in her own thoughts, and heedless of the second letter which she had not opened yet, until Kirke's return.

He stopped on the landing outside, and, opening the door a little way only, asked, without entering the room, if she wanted anything that he could send her. She begged him to come in. His face was worn and weary; he looked older than she had seen him look yet. "Did you put my letter on the table for me?" she asked.

"Yes. I put it there at the doctor's request."

"I suppose the doctor told you it was from my sister? She is coming to see me, and Miss Garth is coming to see me. They will thank you for all your goodness to me, better than I can."

"I have no claim on their thanks," he answered sternly. "What I have done, was not done for them, but for you." He waited a little, and looked at her. His face would have betrayed him, in that look; his voice would have betrayed him, in the next words he spoke—if she had not guessed the truth already. "When your friends come here," he resumed, "they will take you away, I suppose, to some better place than this?"

"They can take me to no place," she said gently, "which I shall think of as I think of the place where you found me. They can take me to no dearer friend than the friend who has saved my life."

There was a moment's silence between them.

"We have been very happy here," he went on, in lower and lower tones. "You won't forget me, when we have said good-bye?"

She turned pale, as the words passed his lips; and, leaving her chair, knelt down at the table, so as to look up into his face, and to force him to look into hers.

"Why do you talk of it?" she asked. "We are not going to say good-bye—at least, not yet."

"I thought——" he began.

"Yes?"

"I thought your friends were coming here——"

She eagerly interrupted him. "Do you think I would go away with anybody," she said, "even with the dearest relation I have in the world—and leave you here, not knowing and not caring whether I ever saw you again? Oh, you don't think that of me!" she exclaimed, with the passionate tears springing into her eyes—"I'm sure you don't think that of me!"

"No," he said; "I never have thought, I never can think, unjustly or unworthily of you."

Before he could add another word, she left the table as suddenly as she had approached it, and returned to her chair. He had unconsciously replied in terms that reminded her of the hard necessity which still remained unfulfilled—the necessity of telling him the story of the past. Not an idea of concealing that story from his knowledge crossed her mind. "Will he love me, when he knows the truth, as he loves me now?" That was her only thought, as she tried to approach the subject in his presence without shrinking from it.

"Let us put my own feelings out of the question," she said. "There is a reason for my not going away, unless I first have the assurance of seeing you again. You have a claim—the strongest claim of any one—to know how I came here, unknown to my friends, and how it was that you found me fallen so low."

"I make no claim," he said hastily. "I wish to know nothing which it distresses you to tell me."

"You have always done your duty," she rejoined, with a faint smile. "Let me take example from you, if I can, and try to do mine."

"I am old enough to be your father," he said bitterly. "Duty is more easily done at my age than it is at yours."

! His age was so constantly in his mind now, that he fancied it must be in her mind too. She had never given it a thought. The reference he had just made to it, did not divert her for a moment from the subject on which she was speaking to him.

"You don't know how I value your good opinion of me," she said, struggling resolutely to sustain her sinking courage. "How can I deserve your kindness, how can I feel that I am worthy of your regard, until I have opened my heart to you? Oh, don't encourage me in my own miserable weakness! Help me to tell the truth—*force* me to tell it, for my own sake, if not for yours!"

He was deeply moved by the fervent sincerity of that appeal.

"You *shall* tell it," he said. "You are right—and I was wrong." He waited a little, and considered. "Would it be easier to you," he asked, with delicate consideration for her, "to write it than to tell it?"

She caught gratefully at the suggestion. "Far easier," she replied. "I can be sure of myself—I can be sure of hiding nothing from you, if I write it. Don't write to me, on your side!" she added suddenly, seeing, with a woman's instinctive quickness of penetration, the danger of totally renouncing her personal influence over him. "Wait till we meet; and tell me with your own lips, what you think."

"Where shall I tell it?"

"Here!" she said eagerly. "Here, where you found me helpless—here, where you have brought me back to life, and where I have first learnt to know you. I can bear the hardest words you say to me, if you will only say them in this room. It is impossible I can be away longer than a month; a month will be enough, and more than enough. If I come back——" She stopped confusedly. "I am thinking of myself," she said, "when I ought to be thinking of you. You have your own occupations, and your own friends. Will you decide for us? Will you say how it shall be?"

"It shall be as you wish. If you come back in a month, you will find me here."

"Will it cause you no sacrifice of your own comfort, and your own plans?"

"It will cause me nothing," he replied, "but a journey back to the City." He rose and took his hat. "I must go there at once," he added, "or I shall not be in time."

"It is a promise between us?" she said—and held out her hand.

"Yes," he answered, a little sadly. "It is a promise."

Slight as it was, the shade of melancholy in his manner pained her. Forgetting all other anxieties in the anxiety to cheer him, she gently pressed the hand he gave her. "If *that* won't tell him the truth," she thought, "nothing will."

It failed to tell him the truth—but it forced a question on his mind, which he had not ventured to ask himself before. "Is it her gratitude, or her love, that is speaking to me?" he wondered. "If I was only a younger man, I might almost hope it was her love." That terrible sum in subtraction, which had first presented itself on the day when she told him her age, began to trouble him again, as he left the house. He took twenty from forty-one at intervals, all the way back to the shipowners' office in Cornhill.

Left by herself, Magdalen approached the table, to write the line of answer which Miss Garth requested, and gratefully to accept the proposal that had been made to her.

The second letter, which she had laid aside and forgotten, was the first object that caught her eye, on changing her place. She opened it immediately, and not recognizing the handwriting, looked at the signature. To her unutterable astonishment, her correspondent proved to be no less a person than—old Mr. Clare!

The philosopher's letter dispensed with all the ordinary forms of address, and entered on its subject without prefatory phrases of any kind, in these uncompromising terms:—

"I have more news for you of that contemptible cur, my son. Here it is in the fewest possible words.

"I always told you, if you remember, that Frank was a Sneak. The very first trace recovered of him, after his running away from his employers in China, presents him in that character. Where do you think he turns up next? He turns up, hidden behind a couple of flour barrels, on board an English vessel bound homeward from Hong-Kong to London.

"The name of the ship was The Deliverance; and the commander was one Captain Kirke. Instead of acting like a sensible man, and throwing Frank overboard, Captain Kirke was fool enough to listen to his story. He made the most of his misfortunes, you may be sure. He was half starved; he was an Englishman lost in a strange country, without a friend to help him; his only chance of getting home was to sneak into the hold of an English vessel—and he had sneaked in, accordingly, at Hong-Kong, two days since. That was his story. Any other lout in Frank's situation, would have been rope's-ended by any other captain. Deserving no pity from anybody—Frank was, as a matter of course, coddled and compassionated on the spot. The captain took him by the hand, the crew pitied him, and the passengers patted him on the back. He was fed, clothed, and presented with his passage home. Luck enough, so far, you will say. Nothing of the sort; nothing like luck enough for my despicable son.

"The ship touched at the Cape of Good Hope. Among his other acts of folly, Captain Kirke took a woman-passenger on board, at that place—not a young woman, by any means—the elderly widow of a rich colonist. Is it necessary to say that she forthwith became deeply interested in Frank and his misfortunes? Is it necessary to tell you what followed? Look back at my son's career; and you will see that what followed was all of a piece with what went before. He didn't deserve your poor father's interest in him—and he got it. He didn't deserve your attachment—and he got it. He didn't deserve the best place in one of the best offices in London; he didn't deserve an equally good chance in one of the best mercantile houses in China; he didn't deserve food, clothing, pity, and a free passage home— and he got them all. Last, not least, he didn't even deserve to marry a woman old enough to be his grandmother—and he has done it! Not five minutes since, I sent his wedding-cards out to the dust-hole, and tossed the letter that came with them into the fire. The last piece of information which that letter contains is, that he and his wife are looking out for a house and estate to suit them. Mark my words! Frank will get one of the best estates in England; a seat in the House of Commons will follow as a matter of course; and one of the legislators of this Ass-ridden country will be——My Lout!

"If you are the sensible girl I have always taken you for, you have long since learnt to rate Frank at his true value, and the news I send you will only confirm your contempt for him. I wish your poor father could but have lived to see this day! Often as I have missed my old gossip, I don't know that I ever felt the loss of him so keenly, as I felt it when Frank's wedding-cards and Frank's letter came to this house.

"Your friend, if you ever want one,

"Francis Clare, Sen."

With one momentary disturbance of her composure, produced by the appearance of Kirke's name in Mr. Clare's singular narrative, Magdalen read the letter steadily through from beginning to end. The time when it could have distressed her, was gone by; the scales had long since fallen from her eyes. Mr. Clare himself would have been satisfied, if he had seen the quiet contempt on her face as she laid aside his letter. The only serious thought it cost her, was a thought in which Kirke was concerned. The careless manner in which he had referred, in her presence, to the passengers on board his ship, without mentioning any of them by their names, showed her that Frank must have kept silence on the subject of the engagement once existing between them. The confession of that vanished delusion was left for her to make—as part of the story of the past which she had pledged herself unreservedly to reveal.

She wrote to Miss Garth, and sent the letter to the post immediately.

The next morning brought a line of rejoinder. Miss Garth had written to secure the cottage at Shanklin, and Mr. Merrick had consented to Magdalen's removal on the following day. Norah would be the first to arrive at the house; and Miss Garth would follow, with a comfortable carriage to take the invalid to the railway. Every needful arrangement had been made for her: the effort of moving was the one effort she would have to make.

Magdalen read the letter thankfully—but her thoughts wandered from it, and followed Kirke on his return to the City. What was the business which had once already taken him there in the morning? And why had the promise exchanged between them, obliged him to go to the City again, for the second time in one day?

Was it, by any chance, business relating to the sea? Were his employers tempting him to go back to his ship?

CHAPTER IV.

THE first agitation of the meeting between the sisters was over; the first vivid impressions, half pleasurable, half painful, had softened a little—and Norah and Magdalen sat together, hand in hand; each rapt in the silent fulness of her own joy.

Magdalen was the first to speak.

"You have something to tell me, Norah?"

"I have a thousand things to tell you, my love; and you have ten thousand things to tell me.—Do you mean that second surprise, which I told you of in my letter?"

"Yes. I suppose it must concern me very nearly—or you would hardly have thought of mentioning it in your first letter?"

"It does concern you very nearly. You have heard of George's house in Essex? You must be familiar, at least, with the name of St. Crux?— What is there to start at, my dear? I am afraid you are hardly strong enough for any more surprises just yet?"

"Quite strong enough, Norah. I have something to say to you about St. Crux—I have a surprise, on my side, for *you*."

"Will you tell it me now?"

"Not now. You shall know it when we are at the sea-side—you shall know it, before I accept the kindness which has invited me to your husband's house."

"What *can* it be? Why not tell me at once?"

"You used often to set me the example of patience, Norah, in old times —will you set me the example now?"

"With all my heart. Shall I return to my own story as well? Yes? Then we will go back to it at once. - I was telling you that St. Crux is George's house, in Essex; the house he inherited from his uncle. Knowing that Miss] Garth had a curiosity to see the place, he left word (when he went abroad after the admiral's death) that she and any friends who came with her, were to be admitted, if she happened to find herself in the neighbourhood during his absence. Miss Garth and I, and a large party of Mr. Tyrrel's friends, found ourselves in the neighbourhood, not long after George's departure. We had all been invited to see the launch of Mr. Tyrrel's new yacht, from the builder's yard at Wivenhoe in Essex. When the launch was over, the rest of the company returned to Colchester to dine. Miss Garth and I contrived to get into the same carriage together, with nobody but my two little pupils for our companions. We gave the coachman his orders, and drove round by St. Crux. The moment Miss Garth mentioned her name, we were let in, and shown all over the house. I don't know how to describe it to you : it is the most bewildering place I ever saw in my life——"

"Don't attempt to describe it, Norah. Go on with your story instead."

"Very well. My story takes me straight into one of the rooms at St. Crux—a room about as long as your street here; so dreary, so dirty, and so dreadfully cold, that I shiver at the bare recollection of it. Miss Garth was for getting out of it again, as speedily as possible, and so was I. But the housekeeper declined to let us off without first looking at a singular piece of furniture, the only piece of furniture in the comfortless place. She called it a tripod, I think. (There is nothing to be alarmed at, Magdalen; I assure you there is nothing to be alarmed at!) At any rate, it was a strange three-legged thing, which supported a great pan full of charcoal ashes at the top. It was considered, by all good judges (the housekeeper told us), a wonderful piece of chasing in metal ; and she especially pointed out the beauty of some scroll-work running round the inside of the pan, with Latin mottoes on it, signifying——I forget what. I felt not the slightest interest in the thing myself, but I looked close at the scroll-work to satisfy the housekeeper. To confess the truth, she was rather tiresome with her mechanically-learnt lecture on fine metal-work—and, while she was talking, I found myself idly stirring the soft feathery white ashes backwards and forwards with my hand, pretending to listen, with my mind a hundred miles away from her. I don't know how long or how short a time I had been playing with the ashes, when my fingers suddenly encountered a piece of crumpled paper, hidden deep among them. When I brought it to the surface, it proved to be a letter—a long letter full of cramped, close writing.—You have anticipated my story, Magdalen, before I can end it! You know as well as I do, that the letter which my idle fingers found, was the Secret Trust. Hold out your hand, my dear. I have got George's permission to show it to you,—and there it is !"

She put the Trust into her sister's hand. Magdalen took it from her mechanically. "You!" she said, looking at her sister with the remembrance of all that she had vainly ventured, of all that she had vainly suffered, at St. Crux. "*You* have found it!"

"Yes," said Norah, gaily; "the Trust has proved no exception to the general perversity of all lost things. Look for them, and they remain invisible. Leave them alone, and they reveal themselves! You and your lawyer, Magdalen, were both justified in supposing that your interest in this discovery was an interest of no common kind. I spare you all our consultations after I had produced the crumpled paper from the ashes. It ended in George's lawyer being written to, and in George himself being recalled from the Continent. Miss Garth and I both saw him, immediately on his return; he did, what neither of us could do—he solved the mystery of the Trust being hidden in the charcoal ashes. Admiral Bartram, you must know, was all his life subject to fits of somnambulism. He had been found walking in his sleep, not long before his death—just at the time, too, when he was sadly troubled in his mind on the subject of that very letter in your hand. George's idea is that he must have fancied he was doing, in his sleep, what he would have died rather than do in his waking moments —destroying the Trust. The fire had been lit in the pan not long before, and he no doubt saw it still burning in his dream. This was George's explanation of the strange position of the letter when I discovered it. The question of what was to be done with the letter itself, came next, and was no easy question for a woman to understand. But I determined to master it, and I did master it, because it related to you."

"Let me try to master it, in my turn," said Magdalen. "I have a particular reason for wishing to know as much about this letter, as you know yourself. What has it done for others? and what is it to do for me?"

"My dear Magdalen, how strangely you look at it! how strangely you talk of it! Worthless as it may appear, that morsel of paper gives you a fortune."

"Is my only claim to the fortune, the claim which this letter gives me?"

"Yes—the letter is your only claim. Shall I try if I can explain it, in two words? Taken by itself, the letter might, in the lawyer's opinion, have been made a matter for dispute—though I am sure George would have sanctioned no proceeding of that sort. Taken, however, with the postscript which Admiral Bartram attached to it (you will see the lines, if you look under the signature on the third page), it becomes legally binding, as well as morally binding, on the Admiral's representatives. I have exhausted my small stock of legal words, and must go on in my own language, instead of in the lawyer's. The end of the thing was simply this. All the money went back to Mr. Noel Vanstone's estate (another legal word! my vocabulary is richer than I thought), for one plain reason—that it had not been employed as Mr. Noel Vanstone directed. If Mrs. Girdlestone had lived, or if George had married me a few months earlier, results would have been just the other way. As it is, half the money has been already divided between Mr. Noel Vanstone's next of kin; which means, translated into plain English, my husband, and his poor bedridden sister—who took the money formally, one day, to satisfy the lawyer, and who gave it back again generously, the next, to satisfy herself. So much for one half of this legacy. The other half, my dear, is all yours. How strangely events happen, Magdalen! It is only two years since you and I were left disinherited orphans—and we are sharing our poor father's fortune between us, after all!"

"Wait a little, Norah. Our shares come to us in very different ways."

"Do they? Mine comes to me, by my husband. Yours comes to you ——" she stopped confusedly, and changed colour. "Forgive me, my own love!" she said, putting Magdalen's hand to her lips. "I have forgotten what I ought to have remembered. I have thoughtlessly distressed you!"

"No!" said Magdalen. "You have encouraged me."

"Encouraged you?"

"You shall see."

With those words, she rose quietly from the sofa, and walked to the open window. Before Norah could follow her, she had torn the Trust to pieces, and had cast the fragments into the street.

She came back to the sofa, and laid her head, with a deep sigh of relief, on Norah's bosom. "I will owe nothing to my past life," she said. "I have parted with it, as I have parted with those torn morsels of paper. All the thoughts, and all the hopes belonging to it, are put away from me for ever!"

"Magdalen! my husband will never allow you; I will never allow you, myself——"

"Hush! hush! What your husband thinks right, Norah, you and I will think right, too. I will take from you, what I would never have taken, if that letter had given it to me. The end I dreamed of has come. Nothing is changed, but the position I once thought we might hold towards each other. Better as it is, my love—far, far better as it is!"

So, she made the last sacrifice of the old perversity and the old pride. So, she entered on the new and nobler life.

* * * * * *

A month had passed. The autumn sunshine was bright even in the murky streets; and the clocks in the neighbourhood were just striking two, as Magdalen returned alone to the house in Aaron's Buildings.

"Is he waiting for me?" she asked anxiously, when the landlady let her in.

He was waiting in the front room. Magdalen stole up the stairs, and knocked at the door. He called to her carelessly and absently to come in—

plainly thinking that it was only the servant who applied for permission to enter the room.

"You hardly expected me so soon?" she said, speaking on the threshold, and pausing there to enjoy his surprise as he started to his feet and looked at her.

The only traces of illness still visible in her face, left a delicacy in its outline which added refinement to her beauty. She was simply dressed in muslin. Her plain straw bonnet had no other ornament than the white ribbon with which it was sparingly trimmed. She had never looked lovelier in her best days, than she looked now—as she advanced to the table at which he had been sitting, with a little basket of flowers that she had brought with her from the country, and offered him her hand.

He looked anxious and careworn, when she saw him closer. She interrupted his first inquiries and congratulations to ask if he had remained in London, since they had parted—if he had not even gone away for a few days only, to see his friends in Suffolk? No; he had been in London ever since. He never told her that the pretty parsonage-house in Suffolk wanted all those associations with herself, in which the poor four walls at Aaron's Buildings were so rich. He only said, he had been in London ever since.

"I wonder," she asked, looking him attentively in the face, "if you are as happy to see me again, as I am to see you?"

"Perhaps, I am even happier, in my different way," he answered, with a smile.

She took off her bonnet and scarf, and seated herself once more in her own arm-chair. "I suppose this street is very ugly," she said; "and I am sure nobody can deny that the house is very small. And yet—and yet, it feels like coming home again. Sit there, where you used to sit; tell me about yourself. I want to know all that you have done, all that you have thought even, while I have been away." She tried to resume the endless succession of questions by means of which she was accustomed to lure him into speaking of himself. But she put them far less spontaneously, far less adroitly than usual. Her one all-absorbing anxiety in entering that room, was not an anxiety to be trifled with. After a quarter of an hour wasted in constrained inquiries on one side, in reluctant replies on the other, she ventured near the dangerous subject at last.

"Have you received the letters I wrote to you from the sea-side?" she asked, suddenly looking away from him for the first time.

"Yes," he said, "all."

"Have you read them?"

"Every one of them; many times over."

Her heart beat as if it would suffocate her. She had kept her promise bravely. The whole story of her life, from the time of the home-wreck at

Combe-Raven, to the time when she had destroyed the Secret Trust in her sister's presence, had been all laid before him. Nothing that she had done, nothing even that she had thought, had been concealed from his knowledge. As he would have kept a pledged engagement with her, so she had kept her pledged engagement with him. She had not faltered in the resolution to do this—and now she faltered over the one decisive question which she had come there to ask. Strong as the desire in her was to know if she had lost or won him, the fear of knowing was at that moment stronger still. She waited and trembled : she waited, and said no more.

"May I speak to you about your letters?" he asked. "May I tell you——?"

If she had looked at him, as he said those few words, she would have seen what he thought of her, in his face. She would have seen, innocent as he was in this world's knowledge, that he knew the priceless value, the all-ennobling virtue, of a woman who speaks the truth. But she had no courage to look at him—no courage to raise her eyes from her lap.

"Not just yet," she said, faintly. "Not quite so soon after we have met again."

She rose hurriedly from her chair, and walked to the window—turned back again into the room—and approached the table, close to where he was sitting. The writing materials scattered near him, offered her a pretext for changing the subject; and she seized on it directly. "Were you writing a letter," she asked, "when I came in?"

"I was thinking about it," he replied. "It was not a letter to be written, without thinking first." He rose, as he answered her, to gather the writing materials together, and put them away.

"Why should I interrupt you?" she said. "Why not let me try whether I can't help you, instead? Is it a secret?"

"No—not a secret."

He hesitated as he answered her. She instantly guessed the truth.

"Is it about your ship?"

He little knew how she had been thinking in her absence from him, of the business which he believed that he had concealed from her. He little knew that she had learnt already to be jealous of his ship.

"Do they want you to return to your old life?" she went on. "Do they want you to go back to the sea? Must you say Yes or No at once?"

"At once."

"If I had not come in when I did, would you have said Yes?"

She unconsciously laid her hand on his arm ; forgetting all inferior considerations in her breathless anxiety to hear his next words. The confession of his love, was within a hair's breadth of escaping him—but he checked the utterance of it even yet. "I don't care for myself," he thought. "But how can I be certain of not distressing *her?*"

"Would you have said Yes?" she repeated.

"I was doubting," he answered—"I was doubting between Yes and No."

Her hand tightened on his arm; a sudden trembling seized her in every limb—she could bear it no longer. All her heart went out to him, in her next words.

"Were you doubting *for my sake* ?"

"Yes," he said. "Take my confession in return for yours—I was doubting for your sake."

She said no more—she only looked at him. In that look, the truth reached him at last. The next instant, she was folded in his arms, and was shedding delicious tears of joy, with her face hidden on his bosom.

"Do I deserve my happiness?" she murmured, asking the one question at last. "Oh, I know how the poor narrow people who have never felt and never suffered, would answer me, if I asked them what I ask you. If *they* knew my story, they would forget all the provocation, and only remember the offence—they would fasten on my sin, and pass all my suffering by. But you are not one of them? Tell me if you have any shadow of a misgiving! Tell me if you doubt that the one dear object of all my life to come, is to live worthy of you! I asked you to wait and see me; I asked you, if there was any hard truth to be told, to tell it me here, with your own lips. Tell it, my love, my husband!—tell it me now!"

She looked up, still clinging to him as she clung to the hope of her better life to come.

"Tell me the truth!" she repeated.

"With my own lips?"

"Yes!" she answered eagerly. "Say what you think of me, with your own lips."

He stooped, and kissed her.

THE END.

EXPLANATORY NOTES

Note: Volume breaks occurred at the end of the Second Scene (Chapter III), page 170, and at the end of Chapter XI in the Fourth Scene, page 350. In the serial, instalment breaks occurred on the following pages: 16, 30, 44, 54, 64, 73, 82, 94, 105, 121, 132, 145, 158, 170, 182, 193, 204, 215, 224, 237, 251, 273, 285, 297, 319, 331, 342, 353, 369, 379, 394, 405, 417, 431, 443, 458, 470, 483, 497, 509, 523, 535. All but three of these breaks are at the ends of chapters: the exceptions occur on page 82 (after line 25: 'The servant opened the door; and Mr Pendril went in'); page 94 (after line 23: '"Yes: on Michael Vanstone"'); page 497 (after line 16: 'old Mazey').

Dedication: Francis Carr Beard was Collins's friend and doctor, who probably started Collins on his lifelong opium addiction during the severe illness that accompanied the last part of the writing of *No Name*. In late 1862 Collins became so dependent on Beard's support that he was not only swallowing his medicines but dictating portions of his novel to him. Beard was the first to be told of its completion on Christmas Eve, 1862.

1 *The day was the fourth of March . . . forty-six*: in a letter to his friend Charles Ward, who worked in Coutts's Bank in London, Collins put the first of many questions about exact dates, postage and shipping times, details that he wanted to have right for this novel: 'What *day* of the *week* was the 4th of March 1846? . . . If [it] was a *Saturday* or a *Sunday*, it won't do for my purpose.' (Letter dated 11 September 1861, held in the Pierpont Morgan Library and quoted here by permission of the Trustees.)

7 *Magdalen*: possibly pronounced as it was sometimes spelt, 'Madlin', from the French form, Madeleine. The name Magdalen is identified with the sinner of Luke 7: 37.

'"*Men some to business . . . at heart a rake*"': Alexander Pope, *Epistle to a Lady* (1735), 215–16.

13 *the mixed train*: in the 1840s this term referred to a train carrying different classes of passengers; later it came to mean one made up of both passenger carriages and goods wagons.

Mr Vanstone's family: in his manuscript Collins often directed the printer to insert an extra white line between paragraphs in order to mark a pause or a change of pace. Some of these were lost in the transmission of the text from one printed version to the next if they happened to coincide with the foot of a page in the setting copy. One has been dropped here; other instances that I have noticed occur on pages 82 (after line 14), 164 (after line 12), 358 (after line 25) and 537 (after line 29).

22 *Diogenes . . . Rochefoucault*: Diogenes, Greek philosopher of the fourth

century BC, a Cynic who ridiculed and despised all intellectual pursuits which did not directly and obviously tend to some immediate and practical good. The Duc de la Rochefoucauld (1613–80) is chiefly remembered for his pithy *Maxims* which trace all human motives to self-love. Horace, Pope, Hobbes and Voltaire are, likewise, all satiric writers.

were received on the foundation of a well-reputed grammar-school: many grammar schools were subsidized by rich endowments dating back to their foundation in the sixteenth century.

28 *the famous what's-his-name*: Richard Brinsley Sheridan (1751–1816). *The Rivals* was first produced in 1775.

36 *Argus*: surnamed 'Panoptes', 'the all-seeing', because he had a hundred eyes. He proved an ineffective guardian of Io, desired by Zeus.

53 *the parliamentary train*: a slow train on which passengers were charged a fare not exceeding one penny a mile. By Act of Parliament every railway company was obliged to run one such cheap train every day over its system.

88 *One of Andrew's superior officers . . . found him*: Major Kirke's name was not mentioned at this point in the serial version. Its insertion in the first volume edition (1862) brought the plot into line with the claim made in its Preface that this novel does not depend upon secrets.

97 *As children born out of wedlock*: in the serial version this read: 'It is the cruel particularity of the English law, that the marriage of the parents does not legitimatise children born out of wedlock' (*All the Year Round*, 10 May 1862). But, as Collins must have learned later, even the laws of other European countries did not legitimize the offspring of subsequently married parents *when one of those parents was married to someone else when the children were born*. In hastily trying to rectify the damage caused by the removal of this blunder, Collins was forced to introduce the circumlocutory paragraph in which Pendril explains to Miss Garth 'a shocking peculiarity in this case' (p. 98).

129 *she and her sister had No Name*: this, and a less oracular reference to the title of the novel (in Magdalen's letter to Norah on p. 130), were written in only after the title had been settled upon early in 1862. They do not appear in the manuscript.

132 *the country theatres are in a bad way*: a true comment, since provincial theatres in England had declined rapidly after reaching their heyday in the second half of the eighteenth century. Collins's own interest in the theatre would have made him well aware of the many reasons that were postulated for this decline, including the rise of Methodist opposition and the poverty of the drama itself. The 1843 Act for Regulating the Theatres, by removing the monopoly of the more flourishing country theatres, in fact provided a death-blow to them all.

needle in a bottle of hay: in this expression bottle derives from a diminutive of the French *botte*, a bundle.

as soon find the North-West Passage: famous searches for this route to the East round the north of the American continent had gone on since Cabot's voyage in 1509, and were not successful until the early twentieth century.

134 *The railway mania of that famous year*: in 1846 there was a great boom in railway investment. The crash came in the spring of 1847.

135 *Leaving the station . . . North Street Postern*: York railway station was until 1877 situated inside the city walls, with closer access to the river than it has today. The ferry was replaced by Lendal Bridge in 1863.

139 *a rope-walk*: a piece of open ground used for the making of ropes.

143 *a hit, a palpable hit*: loosely quoted from *Hamlet*, V.i.295.

155 *mendicity officers*: the Society for the Suppression of Mendicity, founded in 1818, employed officers as professional investigators into the validity of claims for relief.

Rothschild or Baring: names of well-known banking dynasties.

166 *your first benefit in a London theatre*: the famous actor Charles Macready had a London benefit as late as 1848, but in fact the much-abused practice of paying actors by a share system and letting them rely for their support chiefly on the proceeds of a monthly performance held as their 'benefit' had largely been abandoned in London, though it lingered on in the provinces.

171 *Charles Mathews, comedian*: Charles Mathews (1776–1835), actor and entertainer, was best known for his one-man performances called 'At-Homes' in which he assumed a succession of extraordinarily different characters.

189 *Belshazzar . . . Writing on the Wall*: Belshazzar, son of Nebuchadnezzar, was the last king of Babylonia. He was killed in the sack of Babylon, a doom foretold by writing on the wall which appeared at his Feast (Dan. 5).

deserted dead body of Vauxhall Gardens: Vauxhall Gardens was a fashionable pleasure spot from the middle of the seventeenth century to the early nineteenth. The Gardens were finally closed in 1859.

194 *the material called "alpaca"*: a shiny wool mixture material invented by Sir Titus Salt in 1838, using wool from the Alpaca goat.

200 *Chemisette*: a 'fill-in' to the bodice of a day-gown cut low in front.

236 *"Joyce's Scientific Dialogues"*: first published in 1807 as *Scientific Dialogues for the Instruction and Entertainment of Young People; in which the first principles of Natural and Experimental Philosophy are fully explained and Illustrated*, by the Rev. J. Joyce, was many times reprinted. All of Wragge's subsequent display of scientific information is indeed, as he says, lifted straight from Joyce.

237 *Verbum sap.*: '*Verbum sat sapiente*' 'A word to the wise is sufficient'.

Esto Perpetua: 'Be thou everlasting'.

238 *Aldborough, Suffolk*: usual spelling 'Aldeburgh'. The sale catalogue of books

from Collins's library, published in 1890 by M. L. Bennett, lists as Item 76 a *Guide to Aldeburgh and adjacent places*, an illustrated presentation copy from the writer, 1861. The British Library holds *A Guide to Aldeburgh, with a brief description of Adjacent Places*, published anonymously in 1861, which would appear to be the same book since it contains all the information drawn upon in the descriptions of the district given in the novel.

German Ocean: now known as the North Sea.

the poet CRABBE: George Crabbe (1754–1832), son of a collector of salt duties in Aldeburgh, wrote narrative poetry based on his observations of Suffolk rural life.

246 *Ars longa . . . vita brevis*: 'Art is long, life is short'. A translation of the first of Hippocrates' aphorisms.

262 *a complete suit . . . nankeen*: nankeen was a cotton cloth of yellowish-brown colour, usually used only for trousers.

284 *Mesmerism . . . in these cases*: mesmerism, or hypnotism as it is now termed, based on the methods of the Austrian physician Friedrich Anton Mesmer (1733–1815), was a fashionable medical treatment in the middle of the nineteenth century, particularly for nervous disorders.

295 *suaviter in modo . . . fortiter in re*: 'gentle in manner, resolute in deed.'

310 *settlements*: daughters of wealthy families would generally have legal settlements drawn up when they were married, making separate provision for them. Otherwise, all married women's property belonged by law to the husband.

318 *Figaro in the French comedy*: Figaro, the barber in Beaumarchais's *Le Barbier de Seville* (1775) and the valet in its sequel, *Le Mariage de Figaro* (1784), is the type of an ingenious and cunning rascal.

ten days . . . by post: when Collins asked Charles Ward (see note to p. 1 above) to check postage times to and from Zurich he was astonished it took so long; hence the labour to make it plausible here.

326 *The date*: i.e. the postmark.

331 *home on the spot*: this is the only instance where an alteration was made to the ending of a serial episode for volume publication. The last paragraph of the serial version was omitted in the 1862 three-volume edition. It read:

Captain Wragge retired to rest that night in high spirits. He jocosely apostrophised the extinguisher in his candlestick, as he raised it to put the light out. 'If I could only drop you on Mrs Lecount,' said the captain, 'I might bid good-by to the last anxiety left, on this side of the wedding-day!' [*All the Year Round*, 20 September 1862].

352 *out of the place*: a misprint for 'out of place' (i.e. unemployed), which first occurred in the 1862 edition.

356 *in the locks, she rose*: a misprint for 'in the lock, she rose'. Correct in the serial version, it was misprinted in 1862 as 'in the locks, he rose'. Since the subject

is clearly a woman, 'he' made no sense, so 1864 'corrected' to 'she' but retained the error of the plural form for 'locks'. Apparently sensible but uninformed corrections like this indicate the absence of authorial intervention.

368 *Spud*: the iron head or blade fixed to a long handle and used for clearing mud from certain parts of a plough.

408 *had entered the room*: a misprint carried over from 1862. This should read: 'had left the room'.

429 *marriage . . . in Scotland*: in Scotland there is official recognition of what is termed 'a marriage by cohabitation with habit and repute'.

442 *P.S. . . . in the North*: this postscript was added in 1862 after serialization.

460 *coxswain*: the one in charge of the boat and its crew.

461 *Brutus and Cassius*: Julius Caesar's right-hand men, who conspired in his murder.

462 *made-dishes*: stews or casseroles composed of several ingredients.

477 *revolution . . . France*: this was the revolution of 1848; Louis Philippe fled to England in late February of that year (i.e. about the time this scene is set).

497 *list slippers*: 'list' was the border or selvage of cloth; in the eighteenth and nineteenth centuries, these strips of selvage joined together were used to make slippers.

Jezabel: Jezabel, wife of Ahab, King of Israel, was supposedly a flaunting woman of loose morals (2 Kgs. 9: 30).

501 *carneying*: smooth talk or flattery.

515 *Aaron's Buildings*: Aaron was the patriarch of the Jewish priesthood (Exod. 28); possibly connected with *haaron*, 'the ark'.

519 *surgeon in general practice*: the sense of pride in Merrick's insistence on the distinction comes from its being an assertion of his professional reliability and competence and an eschewing of the higher social status conferred upon physicians.

522 *Lady Day*: the feast of the Annunciation, 25 March, one of the four quarter days in the year when rents fall due.

tan: bark fragments left over from the process of tanning hides.

525 *Dum vivimus, vivamus*: 'While we live, let us live'; the maxim of the Epicureans.

Aloes, Scammony, and Gamboge: all strong purgatives.

THE WORLD'S CLASSICS

A Select List

A complete list of Oxford Paperbacks, including The World's Classics, Twentieth-Century Classics, OPUS, Past Masters, Oxford Authors, Oxford Shakespeare, and Oxford Paperback Reference, is available in the UK from the General Publicity Department (JH), Oxford University Press, Walton Street, Oxford OX2 6DP.

In the USA, complete lists are available from the Paperbacks Marketing Manager, Oxford University Press, 200 Madison Avenue, New York, NY 10016.

Oxford Paperbacks are available from all good bookshops. In case of difficulty, please order direct from Oxford University Press Bookshop, 116 High Street, Oxford, Freepost, OX1 4BR, enclosing full payment. Please add 10% of published price for postage and packing.